I0583580

THE TRIALS OF TRISTHOLM

THE TRIALS OF TRISTHOLM

RISE OF THE GRANDMASTER™ BOOK TWO

BRADFORD BATES

MICHAEL ANDERLE

This book is a work of fiction. All of the characters, organizations, and events portrayed in this novel are either products of the author's imagination or are used fictitiously. Sometimes both.

Copyright © 2020 by LMBPN Publishing

Cover Art by Jake @ J Caleb Design

http://jcalebdesign.com / jcalebdesign@gmail.com

Cover copyright © LMBPN Publishing

A Michael Anderle Production

LMBPN Publishing supports the right to free expression and the value of copyright. The purpose of copyright is to encourage writers and artists to produce the creative works that enrich our culture.

The distribution of this book without permission is a theft of the author's intellectual property. If you would like permission to use material from the book (other than for review purposes), please contact support@lmbpn.com. Thank you for your support of the author's rights.

LMBPN Publishing

PMB 196, 2540 South Maryland Pkwy

Las Vegas, NV 89109

First US edition, July 2020

eBook ISBN: 978-1-64971-029-1

Print ISBN: 978-1-64971-030-7

THE TRIALS OF TRISTHOLM TEAM

Thanks to our beta readers
Kelly O'Donnell, John Ashmore, Larry Omans, Allen Collins, Billie
Leigh Kellar

Thanks to the JIT Readers

Allen Collins
Angel LaVey
Billie Leigh Kellar
Dorothy Lloyd
Jeff Eaton
Kathleen Fettig
Kerry Mortimer
Rachel Beckford
Veronica Stephan-Miller

If I've missed anyone, please let me know!

Editor
The Skyhunter Editing Team

CHAPTER ONE

"Whose bright idea was this?" Tim shouted at the group.

"Yours," Cassie growled as she pushed her back against the door to keep it closed. "Only one of your dumbass ideas could go so wrong."

Tim doused her with a healing orb. He felt a little hurt by her characterization of his planning abilities. His plans never went awry. "I don't remember waking up this morning saying, let's go to the creepy cottage at the edge of the slums to check things out," he groused. "All I had on the docket for the day was to pick my new class and sign up to be an adventurer."

JaKobi summoned a ball of flame into his hand. "Let's just get it out in the open. This is probably my fault." He smiled sheepishly.

"Probably?" ShadowLily snarled as she turned to look at the mage.

The fire mage spun and pointed his finger at Tim. "Hey, he was the one who told me to search for areas with suspicious deaths or disappearances. And," JaKobi said and then pointed at Cassie, "she was the one who said let's go check it out."

The bathroom door almost buckled as Cassie fought to keep it closed. "At least we discovered why people tell stories about this place." She gritted her teeth as the door opened just a crack. With a grunt of effort, Cassie slammed the door closed. It wouldn't hold much longer.

If the ghoul got in the room with them, they'd all be taking a trip to meet their caseworkers, and she wasn't ready for another trip back to what felt like too much reality. Cassie scowled at Tim. "Use that big ass brain of yours to get us the fuck out of here."

"I'm more of a leap before looking kind of guy." JaKobi shrugged. "Point at something, tell me to light it on fire, and I got you covered. Escaping from a room with only one door isn't exactly my thing."

Cassie frowned at the mage's smiling face hoping to wilt a little of the man's good humor. "It's cute that you think I was asking you." She turned her attention away from JaKobi and focused on her best friend. "Maybe you could do something to help facilitate things?"

ShadowLily slammed her shoulder into the door to help Cassie. "Trust me, when I start to facilitate things, his big brain turns off." Pushing against the door with her entire body weight, she turned her attention to her boyfriend. "But Cassie isn't wrong. What we need now is one of your plans."

The hint of panic in her eyes spurred Tim's brain into action. Turning away from the door, he scanned the room they were trapped in. There was one tiny window in the upper corner of the back wall. Cassie might be able to fit, but the rest of them would be screwed.

There had to be something he was missing.

Trying to stop his heart from jumping out of his chest like a jackrabbit over a garden fence, Tim took a few deep breaths and looked around the room again.

Not a fucking thing.

"Why couldn't it have been a zombie?" Tim whispered to himself.

Zombies were the walking epitome of an easy farm. The walking dead were slow and easy to kill. Zombies won in numbers and stamina. The undead never sleep, and they don't give up. If they surround a building, you might as well write a letter to your family because you weren't getting out.

Ghouls, on the other hand, were fast and agile.

Tim thought of ghouls as corpse garbage disposals on steroids. The monsters feasted on the remains of the recently deceased. That meant they tended to stay near larger settlements with cemeteries. Sometimes they even followed armies to war. When corpses couldn't be readily obtained, ghouls would kill and bury their food for later, like how an alligator pins a carcass under a rock to make the meat tender.

The door rattled, and he heard one of the timbers crack.

Tim had to find a way to get them out of there. If there wasn't an obvious or sneaky route, they probably had to kill the damn thing. JaKobi's fireballs only seemed to make the ghoul mad, and he was pretty sure none of the rest of them could get close enough to stab it without getting ripped apart. So that left him.

Maybe he was looking at this all wrong. The Goddess Eternia had given him a quest to eliminate an outbreak of wraiths before their attacks could destabilize Promethia. While a ghoul wasn't a wraith, they were both undead monsters touched by darkness, so maybe his newest spell would work.

Looking back on it, the group had been overconfident because of how Tim handled the wraiths at Cardinal Jepsom's ceremony. They'd walked into the little cottage expecting to find one of the wraiths nesting. Cassie was going to distract it while Tim took it down. It was a simple plan.

Sometimes even the simplest of plans can go catastrophically wrong.

Their plan took a turn for the worst when one of the interior walls exploded in a shower of wooden shrapnel. Gaston was the only one who managed to stay on his feet, and without his help, they wouldn't have made it to the bathroom they were trapped in now.

They would have been dead.

Time seemed to slow as an eerie sense of calm settled over his mind. Tim didn't know how to control it, but every now and then, he found himself in what he liked to think of as "the zone." His mind was homing in on an answer to their problem.

A grin spread across his face before he could stop it. When he turned toward his tank, Tim saw the look of worry on her face, but he had just the right words to calm her down. "I've got an idea."

"Oh, shit. He's got that look in his eyes." JaKobi started to grin. "This is when things get interesting."

Gaston nudged ShadowLily out of the way, putting his bulky frame against the door as it groaned in protest. "Don't do anything too crazy. I've only got the one life."

Tim nodded at the assassin. What was once considered insanity was often proved correct as science progressed. The world wasn't flat, and the earth orbited the sun, but sometimes you still had to take a leap of faith. While a scientist in a lab couldn't take a leap if they wanted their work to be published, Tim had no such qualms about rolling the dice.

"Cassie, when I tell you to, I want you to let the ghoul in." Tim tried to reassure her with his smile.

"Fuck that," Cassie shouted. "If it gets in here, we're all dead."

"That door isn't going to last forever," Tim implored. "Just trust me."

Tim didn't wait for a response. Instead, he turned toward JaKobi. "After I hit it with weaken undead, I need you to cast your flame shield to hold it back. After that, we both hit it with everything we've got."

The ball of flame JaKobi had been juggling winked out of existence, and he focused on the door. "I'm ready."

Tim pointed at Cassie and gave her the slightest of nods. "I changed my mind. We go when you're ready." His fingers started working through the motions of his weaken undead spell.

"I still think this is a shitty plan." Cassie motioned for Shadow-Lily to get clear as the ghoul hit the door again. "I don't want to die in a bathroom."

JaKobi snorted. "Elvis died in the bathroom. If it's good enough for the King, it's good enough for me."

Gaston moved away from the door and stood under the small window. He looked at it furtively. "You think I can fit?"

Cassie smiled at the assassin. "You'll only get stuck if you try to squeeze those big beautiful shoulders through there." The glare he gave Cassie bounced off her as harmlessly as a raindrop. "Hey, it's not my fault you're all big and muscly."

"No one ever talks about my shoulders that way." Tim pretended to be hurt as he spared a quick glance at ShadowLily.

One of ShadowLily's eyebrows quirked up. "That's because your shoulders aren't your best asset."

"Ouch." Tim put a hand over his heart.

JaKobi started to laugh. "That was just cold."

"She did imply that I had a best asset." Tim was smiling again.

"I don't like it when people fish for compliments." ShadowLily huffed. "But if he gets us out of here, I might just tell him which of his assets I like best."

"Gross. You two make me wanna barf sometimes," Cassie grumbled.

Tim held up a hand to stop everyone from talking. "Cassie's vomiting potential aside, I'd like to hear more from ShadowLily."

Gaston growled. "Don't we have more important things to worry about?"

ShadowLily just winked at him. "How do you know I wasn't just using sex as a motivator when I was really talking about his brilliant mind?"

"But the other day, you were going on and on about..." The door behind Cassie shattered. The tank managed to whip her bō staff around in time to avoid the ghoul's claws. Planting a foot in the monster's chest, she threw herself backward, pushing the undead monster a few feet outside of the door.

Tim's weaken undead spell flew straight at the ghoul. It slammed into the ghoul's chest, making it stagger back another step. The creature looked from its chest to Tim and let out a bellow of rage that shook the cottage. It was the kind of sound that if you heard it walking home at night, your legs would start running on their own. The howl of anguish and fury was the sound of death coming.

A wall of flames appeared in front of the ghoul, which cut off its most direct path to Tim. The shield would only last for a second against the monster, but a second was all he needed to get off his next spell. His fingers worked their way through his divine light spell as he waited for the shield to fail.

Instead of trying to run through the flames, the ghoul ran out of their line of sight.

Tim looked at JaKobi. "That was unexpected."

A huge green and brown chair flew through the door, taking part of the doorframe with it. JaKobi's flame shield shattered as the ghoul ran forward to rip them apart. The undead monster's eyes locked onto Tim, and saliva dripped from its jaws as the ghoul closed the distance.

Tim's divine light spell hit the ghoul dead center, but it wasn't enough to stop it. Tim stumbled back, trying to work his hand through the motions to cast it again. There was no way he'd get the spell off before the monster ran him over. Despite him weakening the ghoul, it was just too strong. His back hit the wall. Was he really going to die like this? Right before he signed his papers to become an adventurer?

The ghoul leaped into the air. Tim watched in horror as the creature descended on him from above. One strike from those claws would cut through his robes and slice him to the bone. He wished now that he had just picked a damn class and signed his papers instead of stalling.

Looking up at the ghoul, Tim wondered how long it would take him to get to level ten again and shuddered.

JaKobi screamed something that sounded oddly like "you shall not pass," and the ghoul erupted into flames.

Ashes brushed across Tim's checks like the first sprinkles of snow in winter. He looked at JaKobi. "Cut it a little close, don't you think?"

"If the deed isn't dramatic, you don't receive the proper credit. You never hear about a person lifting a car off of another person in the news. If the car is on fire and a kid is trapped under it, all of a sudden, its national headlines. It's really just a matter of perspective."

Tim brushed at his cheek, leaving a dark gray smear. "Next time, just toast the fucker right away and know that I will be immensely appreciative."

"You got it, boss." JaKobi leaned against the wall looking exhausted.

Tim wondered just how much the spell took out of the fire mage as he turned to face their tank. "I don't know if there was some kind of bounty for this creature or not but find out. A little extra gold never hurt anyone. Plus, he might have a stash in here."

He turned and started toward the door, then paused once he reached the exit. "JaKobi, why don't you meet me at the temple in an hour or so? We can talk to Brother Colton together. Hopefully, the priest can give us something to help us zero in on potential locations for the wraiths."

"I'm going to tag along." ShadowLily nudged JaKobi. "Make sure this one stays out of trouble."

"Hey, that was one time and that sheep had it coming," JaKobi whined.

"Repeat after me." ShadowLily tapped him on the head. "I will not incinerate the livestock of merchants, even if they are assholes."

"Fine, fine. Come along and make sure I don't lose my temper and burn down half the city." JaKobi crossed his arms over his chest and started to pout.

"Oh, I'm sure if you need something to burn, we can find a better outlet than the innocent sheep of Promethia." ShadowLily wrapped an arm around his shoulder and guided him past Tim and out into the hallway. "Maybe while we're out, we can do something about those clothes."

"But I like my clothes," JaKobi pleaded as their voices trailed out of earshot.

Tim looked at his two remaining party members. "Feel free to join us after you finish searching the place, or we'll meet you back at the inn when we're done."

Cassie waved him off. "I doubt we'll find much here, but it's worth a look. I'll see you when you get back to the inn."

Gaston had his hands on his hips. "I've got a few other jobs to take care of today. Just fill me in tonight over beers."

Tim gave them a wave. "See you guys later."

This was it; he was really going to do it. In the next hour, he would select his advanced class and become an adventurer. After walking to the temple with his friend, it was time for his appointment with his caseworker to make his status official. When he stepped back through the portal, he should be at the temple and ready to continue his quest.

CHAPTER TWO

"Come on, lady, all I wanted was a taste." A man with tattoos down his arms laughed as he looked at his friends.

The woman he was talking to recoiled and wiped at her check as if the man had licked her. "I told you, I'm not interested."

"This one is playing hard to get lads." He took a step forward and reached out to grab the woman.

JaKobi stopped in front of the stall and cleared his throat loud enough that the larger man turned to stare at him. The mage held his ground. His feet were spread wide, and his staff was planted between them.

"Look, Gil, a hero." One of the men standing behind Mr. Tattoos pointed at JaKobi and started to laugh.

A cruel smile spread across Tattoo's lips as he replied to the man. "Looks more like a beggar to me." He turned to face JaKobi. "This doesn't concern you, fuck off."

"He's right. This really doesn't concern us," Tim said as he continued walking past. He hoped JaKobi knew he didn't mean it. All he wanted to do was get behind the other two without them thinking of him as a threat.

Gil grinned wider while the merchant stared at Tim in disbelief. "Listen to your friend, beggar. Time to move along."

Dropping his hood to reveal his own smiling face, JaKobi summoned a ball of flames into his hand. "I don't think I'll be going anywhere."

The two thugs gave Tim and ShadowLily a long look before they moved to back up their leader. Sticking to his role, Tim continued to talk to ShadowLily about what he hoped to find at the temple. They rounded the corner of the stall and disappeared from sight.

Gil pulled a giant double-bladed axe from the harness on his back. "One last chance to flee with your life, magic man."

Tim peeked around the corner of the stall to see if the two thugs had forgotten about them. As he expected, the two men were hyper-focused on what Gil was doing and the immediate threat posed by JaKobi. They had completely failed to pay attention to the Fire mage's friends.

"I almost slapped the shit out of you back there, but then I realized what you were doing." ShadowLily grinned as they crept around the back of the stall in a crouch.

"That would have given away the plan," Tim whispered back as they edged into position.

"Would have served you right. Did you see the look on her face when she thought we were going to abandon her?"

Tim's knuckles flared white as he gripped the hilts of his daggers. "I surely did."

Both of them dropped into stealth and continued moving forward. Once they were in position behind the two men, they shared a brief look before lashing out. ShadowLily's man went down in a lump, barely making a sound. Tim's victim wasn't so lucky.

Blood sprayed out from the wound in the man's neck as he spun around, clutching at it desperately before falling over.

ShadowLily frowned over at Tim. All he could do was smile and shrug his shoulders. "What?"

"As long as you weren't going for silent, you did a great job," ShadowLily snapped.

Gil spun around and looked at the bodies. His mouth hung open in shock.

Tim glanced at the man whose throat he'd sliced. When he finally stopped kicking, Tim turned his attention back to his girlfriend, ignoring the axe-wielding stranger. A little sheepishly he admitted, "You're right. I'm going to have to work on that."

"Only if you don't want to be the worst assassin ever," Shadow-Lily mocked.

"Hey, I'm a healer," Tim replied, sounding wounded.

Finally processing what happened, Gil stammered, "You killed them."

"This guy's not the brightest," JaKobi said.

Gil spun back around, axe raised above his head. With a bellow of rage, he started to swing, and the haft of his axe burst into flames. A fraction of a second later, the wood was consumed by JaKobi's spell and the head fell harmlessly to the ground. Realizing this was a fight he couldn't win, Gil looked for any direction he could get away in.

The warrior didn't make it more than a step before finding himself impaled on the merchant's dagger. "I just wanted a little taste," she screamed as she stabbed him again.

Tim motioned for the others to join him as the woman finished the man off. "Things seem to have changed since the dark goddess Vitaria made her plans to claim the city known."

"You're right, everyone seems on edge," JaKobi replied he danced a flaming coin across his knuckles as they walked.

"Hopefully, Brother Colton will help us put an end to that." ShadowLily snatched the coin from JaKobi's hand with a grin. "Show off."

"If you've got it, flaunt it." The fire mage tried to snatch the coin back from ShadowLily, but she only giggled and danced away from him. Turning to Tim, he pleaded, "Help me out here."

They reached the temple steps, and Tim turned to his girlfriend. "Might as well give him the coin back. He's going to need something to entertain him while I'm gone."

ShadowLily flipped the coin back to the fire mage. "Try to make this quick. He's not the only one who doesn't like to be kept waiting."

Tim gave her a quick kiss. "Stay out of trouble while I'm gone. I'll meet you at Brother Colton's as soon as my appointment is over."

"See you then." ShadowLily turned away from him and grabbed JaKobi's arm, pulling him along with her. "Why don't you show me this library you're always talking about."

The mage grinned. "Really?"

"No," the assassin said with a laugh. "But I will buy you something to eat while we wait."

"Free food is my favorite kind." JaKobi started to pick up his pace. "Where are we going?"

"Oh, I know a place," ShadowLily said with a smile in her voice.

Tim frowned as he stepped into the temple. Those bastards were going to Joe's without him. Sometimes life was so unfair.

Tim pulled the class change token from his inventory.

This was it, the moment of truth. He had finally decided what advanced class to pick. It wasn't as if this afternoon's scheduled meeting with his caseworker pushed him to make a choice or anything. In the end, Tim decided his path through the game was going to be a little less traditional, and his class should reflect that.

Holding the token in his hand, Tim rubbed his thumb against the upraised knob like he had a thousand times before. This time he was really going to go through with it. He depressed the little button and said the class he wanted to play.

"Battlesworn."

A message appeared in his vision.

Update class from Healer to Battlesworn. Please confirm the changes. <Yes/No>

Tim selected yes.

His body was lifted into the air, and golden motes of light swirled around him as he was lowered gently back to the ground. As Tim's feet touched the cobbles, a spell book appeared in his hand. He looked down at the book, excited to have received more than one new spell.

Battlesworn Spells for Novices.

There was really no time like the present to see what he'd gotten himself into. Tim opened the book to find four spells listed. He had also been granted two different stances. The stances appeared to give him the choice of focusing his healing on a single target or the entire group. Each stance also gave any of his damage-dealing abilities the ability to return health to a single target or the entire party at a reduced rate. Now Tim could damage monsters to heal his party.

How fucking cool was that?

The first stance was called the Way of the Boulder. It provided a ten percent damage reduction buff to a single target. Damage caused by your curses would be returned to the target of your stance at one hundred and fifty percent of the damage done, he read. All other damage inflicted would be returned to your target at the rate of ten percent.

Tim's second choice for a stance was the Way of the River. This stance spread his healing across the entire group. The amount of healing his curses returned as health was once again buffed to one hundred and fifty percent, but the damage inflicted by any of the other spells would be returned at a rate of fifty percent instead of ten. The health generated from his attacks would then be split by the party evenly.

If he was reading the tooltips right, the Way of the Boulder stance reduced damage taken by a single target by ten percent, and his damage-dealing capabilities would allow healing with curses, providing a larger benefit.

Thankfully, neither of the stances restricted his access to his regular healing spells. He could slowly try to weave these new techniques in while having a damn good backup plan. From a healing perspective, things were looking great.

It felt to Tim like his capabilities just got a major boost. It was time for the Blue Dagger Society to start running more dungeons. Now that he could heal his entire party just by attacking the enemy, things were about to get real interesting fast. The kind of utility his new class provided would come in handy for all types of situations.

Tim smiled to himself as he thought about how worried he'd been about picking the right class. He shouldn't have agonized over the decision, just listened to his gut when he hit level ten. His choice seemed perfect, and it would be a hell of a lot more interactive than just sitting back and splashing healing spells at people. Now he would have to manage his stances and make sure to keep his curses, *whatever those were,* on the enemy at all times.

Maybe it was time for him to figure out what his new spells could do instead of just speculating. Tim knew he had a tendency to dive down the rabbit hole of his imagination without always having the facts. He couldn't risk screwing up in combat and hurting his team. He opened the spellbook, determined to understand every facet of the skills being given to him.

Curse of Giving: Is it really giving if you just take what you want? This curse applies a damage over time effect to the enemy target. With each tick of the damage over time effect, the recipient(s) of your current stance will be healed.

Rank: Novice level one

Behold My Power: It's not your power we're interested in, but that of your companions. This spell will drain 1% of your group's health every second for ten seconds. When the timer runs out, the health taken from your party will be transferred to the enemy target as damage and apply a debuff. The debuff increases the damage the target takes from all sources by five percent for ten seconds. This ability has a longer than average cooldown.

Rank: Novice level one

Who Needs a Shield: We all know you could really use a shield, but we gave you a staff instead. This spell applies a 10% damage reduction to all of the targeted enemy's attacks for the next ten seconds. This spell cannot be stacked in conjunction with any other damage reducing spells. This ability has a longer than average cooldown.

Rank: Novice level one

Advanced Cleanse: Sometimes it's not about the health you can add back to your party, but what you can take away from them. No one likes to suffer from the debilitating effects of a nasty debuff, and thanks to this nifty little spell, when you're around, they won't have to. Using this book should complete your knowledge of the cleansing process and increase the spell's effectiveness when used outside of combat.

Rank: Apprentice level seven

"Makes sense," Tim grumbled to himself as he thought about who needed a shield. Stacking debuffs would make things way too easy, especially if everyone had a damage reducer. That or the DEVs would have to balance fights. If everyone didn't cast their damage reducer, the bosses would one-shot people. Not letting the debuffs stack was a much simpler option for the developers to make. Plus, the spell was powerful enough. It was the kind of thing that might make the difference in the tank living or dying when a boss used a cleave type attack.

When they finally progressed into raids, he was going to kick so much ass.

Tim's favorite part of group content was the sense of accomplishment that came with working together as a team to take down a boss for the first time. Hours of wipes, endless nights spent cursing everyone in the group with your mic, all leading up to the big moment.

The win.

From there, it was a simple matter of doing it again and again until you could beat that boss fight with one hand tied behind your back. You could apply the lessons learned in gaming to anything in life. Like any other team-building activities one could do, gaming could be a great way to teach people how to work together. Tim always thought it would be cool to get kids who weren't into sports into team-based games.

What if there was a youth center you could send your kids to after school? One that helped them get all their homework done, and then provided additional free team-building exercises via popular games.

Kids who weren't on the field or in the gym could get their homework done. Get a little time in on the playground, and then learn about teamwork via dungeon crawls and raids. It'd be a blast, and the kids could decide what they wanted to get out of it. Some would pick up leadership skills, and all of them would learn how to deal with winning and losing the right way.

It could be a fun little program if he ever found a way to pay for it.

The spell book disappeared as Tim absorbed the knowledge it contained. Before picking his class, Tim had felt like he needed a little break to re-energize himself for the rigors of adventuring. Now he was ready to put his new spells to the test. Before he could rejoin his crew and find something to kill with his new bag of tricks, Tim had to meet with his caseworker.

With his new class selected and the business he was running in the game, there was no way he could risk getting deleted after death anymore. He'd come too far in the game not to take the plunge and become an adventurer. Once the meeting was over, he wouldn't have to worry about losing all his progress if he died.

You couldn't become a Grandmaster if you never got past level ten.

Or maybe you could if you adjusted your goals. If you liked eating and vegging out, maybe you could work to become the Grandmaster of Couch Potatoes. Tim wondered if there were weird skills like that in the game. He could just imagine Seth Rogan coming into the world as Grandmaster of Joint Rolling. He started to laugh out loud. The priests walking by looked at him as if he might have lost his mind.

There would be time to look into the weirder side of life in *The Etheric Coast*, but for now he had to stay focused on what was right in front of him. One step at a time. Meet the caseworker, find the wraiths, and eventually put an end to the dark goddess Vitaria.

Tim took a step back as the shimmering portal opened next to him. He was about to sign up for his next big adventure.

CHAPTER THREE

Lorelei stumbled and narrowly avoided the dark outline of a tree that came out of nowhere.

Not that trees could move.

At least, she hoped the trees couldn't fucking move. Lorelei was having a hard enough time avoiding what she assumed to be firmly rooted trees. Plus, she had the feeling if the trees could move, they would be moving out of her way. Who in the hell would want some idiot blundering into them every five seconds?

If Lorelei was going to make like a tree, she would have gotten the fuck out of the way.

Apparently, the hardy vegetation of this forest had different ideas. A branch clawed her cheek, leaving a small scratch as she pushed her way past another one of a seemingly endless supply of tormentors. Who would have thought there would be so many trees in the forest? Whatever madness spurred her into the woods at night had worn off, and now she was starting to question her sanity.

Venturing out of the safe zone around the city was a sure-fire way to wind up dead.

"Stay close to home" was the kind of simple rule Lorelei normally would have followed, but she had been too pissed off to care about running into some imaginary serial killer in the woods.

That kind of thing only happened around Camp Crystal Lake.

The real reason she shouldn't have gone traipsing through the woods at night was simply that it was hard as fuck to walk around in the dark. It was all Lorelei could do not to keep her hands in front of her like a mime pretending to be trapped in a box.

What she really needed was a light.

Since a light wasn't going to magically appear in her hands, Lorelei had to keep moving forward. Her growing frustration made her move faster, which only led to her running into more of the damn branches. While she knew running down the hill in front of her would only make things worse, she was half tempted to say fuck it and start sprinting.

The only thing that stopped her from taking off full tilt was thinking about what would happen if she broke a leg. Dying from starvation in the woods sounded worse than the time she watched a movie about a guy trapped in a coffin.

How would she ever explain it to her caseworker if she died from running into a tree headfirst in the dark?

Forcing herself to walk down the hill slowly, she wove from one inkblot tree to another. A flicker of color on the horizon caught her eye. Out in the darkness, a hint of color could only mean one thing.

Fire!

Stopping in place, Lorelei waited to see the flare of color again, praying it wasn't just a figment of her imagination. When she saw the flicker of orange for the third time, she finally let herself believe it was real. Fire meant people, fire meant warmth. Her salvation might be waiting for her just ahead.

Leaning against the trunk of a tree, Lorelei paused to watch the flames. It was clear as day below her now. Someone had lit a huge bonfire. With an unconscious gesture, she tapped her index finger against the center of her lower lip and thought about what the flames meant.

"Let's not get ahead of ourselves." *Light didn't have to mean friends.*

A quick check of her map didn't show anything up ahead. That was part of the problem. Things on the map looked a lot closer than they were, and she suspected the city of Tristholm was at least a day away.

"This would go a lot faster if I had my VW," Lorelei grumbled to herself as she continued watching the horizon.

One of the only things she missed about the outside world was being able to disappear on weekend excursions in her fully rebuilt '76 VW Microbus. She'd had a mechanic take the husk from a junkyard and replace everything. It was basically a Tesla wrapped in a VW bus shell. Maybe she'd find a cooler form of transportation in the game.

Maybe something that could fly.

Lorelei looked at her map. "Legends are such bullshit."

Maps needed disclaimers, like the side mirrors on cars. An inch could be a block, a mile, a hundred miles, or a thousand. It was all a matter of perspective and how far you had the damn thing zoomed out. She might have been drinking when she'd started this little jaunt. The casual stroll she planned on had turned into a two-day toil through the forest.

It was obviously the map's fault. She never made bad decisions while drinking.

Now she was frustrated, tired, and cold. Not to mention starving. Maybe Lorelei should have waited to join an MMO when the science fiction game NPC Corp was working on came out. She would have contemplated killing her bestie right now for one of those *Star Trek* microwaves that made whatever you wanted to eat appear out of thin air.

The delicacies of the future might be out of reach for her right now, but at this point she'd settle for a decent place to sleep, a bowl of slop, and a road to follow in the morning.

As if on cue, it started to rain.

Lorelei had noticed that when you were down in life, fate liked to pile as much on you as you could handle. It didn't matter what that bitch threw at her, Lorelei always came out on top. Although the drizzle was starting to make her think she should spend a little more time planning things and less time bouncing from one idea to the next, or one woman to the next.

When was she going to learn not to fall in love in an instant? It never worked out. The latest case in point was why she was out here now. It was always picking the wrong person to put her trust in. Tammy was just another example of her failures in love.

Why was it always easier to see your mistakes after they happened?

She'd let herself get all wrapped up in that new relationship glow and missed the warning signs. After three days in the game, she'd been kicked to the curb faster than a Christmas tree after New Year's.

Joke's on that bitch.

What Tammy didn't know was that Lorelei had only paid the POD fees for the first year upfront. So unless Tammy suckered some other girl into picking up the rest of the tab, that bitch was going to have to get a real job to stay in the game. Lorelei for one wouldn't mind watching Tammy clean up refuse off the streets. She might even throw some trash out for her to pick up.

Not because she was bitter. Just to give that bitch job security.

"All sizzle and no rizzle." Being a little silly helped take the sting off being dumped. What Lorelei really needed to do was stop settling for the right now girl, and start looking for her forever woman.

None of those problems mattered right now. What she really needed to do was get closer to the source of the fire and see if there was any shelter from the rain. It was too bad her map didn't have a weather feature. She would have saved herself a lot of hassle if she had purchased a coat.

With the clearing below her coming into sharper focus, the hint of a structure started to reveal itself. She took a few more steps down the hill, trying to figure out what it was she was seeing.

Was that a cabin?

Nothing scary about a cabin out in the middle of nowhere. "Can you just check to see if my oven is hot enough? All you have to do is lean over and reach inside." Lorelei grinned as she pulled her newly purchased bow from her shoulder. "Not going to work on this Ranger. I know all about the gingerbread house."

Looking at the cabin, Lorelei saw she only had two choices. Keep moving and give it a wide berth or take a risk and approach the creepy cabin in the woods.

Lorelei continued moving down the hill. If there was a chance to get out of the rain and dry off by a warm fire, she was going to take it. She dipped into a crouch as she held her bow sideways, slowing her pace to a snail crawl as she continuously scanned the area for threats.

"Activate tracking." Lorelei's vision blurred for a moment, and then the world turned almost gray. The tracks of animals who had passed close to the cabin appeared with faint blue outlines around them. She saw a lot of the normal tracks you would expect: deer, rabbits, and wolf prints. Some of the wolf tracks were bigger than they should have been, and it made her doubt the effectiveness of her skill.

Narrowing her vision, Lorelei let the skill work to isolate footprints around the cabin. There were at least eight sets of boot prints. A few of them were smaller and probably belonged to children.

There was no way to tell how recent the tracks were, at least not with her tracking skill ranked where it was. She'd always imagined herself more of an elf, jumping from rock to rock, killing orcs with each shot of her bow, than a ranger tracking animals. It was no surprise that her tracking skills were under-leveled while her skill with a bow was pretty damn solid. If you needed someone to hit an apple from seventy-five yards away while running full speed, she was your girl.

Not so much if you needed to know how many people were inside a cabin.

The small building in front of her could have belonged to cannibals, cultists, or cuddlers. There was no way to know, so she tried to prepare herself for anything. The fire was roaring, and the flames were so bright they might as well have been an outdoor lighting system. The hog on a spit over the fire made cannibals a less likely outcome, so she at least had that going for her.

Pulling the bowstring to her cheek, Lorelei crept a little closer and tried to angle herself so she remained downwind of the smoke. The smell of roasting pork hit her a few moments later, and she couldn't stop herself from salivating. A grumble escaped her stomach, and she wondered how long it'd been since she'd eaten a proper meal.

"At least I'm far enough away no one could have possibly heard that." Glancing down at her rebellious stomach, she willed the organ to remain silent just a little bit longer. "There will be plenty of time for food once we find out if the inhabitants are friendly."

Stepping into the clearing, Lorelei examined the pig, noting that whoever was cooking the animal didn't seem to have any sides laid out on the table next to the massive spit. One thing she'd learned quickly was meat in *The Etheric Coast* was a bigger staple of her diet than it ever had been in the real world. It was easier to carry dried meat when traveling, and every meal she ordered at the inn had been meat stew with crusty bread.

Right now, she'd kill someone to get her hands on a damn good salad. It wouldn't be too much longer before some enterprising young chef opened a restaurant with greens on the menu. Whoever took the initiative to focus on leafy greens first might even be able to take over the entirety of Promethia's salad market before anyone else had the chance. Maybe they could make it as good as her favorite salad place in the real world.

Salad and Go sold hand-squeezed lemonade for a dollar.

For a fucking dollar.

Maybe she should start Promethia's first salad shop. It sounded a lot easier than traipsing around in the woods, hoping she wouldn't get eaten. Lorelei needed to start focusing on the problems right in front of her. Being a big dreamer, her mind tended to wander toward the things she'd like to do, and not on the things she needed to be doing to get there.

The fire crackled as the fat dripped off the pig and hit wood below. The entire area smelled so good Lorelei was surprised it hadn't attracted more animals. Her brain kept screaming this was a trap, but part of her also wanted a slice of meat. Bacon was the kryptonite of every diet she'd ever been on.

Bacon got her.

EVERY.

FUCKING.

TIME.

As a health-conscious individual, she knew eating an all bacon diet would send her to an early grave, but that didn't stop her from thinking it might just be the perfect way to go out.

Plus, bacon came from the store already cut into perfect little strips, no additional butchering required. If Lorelei had to butcher her own meat, she probably would have become a vegetarian. It was so much easier to enjoy meat when you thought of it as just a thing that came served on a plate, and not a cute little animal down at the farm.

Not that this hog looked cute.

The big fucker had tusks that looked like they were made for ripping an unsuspecting Ranger to pieces. Forcing her mind off the pig and back to the business at hand, Lorelei looked around the clearing. She noticed what might have been pens built further away from the cabin. Whoever lived here might be a pig farmer.

But cooking a pig this big didn't make sense. It was wasteful to the extreme unless you were trying to feed an army or lure someone in. Based on the tracks Lorelei saw earlier, there wasn't an army waiting inside of the cabin, and it wouldn't be very effective to try to lure people in with a pig cooking out here.

Although she had found the cabin easily enough.

The thought didn't fill Lorelei with a ton of confidence, and she decided to take things slow. For now, she'd have to be content with hunkering down to watch the clearing until something moved, or she just couldn't take it anymore.

She'd never been known for her patience.

Seeing how long she could wait would be a perfect chance to see how much progress she'd made at being patient since entering the game. Standing in the cold drizzling rain, being gently bathed in the most delicious smoke ever created, wasn't exactly what Lorelei had in mind when it came to fun ideas on how to spend an evening, but she hated the thought of returning to her caseworker again so soon.

Since becoming an adventurer two weeks ago, Lorelei had died four times. A mace to the head, thrown off a cliff, stabbed in the back, and her personal favorite, poisoned by her lover.

That was one hell of a breakup.

She'd come back into the game to find their shared rooms empty, and all of her stuff gone. It reminded her of the time her friend Susan brought a guy home from a bar only to wake up and realize he'd stolen her car.

Who in the fuck did that kind of shit?

Was it so naïve to think that romance should mean forever?

Two weeks into her new existence and Lorelei was on her own. She couldn't remember a time in recent memory when she'd been single. For the first time in her life, Lorelei was going to sit down and really think about what she wanted, instead of just dashing from one great experience to the next. Not being surrounded by people actually felt pretty good.

Being alone with her thoughts was a refreshing change of pace.

Lorelei always imagined herself as better off alone. Maybe she was just a bitch, or she liked it better when she was the one doing the leaving, but she'd ended more than one relationship before the flames petered out. Sometimes she just wanted the freedom to do her own thing. If her lover wanted to come along for the ride, awesome. If they didn't, sayonara honey.

Who hasn't had a messy breakup or a dozen before finding the right one? Sometimes kissing a toad doesn't turn it into a princess, but there was always hope. That hope was what kept her relentless search for love moving forward.

Like her dream for an all-female revival of *Footloose*.

Lorelei would be kicking off a little more than her Sunday shoes with a gym full of hot ladies at her disposal. Although, most nights Lorelei was happier with a bottle of wine, a hot bath, and a good book on her Kindle. It always felt like all of her problems could be fixed with a good soak and a little bit of vino. Lorelei thought if the leaders of the world would all just slip into a hot bath before taking their conference calls, the world would be a much safer place.

It took everything she had not to giggle at the mental image of the president slipping into a tub before a man came in with a golden phone. "Sir, Congress is on the line."

Turning her attention back to the scene in front of her was hard. Lorelei had always enjoyed creating little fantasies and getting lost in her thoughts was a common occurrence for her. Knowing that she didn't want to go back to her old life in the real world helped ease her mind. Why would she want to go back to her cube, when in here she could fight off the forces of evil and save the world?

Sometimes things just needed doing.

It wasn't like a broken heart, and an empty bed were the worst things that ever happened to her. Instead of pitying herself and what she left behind, it was time to get back to work. There was a puzzle to solve here, and she wasn't getting any younger standing around.

Lorelei took a step forward quickly and dropped to a knee, aiming her bow at a shadow she saw emerging from the cabin.

A man poked his head out of the large wooden door. He looked around nervously for a moment before taking a hesitant step toward the fire. Pulling a knife free from his belt, he cut several large slices of meat before fleeing back to the safety of the cabin.

So there was at least one man inside of the cabin, and he was armed with a blade. He might only be a pig farmer with a knife, but he could also be a warrior who just happened to have a few pigs. She remembered from her history lessons that in the early Roman Empire, all men served in the military, but most of them weren't career soldiers. Her guess was a man living way out here had more than a knife laying around for protection, and at least a halfway decent idea of how to use it.

There was a good chance based on the tracks that there was at least one other person inside. There could be eight people for all she knew. Huffing, Lorelei let out the breath she'd been holding.

She could go down there and risk it, but what if there was a band of killers waiting inside? She might only lose a little bit of experience when she died, but she also lost time. If she wanted to show Tammy how bad she screwed up by dumping her, Lorelei couldn't keep dying.

It was time to take a risk.

Rising from where she had been kneeling, Lorelei started moving forward again. She kept her bow held sideways in front of her, with an arrow aimed at the door. She wasn't as comfortable shooting like this, but it was easier if she needed to fire off a shot in close quarters.

Lorelei waffled for a moment as the cabin drew closer. Part of her imagined what it must have been like to be one of the early American settlers. You never knew what someone wanted when they showed up at your door. For all she knew whoever was inside was just as scared as she was right now.

A branch broke in the forest behind her, and Lorelei spun around, scanning the darkness for threats. She'd been staring into the fire for so long she couldn't see shit. Eventually, she hoped to find a trainer who could teach her how to see in the dark, but she hadn't been able to locate one yet. As she turned back toward the cabin, a howl sounded from the forest on her right and was immediately answered from another animal on her left.

The wolf's howls distracted Lorelei enough that she didn't notice the cabin door opening again. The man she had seen earlier was standing there with a big ass crossbow in his hands. He had the bow pointed at her chest. There was no way she could get away if he pulled the trigger.

The man's nerves seemed to ease as he looked at her. Without a thought to his own safety, the man lowered his weapon and motioned frantically for her to get inside. When Lorelei didn't move, he spoke in a hurried whisper. "Hurry up, they're coming."

Lowering her bow, Lorelei took a few nervous steps closer. "Who are they?"

The man looked at her as if she were the dumbest person on the planet. "The fucking werewolves, girl. Now get inside. Once the bastards are here, I won't be opening the door again no matter how much you scream."

The howls sounded again, only this time they were closer. Hooking a thumb at the pig, Lorelei grinned. "Maybe the pig isn't such a good idea with all the…" She slung her bow over one shoulder and lifted her hands in the air, making a gesture that encompassed the area surrounding them. "Big furry beasts out there. If you know what I'm saying."

"Think of it as an offering." He clearly did not want to be outside any longer than necessary. "Are you coming or what?"

Lorelei took one last look at the man. Outside of the crossbow and knife at his waist, he didn't seem to be an immediate threat.

She also liked her chances against a man better than her chances against two werewolves.

Stepping up to the door, Lorelei peered inside before committing to crossing the threshold. There was a woman huddled by the fireplace with a small boy clutching at her waist. She couldn't see anyone else waiting to spring out at her, so she decided to roll the dice and step inside.

The woman looked almost as scared as the boy, and now that the man wasn't facing her down with a bow, she could see lines of worry etched deeply into his forehead. It took a lot of courage to open the door to a stranger, especially when you knew werewolves were close by. It was a kindness she wouldn't soon forget.

"Thank you for taking me in." Lorelei smiled as she extended her hand.

Her savior slammed a large wooden beam into the bracers over the stout wooden door before turning to face her. "What in the hell are you doing way out here?"

"Fleeing from a bad decision," Lorelei said sheepishly, hoping the tone of her voice made it sound more funny than serious.

"And stepping right into another one." The man chuckled good-naturedly as he reached for her extended hand. "That was something my father used to say. He liked to remind us that running from your mistakes only tends to make them worse."

The farmer dropped her hand. "Not that you came here for a lecture." He looked at his wife and then back to Lorelei. "Why did you come here, anyway?"

"Earl." The woman by the fire chastised her husband in the way only a wife can.

Looking a little guilty, Earl turned back toward Lorelei. "That's my wife, Evelyn, gently prodding me to mind my manners. We don't have much here, but you're welcome to be our guest until the morning."

"Thank you for your hospitality, Earl." She turned to look past him toward Evelyn. "And you ma'am." Returning her eyes to Earl's, she smiled. "I'm Lorelei, by the way."

"If they're gone in the morning," Evelyn said, bringing their attention back to the werewolves outside as she stared into the fireplace.

Earl scratched his head. "These attacks do seem different. Normally the werewolves kill a pig or two and move on, but now they come every night. That's our last pig out there. I have no idea what we are going to do tomorrow. We can't make it all the way to town before nightfall. Not without horses."

"What we need is someone to drive them off or kill them." Evelyn pointed at Lorelei. "She looks handy with a bow, maybe she is just the hunter we've been praying for." Evelyn gazed at her husband, imploring him to do something.

"Earl," Lorelei smiled as she tried to turn the conversation away from her fighting werewolves, "I'm not sure I'm the right person for a job like this."

Evelyn rose from her place by the fire. She took a moment to tuck her son into the blankets before coming to stand in front of Lorelei. "We don't have much, but my father was an archer in the army and won the annual contest three years in a row before he passed away. If you agree to help us, you can have his bow."

Quest Received: Saving the three little pigs.

Make sure the werewolves surrounding the cabin are dead or escort the family to the nearest town. If any of the family is hurt or killed, your reputation will suffer, and the reward for the quest will be nullified.

Reward: Evelyn's father's bow.

Failure: Fail to kill the werewolves or to protect the family.

Accept Quest: <Yes/No>

Coming this far north had never really been in her plans, and werewolves certainly hadn't been on the table when Lorelei started this journey. She also knew better than to turn down a quest when there was a shiny new weapon on the line. Who knew when she fled the city looking for a Tammy-free zone to set up shop, Lorelei would have ended up here?

Now she was in a little bit of a pickle.

Something heavy slammed into the side of the cabin, making the entire structure shake. Evelyn screamed, and her son started crying. Earl reached for his crossbow and pointed it toward the door. A prayer tumbled from his trembling lips as he begged for help from the goddess.

All things considered, Lorelei was just happy to be inside. If she hadn't stumbled across this cabin, the werewolves might have ripped her apart before she even knew they existed. She started to check her weapons, wondering if her bow and dagger would be enough to take down a mythical beast like a werewolf. Looking back on her night, the rain and the trees hadn't been so bad after all.

Knowing she could never live with herself if she left this family behind after they'd taken her in, Lorelei accepted the quest.

What was the worst that could happen?

CHAPTER FOUR

Werewolves in this game better be like those big cuddly fluff balls from Twilight.

Lorelei looked at the shaking door, already knowing her wish was too good to be true. The things waiting for her outside were probably much closer to the monsters she'd grown up being terrified of after watching *Underworld*. How Jenny had talked her into watching so many scary movies was just beyond her.

Thinking about Jenny's beautiful pouty lips cleared up the how part of the question. With lips like that, her super sexy ex could get her to do just about anything. That was part of the problem. She wanted to stop making decisions based on her lovers' wild sex appeal, and start making them with a more rational part of her brain.

At least thanks to Jenny, Lorelei had a good idea of what was waiting for her outside. The werewolves she pictured were eight to ten feet tall when standing on their back legs, and just as comfortable using their hands as if they were still human. Forget the fact they could drop to all fours and run faster than a goddamned horse.

At least she wouldn't have to worry about running away.

Running from a werewolf was just about as useful as trying to outrun a car. If one of those big furry bastards caught her, she was dead—no question about it. The only chance Lorelei had was to try to fight them from a distance.

Turning her head, Lorelei looked at the sturdy cabin walls and snorted. "Fat chance of that."

It was too bad she didn't have her ride, but her Micro-Bus didn't exactly fit in *The Etheric Coast*. Lorelei hadn't even seen so much as a steam engine. The best you could do in this world for comfort on a long trip was to hire a coach. While riding around on a comfy seat beat riding on horseback for days at a time, it also brought with it the risk of being attacked by bandits.

Bandits she could handle, but werewolves…

Earl watched the door as it rattled in the frame. "What's the plan?"

"Is there another way out of here?" Lorelei asked as she rubbed her index finger against the arrow. Watching the front door wasn't doing anything to settle her nerves. What she needed to do was figure out how to tackle this quest. There was no telling how effective her bow would even be against a werewolf that could probably regenerate.

What if she needed silver to kill them?

"Are you going to try to leave us here?" Earl asked, sounding wounded, but not surprised.

"Doesn't sound like the kind of thing a hero would do." She spun away from Earl and fired her arrow toward the door. The arrow made a hearty thump as it slammed through the door and into the frame.

The rattling stopped, giving her a chance to think.

Evelyn moved away from them to sit beside her son on the blankets in front of the fire. "How much of a hero you are remains to be seen."

Lorelei looked toward the woman with a little bit of a glare.

Not that she could fault Evelyn for doubting her. The chances of running into a person capable of tangling with a couple of werewolves had to be infinitely small. Maybe if Lorelei was lucky, there would be an entry about werewolves in the user interface, which would save her the embarrassment of asking for help.

Hey, I know I took this quest, but how do you actually hurt a werewolf?

Wincing at the thought of how that particular conversation might go, Lorelei pulled up her interface and started searching for information. A quick check of the monster manual revealed she might have been a smidge too hopeful about what to expect from the game developers. The entry provided wasn't very useful at all. The handbooks' entry for werewolves amounted to saying the monsters were fast as fuck, and to avoid the snarly end at all costs.

Since there was no way to find out more about the werewolves without asking, Lorelei bit her lip and decided to bite the bullet. It was ask for help or end up taking a quick trip to visit her caseworker.

Despite the fact Lorelei's caseworker Jessie felt more like a friend than an employee paid to monitor her, she didn't want to see her too often. Repeated visits probably just added to Jessi's workload, and it also meant she lost a fight. If there was one thing she hated more than anything, it was losing.

It wasn't as if the small crush she had on the cutest caseworker around had anything to do with her not wanting to die. It was a tricky tightrope to walk. On the one hand, she had to die to see Jessi. On the other, she didn't want to die so many times she looked totally inept and unworthy of her time. Plus, if Lorelei was going to throw a fight to go see Jessi, she'd make sure it was a quick death.

Getting ripped apart by werewolves seemed like a big ask for a cup of coffee and a little pleasant conversation.

Lorelei paused and took a moment to get back on track. She had to figure out how to survive this, and the only way she could do it is by asking. "Can you tell me anything about how to kill them?"

Evelyn snorted. "Shoot them full of arrows."

Lorelei narrowed her eyes at the woman. Shit was about to get real. "Well, that was my original plan, but I wanted to make sure sticking them full of arrows would actually kill them, and not just piss them off." She frowned as she continued to get worked up. "You know before I try to save your asses from the monsters that are trying to kill you."

Earl jumped in before his wife could retort. "The only thing I've ever seen bring them down was her father's bow. When he was alive, the werewolves left us alone."

Maybe the bow is enchanted?

There had to be a reason Evelyn's father's bow worked when others might have failed. "Can I see it?" Lorelei asked with a hungry expression on her face. Maybe she'd make it out of this alive after all.

Evelyn glared at the Ranger. "The deal was you get the bow afterward."

Earl moved to a chest at the far side of the room and opened it. "It's a little too much bow for me. That's why I stick with the crossbow." His wife's glare bounced harmlessly off of his back as he rummaged around inside the chest.

Pulling the bow free, Earl turned to look at his wife. "What? It isn't like she has anywhere to go."

Lorelei took the bow from him with reverence. She wanted to treat the weapon with the respect it deserved in front of the family the weapon protected for years. A quick inspection revealed the bow's name as Wolfsbane. The description of the weapon's special ability was simple and to the point.

Any normal arrow fired by this weapon will have the arrowhead coated in wolfsbane.

"Explains why the damn thing is so effective," Lorelei muttered to herself.

"What was that?" Earl asked as he looked from the weapon to her.

Lorelei held out the bow to Earl but kept her eyes locked on his. "If you really want to get out of here, I'm going to need this."

"Not a chance," Evelyn roared from beside the fire. "You could just sneak off into the night and leave us here to die."

The thought of doing something dramatic like throwing her dagger so it stuck into the fireplace by the woman's head and screaming, "I could kill you and take the damn bow anytime I want" ran through Lorelei's head. Instead of acting on her impulses, she removed her bow from her back and set it on the table.

"I'll leave my bow here." She turned to face Evelyn after setting the weapon down. "Worst case for you is the werewolves rip me apart, and in the morning, you have two bows."

"Two bows?" Earl asked.

Lorelei's lips ticked up in one corner, giving her smile a sarcastic twist. "I doubt the werewolves will take the other one with them."

"Oh," Earl stammered, looking a bit shocked. Despite the dire situation, it seemed the thought of someone dying hadn't quite hit him yet. He fell into the chair he was standing beside more than he sat in it. "I say we give it to her."

"Fine, but if she runs off it's on you," Evelyn growled as she turned away from them to look into the fire.

"I'm sure I could live with guilt for the few hours it takes the werewolves to break down the door." Earl held out the bow. "Please don't let us down."

Lorelei slung the bow over her shoulder and tried to look confident. "I've got this."

Climbing from his chair with all the motivation of a bear waking up from hibernation, Earl stood up. He pulled the corner of the lone rug in the room up to reveal a hidden door. The hidden cellar might have worked well against bandits, but it probably wouldn't do much against a werewolf.

Wolves had an extraordinary sense of smell.

"There is a tunnel out of the back of the cellar. It comes out on the hill behind the house. Should be just what you need to get the drop on them." Earl had a hopeful look in his eyes.

He moved toward the fireplace and lit a small torch before returning and handing the torch to Lorelei. Earl pulled open the trap door for her. "Thank you."

"I don't want them to see me coming." Lorelei handed the torch back and gave the pig farmer a quick nod. "See you on the other side."

"Praise the Lady," Earl replied with a sad smile as he closed the trap door, sealing the Ranger in the darkness below.

The cellar floor was muddy.

No big surprise with the rain. It wasn't like a house out in the wild was going to have a concrete foundation. The only scent to hit her nose was stagnant water, and there wasn't a single trace of wet dog. Lorelei took a few squelching steps into the pitch-black cellar and wondered if she should have taken the torch.

A little light wouldn't be such a bad thing, but it also didn't sound nearly as cool. Right now, if she were back at home, she'd be blogging about how she survived the descent into darkness. Here, climbing into the creepy cellar was just the beginning of her adventure.

Now it was time to hunt.

At least it would be once she found her way out of the cellar and back into the woods. Still, Lorelei felt pretty good about how things had gone so far. Everyone had seen the movie where the first person into the dark basement got torn apart by the monsters. She hated those goddamned movies and had seen more scenes like that than she ever cared to remember. Thankfully, the cellar was werewolf free, and she was ready to put the flimsiest of plans into motion.

Standing at the base of the ladder, Lorelei waited for her eyes to adjust to the lack of light after being inside the brightly lit cabin. When she couldn't see any better after a minute of staring into the inky darkness, Lorelei did what anyone would do. She put her hands out in front of her and inched forward until she ran into the wall.

Moving to her right, Lorelei ran her hands over the rough stone surface at about waist height. After a minute of searching her hand bumped into the metal grate. The damn thing wouldn't move, so she felt around the edges until she found a lock. Earl hadn't given her a key. He either didn't know about the lock or didn't think it would be a problem for her.

Closing her hand around the lock Lorelei gave it a firm tug. Some of the metal flaked off, but nothing happened. "If I have to go back up there and get a key, I'm going to be so pissed." Lorelei tugged at the lock a few more times. On the fifth try something snapped, and the lock opened.

A howl reverberated through the cellar.

"If that bastard sent me down here to become a werewolf snack, I'm going to rip his balls off." Lorelei tugged on the grate and wished she could see more of what she was doing.

Skill received: Night Vision

Rank: Novice level three

No one can ever tell you that walking around aimlessly in the dark doesn't have its benefits. Your determination to see in the dark while others use a torch has unlocked this skill.

You can now see in the dark 3% more effectively.

"Awesome." Lorelei smiled as she looked down at the grate again and could just make out enough of the hinges to see she had to lift it up to get inside of the tunnel.

Sometimes little things really do make a big difference.

Lorelei pulled on the grate and lifted it high enough that she could crawl into the tunnel behind it. The solid iron grate slammed back into place with an eerie finality. The tunnel was werewolf free. She didn't fancy her chances in an enclosed space with only her dagger for protection. To have any chance of making it out of this alive, she was going to need to get out into the forest first.

Earl had implied the tunnel wasn't very long, but hunched over in the dark, with howling noises coming from above, every foot felt like a mile. She'd never understood how people went caving. The thought of winding up trapped underground terrified her. If there was one thing she was determined to do in life, it was not to die doing something stupid.

Like fighting werewolves.

Shaking her head to clear it, the grin she'd been fighting returned to her lips. "It's only stupid if you can actually die." This was just a game. No reason not to risk it. The worst that could happen was a trip to see a cute girl with good coffee. With her tracking skills, Lorelei was sure she could follow the werewolves back to their lair, even if it took her a few days to return.

Not that hunting down the weres would do much for Evelyn and Earl. By the time she got back both of them would be dead.

Death wasn't much of a consolation prize.

Lorelei could be wrong, but she was pretty sure the NPCs in the game died for good. It'd be shitty for her to let them all die, especially when the family paid for her services in advance. It wasn't every day that contract labor got paid before the job was fulfilled, and she didn't feel like dying.

There was a small glow in front of her. Thirty seconds later, Lorelei was crouched under a tree looking down at the cabin from a distance. She hadn't even realized the tunnel had been moving upwards.

The cabin's wall's shook, and she heard a scream from inside. It didn't look like the werewolves had gotten in yet, but she understood why Evelyn was worried. These werewolves were as big as fuck, and they didn't seem to feel any pain as they rammed into the building. Lorelei couldn't imagine an old man facing down these creatures just so he could raise some pigs.

If some geriatric pig farmer could fend off a bunch of monsters, then so could she. Pulling Wolfsbane from her back, Lorelei threaded an arrow against the string. It would have been nice to take a few test shots with the bow before trying to hit a moving target, but she could compensate if her first arrow went astray. It just meant no fancy shooting.

And fancy shooting was her specialty.

Lorelei watched as one of the werewolves threw its body at the cabin with the ferocity of a rabid grizzly. She heard a snap as the monster hit and thought one of the timbers had broken, but the creature had just broken a bone in its shoulder. The werewolf stood up and shook off the pain.

With a smooth and practiced movement, Lorelei drew her bow. The brush of her fingers against her cheek sent her to that secret place in her mind that narrowed her focus to only the task at hand. The world seemed to slow down as her vision took over, and every other one of her senses dulled.

The second werewolf hit the cabin and stood up, roaring in rage. The bones in the creature's shoulder snapped back into place, and it howled into the night sky. The werewolves' cries cut off, and the creature's head snapped around. If Lorelei didn't know any better, she would have thought the werewolf was looking straight at her.

Oh, shit, it is *looking straight at me.*

The massive creature's nostrils flared, and Lorelei let the arrow go. Her arrow hit the werewolf in the center of the chest, and the world around her snapped back into focus. Before drawing another breath, she nocked an arrow and started running. As a Ranger, she could hear the other werewolf charging her. She didn't even need to look around to know which direction it was coming from.

From the sound of the werewolf's footsteps it wouldn't be more than a few seconds before it had her. This was the moment of truth. Her entire plan hinged on her execution of a singular ability.

"Mirage," she whispered, and the spell took hold.

She watched as the werewolf slammed into the magical projection of herself nearly twelve feet away. She hoped as the spell gained levels, it would also teleport her further from her starting position. With a bow in hand popping up further away from the target was ideal.

The magical projection was only a mirage, but the tree behind it was very real. Running face-first into a tree had about the kind of effect on the werewolf one would have expected. The monster fell to the ground clutching its head. The beast stood up, shaking its muzzle from side to side as if to clear its vision.

The werewolf wobbled in place for a moment and then turned in search of its missing prey.

"Split," Lorelei commanded as she fired an arrow.

From further away, the skill would have been able to hit three individual targets simultaneously. From twelve feet away, her spell split her single arrow into three arrows, right before all of them slammed into the werewolf, pinning it to the tree.

The creature let out a pitiful whine. It was the kind of sound that would have broken any dog owner's heart in two. The sound of an animal in pain was one of the worst things she'd ever heard. For now, she shoved aside her instinct to help, and launched another arrow, hoping to silence the werewolf for good.

The arrow struck home, and a few moments later she was looking at a naked man pinned to the tree by her artistry. She'd done it. Lorelei, the most badass of rangers, had killed her first werewolf. Now all she had to do was finish off the other one. Nocking another arrow, Lorelei turned to scan the cabin.

The werewolf was gone.

She dropped to a knee to make herself a smaller target as she scanned the forest. The reflexive move saved her life, as the claw trying to disembowel her slammed into her shoulder instead.

She found out what a bug felt like right before it crashed into a windshield.

The bow tumbled from Lorelei's numb fingers as her arm went limp. Her right arm hung uselessly against her side as she rolled back to her feet. Somehow her dagger found its way into her left hand, and she wove the tiny iron bade through the air in front of her with all the skill of a back-alley snake charmer.

Her eyes finally came back into focus, and she realized the body was gone, and so was the other werewolf. Her wound stopped bleeding. It wouldn't be a very fun game if you could bleed to death from a few cuts. In Lorelei's experience, it took something with a little more oomph to take her out.

That didn't stop her shoulder from burning from where the creature's claws had torn through her flesh. Fumbling the dagger back into its sheath Lorelei used her one working hand to pull her only cleansing potion from her belt. Using her teeth to pull out the corked lid, Lorelei chugged the potion down.

"Ugh, kinda tastes like Jägermeister." Lorelei made a face as her wounds healed.

The potion had cost her an arm and leg, but if it healed her wounds and kept her from becoming furry, then it was worth it.

It took her a second to find her bow in the dark. With the weapon secure, Lorelei started making her way back to the cabin. Things hadn't gone perfectly, but she was still alive and knew for certain that her new bow was going to be the key to her success in the region.

Letting out a weary sigh, Lorelei murmured, "I wonder if they have any bacon?"

CHAPTER FIVE

Barbara entered the lobby wearing a shirt with Tim's face on it.

"Like the shirt?" Barbara turned so he could see the back. It was a picture of Tim firing off a healing spell. There was a little chat bubble by his head that said, *"hope you like getting wet."*

He stood for a few moments, unsure of what to say. He looked from the shirt up to Barbara's searching gaze, and then back at the shirt three times before he tried to speak. What did you say to someone when they were wearing a shirt with your face on it?

"Urr." Tim hesitated.

His caseworker held up a hand. "Say no more, I already knew it was too much." Barbara flicked her hand, and the shirt shimmered for a moment before returning to a solid color. "That's better." She turned and opened the door. "Follow me."

"The shirt was kind of cool," Tim added lamely as he followed her through the door. He felt kind of bad that he didn't just let her have the moment. She'd taken the time to make the shirt, which was kind of nice, even if it was also a little creepy.

"Just something I put together for our meeting." Barbara continued down the hallway toward her office.

She stopped at a door with her name stenciled in gold against the frosted glass. "When you died so early in the game and then miraculously turned things around, well, you've kind of made me the office celebrity. People are always coming up and asking how my little project is going."

Barbara motioned for Tim to come inside and take a seat. "I tried to tell them I didn't have anything to do with your success." She paused, looking flustered. "But you know how hard it is to tell someone who's giving you a compliment that you don't deserve it. It just makes things awkward for everyone."

Tim could understand. He was the worst at taking compliments. Leaning forward, he looked around the small office like he had a juicy piece of gossip to drop, and he didn't want anyone else to hear it. "I don't mind if you take the credit, and I think you should keep wearing the shirt."

Tim was always wearing some kind of nerdy shirt with a character from a movie, game, or book on it. It was kind of his thing. Now he was having issues with making the leap from being a normal guy to being the character on the shirt. Tim was the one people were watching, and it was surreal.

He had mini freak out. "Wait, you can watch us in the game?"

Barbara's face turned serious. "Only when you are out adventuring. All bedrooms and bathrooms are strictly off-limits unless there is an emergency. Even then, it takes two people to verify the status of the emergency before they can view it. All viewings of emergency situations are then sent to compliance before being deleted permanently. Anyone just trying to catch a sneak peek of your character in more intimate moments would be fired immediately."

She tapped a few times on her tablet. "We take your privacy very seriously."

Tim sat back in his chair. It was good to know someone wasn't watching him every time he sat down on the can. He had a hard enough time farting in a public restroom when there was someone in the stall next to him. Sometimes he wished a few more people shared that same fear.

At least he could sleep easier knowing a million people weren't tuning in to see him take a dump.

There was part of him that wondered if it mattered. It wasn't exactly his body after all. The logical part of his brain knew a viewer wasn't seeing his real body, but the illogical side of his brain screamed, "I'm naked, get the fuck out."

Tim forced a weak smile. "I just never thought of people being able to watch us play before."

Tim knew that every solid MMO on the planet had a viewership. He'd personally watched how the Game Masters in MMOs could view what the players were doing while monitoring their keystrokes to try to figure out if they were playing or running a program to play for them. That was how the developers caught the bots and people trying to break the rules.

Barbara tapped a few more screens and set her tablet aside. "You can imagine how we have to kick things up a notch in certain situations. No player in our game will be subject to any kind of sexual assault. In fact, no form of continued harassment is allowed if it falls outside of normal game activities. We have no qualms about kicking offenders out of the game permanently."

Knowing there was someone watching the actions of the players to make sure they didn't step out of line with each other made him feel better about the whole system. He knew that you could kill, steal, and destroy in the game, but the company had to draw the line somewhere. He was happy with where they decided to do it. Being bullied, harassed, or assaulted in the game would feel just as real as it would out in the real world, making it completely unacceptable.

He probably read about those protections in his pamphlet, but they hadn't been as interesting as learning about the game, so he'd just skipped over them and moved onto the good stuff.

His caseworker smiled at him warmly. "Now, to the business at hand, I understand you are considering becoming an adventurer."

Tim felt a rush of excitement. "Yes, ma'am."

"You understand when you sign the paperwork, you will be giving up all of the free perks that came with your employment and will have to pay a monthly fee to maintain your POD use?"

Even the thought of paying a monthly fee couldn't take the shine off becoming an adventurer. "I do. I'm just not sure what all of the particulars are." Tim kept his eyes focused on Barbara. He didn't want to miss anything she said. While he had a basic idea of what he was getting into, now he was going to hear all of it.

"The POD fee is ten thousand dollars a month. The price is not negotiable. That keeps you alive and plugged in for a month. If you can't meet your monthly obligation, you have two choices. You can get unplugged, or you can be placed into whatever job we have available for you at the time."

Tim held up his hand to signal he had a question. Barbara nodded, so he jumped right in. "I was going to ask if I kept my job at the forge if it would waive the POD fees?"

Barbara grinned and wiggled her finger at him. "Oh, you are a sly one." She looked at her tablet to confirm something. "No one has ever asked me that before. It looks as though you can keep your position, but it only reduces the fee by fifty percent."

Looking at her tablet Barbara nodded to herself as she confirmed something else. "I actually have another option for you."

He couldn't wait to hear what this was going to be. "You've got my full attention."

"All of us have been asked to comb through our assigned clients and find one or two people who might be interesting enough to offer a streaming contract to. I was hoping you would be interested in applying to join." Barbara watched him for any indication of how he felt about the idea.

Tim didn't know what to say. Not being obligated to work at the forge would be a relief, even if he still wanted to learn more from IronBeard, but he wasn't sure he wanted people watching his every move. The last thing he wanted to do was give away all his secrets. "Tell me what I would need to do."

"What we need from you is four hours of in-game hours a day of content. You turn the stream on in your interface, do four hours of content, and log off. If you don't have four hours of constant content, you can break it into sections, but viewers don't like that as much." Barbara looked him over to make sure Tim was keeping up with what she was saying. "There is a countdown timer located in the stream tab, so you know when you've completed your required content for the day. You don't have to talk to the viewers. This is just a chance for us to highlight what people are doing in the game, and have our commentators talk about it." She gave him a knowing smile. "And for marketing purposes of course."

Tim wanted to make sure he understood her correctly. "So if I stream for four hours a day, you'll cover my POD fees. Anything else I need to know?"

"The contract covers you for a year. After that, it will be renewed or declined based on your viewership or the quality of marketing materials we can make from your content. Your stream isn't available in-game, so you don't have to worry about giving up too many of your secrets. By the time anyone from outside of the game catches up with you, it won't matter."

He nodded. "Because they can't see the stream in-game," Tim repeated to himself. That made him feel a little bit better. People coming into the game could still relay information to others, but that seemed like an expensive way to try to get ahead.

"Exactly." Barbara scrolled through a few screens. "The contract also comes with upgraded accommodations or a small stipend of gold."

The extra gold would always be nice. He wondered if he could have the stipend of gold converted into cash and sent directly to his family. It would take a huge load off his mind to know they were getting a few hundred extra dollars every month.

He felt like the contract was too simple. "What's the catch?"

"No catch." Barbara smiled warmly. "You get one year of free fees with the perk of your choice, for four hours a day of content. In a year if you do well, and I know you will, there will be another choice you have to make. You'll have to re-sign, go back to work, or pay your fee directly. There really isn't a downside. If you hate the job all you have to do is quit, and things will go right back to the way they were before you signed up."

Was there really an easier job in the world than streaming? All he had to do was turn his camera on for four hours a day, preferably when the group was doing something exciting. As an adventurer, coming up with four hours of content shouldn't be too difficult, especially when he didn't have to talk. Four hours was running a few bounties with the guild, or maybe a solid dungeon run. He could handle this but would need the help of every one of his guild members to make it work. Maybe when he renewed, he could try to get contracts for the rest of his team.

If he put in a good word for his guildmates now, Tim could at least get the idea of them also receiving streaming contracts on Barbara's radar. "What about the other players in my group? Will they be able to get contracts too?" It wasn't exactly subtle, but Tim hoped he'd done it in a way where she didn't feel pressured to say yes. Getting his guildmates streaming contracts was the best-case scenario for him, but it wasn't mandatory for his acceptance of the deal.

Barbara frowned at her tablet. "The contract is just for you, although if you took the monthly stipend of gold you could split it between your team."

"Can I just set up the gold to be converted at the going rate and have the money sent to my parents?"

Once the market kiosk was set up, he would have more than enough gold to handle all of the guild's incidental expenses, and maybe even be able to give the members a small stipend. Things were working out perfectly, but knowing his parents were taken care of too was the icing on the cake.

"I don't see why that would be a problem," Barbara bubbled.

Now Tim could focus on ways to get his guild the same contract he had. None of the guild mentioned problems with covering their monthly POD fee yet. If the fee was covered for his group, and they all had a little extra gold in their pockets, it would make life so much easier for all of them. Tim was pretty sure viewers would like watching battles from multiple points of view.

Until his team reaped the benefits of their own contracts, Tim was going to have to contribute more to the guild than he had before. It wasn't fair to split the quest rewards evenly when they were all taking on more risk than he was. If he couldn't get them streaming contracts, Tim could at least make sure none of them had to struggle with any in-game expenses.

"Is it possible for my group to earn contracts based on the quality of the content I provide?" Tim asked, hopefully.

"There is always a chance we could get fans asking for more. If that happens, it's a no brainer for us to sign them." Barbara smiled sheepishly. "Personally, I want to know more about what Cassie is doing."

"Wouldn't we all." Tim laughed. Sometimes he felt like such a bad friend. He really needed to spend more time learning about what his party wanted to get out of their time in the game. Some of them might not want to stream or might not need to. The choice was going to be up to each of them when the time came.

"I'd like to talk to them about it first, but I get the feeling this is a decide right now kind of position for me." Tim watched Barbara, hoping he was wrong and could talk to his friends before he agreed to put them on camera.

"Since we only have limited contact, it's a sign-now-or-never-get-the-chance-again kind of deal." She tapped the clock on her tablet. "Time's a-wastin'. Speaking of time, our stipend is based on real-world months, not in-game, so you will receive one hundred gold every three months to do with as you will."

Splitting the gold between his guild members would be ineffective. He could make more gold for them just by grinding content with the group. Twenty-one months in the game might as well have been an eternity, considering how much they had accomplished since entering *The Etheric Coast.*

Tim knew sending the money home to his parents was the right call. A quick check of the currency exchange showed that one hundred gold was worth about three thousand real-world dollars. It was a good deal, and more than Tim had expected, but he knew in a year, that number would be closer to three hundred bucks.

Inflation was a real bitch.

In-game currency values had a way of decreasing the longer the game was active. For now, a thousand dollars a month would make things infinitely easier for his parents. It was amazing how much that amount could change someone's life. It was enough to take care of the unexpected, and it gave them a safety net. It wasn't enough to put them on Easy Street, but they wouldn't struggle.

Knowing his family was going to be better off made accepting the job a no-brainer. "Count me in."

Holding out her tablet, Barbara stated, "Just put your thumb on the green circle."

He pushed his thumb against the tablet and the screen flashed green. Barbara turned the tablet back around to face her and started working her way through a few screens before looking up. "Looks like we're all set. When you get to Promethia, you will find a streaming tab in your user interface. It's pretty user-friendly, so I doubt you'll have any issues."

She stood up and extended her hand. "Until next time." They shook. "Now go do something cool, so I can rub it in my coworkers' faces." She tapped her shirt with her pen, and the image of Tim reappeared.

Barbara stepped around her desk and opened the door, revealing the portal back to *Etheric Coast.*

Tim stopped at the door and shook Barbara's hand again. "Thank you."

"Don't think anything of it." She angled her body so Tim could move in front of the door, then she pushed him into the portal. "If he keeps this up, I'm going to get a promotion."

A quick tap of her finger on the screen of her tablet closed the portal. Barbara looked down at the screen. "Who's up next?"

CHAPTER SIX

"I think I'm going to puke," Tim said as he swayed unsteadily.

ShadowLily placed her hands on her hips and frowned. "Just hurry it up already. We've been waiting here for hours."

"Don't worry, boss, I can incinerate it. No one has to know." JaKobi grinned.

Tim waved the mage away. "Let's try not to burn the temple down before we meet Brother Colton." Taking a deep breath, Tim stood up. A quick flick of his wrist and his cleanse spell washed over him, taking away the worst of his pain.

"You wound me." JaKobi sounded affronted. "My control of the eternal flame is so precise, nothing burns unless I want it to."

Thinking about how much he hated traveling back into the game world from visiting Barbara, Tim focused his attention on JaKobi. "Are you sure?" He squinted at the mage, looking for any sign of deceit. "I hear things."

JaKobi spun around and fixed his eyes on ShadowLily. "That was one time, and it was only an outhouse."

"An outhouse you had to pay to rebuild," the assassin replied casually as she turned away from the mage to look at Tim. "To be fair, he *has* been getting better."

"See!" JaKobi gestured wildly at Tim. "I told you so." He pointed at the ground. "Now puke. I want to see if I can burn it before it hits the pavers."

Tim shook his head. "As delightful as that sounds, I really am feeling better."

The toe of JaKobi's boots scuffed the worn tiles as he kicked at them. "I never get to have any fun."

Not wanting to steal the man's thunder, Tim decided to give him a little boost. "How about we set up a time and you can show me your improved control? I know Ernie would be keen for any kind of anti-vomit help."

"I'm not sure cleaning up vomit from the bar floor is the best use of my skills. Maybe I could get some wooden stakes and have ShadowLily throw them at me. I could burn them out of the air before they hit." JaKobi looked excited now. "You know, put on a real show."

The assassin gave him a wicked grin. "I kind of like that idea."

"You just want to see if you can hit him," Tim said with a laugh as they started walking the short distance to Brother Colton's chambers. "But if he's willing to risk it, I'm not going to stop you."

"Booyah!" JaKobi leaned back with his elbows at his side. His hands were shaped like little guns. The fire mage made a couple quick shooting gestures, and little pops of fire snapped into existence three feet in front of him like little fireworks.

Tim couldn't help but grin. The small display showed him all he needed to know about the mage's control over his magic. Maybe he'd been underestimating the man because of his rocky start with the guild. Since then, JaKobi had proven himself as a not only loyal but competent companion. He was going to have to find a proper way for the fire mage to show off his talents.

Like when he saved my ass this morning.

Until he found the right place to showcase JaKobi's talents, Tim was happy to let him have his little moment at the bar. If Shadow-Lily found a way to hit the fire mage, and Tim was sure she would, then at least it wasn't his ass on the chopping block this time.

After the teacup incident, he'd never been the same.

Tim thought of what viewers would have thought if they had been able to watch that particular debacle. He started to chuckle and noticed ShadowLily's questioning gaze. Quickly turning the chuckle into a cough, he checked his map and pointed ahead of them. "This way."

The group followed Tim until they were standing outside of Brother Colton's annex. He'd spent the walk thinking about how to tell them about his streaming contract. When they reached their destination, Tim was kicking himself for not telling them right away. There was no way his friends wouldn't be happy for him.

Pausing at the door, he turned to look at his girlfriend and then shifted his gaze to the fire mage. "Before we go in there is something I want to tell you."

JaKobi grinned. "When you say it like that, it sounds like you're about to die."

Tim let out a laugh and felt the tension fall from his shoulders. The fire mage was right. He was setting this up for some kind of dramatic reveal like Elon with a baseball in hand and a panel of unbreakable glass in front of him.

"Dying isn't on the agenda," Tim said, feeling more relaxed by the moment. "I did however receive a streaming contract."

"No way!" ShadowLily jumped into his arms. "That's amazing!"

JaKobi leaned back and examined Tim as if seeing him for the first time. "Makes sense, I guess."

ShadowLily gave Tim a kiss and then backed up a step. "Wait, are we on camera right now? Oh, shit, how does my hair look?"

"Your hair looks great," Tim replied with the knowledge of a much older man. He learned a long time ago that when a woman asked you a question about her outfit, hair, or weight, the answer was always, you look amazing. "But you don't have to worry yet. I only need to get four hours of content a day. The reason I bring it up is because filming the questline would be the easiest way to do it."

A mirror appeared out of thin air and hovered in front of ShadowLily. She quickly checked all of her buckles and straps to make sure they were tied and looking good before tying her hair into a ponytail. Happy with what she saw, ShadowLily dismissed the mirror. "I'm ready."

JaKobi looked at her in awe. "You have a magic mirror?"

"Bonus item." ShadowLily shrugged. "Comes in handy."

Tim smiled. He was thinking of a million ways a mirror could be handy, but none of them were about checking out his look. He realized that since coming into the game he hadn't been self-conscious at all. His body looked the way he wanted, and the only time Tim worried about clothing was when he changed outfits to avoid detection.

Plus, as long as the others didn't have contracts he wouldn't be on film anyways. It kind of took the sting out of the old adage of the camera adds ten pounds. *Wait, did that even happen in games?* Tim brought his thoughts back on track. "So you guys are ok with being on camera?"

"Whatever you need, boss." JaKobi grinned. "I'll get to show off my mad skillz."

ShadowLily gave him a sassy look. "I already told you I'm ready to be famous." She pretended to pose for a few photos. "But seriously, we're just business as usual, right?"

"The only difference is the world gets to watch us get crushed if we fail." Tim smiled. "No pressure."

It wasn't like viewers weren't used to watching wipes. He'd watched plenty of people get steamrolled in raids, hoping to find one little tip that might push his own group past the encounter. It got to the point as a viewer that you found yourself rooting for a win, and if the players died, it felt like you died with them. But when they won, you felt like part of it. It was the same rush he got from cheering for his favorite sports team.

There was really something in games for everyone.

A few seconds later, Tim was going through the menus on his user interface. The last thing he wanted to do was screw up his stream before it even got started. Tim found the tab Barbara said would be there, quickly checked all the settings, and turned the camera on. He pointed at his two friends. "We're live."

"Like live, live?" ShadowLily asked.

Tim looked into his settings and found that he didn't have the ability to do any editing. There did seem to be some grayed-out tabs for those kinds of features in the future. So live meant live. No retakes, no do-overs.

Tim was about to respond when the door to Brother Colton's annex opened, and a very unhappy priest snapped at them. "Do you mind? I'm trying to get some work done in here!"

"I'm sorry for the interruption," Tim said, trying his best to sound sincere. Smiling warmly at the infuriated priest, he continued speaking, "But you might just be the man we're looking for."

The priest laughed. "I doubt that. My research isn't very interesting to most people. If you need help finding someone though, I'd be more than happy to help." He winked. "Especially if it speeds you on your way."

Tim wasn't exactly sure what to make of the man. After his initial outburst, he seemed friendly enough. He kind of reminded him of the students in the library. You so much as farted, and half of them couldn't study for the rest of the day. The other half snickered to themselves and carried on.

"Maybe you can help me." Tim watched the priest in the doorway to see his reaction. "The high priest tasked me with seeking out a Brother Colton for information."

"Oh, you are the warrior of light he mentioned." Brother

Colton looked Tim over. "Forgive me. I was kind of expecting more."

Tim's cheeks flushed red as he looked at ShadowLily. "This game sure has a way of making sure your ego never gets too big."

"Don't worry, I still think you're pretty great," the assassin gushed. "Even if you're not all that impressive."

"Bam-snap," JaKobi said with a grin.

Laughing, Tim turned back to Brother Colton. "Why don't you show us what you've put together before my looks take any more hits?"

Looking at the three of them like they might have lost their minds, Brother Colton took a step back into the room and waved for them to follow. "I was just putting the final touches on my presentation. Please follow me."

Casting a quick glance at the others, Tim nodded and started to walk into the room. His chest ran into something hard, and he looked down to see ShadowLily's arm blocking his path. His eyes followed the path of her arm until he was looking in her eyes. He was trying to figure out why she was standing in his way.

"It wasn't too long ago that a lot of these priests wanted to see you dead." ShadowLily shoved him back a step. "Maybe I should go first."

Tim didn't think anyone in the temple still wanted him dead, but maybe that was wishful thinking. He'd personally killed several high-ranking officials. Most people probably didn't know about that though. He kind of hoped the people in the temple would remember him as the returner of their precious artifacts, and the man who vanquished Cardinal Jepsom's killers.

As far as anyone else knew, Tim had been there to watch the Cardinal's promotion, not to assassinate him. So when he killed the wraiths, it should have made him the least likely target inside of these walls.

But he'd also learned a long time ago not to interfere with ShadowLily when she was determined to do something, and he really didn't want to die. Instead of trying to push past her, Tim took a step back and gave her a not so subtle wink. "As you wish."

JaKobi pushed between them. "Cassie was right about you two. Get a room already." A flame ignited in his hand as he strode into the annex. "I'll take care of this."

ShadowLily rushed in after the mage. "Try being a little more subtle," she whispered in his ear before disappearing from sight.

"I can do subtle," JaKobi hissed with mock outrage. The flames roaring in the palm of his hand extinguished, and a single tiny flame sprouted from the end of his index finger.

Tim sent a healing orb at the flames, extinguishing them as he stepped past the fire mage.

JaKobi shook the water from his hand and yelled at Tim's back, "Everyone's a critic!"

Once they reached Brother Colton's rooms inside the annex, Tim realized there was nothing to worry about. The room was much too small to hide an assassin. With the four of them, the space already felt cramped, and it wasn't like there was a ton of furniture. The room had a cot in one corner, a writing desk against the opposite wall, and a chamber pot.

Along one of the chamber's four walls was a giant map of the city. Brother Colton was standing in front of it looking rather annoyed.

"As you can plainly see on the wall, this is the city of Promethia." He looked at all of them to make sure they at least had a basic understanding of where they were. When none of them appeared confused Brother Colton continued. "I've isolated three outbreak locations. All of them need to be dealt with posthaste."

Tim watched as Brother Colton tapped the map in three places. Each of the locations instantly had a picture of a wraith above them with a number next to it. The first location was a warehouse building located off the docks to the north of the market. Across from the warehouse on the other side of town looked to be an abandoned wharf. Tim hadn't spent too much time out of the slums or the market district, but he thought it was a little odd for any wharf in this city to be abandoned.

He scanned the map for a few more minutes before zeroing in on the third mark. This one hit a little close to home. The wraiths weren't currently in the slums, but this location was closest and probably looking to branch out. There was a lot less protection in the slums and zero help from most of the player base. With his district at risk, Tim knew where he would be going first.

Leaving the people of the slums to fend for themselves wasn't going to happen on Tim's watch. Most of the city guards didn't enter unless it was to arrest someone. Joe's new restaurant was starting to turn some heads, although a fifteen percent discount for city guards might have had something to do with it. But most of the people couldn't care less if the entire slums burned down.

But Tim cared. He'd invested his entire future in the slums.

If no one else was going to look out for the poor, hard-working people of Promethia, then Tim would be their champion. The city guard and the temple priests could keep the rest of the areas secure until they removed the threat to the slums. Reaching out, he shifted the marks on the map until the wraith with a one over its head was where he wanted it.

That looks a little better.

"I've created these little indicators for two purposes." Brother Colton pointed toward the picture of the wraith on the first building. "One to indicate the type of creature we believe to be inside, and secondly to account for the building's importance to the city."

The priest looked at the map for a moment. "These seem to be out of order." He t frowned at Tim.

JaKobi grinned, ignoring Brother Colton's comment. "So, we should go to the building marked with a one first." He reached out and touched the location on the map. "Close enough to home that we can walk there."

Brother Colton looked shocked by JaKobi's statement. He was

clearly wondering how three adventurers from the slums could be responsible for such a huge undertaking.

"Maybe we could stop and get a strawberry shortcake from Joe's first," JaKobi said, thinking about the best dessert in the city. "You know I fight better with a belly full of deliciousness."

Tim looked at the map for a second and back to the fire mage. "Let's head back to the inn and round up the others. I'm thinking we save the dessert until after the fight. Something sweet to celebrate the victory."

The priest nodded his head as if he liked Tim's plan better. "At least one of you seems to understand the importance of the issue. These hubs of infestation cannot continue to be ignored. Over time their influence will grow and further corrupt the city."

Brother Colton seemed to think for a moment and then leaned closer to Tim. "Right now, the city guard and my fellow priests are containing the outbreak, but we need someone to shift the tide in our favor or the city could be overrun."

Now the priest was almost whispering. "Can I trust you with something I haven't told anyone else?"

Motioning for the others to give them a moment alone, Tim focused on the priest. "Of course you can."

When the others had left the room, Brother Colton closed the door. He turned and looked at Tim. "It is of the utmost importance that what I am about to tell you never leaves this room." Wringing his hand nervously, he continued. "We've been able to isolate the worst of the attacks to these three locations, but we still haven't been able to find the source of the outbreak. Until we find the source and stop it, the entire city is at risk. Will you help me?"

Quest Received: Panic at the Temple

Wraiths have been spotted in the city, and for the most part, have been contained to three separate buildings. The source of the wraiths has yet to be found. Find the source of the wraith outbreaks and put an end to it.

This quest must be completed after Get the Wraith Out of Here for the highest possible rewards.

Reward: Variable

Accept Quest: <Yes/No>

Tim quickly accepted the quest. "I'd be delighted to help."

Rushing to the door to hurry the adventurer along, Brother Colton flung it open. The priest looked happy for the first time since opening his door to scream at them. "No time like the present to get started. I'll let you know if I have any other news."

Reaching out to shake Colton's hand, Tim replied, "I can be found at the Blue Dagger inn. If anything comes up, look for me there."

"In the slums." Brother Colton shook his head. "If I have need of you, I'll send someone to fetch you or deliver a letter." He waited just long enough for Tim to step outside before slamming the door shut.

Looking over at his teammates, Tim almost giggled. "He's a bit of a strange fellow."

JaKobi smiled and started walking back toward the inn. "You can say that again."

ShadowLily grabbed Tim's hand and yanked him after the fire mage. "So, what was with all the secrecy?"

Tim quickly filled the two of them in on the details. When they got back to the inn, he'd try to share the quest so they could all benefit from the reward. It didn't seem right for his team to be missing out on extra rewards and experience when he literally couldn't do the quests without them.

If this worked, the guild would benefit from all of his crazy quests as much as he did, but he didn't want to try to share the quest until they were all together. "Let's get back to the inn, I have an idea."

"Don't let Cassie hear you say that," JaKobi said as he casually tossed a fireball back and forth between his hands.

"Hey, she loves my plans," Tim protested as he hurried to catch up with them.

"Love might be too strong of a word." ShadowLily elbowed him in the ribs.

"Ow." Tim rubbed his side. "It's not my fault I'm flawless."

"Just keep telling yourself that," ShadowLily said with a squeal before she started running.

Cackling like a witch, Tim rushed past JaKobi as he chased her. "I'll get you my pretty," he shouted as he ran down the street. Tim turned off his stream. No one got to see what was coming next except for him.

JaKobi watched the two of them as he started to whistle a tune. "Looks like I've got plenty of time for that strawberry shortcake now."

CHAPTER SEVEN

"Four hours," Cassie muttered. "I thought this was important."

"It is," Tim stammered, a blush creeping up his checks.

ShadowLily sauntered into the room. She grabbed a rumple-berry off the table and sliced it open with her dagger. She looked up and realized everyone was staring at her. "What?"

JaKobi pointed at Gaston and held up four fingers as a smile broke out on his face. The burly assassin nudged him, almost cracking up. Tim watched all of this in horror as Cassie rounded on her best friend.

"Four hours!" Cassie roared.

"Don't be jelly," ShadowLily retorted before slipping another slice of rumpleberry into her mouth.

Cassie's eyes bulged. "You know I've got things I'd like to do too. I can't always just be waiting around for you two to get started."

Setting down her knife and the remains of the rumpleberry, ShadowLily stood up and embraced her friend. "I'm sorry I kept you waiting." She smiled at Tim over Cassie's shoulder. "It was his fault, I swear."

Cassie broke away from her friend and turned to glare at Tim. "I knew it!"

Tim couldn't stop himself from blushing again. There wasn't anything more embarrassing than going downstairs to a room full of people after having sex. It was like being back in his house on campus all over again. Trying to sneak a girl down the stairs was the new walk of shame. Thankfully for him, he wasn't ashamed of this girl one bit.

He was a little bit upset with himself for getting carried away.

Trying to smile but mostly feeling awkward, Tim just shrugged his shoulders as if to say what else could I do. "I'm sorry I kept everyone waiting." The two guys burst out laughing, and even Cassie had a grin on her face.

"And you said I couldn't do it." Cassie pointed at JaKobi.

The fire mage held up his hands in protest. "That wasn't me. My exact words were," he paused to make air quotes for each of his next words. "'I don't think you should do it.'"

"But you still bet on if I could," Cassie protested.

"Gold before bros," JaKobi said as he slipped a small stack of coins to Cassie.

Gaston tossed his own bag toward the tank. "I really didn't think she could do it, or I wouldn't have suggested it."

Tim snorted. What else did he expect from his friends? He'd left them alone in the presence of Gaston for too long. The assassin wasn't good at waiting around. It probably took him all of ten minutes to start taking bets on how long before they reappeared. He made a mental note to save the bedroom activities until after guild business was completed.

Motioning for everyone to start heading toward the door Tim said, "Let's get going."

"Wasn't there something you wanted to do before we left?" ShadowLily asked as she finished her snack.

"Not this again," Cassie said, rolling her eyes.

It took him a moment to remember what she was talking

about, and then it hit him. "When we went to see Brother Colton, he gave me a quest. I wanted to see if I could share it, but I wanted to wait until we were all together in case I could only share it once."

"He gave you a quest?" JaKobi looked confused. "I thought that bastard just wanted to get rid of us."

"Maybe that's why he gave you the quest." Gaston chuckled. "I do that to my crew all the time. Idle hands and all that."

Tim pulled up his user interface and located the quest **Panic at the Temple**. A quick double-check confirmed everyone was listed in his group so he clicked on the quest to check for options. On the bottom right-hand corner there was a small button with a plus sign on it. Tim hovered over the icon and smiled as the tooltip came up, **Convert To Group**. There didn't seem to be a traditional share button, so he decided to give it a try.

Panic at the Temple has been converted to a group quest. Rewards and challenges will be scaled based on the number of players in your party.

Would you like to proceed: <Yes/No>

Looking around the room, he could see that everyone was reading a notification except Gaston. He lifted an eyebrow in question. "Are you not eligible for the quest?"

"While I can tag along on your adventures, I can't accept quests. The system has also banned me from receiving rewards meant for players, such as items from chests. Apparently, I broke a few rules when I helped during our dungeon run."

Gaston grinned like a fox. "On the plus side, I also can't harm you and take all of your stuff." His smile took on a more shark-like appearance. "Be thankful for that. All of you are pretty easy targets."

ShadowLily pulled a throwing knife free and threw it so it stuck in the wooden planks at the assassin's feet. "We'll see about that."

Plucking the blade free with casual ease, Gaston sauntered

over to ShadowLily and placed the hilt in her hand. Without saying a word, he continued past her. When he was standing next to Tim at the door, he leaned in close and whispered, "She's good with a blade. You better keep her happy at all times muchacho."

Tim slapped the assassin on the back as he followed him outside. He didn't know how the system controlled what the NPCs said, but somehow when an NPC gave him a nudge, it was rock-solid advice. Keeping your woman happy was relationship 101.

Not that it was an easy task.

As a man, he was woefully unprepared to deal with the trials and tribulations of womanhood. All he could do was hang on, make sure she was safe, and love her like there was no tomorrow. Tim was prepared to do every one of those things until the day he died.

Pulling up his quest log, Tim looked it over to see what changes happened once the quest had been converted from a single-player quest into a group one.

The Quest Panic at the Temple has been successfully converted to a group quest. Because this quest is part of a chain, including the quest Get the Wraith Out of Here, both quests have been converted into group quests.

Players required for completion.

Cassie

ShadowLily

JaKobi

Tim

Difficulty and rewards have been balanced for four players.

"I guess you guys are in this for the long haul now," Tim smirked. Finding a way to get his guild members extra rewards by joining in on his quests as full participants was awesome.

"Wouldn't have clicked yes, if I wasn't down to kick some wraith ass." JaKobi created a circle of fire and jumped through it. "Let's get started."

Cassie was grinning. "And the bass keeps running, running and running, running."

ShadowLily tucked her throwing knife back into her bandolier. "That shit was my jam back in the day. I wish I could link my music library into the game. Kicking ass is so much easier with a great soundtrack."

Tim followed them out the door as he turned the stream back on. "I'm sure I could hire a few musicians to follow you around."

Cassie nudged her shoulder into ShadowLily. "Are you sure you love this guy?"

"He's a keeper," she said as they stepped out into the cool night air.

Tim ran past them, screaming. "You hear that, Promethia? I'm a keeper!"

"Maybe you should rethink things." Cassie delivered the jab with a playful grin.

"No takesie-backsies." JaKobi chuckled as he watched Tim leave confused citizens in his wake. Life must have gotten so much stranger for the citizens of Promethia since they arrived.

The building looked bigger than it had when Brother Colton pointed it out on the map.

Tim looked at the structure and wondered just how many of the wraiths were inside. How many of the monsters could they tackle when Tim was the only one who could hurt them? If the others could hold the wraiths off so Tim could blast them one at a time, things would be fine, but if any of the wraiths got past his defenders, they would all be overrun.

He should have thought about this before, but he'd been preoccupied with his class change. When they returned to the inn, Tim had been distracted by other things. Instead of doing his job and setting the guild up for success, he'd been relaxing like this was going to be easy. If his first series of quests in the game were any indication of how things would go, it would only get harder from here.

I'm really going to have to start paying more attention and stop winging it all the time.

If Tim had spent his time preparing properly, he would have thought of using the one skill the goddess had given him specifically to use in times of need. When Eternia brought Cassie back to life, she'd wanted something in return.

What would he have to give her this time?

It didn't really matter what she requested of him if the benefit was big enough to his group. He wanted all of them to be able to participate in the fight. What good was a group quest if only one person could do any real damage?

Not sure exactly how to activate the skill appeal to the goddess, Tim knelt on the broken cobbles, thought about what he wanted, and prayed for something to happen.

The world seemed to freeze around him, and Tim wondered if only gods could slow time, or if that was something he might learn on his journey to becoming a Grandmaster.

How cool would that be?

Tim didn't care if a spell like that was overpowered as long as he had it to use, and other people didn't. That might seem selfish, but the last thing he wanted was some boss monster slowing down time and taking out his whole team. If he could flip the script, it would be an easy experience all day, every day.

His mind hit pause on his ramblings as the goddess appeared.

Eternia floated down from the heavens. Blue motes of light swirled around her, almost seeming to slow her lazy descent to the ground. Hovering with her toes inches above the cobbles, she walked toward Tim as if on solid ground.

Right before she spoke, the goddess' feet touched the earth. "My time here is short. Vitaria is calling her army to her, and I must do what I can to stop them."

Tim stayed down on one knee, unsure how he should address a goddess. He decided wasting her time with a giant explanation might anger her, so he decided just to ask for what he needed to get the job done. "While I have the ability to fight the wraiths, none of my guild members can hurt them. I need a way to change that."

Eternia looked down at her follower, and a small smile tickled at the corners of her lips. "A wise man asks for a favor that benefits both parties. Because your cause acts to further my own in this realm, I shall give you a gift."

The goddess placed a hand on Tim's shoulder. "Rise warrior of the faithful and accept the gifts that have been given."

Tim climbed to his feet, and two notifications slammed into his vision.

Buff Granted: Armor of Eternia (Novice 1)

A little divine protection for when normal armor just won't do. This spell reduces the damage taken by anyone in your party by all dark magic by 5% and reduces the chance of succumbing to weakness by 5%. Lasts for one hour, can be canceled at any time via the status effects menu page.

Tim knew two things almost instantly. The first was that this spell would come in handy, and with the quest they were on now, he'd be able to level it fairly quickly. He also picked up on the fact there was a status effects menu page. He wondered just how many things he was missing by not digging into more of the game's systems?

Now wasn't the time to worry about extra menu screens. Not knowing about the screens hadn't stopped him from progressing and being offered a streaming contract, so why worry about them now?

Buff Granted: Attacks of the Faithful. (Novice 1)

When fighting the forces of darkness, a soldier of the light needs a proper weapon. Since weapons of divine providence are in short supply, the goddess has bestowed upon you the

ability to convert weapon damage into holy damage. Attacks of the Faithful convert fifty percent of normal weapon or magic damage into holy damage. This ability affects the entire party and can be canceled at any time via the status effects page.

Tim looked into the goddess' eyes, feeling immensely grateful. The gifts she had just given him were more than he ever expected. Eternia's generosity inspired him to take this task seriously. The fate of Promethia hung in the balance. It was time to stop fucking around.

"Thank you, Eternia. I promise not to let you down."

The goddess smiled as she reached out to take Tim's hands in her own. "Use my gifts well and secure the city quickly. Darkness is coming."

"As you command." Tim inclined his head in a show of respect.

Eternia let go of Tim's hands. He expected her to fly off in the same manner she had descended, but instead, her body burst apart in a brilliant explosion of blue light. He was left standing with his hands in the air, looking at nothing.

"What in the hell are you doing?" JaKobi asked as he watched Tim with concern.

"Time to get your head back in the game, lover boy. We've got a quest to complete," Cassie said with a grin.

ShadowLily was watching him intently. She knew Tim well enough to read him like an open book. Something had happened, and she wanted to know what it was. "Spill it."

Hastily putting his arms back down to his sides, Tim faced his group. "I asked the Goddess Eternia for help, and she gave me a few new skills to help us on our quest."

"No way." JaKobi snorted in disbelief and then started looking around. "She was here? Just now?"

"She was." Tim smiled at the looks on their faces. None of them had interacted directly with one of the game's deities as far as he knew, so they didn't understand the nature of the experience.

Goddess here one second, gone the next.

"Let me show you." Before anyone could protest, Tim cast the first of his newly acquired buffs. While everyone was trying to figure out what he'd done, he cast the second spell.

ShadowLily dove into his arms. "I can hurt them now."

"I still don't know if you can kill them. My guess is yes, but when we enter this building, I want to take it slow and steady. One room at a time, nothing left alive behind us, and none of the wraiths can escape."

Pointing vaguely in the direction of the two other wraith nests, Tim continued, "The last thing we want is for the others to find out we're coming."

"Wow, so Eternia was really here?" JaKobi looked impressed. "Do you think I can meet her next time?"

"It doesn't hurt to ask." Tim patted the fire mage on the shoulder. "I'm sure you'd like her."

JaKobi's eyes were distant as if lost in a daydream. "A real goddess! That's so fucking cool."

"How about you stop fanboying over Eternia and get ready to kick some ass," Cassie growled. With her buffs in place, she was ready to bash some wraith heads together.

Tim looked at their tiny tank and took a slight bow. "After you, milady."

Cassie sprinted toward the building. Six feet away from the door, she jumped and launched a kick at the cracked door. When her foot connected, it shattered. Turning, she waved at the group. "Time to sack up."

JaKobi sprinted after her. "This sack's for you."

Laughing, the rest of the group followed the fire mage into the building.

CHAPTER EIGHT

"Thank the goddess, we're saved!" Evelyn shouted.

The pig farmer's wife started sprinting down the hill with her son in her arms. She was making a beeline straight for the front gates of Tristholm. Her husband chased after her, his crossbow in hand, as Lorelei scanned the trees to either side of the road for an attack.

Since leaving the pig farm, they had been running and walking almost nonstop. They hadn't dared to stop moving for long after the first attack. Two more werewolves tried to take them by surprise as they drew closer to the city. Lorelei knew how appealing the safety of the solid stone walls looked, but she also didn't want to die before they reached them.

Running straight down a road carved out of the forest seemed like a good way to die.

Lorelei's sense danger ability triggered, and her eyes tracked toward movement along the right side of the road. There wasn't time to call out. Instead, she nocked an arrow and took aim. There wasn't a flag or anything handy for her to judge the breeze by, so she just had to guess.

The arrow jumped from her bow, sailing high into the air above the running couple.

To anyone watching from the walls it must have looked like Lorelei was firing at a woman and her child as they ran away in fear, but that wasn't the case. The arrow reached its zenith and started its mad descent back to earth. With each passing second, the arrow picked up deadly velocity.

A snarl sounded from the right side of the path. Earl pushed Evelyn behind him as he leveled his crossbow at the forest. Lorelei started sprinting toward them. With dexterity that would have made Robin Hood blush, she pulled the next arrow from her quiver and let it loose as the werewolf burst from the trees.

Earl fired reflexively and missed the monster by a country mile. He tossed the useless crossbow to the side, knowing he'd never be able to load it again in time. Sporting a hatchet and a small skinning knife, Earl faced down the nine-foot werewolf alone.

The werewolf watched the man for a moment, almost mocking him for the weak display. The creature's hind legs tensed as it readied to lunge for the kill.

"Not today, fucker," Lorelei whispered as she let the next arrow fly.

The werewolf jumped just as Lorelei's first arrow plunged into its back. Earl managed to cover his family as the snarling wolf skidded to a halt. Pulling the arrow free from its spine, the beast turned to see the archer running toward it. The werewolf almost seemed to be smiling, excited about facing more of a challenge.

Then her second arrow plunged into the werewolf's eye, killing it instantly.

"Keep running!" Lorelei shouted as she scanned the woods on either side of them. Where there was one werewolf, there could be more. Wolves were known as pack animals for a reason.

Earl didn't bother picking up his crossbow. He just pulled Evelyn to her feet and started running.

Passing the naked man lying in the road with an arrow sticking out of his eye, Lorelei dipped to pick up the crossbow. Her movements were so smooth she didn't have to break stride. With a quick flick of her wrist, she placed the bulky weapon in her inventory and kept her own bow at the ready as she continued chasing after the fleeing family.

A howl sounded from behind Lorelei as she sprinted toward the city gates. Multiple werewolves responded to the call, letting loose with their own cries. The sun dipped over the horizon and turned the sky a dark pink. Lorelei could hear the wolves running down the road behind her, but she refused to look back. On top of the walls torches were being lit, and she could see Tristholm's giant ballistae turning in her direction.

A thunderclap rolled over the valley as one of the giant ballistae released its payload. Lorelei crouched reflexively as the giant bolt flew over her head. The ground shook when a bolt as big as her hit the road behind her. Her balance wavered for a moment when she heard the pinned werewolf thrashing on the ground behind her.

"Holy furballs that was close." Her breath was coming in ragged gasps, but Lorelei forced herself to keep moving.

Evelyn reached the first set of gates, and a small door opened. She shoved her son into the waiting arms before rushing inside. Earl followed her through the door half a heartbeat later. The door started to close, and then Earl reappeared in the gap. Lorelei put everything she had into her sprint as two more bolts flew overhead.

Skidding to a stop just outside the gate, Lorelei looked back. Three men were pinned to the road by the giant bolts fired by the ballistae. Her eyes moved past the dead men toward the hill she'd just sprinted down. Standing on the peak of the hill was a lone werewolf. The setting sun outlined his silhouette against the pinkish sky. The creature reared back and let out a howl that shook the entire valley.

The werewolf gave the guards a very human gesture involving a single finger before turning and running the other way.

Earl reached out and pulled Lorelei inside. The wooden door slammed back into place, and two huge iron bolts were slotted through thick brackets on either side to hold it shut. Earl's face was pale as the shock of almost being torn apart flooded his system. He fell to his knees, retching. When he finished vomiting, the guards pulled him roughly to his feet.

A fourth man came into view. This guard was different. His helmet had a stripe of purple hair down the center, almost like the red horsehair that adorned helmets of the Roman centurions. As he continued toward them, Lorelei noticed that six grim-faced soldiers were spreading out behind him, and all of them had hands on the hilts of their swords.

Lorelei looked at the seven men coming their way and the two guards already holding Earl up, while a third tended to Evelyn and her son. There was no fighting her way out of this without risking her life. She took the arrow from her bow and noticed one of the guards flinch, but all she did was place it back in her quiver to show she wasn't a threat.

The man with the adorned helmet stopped abruptly and shouted. "Has anyone been bitten!"

The guards helping Earl and Evelyn stopped immediately and backed away as if they were lepers. Four of the soldiers drew their swords and fanned out, blocking any route of escape further into the city. Part of her was regretting putting her arrow away, but the odds of survival in a straight-up fight against so many with no help weren't that great.

Earl held up his arms to show he hadn't been bitten. Evelyn and her son did the same. A guard stepped forward and whispered something to the man in charge, then stepped back into formation.

Looking at the frightened family, he roared, "Strip!"

Lorelei had heard enough. "Fuck that." Two arrows found their way into her hand in an almost unconscious gesture. With one arrowhead shining off either side of the bow, Lorelei hoped she could take two of them out on her first shot. That might make the others pause.

"I, Jon VanSutton, captain of Tristholm City Guard, command you to strip or be slain where you stand!" He held out a hand, and one of his men stepped forward to place a blade into his waiting palm.

"I'd rather die than be forced to strip in the street for your fucking amusement! The real question is, how many of your men are you willing to let die to get a chance at seeing my tits?" Lorelei smiled as her bitchy side flared to life. She wasn't going to take any shit from this clown just because he had a shiny helmet.

Jon VanSutton looked at her for a moment, a sneer curling at the corner of his mouth. "Then die."

Lorelei was shocked, but she shouldn't have been. Werewolves had obviously been attacking this city for a long time. Something like that would make you wary of strangers. Especially when the human could turn into a nine-foot-tall killing machine if you let the wrong one in. That didn't mean she was going to strip in the street like she was about to be marched off to some kind of extermination camp.

Two of the guards started moving forward, and Lorelei pulled back on the string of her bow. She was going to have to be quick and keep moving. If they pinned her in, the Ranger was dead. Maybe if she killed enough of them, there would be time to try to scale the gate and run away. With a little luck she'd make it back to Promethia and never come back here again.

Slowing her breathing, Lorelei narrowed her vision and prepared to lose.

Lorelei had the presence of mind not to fire, as the guards stopped moving and turned their heads to look up at a woman upon the ramparts. A woman's voice called down. "What is going on?"

VanSutton called out. "Sister, I did not expect to see you here."

The woman's raven black hair streamed out behind her in the breeze. She was wearing a pair of tight leather pants and rocking them to their fullest potential. The tight leather vest patched with chainmail didn't do anything to hide her shapely features, and the sword on her hip was slender.

Built for speed, just like the woman herself.

Leaping from the wall, Jon's sister took the fifteen-foot fall as if she stepped off a big curb in the city, instead of falling farther than the height of a single-story house. She landed and bounced slightly on the balls of her feet before walking toward them. "You still haven't answered my question."

"We were trying to check them for bites when this one refused to comply with my orders." He thrust a finger in Lorelei's direction.

The woman turned her piercing blue eyes in Lorelei's direction. "It seems she was about to attack you with a bow instead of turning into one of the beasts you fear so much."

"I am not afraid of those mangy dogs, Camilla," Jon growled at his sister. "I am worried about how many of our citizens would die if one of the monsters was set loose inside of the city walls."

Camilla rounded on her brother. "So you force two women and a child to strip down in the streets! We are better than this. You are better than this."

To Lorelei's great surprise, Jon dropped to one knee. "You are right sister, I have forgotten myself."

"Nothing has happened that can't be forgiven, eh, stranger?" Camilla winked at Lorelei as she reached out to help her brother to his feet.

Feeling like Camilla might be flirting with her, Lorelei threw caution to the wind and released the tension on her bowstring. Flipping the arrows back into her quiver, she returned Camilla's wink with a saucy smile of her own. "I don't see why we couldn't still be friends."

"Well said." Camilla started to grin. "I hope the four of you wouldn't mind following me to the castle. There we can get you cleaned up and make sure you are bite-free in privacy."

Earl and Evelyn nodded in agreement. They would have stripped down in the streets without question, too scared to say no. Being thrown out of Tristholm at this point would have been tantamount to a death sentence for the three of them.

Saying no to Camilla now wouldn't help her out of this mess, plus, she was looking forward to following her to the castle. Those leather pants were doing all the right things in all the right places.

Lorelei swung her bow over one shoulder and hit Camilla with her brightest smile. "Lead the way."

Camilla took her hand to pull her forward. Earl, Evelyn, and their son followed closely behind them. The guards brought up the rear to make sure if any of them tried to escape, they would be cut down before making it into the city.

"That was some fancy shooting," the raven-haired beauty said as they followed the winding road toward the castle.

"I just got lucky," Lorelei replied casually, not sure how much of her skillset to share with Camilla just yet.

Pausing in the center of the street, Camilla turned her piercing blue eyes on Lorelei. "Oh, I doubt that very much. Thankfully for you, we've been looking for someone with just your particular skill set for a very long time."

"Sounds like you are offering me a job?" Lorelei took a moment to pull Earl's crossbow from her inventory. She handed the weapon to the shocked pig farmer and turned to continue following Camilla toward the castle.

"It's not my place to formally extend offers of employment, but once I verify that you haven't been bitten, I believe my mother will have a job for you."

"Wait, you're going to check to see if I've been bitten?" Lorelei smiled coyly. In a much lower voice, she said, "I like the sound of that."

As they continued to walk, Lorelei's mind drifted to scenarios involving a very big bathtub and the two of them checking each other for bite marks.

Camilla laughed. The sound was bright and infectious. "Unless you'd prefer for one of my brother's men to do it."

Lorelei wasn't able to stop a bit of huskiness from creeping into her voice. "Oh, I think I'm quite fine with the current selection." Lorelei wasn't a hundred percent sure, but she thought Camilla sounded just as excited about the prospect as she was.

They slipped into a comfortable silence after that. Lorelei was content to watch Camilla lead the way to the Castle. The castle itself turned out to be a large two-story building, with smaller single-story wings to either side. After seeing the magnificent castle that dominated Promethia, she'd been expecting a bit more.

Considering this was a small city, it made sense that the castle wouldn't be bigger than the one in the capital. Maybe she'd just been expecting every dot on the map to be as big as the city she'd started in. Obviously, that wasn't the case. Still, Tristholm had stone walls and armaments, so it wasn't just some podunk village.

The guards trailing behind them faded back as they passed under the portcullis, and men from the castle's personal guard took their place. Camilla didn't slow down as she walked to the castle's main door, but once they were inside of the lobby she stopped and faced them. Two women and a man descended the dual staircase behind her.

As the people dressed in white reached the floor, they headed toward Evelyn and Earl. The couple and their son were led away, and one of the castle guards followed at a discreet distance. Lorelei turned from watching the departing family to see a smiling Camilla standing very close to her.

"I formally request to handle your inspection myself." Camilla grinned as she took Lorelei's hand in her own. "Please follow me to the baths."

Lorelei squeezed Camilla's hand and let herself be led away.

This was just like the fantasy she had on the way to the castle. Was the game trying to help her get over her recent heartbreak by offering her a viable alternative? She took one look at Camilla's ass, and only one thought resonated in her mind.

Who the fuck cared if she was being manipulated?

CHAPTER NINE

Camilla's mother wasn't what Lorelei expected at all.

The woman descended a small raised dais, plucking a sword from the side of the throne as she came. Holding the sword by her side, she walked to the waiting pair. The tip of her blade trailed against the tile for a moment before she came to a stop. Looking at Camilla, her mother spoke. "This is the one."

"It is, Mother." Camilla bowed her head in a show of respect.

Lorelei kept her head up and her eyes on her lover's mother. The unsheathed blade made her nervous, but her own blades were only inches from her hands. Unsure of how to address her, she decided to go with something safe. "It's a pleasure to meet you."

It dawned on her then that she should have asked Camilla more about what was going to happen next. She'd been too busy indulging in her beautifully tanned skin to ask about her mother. Now she was regretting that decision immensely. Was the woman before her just the leader of the city, or was she some kind of royalty?

Whatever Camilla's mother was, Lorelei refused to wilt under her gaze.

Before either of them could speak Camilla continued. "Mother, may I introduce you to Lorelei." Turning from her mother to look at her newest crush, Camilla's cheeks flushed with heat. "Lorelei, this is my mother, Seraphina."

Seraphina smiled, a glint of mischief in her eye. "Is it true you killed one of the beasts with an arrow from a distance?"

"It was a lucky shot," Lorelei responded with a coy smile.

"Camilla seems to think it was more than luck. I propose a test." She spun around, lifting the sword and laying the flat of the blade across her shoulders as she strode back to her chair. "Show me your talent with a bow, and I might just have a job for you."

It sounded like there might be a downside if she failed to impress, but neither of the women elaborated on what that might be. Since entering the game she'd tried to be what other people wanted her to be, but now she was ready to show everyone who she really was.

A grin ticked up on the right side of her face as she watched Seraphina. "What did you have in mind?"

Camilla walked up the steps to her mother's side, as a steel cage lowered from the ceiling to fit into place perfectly around the raised dais. As she placed one hand on her mother's shoulder, her eyes settled on Lorelei's. "Good luck."

Her sense danger ability flared to life almost instantly as a roar issued from the far side of the room. Lorelei knew the sound of a werewolf when she heard one. Moving away from the noise, she tried to use the pillars lining the side of the room for cover. "Not exactly the honeymoon I was expecting."

The werewolf launched itself into the middle of the room and struck the steel cage with ferocity. Sparks splashed off the steel with each strike of the beast's claws, but the women inside of the cage didn't flinch. Instead, they watched the monster with icy detachment.

With her bow in hand Lorelei stepped out from behind the column and activated the ability eagle eye. Her vision zoomed in to the point she could make out the individual hairs on the were-wolf's hide. A sense of calm spread through her body and Lorelei slowed her breathing.

She waited for the moment in-between heartbeats and let the arrow fly.

The arrow crossed the small space in an instant.

Camilla let out a scream as the arrow burst out of the were-wolf's eye. The creature fell to its knees, its body switching back to human. Slowly the human body toppled over until his face was pressed against the bars of the cage.

Seraphina let out a gasp of recognition. "Rothar."

"Mother, if they converted him, then they know all of our defenses. The city isn't safe." Camilla made a gesture with her hand, and the cage started to lift.

Rising from her seat Seraphina gestured. "Go, meet with your brother, and prepare as best you can. We have to assume some of them may already be inside of the walls, so be safe."

Camilla ran past Lorelei for the door before skidding to a stop and coming back. Stepping in front of the ranger, she lingered for a moment before kissing her on the lips. "I'll see you when all of this is over."

Lorelei kissed Camilla back, hoping she would see her again. The game wouldn't be so cruel as to take her this soon. "I'll keep the bath warm for you."

A hungry look formed in Camilla's eyes. "I'm going to hold you to that." Without a word or a look back Camilla left the room, leaving Lorelei alone with her mother.

"She really does believe in you," Seraphina spoke, drawing Lorelei's attention away from the empty doorway. "I've always trusted my daughter's judgment, and despite her obvious interest in you, I have no desire to start doubting her now. If she thinks you are good enough to get the job done, then so do I."

Quest Received: Breaking the Pack

The newest Alpha of the Tristholm Forest Pack is deter-

mined to destroy the city. Seraphina is requesting your help to kill the werewolf alpha known as Silver. Bring back his head to claim your reward.

Accept the quest: <Yes/No>

Lorelei accepted the quest.

"I don't care how you do it, just get it done," Seraphina said from her seat. Her smile had a deadly glint to it. "If you are successful, I may have more work for you."

My first quest chain.

Lorelei gave Seraphina a firm nod. "Expect me to be back soon."

"Oh, I do." Seraphina's smile turned from deadly to amused as if she thought the only way Lorelei would be returning was at the castle respawn point.

Sometimes it was easier for Lorelei to keep her emotions in check than others. This was one of the times she surprised herself. Instead of snapping, Lorelei gave Seraphina a curt nod and headed for the door.

Walking around the castle felt better now that she wasn't being trailed by guards all the time. Sleeping with the ruler's daughter had its benefits. Although not having bite marks probably had more to do with her recent increase in freedom.

How was a girl supposed to think with all that clanking metal following her around?

She started to pick up speed with the exit in sight but stopped when someone called out. She saw Evelyn standing in a doorway, her son clutching at her leg. Lorelei stopped walking and headed in their direction. To her immense relief, Earl walked up behind them a moment later. For a second, she thought maybe her arrow had been too late.

Earl stepped around his wife and extended his hand. "Thank you for all that you've done for my family and returning my crossbow."

"Once I questioned if you were a hero. I know the answer now.

Thank you for saving us." Evelyn pulled her into a hug. "Use my father's bow to end this."

Stepping back, Lorelei stared into her eyes, not knowing exactly what to say. "I'll do what I can."

Earl wrapped an arm around his wife and son. "Which has already been more than enough. Good luck to you, Lorelei."

"And to you." With their final words spoken, Lorelei turned for the door. She would miss the couple. Without her new bow there was no doubt in her mind none of them would have made it to Tristholm, but as comfortable as she was in the city, all she wanted to do now was get her quest taken care of.

Baths didn't take themselves.

Being outside again felt good. Who knew after a couple days in the forest she would miss it so much? Maybe that was a feeling that came with her class as a Ranger. Her thoughts turned away from the family, and Lorelei tried to focus on the problem at hand.

Was it even possible to sneak up on a werewolf? Let alone an alpha?

She expected the alpha to have some kind of guards that never left his side. That would be their human nature overriding the wolf. A true alpha in the wild had no need, as the alpha was the protection for the entire pack.

So how was she going to get past the other wolves to take her shot?

What she really needed was a distraction. Something for the werewolves to focus on, so she could take him out. Should she wait until the monsters attacked the city and then try to find the alpha in the chaos? Maybe it was finally time to work on her sneak skill. Despite not having worked to level the skill before, she knew sneaking around had unlimited potential in the wild.

Back in the tavern when she was doing trick shots, not so much.

The choice before Lorelei now was to wait and hope for the

best or to try to search for the alpha in his lair. If searching for his lair meant going into the forest, then that was what it would be.

The sun felt good, but there was a hint of moisture in the air. The clouds overhead were dark but fluffy. It wouldn't take much for them to bunch together and release a torrent of rain. Torches were already being lit on the walls, even though sundown was hours away. Soon enough, the city would be plunged into darkness, and the werewolves would attack in earnest.

If Lorelei wanted to attack the alpha in his lair, then she needed to be out of here before the attack on Tristholm started. There was no way she could focus on the alpha with all the commotion. Plus, she'd never be able to live with herself if she let someone get killed just to take the shot on her target.

Better not to be here when people start getting ripped in half.

"Get these people to the castle!" Jon bellowed as he walked up beside her. He turned and pointed to a few men. "You two get to the smithy and make sure we have everything in place for tonight."

Jon was the last person Lorelei wanted to run into. Just because she was sleeping with his sister didn't mean she wouldn't put an arrow in the fucker if he pushed it. The thought of him demanding she strip in the street was still fresh in her mind.

"I wanted to extend my sincerest apologies about before." Jon looked down at the ground. "We've lost so many good people, and anyone could be one of those things. I let myself get carried away and forgot that how we treat each other is just as important as the mission itself."

Jon paused, dropping to one knee in the street. "I hope you can forgive my rudeness."

Rude was one thing to call it. Terrifying and demeaning was another.

Still, if Lorelei didn't give people the chance to grow when they wanted the opportunity, what kind of person would she be? If Camilla was the one bending the knee, she would have forgiven her in a heartbeat.

So why couldn't she do the same for her brother?

Reaching out, she pulled Jon to his feet. Their hands were around each other's wrists, and all Lorelei could think of was her favorite fantasy films. For some reason, the men always grasped at the forearm in a sign of camaraderie, where real knights shook each other's hands to make sure the cheating bastards weren't hiding any weapons.

"All has been forgiven." Lorelei tried to smile but found it didn't quite happen. She let it drop instead of trying to force it. "But if you'll excuse me, I have pressing business on behalf of your mother."

"Then, don't let me stop you." Jon reached behind his back and pulled out a sheathed kukri. He handed it to Lorelei. "I noticed that your knife could use an upgrade." He waited for her to accept the weapon and then turned to shout at some men on the wall.

Jon looked at Lorelei with a sheepish expression on his face. "I swear if I don't line them up myself, it will never get done. I bid you farewell." He turned and stomped off in the direction of the men he'd just been chastising.

Lorelei pulled the kukri out of the sheath and examined it.

Ranger Kukri +3 slicing damage

Many adventurers have made this curved weapon their armament of choice because of its vast utility in the field. Not only can it be used for killing monsters, but this weapon is just as useful for clearing the path or digging a hole.

The previous owner of this weapon has taken magnificent care of it, bestowing on it a permanent bonus of plus three to slicing damage.

It was a better gift than she had been expecting. Lorelei turned to thank Jon only to realize that he was long gone. She smiled at the knife as she tied the sheath to her belt. Her old dagger went into her inventory, just in case she didn't like this weapon. It would have been nice to test the blade in light combat first, but she was more of a learn-on-the-fly kind of girl anyway.

The guards at the gate started to pull the heavy iron bars free of their housings, but Lorelei stopped them. "Just be ready to let me back in."

She started running toward the wall. The two guards looked at her mystified as she jumped into the air. She landed on the wall, ran for three or four steps up the side, then leaped over the top.

Lorelei landed heavily on the road leading out of Tristholm. The two guards poked their heads over the wall to make sure she hadn't tumbled from the top of the gates and gotten injured. Once they realized she was all right, the two men disappeared from view.

Maybe that was a little too flashy. When the locals were paranoid about werewolves, people with superhuman strength running up a wall perhaps wasn't the best way to stay off the radar.

But it was cool as fuck!

Lorelei ducked into the forest and started toward the waypoint listed on her map. Part of her wanted to make a beeline from Tristholm to the location, but her training told her to take a different approach. Never come at an enemy from the front when you could sneak behind them. It might take her longer to get there, but she'd have a better chance of living if she did.

It didn't take long for her to track down the small stream on her map. She stepped into the water, grumbling a bit at the cool temperature as it soaked through her boots. *When I purchase my next pair of boots, they are going to be fucking waterproof.* The quick-moving stream only came up to her calves, but she thought it would be enough to mask her scent.

At the very least, it should keep the werewolves chasing their tails for a bit trying to figure out where she exited the stream.

The sun continued to set, and a few howls sounded off in the distance. The wolfmen scouts were on the move. Lorelei put her head down and willed her legs to work just a little bit harder. Walking through foot deep water was no joke on leg muscles after thirty minutes. All of her efforts would be for naught if they found her now.

Five minutes later, Lorelei flopped down onto the bank. Her legs were shaking with exhaustion, and her breath heaved in ragged gasps. Not sure if her plan worked or not, she checked her bow and arrows for damage while trying to slow her breathing to a respectable, and much quieter, level. With her weapons ready to go, it was time to make sure all of the buckles and straps on her leather armor were tied down.

Jingling all the way to the alpha was a sure-fire way to wind up being his next chew toy.

With her armor muffled and her bow ready, Lorelei began working her way deeper into the forest. As she moved silently between the trees, one thought kept resonating through her mind.

This fucker was never going to know what hit him.

CHAPTER TEN

Torchlight covered the entrance to the cave in flickering shadows.

Lorelei watched from the trees nearly two hundred yards above the entrance. Two werewolves stood in the cavern opening below her. The monster's eyes moved across the forest in front of them, watching for any sign of intruders.

"No one ever looks up," Lorelei mumbled to herself as she took three arrows out of her quiver.

She drove two of the arrows into the earth in front of her while nocking the third one. It took her two or three seconds to calculate how the arrow would change flight as it entered the canyon below. Deep calming breaths slowed her heart rate, and she let the first arrow fly.

There wasn't time to watch the flight of her first shot. Her eyes picked out her next target as she reached for another arrow. Slowly exhaling, a second ticked by before the next arrow took flight, and she was reaching for the third arrow.

Rinse and repeat.

After the third arrow was in the air, Lorelei took a moment to

"

focus on what was happening below her. One of the werewolves was dead or dying with an arrow sticking out of its throat. The other was trying to pull an arrow from its stomach as her third arrow plunged into its leg.

Standing, she reached for a new arrow from her quiver. From this distance, she was happy with the results. Three solid hits were more than she had expected at her skill level. Maybe it was time she started giving herself a little more credit. This wasn't shooting apples off heads at the tavern, but it took the same skills.

The fourth arrow launched from her bow like a rocket. Lorelei's heart started to hammer as she listened to the slight whistle made by the arrow's feathers. It was the sound of racing death. Silence descended over the canyon as the last werewolf met its fate.

"Robinhood's got nothing on me, bitches!"

Grinning, Lorelei started moving down the hill, keeping her eyes locked on the cave's opening. If she was right, only the alpha was left in the cave, but that almost seemed too easy. The bodies of the dead werewolves shifted back to human as she continued the descent.

"I'm never going to get used to that shit." Lorelei gritted her teeth and continued moving.

Seeing the bodies of the fallen beasts turn back into men left an impression on her. Was there a cure, some way to reverse whatever forced the change? That was always the conundrum with werewolves.

Was it the man or the monster who was at fault?

The answer varied from film to film, book to book. There was no real way to know for sure how much of a person was left once the change took control of them unless you became one. Lorelei wasn't ready to take that particular plunge in the name of science just yet. Instead, she would rely on what she saw and assume these men retained most of their human consciousness while changed.

The alpha flipping off the city earlier basically confirmed it.

So she was facing human-level intelligence wrapped in the package of a regenerating killing machine. Not having eyes on the alpha was starting to make Lorelei nervous. Did the bastard not care that she'd just slain two of his men? Was he even here? At least they didn't have radios or walkie talkies to call for reinforcements.

Fuck!

She'd been expecting the alpha to storm out of the cavern foaming at the mouth with rage at the loss of his men. The fact that Silver could stay rational and not rush headlong into danger was impressive. It made her wonder if the alpha might have had military training, possibly with the Tristholm city guard.

Reaching the canyon floor, Lorelei started to circle the perimeter slowly, her eyes locked on the entrance to the cave. Creeping across the space revealed more of the interior of Silver's hideout. Two human corpses littered the cavern's entryway. Behind them just inside of the cavern, two torches were burning brightly.

There was no way in hell Lorelei was going into the cave. One on one with Silver in a confined space only benefited the werewolf. She had to find a way to get him to come outside. It was time to put her thinking cap on.

"So the bitch finally found someone dumb enough to come after me," a man's voice called out from inside of the cavern.

Lorelei didn't want to give up her position by speaking, but she still couldn't see Silver and needed to draw him out. "Says the guy hiding in the cave."

A cruel chuckle drifted out of the cavern. "I hope you brought reinforcements." The last of the alpha's words turned into a scream as he started the transformation.

The sound of ripping leather and snapping bones poured out of the cavern's entrance. When the horrible noises stopped, a howl pierced the night air. Silver walked out of the cavern on all fours, but he wasn't like any of the other werewolves Lorelei had encountered. Standing on all fours, Silver was almost as tall as a person.

And then he stood up.

The alpha was at least twelve feet tall. With his curved back legs, Silver stood several feet taller than a man. All of the werewolf's fur was silver in color, which made it hard to see the twinkle of some kind of armor pressed tightly against his fur. It was the eight-foot long sword he held casually in one hand that demanded Lorelei's attention.

What a tricky fucker.

Silver surprised her by speaking. None of the werewolves Lorelei had encountered thus far did anything but snarl. His words came out harsh, almost as if he were growling them. "So what did the bitch offer you to kill her son? Maybe a chance to marry the younger brother?"

"Not my type," Lorelei called from where she was hidden in the trees at the edge of the clearing.

Activating the skill delayed shot Lorelei got to work. It was funny. When she'd received this skill, there wasn't one situation where she thought it would come in handy. Now she was in her first real fight and calling on it for her first salvo.

Sometimes you just had to trust your gut.

The arrow flew from her bow, and then she was running to a spot on the other side of the clearing. Silver's ears had already pinpointed the location of her voice. The twin radars locked in on the spot, and he started to charge.

Delayed shot's count down timer expired, and the arrow that had been hovering magically in place released. The arrow flew from the spot as if Lorelei had just fired the shot herself instead of being twenty feet away already.

Growling as he sprinted toward his newest victim, Silver lifted his massive sword. The arrow clattered off the blade and flew harmlessly off into the night sky.

Fuck, he's fast.

Lorelei's little plan had done the trick. Silver was still running toward the spot she'd left, letting her get a good look at him while she contemplated what to do next. The armor the alpha was wearing certainly didn't help things. What she needed to do was trust herself to make the shot.

Silver's head was completely unprotected, as well as his stomach and his entire back. The alpha's shins, thighs, and chest all showed hints of the dull steel plates that were magically attached to the alpha's flesh.

Getting a headshot on the alpha with how quickly he moved seemed like an impossible feat. Still, the city was being attacked, and they were counting on her to take him out. Lorelei had been so focused on the battle she almost hadn't paid attention to what Silver had said.

Wait, did he say "Mother?"

"Why would you attack your home?" This time Lorelei didn't fire, but she continued moving around, trying to keep as many trees between her and the alpha as possible. Using all of the stealth she had available, she circled around until she was almost on top of the cave.

Silver lunged into the spot Lorelei had most recently vacated. His massive sword whistled as it sliced through the air. The blade slammed into a thirty-foot tall pine tree and got stuck halfway. Yanking the blade free with a snarl Silver shouted, "Home?"

The alpha barked with bitter laughter. "Maybe it was once, but when I saved our supply caravan from attack everything changed."

With an impressive show of strength, Silver toppled the tree with a single punch. "Tristholm is no longer my home," the alpha raged. "When Seraphina found out what I was, she cast me out into the cold with nothing. Said the sight of me disgusted her."

He walked back into the clearing, scanning the edges of the forest with his eyes as his ears swiveled to pick up any hint of sound. "We could have started our own werewolf legion. Our city's warriors fighting alongside my hand-picked pack of elites. We would have finally been able to turn the tide of the war, but she threw it all away for tradition."

Not seeing any hint of his target, Silver continued. "Even then, I might have forgiven her. It wasn't until the first assassin came that I started plotting my revenge." The alpha held his arms out wide. "I ask you this, what kind of mother tries to kill her own son?"

The alpha brought his sword up like a knight in a duel. He moved through a series of motions and then stopped. "I was Tristholm's finest warrior, and then its greatest shame, at my lowest when the Goddess Vitaria came to me. She blessed me and promised to help with my vengeance."

He barked bitter laughter into the night sky. "Mother always taught us to seize every opportunity."

Part of her felt sorry for Silver. Lorelei knew a thing or two about how much it hurt to be rejected by your parents. Granted, her mother had never tried to kill her, but she had been more than happy to condemn her mortal soul to the fiery embrace of hell for eternity. While she'd heard others say the same thing, Lorelei hoped it wasn't true. True love between two people should always be celebrated.

Not that she'd stumbled onto true love yet.

Family making you feel shitty for your life choices was one thing, but to send an assassin after you was another. Still, it didn't matter how fucked up their family life was, innocent people were caught in the crossfire now, and Silver had to be stopped. Lorelei didn't know much about this world's religion, but Vitaria didn't sound like any kind of goddess she'd heard of before.

Well, maybe that wasn't true.

The Greek gods had been pretty vengeful and screwing with mortals was their favorite pastime. It was why so many people worshiped and cursed the gods back then. The gods of their time had represented humanity, and had the same dual nature as all humans.

Lorelei didn't know what dark goddess Vitaria's desires were, but based on the actions of her chosen, she had to assume she wasn't well-intentioned. The good guys didn't try to kill an entire city full of innocent people.

Maybe she should just kill the fucker and be spared the rest of his monologue.

Long-winded sermons were always about how bad things happened to them when they were young, and how they couldn't take it so everyone had to pay. She didn't believe that shit for one second. Lorelei had watched too many broken people turn their lives around and find happiness to be that cynical.

Sometimes you had to be willing to leave the past where it was. People who held on to the dead weight of the past bogged down their futures with what-ifs. It was okay to cherish those moments when they were sad, but you couldn't build your life around suffering and give in to despair.

Sometimes you just had to keep moving.

Lorelei ran toward the edge of the outcropping and jumped. The alpha started to turn, but there was no way for him to avoid the death raining down on him from above. The string of her bow thrummed as the arrows flew. Never had her hands moved so fast, and with such purpose.

Two arrows tore into the alpha's exposed arms as he tried to dodge out of the way. A third arrow struck his chest armor and bounced away harmlessly before the fourth slammed into the top of his head.

Tossing her bow to the side as she hit the ground, Lorelei rolled to keep her momentum moving forward. The kukri found its way into her hand, and she rose to her feet. One step later, the blade sliced through the air, opening up Silver's throat from ear to ear. The alpha clutched desperately at the wound as he tried to keep it closed so he could heal, but his body was already transforming back to human.

As Silver's blood gushed from between his fingers, his massive claws turned back into hands. He wore an expression of disbelief on his face as he fell to the ground at Lorelei's feet. Blood bubbled from his lips as his last words formed. "It wasn't supposed to end like…"

Looking down at the corpse Lorelei just felt sad. All of this could have been avoided if Seraphina had just accepted her son for who he was. "At least I know why she wanted the head. Can't have the villagers finding out about this." Lorelei set to the grisly task of cutting off a very human head to complete her quest.

Not wanting to linger in case other wolves in the pack started to return from their battle with Tristholm, Lorelei rushed into the cavern to scavenge anything of worth. Emerging from the cavern a few gold pieces richer, and with a matching kukri, she started her long walk back to the city.

Hopefully, the walk would take long enough for her to figure out the best way to hand a son's head to his mother.

CHAPTER ELEVEN

One of Tristholm's main gates had been ripped off its hinges. Corpses littered the landscape as Lorelei made her way into town. Some of them were naked, signaling that they used to be werewolves, while others had on armor. A few women dressed in black moved among the corpses with daggers in hand. They stopped next to each of the armed men and rammed a blade into their skulls before moving on.

Seraphina was making sure that none of the injured or dead had a chance to come back as a monster. Lorelei wondered how much of this disaster was the woman's own making. If she had embraced her son and tried to help him, there was a chance none of this would have happened.

There was also the chance Silver was just a giant douche who wanted nothing but power. If he had been allowed to take over Tristholm and convert its populace to werewolves, he would have led an army of monsters to the gates of the capital.

Whatever.

It didn't matter what Lorelei wished for Seraphina's relation-ship with her son. Once their family squabble started killing innocent people, she had no problem picking a side. Attacking a city over your mommy issues was so cliché. Get over yourself already.

Being a werewolf could have been fucking awesome. Imagine how fun it would be to run through the forest, to have the strength to jump across rivers. Lorelei was sure being transformed didn't automatically turn you into a raving killer. The alpha seemed completely aware of his actions.

And who was the Vitaria?

Lorelei had never heard of her. The only temple she had ever seen was erected to the Goddess Eternia. She had assumed there were other deities in the game, but one thing she learned early in life about facts was, if you don't know, don't guess. So while there hadn't been any evidence of other gods until now, she'd been keeping an open mind.

Being prepared for anything lessened the shock when the unexpected happened.

The castle gates were blocked by a battalion of guards. Jon was standing in the center of the men looking out over the city as if it wouldn't be long before the next attack came. Lorelei hoped Seraphina was right and that with the alpha dead, the rest of the pack would scatter, and stay scattered.

"I have urgent business with Seraphina," Lorelei called out as she drew closer.

The men behind Jon tightened their hands on the hilts of their swords, but their leader walked forward with a casual gait and a smile on his face. "Thank Eternia!" He extended his hand. "If you hadn't killed the alpha, the rest of us were done for."

Grasping Jon's hand Lorelei gave it a firm shake as she scanned the area behind the guards for Camilla. "I have to deliver proof to your mother." She continued searching the crowd.

"She will be pleased. All of us need to see more of the light after today's dark events." Jon turned away from her and motioned for his men to make room for Lorelei to pass. "Thank you for your service to Tristholm."

A pit of worry was working Lorelei's stomach into knots. Where was Camilla? Had she been hurt, or worse, been killed? It seemed cruel for the game to have given her a glimpse of such a sweet woman only to snatch her away.

It took Lorelei five times as long to reach the throne room as it had before. It wasn't that the walkways were crowded or that any of the guards stopped her. She was holding herself back. Part of her wondered if this is what it felt like when they asked someone to identify the body of a loved one.

She couldn't imagine the hope that must flood into someone's heart right before the sheet was pulled back. There had to be a moment where, despite all odds, the person hoped it wasn't true. Then they'd see the face they hoped not to see, and the reality of the moment would come crashing down around them.

Lorelei was trying to avoid the crash.

Despite her best efforts, she was paralyzed by the thought of what could have happened. There was a feeling in the air that something was wrong, and she knew it couldn't be avoided for much longer. It was time she started to follow her own advice and keep moving forward. Dwelling on the recent past could be just as bad as digging into the Wayback machine for answers about how and why you are who you are. Lorelei refused to give in to the weakness she felt. Her will became a juggernaut, keeping her feet moving forward despite the fear.

Standing outside the throne room door, she took one deep breath and then shoved it open.

Seraphina's screams filled the chamber. The ruler of Tristholm wasn't in mourning, she was fucking pissed. The woman's cheeks were stained red from her last outburst. The man she'd been screaming at fled from the room as if his very life depended on how fast he could scurry away.

Lorelei was reluctant to draw Seraphina's attention to herself after seeing the display, but she had a quest to turn in. Clearing her throat, Lorelei muttered, "I have returned."

Seraphina stood up, clapping her hands. "Oh, goodie, maybe we should throw a party."

It wasn't so much what she said to Lorelei, but the sarcastic manner in which the comment was delivered that upset her. Reaching into her inventory, she pulled the alpha's head free and threw it toward the bottom of the steps. The head bounced along the floor and stopped just short of its intended destination.

It wasn't as if she had a lot of practice throwing heads around.

The man formerly known as Silver's milky white eyes stared accusingly at his mother. The head seemed to be screaming, "You did this to me," but the throne room was silent.

"I've completed my quest." *And you better have a damn good reward for me,* Lorelei thought silently before continuing. "I'd like to see Camilla, and then I will be on my way."

"See Camilla," Seraphina screeched. "Well, you can't fucking see her because she's gone."

Lorelei felt her heart drop. Her worst fears had been confirmed. She stood for a moment, chest heaving as her mind raged. How could Camilla be gone? They'd just fallen for each other. Would the developers really be so cruel?

Guilt flooded Lorelei's system as she realized what she'd just done. Seraphina was grieving the loss of a child, and she'd just tossed the head of another at her feet. It didn't matter how big of a bitch you were, no one deserved that.

Then it dawned on her. Seraphina had said Camilla was gone, not dead.

"What happened?" Lorelei asked, dreading what was coming.

"What happened? I'll tell you what fucking happened. One of those mangy animals bit her, and now she's gone forever." Seraphina lowered her head into her hands. "What am I going to do?"

"How did she die?" Lorelei was pretty sure Camilla had just been turned, but dragging the information out of a grieving mother was harder than she would have liked.

"She's not dead. Camilla is one of those *things*. One of those goddamned monsters." Her eyes blazed with barely contained rage. "For a thousand years, my family has stood between the land of the living and the darkness from beyond the mountains, and for what? So it could all end now?"

Seraphina rose and started walking down the steps. When she reached her son's head, she kicked it out of the way. "Burn this," she shouted.

Stopping in front of Lorelei, Seraphina took her hands. "I will not be the one to fail our line, our sacred duty, but for Tristholm to stand, we need help. The Goddess Eternia can only do so much for us. What we really need is something to turn the tide of battle in our favor. There is a man in Promethia who can help us. Find him and secure his services for us."

Quest Completed: Breaking the Pack

You have returned the head of the Alpha known as Silver to Seraphina. Things have not gone as expected. Camilla has been bitten, forcing her to flee the city of Tristholm.

Reward: Twenty gold coins and the Pin of the Hunt.

Item received: Pin of the Hunt.

This pin is given to the fabled hunters of Tristholm when they pass the final trial of initiation.

While wearing this pin, you receive a 5% bonus to your critical hit chance.

Quest Received: Find the Poison Master

You must travel back to the city of Promethia and find the Poison Master. He works out of an inn at the slums. Show him the token Seraphina has provided you and say the words, "Honor the shadows."

Accept Quest: <Yes/No>

Lorelei was torn. On the one hand, she didn't want to condemn the entire city of Tristholm to death because Seraphina was a stone-cold bitch who would rather kill her bitten children than use them to save the kingdom. Then there was the part of her that wanted to scream *"FUCK YOU"* in her face, find Camilla, and make sweet little wolf babies together. Maybe there was a cure, maybe she didn't care if Camilla was cured. Having your significant other turn into a killing machine at the drop of a hat was a pretty badass advantage in life.

Not that they'd made it to the significant other phase yet.

If she took this quest, it would put her on the opposite side of the battle from Camilla and ruin her chances at a burgeoning romance. On the other hand, was she willing to sacrifice all of these people's lives just so she could be happy? How could she choose between love and responsibility?

Wasn't that always her problem?

For most of her life, Lorelei had been a creature of spontaneity. She bounced from one job to the next as easily as she did lovers. Maybe it was her thirst for life that drew people to her, but she was always living in the moment, blinded by the next great thing. Sometimes the next great thing turned out to be a big pile of shit.

The grass wasn't always greener.

This time, Lorelei decided that instead of following her heart, or possibly her insatiable libido, she was going to take the path she never traveled. The dreaded road of responsibility. Who in the fuck wanted to be responsible anyway? She wanted to show up when she wanted and leave twice as fast. Drink like a sailor, and fuck like a porn star.

Maybe it was time for a change.

Lorelei continued working the quest over in her head, thinking about Camilla's soft tan skin the entire time. While her love life might have been messy, she never set out to hurt anyone, and now she was contemplating taking a quest to track down a man who could help kill her lover.

Something didn't feel right.

What if Lorelei took the quest and stalled for time, or better yet, found a way to complete it and save Camilla. There was always a chance she could make it to Promethia and back before things between mother and daughter deteriorated to the point they had with Silver. A quick glance at Seraphina's face told her that might be extremely wishful thinking.

Was it possible the game had a purpose for her, and that it was trying to bring out the best parts of her character? Maybe Lorelei was just trying to find ways to justify the quest to herself so she wouldn't have to feel guilty. It wasn't working. If she was going to feel guilty anyway, she might as well at least get paid while brooding. She accepted the quest, vowing to herself that if there was a way to help Camilla, she would before she let the poison master do his job.

Seraphina placed a coin in Lorelei's hand. "Give this to him and say these words." She closed the ranger's hand around the coin and then turned back toward her seat. "All our hopes rest with you."

Hearing the defeat in Seraphina's voice was hard. The woman had lost a son and a daughter today. It didn't matter how it happened, the death of a child for a parent wasn't an easy burden to bear. Lorelei wanted to offer her some kind of condolence but was unsure of what to say after tossing her son's head at her a few moments ago. Anything she said now would just ring hollow.

Instead of saying anything to comfort Seraphina, Lorelei kept the topic on the job at hand. "I'm going to need a horse."

"Talk to Jon." Seraphina put her head into her hands and started sobbing.

Taking that as her cue to leave, Lorelei turned away from the grieving mother. She pinned the talisman she received as a quest reward to her leather armor as she stepped back into the light. To her surprise, Jon was waiting for her with a beautiful chestnut-colored horse.

His smile was dark, but he at least seemed happy to see her. "It was Camilla's favorite." He handed her the reins. "I know what my mother has asked you to do, and I'm sorry it has come to this."

Lorelei took the reins and vaulted onto the back of the horse.

"All is not lost. If there is a way to help your sister, I will try to find it."

The knight looked up at her, a single tear trailing down his cheek. "May the goddess protect you on your journey."

"May her light shine down upon us all," Lorelei completed the saying. Without another word, she spurred the horse toward her destiny.

CHAPTER TWELVE

Tim came to a stop just inside the door.

Cassie had her bō staff out wide, blocking any of them from getting around her. It took him a few moments to figure out why, but then he saw what the interior of the building looked like. Tim had been expecting to fight a bunch of the wraiths like they had already encountered or maybe even more of a traditional dungeon crawl, going from one room to the next until they fought the boss monster at the end.

Instead, they'd almost run into the boss. There was a shimmer in the air about a foot in front of Cassie. The boss was on the other side. Thankfully, it looked as if the monster contained within couldn't see them through the shimmer. The downside was that Tim also couldn't glean any information about the boss from this side of the veil.

The rough shadow showed something moving around, something big. Tim was so happy he decided not to play a tank. What a thankless job. If the group dies it's your fault. If the group succeeds with ease, no one knows your name. Either way, you have to get the shit knocked out of you.

Kind of like being Connor McGregor.

Sure, that spunky Irishman dished out a lot of pain, but he also came out bloody most of the time. Sometimes it felt like cage fighting was a war of attrition. All they did for the first few rounds was to feel each other out, trying to do some damage while waiting for that one mistake, and then…

BAM.

Tim wanted to make sure they didn't end up being what was left on the mat to scrape up after the BAM happened. He looked over his team. "Everyone ready?"

Four pairs of determined eyes met his own, and Tim felt a grin break out on his face. "Then what in the hell are we waiting for?"

Cassie reached out to touch the shimmering haze. She pulled her hand back the haze sticking to it almost like water. "This is so cool." Her face grew concerned. "Hey, what the fuck?"

The liquid attached to her fingers spread up her hand before grabbing Cassie's wrist. She tried to pull away and was yanked forward. Panic spread across her features as she squatted down, setting her feet like the anchor of a tug of war team. Grabbing the entangled forearm, Cassie pulled back with every ounce of strength she could muster.

When Cassie didn't move an inch, she turned to her friends. "Somebody help me."

JaKobi pointed to himself. "Not it."

"You mother fu…" And then Cassie was sucked inside of the boss' chamber.

Gaston grabbed JaKobi by the back of the robes. "You're up next." He ran forward, pulling the mage with him.

Smiling, Tim reached out for ShadowLily's hand. "See you on the other side." He took a step forward, unsure of what to expect.

The portal reached out to grab him, and Tim popped out the other side. It was almost like being the cork in the bottle except there was no momentum. One second, he was on one side, and the next he was on the other, with Cassie waving for him to duck.

There wasn't time to think, so he just threw himself flat and hoped for the best.

When he didn't hear anybody scream and didn't end up back with Barbara, Tim knew he'd gotten down in time. Ever so slowly, he raised his head until he could see Cassie watching him. She peeked over a crate and motioned for him to join her. As Tim got closer, he saw JaKobi was squatting behind another of the crates, but Gaston was nowhere to be seen.

"Fucking assassins," Tim grumbled to himself a little jealously. He could sneak around, but he couldn't flat out disappear like the two of them. He was pretty sure if he tried to use his fledgling skill against a boss ranked monster, he'd end up ruining his stream before it even got started.

Tim waited until Cassie gave the all-clear, and then he poked his head over the crate to catch a peek of the boss. The monster wasn't what he'd been expecting at all. This wasn't some kind of gothic dungeon crawler, this was a fantasy game set in Eternia. The trouble in this land came from kobolds, orcs, and goblins.

The boss waiting for them on the other side of the crates was nothing like what he'd seen in the movies. Apparently, someone on the development team said fuck all this easy shit, let's give them a heart attack. Tim didn't like the idea of going from the more classic fantasy setting to being trapped in a *Silent Hill* remake one bit.

Cassie got his attention and mouthed. "What do we do?"

Tim just shrugged his shoulders.

What in the fuck were they going to do? He'd never seen a monster like this in Eternia before, but this was a game, and there had to be a way to win. Meeting Cassie's hopeful eyes, he mimicked hitting something with a stick. It was all he could think of to do. They came here to fight, and they had to defeat the boss if they wanted to complete the quest, so there really wasn't much of a choice. He focused on the tank. "Let's just take this slow."

Cassie nodded, and Tim looked back over the box. He was

happy he wasn't the one running straight at a boss named Knuck-lebones. Not when his knuckles were covered by huge blades. He kept his head low when the boss started another slow circle of the room.

How was he going to get them through this?

It was one thing to be facing down a giant wraith, it was quite another to be facing something that might have walked out of hell. Knucklebones was easily ten feet tall, and his shoulders seemed as wide as the front of a bus. It wasn't the boss' heavily muscled shoulders that had grabbed Tim's attention though.

It was the giant metal blades bolted through his forearms.

The razor-sharp metal blades looked to have been attached to the boss' arms by giant silver bolts. The pain of having those driven through the bones must have been excruciating. Not to mention how much it had to hurt hitting someone with them.

Blood dripped down the boss' arms, the few shredded bandages it had in place not enough to stop the black liquid from seeping out. Carrying the weight of those massive blades explained the crazy strong arms and shoulders. Tim was pretty sure if Knuckle-bones hit any of them, they would have a real bad day.

Not the auspicious start to the quest Tim was looking for. Instead, he had to find a way to use his new skills for the first time against a boss-level monster. Whatever happened to planning and taking things slow? He felt a little out of his element. Winging it wasn't really his thing.

It appeared as if the boss was alone in the room. *At least they didn't have to worry about minions.* Tim slipped into his Way of the Boulder stance. Cassie was going to need all the damage reduction she could get, and the majority of the heals. If the little tank did her job right and kept the boss' attention, things should work out just fine.

Cassie held her hand in the air with four fingers up. She made sure they all had time to see it and then lowered one finger. She did a quick double-check with JaKobi and Tim before lowering the second finger. With two fingers still in the air, Cassie took one last look before vaulting over the crates.

Tim jumped to his feet, wondering if he had somehow missed the count. He scrambled over the crate with much less agility just in time to see Cassie charging at the boss with her bō staff held high above her head.

"Come and get some you big ugly fuck!" Cassie roared as she picked up speed.

Tim noticed that metal plates were bolted into Knucklesbones' thighs and shins. From a distance, the metal just looked like armor. Now that he knew the difference, he felt kind of bad for whoever the man used to be before the dark goddess Vitaria had twisted him into something unnatural.

That was the sad thing about wraiths, they used to be people.

A wave of energy radiated out from the boss as he cried out in agony. The wail of pain staggered every member of the party and sent at least three of them to their knees. The assassin's stealth was shattered, and the boss' skin took on the slightly red tint of an enraged monster.

"How in the fuck can he be enraged, we haven't even hit him yet?" Cassie griped as she lifted her bō staff in the air to land the first blow.

"Just be careful," Tim called out as if he needed to remind Cassie getting cut in half was a bad thing.

His go-to move at this point would normally be to cast a healing orb. Since his main healing spell received a healing over time component, it had become incredibly handy. Now Tim had a new option, although at novice level one it was a comparatively weak option. At least he could fall back on his older healing spells if things got out of control.

For the first time ever, Tim cast curse of giving.

One percent of the damage the spell dealt would be returned to Cassie as healing. With his buff from the stance, that amount jumped to two percent. All he had to do was get the skill up to where it would do fifty percent of the damage returned as health, and his stance would buff it to one hundred percent. That day was a long way off, but he'd get there.

Maybe at Grandmaster rank the spell would return more health than damage or add an additional perk, like a cleanse. He didn't want to be super-overpowered, but the benefits of a spell like this seemed infinite. Especially when he could switch stance and heal more than one person with the same single cast.

Cassie's staff cracked against one of Knucklebones' blades. The boss shrugged off the attack and spun his fist around to decapitate her. Cassie managed to dodge his blade-like hands, but it had been closer than it should have been. The tank was normally much more agile than this. Why was she moving so slowly?

He could have slapped himself for not even thinking to check. With a quick thought, he pulled up his status effects to see if the boss had applied a debuff to them when they had staggered.

Agony: movement speed reduced by twenty percent.

Tim had never used his cleanse to try to remove anything but a hangover. In other games the same spell worked to cure a number of maladies. He personally hated it in games when the developers made a choice to have each class only able to remove some of the debuffs. People don't want to be shoehorned into a class or role just because they need one buff or cleanse for the group to be successful. They want to play what they want to play.

Hoping the mega geniuses running *The Etheric Coast* felt the same way he did Tim cast cleanse on Cassie hoping for the best. The spell took shape, and a bolt of shimmering light flew toward the tank. When the light reached her it exploded like a firework over her head, and the sparks rained down over her shoulders. A quick check of his status window confirmed the debuff had been removed, and Cassie was free to kick ass as usual.

"That's going to come in handy." Tim worked on cleansing ShadowLily next.

A sharp pain drove him to his knees. Tim didn't bother

standing up. He just stayed on his knees and cast like his life depended on it. His curse of giving was taking care of Cassie, but the rest of them were taking damage from the boss. Maybe his agony skill also applied damage over time to the entire party?

This entire fight might as well have been a giant healing check. Tim switched his stance to Way of the River and recast curse of giving. Now the healing should spread to the entire party. While their health was relatively full, he decided to cast who needs a shield to reduce the boss' damage while they tried to figure out his attacks.

"My time to shine." Tim cracked his knuckles and got to work healing while the rest of the team delivered damage to the boss.

"Hate to break it to you, but I'm the only shiny one here." JaKobi grinned as he sent a fireball racing toward Knucklebones.

The flames broke over the monster's skin, leaving it singed. Turning away from Cassie, Knucklesbones crossed his forearm blades in front of himself and knelt. Tim knew what was coming next. The boss was going to charge. Orienting himself on the fire mage, Knucklebones dug his feet into the ground and started running forward.

JaKobi was too busy casting his next spell to notice what was going on. Tim ran toward the mage and tackled him to the ground as he felt the wind rush past his feet. He had to look down to reassure himself his feet were still there. The building started to shake as Knucklebones hit the far wall before turning to face the group of fighters.

Scanning the room, Knucklebones' head tilted back to let out another wail of agony.

Tim was ready for damage this time and knew that the spell would hit them with at least one more wave of pain before it dispersed. What he had to worry about now was getting the debuff off their tank. His cleanse hit Cassie, JaKobi, and ShadowLily before the next wave of pain hit.

At least the second wave didn't apply the speed debuff again. It only reduced everyone's hit points. Tim quickly cast cleanse on himself and Gaston before recasting curse of giving. He had to admit that having his first real group heal was amazing, even if his healing mostly came from doing damage. Maybe his flame burst spell would finally be useful.

For the first time since she joined their party, Tim saw the benefits of Cassie's class. Being an avoidance tank meant she didn't take a shit ton of upfront damage. The bad side was that a critical hit put her damn near on the verge of death. In this fight, her ability to dodge was what gave him the chance to get everyone's health and status effects where they needed to be. If he was only able to focus on the tank, they would have all been in trouble.

Cassie kept moving, using her bō staff to harass Knucklebones. The boss grew frustrated with her, and the red around him started to grow darker. Tim started to worry that maybe she hadn't noticed the change, but he should have just kept his mind on his own business. Cassie was a professional.

The tank easily skipped to the side as the blades on Kuncklebones' arms detached, and shot forward with incredible speed. The two blades stuck in the ground, and despite Knucklebones pulling on the chains attached to them, they wouldn't come free.

ShadowLily and Gaston jumped into action, using their throwing knives to start whittling down the boss' health. JaKobi let loose with a howl of his own and sent a fireball flying into Knucklebones. It would have been fun to join the party, but Tim took the time to let his mana pool regenerate, while the others focused on the real work.

Keeping at a distance seemed like the prudent thing to do, even if it made their DPS slower. There was no telling what Knucklebones would do next. The whole dynamic of the fight would change if he could start launching his blades at people from a greater distance. Cassie smiled at the group and started to circle the boss, ready to jump in as soon as Knucklebones was free.

It seemed creating some distance was the right thing to do. The red around the boss grew dark and began pulsing almost black in color. Knucklebones finally managed to rip his blades free from the ground. Instead of pulling the weapons back toward himself and attacking again, the boss started to spin around, creating a whirling circle of razor-sharp death.

"Cyclone!" Tim yelled out, hoping everyone got the reference.

Every fantasy game on the planet had one class that spun in circles to hit a bunch of enemies at the same time. The problem was that when a boss monster did it, the damage was normally unavoidable and catastrophic. All you could do was get the fuck out of the way.

Thankfully, the group had been willing to take things slow or else three of them would probably be dead right now. Tim shuddered to think what would have happened to the two assassins and the tank if they had been in close range when the attack started. By all rights, everyone should have been in close to inflict maximum damage, but they had stuck with the plan, and it was paying off.

Things were going better than expected.

His last thought must have been a kiss of death because as soon as Tim mentally patted the party on the back, everything went to shit. The boss stopped spinning and pulled the blades back to himself, where they magically reattached to his forearms. With a grunt of effort, he charged toward the tank, ready to start their deadly dance again.

Cassie dodged two of Knucklebones' attacks and even landed one of her own before his mouth opened and changed the dynamics of the entire fight.

The same snake-like feeder the warden had used shot out of Knucklebones' mouth and grazed Cassie's shoulder. Her arm must have gone numb because the tank's staff clattered to the ground. All Cassie could do was dodge out of the way as Knucklebones started to chase her around the warehouse.

Tim cursed. He should have realized his buff against weakness wouldn't do much against a boss level monster. Not at the lowest of skill levels. He'd been a little overconfident in the buffs he'd received from Eternia and his own new class. It was time to get back to basics and make sure they survived this fight.

JaKobi was casting some kind of root spell, but the boss seemed to be immune to the effect. Tim thought about trying to cast his own low-level root spell and decided it was a waste of time. Instead, he worked on doing something he knew would help. A quick flick of the wrist and his cleanse spell enveloped Cassie. Her arm started working again almost instantly, but she still didn't have her weapon.

ShadowLily and Gaston chose that moment to strike. The two assassins leaped from the shadows to attack the boss from opposite sides in near-perfect unison. Their daggers clanked off of Knucklebones' forearms, and Tim started to wonder if they were in over their heads. His next set of heals went out just as the damage from agony staggered them again.

ShadowLily and Gaston went down, but Cassie had been out of the area of effect. The tank picked up her staff before charging back into the fray to save her friends. Her bō staff caught a blow that would have taken ShadowLily's head off and redirected it into the dirt.

Letting out a sigh of relief, Tim took a moment to think about what to do next. Their health was never going to get any higher than it was right now, so it was the best time to try out his new spell.

"Sorry, guys." Tim cast behold my power, sending the first of ten small waves of pain through his team.

Trying to buy them some time to recover, Tim quickly cast weaken undead. The spell hit the boss, and he stumbled for a moment. That one errant step was enough of an opening for Gaston and ShadowLily to dive right back into the fight. Their daggers repeatedly found purchase on the wraith's unprotected flesh, and his health bar started dropping in larger chunks.

Tim wanted to call on his divine light spell to try to end the fight, but he knew they were about to get hit with another wave of pain, and his team's health was already dropping more rapidly than he would have liked. Tim dropped to one knee in exhaustion, his mana reserves plummeting below ten percent. His group heal was keeping the team alive, but with the damage he was doing to them, he couldn't come out ahead.

Hearing a new guttural form of chanting, Tim wondered what was about to hit them next when he realized it was coming from JaKobi. The crazy bastard had a mirror held out in front of him, and he was babbling some nonsensical words while looking into the glass. The fire mage's voice sounded different, and Tim couldn't keep his eyes off of him.

Tim's spell behold my power finally kicked in, and all of the health that the spell had taken from his party was transferred to Knucklebones in one fell swoop. The boss staggered, and the debuff icon appeared over his head, indicating the boss would take more damage from all sources.

Flames erupted from JaKobi's robes, flowing out behind him as he walked toward the boss with deadly purpose. His chanting stopped, and he flipped the mirror around. White light erupted from the mirror. The glass shattered into a million pieces as a light raced straight for the boss. The beam of solid energy tore a hole through the boss' chest, leaving behind a trail of smoking flesh.

Knucklebones crumpled to the ground, his last breath coming out as a ragged gasp. The boss' hit points reached zero, and the battle was over. The body slowly dissolved into a brilliant swirl of golden motes. When they could see again, there was a single chest waiting for them in the center of the room.

"One down, two to go," Tim said, and the group groaned.

"How about we see if this loot was worth it," Cassie said deviously as she walked toward the chest.

"I just hit level ten. Loot is only a bonus," JaKobi said, grinning from ear to ear. "All I have to do now is go and see the trainer for my new class."

"Wait, you don't have to do a quest?" ShadowLily asked, sounding put out.

JaKobi laughed. "You didn't think I was spending all that time at the library for fun, did you?" He lifted his hands in mock surrender as the guild glared back at him. "Okay, so not just for fun. It's not my fault you all had to do some kind of quest and all I had to do was prop open a book and learn a few things."

Tim clapped the fire mage on the back. "Well, whatever that last spell was, it was fucking awesome!"

"It was pretty awesome," Cassie admitted grudgingly. "And you just hit level ten, so I guess you should go first." She pointed at the golden chest. "Hurry up and open it before I change my mind, Fireboy."

JaKobi placed his hand against the chest, and a moment later a look of joy spread across his face. He looked at the group as a bright red wizard hat appeared on his head. "I've always wanted one of these, but this one actually increases my affinity with all fire spells by a level. You may now refer to me as JaKobi the Red, second only to Gandalf the White."

"Put your nerd boner away and let me see what's in the chest for me." Cassie touched her hand to the chest. She frowned as she looked at the item she received. "Headband of Zula, for when your head is as hard as a rock?"

She looked at JaKobi. "Explain."

The fire mage looked around the group and quickly realized that either no one knew who Zula was or they were all playing dumb so they wouldn't have to say. The look of panic on the man's face told Tim the poor mage was trying to figure out how to phrase his answer in a way that didn't end with him being throttled by Cassie.

Poor bastard. Was it wrong for him to be smiling?

"Zula was this super badass warrior woman in *Conan the Destroyer*. When he tried to grab her, she head-butted him to get away." JaKobi gave her a smile. "She fought like a true warrior and kicked ASS just like you."

Cassie kept her eyes locked on him. "I'm going to look this Zula up so you better not be lying to me."

"Don't be mad at him for spending weekends locked in the basement. Being a nerd is cool as fuck. There's a rumor they run the world." ShadowLily grinned as she held her arms out as if to say, see, we're standing in it right now.

"Plus, you totally needed something to protect your dome. The last thing we want to do is start calling you concussion protocol." JaKobi tapped his knuckles against his own head.

Cassie stuck her tongue out at the fire mage and flipped ShadowLily the bird.

"Just be thankful you didn't get stuck with a full-on helmet, that shit's hard on the hair." ShadowLily walked up to the chest and put her hand on it.

"Wicked." She pulled out a dagger with a straight blade. It was the kind of thing you would use to stab between the chinks in a set of armor. The steel tip of the knife was almost green in color. "Five percent armor penetration, and it makes my poisons five percent more effective."

Gaston eyed the blade jealously. Tim felt a little bad for the guy. Last time he went on a dungeon crawl with them he was allowed to take loot. Apparently, that was a no-no now making these trips not very profitable for the assassin.

Tim made a mental note to ask Ironbeard if he could make Gaston a similar dagger. Their party wouldn't have been able to make it this far without his help, and he deserved to get something out of these quests besides the pleasure of their company.

Stepping up to the chest, Tim put his hand against the lid. "Boots of Swift Regeneration. Increases base movement speed and mana regeneration by one percent."

Everyone's gear seemed to have bonuses, but Cassie hadn't

spoken about hers. Tim couldn't help but wonder what she was hiding. "Hey, warrior princess, what's the bonus on your helmet."

The group turned to look at Cassie, and she glared at Tim. "It says the item provides an aura called "Hard Headed," which makes the wearer immune to being stunned."

Tim shook off her glare with ease. "Seems like an awesome bonus for a tank that needs to keep moving to survive."

Cassie looked at the circlet with newfound respect before placing it on her head. "Just because it's awesome don't think I'm not looking up this Zula chick the first chance I get. If you fucked with me, you're going to have a real bad day." She pointed at JaKobi. "I will end you."

Looking over his group, Tim came to a decision. "I thought this was just going to be us rounding up a few of the wraiths before we reached a boss, but now I think we have to treat this like a dungeon where each encounter is an instanced fight."

ShadowLily nodded. "Sounds about right. I wasn't expecting a boss-type monster to be waiting for us at what Brother Colton described as the least important location."

"To say I nearly shit my pants would be an understatement," Cassie said with a laugh.

Tim grinned as he thought about her kicking the door to the warehouse down and almost stepping right into a boss encounter. Luckily, the game saved them from that particular fate, giving them enough time to get set before the fight started.

"If everyone agrees, this is what I want to do." He turned to JaKobi. "Go and get your class upgraded. We're going to need all the firepower we can get."

Tim looked around the room at the weary faces. It had been a long day, and he was pretty sure selling a quiet night back at the inn wouldn't be too hard. "As for the rest of us, I propose a good meal and an early night. If we start early enough tomorrow, we should be able to knock out the remaining encounters."

"Sounds good to me, Boss," JaKobi shouted as he ran for the

door. The last thing the fire mage wanted was for someone to stand in the way of his class change.

Cassie grinned as she watched JaKobi. "I guess that answers the question for all of us."

"Just be happy there aren't more fish guts in store for your future," ShadowLily said with a smirk as they headed toward the door. Her class change quest had been a smelly one.

"I had to throw those boots away. Even the game couldn't get the smell out of them," Cassie replied as she stepped out into the late afternoon sun. "Although I did make a nice profit on the trident."

Tim wrapped his arms around both their shoulders and started steering them back to the inn. "Let's continue this stimulating conversation with a beer."

Gaston thumped him on the back before darting around the group. He was jogging lightly backward in front of them. "Did you say something about beer?"

Tim nodded, and Gaston started running away from him as fast as JaKobi had. He shouted after the fleeing assassin. "Just tell Ernie to put it on my tab."

The assassin lifted a fist in the air to signal he'd heard as he raced down the street. Tim could have sworn he heard Gaston shout "already done," before he sprinted around the corner.

"Guy really likes his beer." Tim chuckled.

The three of them broke out in laughter. Life was good when you had wonderful people to share it with and enough coin to take away the sting of everyday burdens.

CHAPTER THIRTEEN

The third cup of coffee really does the trick.

Tim smiled as his body relaxed from the blast of caffeinated goodness. The only thing that would make this better for him was a giant cinnamon roll, or better yet, a stack of cinnamon roll pancakes. Was there anything cinnamon, sugar, and butter couldn't make better? Tim checked his waistline, loving every minute of being in the game.

Ryan Reynolds isn't the only one with abs you want to eat pizza off of now, right, world?

The warm coffee spluttering out of his nose woke him up quicker than drinking it. Why in the fuck was he daring the world to eat pizza off his abs, and why of all the people he could be imagining feeding him a slice was it Ryan Reynolds? It just wasn't realistic.

The fucker didn't eat carbs.

Thankfully for Tim, he could eat all the carbs he wanted. It didn't seem as though he could gain weight in this game. He had heard of a service where you could change your appearance, and make yourself older, younger, thinner, fatter, whatever you wanted, was only a few dollars away. So much easier than out in the real world where you had to work your ass off to lose a few pounds.

Being committed to a healthy lifestyle took a lot of work. Tim would be the first to admit he liked his pizza a little too much, and his exercise a bit less than he should have. He'd let things get out of control once, but he vowed to never do it again. Here he didn't have to worry about his weight.

Which meant eating for pleasure came without the guilt trip.

Just one more reason living inside of the game was better than reality. If Tim had taken the job offer he received, at this very moment he'd be stuck in a cubicle trying to discern patterns from graphs to make people an extra few cents. Instead, he was going to kill two wraith bosses and celebrate victory with his friends at the inn.

A life of adventure was hard to beat.

He looked up from wiping off his face to see the most beautiful woman in the world walking down the stairs. Tim knew it wouldn't matter how long he was alive, she would always be perfect. It wasn't just that bitchin body he was into either. It was the fact they could sit in a room together in complete silence and still feel connected.

He never wanted to give that up.

"Ready to kick some ass?" Tim asked as he poured her a cup of coffee from the silver carafe on the table.

She snatched the coffee and took a sip before setting the cup down. ShadowLily arched her back then let out a long sigh before sitting down. "I'll let you know after breakfast."

"Sorry milady, but today we've got meals on wheels," JaKobi said as he returned from the kitchen with his arms full of little bundles of butcher's paper.

"What are those?" Cassie asked as she pulled up a chair and poured a glass of rumpleberry juice.

Grinning from ear to ear, JaKobi set the small pile of wrapped packages down on the table with reverence. "Breakfast burritos."

"Get out!" Cassie screamed with delight.

ShadowLily had a knowing smile on her face. "My dad showed the inn's cook how to make them for us, but he also insists that we come to the restaurant more often. He holds an open table for anyone in the guild."

Gaston rubbed his belly and smiled. "I can attest to that. Joe is a great man, a man who should be honored by his daughter."

"See, I told you he missed us," ShadowLily said to Tim.

Tim smiled mischievously. "I might have some people looking into how to connect his inn to the restaurant, and Ernie is building that new wing with updated bathrooms for us."

ShadowLily shrugged. "I still think we should have dinner at his place tonight."

"You never have to twist my arm to eat whatever Joe is cooking." Tim picked up his burrito. "Let's hit the road."

Cassie picked up hers. "What's with the butcher's paper?"

Flames curled the paper around JaKobi's burrito to ashes, and he took a bite. "I don't think anyone's invented tinfoil yet."

"Or manners," Cassie snapped as she headed for the door.

Laughter broke out amongst the group as JaKobi tried to reply with a full mouth. He finished his bite and then chased Cassie toward the door. "I'm sorry. I was just so hungry."

He took another bite, this time keeping his mouth closed until he was done chewing. "It's super-good, just so everyone knows!" The fire mage ducked out the door.

Tim tapped his burrito against ShadowLily's. "After you."

She let out a mock groan but climbed to her feet quickly. Each step the assassin in training took toward the door, she looked more alert than the next. Turning away from the magnificent view, Tim picked up the last burrito and tossed it to Gaston.

"Ready to roll?" Tim noted the solemn look on the assassin's face.

Gaston wrapped his arm around Tim's shoulders and herded him toward the door. "Let's try to get this business wrapped up today. With Malvonis still out of the picture, the city's underworld needs a leader. I can't spend all my time helping the goddess' chosen."

Tim defaulted to his go-to burrito tap. "Then let's go get this shit done, so you can get back to ruling the dirty underbelly of the city."

"It's not so dirty," Gaston replied incredulously. "Most of the filth left town." He slid a finger across his throat as they stepped out into the sun. The assassin took a bite of his burrito and looked at Tim. "Hey, these are good."

Tim shook his head in wonder. His life was kind of strange now, but it was also fucking awesome.

The second location on the map made the slums look good.

Not knowing when the fight might start, he activated his stream, not that people would get to look at much. Tim would have thought there couldn't be a worse side of town than the slums until he came here. He wasn't sure how long it took a full pier of ships to rot into the ocean, but somehow it was happening. The only people happy about the state of this pier were the fish.

How was it that the main docks of Promethia had so many ships the captains had to take turns docking, and this pier, mere miles away, was empty? It didn't make sense. Something had gone wrong in this section of town long before the wraiths had shown up, and his group was going to have to deal with it now.

Rotten timbers shifted under their feet as they slowly moved along the wharf, looking for clues. Brother Colton had clearly marked this as the location, but all that was here now was the wreckage of ships just under the surface.

"Holy shit, is that an arm?" Cassie pointed down the wharf, drawing their attention to something white lying on the sandy shore.

Tim almost gagged at the smell as they drew closer to the object. Twenty steps later and Tim could tell it was a hand sticking out of the ground, all five fingers splayed as if hoping someone would pull them from the seas before they drowned.

Fuck, this is dark, even for a game.

The arm marked the center of Brother Colton's marker on the map. Tim didn't see the shimmer they'd encountered at the last location. The only thing here was a half-rotted arm, which smelled worse than it looked but not by much.

Everyone else was facing outward, keeping an eye on the water and the alleyways leading to their location. There didn't seem to be any movement, and he couldn't think of anything to initiate the fight, unless…

"Guys, I think this is going to suck." Tim motioned for them to back up. "And I really hope I'm not wrong."

Moving toward the hand, Tim gave it a quick slap before sprinting back to join the others. The wooden timbers of the wharf started to rattle, and everyone scrambled away from the source of the disturbance. The last thing any of them wanted was to get thrown in the rancid water.

"Get behind me!" Cassie roared.

Get behind the tank, that's a good fucking idea.

It wasn't as if they should have needed a reminder, but all of them had forgotten themselves as they watched the wharf falling apart around something huge. Cassie's command brought them back on track and reminded him of something important. Don't stop and stare until you're in position.

Anything else was a death sentence.

Heeding his own advice, Tim started running and didn't stop until he skidded into place behind the group. There was no way to know what was going to happen next, but he had a healing spell ready to go. They hadn't lost a fight yet, and he wasn't ready to start now.

The Blue Dagger Society had a stellar track record of figuring things out on the fly, which always kind of surprised him because he thought of it as a weakness of his own. Every member of the team brought something different to the table, and all of them executed their jobs at a high level.

Cassie had her bō staff in front of her, and her legs spread in a defensive stance. When she started shuffling backward, the group followed her step for step. She was giving whatever was trying to emerge from under the toppled wharf room to spare, and Tim didn't blame her one bit. It never paid to run heedlessly into battle when you could take a second to plan.

An arm stuck out of the rough wooden planks and started to jiggle back and forth like some kind of perverse tube man. The limb flopped more violently as the timbers around it started to push upwards. Cassie backed up another few feet. She wanted to fight the boss on a level surface.

"Is that a hat?" JaKobi snorted as he pointed at the arm.

Tim almost laughed, but it would have been the nervous kind, and not what his team needed right now. The fire mage didn't need to point, none of them were looking anywhere else, but JaKobi was right. What was coming out of the ground did look like a hat.

A giant fucking pirate hat.

And instead of a cute little adornment like a feather, there was an arm. How big did the thing coming out of the bay have to be if it could wear a human arm on top of its hat like a feather?

Maybe we should back up a few more feet.

The boss started to reveal itself, and Tim wasn't quite sure what he was seeing. The creature was man-shaped for the most part but had a lower half like a giant crab. The pincers looked to be covered in some kind of razor-sharp barnacles, while the rest of his limbs had sturdy shell plating.

From a distance, it might have looked like the boss was just some crazy pirate riding a crab. All you had to do was get a little closer to know that wasn't right. A hot female torso on a spider's body he could get behind, but a big smelly pirate chest on top of a crab offended his sense of joy for the encounter.

Or maybe it was the smell.

Tim rubbed his eyes and tried to decide the best way to take it down. So far, all he'd managed to do was figure out the creature's name, Captain Orlof. He wondered if the man had been cursed or if somehow, when he was attacked by a wraith, it twisted him in a way they didn't know was possible.

In other words, I've got no fucking clue what to expect, as usual. His mind jumped into overdrive as he prepared himself for the fight.

"Who disturbs my slumber!" Captain Orlof roared as he circled around, scanning the wharf in front of him for someone to kill.

When Orlof looked up, Tim realized the captain only had one eye. There was a patch over the other one. Whatever artist had thought this creature up had done a good job. The crabman hit all of the pirate tropes, but it was scary as hell.

Like, run straight to therapy, do not pass go kind of shit.

The good news for them was that unlike in the real world where you had to work through your problems with words, and show empathy to others, here all they had to do was kill the fucking thing. Tim reached out and patted Cassie on the back. "Go get 'em, tiger."

The tank gave Tim a quick glare before facing the boss. Cassie rested her bō staff against her shoulder for a moment as she spit on her leather gloves. After rubbing her hands together, she picked up the staff and set her feet. "Time to get some."

Without another word, she ran at Captain Orlof. Cassie rolled through his first attack and then dodged past his second one. Her bō staff slammed into the crab's underbelly and bounced back toward her. Cassie used the momentum to change directions, barely missing another swipe of the Captain's chitinous legs as she worked to turn him around for the DPS.

JaKobi didn't waste any time and went straight for the kill with his mirror spell. Tim wasn't sure if the spell would make it past the crab's armor. He also wondered for the first time if maybe the wraith had inhabited an undiscovered boss and corrupted it. Most players didn't venture through the dilapidated parts of the city and would have avoided this place.

Big mistake.

Tim managed to cast his weaken undead spell right before JaKobi's ray of brilliant light shot forward. He might as well have not wasted the effort. The spell bounced harmlessly away like an underfilled balloon in a water balloon fight. Sadly, the fire mage didn't fare much better. The spell he'd used on the last boss with such great effectiveness barely left a scorch mark on the captain's shell.

"We have to break his shell open," Tim called out to the others.

Captain Orlof spun around and knocked Cassie to the ground with his back legs as he rounded on Tim. "So you are the one our dark queen seeks to vanquish." He rose up on his hind legs as the two razer covered pincers in front turned into whirling blades of death. "Do you hear the cries of the damned? They are calling you home."

The boss' claws came crashing down in a flurry of attacks. Tim managed to dodge the first two but was grazed by the third. Captain Orlof's pincers shredded through his robes like tissue paper, leaving a gash down his side. The attack could have been a lot worse. If he hadn't been moving, Tim might have lost an arm instead of having the worst case of road rash ever.

Blood leaked from his wounds, and Tim started trying to heal himself. It was a lot harder to concentrate when he was the one bleeding. He made sure to take note of this for later. It was going to suck, but he was going to have to practice casting while hurt if he wanted to get any better at it.

Something crashed into him from behind. Tim hit the wooden planks hard, sending a jolt of pain through his injury. He couldn't stop a cry from escaping his lips, and he not so silently cursed at whoever tackled him to the ground.

Tim's anger only lasted until he rolled over and saw the area he'd just occupied shattered and broken by Orlof's massive body. The boss must have launched into the air and come down on the spot with enough force to splatter Tim like a bug. A healing orb took the edge off his wounds as he scrambled to his feet.

JaKobi stood up next to him, grinning ear to ear. "That was a close one."

"He's stunned!" Tim cried out, hoping to draw everyone's attention to the unmoving boss, and away from the fact he almost got turned into paste.

ShadowLily appeared on top of Captain Orlof's shell and stabbed her daggers into his unprotected torso from behind. Gaston mirrored her attacks from the other side. JaKobi ran forward, a sword created purely out of fire appearing in his hand. The fire mage rushed at the boss, only to stop just short of attacking him.

Tim was about to ask JaKobi what in the fuck he was doing when he noticed the fire mage's health bar plummeting. He cast a healing orb on the fire mage and started sprinting toward him to find out what was going on. Tim couldn't see whatever was happening to JaKobi from this angle.

He reached JaKobi's side and saw the problem instantly. Captain Orlof's eye patch was gone, and the feeder Tim normally associated with a wraith's mouth had launched out of the socket and struck JaKobi in the chest.

Pulling his own dagger free, Tim started hacking at the feeding tube. Every few seconds he had to stop and heal JaKobi. "Can I get some help down here?"

ShadowLily was by his side in a flash and cut JaKobi free with a single strike of her blade. Sometimes he was a little envious of how fast someone with dedicated DPS could do something that took him forever.

But now he got to do the thing that made him special.

Tim knelt next to the fallen mage and focused all of his attention on bringing JaKobi back from the brink of death. It would take everything he had to try to get rid of the wraith's poison. Healing him only seemed to stall the inevitable. Every time he had to heal the mage, he lost progress on cleansing the poison from his system.

"Who wants some fucking crab cakes!" Cassie yelled as the boss went down.

Tim hardly even noticed the encounter was over. He was too busy trying to keep JaKobi alive. The fire mage groaned, but his color was improving. Slowly the target of his cleanse started to look more like himself.

JaKobi's eyes fluttered open, and he looked up at Tim. A small frown formed at the corners of his lips. "I always thought that if I ever passed out, I'd wake up in the arms of a beautiful woman."

Tim shoved the man off his lap. "Keep dreaming."

"That's my biggest problem. The good-looking ones only like me in my dreams," JaKobi said as he stood up and brushed his robes free of dirt.

Cassie was starting to work herself up, but instead of going off she gave the fire mage the finger. "Probably because you refer to them as the good-looking ones, implying you only care about one thing."

JaKobi looked wounded. "Think of the looks as the gateway. Once we've established that you meet the base requirements, we delve deeper into the heart and soul."

"Ah, so you're only shallow at first," Cassie chided.

"Let's just say I like to have my cake and eat it too." The fire mage wiggled his eyebrows at the group.

"I'm just going to call that creepy." Cassie brushed past him. "Let's get our gear and get the hell out of here."

"I'm with her," Tim replied.

"Me too," ShadowLily said with a smile as she joined Tim by the treasure chest.

Gaston looked at JaKobi. "You'll always have me."

The fire mage lowered his head. "That's what I'm afraid of."

Cassie tapped her hand against the chest and a grin that would have made the Grinch jealous spread across her face. "Bō Staff of Thorns. Every third hit, thorns will appear on the end of the staff, causing a bleeding-over-time effect."

"Nice." ShadowLily stepped to the front of the group and placed her own hand on the chest. "Leggings of Endless Night. Adds a level to all skills executed in stealth."

Tim waved JaKobi forward. "Let's see if you get something to go with that hat."

The fire mage smiled. "I hope so. My new class is called pyromancer, and I need a few things to really make it shine."

The newly minted pyromancer looked down at the chest. "I doubt I'll get anything special. I kinda feel like I've exceeded my luck quota for the week already." He put his hand on the chest. "I mean, without you guys I'd just be throwing fireballs at targets back in town, too scared to try anything else."

"Let's just call it even," Tim said as he clapped JaKobi on the back. He thought about the times since that first encounter where his fiery friend helped them win a fight and knew their kindness had been paid back a hundredfold.

Tim placed his hand on the chest as he watched JaKobi's simple robes were replaced with a set of red robes trimmed in gold that matched his new wizard's cap. "So much for your luck running out."

"What can I say?" JaKobi danced around the wharf. "These Robes of Undying Flames make me look good." He stopped his shuffling hop step of a dance and faced the others. "They also extended any damage over time abilities I have by five seconds.

Tim looked down at his white and blue robes, a little envious of the pyromancer's pizazz. Maybe there was a merchant somewhere that could dye clothes? There was so much he didn't know about the world around him. Things always seemed to be happening so fast. It was like his life just went from one crazy event to the other.

Not that those events weren't highly profitable and full of great loot.

"Wristband of the Goddess. It provides a ten percent damage reduction against all attacks of a dark nature."

Cassie started leading them back into town. "What does that even mean?"

"I'm not eager to find out." Tim shook his head as if banishing a bad thought. "Just imagine if I couldn't cast during a fight because I got hit with one of those feeders. I'm hoping this wristband makes that outcome less likely."

"Let's just go with that and call it a win." JaKobi tipped his hat back. "Now hurry up. I want to finish off this last boss to get the quest done."

ShadowLily popped out of the darkness next to the pyromancer, scaring him so badly he fell to the ground. Laughing, she helped him to his feet. "Last part of the quest, and we are still no closer to figuring out where the big baddie is hiding."

Cassie directed the group onto one of the main thoroughfares as she led them to the next waypoint. "I've been wondering about that. It isn't like the bosses are dropping clues."

"After we handle whatever is waiting for us at the next location, we'll go back to the inn and see what we can come up with. If we are still drawing a blank, we'll go back to Brother Colton and see if he has anything else for us to go on." Tim hoped they didn't have to go back to the priest with their hats in hand. He had the feeling there might be a better reward if they figured out the location on their own.

Gaston interjected. "With beer and girls after we're done?"

Tim waved his finger at the assassin. "You know the inn's policy on contractual lovemaking." He smiled at Gaston's crestfallen expression and took pity on him. "But other establishments don't have those restrictions. I'm sure we could wrangle up some gold for you to indulge yourself."

"When my guys ask why I keep helping you out, this is the stuff I tell them." Gaston chuckled. "I'm sure more than one of them wants to take my place."

"I thought you said I'd always have you?" JaKobi pouted.

Cassie elbowed Gaston in the side. "This is where you say, fuck you."

"Fuck you, JaKobi!" Gaston roared with the relish of a man accusing someone of cheating at poker.

"Now he's getting it." Cassie put an arm around the pyromancer's waist and gave him a little hug. "Not that you're all bad."

"Holy shit, was that a compliment?" JaKobi prodded.

"No," Cassie said, pulling away from him. "It most certainly was not. Saying you aren't shit isn't like saying you're good at something."

Tim and ShadowLily walked by, hand in hand and said almost simultaneously, "Sure sounded like a compliment to me." They looked at each other and giggled the way only those young and in love can and kept walking.

"Wasn't," Cassie grumbled.

JaKobi reached out to pull Cassie into an awkward hug. Her reaction reminded Tim of his attempts to escape his aunt's famous cheek pinches.

Who in the fuck pinches people's cheeks?

Cassie sprinted past the strolling couple. "All I said was, you're not completely worthless."

ShadowLily nudged Tim in the side. "Just what every girl wants to hear."

"Baby, you're not shit," Tim managed to say with a straight face.

The two of them broke into laughter, leaving a confused JaKobi trailing behind with Gaston bringing up the rear.

The guild really felt like an extension of Tim's family. At this point, he couldn't imagine spending a day in the game without any one of them. Things were looking up for the Blue Dagger Society, and he was excited to see what the next encounter had in store for them.

CHAPTER FOURTEEN

"What's all that commotion?" someone called from a window overhead.

The sound of cheers and jeers could be clearly heard from down the street. Tim hadn't spent much time on the north side of the city outside of his trips to visit Lady Briarthorn, but he didn't get the feeling shouting crowds were commonplace around here. Whatever was happening up ahead, it wouldn't be long before the city guard was involved, and that was a hassle he'd like to avoid.

Although he had been cleared of all charges, his last interactions with guards had him being tossed in prison because Cardinal Jepsom was rich and connected. At least the Cardinal was a problem Tim didn't have to worry about anymore.

The noise up ahead grew easier to make out. There seemed to be some kind of fight going on, and people were betting on it. Tim hadn't seen anything like this since coming to Promethia. He'd assumed fighting in the streets wasn't a socially acceptable pastime. It was the kind of thing that should have taken place in an underground fight club, and not on a city street. Still, the thought of a street brawl kind of intrigued him.

A small opening appeared in the crowd as they drew closer. Gaston took a quick look around. "Watch your coin purses."

Tim wasn't worried about his gold. He didn't keep any in a purse. It was all tucked away in his inventory or locked in the bank. Not having to worry about being robbed made pushing up to the front of the crowd a much less risky proposition.

The fight playing out in front of him was something he hadn't seen before. The fighters in the street had their left wrists attached by a three-foot length of cord. In their right hands, they held daggers reversed for slashing. The two combatants moved around each other, and the crowd roared as they slashed and parried.

"You should have just paid up, Jules," the man growled. He was bleeding from a slash on his arm and one on his leg.

"I offered you the coin, Larson, but you wanted more." Jules dodged around a clumsy strike of his blade. "And now you'll pay for your greed with humility."

Larson let out a fierce growl and grabbed the cord with both hands, yanking the woman toward him. Instead of trying to resist the pull, she threw herself into a roll and came up behind him, slashing at his hamstring. Larson cried out in pain. He tried to stab downward between his legs but couldn't reach her.

Pulling the cord hard, Jules flipped the man over. As his back hit the ground, she sliced the rope binding them together and sneered. Blood dripped down her left forearm from the only wound she'd received. "First to three touches. The victory is mine."

"You're a cheating bitch," he growled. "No one moves like that without help."

To Tim's great surprise, Gaston stepped into the circle. "You two should be ashamed of yourselves. The ritual of Qwark isn't done in the streets. It is sacred."

"Says the man too good to spend time with his own kind." Larson spat on the ground. "The vote's in three days, and then you're out on your ass."

The woman tucked her dagger away and dabbed at her

wounded forearm with a swatch of clean cloth. "Not everyone believes in Malvonis' promises. There are those of us that stand with you."

"Whatever you believe, you better get out of here before the guards show up," Gaston warned.

A trumpet sounded in the distance, and the group of thieves and assassins scattered. Tim looked up at his burly friend. "What was all that about?"

Gaston started walking again. "Just our old friend up to some new kind of trick."

Tim realized whatever was going on, Gaston didn't want to talk about it. If they didn't have a job to get done, he wouldn't have let the issue drop, but as it was, he decided to stick a pin in it so he could circle back when they had more time.

"If you need our help with something, all you have to do is ask," Tim stated as he followed Gaston toward their destination. He needed the assassin to know their friendship was a two-way street.

"All of us have your back," JaKobi added helpfully. "Nobody fucks with my best bro."

"There may come a time when I need your help, but for now, I've got it handled," Gaston rumbled, but the look on his face was anything but confident.

"As long as you know we are here for you, big guy." Cassie nudged Gaston with her elbow, smiling up at the assassin. "I mean, I should probably be paying you for getting to look at those arms all day."

ShadowLily snorted as she pulled out one of her daggers and spun it around in her palm before slamming it back into the sheath on her hip. "Screw all these happy thoughts. If those bastards want to take you out, they are going to have to get in line behind me." The look in her eyes let everyone know she was just being playful.

JaKobi nodded in solemn thought. "There can be only one apprentice and one master."

"This isn't a Darth Bane novel, and she doesn't have to kill him to take over." Tim laughed, clearly enjoying the chance to geek out.

"Well, she wouldn't have to kill me." Gaston grinned. "But the only way to become the Grandmaster of Assassins is to kill the one at the top."

"Are you serious?" Tim asked, sounding incredulous.

"It's our way," Gaston replied casually. "Just like Qwark is used to settle small disagreements to prevent further bloodshed."

ShadowLily nodded along as if she had heard all of this before. When she noticed Tim looking at her, she shrugged. "What? Our whole profession is based on killing people. There were bound to be a few quirks."

"I'd say that's disgusting, but if all I could do was log in and build houses and play with furniture, I wouldn't be here. A cool housing system is really just a bonus in any game. I mean, who would want to be a virtual farmer when they could also be a knight in shining armor?" Tim kept his feet moving as they drew closer to their destination.

"Says the guy in a faded bathrobe with a wooden stick in his hand." Cassie grinned and held up a finger to indicate she'd scored a point.

"Just remember this bathrobe wearing dude. is the one in charge of keeping you alive." Tim growled.

"Did I say bathrobe?" Cassie paused. "I think I meant to say, robe so luxurious the Pope would be jealous."

"That's more like it. Now let's hurry up and get there before we run into anything else." Tim stepped in front of the group and picked up the pace to the warehouse.

Warehouses on the rich side of town sure didn't look like warehouses.

The building might as well have just been another bank of the three-story houses lining both sides of the street. The warehouse fit in so seamlessly with the neighborhood it might as well have been invisible. It reminded Tim of his best friend's kitchen. The fridge looked just like all the other cabinetry. Unless you knew where to look, the probability of finding something to drink was low.

This building was just like the mystery fridge. If the warehouse had any large doors for wagons to bring or deliver packages, they were in the back. Anyone walking down the street would be none the wiser. It was actually kind of ingenious.

The people in this neighborhood wanted fancy things. The shops closer to the castle were smaller because of the price of real estate, which meant they couldn't keep a lot of inventory on hand. Move a mile south, and the real estate was cheap enough they could afford to store goods closer than the larger warehouses at the docks. Most merchants learned quickly that people don't like to wait for the things they've purchased.

A company called Amazon figured out the same thing.

You could get packages delivered to your house in days, less if you lived by a hub. Tim remembered seeing free same-day delivery on things for the first time and freaking out. Once he ordered something at 10 p.m., and it was waiting on his doorstep when he woke up. The wonders of the world never ceased.

This elite group of merchants found a way to get the same kind of delivery service available using horse-drawn carriages. Granted, these merchants would offer a limited selection of goods, maybe even forcing someone to shop at more than one store. Unlike The Zon, which pretty much had everything you could ever want one click away.

Maybe life was simpler without all the shiny things. Who needed access to four thousand kinds of jelly beans at two in the morning? Having the power to order anything at any time led to a lot of bad decisions.

Like a five-pound tub of M&Ms and a month of regret when looking at the scale.

Promethia might not have had infinite supplies of jelly beans, but they now had a real-world restaurant. ShadowLily's dad Joe was slowly working his way through the markets and finding the things he needed to bring everyone the culinary delights they were used to. While Joe's didn't have everything on the menu that they did back home, the restaurant here had one major advantage: customers could eat there every day and never gain a pound.

How fucking cool was that?

You could eat pancakes with corned beef hash for breakfast, followed by a Reuben for lunch, and a steak with mashed potatoes for dinner. Top it all off with a slice of cake big enough to gag a camel, and you still wouldn't gain a pound. For anyone in the real world who was a foodie, *The Etheric Coast* was the place to be.

"Earth to Tim," ShadowLily called from behind him.

He looked back at the group a little sheepishly. "Sorry. I kind of zoned out."

"We hadn't noticed," Cassie replied, faking a yawn.

"Food or porn?" ShadowLily's eyebrow shot up in ritual challenge.

Tim held a hand to his chest. "You wound me. Why must a man always be reduced to his basest needs?"

The two girls looked at each other and then turned to Tim. "Porn," they said at the same time.

"It was food, I'll have you know," Tim said with mock outrage. "I hate the implication it could only be one of those two things I was thinking about."

JaKobi brought them back on task. "So, how are we going to handle this?"

"Let's get inside and take a look around. We started the other fights. There is a good chance we can take a peek around the place before anything happens." Tim walked toward the building.

"Spoken like a man who's about to die because his girlfriend found his porn stash," ShadowLily mocked. "Why don't you let the ladies go first? Someone has to be responsible for protecting the menfolk."

Tim bowed to the two women. "I have no problem with a woman going first."

"Especially when death is on the line," JaKobi snarked as he brought up the last spot in the group.

"Or paying a bill," Gaston chimed in.

"God, we can't take these guys anywhere." Cassie rolled her eyes as she reached for the doorknob. She hesitated a moment before pulling her bō staff out of her inventory. "Just in case." She looked back at the rest of her party and gave them a quick nod before pushing the door open and ducking inside.

Tim watched as the rest of the group filtered in. He took deep, even breaths. After this, the first part of their quest chain was done. He really wanted to know what was going to happen next.

Casting a quick glance up and down the street to make sure no one else was watching, he stepped inside.

CHAPTER FIFTEEN

"Holy shit!" Tim gasped.

"I know. Isn't it beautiful?" ShadowLily replied.

Looking around the warehouse, Tim couldn't agree more. It was the kind of thing he'd seen on TV a million times: take an old industrial building and convert it into a living space. While this space hadn't been converted yet, Tim could see the potential.

There were hardwood planks on the ground, and most of the ceilings vaulted all the way to the third floor, exposing the lattice-work of beams all the way up. On the other side of the expansive space, it looked as if the floors had been walled off to provide an area with a little more privacy.

The one thing Tim wasn't seeing was the shimmer that led to a boss, or anything that would activate a fight. He wanted to tell the team to spread out and look, but that seemed like suicide. If any of them triggered the fight alone, they'd be taking a quick trip to meet their caseworker.

"Let's group up and sweep the place. If we don't find what we're looking for, we can consider other options." Tim pointed off to the left and the wide-open side of the warehouse. "Let's start this way and work our way in."

Cassie shrugged and not having a better idea headed in the direction Tim indicated. "You know what has me really weirded out?" She paused for a bit of theatrics. "Why aren't there any employees or any stuff?"

Tim stopped walking. Slowly he turned to scan the warehouse from side to side. Why wasn't there any stuff? A building this size in this part of town must have cost a fortune. Leaving it empty would be a ridiculous waste of money. The tank was right, something was wrong here.

Jogging to catch up with the group, Tim shouted, "Stay alert, something doesn't feel right."

"I know. That's what I've been saying," Cassie retorted.

JaKobi thrust his arm into the air. "Lux!" A bright orange orb floated fifteen feet into the air and hovered to provide the group with extra light. "I'm not seeing anything as obvious as an arm sticking out of the ground. Anyone else find anything?"

Cassie snorted. "Just dust and...wait, there is something. No, it's just more dust."

ShadowLily looked at the massive space around them, feeling like she was stepping into a hollowed-out Walmart Supercenter. "Maybe we should split up?"

"Famous last words," Gaston replied with a chuckle.

"It's going to take us forever to search this place from top to bottom in a group," ShadowLily replied. "I know we have the time, but I'd rather get to slicing and dicing than poking around."

"It's a good thing you specialized down the assassin path and not the thief one," Tim said with a laugh. "More stabby-stabby and less slinky-slinky."

"Hey, I thought you liked it when I was slinky?" ShadowLily chided.

"What happens in the bedroom stays in the bedroom," Tim stated as a fact, but his cheeks burned bright red.

"Gross, you two, just fucking gross," Cassie snarled as she stomped away.

The sound of metal grating on metal made the entire group pause. All of their heads turned slowly to zero in on the sound. At first, Tim thought it might be coming from one of the huge doors along the back of the building, but the more he listened, it was easy to tell his first impression was wrong. The sound was coming from the center of the warehouse.

But the space was empty.

"Cassie, get in front of us and get ready." He turned to address the two assassins only to realize they had already used their stealth abilities and were moving into position on either side of the room.

"JaKobi, stick with me and unleash hell." Tim clapped the man on the back and started casting his buffs for the group. With armor of eternia and attacks of the faithful cast, Tim dropped into his Way of the River stance. This stance had proved to be incredibly effective during one of his earlier fights, and he could switch back mid-combat if Cassie needed extra help.

"You got it, boss," JaKobi replied as he prepared one of his own spells.

It was nice knowing the mage was going to be by his side. Not because he needed the pyromancer's protection, but because during the chaos of battle, he wouldn't have to think about where one person was for heals. Everyone else would be running and dodging and hiding, but all he had to do to heal JaKobi was turn around.

If only healing were always that easy.

Cassie walked forward and stopped about twenty feet in front of the two men. The tank spread her legs wide in a defensive stance and held her bō staff across her back diagonally in a classic ninja warrior pose.

The metal scraping sounds stopped, and the floor in the center of the room started to shake. The wooden planks rattled as if there was an earthquake happening, but the rest of the warehouse looked like the same calm empty space they'd entered minutes before. Slowly the shaking floorboards subsided, and the warehouse grew quiet again.

Tim shook his arms to keep them loose. The tension was killing him.

Thankfully, he didn't have to wait long. The wooden planks in the center of the room burst upwards, and Tim realized that there was a door built into the floor for some kind of underground storage. A man nimbly jumped out of the hole and landed in front of them.

He didn't look like anything impressive. He was of normal size, and he had purple robes on with a foppish merchant hat. If Tim had run into him at the market, he wouldn't have been surprised one bit. The real question was, what was he doing here?

And how did he jump out of that hole?

"I'm sorry, this is private property. I'm afraid I'm going to have to ask you to go." The man started wringing his hands nervously.

It was almost laughable to ask him the question, but it had to be done.

Tim stepped up behind Cassie. "We are on a mission from the Goddess Eternia. Her light guided us to this location. Can you tell me, is something amiss?" Tim kept his eyes on the man and tried to investigate him to reveal his nameplate. A box appeared above the man's head declaring him as the Proliferator.

"Only that you are standing inside my warehouse uninvited," the Proliferator mumbled almost to himself. "That won't do, that won't do at all."

The Proliferator's purple robes rippled as he jumped across the twenty-foot gap created by the hatch in the floor. He landed deftly on the other side. "Why must things always be so difficult? All I wanted to do was multiply."

"I don't like the sound of that," Tim whispered to Cassie as he started edging further behind the tank.

Cassie took a couple steps forward. "Pretend like you have a pair and get ready for whatever comes out of that fucking hole."

"She really has a way with words, don't you think?" JaKobi said with a grin as he created a fireball in his right hand.

"I heard that," Cassie called over her shoulder. The feisty tank was too disciplined to look away from a possible foe to properly chastise the pyromancer.

"Profits!" the Proliferator roared. "All they cared about were profits, but I showed them the error of their ways. Now they all work for me. BUAHAHAHAHAHA!"

Tim started to move off to one side, hoping to get a better look at what was waiting for them in the hole. "I'm not sure this guy is all there."

"He's clearly batshit," JaKobi added from behind him. "In my eyes that makes him even more dangerous."

Pacing, the Proliferator started mumbling again. "How many should I send? One. No, no. Two." He paused in his pacing, looking up as he wrung his hands together. His eyes settled on the group. "Oh, yes, three for three."

Reaching inside of his robes, the Proliferator pulled a riding crop from an inner pocket. He smashed the crop against the wooden floor three times and stood back. "How many more? How many must I make?"

Three wraiths jumped out of the hole and landed next to each other. All of the men were wearing tattered silken robes. Their flesh had turned gray from lack of exposure to the light, and their feeding tubes snapped back and forth, hungry for human flesh.

Tim couldn't stop thinking about how ugly the wraiths were. It was like the mouth from *Aliens* was attached to one of the monsters from *The Strain*. He would have called them Vampires, but the wraiths didn't suck out a person's blood.

A wraith sucked out a person's soul.

Cassie didn't appear to be worried about the wraith's poor

fashion choices. All she cared about was stopping them from ripping apart her friends. Without any thought to her own personal safety, she charged the pack.

Tim cast curse of giving. He'd save his more powerful spells until he knew if there was a boss monster or if it was just going to be wave after wave of the wraiths. If this was some kind of challenge to see how long they'd last, he would be a fool to waste too much of his mana reserves this early.

Cassie hit the wraiths hard, but she wasn't going to last long without some help. JaKobi couldn't launch his spells without hitting everyone, so he started to circle around to the side. Tim trailed behind the pyromancer. Keeping stacked helped save lives as far as most healers were concerned. When the entire party was scattered all over the place, it made things much more difficult.

Gaston and ShadowLily appeared, seemingly out of nowhere, hacking at the wraiths from behind. Two of the monsters fell under their continued assault. Cassie shoved the third monster away from her. With a growl, the wraith gathered its feet underneath itself and prepared to launch.

The two assassins blinked out of existence just as the last wraith leaped into the air. JaKobi reached above his head, clapping his hands together. As his hands met, a burst of flames shot out. The indistinct flames turned into a Phoenix, which closed the distance between the mage and wraith with one brilliant flap of its wings. The wraith burst into flames and fell at Cassie's feet.

Her bō staff crashed down on the wraith's skull, ending the creature's pitiful existence. "Nice one!" Cassie called out with a grin.

"Five of them!" the Proliferator shouted. "Well, five is better than three, but only if you have to pay once."

"Questions, questions. How many? What size?" His purple robes swished as he strutted back and forth, deep in thought. The Proliferator turned to stare at the party of adventurers before coming to a decision. "Yes, yes. Two in the air, and three with feet, won't that be a tasty treat." Drool started leaking from the corners of the boss' mouth as he thought about the meal to come.

Instead of jumping across the gap in the floor himself, the Proliferator tapped a series of rhythmic beats against the wooden boards as he called more creatures forward. Slipping the riding crop back into his coat, the Proliferator raised both arms high into the air and began shouting. "Rise my pretties, rise!"

Two more wraiths leaped out of the hole in the floor. They landed gently and then turned to hiss at the group, forcing them to move back a few steps. There was a noise from behind the new arrivals, and Tim couldn't quite make out what it was. It was almost like the flapping of wings but faster.

Much faster.

Two giant wasp-like creatures emerged from below the floor. Instead of a stinger on their tails, they had one of the feeding tubes. They continued to rise up, and Tim wondered why they were struggling so much. A wasp three feet across should have been able to zip around the building in an instant.

It was almost as if they were carrying something.

The wasps continued to fly higher, and the party could see fine chains had been tied to their legs. Whatever they were pulling up from below was big and heavy. Tim wasn't sure if they should start attacking now or if they should wait and see what was in store for them. He was about to call out when the head of the creature the wasps were lifting breached the surface of the pit.

Tim wasn't exactly sure what he was looking at. It was a human with the head of a toad. *Maybe calling it human was going too far.* The creature's skin was green, and its hands and feet were webbed. When the wasps dropped the wraith to the ground, he landed with his arms out in front of his knees like a frog.

The two more traditional wraiths climbed out of the hole to stand behind the green man.

Tim didn't know a lot about frogs. His school didn't do the whole dissect a frog thing. He'd always laughed when they did it in movies and wondered if it was something that ever happened outside of a Hollywood script. Still, it didn't take a genius to know that toads ate with their super-long tongues.

"Expect the toadman to have extra-long reach!" Tim shouted as the battle started to unfold. He quickly cast curse of giving and tossed an extra healing orb in Cassie's direction. Being one of the only members of the group with ranged attacks, Tim shifted his focus from healing to trying to kill one of the wasps.

JaKobi grimaced when his fireball flew wide of the wasp on the right. "Those suckers are fast."

It didn't take Tim more than a second to figure out the same thing when his first cast of divine light missed the wasp by a country mile. It was scary to think how much faster the wasps would be if they didn't have chains dangling from their legs.

The two normal wraiths died under the assassin's attacks, leaving the group with the two wasps and Toadie to deal with. Tim wondered where his attention should be focused next. Hitting one of the flying fucks from range was out of the question. "Unless I have a spell that doesn't need to be aimed." A smile broke out on his face as he cast his newest acquisition, behold my power.

He saw JaKobi wince as the first percent of his health was whisked away. The pyromancer was able to ignore the damage and finish his cast with ease. Tim followed the spell and watched as a flame shield sprang out of thin air just in time to stop the wasp from attacking ShadowLily.

Gaston didn't have the same luck in partners as ShadowLily, so instead of the wasp getting blocked, it managed to strike the assassin's blade with its feeder. Gaston was able to weave his remaining dagger around in a way that kept the creature from trying to attack him again, but if the creature did manage to hit him, the group was going to be in real trouble.

Diving deep into his bag of tricks, Tim cast snare. The weak level of the spell wouldn't hold the wasp for long, but he hoped it would be enough time for what he had in mind. Turning his attention away from the monster, he cast cleanse on Gaston.

The assassin did a backflip away from the wasp he'd been fighting. Somehow, he twisted in the air and avoided the feeding tube before landing on his feet and rolling under the flying bastard to pick up his fallen dagger.

A flick of Gaston's wrist sent his blade flying at Toadie. Cassie glanced back at the assassin as her target fell to the ground with a dagger sticking out of his head, but Gaston hadn't stopped moving. Sprinting toward the fallen wraith, the assassin started throwing knives at the wasp on the other side of the flame shield.

Several of the small blades nicked the bound wasp as Gaston plucked his dagger free from toadies' skull, then flipped over the flame shield to face the wasp in single combat.

Tim cast snare again to give him time to scan the battlefield. Everyone's health looked ok, and he didn't see any negative status effects. ShadowLily made sure that both wraiths and Toadie were dead, while JaKobi kept them encircled in a wall of flames so she had the time to handle it.

"Cassie, help Gaston," Tim shouted. He stared in wonder as a doorway sized hole opened in the flame shield so Cassie could sprint out.

The tank gave him a questioning look but ran off to help Gaston just as JaKobi's flame shield came crashing down. Tim hoped he was right and didn't screw up by sending Cassie to help, leaving the others unprotected.

The tank and Gaston were doing their best to fight one of the wasps. The other wasp noticed that the flames were gone and started beelining for his girlfriend. If his new spell didn't activate soon, he was going to have a lot of explaining to do before bed tonight. Tim didn't like to leave things up to chance and preferred his bed be used for something besides a battleground, so he started preparing for the worst outcome possible.

The wasp buzzed closer to the group, its feeding tube ready to strike out at the unprotected assassin, when it burst apart with a wet pop, splattering the ground with dark liquid.

"It fucking worked!" Tim cheered as he slid to a stop.

"Just what every girl wants to hear," ShadowLily mocked as she started running to help the others.

Tim wanted to cast the spell again to take out the other wasp, but the spell was on cooldown. Knowing he couldn't cast again right away was killing him. The spell took life from his entire party enough to control how many times he could cast it safely, making him unable to use it for long periods of time.

"Maybe later on it will get a cooldown reduction," Tim griped to himself as he worked on bringing the group back up to full health.

The last wasp fell to the combined fury of their efforts. Tim once again made sure everyone's health was topped off, and they were free from status effects.

The Proliferator started pacing again.

"No, no, this won't do at all. When one can't count on the help to do their job correctly, one must simply handle matters oneself," the boss chattered to himself.

"Never count on a person when you can count their coins instead." The Proliferator stopped pacing and stared at the group. "The dead have no need for money."

His purple robes ripped as the boss grew in size. Drool dripped from his jaws as they extended. Three of the wraith's feeders came out of his mouth as he looked over the party with hungry eyes. "Don't even think about leaving. My best merchandise is still to come."

The Proliferator jumped to the center of the warehouse, forcing the group to follow him. In one hand, he held a giant version of his riding crop and in the other, a simple dagger. Simple being a flexible word when the blade of said knife was three feet long.

Tim wasn't sure what to expect, but he knew the man in light robes with one knife and a couple extra feeders wasn't going to be the only challenge to this fight. It felt too simple, even if they had been locked in active combat this entire time, reducing his mana regeneration by more than half.

A quick check confirmed his mana was in a good place so this fight wasn't nearly close to over as it seemed. "Remember the plan!" Tim called.

Cassie turned to look at him. "We had a plan?"

"Slow and steady wins the race." He almost laughed as he said it. It was funny when you heard the things your parents used to tell you coming out of your own mouth.

"That's not a plan," Cassie said in her best *Crocodile Dundee* accent. "This is a plan." With a roar, the fierce little tank charged into the fray.

"I guess that means go." JaKobi focused on the Proliferator, his hands rising above his head. A phoenix burst forth from his clap and flew across the room.

The Proliferator laughed as he cut through the spell with his riding crop. The boss' moment of distraction was all Cassie needed to close the distance. With all of her weight behind her, she slammed her bō staff into his knee. A crack sounded, and the boss stumbled to the side.

Gaston was waiting, but as he tried to lash out, his arms were pierced by the feeding tubes. His daggers clattered to the ground, and the third feeder bit deep into his chest.

Tim stopped thinking about doing anything offensive and started healing the fuck out of the assassin. Thankfully, the rest of the group hadn't stopped moving, and now the Proliferator had more to deal with. Tossing the weakened assassin to the side, the boss returned to fighting Cassie.

A quick cleanse and a few heals got Gaston back into the fight.

They were making good progress now that all of them were working together. The boss' HP was nearing the fifty-percent mark. Tim felt like if something was going to happen, it would have to be soon. Maybe the boss had an enraged burn phase.

He could just imagine hundreds of mini-bosses coming out of holes all over the warehouse floor and overwhelming the group.

Fuck that!

"Get ready for it!" Tim roared as he cast a round of healing orbs on the party.

ShadowLily started running for the boss. Gaston knelt in front of her, and she sprang off of his back like a world-class gymnast hitting the vault before she flew through the air. She rose up like an avenging angel, her poisoned daggers ready to plunge deep into the Proliferator from above.

The boss' HP hit fifty percent, and a shield snapped into place around him. ShadowLily hit the shield hard and bounced off before crashing to the ground. Tim was there a moment later to make sure she was at full health.

"What in the fuck was that?" Cassie gasped, bringing all their attention to an egg-like sack on the other side of the room.

"DPS now!" Tim cried as he cast weaken undead. He didn't want to know what was in the creepy pulsating egg sack, but he'd played enough games to know that if they killed it fast enough, they'd never have to find out.

He fired weaken undead and divine light. Two of JaKobi's spells hit the sack a moment later, and then the two assassins were on it.

ShadowLily was covered in green slime from head to toe when she turned to look at Tim. "There's another one."

"Maybe they just keep coming until he comes out of the shell?" Cassie called as she ran at a third sack.

"Let's get two teams going," Tim yelled. "Cassie, go with Gaston, and JaKobi, you go with ShadowLily. I'll try to soften them up for all of you, and make sure you stay healed."

The group split up into their assigned teams and started

hacking at the sacks as they appeared around the room. Tim did his best to help, but he also knew there was a good chance he'd need his mana ready for when the boss broke out of this phase. He let the magic inside of him continue to build as his team worked to empty the room.

The eggs stopped spawning, and the Proliferator stepped forward. "None of my pretties made it. That makes me so mad! Displays are made to be shared, but you better keep your hands off before I cut them off."

A broken cackling laugh escaped from the Proliferator's mouth. The laughter turned into a gurgle, almost as if the man were melting. There was a sick wet popping sound, and then there were two smaller versions of the boss waiting for them.

"Well, that was fucking disgusting," Cassie grumbled as she ran forward.

Now that the boss was smaller, he was easier to manage, but the problem was there were two of them. Keeping both of the Proliferators busy became Cassie's full-time job, just like keeping her cleansed became Tim's. The others more than made up for the difference of their reduced utility, and slowly the boss' health continued to fade.

Tim was thankful that the separate parts of the boss shared a single health meter. It seemed like a lot to ask this early in the game for them to be able to whittle down two bosses' health pools simultaneously. Those fights could be fun, but they also normally required more than one group and sucked major ass when you couldn't balance the parties correctly.

When the Proliferator's health hit ten percent, two things happened. The twin version started pulling at itself and then somehow split into three. The boss was still the size of a normal human, but there were fucking three of him. Eggs also started spawning around the room, and Tim saw they had bars over them that were shrinking rapidly.

"Everyone on the boss!" Tim cast behold my power, hoping that they had ten seconds to spare. "JaKobi if those eggs start breaking open, I want a shield up around the group, until then, give him everything you've got."

Tim felt a smile break out on his face as JaKobi pulled a small mirror out of his bag. He'd seen the spell work before, and it had been awesome. The three melee-ranged players were battling for their lives, so he started blasting away at the eggs in the room. There was no way he could stop them all from hatching, but he could buy them some more time.

One of the eggs burst, and a spiderlike version of the Proliferator came running out on eight legs. It charged toward the players attacking its daddy like a bat out of hell. A squeal burst from the creature's throat as it leaped for Cassie's back.

A wall of flame roared to life in front of the creature, and it was incinerated. "Nice one, JaKobi!" Tim called as more and more of the eggs eluded his grasp. This was it. They were either going to get the Proliferator down or they were going to die.

The spiderlike creatures had them surrounded, and JaKobi's flame shield started to sputter out.

"THERE ARE NO DISCOUNTS ON SUNDAYS!" the three heads screamed as one before the boss started to dissolve. "You'll find out soon enough." The last of his words slurred as the Proliferator turned into a puddle of steaming goo.

Tim sat down in the middle of the floor, heaving for breath. His hands were covered in the green slime from the burst eggs. "That was unexpected." Cassie started running toward him, and he held up his hands in horror. "No!"

The tank slammed into him and knocked him into the slime and spider guts. "Now you are one of us."

"One. Of. Us," JaKobi said slowly with a deadpan expression.

"Now I get what they mean when they say don't follow the group mentality. I was quite happy alone and slime-free," Tim complained as he stood up.

"Well, then you certainly aren't going to like this." ShadowLily bent down to pick up a handful of the viscous fluid and flung it at Tim. Before anyone could react, she grabbed another handful and threw it at Gaston. "Slime fight!"

For the next five minutes, they left the dangers ahead of them behind and celebrated the victory.

CHAPTER SIXTEEN

Throwing the slime was fun.

Getting hit with the vile stuff was another story. By the end of the fight, the entire party was covered from head to toe in the rancid gunk. JaKobi was making a retching sound like some got in his mouth, and Gaston was busy trying to clean out one of his ears.

Tim wanted to laugh, but he was afraid to open his mouth. Instead, he stripped out of his robe and used the clean inner portion to wipe off his face and hands. He replaced the robe in his inventory and pulled it back out clean. He felt better now that he wasn't covered in slime.

Most of the group quickly followed suit, but Gaston couldn't do the inventory trick. Instead, Tim had to splash the assassin with a few healing orbs to help clear the worst of the gunk off of him. Then he used his own clean robe to wipe him off. It was simple enough for him to put the item back in his inventory again before reequipping it.

"As much as I appreciate a clean face, if I ever see you walking toward me again wearing only your underwear, we are going to have big problems," Gaston grumbled as he side-eyed Tim suspiciously.

"Are you saying you don't trust me?" Tim batted his eyes at the assassin.

"I don't trust anybody with a dick and no clothes." Gaston smiled. "But, I have a simple way of fixing one of those problems." He made a quick cutting gesture that left Tim wincing.

"Note to self: no streaking by Gaston's room." JaKobi grinned at the group as they all turned to look at him. "What do you say we see about this loot and get back to the inn for some real clean up?"

"I second that," Cassie replied quickly, ever eager to earn her next shiny.

Gaston smiled at Tim. "Can I assume my drinks are on you?" When Tim nodded, he continued. "Then I'm going to get out of here, and get a head start on the festivities."

"Just don't overdo it. We have one more boss to hunt if we can figure out where it's hiding." Tim patted the man on the back and handed him a small pouch of gold coins. "Just a little something to make up for your lack of rewards. We really couldn't do this without you."

Gaston crushed Tim against his chest. "Beer and money. Maybe I have to reevaluate my stance on your naked advances."

Tim pushed away from the assassin hard enough he landed on his ass in the goo. "How about you just go and enjoy a few drinks on me and save those big muscles for someone who can appreciate them."

Hefting the bag of coins in his hand, Gaston raised one eyebrow toward the sky. "With this kind of money, I could just pay someone to compliment me, but I think I'll settle for a night at the Twix Thine Pixie."

ShadowLily moved away from the assassin toward the loot chest. "I don't even want to know."

"Make sure you're back at the inn tonight so we can plan tomorrow's adventure before we hit the hay." Tim stood up. "And one more thing." Gaston looked at him like he was about to be chastised, but Tim's smile just grew wider. "Try to have some fun."

Gaston spun on his heel and headed for the door. "That won't be a problem."

When Tim reached the trunk, Cassie was already gushing as she looked over her new chest piece. JaKobi had a pair of gloves to match his hat and robes, and ShadowLily was now sporting a matching dagger to the last one she'd received. All of them looked incredibly satisfied, so he wondered what was waiting for him.

Tim took the last few steps toward the chest and placed his hand on it. Pulling up his inventory revealed that he'd received some gold, and a weapon augment.

"Leather wraps of divergent health." Tim looked at the tooltip and couldn't stop grinning. "These wraps can be applied to any staff. Any single-target healing spell cast will have a ten percent chance of jumping to the next closest friendly target, healing them for fifty percent of the value of the original heal. Apparently, it's upgradeable."

"I wish these bosses were repeatable like the dungeons. It'd be nice to get a few more rolls for a chance at an augment for our classes," Cassie said, looking wistful.

"Hey, we've still got one more shot if we can figure out where the next big baddie is," ShadowLily reminded her friend of the loot that might be coming their way soon enough. "Now let's get out of here, I want a bath." She grabbed Tim's hand and started pulling him toward the door.

"Just try to keep it under four hours," Cassie called after them.

JaKobi snorted and held out his hand for a high five. "Good one."

"It's what I do." Cassie grinned. "If your friends can't bust your balls, who can?" Turning, she jammed a finger in his chest. "Don't you even fucking think about saying something like you can bust my balls anytime or I'm going to hit you really fucking hard."

The pyromancer looked wounded. "I would never say such a thing. If I wanted to ask you to touch my balls, I'd be much more creative."

"Well, it's about time someone around here was willing to up their game." Cassie walked to the door, leaving the stunned pyromancer behind her.

"Wait, does that mean what I think it means?" JaKobi called after her. Did he have a shot, or was she just messing with him? He stood in the darkness of the warehouse for a moment before running to catch up.

If he had a shot, he wasn't going to miss it.

An hour later, Tim headed down the stairs to meet the others.

A bath wasn't something he used just to get clean, it was his happy place. It was also the place where he went to think. If going for a walk didn't give his mind the chance to work out a problem, hopping in the bath always did. He'd spent most of this bath trying to figure out where the last boss was hidden, while the last fifteen minutes were used for something else entirely.

Warm food was waiting for him at the table in the corner. JaKobi had a map up on the wall and was going over the marked locations. He'd drawn a line connecting them all by following the roads. Everyone was trying to decide if it had meaning.

Tim sat down and picked up his fork to dig into what looked like meatloaf and mashed potatoes with tomato sauce. The food was incredible and made him wonder when his girlfriend had found time to run to Joe's. Had he really stayed in the bath that long after she left?

After finishing his first plate, Tim grabbed another slice of meatloaf and a big spoonful of mashed potatoes. This time he also added a roll into the mix and made himself a little sandwich as he stared up at the map.

The conversation waged on around him, but it was like he was there alone. His eyes moved between the three locations as he ate his sandwich. Tim didn't feel like he'd spent enough time in the city to be an expert on the possible locations where the leader of the wraiths could hide. The only place he knew of was the prison.

His mouth hung open for a second before Tim realized it was full of food. He chewed as quickly as he could and took a sip of beer as he approached the map on the wall. It all made sense. He'd thought the Sheriff was the big issue when really, he had been sitting on top of it.

Placing a finger on the map, Tim marked the location so they all could see.

"The prison? It can't be there. We already killed Jon Hobbs," Cassie replied. "We should just bite the bullet and go see Brother Colton again."

"What if the sheriff was just the tip of the iceberg?" Tim looked at the group as he started to warm to the idea. "That would mean the big problem is still there waiting for us."

"It's not like they are just going to let us go back inside and poke around." ShadowLily frowned. "Getting you out of there the first time was hard enough."

"You're right. We are going to need help." Tim fired off a message to Lady Briarthorn. "But the boss is there, I can feel it."

"Well, you haven't led us wrong so far." JaKobi poured himself a beer. "And now that the thinking part of the night is over, I plan to indulge myself. Anyone care to join me?"

Cassie poured herself a beer. "Darts?"

"As long as you promise not to beat me too badly." JaKobi grinned as he picked up the pitcher and headed for the dartboard.

Cassie trailed behind him. "I make no such promises."

Tim felt good about how things were progressing on their first group quest. All he had to do now was wait for Gaston to get back so he could fill him in on the details. By then, he should have a response from Lady Briarthorn and know if they could complete this quest the easy way, or if they would have to break into the prison to get the job done.

Tomorrow was going to be an interesting day.

CHAPTER SEVENTEEN

One sleepless night in the woods was all it took for Lorelei to wish she hadn't left Tristholm in such a hurry.

It turned out that while the werewolves were content to leave Tristholm alone for the time being, they also weren't going to let people come and go as they pleased. The forest was covered in roving packs of the furry fuckers. As much as she hated to admit it, the werewolves were just as smart as she thought they would be.

It's easy to forget how smart something is when it's nine feet tall and trying to rip you apart with razor-sharp claws.

The concentric circles of the patrols Lorelei continued to dodge were enough to remind her to be on her guard at all times. Despite losing their Alpha, the pack was well organized. A little more disarray might have been nice, but it seemed the werewolves had decided to mourn later and to keep as many of their tasty snacks trapped inside of the city as they could.

Sneaking through packs of angry werewolves with an absurd sense of smell wasn't easy, and it wasn't something she could do on horseback. As much as it pained her to do so, at the first sign of trouble, she'd jumped off the horse and sent it fleeing back to town as a distraction.

Now that the sun was up, it was time to move, and for the real work to begin.

It didn't take her long to reach the stream she'd crossed while tracking the alpha. From there, it was simple enough to cover all of her exposed skin with mud. For good measure, she also rubbed as much of the stuff on her clothes as time permitted. The next part of her plan wasn't going to be fun, but it was vital for her to make it out of the woods alive.

Twenty minutes later, she found what she was looking for, a couple of big piles of shit. Her tracking ability told her this area had been slept in recently. The forest floor was disturbed. There was a smell of piss around the clearing and claw marks on the trees too high for anything but a bear or werewolf to make.

Lorelei hadn't seen any fucking bears.

Knowing she was going to hate this next part, no matter how long she waited to do it Lorelei got to work. "Thank the goddess for gloves." She mumbled to herself as she plunged her hands into the first pile of cold shit. Touching the stuff wasn't as horrible as she'd expected, and it wasn't as if she hadn't walked a few dogs in her day.

But touching wasn't all she had to do.

Lorelei started grabbing handfuls of the werewolves' shit and rubbing it on her mud-covered clothes. It was the only thing she could think of that would mask her scent enough to make it past the patrols. She wondered if this was how Rick had felt the first time he had to cover himself in zombie's guts.

With her shit covered clothes in place, Lorelei started running through the woods. As part of her continued training, she tried to keep her heartbeat and breathing regular so she could listen to the sounds of the forest as she ran. All Lorelei had to worry about was staying silent and not leaving a trace of her passing. Thankfully, she had a skill that helped her with both.

Lorelei thought she was being super successful at the tasks she'd set out for herself. At this pace, she might reach the cabin by nightfall.

A slim werewolf with jet-black fur stepped into the clearing. It looked around for a moment and let its nose do most of the heavy lifting, but wary of a trap just the same. Walking slowly around the clearing, the werewolf stopped at a pile of scattered droppings.

Tilting her head back, she howled. Her prey was close, the hunt was on.

Lorelei crossed a small stream close to Earl's cabin.

From there, she ran five miles next to the stream before hopping back in. This time she quickly unequipped all her gear and put it in her inventory. Using the slow-moving water, Lorelei scrubbed any remaining mud and filth off of her before reequipping her clothes.

Quickly scanning the forest and not finding anything, she started to run. Lorelei tried to pick up the pace. Running wasn't her thing, and running fast wasn't fun unless she was being chased by a woman with a bottle of champagne and a bucket full of strawberries.

Then she could be as fast as she wanted to until it was time to get caught.

For Lorelei, drinking late night cosmos and building drunken Lego towers was more of her thing than a night watching the Oscars. Not everyone was into her way of adulting, but fuck 'em, that was why there as a whole sea full of fish.

And she could reel them in like a pro.

The problem was that she had a penchant for reeling in the

wrong type. Types like Tammy Two-Twats. That bitch was the kind of girl who would use a person for everything they were worth and leave them when it mattered. Not all of the women she'd dated were like that, just the ones she really liked.

What was her obsession with fixing people?

People could change over time, but most folks were content with who they were. Why Lorelei was determined to only date the women she deemed fixer-uppers was something only a therapist could tell her.

And who had time for that shit?

She was a mile further up the stream than where she originally went in. Her little plan had cost her a couple hours of time and drained most of her stamina, but if it worked, it was worth it.

Her clothes came off just as quickly as before, and she was running through the woods naked as a jaybird. She almost laughed. If any of her friends in the real world saw her now, they would have said she had finally found her true home. As exhilarating as it was, running naked wasn't her thing either.

She felt too exposed.

Lorelei didn't even break stride as her clothes magically appeared back on her body. Getting dressed in this game was so easy. When she had to go back to the real world, it was the thing she would miss the most. That and how easy it was to clean her clothes.

Dry cleaning was fucking expensive.

It didn't take her too long to track down Earl's cabin once she started following the waypoint on her map. The door was ripped off, but she was pretty sure there would be something inside she could use to nail the door in place, or some piece of furniture she could cover the opening with.

If her plan worked, the door wouldn't be much of an issue. The patrols seemed to be passing her locations less frequently. She was pretty sure the werewolves would be more aggressive at night, so she'd hunker down until morning.

After the sun came up, she would make the final push to Promethia. Until then, it was time to eat a little of the food she'd brought with her and get some rest. It was going to be a long day tomorrow if Lorelei was going to make it to the city before nightfall. It would probably involve more running.

Fucking great.

The dried beef and fruit she had wasn't a great meal, but it was enough to ensure her stats would be at full strength when she woke up. The food would also give her enough energy for a final burst of action before lying down.

The front door was in ruins, but there was a chest full of dishes in the corner that had been toppled over. Getting the chest upright took more time then she would have liked, but the bulky piece of furniture covered the doorway perfectly. Knowing she'd done as much as she could for the time being, Lorelei pulled a blanket from her inventory and went to sleep on the trap door to the cellar.

Sleeping on the floor wasn't comfortable, but knowing she was next to a secondary exit made her feel safer. If a werewolf burst through the chest blocking the door, she was confident she could get in the cellar before it found her. It wasn't guaranteed, but it beat sleeping outside.

"This Poison Master asshole better be fucking worth it," Lorelei mumbled to herself as she closed her eyes.

CHAPTER EIGHTEEN

Camilla's voice whispered, "We can still be together."

They were in the bathtub again. God, she couldn't get enough of this woman. There was a twinkle in her eye that said she would take it as far as Lorelei wanted to go and love every fucking second of it. It was a look that promised a good time but also threw out major red flags.

Lorelei had never concerned herself with being cautious.

She pulled Camilla toward her and kissed her lips with desperate need. Her hands moved up and started running through her thick black hair before moving down her naked back. The woman had an ass that went on for days. It must have been all the horseback riding.

Their kiss deepened, and a moan escaped Lorelei's lips. Her eyes opened, but this time they weren't in the bathtub back at the palace, they were inside of Earl's beat-to-shit cabin. The chest blocking the door had been shoved out of the way, and the woman in front of her was real enough.

"What in the fuck is going on?" Lorelei scrambled away from Camilla like she'd woken up in the arms of a serial killer.

Her lover was here. The woman had tracked her down. That was kind of awesome, but wasn't she a werewolf now? Lorelei's heartbeat started to slow as she realized how her rejection must have made Camilla feel. It wasn't every day you got thrown out of your home and rejected by your latest lover.

Moving closer, Lorelei reached out to touch Camilla's arm. The woman jerked away from her touch, but the ranger kept coming closer until she pulled her into an embrace. The two of them sat on the rough wooden floorboards while the new werewolf cried.

There was no way to know how long they huddled together letting their emotions power out, but it was long enough for Lorelei to have to stretch her legs when she stood up. Looking down, Lorelei didn't feel anything but sympathy for what happened to her lover. "I'm so sorry about what happened to you. Your mother should have never made you leave."

Camilla brushed her hair back and reclined on one elbow, looking up at Lorelei with affection. "She had to. There are rumors of a man and his pet witch. Apparently, she can control the werewolves. If I'd stayed, I could have been commanded to change and kill anyone."

"So, she did it to protect you?" Lorelei was confused. The woman she'd left behind in the throne room of Tristholm hadn't given her the impression of someone doing the right thing. In fact, Camilla's mother seemed to feel rather guilty about the situation.

"Are you sure the werewolves aren't just happy to follow them because of how your mother treats their kind? If they found a leader who would offer them a place they could be themselves and not have to be ashamed, that could hold a strong allure," Lorelei pondered out loud.

"We could find out together." Camilla sounded hopeful.

"But I'm not a..." Lorelei's voice trailed off at the hungry expression on her lover's face.

"You could be if you wanted to. All it would take is just one bite, and we could face this world together." Camilla grinned. "You can't imagine how amazing it feels to run through the forest on four legs, to feel the call of the moon as you hunt your prey."

Those prey used to be your friends.

Lorelei was too smart to say what she was thinking out loud, but she also needed to find a way to get the hell out of here without provoking an incident. Getting out of relationships without creating fireworks was sadly not one of her many talents. She liked Camilla, but life as a werewolf wasn't for her. Not if it meant tearing innocent villagers apart for fun.

Lorelei tried to play it cool. "I don't think I'm ready for that kind of commitment."

"Shame," Camilla said with icy detachment as she climbed back to her feet. "It would have been so much nicer if you came willingly."

The bones in Camilla's hands started to break as the transformation started working its way through her body. "But I also can't let you leave. No one gets out. That is what the master says." Her voice cracked as a scream tore from her throat.

Lorelei started backing away.

She had fallen for Camilla hard, but she had been on the rebound, so that was to be expected. What wasn't expected was for her lover to become corrupted so easily by whoever the Master was. Somehow this Master had taken a defender of the land and broken her to the point she worked for him in less than a day. That was the kind of man that needed to be stopped.

Like with all good stories, the road to fixing things starts with a woman doing what was right over what was easy.

Summoning her bow into her hand, Lorelei rolled away from her ex-lover. Being close to a naked woman was one thing, but she wasn't into bestiality. When her roll stopped, she swung back around to face Camilla, keeping one knee on the ground to stabilize her shot. A heartbeat later, an arrow was in her hand, and by the time she'd finished releasing the breath she'd been holding, the arrow had torn a hole through Camilla. The next two sank into the half-formed werewolf's chest.

Standing, Lorelei put her bow back into her inventory and moved to Camilla's side. She knelt next to her and brushed her eyelids closed with a gentle touch. "I'm sorry how things turned out."

Looking to the door, Lorelei wondered if Camilla had come alone. There would be time to worry about that later. She stopped in the doorway and looked back at the body. "You deserved a better fate. I won't stop until I find the werewolf responsible for this and put them down. That is my promise to you."

She watched as her lover's body returned to human, and then stepped out of the cabin. There would be time to mourn her later. Now it was time to run.

The forest brought her a sense of calm as she started winding through the trees. It was still dark out, but dawn wasn't far off. Lorelei would find Ernie and bring back whoever else wanted to come. Together they could take back the city of Tristholm from the darkness that surrounded it.

"This Master of Poisons, he better be fucking worth it." Lorelei oriented herself toward Promethia and focused on putting one foot in front of the other.

It was going to be a long day.

CHAPTER NINETEEN

Ernie fished the lightweight ball out of his glass and chugged the contents.

"I love whatever this game is called." He tossed the ball back across the table, splashing it into his opponent's last cup. "And I love winning."

"As long as the stakes stick to drinking, I'm ok with that." Tim gently reminded Ernie that he and gambling weren't the best of friends.

The innkeeper finished setting up the table for another round. "On that count, I've learned my lesson. Now get over here and put up or shut up."

ShadowLily leaned next to Tim and whispered in his ear. "Cassie's been trying to teach him slang."

"It's the putting up I have a problem with, Ernie." Tim wasn't sure if the innkeeper knew he'd just asked him to place a wager or if he was confused by Cassie's teachings and only challenging him to a game.

"I thought that was getting it up," Gaston called.

As everyone in the room started laughing, ShadowLily rose to her feet. Turning toward Tim, she extended her hand. "Let's go see if that is going to be a problem or not."

Tim jumped to his feet and pulled ShadowLily into his arms. "Sorry, Ernie, I'm out." He made his voice a little more serious. "And no gambling."

Ernie had a look on his face that said, who me? I'd never. Tim was about to remind him what had happened to the inn the last time he went off the rails when someone burst through the front door.

A woman they'd never seen before stood in front of them, water dripping off her travel-stained cloak. "I'm looking for Ernie."

"Probably another paternity case," Gaston roared. When he realized no one was laughing, he took another sip of his beer. "Tough room."

Tim had already figured out that the new person was another player. He thought it was odd the game would send someone else to Ernie for a quest when Tim was already working with him. It was normal in other games, but he hadn't encountered it here unless you counted IronBeard's running quest for metal.

Other merchants probably offered the same kind of quests, but Tim had a feeling they had secret quests as well. This game seemed to have a penchant for making you work for it. Become enough of a benefit to the quest giver, and the number of quests available, as well as their rewards, went up.

At least that was what it felt like to Tim.

How else could he explain his windfall for helping the temple recover their lost artifacts? He was sure not every player received the same quest, or else it would have ruined the economy. The amount of money received from exchanging gold to cash would have plummeted as well. Those things hadn't happened. So, Tim had to wonder if he was benefiting from a little divine intervention.

Maybe it was better not to ask questions.

As far as Tim was concerned, the game was treating him just right. Plus, he had the one thing he cared about more than anything else standing next to him. Not that the woman who just burst into the inn and ruined his alone time cared one bit.

The player's expression was haggard as if she hadn't slept for days. Tim wasn't sure if he'd seen anyone look so exhausted in his entire life. Despite the fact she clearly wasn't at her best, and her wet hair was plastered to her skull, Tim found that she was stunning.

So was her smell.

Tim spared a quick glance at ShadowLily and wondered if she could read his last thoughts. Knowing how his woman's mind worked, she'd zero in on the stunning part and not care that he also thought she was smelly.

Deciding taking chances wasn't worth the risk, Tim quickly started chanting the words "not hot" in his head while desperately trying to figure out what to say. Thankfully, he didn't have to say anything. The innkeeper saved him the trouble.

Ernie moved away from the table game and came to the front of the room to face the traveler. "I'm Ernie."

Tim noticed the man had a vial of something in his hand. Knowing the poison master, it was probably some kind of knockout gas. Despite his title, Ernie seemed to be more of a kill-as-a-last-resort kind of guy, although he'd probably ended more lives with his concoctions than all the people in the room combined.

The woman let out a sigh as if the man in front of her wasn't what she had been expecting. Her look said she'd been expecting a warrior of renown and not a drunk innkeeper. "Lorelei," she said flatly.

With a flash, her wet cloak was gone, and she had a towel in her hand. The ranger quickly dried her hair, then the towel vanished as well. Lorelei looked at all the expectant faces. "I could really use a drink."

Ernie looked a little put out as if he wanted to yell at her. Instead, he channeled his inner calm and called out, "Someone get the lady a beer."

"Wine if you have it!" Lorelei requested as Liz ducked behind the bar.

Motioning toward a table, Ernie continued, "Now, why don't you take a seat and tell me what's going on."

Lorelei sat down. Despite being cleaned up, she still looked exhausted. Reaching inside of her leather vest, she pulled out a small sealed letter and a coin. "I have a letter for you from Seraphina in Tristholm. She told me to impart to you that the situation is dire, and you should remember the shadows. Also, I was supposed to say, 'Honor the shadows' and 'All our hopes rest with you.' That was Seraphina. "

Ernie accepted the letter and the coin and unfolded the document, a frown growing on his face as the words sank in.

Tim watched his face for a moment, then turned back to Lorelei. "I haven't heard of Tristholm. Is it far away?"

"Maybe a day and a half on horses, double that walking. More if you get attacked by werewolves." She accepted the glass of wine from Liz with a flirty wink before taking a sip and leaning back in her chair with a look of contentment.

"Werewolves." Cassie took a seat at the table, sounding excited. "Tell me all about that shit."

A dark shadow seemed to pass over Lorelei's face. "I'd rather not."

Tim was happy when Cassie didn't push for more information. If it had been anyone in the guild, she wouldn't have let up until they talked, but being an outsider had its privileges apparently.

Ernie looked up from the letter. "Is it true what Lady Seraphina says? Has the mountain pass opened, and have the werewolves attacked Tristholm?"

Lorelei finished her glass of wine in a single giant gulp. "It is true, and with two of her children dead, she begs your assistance."

Ernie set down the letter, his hands starting to shake. "I promised myself I'd never go back there." He looked down at the table. "I moved here and forgot that life."

"I don't know what happened between you and Seraphina, but she needs your help. For some reason, she thinks you can help save the city." Lorelei let out a little snort. "Although I can't see why."

Gaston rose from his seat and swaggered over to the table with all the machismo of a sex-starved bull. "That's because our little innkeeper here is also a poison master." He set his beer on the table and stared dreamily at the newest arrival. "Can I get you another drink, or maybe a key to my room?"

Lorelei started to giggle. "Not unless you're packing a vagina down there, big guy."

Gaston backed away, a hand over his crotch. "Message received."

Cassie started to laugh. "I should have used that response a long time ago." She watched the assassin go to the bar and pour another beer for himself, the one he had been drinking left behind in his haste to get away. "But those muscles." Cassie licked her lips. "Me likes."

"Well, the softer side of Sears isn't for everyone." Lorelei lifted her glass to indicate she could do with a refill. Turning away from the tank, she focused on Ernie. "The real question is, will you set aside the past and help an old friend in a time of need?"

"I don't know how I could refuse." Ernie looked like he might pass out. "Before we go, I have to get a few things ready. It will take a few days."

Lorelei grimaced. "We can wait for a few days, but by the time we get back to Tristholm, the city could be under attack. The werewolves are already patrolling the forests." She paused to take a sip from her new glass of wine. "The last attack didn't go well for them, so it might take them time to regroup."

"It will take me at least a day to get the bare minimum of what we need, and we'll have to hope Seraphina stockpiled the other ingredients as I recommended." Ernie went to the bar, grabbed a slate and a piece of chalk, and started making a list.

Tim looked from Lorelei to Ernie and realized the innkeeper was about to run off with a complete stranger. He knew a Poison Master probably had a few tricks up his sleeve, but running off without the group into werewolf-infested territory sure seemed like a good way to die.

The last thing Tim wanted was for Ernie to perish on some fool's errand.

"Ernie, are you sure this is a good idea?" Tim hedged. He didn't want to start a fight with the other player over this. He was sure Lorelei was just following a quest, but he didn't want any harm to come to his friend.

The innkeeper faced the room. "I'm pretty sure this is a terrible idea, but I have to go. If what this young lady is saying is true, there is more at stake than just my inn."

He started pacing. "The werewolves of Tristholm Valley have had a long and sacred relationship with the people who live there. The city pays tribute to the clans with livestock, and the werewolves protect the city from what lies beneath the mountain."

Taking a heavy pull from his beer, Ernie let out a deep sigh. "All it took to shatter the bonds of friendship was the attack of a single rogue werewolf and the death of a prince. The last hundred years have only left one question in many people's minds."

Everyone in the room waited to hear what Ernie would say next, but the innkeeper was savoring the tension.

"What happens when the war starts and what's under the mountain is allowed out into the world?" Ernie continued with a frown. "All I know is whatever waits under the mountain is worse than werewolves. If it's made a deal with them or taken control of the clans, we're in real trouble."

"End of days," Gaston rumbled from behind them. "The darkness spreads from below, and the seeds of light wither and die."

JaKobi was the only one who smiled. "From the Book of the

Goddess. She talks about the evil goddess Vitaria being contained in a chamber below the earth, and how one day she will break free."

Cassie threw her hands into the air. "Well, we already know that happened from her little appearance at the temple."

"So Ernie *has* to go." Tim didn't like it. The innkeeper had trouble thwarting a couple of kobolds. He wouldn't fare well in the forest. Lorelei looked like a capable enough adventurer, but how much could one person do against a pack of werewolves?

"I'd feel a lot better about this if we could come with you." Tim looked at ShadowLily, hoping for some help.

"How long will it take you to round up what you need?" ShadowLily asked the innkeeper.

Ernie looked at his slate and then moved his head as if he were trying to discern a hard problem. "Most of the day, if not all of it."

"Why don't we plan on leaving the morning after? It's not as quick as Lorelei would like, but then we should be able to tag along." ShadowLily looked at the Ranger to see if she thought the offer was acceptable.

"Don't look at me," Lorelei smirked. "I'm not anxious to head back into werewolf infested territory without help. You all are saving me the trouble of trying to round up an escort tomorrow."

Tim felt like this might be the right time to find out more about their mysterious new companion. "We have a quest we need to finish in the city before we leave, or it might not be here when we get back." He looked around the room, then made the offer before he asked for anyone's input. "Would you like to tag along?"

"Hold up," Cassie stated flatly. "If she gets to come, who will stay here?"

Tim held out his hands in surrender. "If I'm not mistaken, Gaston has some personal business that needs to be handled, and that would have left us one short."

Everyone turned to look at the assassin, who finished his beer before nodding.

Ernie tossed a room key to Lorelei. "Then it's settled. Tomorrow we prepare, and we leave with the first rays of the next morning's light."

The ranger snatched the key out of the air. "Anywhere to grab some half-decent food around here?"

"Actually, we have a standing table at the best restaurant in town." JaKobi bowed with a flourish. "And I could do with another slice of pie."

"You've already had three slices today. Joe's going to start charging you pretty soon." Cassie poked the pyromancer in the belly. "Good thing you can't gain weight."

JaKobi touched his chest, pretending to be wounded. "I'll have you know, Chef Joe and I have worked out our own deal, and I pay him a weekly stipend to ensure my pie habit is attended to."

Cassie motioned for Lorelei to follow them. "Let's go. I'll save you from having to watch this jackass finish a pie by himself."

"Now that's something I'd like to see," Lorelei replied with a casual smirk.

"Oh, I've seen it." Cassie put an arm around the ranger's waist like they were old pals and started escorting her from the room. "It's when he dumps a gallon of vanilla ice cream in the center of the pie before he starts eating it, well, that's when things get interesting."

Tim watched them leave with a smile on his face. Lorelei hadn't run off screaming, so there was a chance she could fit in. He refocused his attention on Ernie. "Anything you need help with tonight?"

"Nothing can be done until the morning, and by then I'll have all the help I need." Ernie started to shuffle off in the direction of the kitchen. "But, I do have a few things I need to attend to before we go."

ShadowLily waited for the innkeeper to disappear before extending her hand to Tim. "I believe we were shortchanged on our time together this afternoon. Care to join me for another bath?"

If there was one thing Tim never had to be asked twice, it was if he wanted to go upstairs and get naked with his girlfriend. He pulled ShadowLily into his arms and lifted her. Cradling her against his chest, he ran for the stairs with the speed of an Olympic sprinter.

Gaston poured another beer from the tap and returned to his table. He sat deep in thought, knowing what needed to be done but not sure if he actually wanted to do it. After his third sip, he smashed the mug onto the table. "Grahhhhhhhhhhh!" he cried out in frustration and climbed to his feet.

"If they want a leader, I'll give them a fucking leader." The assassin tossed a coin on the table and headed for the door.

CHAPTER TWENTY

Gaston filtered into the back of the crowd like a ghost.

Everyone was too busy drinking and gambling on the match of Qwark going on in front of them to pay him any attention. His first thought was to grab another beer, but if his nerves weren't settled by the ten he'd tossed back at the inn, an eleventh wouldn't help. He found a spot where he could lean against the wall and watch the fight in front of him.

"Kill him, Fernando."

"Gut him like a fish, Charles."

The crowd was in a bloodthirsty mood tonight. Already the ritual of Qwark had been corrupted by betting. It wouldn't be long before the fights became deathmatches. There was a time when the Brotherhood had watched the combatants in stony silence. It was their job to observe rituals to make sure no one cheated.

The Brotherhood had lost its way.

Assassins weren't common thieves. They didn't steal while on the job. That brute Malvonis had blurred the lines, accepting members that shouldn't have been allowed in to clean their boots.

The filth had polluted their ranks for long enough. It was time for a change.

The fight in front of him deteriorated into a battle for survival as both men changed their daggers from being held for back-handed slashing to a more traditional stabbing grip. Cries sprang up as new wagers were called out and accepted across the room. Gaston had seen more than he cared to watch in a thousand lifetimes.

"Enough!" the assassin roared.

The fight stopped, and all eyes turned to Gaston. "You have forgotten the way of steel and shadows. I am ashamed to call you my brothers."

Some of the men in the crowd looked ashamed, but even more, looked at the assassin as if he had lost his mind. A few in the crowd looked downright hostile. A burly man pushed his way to the front of the pack to stand in front of Gaston. He had hard eyes, the kind of soulless eyes that let you know he'd just as likely kill you as say good morning.

"Your time is over, old man. The Brotherhood has moved on. Relics like you should be buried in the dust." He pulled twin daggers from behind his back, and a shark-like grin spread across his face.

Gaston knew before coming tonight that it would come to this. He'd sat idly by and watched as the Brotherhood was corrupted when he should have been fighting tooth and nail to preserve their way of life. With Malvonis out of Promethia, it was time to start righting some wrongs. The time for words was over.

Now it was time for death.

The first of his throwing knives pierced the young assassin's shirt button at the navel. The next four dug into his chest at each button in ascending order. The man looked down at the five blades sticking out of him with an expression of shock on his face.

Gaston started running as the dying assassin fell to his knees. Pulling his daggers free from the sheaths behind his back, he spun around the corpse. With a move that would have made Neo jealous, he leaped into the air, flipping at the apex of his jump to slow his momentum.

The daggers flew from his hands too fast for anyone in the crowd to follow.

Landing in the center of the arena in a superhero pose, Gaston slowly rose to his feet as the bodies of Fernando and Charles hit the ground. He turned to face the crowd, knowing that if they all came at him together, his life was probably over. A few friendly faces poked out of the sea of hostile ones, but not enough to lend him any confidence.

"Brothers, we have ignored our duty to the code for too long!" Gaston called out to the assembly.

Not wanting his nervousness to show, the burly assassin moved toward one of the corpses to pull a dagger free. "We have forgotten the path of the masters who came before us, and it is time for us to remember our oaths. We are not thieves, we are not thugs. We are above that, we are assassins!"

His eyes moved around the room, looking for potential allies.

"One contract, one death. We are the shadows, death is our pact!" A man called out from the back of the room.

More than half of the room responded to his call. "We are the shadows!"

Gaston moved to the second corpse in the arena and wrenched his dagger out of the man's breastbone. "I plan to see our noble profession restored to its glory. Once we worked for kings, not just the highest bidder."

With his daggers back in hand, Gaston slashed the blades together, making them spark. He loved doing that. It was dramatic, but it also let everyone around the room focus in on his legendary blades, The Twins.

Two snakes' mouths made up the edges of the crossguard. The serpent's bodies wove around the grip. Instead of a pommel at the bottom for balance, the twin snakes' tails formed a forked blade, making the dagger just as deadly from either side. The blades had been handed to him by the only living Grandmaster.

Turning slowly, Gaston met every eye in the room. "We will be returning to the ways of old. Anyone who has a problem with that can leave now without fear of reprisal. Stay and fail to honor the way of steel and shadow, and you will be cut down."

A few men started to filter out of the room. He didn't know their faces, as not many of Malvonis' new recruits warranted his attention. There was one man who seemed to have collected a following of ten or so others and was now moving toward Gaston with murder in his eyes. When he could finally make out the man's features, he swore.

Fucking Barnabus.

"Malvonis will hear about this." Barnabus pointed his finger in Gaston's direction. "And he won't be pleased."

"Is he ever?" Gaston set his feet and prepared himself to face the men alone. "My offer still stands. Leave now, and I won't come for you."

The men behind Barnabus started laughing, and Gaston was forced to pivot to look behind him. Another twenty men had gathered in silence. All of them had daggers in their hands, and none of them had friendly faces.

Thirty on one. That's going to be a lot of dead bodies.

One of the men behind him stepped forward, his eyes hard as cold-forged steel. "We are with you, Gaston. We are the shadows, and death is our pact."

Turning back to Barnabus, Gaston was grinning from ear to ear, his eyes matching the joy he felt. It was time to reclaim their honor, and it would start as rebellions always did, with blood.

"Should have accepted my offer." Gaston slid the dagger in his right hand back into its sheath and reached for his throwing knives.

Three deaths were all it took for the men to break. As they ran, all of them were cut down by the men assisting Gaston. Only

Barnabus was left standing before him. More than a few of the men in the room still looked unsure of which side to choose. It was those men Gaston tried to reach when he spoke.

"I again offer anyone unsure of their future as an assassin the chance to leave now." He swept their amphitheater with his gaze. "If you stay, expect to work harder than you ever have before. Contracts will be earned through merit and dedication to your craft. The assassin's way of life isn't for everyone. Make your choice!"

A few more men shuffled out, and a few looked unhappy about the new direction, but they wouldn't be a real problem. Gaston marked three other men who were probably Malvonis' spies and knew he was missing at least two more. It wouldn't happen overnight, but eventually their guild would be back in order.

Even if it cost him his life.

Gaston motioned for the remaining assassins to be seated as he turned his attention back to Barnabus. "Since you have neither fled nor killed yourself, I can only assume you have something else in mind."

"So kind of you, brother." Barnabus sneered. "Not to cut me down like the rest." He let his words hang thick and heavy with sarcasm. "Am I to be your final spectacle?"

Turning to the crowd, Barnabus pleaded. "This man who cares so much about our rights, our honor, hasn't even offered me the chance to settle our dispute via Qwark. Which is our oldest law."

Before Barnabus could try to sway any more men to his cause, Gaston cut him off. "I have another ritual in mind for you, one that will dissuade others from abusing the code."

"You don't mean…"

"A thousand cuts," Gaston replied coolly. "A punishment reserved for traitors. I have yet to administer the entirety of the punishment. My record stands at only nine hundred and thirty-two."

"This is madness," Barnabus pleaded as he looked around wildly. "Would you really let him do this to me, brothers?"

Gaston laughed. "You did this to yourself. Be thankful that your death will be an example to others." He turned to look at the men behind him. "But I will not throw tradition by the wayside. You will have your match of Qwark, and then you will meet your fate."

The men started to cheer. Everyone but Barnabus was excited to see the old ways return. Any idiot could be a thief, but it took a true master of the shadows to be an assassin. Gaston knew something was wrong when the tone of the crowd changed. He whirled to face the threat, but he needn't have worried.

Barnabus' body hit the ground with six different blades sticking out of him. "I guess that settles that." Gaston rumbled with gratitude. "Tonight we drink, tomorrow we train."

The men cheered and called for the cellar to be opened and the kegs of ale to be brought up. Gaston looked around the room and thought about how long it was going to take to undo the harm Malvonis had done to their organization and their reputation. Thankfully, he'd recently learned patience and long-term planning from a friend of his.

He didn't have to win in a day, he just had to keep fighting for what he believed in. Gaston accepted the first cup of ale and then waited until everyone had a drink in their hand. Lifting his glass high in the air, the assassin shouted, "We are the shadows!"

The room broke out into cheers for the new head of the assassins guild of Promethia.

CHAPTER TWENTY-ONE

Lady Briarthorn exited her carriage with the grace of a ballerina.

It was the kind of thing only a person who had trained for countless hours could do. Dedicating a portion of one's life to learning how to be perfect in every action or mannerism lest it sully the family name was a heavy burden, but she wore it well.

Beckoning Tim to her with a white-gloved hand, Lady Briarthorn spoke. "After speaking with the high priest, I've made all the arrangements. Still, I thought I'd better come down and make sure you didn't run into any problems. You should be free to come and go as you please."

She didn't slow down as she passed Tim. The good Lady Briarthorn was in business mode today, she didn't have time to waste on pleasantries. Her pace toward the gate was brisk, her manner abrupt. Tim was just happy it wasn't going to be him on the end of whatever storm was brewing beneath the surface of the good lady's normally calm demeanor.

Reginald followed closely behind her, and when they reached the gate, he beat his cane against the iron bars until one of the guards emerged from the tower. "If you were told to expect the Lady this morning, why is she waiting?"

The guard, deciding discretion was the better part of valor, ignored the question. "So sorry for the delay. The new sheriff was just finishing his briefing as you arrived."

"Just give him a gate key." Lady Briarthorn pointed at Tim. "I want to make sure he can move in and out of this facility like the wind."

Pulling a key from his chain, the guard handed it to Tim without hesitation. "The sheriff requests a moment of the good lady's time before she leaves."

"Please inform Sir Jorgen that I have other business to attend to," Lady Briarthorn stated coolly before turning and heading back to her cart.

Tim flashed the guard a quick smile and gave his group the hold on a second gesture as he followed Lady Briarthorn back to her carriage. "Is there something wrong, Lucy? Do you need help with anything?"

"Not unless you want to get married?" she spat bitterly as she approached the carriage.

Tim was ninety-eight percent sure her question was rhetorical. The other two percent came from the fact Lucy looked so desperate she might have meant it. So he bet on the odds. "Sir Jorgen is on the list of candidates?"

A little growl of frustration escaped her lips. "Father seems to think we'd make a fine match." Lady Briarthorn gritted her teeth as she tried to remain calm.

Tim felt bad for her. He couldn't imagine being forced into an arranged marriage. His heart belonged to one woman, and he'd rather die than be forced to marry another. Lucy didn't strike him as a woman who had her eye on a particular gentleman just yet, but she was a lady that wanted to be able to choose her own fate.

"I don't know how marriage works around here, but I do know

a man who removes problems." Tim was pretty sure she would pick up the hint.

Reginald helped her into the carriage as Lady Briarthorn responded, "Oh, yes, that well-muscled fellow who normally follows you around. Where is he, by the way?"

"Gaston had some private business to attend to this morning, but I wouldn't be surprised if he was back at the Blue Dagger Inn right now." Tim gave her a wink. "He's a man you can count on to handle delicate issues with discretion."

It sounded like Tim was trying to set her up with an escort. At least if anyone was listening, they wouldn't know what the two of them were talking about. Tim tried not to blush as he held the lady's eye. It was hard to do while he was picturing a shirtless Gaston holding Lucy in his arms like one of the covers on a romance novel.

Some of the anger faded from Lucy's eyes, and she seemed thoughtful. "I do have a few itches that need to be scratched. Maybe I will call on that associate of yours." She pulled the door to the carriage closed but leaned her head out of the window. "Thank you, Tim, and good luck."

"It has been a pleasure as always, Lady Briarthorn." Tim gave her a small bow, and Lucy sat back, disappearing from view.

Reginald climbed into the driver's seat and tipped his hat to Tim before spurring the carriage into motion.

As he returned to the group, ShadowLily nudged her shoulder into Tim's and whispered, "What was that all about?"

"Man problems."

"Maybe you should have let me talk to her then. You're not exactly well versed on the issue," ShadowLily chided.

Tim snorted. "Perfection like me is almost impossible to obtain."

"Asshole."

He started laughing in earnest now. "But I'm *your* asshole, and I'm sure Lucy will be fine. I told her to go see Gaston."

ShadowLily slapped his arm. "That buffoon. He's only helpful if you need a beer or want someone dead…" Her voice trailed off.

"Now you're getting it." Tim motioned for everyone to step inside the gate, and then he closed and locked it. Turning, he headed toward the prison and away from The Sheriff's tower.

The guard called out. "The sheriff would also like to see you."

Tim stopped moving and turned to the guard. Part of him was annoyed at the waste of time, but he knew his life would be easier with the current Sheriff on his side. The last thing he wanted was to find the boss and beat it, only to realize they'd changed the locks, and he was trapped in the dungeon.

Again.

"Lead the way." Tim started toward the sheriff's tower.

Looking relieved, the guard picked up his pace so he was leading Tim instead of following. "Thank you. I wasn't looking forward to telling him both parties ignored his request."

"More than happy to help." Tim wasn't, but having the guards in a prison on your side was always a good idea. "I don't remember you from my last visit. Did you work here under the previous warden?"

"I did not," the man stated flatly. "All of those guards have been reassigned."

Tim stepped into the open doorway and waited for his group to enter before pulling it closed. The door to the warden's office was open, but there was no way all of them could fit inside of the cramped office.

Thankfully, they didn't have to try since the warden popped his head out of the room.

"Sir Jorgen," the man said warmly and extended his hand. "I see Lady Briarthorn couldn't make it." He looked crestfallen. "Oh, well, on to the business of the day then. Mind if I walk with you to save some time?"

Would have saved more time if you'd met us at the gate.

Tim smiled at the absurdity as he watched the guard open the door he just pulled closed. "Lead the way."

A quick glance at his party confirmed they were all feeling the same way he was. No one liked it when a quest made you traipse all over the map and back again multiple times. No one wanted to run fetch quests, everyone wanted to fight monsters, and smart developers were shifting their focus.

Once they were back outside, Sir Jorgen continued, "Everything should be pretty much how you remember it from last time, although we have made some improvements to the inmate's daily lives in light of the situation they were in."

"Hopefully, that means better food." Tim's face scrunched involuntarily as he remembered.

"At least once a day," Sir Jorgen replied, sounding pleased. "The budget won't support more than that."

The sheriff stopped outside a door and tapped on it. One of the men inside replied in kind, and Sir Jorgen opened the door. "This is where I leave you. Try not to destroy my prison?" He turned and walked back to his office with the air of a man resigned to cleaning up the worst outcome.

Ignoring Sir Jorgen's lack of faith, Tim stepped inside. He was excited to find out if his idea was right, and finish up this last quest. He turned and looked over his party. The only wildcard in the group was Lorelei. She looked pretty confident with her bow, and he guessed they'd find out soon enough.

Today was going to be a good fucking day.

CHAPTER TWENTY-TWO

The prison was just how Tim remembered it.

If the new sheriff was doing anything to ease the lives of the men down here, it wasn't readily apparent. Tim also wasn't sure how he'd be received by the prisoners. The last time he'd been here more than a few men had died. He still felt guilty about leaving the others behind to deal with Jon Hobbs after he'd been released.

Unfortunately, Tim was going to have to find out how the inmates felt about his return. Otherwise, it could take them weeks to find what they were looking for. *I don't even know how big this place is.* There was no chance in hell the men living down here didn't know which areas to stay away from.

Those were the places they needed to search first.

Tim led their party down the narrow corridors toward the main dining hall. All the areas he'd previously visited were still available on his map, so he knew right where to go in the maze of crossing corridors. The group followed him in silence, probably wondering how he'd been able to spend days underground without going nuts.

If Tim hadn't been trying so desperately to stay alive, he might have.

There was a part of him that wondered if that was how astronauts stayed sane. Keeping busy and sticking to a routine probably kept how small their living quarters were out of their minds. It wasn't like they could just step outside.

It was one thing to stay inside because you wanted to and quite another being trapped because one step out the door was instant death. It was the difference between taking a tour of a cave and being trapped alive.

Personally, Tim didn't care for either option.

The prison didn't bother him nearly as much as it had the first time. He had a pretty realistic idea of what to expect and knew he had a key to get out whenever he wanted. Plus, because none of them were prisoners, if they died, they would respawn outside of the prison. The worst-case scenario was they were only a death away from freedom.

Not that any of them were going to die.

Twenty minutes later, their group walked into the dining hall. There wasn't any singing or laughter going on, but the men looked content enough as they chatted idly over dinner. Tim noticed that the still was gone, so that explained the change in mood. He wondered if these men would rather have better rations or their access to alcohol back?

It didn't take long for the prisoners to realize something was happening. Most of these men probably hadn't seen a woman in twenty years, and now three of them had miraculously appeared in their midst. None of them made a move, but a few of them looked like they were weighing their odds of survival against the well-armed party.

Most of the prisoners looked smart enough to know challenging them would be a death sentence.

One man stood up from his bench and started moving toward them. As he came forward, two other men from opposite sides of the room came to stand behind him. A grin spread across his face. "The healer's back, lads. Just in time to take care of the rash on my ass."

"I thought that rash was on your balls, Skip," the bald man behind Skip said with a grunt of laughter.

"Just keep my fucking balls out of your head, Jim," Skip quipped.

"And out of your mouth," a man called from somewhere in the room, causing everyone to laugh.

Tim relaxed as he felt the tension break. "If anyone needs healing, I'd be happy to help before we continue. All I require in return is some information."

"Tucker knows where the lost city of Tulusia is!" a man yelled out. A second later, he was tackled to the ground.

Apparently, Tucker wasn't thrilled with his friend's secret-keeping ability.

Tim held up his hands for silence as the two men were pulled apart. Before he spoke, he tossed a healing orb at each of them, instantly taking care of their wounds. "I'm not looking to barter for any of your personal secrets."

Tucker took that moment to elbow his buddy in the side, almost starting the entire fight again.

Not sure of how much time was left before things boiled over, Tim continued. "All I want to know is if there is a place you're afraid to go in the prison, or maybe somewhere that seems haunted."

Skip shrugged. "That's simple enough. You're looking for the Lower Ward. Every now and then, some idiot gets the bright idea there is an escape tunnel down there, but no one that ever goes looking comes back."

"Desperation makes some men go crazy," Jim said as he put a finger to the side of his head and twirled it.

"We'll need someone to show us the way there. They don't have to come with us after that." Tim looked at the men, wondering if they would get any takers.

When no one said anything, a grumpy-looking older gentleman stood up. His bushy silver hair poured out of the bottom of a well-worn beanie. "Fuck it, I'll take you. It's not like I've got anything else to do."

"Perfect." Tim clapped his hands in excitement. He could feel the thrill of the hunt building inside him, but first he had to take care of business. "If anyone needs healing, get in a single line."

When Tim noticed people rushing to get to the front behind Skip and his crew, he shouted over the commotion, "I won't leave until I've seen everyone, so no need to hurry."

Things settled down a little bit, but not a ton. It seemed since Barron and Henry died, no one had really stepped up to become a leader down here, but if Skip was what he had to work with, Tim would make do. "If there is anyone that needs help who isn't here, let me know before I leave. I might not be able to make it back for a while."

Skip nodded his head. "We have a couple that could really use you."

"Let's knock out the simple stuff first, and then we'll see to the rest," Tim stated as he started casting healing orb again.

It didn't take long for the world around him to fade away as he settled into a healing rhythm. Coming here had given him the chance to honor his promise, and despite how badly they needed to finish the quest, stopping to take care of the injured felt right. Even if it took hours, he promised himself that he would heal every man down here before moving on.

"That was a real nice thing you did back there," Jessie said through a mop of silver hair.

"Thank you." Tim never knew what to say when people

complimented him. He didn't want to feel like he was taking too much credit. He just did the things he thought anyone else would do, but when someone pointed them out, he got all flustered.

He let the conversation lapse into silence and followed the old inmate as he limped down the corridor. The man wasn't exactly speedy, but even after Tim had honored his promise to heal every wounded prisoner, none of the other men had wanted anything to do with a trip to the Lower Ward. So they were stuck behind Jessie.

If I broke his leg and healed it straight, it might speed things up.

Tim paused, walking for a second, and then stopped himself from reaching out.

No, bad Tim. He mentally slapped himself on the wrist.

Jessie stopped outside of an old iron door that looked like it would fit inside of a submarine rather than a dungeon. He pointed to a bell hanging on the wall. "When you want out, you have to ring the bell. There is a string on the other side."

"So, you're going to lock us in." JaKobi stared daggers at the old prisoner.

"The door stays closed, boy, that's the rule. If you had any fucking sense, you wouldn't be going down there. But you wanted to see the place, there it is," Jessie snapped.

Before the pyromancer could incinerate the prisoner, Cassie stepped in front of the mage and cut off his line of sight. "Open that shit up, old-timer, and we'll get out of your hair."

Laughing as he turned to face the door, Jessie started cranking the circle set in the center of the frame to the left. "Don't say I didn't warn you."

Cassie stepped past him into the doorway leading down. "The only person I ever blame is that guy." She pointed at Tim. "Whenever we get into trouble, it's his fault."

"Ok, lizard bait," ShadowLily replied with a laugh as she followed her friend in the tunnel. The assassin paused in the entrance before looking back at the pyromancer. "We need a light."

Conjuring a ball of white fire in his hand, JaKobi grinned. He tossed the glowing orb into the air above him and started moving toward the stairs. "Coming."

Lorelei just watched the group, probably trying to figure out their dynamic before jumping in with any banter of her own. Tim could see her smile from time to time, so he knew it wouldn't be long before she came out of her shell. Now wasn't the time, though. The ranger pulled her bow free and followed the others.

Tim stopped in the doorway and reached into his inventory. He wasn't sure why, but the last time he was in the market, he'd been compelled to buy two things. He pulled them from his inventory now and handed them to Jessie. "Thank you for your help."

Jessie pulled on the coat and looked a good deal happier than when they first met him. The man looked at the other gift, and a tear leaked from the corner of his eye. "Chocolate."

"Enjoy it." Tim smiled as he stepped into the doorway. It felt like the goddess had led him to this moment, and if that was true, the next fight was going to be epic. The heavy iron door slammed shut behind them, making Tim jump. For better or worse, they were on their way. He started taking the stairs two or three at a time to catch up with the bobbing light.

"Don't forget the healer!" Wasn't that how it always worked? He spent so much time trailing behind people they forgot he was there.

Until they died.

Then he never heard the end of it. Maybe Tim needed to start a healers' support group. *Not only am I the founder of Healers Anonymous, but I'm also a member.* A chuckle escaped his lips as he caught up with his friends.

This was going to be epic.

CHAPTER TWENTY-THREE

A doorway and a choice.

Tim stepped down into the wide and towering alcove. After being trapped in a stairwell barely large enough to walk in single file for the last thirty minutes, the cavernous space felt huge. But it wasn't a cavern exactly.

The room was more like a cathedral.

The walls were made out of stone, but the stone had been smoothed and polished with great care. Walking closer to one of the walls, Tim placed his hand against it. He couldn't even find a seam. The amount of talent and time it would have taken to carve this room without a blemish was impressive.

It was almost magical.

"Dude, this is badass," JaKobi said, looking at the door. "I wonder what these runes mean." He started reaching his hand toward the door.

Cassie's staff smacked his hand away. "Ah, let's not touch anything until we're ready." She looked around the open space. "How is there light down here?"

Rubbing his hand and staring at Cassie with a reproachful look

JaKobi plowed ahead. "I brought the light." JaKobi waved his hand and extinguished his glowing orb. "See."

Cassie laughed when the room they were in stayed the exact same level of brightness. Turning away from the embarrassed pyromancer, Cassie mumbled to herself, "There aren't even any torches."

Tim ignored the question of where the light came from. No game developer wanted you stuck in the pitch dark, that shit wasn't fun. He just wrote off the light as a creepy addition to the ambiance.

It would have been nice if they lit the stairwell.

Stepping around JaKobi, Tim focused on the runes and tried to decipher their meaning. He willed his brain to unlock the secret language, but after a few minutes, he had to admit it wasn't going to happen.

ShadowLily looked equally confused.

The only person without a befuddled look on her face was Lorelei. She was staring at the runes and moving her lips. She shook her head as she stumbled over something and then started mouthing the words as she struggled to figure out the meaning.

Lorelei's face lit up with excitement, and then it turned into a frown. Pointing at the runes as she spoke, Lorelei moved forward and traced them with her fingers as she spoke their meaning to the group. "Purification chamber."

"Sounds ominous." ShadowLily looked at the barrier with newfound respect. "Like something from a cult or a death camp."

"The last thing anyone wants to hear on a first date is 'let me take you to the purification chamber.'" JaKobi gave a nervous chuckle.

"Well, we didn't come down here not to go in, so it really doesn't matter what the door says." Cassie was starting to sound impatient.

That was usually when the fight started.

Tim positioned himself so she couldn't get to the door without going through him. "Let's just take a second and see if our new friend can tell us anything else."

Lorelei was staring at the door, trying to read more, but most of it was beyond her comprehension. "I don't even know how I read the first part. The only other thing I can make out is that it keeps saying salvation lies ahead."

"For an inmate, salvation must feel a lot like freedom." JaKobi looked around. "We've only been down here for an hour, and I already want to get the hell out of here."

"Says a guy who could spend a week in a library," Cassie retorted.

JaKobi grinned. "At least there they have books. All we have here is a creepy ass door, with a giant monster behind it."

Cassie turned from the pyromancer to look at Tim. "So, what's the word? In or out?"

"That's what she said," Lorelei quipped.

Everyone started to smile. Her little joke broke the tension, and it reminded them all of Gaston. While he wasn't here with them now, their newest friend seemed like she might be willing to pick up the slack in the lewd comments department.

"I guess we're going in. Anyone see a way to open the damn thing?" Tim walked up to the door and tried to push it open. Nothing happened. He looked for a handle or a knob, but there wasn't one.

ShadowLily moved off to the side of the door and found a small knocker. She lifted it up and turned to look at Cassie. "You ready for this?"

"Do you even have to ask?" Cassie lifted her bō staff, ready to face anything that might come running out of the door.

ShadowLily slammed the knocker down three times and then made sure to get behind the tank as quickly as possible. The feeling of tension ratcheted up to a nine out of ten when nothing happened immediately. The entire group was glancing around nervously, wondering what was about to happen when a squeal sounded from the door, as well as a series of clicks like tumblers falling into place.

The door popped open just wide enough for a person to be able to reach inside to pull it wider. Cassie looked at the gap. "Yeah, not falling for that shit." Instead of her hand, she pushed her staff into the gap and used the weapon like a fulcrum to shove the door open wider.

All that waited for them on the other side of the door was inky blackness. Even JaKobi's magical light couldn't pierce the interior. It reminded Tim of entering an instanced location in most games. When they left this room, they might be heading somewhere else entirely. There was no way to know without stepping inside.

"Cassie, my fearless compatriot, care to lead the way?" Tim started casting buffs on the group. "I think it's time we ended this."

"Fuck, yeah!" She turned to give Tim a look that said *you better be right fucking behind me* and then ran through the entrance.

JaKobi followed, clearly not wanting to get in trouble for not helping her again.

"Don't worry, I'll make sure only the boss gets hit." ShadowLily went in behind them.

Tim looked at the newest member of their group. "Ready to see what we've been dealing with?"

"Can't be as scary as werewolves," Lorelei said with a shrug as she ran to catch up with the others.

As he rushed toward the black doorway, Tim thought, *You haven't seen anything yet.*

CHAPTER TWENTY-FOUR

"It's so beautiful." Tim couldn't believe his eyes.

Who would have thought that down in the deepest, darkest part of Promethia's most dangerous prison, there would be what could only be described as a bathhouse? The obsidian floor had been polished to a shine, and golden inlays had been set in a pattern around the room.

Following the golden lines, Tim noted that they started in a half-circle, the middle of the circle being the doorway they'd entered from. Lines branching out from the circle split the room into four sections. Each of these sections had one item inside of it.

A golden bathtub.

Each tub was filled to the brim with hot steaming water. Beyond the four tubs was the next section of the room. There, on a dais, sat two bathtubs instead of four, and they were more than twice the size of the first ones. On the next highest level was a single tub bigger than all six of the others combined.

Tim was pretty certain he didn't want to tangle with whoever used the last tub.

Torches hung from the ceiling and lined the walls, bathing the room in a soft wavering light. Tim wasn't sure if they should be bathing or expecting a fight. He was tempted to let his guard down, but then he remembered Jessie saying that no one ever came back. Despite the feigned innocence of the room, he knew something sinister must be brewing under the surface.

"Be ready for anything!" Tim called out as he started looking around the room for something that might trigger the encounter.

Cassie moved out into the center of the room, careful not to leave the semi-circle the group was standing in. "I don't get it. How is a bath considered purification?"

"The same way dunking your head underwater is," JaKobi countered. "Hey, I've seen *The Exorcist*. No way this guy wasn't getting baptized. Always better to be safe."

"As if," Cassie snorted.

"We've all seen things we can't explain, they happen every day. I'm just saying that if there is a heaven or a hell, I know which one I want to be in." JaKobi grinned. "And it's not the hot one."

Lorelei followed their banter as she looked around the room. With her tracking skill activated, she could see footprints leading from the four tubs to the two, and from the two to the one, but nothing else. Not knowing what to expect was making her nervous.

Since no one else seemed to have any bright ideas, there was only one thing Tim could think of to do. "I sure hope I'm right about this." He moved toward a knocker on the door and slammed it down.

Nothing happened.

The silence seemed to stretch out for an eternity, and then from deep inside of the walls there was a click, like an old gear turning over. The entire party turned to stare at the closed door as the clicking noises intensified. Whatever lock they had opened from the outside was sealing them in. He didn't see another door, so there was only going to be one way out of here.

"Welcome to the halls of purification," multiple voices rang out in unison.

Tim spun around his heart racing. There were four men in the room now, one standing behind each of the golden tubs. They were covered from head to toe in hooded black robes. Each had their hands clasped in front of them, and the skin on their arms was milky white and hairless.

Cassie took point as ShadowLily disappeared into stealth. Lorelei and JaKobi fanned out to either side, leaving Tim behind the tank in the center of the circle. From here, he'd be able to see everyone. Normally he would have preferred the ranged DPS to stack, but with four potential enemies spreading out made more sense.

He wasn't sure if Cassie even had an AOE taunt skill yet. He was really going to have to sit down with everyone and find out what their skills looked like now that they'd made the jump to their next classes.

Before now, Tim had just been relying on people to do their jobs, but the encounters were getting more intense. It wouldn't be long before they were wiping in fights and having to learn mechanics again instead of being able to bully their way through. Not that life had been easy so far, but harder encounters as you leveled made more sense.

Plus, the last thing the developers wanted was to be constantly wiping people out before they made it to level ten. Suck the people in and make sure they keep having fun to generate the subscription revenue. Otherwise, people left or just came back for major content releases.

The Etheric Coast wasn't anything like a traditional game. As far as Tim could tell, there wasn't a level cap, just a skill cap. With each skill basically taking twice as long to master as the level before it, reaching the Grandmaster ranks seemed like a pipe dream, but he was sure with enough effort he could get there.

Being the best healer in the game would certainly come with a few perks.

Not that future perks were going to help him get through today.

"Let's take it easy until we find out what these guys are up to," Tim shouted to the group. "Cassie, it's your show."

"It's been so long since we've had anyone to purify. The wait has been most unpleasant." All four of the men spoke as one.

One by one, they lowered their hoods to reveal bald heads covered in the same white skin. Their eyes were red like rats', and for the first time, Tim noticed their hands looked more like claws. Reaching into the tubs, each of the men pulled a sword out of the water.

"We do grow hungry!" the four men roared in perfect unison.

Tim dropped into his Way of the River stance and quickly hit Cassie with a healing orb. The heal over time effect would take care of any little scratches as he monitored the rest of the fight. The four sword-wielding rat-men jumped over the tubs and charged at the players.

Things quickly degenerated into chaos.

Cassie managed to intercept two of the fighters, leaving JaKobi and Lorelei to deal with their own. The ranger took one down with three arrows in the center of its chest. A bright light blinded Tim for a second as JaKobi's target was reduced to a puddle of white mush.

Something didn't feel right.

Could this really be their last fight? It felt way too easy, and as far as Tim could tell, none of these creatures were wraiths.

A third one of the monsters fell to a critical backstab from ShadowLily. Enjoying the chance to sit back and cast for a bit, Tim let loose with divine light. "Cassie, look out!" The tank dove to the side just as Tim's spell reduced his target to a puddle of goo.

He looked around the room and saw that each of the targets had been turned into a puddle of white slime. Part of him was tempted to look for a stick to poke into the mess. The thought reminded Tim of being a kid. Whenever they found something too gross to touch, they always poked it with a stick. It wasn't logical, it was just what little boys did. He started to edge toward one of the puddles as Cassie climbed to her feet.

"Little more warning next time." Their tank brushed off her vest.

Tim reached out and grabbed Cassie's arm, yanking her away as a tendril shot out of the goo and tried to snare her leg. She was still giving Tim a "what in the fuck" look as he let her go and pointed.

Four white blobs slid across the floor. Before Tim could think of trying to take them out, the four blobs had made it into the two tubs on the next level of the room.

Bubbles started forming on the surface of the water and then spilled over the edges. Cassie motioned for everyone to get behind her as they watched the two baths with horror.

"I don't have a good feeling about this." JaKobi held his staff in front of him like he was going to battle the devil himself.

"Just try to remember, when we kill whatever comes out of those tubs we have to try to stop the goo from making it into the last tub." Tim tried to get the group thinking about possible mechanics, and not just the craziness of what was happening.

No one acknowledged what he said, but Tim knew they heard him. Hopefully, it registered, but he wouldn't be surprised if it didn't. Sometimes in a fight, things were too intense, and why games had response timers and long runs back to bosses. That way, everyone could bitch for five minutes before trying the fight again.

Two shapes started to rise from the golden tubs. The creatures no longer resembled men at all. Their faces had elongated, they had tails, and they were twice as big as before. Most of that mass went into muscles.

It looks like they needed them for all that heavy armor.

It seemed kind of unfair that not only would the boss monsters get bigger, but they would also get armor for the second stage of the fight. Tim looked over the giant rat-men. He noted that the armor just covered the large parts of their bodies. There were still plenty of gaps for weapons and spells to do their worst.

Reaching into the tub, the warrior ratman on the left pulled out two double-headed axes, and the one on the right pulled out two shields. Instead of exchanging weapons so they each had a shield and an axe, the two warriors began moving toward the group.

"Focus on the unshielded one first," Tim yelled to the group. "Don't let them work together."

That was a task easier said than done.

The nine-foot-tall ratman jumped into the air and easily intercepted JaKobi's ball of flame. Lorelei's arrow pinged off the rim of his shield. Just an inch higher, and she might have had him. They'd given up their chance at a quick kill, and now the rat warriors were working in tandem.

An axe would chop, and just before any unprotected flesh could be harmed, a shield was there to protect. The two ratmen worked together almost like they were dancing, only in this dance one wrong move would cost you your life.

Tim cast curse of giving on the rat with the axes, quickly followed by behold my power on the one with the shields. As the curse hit, Tim started counting down in his head. Ten, nine, eight.

As the seconds ticked by, Tim cast healings orb on his companions. His mana was getting low, but after they won, he should get a little bit of a recharge before the next leg of the fight.

At least Tim hoped he would.

The two rat warriors were fighting the four of them to a standstill, but they forgot one very important thing. ShadowLily appeared behind the warrior with the axes and sank her daggers deep into his back. The shielded warrior turned to protect his partner, and Tim heard the clap that signaled JaKobi's phoenix spell.

The mythical bird of fire flew across the space in two massive flaps of its wings, slamming into the unprotected back of the shield-bearer. Three of Lorelei's arrows flew past the downed rat warrior and into his twin. The axes dissolved into slime, joining with the puddle created by his body.

The slime started moving back through the room toward the single tub at the very back.

"Attack the slime!" Tim called.

"But what about…" Lorelei's voice trailed off as Tim thrust his finger at the puddle as it picked up speed. "Whatever. It's your ass." Her arrow flew into the puddle of slime, but she couldn't tell if it had any effect.

Tim turned away from watching their encounter to see the shielded rat warrior coming right at him. JaKobi had a nervous look on his face, but his spell sailed past the charging warrior as he followed Tim's instructions. His brain started screaming how bad of an idea this was when the curse took hold.

The shield-bearer hit the ground and instantly turned to slime.

"Have we hurt that one at all yet?" Tim called out.

"Unknown," Lorelei replied as she fired another arrow.

The first bit of slime was about to make it to the tub. If they were going to stop it they needed to switch it up. "Change targets. Give it everything you've got."

Tim wasn't sure what he could do to help, but he was determined to do as much damage as he could. The first thing he cast was snare hoping to slow the slime down. The spell might have worked, but its rank was still so low he wasn't sure. Next up was weaken undead. He wasn't sure slime counted as undead, but if it increased anyone's damage it might help.

Last he called on his old faithful, divine light.

With his rotation complete, Tim slowed to examine the slime as it passed the first set of tubs. It had a few arrows stuck in it and what appeared to be a throwing knife, but it didn't look hurt.

Lorelei was right; this was a waste of time.

"Fall back," Tim called as he gave up his examination and returned to the main part of the room.

Cassie looked back at Tim with a disgusted look on her face. "What the fuck is that shit?"

"No clue, but I think we only need to beat it one more time." Tim was too busy watching the sides of the room for any surprises as Cassie tapped her forehead and mouthed the words, "No duh."

All they could do now was wait to see what came out of the last golden tub. If they beat the boss, their quest was complete, and they could go off to help Lorelei. If not, they'd have to try to do this again with the knowledge they'd gained from this round.

If they learned anything.

Tim still wasn't exactly sure what he was seeing. There was obviously some kind of magic at play, but he had no idea what kind. Were these even ratmen, or was it some kind of slimy shapeshifter that used the water to heal? He had no clue. Up until now, the fight had been relatively easy, which meant things were about to get much worse for them.

The water started bubbling, and it was more violent than before. Dark green liquid sloughed over the edges of the tub and splashed on the black tiles inlaid with gold. Something massive began to rise out of the water. At first, Tim thought it must be a huge shield because of the size, but there were eye holes.

"Holy shit, that's a head!" The words tumbled from Tim's mouth in a breathless rush.

As the boss' shoulders rose out of the water, Tim frantically checked everyone's health and status of effects to make sure they were ready. When he looked back, he could see massive steel spikes sticking out from the armor on the boss' shoulders and forearms. Even the tail was plated with a spike ball at the end.

How in the fuck were they going to hurt it?

The steel plates covering the boss weren't like the ones that had been hammered into the flesh of the lesser warriors. The massive rat was wearing a full set of actual plate mail modified with spikes.

Tim was surprised by how much scarier the steel warrior looked than a regular human in the same garb.

Size really does matter.

There would be no running from the Agent of Purification. At least the boss finally had a name. Everything that came before this had just been preamble as far as he was concerned. They finally had the real deal in front of them, and it was time to take him down.

"Remember, keep it slow and steady," Tim called out as the group started to get into position.

"This isn't my first time behind the wheel, Grandpa," Cassie said and strode to the front of the room.

Seeing their tiny tank walking alone to face a boss that was fifteen feet tall and a good seven feet wide at the shoulders with what amounted to a wooden stick in her hand was all kinds of impressive. Cassie's constant displays of bravery always shored up his own confidence. Tim could imagine the trouble he'd have if this was a one on one fight, where he just ran in circles casting snare and curses over and over again until he went splat.

He was glad he had Cassie to go splat for him.

All Tim had to do was sit back and watch. Hopefully, he'd be able to heal her through any kind of tank buster so they could all live. Just everyday life for a backline healer. Not that it wasn't stressful. One mistake by him and the fight was over. Groups tended not to last long without a healer. Healer dies, tank dies, DPS tries to kite the boss, DPS dies. They were doing so well though, Tim didn't think a full wipe was in the cards.

Victory before death!

Shouting that in his mind like a knight of Winterfell screaming, "King of the North!" Tim got to work. A quick double-check of his buffs told him he didn't need to be worried about them falling off any time soon. For now, there weren't any adds, so he switched his stance to Way of the Boulder so all his heals would go to Cassie, then let the chaos of battle wash over him.

"I've got your fucking cheese!" Cassie roared as she charged at the Agent of Purification.

Their tank looked small as she crossed the space. If Tim was right, Cassie couldn't have been much taller than the boss' knee, who was hunched over looking more like a nervous lab rat than a proud warrior. It also meant the creature's reach was probably longer than it looked.

Cassie jumped over the mace on the end of the boss' tail, slipped under his outstretched fist, and slammed her bō staff into his knee joint. The staff hit his leg, and then Cassie dropped it as her arms went numb from the impact. She might as well have slammed a baseball bat into the side of a steel mountain.

Rolling away from getting stomped, Cassie collected her staff. Now she was playing purely on the defensive, making sure to keep the boss focused on her while the others did their thing. Tim topped off her health as he heard the clap of JaKobi's phoenix spell.

The bird slammed into the Agent of Purification's helmet and left a streak of ash down the side. It also knocked it loose if Tim wasn't mistaken. There was only one way to find out. "JaKobi, try hitting that same spot with everything you have." He forgot he had another ranged player to work with now. "Lorelei, same thing: shoot for the head." A couple of arrows pinged off the boss' helmet, and Tim was sure.

The helmet was loose.

"I was saving this for later, but what the heck." JaKobi pulled a glittering egg from inside of his robes. Cracking the jeweled creation over his head, he sparkled for a moment as the pieces disappeared.

The pyromancer started working on his next cast of phoenix fire. As the words tumbled from his lips, JaKobi started to split in half. Tim realized his fiery friend hadn't actually split in half but had somehow created a clone of himself. The spell finished as the twin mages raised their arms in the air and clapped.

Two of the phoenixes flew across the room, one after another.

They both struck the boss' helmet and knocked it free. One of Lorelei's arrows left a scratch down the Agent's face before he started moving.

The boss was big enough that as he stood on the second dais, he could reach his arms into both tubs at the same time. Lorelei tried to fire an arrow at him, but it bounced harmlessly off an invisible shield. It seemed as if they weren't allowed to stop the boss from whatever it was doing.

The Agent of Purification's health was down by a third.

Knocking his helmet free had really opened an industrial-sized can of whoop-ass on the fucker. Tim was starting to feel like they were on the home stretch, but he didn't want to get overconfident. When a gamer got cocky during a boss fight, it was normally followed by an apology for dying. When this repeatedly happened to his gaming buddies, he liked to fall back on saying he learned from watching the NFL.

Do your job.

The message was simple. Worry about what you were supposed to do and trust your teammates to be where they were supposed to be. The only thing that happens when you leave your position or role is you expose the team to risk. Tim was risk-averse as an investor and even more so as a healer.

Don't stand in the red if you don't want to get dead.

The Agent pulled a massive shield from one of the tubs and an axe from the other. The front of his shield looked like it had one of the warrior rats trapped in it like a chunk of floating carbonite, and the haft of his axe appeared to have the other holding the blade of the axe.

Tim hated to admit it, but those weapons were creepy as fuck.

There was also the added danger they could be made from the same slime and turn back into the warriors. He fucking hated shapeshifters. Nothing in the fight was fair. They always had another trick up their sleeves.

Cassie launched herself back into the fray, and the fight continued.

This part of the fight felt more like a traditional tank-and-spank. Cassie kept the boss occupied, and the group worked together to efficiently wheedle down his health. When the Agent of Purification's health pool reached fifteen percent, he roared, throwing the shield and axe away as he headed toward the four tubs.

Tim cast behold my power on the boss before the shielding went up, but he noticed that the timer hadn't started. Whatever mechanic the boss was enacting now prevented Tim's curse from working. Hopefully, when the shield came down, it would be business as usual, and he wouldn't have to cast the curse again.

Hearing Cassie's scream brought Tim's mind back to the battle. He'd been complacent, thinking that while the boss was protected, the fighting was over, but that wasn't the case. Before he looked to see what was happening, Tim cast healing orb on the tank.

Cassie was bleeding freely from a cut on her arm, but the two warriors were down. Thankfully his party hadn't stopped paying attention. The shield and the axe must have turned back into the warriors when the boss shielded himself. It was the kind of move dickhead developers put in so you couldn't recharge your mana while the boss was powering up to kill you.

His curse should take a large portion of the boss' health ten seconds after he emerged from the shielding. So they had ten seconds to deal with whatever his surprise was before they brought the monster to his knees.

Ten seconds to paradise, baby!

Maybe ten seconds wasn't enough for paradise, but it would complete their quest if they could handle it. Tim had a sinking suspicion the last fifteen percent of the Agent's health was a burn phase. He also knew that whatever came out of those tubs wasn't going to make things easier.

All four tubs started boiling over, but the boss only had his hands in two of them. The group was focusing on the boss, all of them instinctively knowing this was it. The Agent pulled two massive daggers from the tubs and leaped back into the battle.

Tim cast weaken undead, quickly followed by divine light. He was counting down the seconds in his head. When his curse took hold, the fight would be over, and it would be time to break out the beer.

Three.

Two.

One.

VICTORY TASTED SO FUCKING GOOD!

Was that a noise behind him?

Oh, shit. All four tubs had been bubbling, which meant there could be two things unaccounted for. Tim whirled, lifted his staff to protect from an overhead attack, and took a sword to the gut. He looked up into the hooded ratman's eyes as a second blade cut off his head.

CHAPTER TWENTY-FIVE

System Message: You have died

Have a nice day!
3
2
1
...

CHAPTER TWENTY-SIX

Ah, the good old waiting room.

As much as Tim loved seeing his caseworker Barbara, all he wanted to do was get back in the game. He hoped his team had been able to finish off the boss before getting wiped. Thankfully he was an adventurer now and didn't have to worry about losing all of his stuff. Maybe when he got back in the game, there would even be a shiny new piece of loot waiting for him.

Dying wasn't so bad when it came with perks.

With his in-game future secure for the moment, there wasn't a lot to worry about unless the stream tanked because of his death. Tim wasn't sure what the protocol was. He rubbed his throat to make sure his head was firmly attached before looking around the room. He wondered if there was a button he could push to let them know he was ready.

Not seeing any way to speed up the process, he relaxed in the chair. It'd been a while since he felt real pain in the game. Dying certainly wasn't fun, and adding in the pain feedback system sure made you want to do it less. He couldn't imagine what it would be like to be in a raid and dying over and over again to a boss. When wipes physically hurt, they took on a whole new meaning.

Barbara appeared in the doorway, and she had on one of her famous t-shirts. This time the shirt showed Tim's surprised face and a chat bubble appeared with *WTF*. When the chat bubble disappeared, the image changed to a beheaded Tim lying on the ground.

"What do you think?" Barbara asked with a pleased smile.

Remembering how bad he'd felt about hurting her feelings the last time, Tim decided to be more excited about her shirts even if they were replaying his death. "I think it's awesome!"

"I thought so too." Barbara motioned for Tim to follow her. "If you hear anyone say they don't like it, they're just jealous because you are doing so well. My star streamer! I wouldn't have thought you'd make this far after our first meeting, but I'm excited you did."

Tim followed her through the hallway into a much nicer office. "Thanks, I guess."

"Oh, no need to be humble. Just look at your views." Barbara waved her hand, and a graph appeared in the air with an arrow pointing up. "People are loving your channel."

"But I just died," Tim protested.

"They don't seem to care. They just like watching your group. Something to do with your party's witty banter." Barbara looked pleased. "You should see some of these other groups. They take things so seriously. Must maintain battle silence and all that nonsense."

"So, things are going well?" Tim was shocked. Outside of turning his camera on for the big fights and maybe a game of beer ball or two, he hadn't done much. If people enjoyed the content, he wasn't going to complain. It'd just make it easier for him to get the rest of his party contracts.

"Better than well, things are downright fantastic," Barbara

responded. "Which brings me to my next point, it's time for you to get back in the game. You can't make any new fans sitting in my office."

With a wave of her hand, the door behind Tim opened, and the portal appeared. Barbara stood up and pulled Tim into a quick hug before shoving him through. "Go kick some ass."

Tim fell backward into the portal. "*Geronimo!*"

List of Tim's Current Stats and Skills.
"Tim" Level ten magic user

Primary Stats
Strength 12
Endurance 12
Dexterity 16
Intelligence 16
Wisdom 28
Perception: 5
Vitality: 3
Revitalization: 3
Luck: 5

Tim also has two undistributed stat points.

Notable Gear
Circlet of Wisdom +1
Simple Dagger of Dexterity +1 (X2)
Boots of Swift Regeneration Increase base movement speed and Mana regeneration by 1%

Robe of the Everlasting: Wisdom +3

Belt of Wisdom +2

Wristband of the Goddess 10% damage reduction to dark based attacks

Gloves of Wisdom +2

Leather Wraps of Divergent Health 10% chance for single target healing spell to jump targets and heal the secondary recipient for 50% of the value.

Skills

Healing Orb: Apprentice rank nine

Dodge: Novice rank two

Flame Burst: Apprentice rank three

Cleanse: Apprentice rank seven

Appeal to the goddess: Novice rank one

Infiltrator: Novice rank three

Sneak: Apprentice rank two

Small Blades: Apprentice rank six

Throwing Knives: Apprentice rank two

Sneak: Apprentice rank three

Night Vision: Novice rank five

Back Stab: Novice rank seven

Weaken Undead: Apprentice rank one

Divine Light: Apprentice rank one

Healing Storm: Novice level one

Curse of Giving

Behold my Power

Who Needs a Shield

Cleanse

Stance: Way of the Boulder

Stance: Way of the River

. . .

Open Quests
Get the Wraith Out of Here
Panic at the Temple

CHAPTER TWENTY-SEVEN

"To the gates!" Seraphina roared as her sword burst into brilliant white flames.

The leader of Tristholm quickened her pace and put distance between her and the soldiers behind her. The runes carved into her half-plate armor flared with the same energy as her sword, which inspired hope in her followers and fear in her enemies.

That holy energy coursed through her system, powering her muscles past mortal endurance. If she'd managed to sprout wings, Seraphina would have looked like an avenging angel. Instead, the men charging after her had to be content with seeing her leap fifteen feet into the air before crashing into the breach in the wall like a cannonball.

After the dust cleared, Seraphina was already swinging her sword. The ground was wet with blood from the werewolf she'd split in two on her descent. The creatures gathered around the gate were still trying to recover as she cut them down. Her soldiers swarmed around her, killing the rest of the weres.

Nothing made her feel alive like combat against the monsters of the forest. A warrior of Tristholm didn't prove their worth until they killed their first werewolf. It had been many years since that thirteen-year-old girl stood over a corpse with a spear in hand. Since then, she'd stood over many more, and would continue to slaughter the beasts until they fell into line or were extinct.

Seraphina had lost a husband, a son, and a daughter to those bastards. The only thing they deserved from her was death.

The breach in the wall wasn't as bad as it looked from the castle, but it would get worse as the assault continued. What they needed were repairs. She motioned with one hand, and a messenger appeared.

"Get the woodworkers and masons down here to patch this as best they can." Tristholm's leader's eyes burned with intensity. "I will buy them the time they need."

The messenger ran off, and Jon took his place at Seraphina's side. "What's next?"

Placing a hand on her son's shoulder, Seraphina smiled. "I've always been proud of you. Remember to be kind to the people, to try to love them like family." She put her hand on Jon's chest and shoved him away. Looking at the bewildered expression on his face, Seraphina hoped he knew how much she loved him.

Now it was time to act.

Camilla's latest tart would have been jealous at the ease with which Seraphina leaped over the wall. Unlike Lorelei, when she scaled the gate, the Leader of Tristholm didn't need any kind of boost to clear the twenty-foot wall. There was a part of her that felt selfish for what she was doing, but she was tired of watching her children fall in battle while she sat on her throne.

Let someone else sit in that uncomfortable fucking chair. I was forged for battle.

A small crater appeared when she landed on the other side of the breach. Seraphina's husband would have made a joke about her being too heavy in the armor, but he was dead now, slaughtered by the beasts almost ten years ago. The werewolves clustered around her landing site were thrown to the ground, and her sword went to work.

Jon called for archers on the wall, as her sword blazed with the holy wrath of the Goddess Eternia. Seraphina started to spin, the flames from her blade making its range three times as long as before.

As her spinning quickened, Seraphina roved across the battlefield, slaughtering any werewolf she came in contact with. Thirty had fallen by the time she ran out of power, but there were a hundred more.

Had all the clans united against them?

When the accords were shattered, the werewolf clans turned on each other, all thirteen alphas vying to be the true leader of all the clans. As each alpha fell, another rose to replace him, keeping the unending battle raging, all the while bleeding themselves of their best warriors in the process.

The hope of every generation in Tristholm was that the clans would never crown a single alpha and unite.

How cruel were the fates that it should happen in her lifetime?

Defending the gate from this side of the wall without backup was a death sentence, but if her people lived, it was worth it. Saving a life was more important than all the gold in the kingdom. Instead of doing what the horde expected and running back to the sanctuary of the city and its ballistae, Seraphina charged back into the fray. If she was going to die on this battlefield, she was determined to take as many of these mangy furballs with her as possible.

The inscriptions on her armor flared as Seraphina's shoulder slammed into the first werewolf. The creature's body flew back into the press of monsters, and she followed the path it created into the pack. From the wall, it must have looked like she was trying to kill herself, but Jon would know better.

Knowing it wouldn't be long before Jon called for arrows,

Seraphina ducked and pulled two of her recently created human corpses over her for cover.

The werewolves thought it was the opportunity they had been waiting for and sprang forward to rip the woman limb from limb. She felt the first impact, and then the sound of raining death filled her ears. To Seraphina, the sound was as sweet as a summer thunderstorm.

Normal arrows wouldn't be enough to kill a werewolf. They regenerated too fast for that, but they would slow them down. Pulling arrows out of your internal organs wasn't a pleasant experience, even if the wounds healed almost instantly. It also meant Jon's attack would only buy her a little bit of time.

It took all of her augmented strength to burst free of the pile of wounded werewolves. The cheers from the wall filled her with energy as her sword continued its deadly work. White flames flashed in the darkness as Seraphina's blade rose and fell. The horde seemed to be falling back. Maybe she'd overestimated their strength. If the clans were this weak, she should signal for the charge.

It's a trap.

The words slammed into her thoughts with the force of a galloping horse. Seraphina's order to charge died on her lips. She'd learned not to ignore the goddess' warnings long ago. When Eternia spoke, she knew it was time to fucking listen.

Instead of doing what honor demanded and calling for her men to storm the battlefield, she waited to see what would happen. A lone fighter, no matter how imposing, would never have scared off the werewolves. Their animal desires should have overloaded their human thoughts and sent them rushing to attack as mindlessly as a rabid dog.

But the werewolves continued to retreat. The scene was something that would have been perfect for painting as a mural, a picture that said a million words. A lone warrior covered in holy armor standing against an army of darkness as they retreated. This moment would be something that could inspire future generations.

Only if we win.

The werewolves parted like the seas had for Moses and a single figure moved toward her. All of the wolves bowed their heads as the man approached. Seraphina had never seen anything like it. No mere man could cow a pack of slavering werewolves into submission, but this one had the respect of hundreds.

She wondered what secrets the man was hiding. He was shorter than her, easily under five and a half feet tall. The robe he was wearing confirmed she didn't have to worry about his martial prowess. If the werewolf loving bastard was going to attack, it'd be with tricks or magic.

She fucking hated magic.

"I'm surprised to see you out here all alone." He paused just past the line of werewolves, and outside of her range.

Seraphina scoffed. "If you want to take Tristholm away from me, you're going to need more than puppies."

Some of the werewolves behind the man bristled at the insult, but they stayed in formation as he continued to speak. "It's no wonder we got off on the wrong foot, since I've failed to introduce myself properly. My name is Steve, emissary to Malvonis."

Steve? When was anything great ever done by a Steve?

Seraphina watched the man as she tried to figure out what his angle was. Was he trying to parley with her, or maybe buying time to launch a surprise attack on the rest of the city? She trusted Jon to handle Tristholm's defenses in her absence. All she had to do was give them enough time to be successful.

"Steve, you are standing on land belonging to the City of Tristholm, at the head of an army of monsters. Tell me what you've come for, and I might spare you the indignity of running back to your master with your tail between your legs." Seraphina waved her hand vaguely toward the East. "Reinforcements from Promethia will come, and when they do, this will be over."

A sickly smile spread across Steve's lips, and he pretended to check himself for a tail before speaking. "Oh, Promethia has its own problems to deal with for the moment. I wouldn't plan on receiving any help from them."

Motioning to the naked human corpses littering the landscape, Seraphina returned the smile in kind. "We might not need as much help as you think."

Laughter bubbled from Steve's lips. "This is just our opening salvo. We haven't even begun to move against you yet. The only reason I am here is that my Master understands it's cheaper to rule over a conquered city than it is to build a new one."

Instead of backing down from the threat, Seraphina seemed to grow in size as her anger bubbled over. "You little shit!"

A blur appeared behind her, and Seraphina hit the ground hard. Her armor flared, fending off the next strike of Steve's magical attack. Somehow the bastard had created a mace out of magic without even moving his hands. The magical mace tried to batter her into submission, but she refused to give in. With each hit she took a step forward, closing the distance between them as slowly as a glacier floating on the tides of the sea.

The smile on Steve's face faded as he realized the mace itself wouldn't be enough to defeat her. He started backing up, calling on the other spells in his arsenal. All of them bounced harmlessly off her armor. The only thing stopping Seraphina from cutting him down was his mace throwing her off balance. Falling down now would be a death sentence, so she struggled on.

Seraphina growled as the mage's final spell shattered against her. She crossed the distance to Steve in half a heartbeat, and her sword skewered him through the center of his chest. Using all of her strength, she lifted his punctured corpse into the air so she could watch the life bleed out of his eyes.

Kicking the corpse free of her blade, she roared into the night. "Is this the best you've got?"

It looked as if the werewolves were backing away from her unbridled fury until she saw them hunker down. Werewolves didn't split for weak mages, and they certainly didn't kneel for anyone.

What in the fuck was going on?

A woman in a black dress appeared out of the night. The dress was split in the front, so at any time, one of her legs was exposed. The outfit was too provocative for a gala, and very out of place on the battlefield.

Raven black hair swept down around the woman's shoulders, and a golden circlet rested on top of her head. There was a twinkle of the same gold on each of her wrists, and a belt of loose golden rings around her waist.

"He was a decent apprentice but had much to learn." With a casual flick of her wrist, the woman encased Seraphina in a cone of dark energy. "I, on the other hand, am not so easily defeated. You see, when one is fully trained in the art of darkness, they have no equal."

With a sneer, the mage dropped the spell, letting Seraphina gasp for air on her knees as she continued speaking. "My master has more mercy than most. You have three days to open the gates and turn over the city."

"If I refuse?" Seraphina growled.

"Then, we burn it to the ground and use the corpses of your citizens to feed our growing army." She knelt next to Seraphina, her expression tainted with smugness. "When you bow before Malvonis, remember to tell him it was Abigale who brought you to your knees."

Hatred burned in Seraphina's eyes as she stared into the gloating black orbs of Abigale's. "Tristholm bows to no one." Pulling a blade-free from her belt, she lunged forward. An inch from striking the woman, the blade hit an invisible shield and skittered away harmlessly.

"You bitch!" Abigale roared. With two furious motions, her

magic lifted Seraphina into the air and then crushed her breast-plate. She tossed the broken body back toward the city.

Looking at the dead leader, Abigale giggled. "Oh, I shouldn't have done that."

A rallying cry rose from the walls, and a trumpet sounded as the gates opened. Men on horseback poured out into the night racing toward their fallen leader. The witch watched them with icy detachment for a moment before turning and walking slowly back to the army of werewolves.

"Time to go." A massive werewolf rose from where he had been kneeling and moved to Abigale's side. The witch climbed onto the werewolf's back, and the army followed them into the forest.

In moments it was if they'd never been there.

Seraphina struggled to breathe. Why was everything wobbly? She tried to stand up but couldn't find the strength. A face came into view and her body tensed, but it was only her son.

Jon was shouting for a healer and a stretcher as she reached up to touch his face. "My boy." Her hand fell away, and she slipped into darkness.

CHAPTER TWENTY-EIGHT

System Message: You have gained a level

Tim stared at the screen in front of him for a moment. He'd never left Barbara's office and not appeared directly in the game before. It was nice that he was going to be able to allocate his unused stat points before entering *The Etheric Coast*. Having given up his Boots of Wisdom for the extra mana regeneration, Tim decided to place all of his remaining points in Wisdom.

Wisdom was the main stat for his class. Every point he spent in it made his spells hit harder. He would either do more damage or more healing with every cast. Right now, that seemed like the way to go. If Tim's mana regenerated fast enough, then he could brute force his way through some of the encounters.

Next up on Tim's list was his Intelligence. For now, his Strength and Endurance would have to wait. Sure it would be nice to carry more stuff or run faster, but none of that was essential to his role as a healer. Not that he'd let his Dexterity slide too far behind. When you wore cloth armor, being able to dodge away nimbly was a bonus. Not to mention he'd already spent a bunch of time getting his assassin skills up to par. He'd hate to waste all that effort by never using them.

Next on the list to the magical stat of twenty was his Intelligence.

Normally in an MMO, you didn't have to worry about min/maxing your stats until end game. In *The Etheric Coast*, every battle felt like an end game encounter. If you happened to be under level ten and not an adventurer, then it actually was. Thankfully, everyone in their party was past the point of a hard reset unless Lorelei hadn't made the jump.

Tim was going to have to find out more about their new traveling companion as soon as he could. The last thing he wanted was for her to die on his watch and hold a grudge. So far, the only person who'd died on one of his adventures was Cassie, but the goddess had brought her back to life, so maybe that didn't count.

Nervous laughter broke from his lips. Hopefully, everyone hadn't died right after he did. A full group wipe wasn't the type of first impression he wanted the Blue Dagger Society to give a potential new recruit. Not to mention, they would have to fight the boss again before leaving Promethia, and that would slow everything down.

At least he was level eleven now. It might have been a small boost to his stats, but every little bit helped when they were permanent increases. With nothing else holding him back from entering the game, Tim hit the little green button on the side of the screen.

It was time to go home.

The screen disappeared, and the darkness swirled around him. He felt like Batman dropping through a vortex of bats, only instead of fighting bad guys, he was hoping to get a beer. Tim closed his eyes, and when he opened them again, he was standing in the courtyard of the prison. The rest of his guild was standing by the gate, surrounded by guards and looking more than a little pissed off.

Maybe the sheriff wouldn't let them leave until he got the gate key back.

ShadowLily noticed Tim fist. She sprinted across the space and enveloped him in a hug the second they collided. "Took you long enough."

"Barbara wanted to chat for a minute." Tim grinned at the look on his girlfriend's face when he mentioned another woman's name. A little flair of jealousy wasn't a bad thing. It was only when it reached swimfan-level proportions that things started to spiral out of control.

Reaching into her inventory ShadowLily pulled out a ring. "After we all used the chest, this shot out and said bound to player Tim on it." She placed the ring, set with a small Azurite stone, in his hand.

Tim gave the ring a casual glance and then equipped it. He didn't have any real jewelry to speak of, so he didn't have to check and see if it was an upgrade. He'd check out the details later. "Thanks, babe."

They started walking back toward the gate, and Tim couldn't help himself. He pulled up the ring in his inventory and looked at the stats.

Ring of Marginal Transcendence: This item is almost really good, but instead of being the flawless version of itself, this ring appears to be a castoff. Increases wisdom by two and mana pool by 10%.

Whoa, I wonder what bonuses an actual Ring of Transcendence receives?

As they reached the rest of their group by the Gate, the sheriff came bursting out of his office and started running across the space to catch them before they left. Tim unlocked the gate before the sheriff could reach them. When everyone was outside of the prison, Tim turned to wait for the man to catch up. He felt better about being outside of the gate than in while they waited.

So far, the new Sheriff was much nicer than the old one, and

Tim couldn't think of a reason to just leave when the man clearly wanted to speak with them.

The guards pulled the gate closed and locked it as the sheriff came to a stop behind the bars. Looking for something outside, the sheriff's eyes moved across the empty courtyard, his face crestfallen in a way that could only happen to a man in love.

Tim tried not to snicker.

Lady Briarthorn wasn't going to come back, at least not based on her reaction when she helped them gain entrance. Part of him wondered if the good lady had taken him up on his offer to speak with Gaston.

The sheriff was clearly still living, so no assassin had come for him yet.

It was crazy to think they were living in a world where it was easier to kill the problem of an unwanted suitor than it was to tell them to fuck right the hell off. The situation reminded him of watching movies about the political intrigues of the royal court; everyone was a backstabbing bastard in those movies. But the sheriff wasn't Tim's enemy, and he didn't have to make him one. Instead of bringing up Lucy's lack of an appearance, he went with something a little more diplomatic.

"Thank you for your help, Sheriff." He held the gate key out to the man.

"Are you sure you're done?" the sheriff pleaded as he looked between the bars, hoping for a glimpse of a certain noble's carriage.

Tim didn't bother looking at his group for confirmation. They'd beaten the boss, and he'd hear more about how over drinks. Right now, they had quests to turn in, and a poison master to escort to the city of Tristholm.

"Afraid to say we are, Sheriff." Tim gave the man a warm smile. He'd learned a long time ago never to make an enemy when he could make a friend. "I'd also be more than happy to inform Lady Briarthorn of just how integral you were to our success."

The man's cheeks puffed out. "That would be very kind of you. If you ever have need of my assistance, feel free to call on me."

"I'll be sure to do that." Tim stuck a hand through the bars and shook with the sheriff.

Letting go of the sheriff's hand, Tim turned back to his waiting group. "Let's get back to the inn and find out how Ernie is doing. Once we see where he is at with supplies, we'll make a plan for the journey."

"As long as any plan includes turning in these quests we've completed," Cassie said as she picked up the pace. "I don't like seeing a shit ton of rewards and experience just sitting there."

Grinning at his loot hungry tank, Tim replied. "Don't wait on me to turn them in. I just wanted to tell Brother Colton in person before we leave."

"Won't he get the update when we turn them in?" ShadowLily asked as she looked over her status sheet.

"No idea." Tim thought about why he wanted to go in person and could only come up with one reason. "So far, I've had pretty good luck picking up extra quests when I return to the quest giver."

JaKobi grinned as flames splashed out from the soles of his boots with each step. "Aren't we leaving in the morning?" He jumped in the air and landed on his heels. The same amount of flame shot out the back, leaving JaKobi looking disappointed with the result. He'd clearly expected his jump to make more flames shoot out.

After taking a few more steps, the pyromancer's smile returned. "I love these boots." He looked up at the group, realizing he'd sidetracked their conversation. "All I have to do is stop at Joe's and fill up with awesome, and I'm ready to go."

"Well, as long as Ernie is ready, the plan will stand. That means we're leaving in the morning, so get your fill up before then." Tim turned away from the pyromancer and focused on Lorelai. "Is that okay with you?"

"I can't leave without Ernie. So, whenever he is ready to go is when we go." Lorelei grinned at the group. "And I'm not hating on a little downtime. The last few days have been fucking brutal."

Grabbing Tim's hand, ShadowLily started to pull him toward the inn. "At least we get one more night in a comfy bed."

"Gaaaaroosss!" Cassie whined. "But at least at the inn, we can't hear you."

Tim's face went pale. "Wait, you've heard us?"

Cassie stuck out her tongue and blew a raspberry at Tim.

Before their leader could think too much about it, JaKobi slid an arm around his shoulders and steered him away from the ladies. "I'll let you in on a little secret. I think she kind of likes me."

Tim coughed, not sure what to do about the sudden change in discussion. Was he talking about Cassie? Tim must have missed something while he was gone.

"Hey, what are you two talking about?" Cassie called out from behind.

"Nothing," JaKobi replied instantly.

A little chuckle broke through Tim's lips. The last thing you ever wanted to say when a woman asked you what you were talking about is nothing. They knew you weren't talking about nothing, or you wouldn't have been talking. When you say "nothing," it only makes them more suspicious. His fiery friend had a lot to learn about the fairer sex.

Tim felt a little bit of color returning to his cheeks. "So the hearing us thing—that's not real, right?"

"Only if you count that one time you left the door open. Sound enchantments don't work if the room is open." JaKobi stated it as a fact, doing his best not to embarrass his buddy further. "Anyone who shared a house in college has heard far worse."

Tim picked up the pace as the top of his ears began to burn. "I guess that's something."

The freshly painted blue door to the inn was a welcome relief.

Coming home to the Blue Dagger was just the thing they needed to get everyone focused on the next part of their mission. Cassie was going to head into town and buy supplies for their trip. They didn't have tents or sleeping bags, or the animals to carry anything. Tim had never been much of an outdoorsman, so he left the planning up to folks who knew the task better than himself.

Life as a guild leader was so much simpler when you had knowledgeable people around you. All you had to do was put the people with the most experience in charge of their tasks and get out of the way. Once that was accomplished, his main job became focusing on relationships and cutting off any squabbles before they could turn into something more.

A good captain kept all his rowers going in the same direction.

Not that Tim was really their captain. In his mind, they were all on equal footing. He wouldn't be able to do this without them. One thing he knew from experience is you couldn't just replace someone and hope everything would stay the same. Sometimes chemistry was more important than the end result.

Lorelei went with the tank, and Tim couldn't have been more excited about the pair. The Ranger had already made the trip once and would know what they needed to make it again. Maybe setting up camp wasn't advisable, and they would be better off finding something that could keep them on their feet until they reached Tristholm. With all the magic floating around this game, there had to be some kind of super juice.

Maybe Red Bull wasn't the only thing that could give you wings.

There was also a chance JaKobi could find something to speed their journey along. If anyone could find a spell or a secret at the library, it was him. Tim was super impressed with the progress the pyromancer had made since joining their group. It seemed a little nudge had gotten JaKobi out of his shell, and if the rest of them didn't hustle, he'd be the strongest member of their group soon.

Tim took a sip of his favorite brew. It reminded him of Dogfish

Head's famous Red and White. While the company in the real world only released the stuff once a year, in the game, he could have one whenever he wanted.

Perks of living a virtual life.

ShadowLily finished off her own drink and stood up from the table. "I'm going to try to track down our burly assassin and see if he'll help me polish up a few of my skills before we go."

"If he isn't here, you might want to check Lady Briarthorn's manor. I told her to seek him out if she had any problems." Tim finished his own beer and joined her as she walked to the door.

"Let me put her house on the map for you." Tim gently pushed his index finger against ShadowLily's head and transferred the location of Lucy's house to her map. "I'm going to see Brother Colton and then swing by IronBeard's shop."

A small sigh escaped ShadowLily's lips. "Just don't let him put you to work again. Last time you didn't come home until after midnight and couldn't move your arms properly for days."

Tim just smiled as they stepped out of the inn and into the street. A light sprinkle started as they made their way out of the slums. "But there is just so much I want to learn, and our deal is, I work for the knowledge."

"Just try not to work so hard. This is our last night in town for a bit, and I plan on taking full advantage of it." ShadowLily gave him a sultry wink before completely disappearing from view.

Tim looked around for a second, trying to spot her, and couldn't. He was more than a little jealous. He could hide in the dark, or in the shadows just fine, but to be able to disappear in the middle of the day was some next level shit.

Even if it was raining.

"You see that, Chris? This guy's game is so weak he made that girl disappear," Brian stated in a matter of fact tone.

"Didn't Rose do the same thing to you last night?" Chris snickered.

Brian turned and stared daggers at his friend. "What the fuck, man? Save the jabs for the slum rats."

"Right you are," Chris said with a grin as his eyes moved from his friend toward Tim. "Might have better luck if you bathed."

Brian nudged Chris. "That was weak." He turned his attention back to Tim. "What he's saying is, you smell like you just crawled out of a horse's ass."

Tim waved over his shoulder as he walked down the street. He was going to have to find out who this Rose person was and buy her something nice for knocking his friendly neighborhood guard down a few pegs.

He was also a little disappointed. The boys normally had more gusto when they jabbed at him.

Oh, well, there were only so many insults you could hurl at a man before they became redundant.

Smiling to himself as he walked, Tim thought about what he could do for the city guard to get them on the side of the slums. Maybe he could offer them free drinks or food. He'd heard gas stations did stuff like that for police because they were less likely to be robbed when a cop was sitting in the parking lot.

Just like the cops back home, a little incentive might go a long way to get the guards on his side. He doubted people took care of the guards. If he could get them on his side of the wall and willing to help, it would go a long way toward making his business seem legitimate. He'd have to send a letter to Mr. Applebottom to find out what was and wasn't allowed. The last thing Tim wanted was to get on the bad side of the royals for bribing guards.

He added a few things to his mental notes as he walked into the market. A quick change of clothes got rid of any smell he might have had, and he made sure he wasn't being followed. Two more uniform changes and he was back on the streets, heading for Brother Colton's annex.

CHAPTER TWENTY-NINE

The door to Brother Colton's annex was open. Men and women seemed to be coming and going with orders constantly. Tim waited outside for a few minutes, hoping that the flow of people would stop. When it became apparent the tide of people wasn't diminishing, Tim made his way to the door.

Bet Brother Colton hates this.

He cracked a smile as he remembered the man trying to get rid of them as soon as possible. Having all of these people coming in and out of his sanctuary must be driving the priest nuts. Tim was surprised there weren't fewer people now that the biggest threat to the city had been eliminated by his guild.

Tim added himself to the flow of people moving into the building. Once he made it inside it was clear that Brother Colton had really stepped up his operation. There were at least three priests working under him now, but the door to his inner chambers was closed. Tim shoved his way past the milling people until he was next to the door. Not sure if Brother Colton would hear a simple knock, Tim channeled his inner police officer and pounded on the door like he meant business.

Bet the cops have an entire class on how to knock with authority at the academy.

"Go away," a muffled voice said from within.

There was no way to tell if it was even Brother Colton who responded, and he hadn't walked all the way here not to see the man himself. So instead of saying anything, Tim pounded on the door again.

The door flew open, and an exhausted looking Brother Colton stood rubbing the sleep out of his eyes. "What part of do not fucking disturb do you not understand, Samuel?"

"Mostly the part about being Samuel." Tim couldn't help himself. Sarcasm was his natural response to just about everything. His mouth got him in more trouble than he cared to admit.

Brother Colton's furious eyes eased a bit when he saw who was standing in front of him. The man still looked rather put out. Tim understood that feeling well. It seemed like every time he'd tried to take a nap in college, some asshole knocked on the door. Although, with all the people milling around, he was surprised the priest could sleep at all.

"Since you're probably not going to leave until I let you in, we might as well get this over with." He stepped back from the door and waved Tim into his inner sanctum.

Looking around the tiny chamber, Tim's eyes settled on the map. All three of the locations they'd been sent to were unmarked, but little red dots littered the map. All of those little red dots must have been wraiths.

How were there so many?

Brother Colton flopped down into a chair and put his feet up. "So, are you here to help with the cleanup? Samuel could have given you a quest in the other room, and I could still be sleeping."

Quest Received: Scour the City

While the biggest problems facing Promethia have been dealt with, there are still several small pockets of wraiths that

need to be removed from the city. Kill ten wraiths and report back to Samuel.

Accept Quest: <Yes/No>

Tim declined the quest. "I actually was hoping you could provide a little insight into another issue I was having."

Brother Colton's expression changed from hopeful to flustered. "If you're angling for a better reward, the high priest assigns them, so go and bother him."

"Not a very nice thing to say to the man who just saved your ass." Tim did his best to remain calm. He didn't come here for an extra payout. All he wanted was information. Just to make his position clear, Tim turned in both of his pending quests.

Quest Complete: Panic at the Temple

Tim smiled as his experience bar filled up nearly halfway. A quick check of his inventory showed he didn't receive an item, but he did get almost twenty gold. Flipping over to his notifications revealed there was a fifty percent bonus for finishing the quest before any real harm befell the city.

Quest Complete: Get the Wraith Out of Here

Forgetting completely about Brother Colton for the moment, Tim focused on what he'd just received from the goddess. Hopefully, the team would be excited about the five gold they all received, but all he cared about right now was his shiny new weapon.

Staff of Divine Retribution: A little pain goes a long way.

+5 Wisdom

+4 Intelligence

Special Ability: Whenever you are damaged, 5% of the damage inflicted upon you will be returned to your party as health.

That's so fucking cool.

Tim was so lost in his thoughts about the potential uses for the staff he missed Brother Colton trying to get his attention. All he wanted to do now was find something he could fight. Holding the new staff in front of him, he spun it around, enjoying the slightly blue glow it gave off.

Brother Colton cleared his throat. "I'm sorry, it's just been an exhausting few weeks. It's funny when you think about it. I picked this branch of research because it was supposed to be mythical, as in, won't ever happen."

Rising from his seat, Colton let out a weary sigh. "When the world turns upside down, the impractical becomes a necessity, no?" He moved across the room and closed the door. "But why don't you tell me what's bothering you? You've earned that much from me."

Feeling a little better about the whole situation, Tim thought about what he wanted to say. How much information did he want to give the priest? He certainly had enemies in the city, and the last thing he wanted them to know was when he was leaving the protection of Promethia's walls. So far, Brother Colton had only shown interest in getting him out of his office, so he doubted the man cared enough about Tim to blather his business to anyone.

Coming to a decision, Tim met Brother Colton's eyes. "I have urgent business in Tristholm. Apparently, they have a werewolf problem."

"Is that all? My word boy, Tristholm has always had a werewolf problem. Maybe I can save you a trip." Brother Colton reached inside his robes and pulled out a small blue crystal. "This is a communication crystal. It allows me to contact any of the outlying temples."

Holding the small crystal in front of him, Brother Colton started praying to the Goddess Eternia. Light began to shine inside of the crystal and then to pulse, filling the room with flashes of blue light. He let the crystal go, and it floated in the air and hovered just above their heads.

"Temple of Tristholm, this is Brother Colton from Promethia. Can you confirm for me that all is well?" Brother Colton stared at the crystal as the blue pulses sped up.

When no response returned through the crystal, the priest's face fell. "Temple of Tristholm, please respond."

When he didn't receive an answer for the second time, Brother Colton reached up and grabbed the crystal before shoving it in his pocket. "We have a problem."

Tim tried not to laugh. Of course, they had a problem. That was why he was trying to get there but saying that to the crestfallen priest didn't seem like the right way to approach the conversation. "Is it unusual for them not to answer?"

Nodding his head in answer, Brother Colton started rambling. "Each Temple has a crystal. They should be manned at all hours. Not receiving a response is worrisome."

"How worried should we be?" Tim hoped that some young acolyte just ran off with a case of the Hershey squirts, and not that the city had already been overrun.

Brother Colton was already picking up his cloak and heading for the door. "We have to talk to the high priest right away. The Temple in Tristholm helps power the city's defenses. If no one is there, the situation could be dire."

Tim didn't hesitate when Brother Colton flew from the room. He ran after him, hoping the high priest would have the answers they were looking for. So far, he'd just been thinking of helping Ernie get to the city and not about what would happen when they got there. Now his mind was spinning with endless possibilities. In some scenarios, they were the saviors, and in others, he was looking at one of his deaths on Barbara's newest shirt.

There was another part of him that felt excited. Before this had just been a tag-along and hope for the best kind of mission, but now he had a shot of getting his own quest out of it. Coming to see Brother Colton in person was paying off. Even with the priest's surly attitude, today was turning out to be a fantastic day.

Following the priest through the winding paths of the temple made Tim wonder if he'd ever be able to find the high priest's chambers on his own. All of the other priests and the acolytes could find it, but he still had trouble. It was almost as if the temple's interior shifted each time he entered the place. Thankfully, like now, he'd always had a guide.

Having magic shift the corridors was one hell of a security measure. While he didn't have proof, it would explain why his map was basically worthless every time he entered the temple. Plus, it wouldn't be a very good look for the goddess if her high priests were continually getting bumped off.

The golden doors swung open on their approach and quickly closed behind them as the two men entered the room. Paul sat in his normal seat, but this time he had a large tome open on his lap. His eyes didn't look up as he continued reading. "Give me just a minute."

Brother Colton shifted nervously while Tim just let himself relax. He'd been here before and considered Paul his friend. There wasn't anything to be worried about, especially when all he did was pull the temple's metaphorical toes out of the fire on a regular basis.

Paul closed the book with a thump and fastened the silver clasp in place to keep it closed. A man dressed in black moved out of the shadows and took the book from the high priest before disappearing again. With the book out of the way, Paul turned his attention to the two men before him.

"Thank you both for your work in securing Promethia from the wraiths." His smile was so warm it lit up the room. "What can I help you with today?"

Tim was tempted to nudge Brother Colton and tell him, see that's how you thank people, but he kept his mouth shut. What the man had to say was more important than his bad attitude as a quest giver.

Colton dropped to his knees. "Please forgive us for the interruption." He tried to pull Tim down to his knees beside him, but the healer shook off his grasp. "I'm having trouble reaching the temple in Tristholm."

Paul looked from Brother Colton to Tim. "And why does our holy warrior have an interest in the city of Tristholm?"

Tim tried to pull Brother Colton back to his feet. Something about having the man kneeling next to him while he was standing bothered him. He'd never seen Paul request such subservience before. It seemed more like something Cardinal Jepsom would have done before his untimely death.

Tim tried to state the facts as he knew them. "The leader of the city requested help from a friend of mine. We planned on leaving in the morning, but I figured I would come and get as much information as I could before we left."

Brother Colton continued to struggle against him, but Tim managed to finally pull him up. "I asked Colton for help, and he tried to contact the temple on my behalf." He held out his hands in a gesture that said, and now we are here.

The high priest thought about it for a moment and then pulled out his own version of the communication crystal. "Tristholm, this is the high priest. Is anyone there?"

There was a crackling sound, almost like static over the radio. "Help...we've been...graaaghhhh."

Paul's crystal fell from the air, and he caught it before it hit the ground. "That was rather unexpected." Despite his casual reply, the high priest's eyes crinkled with worry.

Making a gesture with one hand, Paul summoned another one of the men dressed in black. "Try to open the gate to Tristholm." The man gave him a quick bow and ran off.

Gate? Did that mean there was a way to quick travel in this game? If they could get from one city to the next without having to slog around the countryside, it would be amazing. All he had to do now was figure out if only the temple had use of them, or if there were others. Once he knew, maybe he could ask Paul for traveling privileges. Despite being in the game for what seemed like forever, Tim was always learning new things about the world around him.

The man ran back into the room. "The gate has been sealed."

Paul nodded to himself. "Sealed to stop something from coming through, or to stop us from rendering aid in a timely manner?"

He stood up and walked down the steps to address Tim as an equal. "I need you to go to Tristholm and reopen the portal. The Temple there is more important to the city than most people know."

Turning away from the two men, Paul began pacing the room. "The real question is, how long have the temple's defenses been down? If it's been too long, the city might already be laid to waste."

His eyes burning with an almost fanatical glee, the high priest focused on Tim. "Will you do this for me? Go to Tristholm and stop whatever is happening. We need that gate open, and for the temple to be fully functional."

Quest Received: Don't Stop Believing

The temple in Tristholm serves as a beacon of light in the darkness. As the people worship, the goddess shines her light of protection down upon them. Go to Tristholm and return the goddess' light to the people.

Rewards: Access to the Tristholm Gate, and an item of your choice from the temple's coffers.

Accept Quest: <Yes/No>

Tim accepted the quest.

He was going to Tristholm with a new quest. It always paid off to multitask whenever possible. Plus, he didn't want to let Paul down. The only reason he'd made it so far in the game was because of the high priest's generosity. All of his future plans could be tied back to the reward he earned for saving the temple's artifacts.

Paul nodded his head. "You will need a priest to go with you, and it seems we have one here to assist you already."

Tim patted Brother Colton on the shoulder. "Surely, he is of better use here, putting his knowledge to use for the benefit of the city?"

Brother Colton smiled warmly at Tim and nodded. "I am not a

man who seeks out adventure unless it can be found between the pages of a good book."

"Then it is time we broaden your horizons," Paul replied with the warm smile parents used when telling their kids to do something they didn't want to do. "I find that one's mind becomes stagnant if it only dwells on the successes of the past, don't you?"

Never one to argue with his superiors, Brother Colton did his best to sound excited. "Of course, your holiness. It would be a great honor to accompany the young warrior to the temple."

"Good, then it's all settled." Paul returned to his chair. His mind had clearly moved on from the task he assigned to whatever else he needed to do for the day.

The golden doors swung open behind the two men, and they turned to leave. Tim put an arm around Brother Colton's shoulders. "We leave from the Blue Dagger at first light. I expect to see you there prepared for a long journey." He made sure to look at the man's sandals, hoping the priest would get the hint to purchase some boots before they left.

"Of course, of course." Brother Colton stammered. "I will see you then."

Tim watched the man scurry away and wondered if he'd ever spent a full day outside of his annex before. Turning away from the priest and heading back to the inn, he couldn't stop thinking about the reward he'd been offered. Would his guild be the first one in the game with access to a quick travel location?

Something as significant as access to a Gate would certainly help with recruitment. Not that he was actively looking to make the guild bigger, but he also didn't want to give off the *fuck you, we're leet,* vibe either. Nothing felt worse than when a guild expected you to dedicate your life to them like it was a second job and more important than family.

He wanted everyone in his guild to have time to pursue their own projects, just as he had the Healing Shack and his real-estate ventures. They would set times to do bounties or quest chains, but there needed to be just as much time for them to branch out and flourish in whichever ways they wanted. Any new skills brought to the table benefitted the entire guild.

There was a little extra bounce in his step as Tim continued walking. All of them thought he was crazy for turning in the quest in person, but now he was coming back with a chance for extra EXP and loot.

It was going to blow their minds.

CHAPTER THIRTY

The smell of coffee brought Tim to his senses.

No one should have to wake up when it's still dark outside. Early mornings should be reserved for the guys mowing the golf course, and farmers. Everyone else should get to sleep in. Maybe that was just his personal stance after working as a groundskeeper over the summer the year before. Getting paid minimum wage to rake sand traps in the dark hadn't exactly been his cup of tea.

Not after a night out with Xander.

Drinking until two a.m. and then having to do hard manual labor starting at five was a recipe for only one thing: a puke in the bushes.

And maybe a little praying in hopes that the world would stop spinning.

At least he didn't have to worry about hangovers in-game. A little cleanse spell before bed, and he always woke up with a clear head. Today being ready to roll was especially important. The guild would start their journey to Tristholm within the hour.

"Colton better be on time, or I'm leaving his ass behind, " Tim grumbled as he made his way to the bathroom.

If this was the last time he could get clean for a few days, then he was going to enjoy as much of his bath as possible before going. The hot water worked to loosen him up. He wasn't sure why he felt so tense, except that Lorelei's picture of Tristholm wasn't very heartwarming. Getting ripped apart by a pack of werewolves wasn't high up on his list of ways he wanted to experience death.

Just like getting eaten by zombies.

There probably wasn't a worse way to go. How long could you live while another person was eating you? It was possible only Hannibal had the answer, and it wasn't something Tim was going to start researching on his own.

Shaking off the thought of hungry werewolves, Tim climbed from the water. Stopping in front of the mirror, he smiled at himself. Not having to shave was fucking awesome. He never realized how much he'd despised that daily chore until he didn't have to worry about it again. That and brushing his teeth. It didn't matter what he ate here, his breath never smelled. A world with no morning breath. It was a wonderful time to be alive.

All of his clothes appeared on him the second he was dry, the entire outfit in place with a single thought. *The real world could use some improving.* Tim felt his energy shifting from nervous to ready to roll. It was okay to be nervous. That just meant whatever he was doing was important to him. At the same time, he had to let those nerves go to be successful.

You think the Wright brothers didn't shit themselves a little bit the first time they flew?

The world was full of scary moments. All Tim tried to do in those times was the best he could. Not everyone was born to play guitar, or sing on stage, but everyone was born with a talent. They just had to find it.

Not that talent was any replacement for hard work.

There were a whole lot of almost somebodies out there. It

doesn't take much to get off track and to lose your way. The world is full of temptations and fantastical delights. Sometimes it was fine to indulge and others it wasn't. It wasn't Tim's place to judge how people led their lives. All he could control were his own actions.

Today that was getting out of bed and riding off to kick some werewolf ass.

The inn's main room was bustling with activity. It seemed Ernie was finally starting to bring in some steady business. It didn't hurt to have the Healing Shack and Joe's attached to the building. Those two staples, along with the few other shops that had moved in, were bringing more people to the slums.

People also seemed to like the market kiosk he had set up. He charged a lower fee than they did down by the docks. He didn't make as much money per sale, but he did make up for it in volume. That was his favorite part of business, finding the sweet spot. There was a perfect intersection between price and profits if you were just willing to take some risks.

One of Tim's friends started a business not too long ago, and instead of maximizing his personal revenue, he chose to help others succeed. It takes a special kind of person to help other people live their dreams, and Tim was happy to know someone like that.

In *The Etheric Coast*, Tim was in the position to do the same thing for his guildmates and friends. Whatever he could do to help them get a streaming contract or to help them financially, he would do. Because every time they succeeded, it felt like he was lifted right up with them. That was how he wanted to live his life.

Lifting other people up.

In the next few days, they'd be able to lift the hearts of the people of Tristholm. Not that their help was coming for free. It wouldn't be a proper quest if it didn't come with a healthy profit and some new shinies. Tim wasn't sure what the others would select from the goods the temple had to offer, but he knew whatever he received would be spectacular.

He found ShadowLily and JaKobi in the corner, nursing their own cups of the goddess brew.

"Our fearless leader awakens." The pyromancer used a spell to heat up the coffee pot on the table before topping off Tim's mug.

"I was about to send a search party," ShadowLily replied with a smirk.

Tim took a sip of his coffee and let the caffeine bring his brain back online. "Not all of us are morning people."

"Pleeeasssee," the assassin snarked. "If you could spend your entire life between the kitchen, the couch, and the bed you'd be perfectly happy."

JaKobi clinked his glass against Tim's. "I hear that."

ShadowLily glared at the mage. "This is why you don't have a girlfriend. You'd actually have to leave the house to meet one."

"Not so. You can meet plenty of them from the comfort of your home. It's convincing them to come over, that's the tricky part."

Laughter burst from ShadowLily's lips. "That's because no girl with an ounce of sense is going to show up at some rando from the internet's house."

"You'd be surprised," JaKobi mumbled. "And I go places. We've been all over the city, and now we're going to another one."

Tim poured the man the last of the coffee. "Maybe if you ask us real nice, we'll take you to the Stiff Tart. I'm sure we can find you a nice wholesome girl there."

"Not my style." JaKobi snorted. "I'd rather go without than have to pay for it."

"Spoken like a true gentleman," Cassie said as she slid into the booth next to the pyromancer. "Everything is ready to go. Lorelei and Ernie are waiting outside with our gear. She said we'll probably have to ditch most of it before we get there."

Tim nodded. "My guess is a werewolf is faster than a horse carrying a person and gear by a good amount." He stood up.

"Might as well get started. I'd like to ride as far as we can before nightfall."

Tim took a quick look around the inn and started making his way to the door. For some reason, he felt like he was leaving home and not coming back. He shook the feeling off. As an adventurer, he could never truly die. Not unless he ran out of money and his time in the POD came to an end.

The rain outside of the inn was coming down in sheets.

Of course, they couldn't leave without getting soaked. It was like the game knew just when to turn on the waterworks. The only pleasant part of the rain was seeing a plump Brother Colton scurrying down the muddy walkway in their direction. The man was puffing hard, clearly worried about being late.

Tim decided to embrace the rain. It made it feel like they were leaving on a grand adventure. One thing he always thought got lost in the *Hobbit* movies was the passing of time. When those adventurers left, they were gone for years. While he might be only going on a trip for a few days, it felt like the beginning of something epic.

It didn't hurt that Lorelei shared her quest with the entire party. Now they were all going to get bonus experience just for bringing Ernie to Tristholm. The Blue Dagger Society hadn't offered her a full-time position yet, but so far, the guild was in agreement that unless some catastrophic personality flaw showed up in the next few days, the Ranger would be a welcome addition to the guild.

Lorelei had proved her worth during their battle with the Agent of Purification, so the decision to let her in really came down to personality. She'd already proven to be resourceful by helping Cassie secure everything they needed for traveling, and after hearing how the Ranger dodged the werewolves looking for her, Tim was pretty sure the woman had an iron will.

Brother Colton, on the other hand, was breathing like a landed fish. The jog from the gate to the inn had completely worn him out. If they had to ditch the horses and run, his stamina was going to be an issue. Tim pushed the thought to the back of his mind. They'd cross that bridge when they had to.

"The rain is an auspicious sign from the goddess. She approves of our venture to Tristholm," Brother Colton wheezed.

"She does seem rather fond of water," Tim added unhelpfully as he thought about what the priest was saying.

All of his original spells were water-based. The priests at the temples wore blue robes. If the goddess did favor water, then maybe this was a divine sign. It could also just be a storm coming off the ocean or down from the mountains. Tim was never one to put too much faith in omens.

Brother Colton grinned. "That she does."

Lorelei looked into the rain. "Let's hope it lasts. The rain will push our scent out of the air and make it hard for anyone to track us. The longer we can keep the horses, the better." She gave a disapproving look at the priest.

Tim felt bad for the man. Brother Colton had clearly dedicated his life to research and delicious food. Part of him wondered what pursuits people would follow if they didn't have to worry about basic needs. Would they become artists, musicians, cultivators, or would they just sit around doing nothing?

He liked to think that people would search out their passions.

It wasn't as though people liked to sit around doing nothing. A lot of people thought they could do it, but after a week or a month, they started going stir crazy. That's why it took a special kind of mental strength to be an astronaut. It was one thing to be at home and have the choice to go outside, and another to know any trip outside would kill you instantly.

Thankfully for the party, they didn't have to worry about lockdowns or the atmosphere. All they had to do was make it to Tristholm in one piece. The werewolves weren't going to make that easy for them.

A small sigh escaped Tim's lips as Ernie pulled around the

corner in a covered wagon pulled by four horses. If the Poison Master needed whatever was in the cart, they wouldn't be able to abandon it and continue on foot. Now it was starting to make sense why they all had horses to ride.

I guess running is out of the question.

"The goddess always provides!" Brother Colton shouted as he ran for the wagon. He jumped up on the seat next to Ernie, clearly enjoying the protection of the awning.

Tim could only smile at the priest. Now that he was out of his stuffy annex, the man reminded him of Friar Tuck. To complete the look, he'd need a cask of ale and a mug the size of Texas. A little bit of laughter almost escaped his lips as he thought of Brother Colton singing drunken ballads, wearing a dark brown robe tied with a simple rope at the waist.

Lorelei motioned for Tim to join her. "This is Daisy." She patted the horse. "She's a good girl, just don't push her too hard."

"Daisy, huh? I was hoping for something fiercer." Tim rubbed the horse's neck, and Daisy turned to snap at his hand almost as if to say, is that fierce enough for you?

He continued to rub Daisy's neck. "Point taken." He looked at Lorelei. "Daisy has the heart of a champion." This time the horse whinnied in agreement.

"Don't forget it." Lorelei smiled as she hopped onto the back of her own mount. "If you treat your mount with respect, you won't end up dumped on your ass in the middle of the road."

"Sounds like good advice," JaKobi said, pulling a carrot from his robes and feeding it to his horse.

Cassie climbed into her saddle and patted her horse's neck. "Just be thankful I didn't switch places with the big guy over there." The horse turned so it could see Cassie and winked at her.

"These horses have a lot of personality," Tim said as he watched everyone's interactions.

He didn't know much about horses except that they were supposed to be pretty smart. Tim felt like he'd read somewhere they were like a four-year-old child, so it shouldn't have surprised him they understood a little of what they were saying. Hopefully, Daisy understood the words slow the fuck down, because he'd never ridden before and wasn't keen to find out what falling off a horse felt like.

Gaston emerged from the inn and looked over the group of travelers as they started to depart. The assassin was sporting a new slash across his right cheek but seemed content enough. "Take care of Ernie for me. I'm going to need him returned in one piece."

Tim splashed Gaston with a healing orb. "I'll guard him with my life."

"We all will," ShadowLily echoed. "Are you sure you don't want to come with us?"

Leaning against the wall, Gaston pulled out one of his throwing knives and started cleaning his nails. "I've got a few things to wrap up here for Lady Briarthorn."

"Don't do anything I wouldn't do," Tim called out as he moved his horse into the street.

"From what I've heard, that isn't much," Gaston replied with a chuckle.

The tops of Tim's ears turned red with embarrassment. "How does everyone always know everything?"

"Don't mind them, they're all just jealous." ShadowLily winked as she started to lead them along the street out of the city.

Lorelei moved to the front of the group. "We can't go flat out the entire way. It would exhaust or kill the horses, but once we are outside of the walls, we need to pick up the pace for as long as we can."

It wasn't often Tim got to take a back seat in the leadership department, but he was happy to have someone else at the helm for this trip. "Lorelei, you lead the way and tell us what to do. We're all counting on your expertise to get us there."

"That's what she said." Lorelei grinned back at Tim. "Just do your best to keep up."

"Keeping it up has never been one of his problems," ShadowLily quipped.

Tim's hand slapped against his forehead. "Ladies! There is a priest here."

Laughing, Brother Colton waved them forward. "Don't worry about me. I'm having a rather good time watching them make you uncomfortable."

"I wonder where I can get my hands on a silencing spell," Tim groused as he nudged Daisy to move a little faster.

Cassie stood up on the back of her horse, balancing like a trick rider at the rodeo. "You know you love us." She flopped back into her seat. "Why don't you get that big brain of yours working on a solution to what we might find at the temple and let Daisy take over the hard work?"

"I think that's just what the doctor ordered." Tim patted Daisy's neck. "Hear that? You're in charge, girl."

Daisy let out a whinny of triumph and started galloping down the street. It was all Tim could do to hang on as the guild's laughter slowly faded.

CHAPTER THIRTY-ONE

Lorelei knew her way around a campsite.

It was a damn good thing she did because none of these other fools seemed to know that the sky was up, and the earth was down. With a sigh, she slapped the wet hair out of her face and got back to work on the last tent.

When she was finally done, Lorelei stood up, feeling exhausted. Nothing wore her out like being on the trail with people clearly used to city life. The constant rain made it worse, and she was starving. Why did everything feel so much more serious when you were hungry?

When this bitch is hungry, you better get out of the way.

Lorelei knew she had what she affectionately labeled the "hungrowls," and the only way to remedy the situation was with food. Not just any food. She needed something hearty, or maybe a slice of cake to take the edge off. It wasn't like she hadn't earned it. Riding for a full day was a lot of work, but it was damn good exercise for her core.

Kinda like working at her desk while she sat on one of those stupid rubber balls.

A flicker of orange lit the campground behind her, and Lorelei spun around to see what was happening. The pyromancer was trying to start a fire in the center of their little camp. Didn't the idiot know werewolves had eyes?

"No fire!" Lorelei snapped.

"But how are we supposed to cook?" JaKobi stared longingly at the fire as he snuffed it out.

Cook? This wasn't a fucking hoedown.

Reminding herself not to let the hunger respond for her, Lorelei went to their supplies and pulled out two small bags, tossing them to JaKobi. "Dinner of champions." She pulled two more bags for herself and took a heavy seat on the muddy ground to start eating.

The mud didn't bother her so much, not when she was already soaked to the bone. The best part for her was she wouldn't have to sleep in wet clothes. All Lorelei had to do to get dry was to place her clothes in her inventory and re-equip them right before stepping into her tent. At least she'd be dry for a few hours before they started the morning slog.

The beef jerky and packet of trail mix quickly took the edge off her attitude. Lorelei didn't understand why she got so mad when she was hungry, but it'd been happening for so long all she could do was deal with it. Normally, she kept little snacks around, but today there really hadn't been time.

Lorelei had pushed them hard, hoping if they covered more than half the distance before they stopped, they could make their final push to the city the next day. With Brother Colton and Ernie's cart to protect, there was no way they'd be sneaking through the forest. So tomorrow there was going to be a fight.

Everyone was eating in silence and staring at the wet logs where there should have been a fire. They all looked exhausted, but Lorelei wanted to sleep first. She wasn't sure how good anyone else was at detecting threats in the wild, and when everyone else was asleep, she wanted to be wide awake.

Even though Tim had put her in charge of getting them to the city, she wasn't sure yet if he was the kind of guy who could take instruction from a woman or the kind who would put her in charge only to micromanage the shit out of her.

There was only one way for Lorelei to find out. "We'll need to set up a watch. I'd recommend anyone with solid night vision take some of the later spots."

Tim sucked some of the salt from the trail mix off his fingers. "Makes sense to me. We'll have JaKobi take first watch, and Cassie takes the early morning. I've got a little skill with night vision, but ShadowLily can practically see as well as she can during the day. I'm not sure where we'd fit in best."

Lorelei smiled as she folded her empty container of trail mix before standing and putting the leather pouch back in one of the saddlebags. She hadn't expected Tim to default to her expertise so readily. He'd also made the easy call to have the people with the least amount of night vision to take the two easiest shifts. She doubted anyone would attack them right now or just before dawn.

Stealth attacks usually happened around the witching hour. It was the time of night when most people were in a deep sleep, and the guards on duty were tired and spread apart. Thankfully for her, their group was small, and one scream would have them on their feet in an instant.

The choice before her seemed pretty simple. She turned from her pack to face the rest of the group. "I think the order should be: JaKobi, Tim, myself, ShadowLily, and Cassie. Brother Colton and Ernie can help out if they want."

Tim nodded. "Our best eyes for the darkest hours." He stood up and stretched his back. "Guess I'm going to crash then." He peered into his tent. "They really need to make these more like the tents in Harry Potter." His clothes disappeared and reappeared dry in a blink before he stepped into the tent.

"Duty calls." ShadowLily made her way to Tim's tent, and then stopped as she realized what she said. Turning, the assassin looked at everyone. "I meant sleeping, so I could be awake later. Not that sleeping with my man is work."

JaKobi grinned. "I'm just hoping to get a relationship to the doing-my-duty phase."

"Well, you're never going to woo a woman's heart if you tell her sleeping with her is your job." Cassie slapped her head. "Might as well just send random girls on the internet dick pics."

Pretending to be shocked, JaKobi replied, "Wait, that doesn't work?"

Lorelei grinned as she stood up and made her way to her own tent. "Why don't you send me one, and I'll tell you if it would help you or not."

"Said the lesbian, nevermore." Cassie giggled.

"Just because I'm gay doesn't mean guys don't send me dick pics." Lorelei laughed. "They seem to think the right dick will make me change my ungodly ways. What they don't know is we post them in our private group and have a good laugh."

JaKobi stood up and sheepishly made his way to his tent. "I think I'll pass on the penis rating. The only woman I want judging me is the one I'm to spend the rest of my life with." He ducked into the tent.

Cassie looked at Lorelei. "That was actually kind of cute."

"Why don't you remind him that he has the watch and that he can't hide those red cheeks forever?" Lorelei asked before disappearing into her tent.

She really liked this group of people. They weren't pretentious, and even if they disagreed with you, they didn't judge. One of Lorelei's favorite things about life was having a diverse pool of friends. Everyone had different experiences that shaped them into the people they were.

Part of her felt sad for people who only hung out with people who thought and felt the same way they did. Those relationships were fragile things. One shift in ideology and they broke apart like a wine glass on the pool deck. She liked hearing other points of view. It was how she made calm, rational decisions. Unless she was hungry.

Then it was time to unleash the Kraken.

The rustling of her tent's flap woke Lorelei.

It wasn't the first time she'd been woken up by a man, but it was such a rare occurrence she almost screamed at him before she realized where she was. Tim was waking her because it was her turn to take watch. A yawn escaped Lorelei's mouth, and all she could think about was diving back under the covers.

Tim waved a cup in front of her, and the scent of warm coffee reached her nose. "What? How?"

"JaKobi found this enchanted teapot at a local store. All you have to do is add water and the container heats itself. Thankfully it will boil whatever you put inside it because only suckers drink tea."

Lorelei accepted the cup of steaming bliss from Tim and smiled as she took her first sip. "You know, I don't mind tea. I don't get the whole tea versus coffee thing. There is no reason you can't like both."

"That is where you're wrong." Tim winked at her. "It's been quiet so far. See you in the morning." He ducked back out of the tent.

A few moments later, Lorelei was standing in the cool night air. It had stopped raining for the moment, but the drips and drops could still be heard throughout the forest. It was the calm after the storm, or maybe just a pause in the action until the next storm rolled through. There was no way to know without a weather channel, and as far as she knew, one of those didn't exist yet.

More rain was probably likely as she couldn't see a star in the sky. Even the moon looked like a blip due to the dark clouds that blanketed the sky. At least it was quiet. It would give her time to think about her next move. Seraphina might not be happy to see her if she found out Lorelei killed her daughter.

Not that killing Camilla was her fault. She could be blamed for a lot of broken hearts and hard feelings over the years, but this time wasn't on her. It wasn't every day you were confronted by a lover turned werewolf who decided working for an evil goddess was better than returning home.

Hasty decisions had been made, but Lorelei stood behind them.

She took a spot by the waterlogged fire pit and sipped her coffee. It was colder out now that the rain had stopped. It wasn't cold enough for snow, but it felt like that could change at any minute.

At least this time she remembered to bring a coat.

Lorelei didn't waste any time walking around the campsite. Even with her enhanced vision, without any moonlight or stars to light the landscape, she couldn't see a thing. It might have been better to have ShadowLily cover this slot, but the next one was going to be just as dark.

Wanting to be ready in case there was an attack, she pulled her bow from her inventory and started looking over the weapon. So far, she hadn't run into any problems with her weapons. As long as she put them back in her inventory after a fight, they basically repaired themselves.

That didn't mean it wasn't prudent to double-check.

The arrows in her quiver were separated into two batches. She had her normal serrated arrowheads. Those particular arrows had two spikes built into the shaft that extended on impact, making the arrow do twice as much damage if someone tried to yank it out. Her other arrows had magical fire. There were only a few of the magical arrows in her quiver, so if she chose to use one, she had to make it count.

With no fire to watch and the silence of the forest around her, it was hard to stay awake. What she really wanted was her vape, but she hadn't seen anything equivalent in the game. Lorelei refused to start smoking. That shit made you smell like walking death or a librarian from the forties. All she wanted was just a few drags on her favorite pen to take the edge off.

Maybe if they make magical teapots, they could also enchant her a vape.

"Wouldn't that be nice," she mumbled to herself.

Lorelei almost missed the sound of a snapping twig because she was talking. Fortunately, she'd mumbled so low it hadn't covered up the noise. Normally a twig breaking in the woods wouldn't be a cause for concern. All kinds of creatures moved around in the forest, but on a dark night after a rainstorm, everything had been still until now.

There was no way to know if the sound was just an animal passing or if they were about to be attacked. The last thing Lorelei wanted to do was to wake everyone up before she knew for certain there was a werewolf stalking them. Pulling one of her arrows out, Lorelei nocked her bow and stood up.

A rustle sounded to her left, and then another one off to her right. If there was only the one sound, she might have talked herself out of saying anything. Lorelei could handle a werewolf on her own, but this sounded like more than one. Keeping her eyes moving along the tree line, she backed up to Tim and ShadowLily's tent.

"I think we're going to have a problem," she hissed into the tent before ducking back out and working her way across the campsite to the next tent in line and repeating the process.

One by one, the group joined her in the center of their campsite. All of them were facing outwards with Brother Colton and Ernie at the center of the five-person circle. Lorelei looked at JaKobi. "How about a little light?"

"I thought you'd never ask." The pyromancer said a few words she couldn't understand and then pointed to the sky.

A small white orb shot up, leaving a trail of light behind it.

When the orb broke through the tree line, it burst into twenty flaring pieces that slowly started falling back toward the ground.

It took all of a second for Lorelei to realize they were surrounded. "Oh, shit."

Tim smiled at the group as he cast his buffs and dropped into the Way of the River stance. "Cassie, why don't you show these furry fuckers why you don't mess with the Blue Dagger Society?"

"It'd be my pleasure." Cassie charged at the forest, screaming, "Time to get some!"

As Cassie continued her mad dash to the edge of their camp, two more werewolves came from the side to try to ambush her. It was like they were fighting fucking velociraptors. Super strength and speed, along with human intelligence, might have made the werewolves an even deadlier opponent.

Lorelei's arrow took out the werewolf on Cassie's right. She turned to see what was coming from behind them. The next arrow flew from her bow before she had time to aim. The loping werewolf took the arrow to the leg and crashed to the ground. Without hesitation, she moved to the next target. At this point, slowing them down was more important than killing them.

The werewolf she kneecapped burst into flames as Lorelei spun for her next target.

Werewolf hunting was a bit easier when all she had to do was knock them down so the pyromancer could incinerate them. Knowing that all of her shots didn't have to be perfect, Lorelei let her bow do most of the work as she moved from target to target.

JaKobi's light was starting to fade, but the battle was almost over. The last werewolf went down to ShadowLily's poisoned blades. Cassie smiled at the group and started walking back to them. A dark shape fell from the trees like a cannonball. The tank didn't even have time to scream as the werewolf's claws tore through her armor like tissue paper.

Flames erupted around the werewolf, erasing its smile in seconds. The beast howled as it was burned alive. It clawed to be free but was rooted in place as its skin started to melt. The fire blazed white-hot before a pile of bones fell to the ground.

Lorelei watched in growing horror as Tim slid to a stop next to Cassie. The tank wasn't moving, but she could see his spells were working. The ragged claw mark down Cassie's back started to heal. After thirty seconds, her skin was like new, but her armor told the tale of what had happened.

Tim's face was haggard. "She's stable, but there is something fighting me. I can't get her to wake up."

Brother Colton jogged to the fallen tank and scooped her into his arms to carry her back to the cart. "We must get her to the temple before the infection spreads."

"They aren't going to let her into Tristholm like that." Lorelei told the group about her first journey to the city, and how diligent the soldiers were when checking for bites or claw marks.

"The goddess will see us through this. In her light we serve, and her servants always find a way to get the job done," Brother Colton responded as he lay Cassie down in the back of the cart as gently as a newborn.

Tim tore his eyes away from the pale, almost lifeless features of his friend as his mind started working on the problem. "Break-down what we can, leave everything else. I want to be on the road in five minutes." He turned to the priest. "Brother Colton, I expect you to get us inside the temple ASAP."

"You get us there, and I'll get us in." Colton jumped up to the driver's side of the cart, and Ernie popped up next to him.

The rest of the party quickly loaded what they could on the horses, and as they left their little campsite, JaKobi incinerated the gear they left behind. Lorelei watched the flames for a moment before turning her eyes back on the darkness of the forest around the road. She gently nudged her horse to the front of the group.

"I'm going to scout ahead. I know this doesn't need to be said, but no talking." Lorelei turned her head toward JaKobi. "And no more lights."

She started to push her horse forward and stopped to address the group. "That was just a scouting party. Be ready for anything. When those dead furballs don't report back, more will come for us."

As she pushed her mount into a gallop, Lorelei could have sworn she heard JaKobi say, "Bring it on. I'll burn down the fucking world to save her."

Soon the noise from behind her faded away, and she was alone in the forest, just the way she liked it. They would get to Tristholm and save Cassie. Her brain tried to tell her their situation was impossible, but in her heart, the job was already done.

She wasn't going to lose someone else, not this time.

CHAPTER THIRTY-TWO

Tim felt like he was strapped to a fucking rocket.

The bounciest, most unsafe rocket on the planet. Maybe he was like that guy who kept showing up in the Borderland's games, always trying to launch himself to the next great destination. For Tim, the best place he could be was on the ground, using his own two feet to get around.

He never knew horses could go so fast.

When you watched the horses on TV race with the hundred-pound guys strapped to their backs, there was no sense of speed. It was like watching NASCAR on TV. The cars just go in circles, and it doesn't look like a big deal. You go see the race in person, and the cars feel like they are only in view for a split second.

Right now, Tim wished the difference between his perceptions and what was happening to him wasn't so different. It turned out horses were fast, really fucking fast, and that was under normal circumstances. When a horse was being chased by an apex predator big enough to rip it in half, they might as well be flying.

The only good news was that he finally found his snare spell useful. His horse was going so fast that even if the spell only slowed the werewolves for a second it was enough to keep their wild caravan in front of the monsters.

Barely.

"There is going to be a path to the right, take it!" Brother Colton screamed from his place on the covered wagon as he snapped the reins.

How in the fuck did you turn a horse to the right?

Tim saw a tiny gap in the trees and leaned to the right, hoping that the horse would follow him. He wasn't sure if it was his legs squeezing against the horse, but somehow he managed to get on the right path. Now it looked as though they had a new problem. The city of Tristholm appeared to be getting further away.

"I hope you know where we're going!" Tim shouted at the priest.

His horse slowed down from flying to a gentle gallop. Somehow, their turn onto this path stopped the werewolves from following, or maybe they'd just bought enough time to catch their breath. He looked back and not seeing any werewolves, urged his horse into a trot.

"How is Cassie doing?" Tim asked as he moved next to the wagon.

Ernie poked his head out of the covered back. "She's still unconscious, but she doesn't seem to be getting worse."

"The virus won't let her," Brother Colton replied as he slowed the horses down to a walk. "The Lycanthropy virus will heal her body, but it will also turn her into one of those things."

Lorelei came up from behind them. "Why are you slowing down? We need to keep moving."

Brother Colton waved away her concern. "This path to the side gate is lined with wolfsbane. It should keep us safe."

Howls of rage sounded behind them, followed by several yips of pain. Then, almost like a trumpet blast signaling warriors to battle, a lone howl echoed across the valley as the sun rose. The call was answered by so many werewolves, Tim couldn't tell if it was a hundred or a hundred thousand. All of their voices cried out as one.

Snapping the reins, Brother Colton looked chagrinned. "Or maybe we should go a little bit faster."

Just like that, Tim found himself strapped to the back of a bouncing rocket again.

The clearing leading to the gate came into view, and it felt like a beacon of light in a coming storm. There didn't look to be any soldiers manning the walls, and Tim wondered how they were going to get inside. Brother Colton better have a way, or they were all going to end up as doggie kibble.

"There should always be a priest at the gate. Something is wrong." Brother Colton looked worriedly at the large stone gate. "Where are they?"

Tim glared at the man. "Probably the same fucking place they were when we tried to call. They're fucking dead." He tried to let some of the anger seep out of his voice, but he just couldn't do it. "You better have a way to get us inside, or I'll feed you to the fuckers myself."

Brother Colton started to grin. "There is that fire the high priest is always talking about. I was starting to think he was pulling my leg."

"Just get us inside," Tim snapped.

Being in front of the cart wouldn't do him any good. They had to protect Cassie until they could get her into the temple and find a way to make sure she didn't become a werewolf.

Tim let his horse drift back until he was riding next to Lorelei and ShadowLily. "I'm not sure what the plan is for when we get there. The only thing I know is we have to protect the wagon until Cassie is safe."

He looked around. "Where in the hell is JaKobi?"

ShadowLily grinned. "He dropped back to leave a little surprise for the werewolves."

"We're here," Brother Colton called from the front as the cart stopped moving. He dashed off the seat and ran for the gate. He had an amulet in his hand. There was a small inset on the side of the gate. The amulet went in the impression, and the gate started to open. Slowly.

Much too fucking slowly.

"Looks like we've got some work to do." Tim watched the gate for a moment before climbing off his horse.

It felt good to be back on the ground, although his legs felt wobbly. It was like the one time he took the ferry to Catalina Island. He hated the rolling sea, almost as much as he'd hated dry land when they docked. His legs hadn't felt right for at least a day.

Now he was wondering if his legs would ever come back together so he could walk like a normal person and not like a cowboy from some demented cartoon.

Lorelei took up position with her bow, and ShadowLily disappeared. Keeping his eyes focused on the path ahead of him, Tim got ready for whatever came around the corner. He almost cast one of his spells the second he saw something, but it dawned on him just in time it was probably JaKobi.

The pyromancer had his head down against the horse's neck. He looked like a jockey coming around the final bend of the Kentucky Derby. There was a smile on his face that would have felt more at home in the movie *Insidious* than it did here. The howls following him meant the werewolves were right on his ass.

Raising one hand in the air JaKobi motioned for them to get down. Tim was about to ask what he was doing when a fireball erupted behind him. Screams of pain could be heard over the sound of the forest erupting in flames.

"I don't know what he did, but whatever it was slowed them down." Lorelei pulled her bowstring taught and kept the weapon pointed at the pyromancer as he charged toward them.

Tim looked back at the gate. "If this thing takes as long to close as it does to open, we may be here for a bit."

"I don't like the sound of that," Lorelei replied as she shifted her focus to the dark gray shape rounding the corner.

"Just get somewhere where you can kill as many as possible and still fall back to the gate." Tim had no idea where ShadowLily was, but he knew she'd probably heard him.

Lorelei let her arrow fly as JaKobi's horse came to a stop. The pyromancer looked angry, but there was a ring of concern around his eyes. Tim knew that he liked Cassie. He wouldn't have been surprised to find out the two had a late-night snog or were dating. Thinking about how he would feel if this had happened to ShadowLily instead, Tim could understand the emotions the man was dealing with.

The cart started to move inside the gate. Ernie ran behind and gathered their mounts and took them inside. The gate rumbled to a stop at the top of the wall. Brother Colton pulled the amulet free and stepped inside the gate. A moment later, the gate started to lower just as slowly as it had risen.

"What in the fuck is up with this gate?" Tim complained as he started backing up.

"Kind of feels like a wave-type mission, where they send enemies at you in bigger groups until you either fall or last long enough to get the rewards." Flames rippled across JaKobi's robes. "I've always loved those."

"I, for one, never wanted to know what the Alamo felt like," Lorelei said as she let another arrow fly.

"No heroic last stands today. We've just got to last a few minutes." Tim watched the corner, wondering just how bad things were going to get.

The ground started to shake, and all he could think of was elephants. Nothing else could make the earth shake like that unless it was a herd of cattle or an earthquake. *Holy fuck.* His mind went numb as he tried to imagine how many werewolves it would take to make the ground quake.

"Forget what I said, everyone inside," Tim bellowed as he ran for the gate.

ShadowLily popped back into existence and ran inside to help Ernie. Tim started backing up as he cast snare on as many of the werewolves rounding the corner as possible. Reaching out, he grabbed Lorelei's belt and started pulling her back while she continued firing arrows into the oncoming hoard.

"JaKobi! Move your ass," Tim shouted as he continued pulling the Ranger back a step or two at a time.

A quick look behind confirmed that the door was still closing at a ridiculously slow pace. They had plenty of time to get inside, but it wasn't unlimited. What in the hell was the pyromancer doing? He needed to start moving now, or he wasn't going to make it.

"Now!" Tim screamed in his best *Full Metal Jacket* voice.

JaKobi waved away his concerns with one hand before he clapped his hands above him, sending a flaming Phoenix toward the werewolves. While they were distracted, he started running back to the gate.

Seeing the mage finally come to his senses, he gave Lorelei's belt one last tug. "Hit them with something big, and let's get out of here."

"I thought you'd never ask." Lorelei pulled three fire arrows from her quiver. "These pack a punch."

There wasn't any need for her to aim. The werewolves lined the road from side to side and extended back as far as Tim could see. It was the very definition of fish in a barrel. Although, unless those arrows had dynamite attached to them, it wouldn't make a huge difference. Even if they killed half of the horde, the other half would overwhelm them.

Tim didn't have a nuclear option in his arsenal.

The arrows came down into the mass of bodies and detonated. Flames spread out from where each arrow hit. Some of the werewolves tried to dodge to the side but then ran into the wolfsbane guarding the road. The others continued on regardless of the flames.

Tim ducked under the descending gate, and Lorelei followed him a moment later. JaKobi was close to the gate but stopped again. This time he pulled an item from his pocket. He gave the object a kiss and then threw it toward the horde with everything he had.

The little jar sailed through the air and then dropped like a rock woefully short of the horde. The ground shook harder as they got closer. There wasn't a chance in the world the pyromancer could survive out there. The gate was almost closed. He didn't have to sacrifice himself to save them.

The first of the werewolves passed the jar and was close enough that he worried JaKobi had some kind of mental break. "Get inside now!"

"Wait for it." JaKobi took a step back.

The gate was only four feet from the ground now and seemingly picking up speed. Lorelei ducked underneath the heavy stone barrier and knelt to get off a few more arrows. She managed to kill two of the front runners while JaKobi stood there like a sacrificial goat.

When the gate was only three feet from closing, Lorelei looked at Tim. "I don't have any clue what he's doing."

Tim stared out of the entrance, as the gate continued to close. The pyromancer lifted his arms in the air as the bulk of the werewolves passed the object he'd thrown. He screamed the final word of his enchantment, and the world turned red.

The shockwave of the blast sent JaKobi back into the gate. His body hit with a crunch and then crumpled to the ground. "Bigger than I expected," he mumbled as Tim and ShadowLily dragged him under the closing gate.

Tim smiled as the gate hit one foot, and then he saw JaKobi's new hat outside of the door. He reached out and snared it. Pulling the hat inside, he stood up grinning as he brandished the hat to the group. "Indiana has nothing on me."

A werewolf hit the gate, and a paw swiped under the barrier trying to reach anything it could. The gate dropped the final ten inches and crushed the arm underneath. Tim was pretty sure there was noise coming from outside, but he couldn't hear it. Whatever bomb JaKobi set off must have destroyed their hearing.

"Healers gotta heal," Tim mumbled to himself, thinking of one of his favorite memes. He loved thinking of the picture because it always brought a smile to his face when he saw the words "douchers gotta douche."

Some people just can't help themselves.

Standing up, Tim started casting cleanse and heals on the others. It took a few tries, but eventually he could hear again. When he was sure everyone else had their hearing back, he turned to the pyromancer. "What in the fuck was that?"

"Just a little surprise from my class trainer. He's going to shit when I tell him how effective it was." JaKobi was grinning like an idiot. "Only use in emergencies and outside was all he said. Glad I followed the rules for once."

Tim thrust the pyromancers' cap at him. "Just try not to blow us all up next time."

"Fire go boom." JaKobi smiled as though Tim's instructions meant nothing to him.

ShadowLily clapped him on the back. "Don't worry. You just saved our asses. I can't wait to tell Cassie how awesome it was."

Lorelei chuckled. "It was pretty awesome."

"We could use a few more of those toys." Tim put his hand against the closed gate. "I didn't think there would be so many."

Brother Colton stepped toward them inside of the narrow chamber. Only the light provided by the magical enhancements was keeping them from being in total darkness. "I don't know what's waiting for us on the other side. The temple itself is like an outer defense for the south side of the city. It has its own wall and gates and is closed off to Tristholm's residents unless you go through the temple."

He shrugged. "It seemed like a good idea when they built the place, but it also means we're cut off from the city until we make it inside the temple and out the other side."

"Are you expecting trouble?" Tim asked hesitantly.

Brother Colton nodded his head. "You were right, they didn't stop answering our calls because they wanted to. Something is seriously wrong here. We have to get inside and get word back to the high priest at once."

Tim looked over his group and knew they were up to the challenge. Every single one of them would do whatever it took to get Cassie inside the temple and healed. Helping the high priest and Brother Colton was just icing on the cake. There was just one last thing to do before they continued.

"Lorelei, I'd like to formally invite you to the Blue Dagger Society. I've been waiting for the right moment, but since we all might die soon, I think this is it."

The Ranger looked from one face to another, searching for confirmation from everyone. All she received in return were smiles. "I'm in."

"Good. Let's see what shitstorm the high priest is sending us into now." Tim looked at Brother Colton. "Let's do this thing."

The priest moved to the inner door and placed his amulet against it, and it started to rise.

CHAPTER THIRTY-THREE

ombies. Why was it always zombies?

Tim watched the open courtyard for a moment before turning back to the group. "It might be better if we leave the horses here until we sort this out."

"We can't just leave Cassie trapped in here," JaKobi pleaded.

ShadowLily pulled the upset mage into a hug. "Of course we won't. Ernie and Brother Colton can stay here until we clear out the courtyard. Once we know it's safe to come out, we'll move her to the temple together."

The hair on Tim's arms stood up as he watched one of the dead priests walk across the courtyard. The man was holding a foot to his mouth and taking bites as he staggered from one wobbly step to the next.

"Just how many men worked at this temple, Brother Colton?" The last thing he wanted to do was remind the man of how many brothers in faith he'd lost, but Tim had to know what they could be facing.

Brother Colton's face went pale. "Maybe fifty brothers, double that in support staff."

"I should have brought more arrows." Technically, she had an unlimited number of regular arrows, but the special ones she reserved for emergencies were running low. Lorelei had a grim smile on her face. It was the kind of look that said she could kick the apocalypse's ass if it got in her way.

Tim was pretty sure his divine light spell would obliterate any of the zombies, and Lorelei's arrows to the head would also probably do the trick. Fire might not work unless they could trap them somehow, or JaKobi could find a way to boil their brains. Their assassin's knives would come in useful if any of the fuckers got too close. He felt the tugging of a rudimentary plan coming together.

"Our first course of business will be to clear out the courtyard. When we have that secure, we can move the horses into the stables, and make our way to the temple itself."

Brother Colton shifted his feet nervously. "Not to add any pressure, but we need to do it soon. The temple's divine energy flows through the walls of this entire city, keeping the werewolves at bay. If that power is corrupted, Tristholm could be overrun."

"I've got ninety-nine problems, but Tristholm ain't one," JaKobi mumbled. It brought a nervous laugh out of the rest of the group as he looked back at the wagon with Cassie tucked away inside.

Tim wrapped an arm around his shoulders. "Don't worry, Cassie will be fine."

"Bitch is too stubborn to die," ShadowLily added.

Lorelei grinned as she let an arrow go. A zombie who had ventured too close to the gate hit the ground with an arrow sticking out of its head. "Plus, what's the worst-case scenario? She gets all furry and fights on our side. Might be kind of badass."

JaKobi chuckled. "I've got enough problems dealing with the tiny sized version. A nine-foot-tall Cassie with claws might be too much for me to handle."

"Oh, shit. I take back my previous statement. Let's clear out this courtyard before we find out." Lorelei looked at the pyromancer. "Don't worry, we got this."

"I always loved watching *The Walking Dead*, but I never wanted to be part of it," JaKobi said. "Guess this will give me a chance to work on my root spell unless someone has something pokey I can borrow."

Tim pulled a dagger from his inventory and tossed it to the mage. "Just try not to lose it."

"Strictly a backup plan." JaKobi grinned. "I'm never afraid to let the rest of you do the heavy lifting."

"Asshole." ShadowLily smiled.

"Typical man," Lorelei snorted. "Always waiting for his woman to take charge."

Tim looked at Brother Colton as if to say, see what I have to deal with? "Close yourselves in, we'll be back."

Ernie's head popped out of the back of the wagon. "Just be quick about it. I'm doing all I can to halt the transformation, but we don't have a lot of time. Something is accelerating the process. Can't you just magic this away?"

Could he cleanse the lycanthropy curse? It seemed like that would be too easy, but he had to try. He cast cleanse on Cassie, and then repeated the spell three more times. A quick look at Ernie's face told him all he needed to know about the effectiveness of his efforts.

Maybe I just need to level up my skill.

"Just do your best." Tim waved at the others to follow him. "Let's get moving, time is a factor."

The four adventurers stepped out into the courtyard, and the gate started to close behind them. There was a finality to the sound Tim didn't like. He wondered if they died here, where they would respawn. Normally, it was back at the square in the city, unless you'd been bound by the game to another point.

Respawning in Zombie central wouldn't be fun for anyone.

Tim moved away from the gate using the stalls set up for donations as cover. The only way they would run into real trouble here is if they were overwhelmed by sheer numbers. Lorelei's single arrow to the head showed them the zombies weren't exactly resilient. All they had to do was take them out in small groups as they moved around the courtyard.

Staying silent would be the key to their success.

On the plus side for the group, ShadowLily could use her stealth to lure the zombies into a trap or to get away if things got hairy. Tim's own limited stealth abilities might let him get away, but as far as he knew, JaKobi and Lorelei didn't have that same capability. It was better to try to go slow, even though Cassie didn't have forever.

"Babe, don't take this the wrong way, but I'd like to use you for bait." Tim looked at ShadowLily and hoped for the best.

The assassin's eyes locked onto Tim's, letting him know he was on thin ice. "Let me guess, get the zombies on my ass, then stealth out while you try to pick them off."

Lorelei frowned. "That sounds like we'll end up as dinner. A horde of charging zombies running right for us, I don't like the sound of that."

"Better than a horde of werewolves. That shit wasn't fun." JaKobi looked back at the closing gate as if the werewolves might find a way through the stone to kill them at any moment.

Tim knew there was a clock running, and it wasn't just for Cassie. If they failed to get the temple back under Eternia's control, the entire city was at risk. Somewhere in his adventures, he'd gone from the guy who took on random bosses to the guy who saved cities on a regular basis.

Was *The Etheric Coast* this intense for everyone?

Looking over the concerned faces of his group, Tim decided he'd better start explaining before they got too worked up. "I was thinking of something a little less risky."

"See those stalls over there." Tim pointed. "I'm not sure what they were for, but they make a nice little U shape, and it looks like an assassin of some renown could slip out the back, loop around, and close the gate before the zombies were any wiser."

Lorelei pointed a finger gun at the enclosure. "Then it's like throwing darts at balloons."

ShadowLily grinned. "I like that. The whole fish in a barrel thing is overplayed. I mean, if the fish are in the barrel, they are already dead."

"So are the zombies," JaKobi said with a snort of laughter.

Tim reached out and pulled ShadowLily close to him. He gave her a kiss. "Be careful and be quick."

"Aww." Lorelei winked at JaKobi. "I'm a sucker for a good moment."

Before the pyromancer could respond, ShadowLily disappeared. All they could do now was wait for the assassin to reappear as she sprinted back to the gated stalls. It was tense for Tim to send her out alone. With no way of knowing how many of the hundred and fifty potential zombies were in the courtyard, he was feeling a little nervous. So far, they'd only seen a couple zombies shuffling around, but he'd seen enough horror movies to know that the damn things came out of nowhere just when you thought it was safe.

Any of the small covered stalls or the stables could have zombies in them. Brother Colton said there were at least a hundred and fifty people here, and that was just the priests and their support staff. Villagers could also be inside. They could potentially be facing hundreds of zombies.

His plan wouldn't stand up to hundreds.

The last thing Tim wanted was for this to turn into one of those games where you placed turrets on the map to try to take down the zombie hordes before they overran your city. In those games you always died. He planned on living through this. He had to. Cassie, and the entire city of Tristholm, was counting on him. If Tristholm fell, Promethia would be next up on the buffet line.

No pressure.

ShadowLily came sprinting around the corner. She turned and faced whatever was following her. "Over here, you smelly fuckers! Come and get your dinner." She waved her hands over her head and stomped her feet before turning and running again.

His woman was ballsy, but that was part of why he loved her. Tim never would have expected that their chance encounter at graduation would have led to such an amazing relationship. He'd followed her into the game, and now he couldn't imagine his life without her.

And critics say video games don't bring people together.

Sprinting into the U-shaped enclosure, ShadowLily picked up a board and started banging it on the wooden frames of the stalls to keep the zombies coming. Tim hoped her antics wouldn't bring any of the hidden lurkers running toward them as well.

Slipping out of the back of the enclosure, ShadowLily kept hitting the boards as zombies continued to fill the space. When the last zombie made it inside, she disappeared. A moment later, she popped back into existence by the wooden gate. With a quick push, she sealed the zombies inside of their makeshift corral.

Tim had seen enough episodes of *The Walking Dead* to know they could probably walk up to the edge of the fence and just stab them in the head, but why get close when you don't have to? He started picking out targets and casting divine light on them. White beams of holy energy filled the air, and soon the lifeless bodies started to pile up.

Nothing in the enclosure was moving as Tim crept closer to take a peek. JaKobi had a ball of flame in his hands, ready to deal with any sudden surprises, but Tim got the feeling they were safe for now. Nearly fifty bodies littered the floor of the stalls, but he didn't see any of the familiar white robes with blue trim he'd come to expect from the priests. All of these had been regular people, and for some reason it made him sad.

He couldn't imagine how it felt to just be out doing your thing, and then to be smack dab in the middle of the apocalypse. A lot of shows and movies didn't cover the days leading up to the break in society. It wasn't sexy like roving hordes of zombies. All that would happen in the initial stages of a zombie outbreak were fear, disbelief, and death.

Thankfully, they hadn't been here to witness the carnage.

While there was no chance he could bring these people back to life, he could find whatever killed them or turned them and make sure it didn't happen to anyone else. It was one thing to lose a loved one to disease or old age, but quite another to have them turn into a ravenous killing machine.

"Lorelei, retrieve your arrows." Tim turned to JaKobi. "When she's done, ash the bodies."

The pyromancer looked over the bodies with grim determination. "You got it, boss."

Tim looked away as the Ranger started picking her way through the corpses. He didn't envy her task at all, or the one he'd assigned to his fiery friend. He would do his best to reassure the citizens of Tristholm that their loved ones had been treated with care.

Walking the half-circle around the tower, Tim and ShadowLily looked for stragglers. When they didn't find any other corpses, Tim gave the signal for JaKobi to start his fire. The rest of their battle would be taking place inside the temple itself.

Stopping in front of the tower's door, Tim pressed his hands against the dark wooden surface. It was almost as if he could feel the evil emanating from within. Whatever was waiting for them inside would be a hundred times worse than what they'd faced out here. The courtyard was just the kind of softball developers lobbed at you, so when the next set of MOBS hit twice as hard, the players weren't ready for it.

Facing the unknown without their tank wasn't the most thrilling of prospects.

Tim's head whipped around as the gate they had come through started to open. Stepping away from the tower, he motioned for the group to follow him back so he could find out what was happening.

Brother Colton emerged, leading the cart and the extra horses into the courtyard. Once their little caravan was inside, he started to close the gate again. "I think the protections are failing faster than previously assumed."

Tim wanted to make a crack about the usefulness of assumptions, but it wasn't the right time. "Maybe we should all head inside to face what's there together." It wouldn't be ideal carrying Cassie into fights where she couldn't help. In fact, she might be more of a hindrance, if other people had to defend her.

The howls of the werewolves shattered the warmth of the morning sun.

A voice cackled from the top of the tower. "Welcome adventurers. I hope you've found the journey to this point a relaxing endeavor."

ShadowLily look at Tim and mouthed, "What in the fuck?"

He just shook his head from side to side. Tim had no clue what was going on, but it felt like they'd just stumbled onto a boss fight.

The disembodied voice continued. "I'm a bit upset about what you've done to my subjects, but more bodies can always be found to experiment on. You see, I find that science is the only way to progress spiritually."

"If we could only unlock the secret to eternal life, then, and only then may we truly open ourselves up to the holy spirit. It is the demands of the flesh that limits us."

Dark laughter pealed from the heavens like thunder.

"There was a time I would have been happy to share my secrets with you. That was before the temple ridiculed me and called me a monster. I've been working for so long, but the answer to eternal life still eludes me. That doesn't mean that I haven't had many other successes."

The sun faded from the sky as dark thunder clouds moved in. A gentle rain started to fall. It was just the thing to set the mood for something terrible to happen. Whatever was in the tower waiting for them was strong enough to control the weather and sounded insane enough to be unpredictable.

"As with all knowledge, it is wise to find out if the pursuer is worthy. Before you enter the temple, you must face my latest creation. I present to you, the Devourer."

Tim scanned the courtyard for some hint of the monster, but he didn't see anything. The sound of a struggle pulled his attention back toward the cart.

Cassie was out on the bench trying to pull her leg free from Ernie's grasp. "I'm telling you. I feel fine." She shook off the innkeeper's hold and sprang down to the cobblestones in one fluid motion.

It seemed like Cassie cleared the distance to Tim in half a heartbeat. "Sounds like you guys are about to need me."

Tim looked past the tank toward Ernie, who was violently shaking his head from side to side. Brother Colton looked just as concerned but didn't say a word. "Cassie, maybe you should sit this one out."

"What and miss all the fun?" The tank strode toward JaKobi. As she reached him, Cassie wrapped her arms around the back of his neck and pulled the pyromancer in for a kiss. "Let's get this show on the road."

JaKobi looked at Tim and gave him a thumbs up. "We're going to need a tank."

Ernie climbed out of the wagon to sit by Brother Colton. "Any activity will only accelerate the virus. She needs to lie down."

"Are you kidding?" Cassie roared. "I feel like a million bucks."

"They always do." Ernie frowned. "Right up until their bones break, and their skin rips off."

JaKobi was smiling from ear to ear, the brief kiss clearly still on his mind. "Kind of dark there, Ernie."

Cassie pointed as something massive jumped off the tower and landed in the courtyard. "You want to fight that thing without me?"

Tim took one look at the Devourer. "Naptime can wait."

CHAPTER THIRTY-FOUR

The Devourer looked at its newest meal and smiled.

"That's one ugly son of a bitch." Cassie stepped to the front of the group.

Tim just nodded in silence as he looked over the monstrosity. What sick bastard would think that making something like this was good science. As far as he could tell, a was made of different body parts held together by some kind of dark magic.

Three torsos were stitched together to make one massive body. The creature had six arms and four legs. Tim thought of it as a monster because it was too horrible to think that this thing used to be a person. Or, from the looks of it, more than one. The Devourer reminded him of an episode of *Hannibal,* where the killer made a totem out of bodies on the beach.

"He seems awfully pissed off," JaKobi said as the Devourer started moving forward.

Tim felt the fog of battle taking over. "Wouldn't you be? Just look at him."

"I'd be in too much pain to be stomping around killing people." Flames erupted around the pyromancer's robes.

"Anyone else feel like they are about to barf?" Lorelei asked as she nocked an arrow.

ShadowLily disappeared. "You aren't the one who has to get close to him."

"All right team, slow and steady. Cassie, I'm going to need you to use as little energy as possible. I don't want you getting wolfie on us." Tim stared at the tank, wondering if she would heed his advice.

"Arrooooooo!" Cassie shouted as she ran forward to meet the Devourer's charge.

A blast of fire flew over Cassie's head and struck the boss in the chest. The tiny tank looked back at the pyromancer. "Wait until I get agro!"

"My bad. I was just so excited to see you." JaKobi grinned from ear to ear.

Lorelei nudged him. "Blowing your load early isn't a sign of affection."

Before JaKobi could respond, the battle roared into full swing. The Devourer rushed toward Cassie, it's six arms and four legs working in unison. The boss didn't have a weapon, but its arms looked like they might have been ripped off Schwarzenegger in his prime, and his thighs were as thick as tree trunks.

Getting a bear hug from this guy would be bone-crushing.

Without thinking, Tim dropped into Way of the Boulder stance. Cassie was going to need all the heals and the extra defense. He quickly cast his buffs just in case the boss wouldn't take normal damage, and then scanned the field for any surprises. Not seeing anything special going on, Tim fired off a bolt of divine light.

He followed the white-hot bolt of holy energy and was impressed to see three or four arrows already sticking out of the Devourer's chest by the time his spell hit. It seemed their new Ranger wasn't one to waste time. A familiar clap sounded next to him, and Tim smiled as the flaming Phoenix slammed into the boss' chest.

Roaring flames washed over the boss, and he staggered backward for a single step. Shaking his head, the Devourer glared at JaKobi before returning his attention to their little tank and her staff. Grinning like a cat who caught the canary, the boss ignored the repeated blows of Cassie's staff. The weapon's extra thorn damage clearly didn't bother him as he swiped at her with three of his arms.

Cassie rolled out of the way, leaping to her feet as she finished the maneuver. Her staff cracked into the back of one of the boss' legs, but the other three kept him upright. As Tim watched, all he could think about was how fast Cassie could move. It was like she'd chugged an unlimited haste potion.

Maybe having her be wolf-y wasn't such a bad thing.

The Devourer roared in frustration as the little tank kept swatting at him. Deciding to ignore the pest, the boss looked at the rest of the group. His eyes settled on JaKobi, and he started to charge.

Thunderous steps shook the cobblestones as the Devourer gathered himself for a leap that would flatten whoever he targeted. Just before he jumped, ShadowLily appeared out of nowhere and slashed her blades across the backs of his legs. Two of the limbs kept working and the boss only staggered. Using his six arms like a bug, he hit the deck and ran out of sight faster than the group could follow.

Tim ran around the edge of the temple in time to see the Devourer's middle chest open like a mouth as he shoved a zombie into it. The wounds on his legs must have started to heal since the boss stood up straighter. JaKobi clearly hadn't had time to incinerate the potential food source.

"Don't let him eat anything else," Tim roared. It was times like this he wished for more offensive capabilities. Such was the life of a healer.

Instead of whining about his general lack of damage, Tim

switched into Way of the River stance before casting his highest damaging ability, behold my power. With the spell cast and his group taking damage, he quickly followed up with curse of giving, and a healing orb for their tank.

JaKobi busied himself burning a zombie they hadn't had time to address before Cassie's reappearance. Tim wondered if the boss fight might materialize more of them, or if by killing the zombies before the Devourer showed up, they'd saved themselves a lot of trouble. Tim decided it only mattered if the bodies reanimated. For now, they had more important things to focus on.

There must have been a few fresh zombies, but Lorelei dropped them quickly, and JaKobi incinerated their corpses before the Devourer could reach them. The boss roared as his food and healing went away. The massive cavity in his center torso snapped open and closed as it demanded more food. The dark energy binding the Devourer together was a hungry mistress.

Cassie kept her bō staff hammering against the boss as it roared in frustration. ShadowLily jumped off one of the stalls and landed on the Devourer's back, leaving twin wounds trailing down its back like rips in a canvas. Tim's curse hit, staggering the boss enough that it fell to its knees.

Black fluid dripped from the Devourer's wounds as it cried out in agony. The boss tried to stand up, but Cassie was ready for it. Her bō staff cracked into the back of one knee, forcing the Devourer back down. ShadowLily started slashing at the arms on the monster's right as it tried to regain his feet.

Lorelei reached into a pouch on her waist and pulled out a tiny bottle. "I was saving this for a celebration, but I guess this will do." She tossed the bottle at the boss, and it shattered over his chest, covering it in clear liquid.

"Time to light him up!" Tim looked at the pyromancer and nodded.

His divine light spell caught the Devourer a split second before JaKobi's Phoenix slammed into its chest. Flames erupted as the liquid Lorelei threw on the boss ignited. The dark energy holding the Devourer together broke apart, and the body parts hit the ground with a wet splash.

Rotted arms, legs, and torsos sitting in a pool of black goo were all that was left of the monstrosity. Tim wanted to say something witty, but he just felt bad for the people the creature was made out of. It must have been horrible for them as they were stitched together in some grotesque experiment.

Cassie wiped dark liquid off her face before falling to one knee in exhaustion. "I vote we never do that again."

"I'd sign that petition." JaKobi's facial features shifted to concerned. "How are you doing?"

Standing up, the tank made her way back to the group. "I'll be fine. Let's just get inside and end this."

Tim looked at the tower and wondered just how many monstrosities waited for them inside the temple. Whatever made the Devourer was still there, and it had to know they were coming for it. Cold rain continued to fall on them as Ernie and Brother Colton emerged from the stables.

Ernie ran forward and handed Cassie a vial. "Drink this."

"This better not make me sleepy, you cagey bastard." She swallowed the drink in one go.

The Poison Master grinned. "I know you're too damn stubborn for that. This is the best I could come up with to slow your transformation."

"Would it really be so bad if she turned into a werewolf?" JaKobi asked.

Brother Colton placed a consoling hand on the pyromancer's shoulder. "In normal circumstances, I'd say no, but there is something controlling the Clans. Someone is driving them to attack, and if Cassie turns, she could be forced to join them."

"It would never happen," the tank said flatly. "No one can make me do anything I don't want to do."

ShadowLily laughed. "I can attest to that."

"Bitch," Cassie retorted.

Tim looked at his team, happy to have every single one of them on his side. The fact they got along better than most families made him happy. You couldn't pick your relatives, but you did get to pick your friends, and he had picked some of the best. Tim was just glad they saw something in him that made them feel the same way.

He was about to say something mushy when it thundered loud enough to make him wince.

"So the Devourer has fallen, but do you have what it takes to face what is waiting inside?" a disembodied voice bellowed from the heavens.

"Your little toy wasn't up to the task!" Cassie shouted into the storm defiantly.

Laughter rumbled like thunder. "Then step into my menagerie of wonders and behold the sights that I have created."

"You mean the monstrosities!" Brother Colton stepped forward. "You are an affront to the Goddess Eternia. Name yourself or face her holy wrath."

"As if your goddess' power holds sway over me. I am eternal, I am darkness, I am the Surgeon. Science will always win over blind faith and lackluster devotion." Thunder echoed through the courtyard. "If giving birth to new life is divine, then I have truly become a god."

ShadowLily put a hand on her hip and had one hell of a sassy expression on her face. "I'm surprised his ego fits inside the temple."

Tim couldn't help but laugh as the temple doors swung open to admit them.

The voice called out one last time. "Death and rebirth await all who enter."

"This must be how it feels to meet Pinhead." JaKobi dropped his voice. "We have such sights to show you, and the suffering, such sweet suffering."

Tim patted the pyromancer on the back. "Let's hope inside doesn't take us to hell. I, for one, could do without a trip to the underworld."

"Praise the goddess," Brother Colton replied.

Cassie looked over the group, grinning. "I can't wait to finish this fucker off." She held up her hand for a high five, and then lowered it as she stared at her forearm. "What in the fuck?"

"Looks like someone is going to need a razor for Christmas," Lorelei quipped as she looked at the hair on the tank's arms.

ShadowLily smiled. "A little hot wax would do the trick."

Cassie looked down at the ground. "I hate you both."

Running forward, JaKobi put an arm around her. "I still think you're gorgeous. Just don't eat me, ok?"

Grinning at the pyromancer, Cassie replied, "No promises."

"Let's find out what the Surgeon has in store for us." Tim took the first steps toward the temple, and the rest of his group followed. He didn't know what was waiting for them. All he knew was they would defeat it and save Cassie from turning into a werewolf. There was no room for doubt. They had to succeed.

Good thing for the high priest and the city of Tristholm, the Blue Dagger Society would never falter.

CHAPTER THIRTY-FIVE

The inside of the temple was bigger than Tim imagined.

He was having trouble rectifying the building outside with the one within. It wasn't quite like the tents in *Harry Potter*, but it certainly felt larger on the inside. The entire back of the temple was built into the wall of the city, blocked by a massive iron gate. Through the bars Tim could see solid wood and iron doors preventing the temple's access to the city.

Maybe the room he was in was so magnificent because it was the main entrance for worshipers attending service. One thing churches liked to have was a grand entrance. Nothing showed a church's devotion to their deity of choice like a jaw-dropping spectacle. While Tim had never been big on the concept of church, he *was* a believer in something bigger than him.

Looking around the temple, it was easy to see why so many people worshipped the Goddess Eternia. In all the paintings around the room, she appeared to be a benevolent benefactor for humanity, righting the wrongs of the world and crushing evil wherever its ugly head rose. Tim knew for a fact which side the goddess was on, and he owed her for everything she had done for him.

Without a little divine intervention, he might not be standing where he was today.

"Anyone else feel like we walked into a tomb?" Cassie said as she poked at an empty row of seats with her bō staff.

Brother Colton looked around nervously. "There are normally many people here. Where are all my brothers? Surely the goddess wouldn't let all of them perish."

"Do you think we can get this gate open? I'm sure Seraphina would like to see me as soon as possible." Ernie looked at the shuttered gate with longing.

Tim took one look at the door and then back at the innkeeper. "I think you're stuck with us until we find the Surgeon and take him out."

"It might be that our talents are better suited toward preparing for what happens after you deal with the threat," Brother Colton replied as he tried to keep his shaking hands hidden from view. "The Poison Master and I should return to the stables and start working on whatever he will need to get us out of trouble."

ShadowLily nudged Tim in the side. "Might be a good idea to get them out of here. In a real fight, they would only slow us down."

Thinking about the time Tim saw Ernie trying to take out a Kobold with a frying pan, he couldn't agree more. "As long as Ernie is okay preparing for the next phase of our adventure, I think separating would be a good idea."

Brother Colton practically grabbed the Poison Master and started dragging him toward the exit. "Just let us know when you're done, and I'll use the temple to cure your friend."

Ernie broke out of the priest's grip and locked eyes with Tim. "Faster would be better."

Nodding was more of a reflex than an answer. Tim already felt the weight of a ticking clock on his shoulders. Cassie didn't have time for them to do this slow and careful. They needed to find the Surgeon and end him.

Tim pointed to the stairs leading up. "Might as well get this show on the road."

"Thought you'd never ask." Cassie leaped up the stairs and took them two or three at a time.

Ernie called out, "I said, go slow."

Running to catch up with his slightly furrier girlfriend, JaKobi shouted, "This is the new slow."

Motioning for everyone to catch up, Tim started his own run toward the stairs. It wouldn't do for the healer to get locked out of the fight. While it was kind of funny to wipe in other games when someone made a silly mistake, in *The Etheric Coast*, a death right now would be a huge hindrance to their plans.

Cassie stopped at the first landing. "All the way to the top and work our way down, or start down here and work our way up?"

Coming to a stop just behind the group, Tim paused to think about it. His initial instinct would have been to go down, but the priest didn't have a dungeon or any underground tunnels as far as he knew. Chances were, they did have some hidden areas built into the temple. Eternia knew there were plenty of them back in the temple in Promethia.

How else would Paul's guards come and go with the golden doors closed?

Since down wasn't the answer, his next choice would be to go straight to the top, but he was sure the Surgeon wouldn't make it that easy for them. One thing Tim knew about deranged doctors was that they needed a quiet place to carry out their work. It wasn't like they could book a surgical suite at the hospital to make a human centipede.

With each floor of the tower being slightly smaller than the last, it would make sense that most of the hidden areas would be on the lower levels. What made sense to most people often seemed to defeat developers, so Tim wasn't sure. This was a game, and they could just add a secret room to the rules of architecture. It didn't have to make sense, but so far everything Tim had seen seemed to build upon the foundation of the real world. If that was the case, they needed to start here.

"Let's start here and work our way up. Look for anything that might indicate a secret room or passage." Before Tim finished speaking, Cassie was moving forward. The werewolf side of her wouldn't let her sit still for long.

Cassie took the lead and led them into the first room. A single zombie fell to one of Lorelei's arrows, and then the group spread out to search the room. Books lined the walls from floor to ceiling. Pulling on each one of them to try to find a hidden passage would have taken days. There had to be a simpler way to do this.

JaKobi looked over the rows of books, a smile spreading on his face. "I could burn them."

A thump sounded as ShadowLily's hand smacked the back of his head. "You are not burning the books."

"You never let me have any fun," JaKobi whined.

Cassie was staring daggers at ShadowLily. "Hands off the merchandise, honey."

Taking one look at her friend's blazing eyes, and slightly longer lower incisors, ShadowLily decided it wasn't the time to talk about being called honey. She'd bring up rude nicknames after her best friend wasn't being a wolfgina. "Won't happen again."

As Cassie turned around, ShadowLily mouthed at JaKobi, "Fire Bad."

Tim watched the interaction and wondered just how much time they had left before Cassie totally wolfed out. JaKobi was right. They couldn't just walk around pulling on any book at random and hoping for the best. There had to be a more efficient way to do it. Tim racked his brain, trying to think of all the ways people found secret passages in movies and books.

It was time to channel his inner *Hardy Boys*.

Those two fuckers unwound puzzles like it was nobody's business, and they even brought their friends or dad along on occasion. Tim looked down at the ground and mumbled, "What would the Hardys do?" and then his head snapped up.

His plan might not work, but then again it could be just the thing they needed to get things moving. Every secret passage or room needed air, and most of the time, that caused a draft. Sure, his plan wouldn't work with a panic room with its own water, power, and air, but back in the Middle Ages they weren't setting up air shafts and independent power.

"Is that the look you guys are always talking about? The one Tim has when he gets an idea." Lorelei scanned the party, hoping she read the situation right.

JaKobi started to smile. "That's the one."

Tim pointed at the pyromancer. "Fire good."

"That's what I've been trying to say." JaKobi started creating a vortex of fire by spinning his arms.

Motioning for JaKobi to stop, Tim replied, "I was thinking of something a little less destructive." He took a few steps toward one of the shelves. "Do you think you could send a stream of fire in front of the cabinets without burning any of the books?"

"Bro, if I can incinerate a fly as it crosses the room, I'm sure I can handle not burning a few books." JaKobi grinned as he let a blast of flames go. "But I'm not sure exactly what I'm doing."

Tim smiled. "I thought it'd take too long for all of us to get candles and search for a draft. With your help, we should be able to find out if there is something a lot faster."

Turning away from the group, JaKobi sent a wave of flames across the room about a foot from the bookcase. When nothing happened, he turned around and looked at Tim. "What exactly are we expecting here?"

"Something incredible," Tim replied casually. When no one laughed or looked amused, he motioned for the pyromancer to keep doing his thing. "Let's keep going. Eventually, we'll find something."

JaKobi shrugged his shoulders. He was always happy to play with fire.

The group searched the second floor of the tower, going room by room. They didn't find anything as they moved through the building. Tim was starting to doubt his plan had merit as they moved to the third floor.

At least they were still getting experience.

The trickle of experience wasn't enough to keep their spirits lifted. Cassie was growing more agitated, and Lorelei kept watching her out of the corner of her eye, clearly ready to put an arrow in her if she freaked out. Guildmates killing each other was a problem Tim never wanted to deal with, so he started walking just a little bit faster.

The third floor didn't reveal any secrets, but the number of enemies increased. As a group, they were able to take out rooms full of zombies. Unless the creatures got stronger or started coming in packs of ten or more, their group didn't even have to put in any effort. Tim was starting to wonder when they would encounter the priests. He was pretty sure all of their retainers and patrons were dead by now.

A man in a white robe charged them as soon as they reached the fourth floor. His eyes were gouged out, and one of his arms was missing. Lorelei hit him in the center of the forehead with an arrow, but he didn't stop running until Cassie tripped him and used her staff to crush his head like a watermelon.

"Finally, a little action," the tank growled. "Please tell me there are more of them."

Tim pointed toward the first closed door on the right. "Let's find out."

Three steps later, Cassie launched into a flying kick aimed at the center of the double doors. Both of the wooden doors slammed open and hit the walls hard enough to dent the stone. Their tank flew around the room like she was using the furniture to set up her own Ninja Warrior contest.

Priests in white robes fell under her relentless assault, as Tim tried to pick off any stragglers left in her wake with his divine light spell. Lorelei's bow took out anything he missed, while JaKobi and ShadowLily leaned against the wall looking bored. It was a first for them not to be the ones dishing out the most DPS, and they clearly didn't like it.

When the room was clear, Tim waved for the pyromancer to do his thing. He went around the edges of the room, blowing streaks of fire in front of the bookcases. On the third wall, Tim thought he might have seen something.

"One more time." He stopped JaKobi from moving forward and focused his attention on where he thought the flames had shifted.

This time when his fiery friend cast the spell, Tim was sure of it. The flames tugged toward the panel. It wasn't as obvious as he thought it would be, but there was something behind this part of the bookcase.

Moving forward, Tim started grabbing books and ripping them from the shelves. He was sure the rest of the group thought he was nuts. They were all acting like they hadn't seen a thing. Part of him was starting to believe they were right, and then his hand snagged on a book that didn't move.

"Bingo!" Tim called out with jubilation.

The bookcase popped open with a click, and Tim started to pull the door aside.

Cassie not so gently nudged him out of the way. "Squishies to the back."

While he might not have liked the implication, Tim moved behind the tank. It didn't make sense to die because you were too prideful to get out of your own way. It was okay to fail, and even better to recognize when you lacked the skill to accomplish a task. Once a person knew where they stood, it was easy enough for them to buckle down and work to become sufficient or to hire someone with the talent to complete the job.

Tim felt a certain sense of pride that he had written every one of his college papers himself. He also knew that without the help of an editor he'd found online, all of those papers wouldn't have done nearly as well.

When it came down to it, he could make numbers sing.

The words, not so much.

Cassie let out a sigh. "This isn't going to help us." She stepped out of sight and then returned a second later, carrying a small chest. She put it on the table and opened it. A few golden coins spilled out on the table

With a thought, Tim directed the game to split the coins evenly and disperse them to the team. Each of them smiled as the two golden coins appeared in their inventory. It wasn't the room they were looking for, but it did mean his plan wasn't a complete waste of time.

They found one more chest on the fourth floor, and four more on the fifth.

By the time the group reached the sixth floor, there weren't even any zombies left. They cleared the floor quickly and made it to the final room without finding a thing. Tim pounded a fist against the wall. "This just doesn't make sense. There has to be something here."

JaKobi let a burst of fire go along the side of the bookcase. The flames sucked inwards so hard the books caught on fire. "What the hell?"

"I thought we talked about burning the books?" ShadowLily smirked. "You are lucky wolf girl has your back, or I'd make you do some punishment pushups."

Cassie grinned. "Actually, I wouldn't mind watching him do some pushups." She pointed at JaKobi. "Gotta lose the robe first, hot stuff."

"Ugh, now you sound as bad as him." Lorelei pointed at Tim as he splashed healing orbs against the books to douse the flames.

One of the books caught on Tim's hand, and an entire section of shelving slid to the side. The hallway was big enough for five people to walk side by side and curved away from them so there was no way to tell what waited for them at the end.

"Told you it wasn't my fault." JaKobi grinned with righteous vindication. "I know how to keep a fire contained."

Cassie snickered. "Passion should never be contained."

"I think we need to hurry," ShadowLily said, trying to stifle a laugh.

Tim nodded in agreement. "Let's find out what's waiting in the creepy passage behind the bookcase."

The group moved inside the passageway, and the door closed behind them, sealing them in darkness.

CHAPTER THIRTY-SIX

Tim was tired of long dark tunnels.

He'd spent more time in them than he would have liked when he'd been imprisoned by Cardinal Jepsom. Maybe it was just that Tim had never seen a horror movie in which someone went underground that ended happily. Normally once a person was trapped in creepy tunnels, it was a death sentence.

Not that his mind was warped by watching too many scary movies.

Horror prepared people for a worst-case scenario. There was no way to tell when you'd meet the next Bundy or have a BTK break into your home. Watch enough horror films, and you'd know all the things not to do pretty quickly by watching all the ways people died.

Thinking about his favorite movies was a coping technique Tim used to deal with stress. As the tunnel continued to descend, he thought about how disappointed some people were with horror. Mostly it was false expectations, but some of the time the movies were just pure shit. He smiled, thinking about how many people thought slasher flicks were about the final girl. No one went to *Halloween* or *Nightmare on Elm Street* because of the hero. Everyone wanted to see the bad guy do his thing.

It was funny how much time Tim spent cheering for killers, but never hesitated to change allegiances for the victims of a supernatural attack. There was something terrifying about the dark and the evil things hidden within. While he liked the thought of the bad guys in movies, Tim decided his life in the game was better spent vanquishing evil.

He hadn't seen anything as evil as the Surgeon.

It took a special kind of monster to experiment on people. It's one thing to be a killer, and something else entirely to take pleasure in hurting others. When a psycho devolved into sewing people together and creating things out of body parts, well, that was some next level shit. The only way to deal with someone that depraved was to end them.

Cassie must have felt the same way because she picked up the pace. They were almost running as they continued moving in a downward spiral. The flames above JaKobi's head were the only thing providing the party with any light. They all felt the tension building and knew that at the end of the path, there was a boss fight waiting for them. There was no way to tell how far down they'd gone, but Tim was sure they passed the ground floor of the temple long ago.

Just as he was starting to feel like Hell was the only thing left below them, the decline of the ramp they were on stopped. The hallway continued to curve until they came to a giant wooden door. Stenciled against the faded white paint of the wall were foot long black letters spelling out the words Surgical Ward.

"The closest thing I've seen to surgery in *The Etheric Coast* is stitches. Everything else is healed magically or you die." Lorelei shrugged at all the looks. "Trust me, I've died more than a few times."

"My guess is the Surgeon isn't interested in curing people," Cassie snapped. "Let's go kick this motherfucker's ass."

Tim felt the same way. After facing down the Devourer, he knew the surgeon was an evil that needed to be cleansed from Eternia. He would have killed this boss for free, but thankfully he was getting paid to be here.

Cassie walked forward and pulled the bolt from the center of the double doors and kicked them open. Inside of the room were rows of cots along both walls. All of them were bloodstained, and they were all empty.

"I hope this isn't where the Brothers ended up." Tim looked at the bloodstained sheets and thought about the mad priests with no eyes who attacked them as they searched the upper floors.

ShadowLily put a comforting hand on Tim's shoulder. "We'll make the Surgeon pay for what he's done."

"I can't wait to light this fire," JaKobi said as flames rippled down his robes. "Let's show this freak the stairway to hell."

Lorelei started laughing. "What? I was just thinking how different the world would have been if Zeppelin wrote that instead of the *Stairway to Heaven*."

Tim felt the calmness of battle settling over him. A little witty banter before the fight always calmed his nerves. Looking at Lorelei, Tim replied, "There are so few people going up they only need a stairway, but for hell you get to take the highway."

Cassie snarled. "Follow me."

Looking back at Tim, JaKobi mouthed, "Oh, shit."

The tank strode into the room with the rest of the group fanning out behind her. Tim smiled at their spacing. ShadowLily was on Cassie's heels, while JaKobi and Lorelei stood to either side of Tim.

Not sure of what to expect, Tim activated his Way of the River stance and cast his buffs on the party. A quick double-check confirmed his stream was still recording from the earlier battles. It was weird to think about having to turn it on or off all the time. Maybe he could talk to Barbara about automating some of the system. He liked playing better when he didn't have to think about flipping on his camera.

At the end of the room, there was a gallery that looked like the place where doctors held surgical theater. It seemed like such a foreign concept to have other doctors watching surgeries, but they didn't have video cameras. If you wanted to learn, you needed to watch someone else do it, or dive right in and hope for the best.

Life had to be easier for surgeons today. Besides the advanced tools, they made training simulations for all kinds of surgeries. With enough time in the simulator, a surgeon could become proficient without ever touching a body. Science and medicine were doing wonders for people's health.

That was back in the real world.

Here in Eternia, it was more like Jack the Ripper was sanctioned to experiment on people. Tim could understand the madness behind the Ripper. It was people like Edward Gein he couldn't wrap his mind around. How a man who had only been proven to kill a single person could be the basis for so many scary movies said something about how batshit crazy he was.

The Surgeon made Ed look like a teddy bear.

There was a priest on the Surgeon's table, and the man standing over him was sewing an extra arm onto his torso. The Surgeon looked up at them, mask covered in blood. The mask twitched a bit, and Tim imagined the boss was smiling at them.

In an interesting departure from normal, this boss was the size of an average man. He was covered in a white robe with blue trim, marking him as a priest. Eyes dancing with amusement, the man went back to work and ignored the adventurers. The Surgeon finished stitching the arm onto his newest test subject, then put down the needle and picked up a scalpel.

"The truest of the goddess' teachings can be found internally." The Surgeon sliced the man on the table from his chest down to his groin. He placed his hands in the open wound on the man's stomach and ripped the slit wider. Pulling some intestine from the man's stomach, The Surgeon looked at Tim. "Amazing, isn't it?"

Trying his best not to throw up, Tim managed a weak reply. "Not exactly the word I would use for what is going on here."

Lorelei's bow thrummed in her hands. The arrow hit an invisible barrier in front of the Surgeon and spun harmlessly away. "A doctor's oath is to save every life!"

Tim noticed something. the Surgeon had six arms. His additional appendages seemed to sprout from his back instead of another arm socket. The other arms were skinnier, almost skeletal in size. The limbs also had a flicker of darkness about them, which let the group know they were made using dark magic. He had a feeling the magical limbs would be stronger than they looked, and maybe faster as well.

The extra arms would be an issue.

One of the Surgeon's extra hands moved up to remove the man's mask. The flesh of his right cheek was missing, showing the inside of his mouth as his tongue worked to form his next words. "My oath is to progress, and the best progress always comes from experimentation."

Laughter echoed from around the room as the Surgeon grinned. "One of my teachers used to say, you don't make mistakes, because with every failure you learn what not to do next."

His eyes locked onto Lorelei. "I've made thousands of mistakes. Monster they called me, abomination they mocked, but when the bastards needed to be saved, they all sought out my services."

The Surgeon's four additional arms all rose in unison with a scalpel in each hand. "Today, they paid for their arrogance, and I furthered my research."

Tim wondered if the temple had any other dark secrets. He managed to stop himself from shrugging. It didn't really matter. When it came down to it, everyone was the same. Just because you held an esteemed profession didn't make you a good person. There were enough documentaries in the world showing the fall of people who had been held to higher standards. It stood to reason there was a crazy asshole out there doing just about everything, from the president's office down to a guy begging for change on the streets.

Tim squared his shoulders and prepared himself for the fight. "They have a saying where I come from, too. Those who have the ability to stop evil also have the responsibility to kick its fucking ass."

JaKobi snickered. "I'm not sure that's how the quote goes, but I like it."

"Let's just kill this bastard!" Cassie roared as she charged at the surgeon.

Tim wasn't sure if the tank hadn't seen the arrow hit the barrier or just didn't care, but he started casting healing orb right away. Their friend wasn't acting like herself as the werewolf side of her fought to take over. All he could do now was try to keep her safe until this was over.

The barrier came down as Cassie passed through, but Tim's healing orb hit it with a wet splash. Water dripped down the invisible shield. Their tank was stuck inside, and none of them could get to her.

JaKobi called on his Phoenix, and the flames spread over the shielded area like a dome. There seemed to be a small gap at the top, but the rest of the Surgeon's shield held firm. Lorelei tried her luck with another arrow shot. When it failed, she arced an arrow into the gap. It fell through the hole in the shield and embedded itself on the surgical table.

The Surgeon never looked away from Cassie. "Beautiful and deadly. I've never had the chance to examine a person going through the change before. How exciting."

Cassie looked back at the group. "Little help."

Appearing next to Tim, ShadowLily looked nervous. "Throw me up there."

"JaKobi, I need you," Tim shouted as he went to stand next to the shimmering shield. "We're going to make a step for Shadow-Lily and try to throw her up to the gap."

Cassie started backing away from the Surgeon as he advanced on her. She did her best to keep the table between herself and the man who wanted to cut her open to see how she worked. "Uh, guys."

Motioning for ShadowLily to go, Tim and JaKobi locked hands, making a cradle for the assassin to place a foot in. She landed in their hands, and both men lifted with everything they had as ShadowLily used their momentum to increase the distance of her jump.

Flying through the air like an acrobat, ShadowLily flipped once to control her motion. It looked like she wasn't going to make it but was high enough that with a few steps, she might be able to grab onto the gap and pull herself in. When her foot hit the barrier, it launched her across the room and into the stadium seating.

Tim was healing her seconds later, as the rest of the group kept their eyes on Cassie.

ShadowLily climbed to her feet. "Let's not try that again."

"Good idea." Tim looked frantically around the room. There had to be a way to bring down the shield. Something this powerful would need a magical power source.

Knowing the woman he loved was alive and well took some of the pressure off, but he needed to find a way to save her best friend. Taking slow deep breaths, Tim tried to keep his eyes off the fight at the center of the room and focus on what he could control. There had to be something he was missing.

Spinning in a slow circle, Tim let his eyes work up and down the rows of seating for anything that wasn't uniform. The stairs were all the same color, and so were the seats. The railings looked to be made out of iron but weren't anything special.

"There has to be something," he muttered, trying not to listen to the sound of the Surgeon's voice as he talked about what was in store for Cassie.

Finally, he saw it, or at least he thought he did—just the barest flicker of light in the top left corner of the room. Tim ran toward Lorelei, never taking his eyes off the spot. He was afraid he'd lose the marker if he looked away.

Tapping the Ranger with one hand, Tim pointed with the other to what he was looking at. "You see it?"

"Fuck me." Lorelei looked at the tiny little square. A second later, her bow thrummed, and an arrow flew across the room.

Tim watched as the arrow flew straight toward the little shimmering square. An explosion of energy erupted from the impact, and the giant shield in the middle of the room wavered. "Look for more of them!"

"On it," Lorelei shouted as she started to circle the perimeter for more of the shield's power sources.

Another burst of energy came from JaKobi's side of the room. "Got one."

Cassie screamed in pain, and all of the group's eyes turned toward the circle. The Surgeon had managed to slash one of the tank's legs, and she was limping. A few moments later, she was disarmed and strapped to the operating table.

"We don't have a lot of time," Tim shouted. As far as he could tell, the power sources were evenly spread around the room. He searched for the one that must be right behind him. His eyes caught a flicker, and he let loose with a blast of divine light.

The Shield in the center of the room wavered but still held strong. Tim pointed across the room to where the last energy source must be hidden. Instead of looking around for it, JaKobi decided to go with the nuclear option and cast fireball after fireball at the corner of the room until something blew up.

The Surgeon used his additional arms like a barrier as he placed his scalpel against Cassie's belly and started to cut. "The wonders of the flesh never cease to amaze me." The wound healed as he cut. "It looks as though I need to dig a little deeper." He plunged the scalpel into the tank's stomach and jerked the blade upwards.

Tim ran forward, casting healing orbs in rapid succession. JaKobi looked on helplessly, having used all of his mana to take out the final power source. ShadowLily sprinted down the stairs, but she would never make it to Cassie in time. He felt the command on his lips for Lorelei to fire when an arrow appeared in one of the Surgeon's eyes.

Turning away from Cassie, the boss looked at his attacker. "How did this happen? The mysteries have not revealed themselves to me yet."

Flames burst from the tip of the arrow lodged inside of the Surgeon's head, and he was consumed from the inside with magical fire. All that was left of him was the scalpel stuck in Cassie's stomach, and his surgical apron lying on the ground.

The heals flowed out of Tim like a river after heavy rain. He plucked the scalpel free when he reached Cassie and started blasting her system with as much power as he could summon. The tank's own body was doing most of the work, but Tim liked to think he was helping.

"Go and get Brother Colton. We'll get Cassie upstairs," Tim shouted at JaKobi. He knew the pyromancer's head was swimming, and giving him a task would keep him focused.

Tim scooped Cassie into his arms, wishing he'd put a few more points in Strength. There was a golden chest resting in the center of the room, but they would have to come back for loot. Right now, all that mattered was getting Cassie upstairs and to the man who could stop her change.

He ran.

Running was his own personal kind of hell. Being trapped alone with only his heavy breathing and thoughts to keep him company wasn't ideal. Tim's legs burned as he ran up the ramp to the exit.

Somewhere along the trip, Tim passed Cassie into Shadow-Lily's arms. By that time, he was so gassed it didn't even bother him that his girlfriend was stronger than him. It wasn't the first time he'd been beaten by a woman, and it wouldn't be the last.

If only it was a burrito eating contest. Bet I'd win then.

Tim laughed at the thought of it. Then he remembered a tiny lady on TV who ate like fifty hotdogs. Now wasn't the time to compare himself to the superwoman who was his girlfriend. It'd be much better for his ego if he just found someone mediocre to compare himself too.

When you set the bar low, you always reach your goals.

Today his goal was to let ShadowLily continue doing the heavy lifting while he tried to keep up. Thankfully, Lorelei was watching their backs. Tim was pretty sure they'd cleared almost the entire tower before finding the secret passage. His arms and legs were trembling too much for him to care.

Dying might actually be a relief.

Whoever invented running was a sadist of the first order. Tim cursed the name of whoever that forgotten asshole was as they burst out of the hidden chamber. Cassie let out a cry of pain. The wound in her stomach was fully healed, so this was something else entirely. A bone in the tank's leg snapped with an audible pop.

The transformation was starting.

ShadowLily looked at Tim. "Just keep healing her. Maybe it will slow the transformation down."

Tim did what he was told and kept healing Cassie as her bones continued to break. They reached the bottom of the stairs as the tank cried out in delirium. The pain must have been excruciating. It was the kind of thing only a monster like Pinhead would enjoy. For Tim, every scream threatened to break the last of his resolve. It was one thing to be in pain yourself but another to see someone you cared about going through it.

Brother Colton strode through the door, Ernie and JaKobi at

his heels. "Get her on the altar." He pointed, and ShadowLily kept running.

"We don't have a lot of time." Brother Colton took Cassie out of ShadowLily's arms and placed her on the altar himself. Prayers tumbled from his lips as he asked the Goddess Eternia to save her.

Cassie's bones stopped breaking almost instantly, but it took another five minutes of prayer before Brother Colton had her stable. He fell to the floor, his body shaking with exhaustion as if he'd fought Vitaria to save the tank's soul.

Tim didn't know what the priest did to save his friend, but he owed him more than a debt of gratitude.

JaKobi looked from Brother Colton to the sleeping form of Cassie on the table. "Is that it, is it over?"

Brother Colton nodded his head, too tired to speak.

JaKobi pulled Cassie into his arms and gave her a kiss. "I'm so happy you're okay."

"Get off me." Cassie came to her senses and shoved the pyromancer away. "I'm not some Disney Princess. And who said you could kiss me anyway?"

"I thought…it's just you kissed me earlier." JaKobi stopped speaking and looked at the ground.

Cassie looked around the room. "It's not true. I didn't kiss him, did I?"

Laughter broke out around the room as Lorelei started making kissing noises. "It was epic."

ShadowLily shoved JaKobi closer to the altar. "You sure did, and you liked it."

Brushing a finger against her lips, Cassie started to smile. "I guess it wasn't that bad."

"Just what every guy wants to hear, you weren't that bad," JaKobi mumbled as he shifted from foot to foot.

"At least I didn't say it was too small." Cassie grinned as the pyromancer tried to back away. Before he could get out of her grasp, she wrapped an arm in his robes and pulled him to her.

"Let's see if I remember this one." She grabbed the mage's head and kissed him like she was Westley returned to Buttercup after becoming the Dread Pirate Roberts.

They broke apart, and JaKobi leaned back. His eyes rolled up in the back of his head. "Now that's the good stuff."

Cassie hopped off the altar. "Don't you forget it." Glancing at the rest of their group, she grinned from ear to ear. "Now tell me, what's a girl gotta do to get some food around here?"

"The kitchen is that way," Brother Colton said with a nervous smile. He was clearly excited that the kissing was going to be moving away from the altar of the goddess. "If you take long enough, I should be able to figure out how to open the doors to the city.

Taking the pyromancer's hand in hers, Cassie tugged him from the room. "Let's eat."

Tim cast a knowing look at ShadowLily, and they both grinned at each other like idiots. All he could think about was the time he jumped on top of his chair at graduation to ask her out. Love always had an origin story, and theirs was pretty epic. He wasn't sure if it held up to saving a person from lycanthropy, but you couldn't do that back in the real.

Holding out his other arm for Lorelei, the three of them started walking behind the new couple. Their guild was going to be great because of the people in it, and the Ranger was one of them. It was his job to make sure Lorelei never felt excluded. She was one of the Blue Dagger Society now and would always be treated like family.

CHAPTER THIRTY-SEVEN

The best thing about a priest's kitchen was the beer.

Tim wondered if Paul had been holding out on him. Not that he would have given up the gold coins for beer, but if the priests in Tristholm had this majestic ale on tap, Paul had to have an even better brew stashed somewhere. Next time he spoke to the high priest, he was going to ask a few very pointed questions.

The first thing he needed to do was find out if they had received any loot from the Surgeon. He scrolled back through his logs and found where the boss died. Tim didn't remember seeing a chest, but bosses didn't go down and leave you nothing; that wasn't how things worked. A few seconds later, he found an entry for ten gold coins.

"Must be because we also had a quest to clear the temple." And the coins they'd found while searching the place.

He could worry about the mysteries of loot after he looked at his skills. It had been awhile and now he wanted to find out how he was progressing before doing anything else.

It was easy to forget about what they'd been through on their journey when everyone was healthy, and the ale flowed like a waterfall. With everyone relaxing, Tim decided it was a good time to check on his alerts and find out which of his skills had updated.

Skill Increased: Armor of Eternia

Rank: Novice rank six

The members of your party sure do like getting hit. Tell them to keep getting smacked around if you want to see bigger increases.

The buff now provides an 8% reduction in damage caused by dark magic, as well as an 8% less chance to succumb to weakness.

Skill Increased: Attacks of the Faithful

Rank: Apprentice rank one

It's amazing how much better your party is at hitting stuff than being hit. Your skill has reached the apprentice ranks and now comes with additional benefits. 60% of normal damage is converted to holy damage, and each attack may now proc Holy Siphon. Holy Siphon has a 5% chance to be applied to a target, adding 10% of the Holy damage dealt as damage over time. The Holy Siphon effect will be applied over five seconds.

Skill Increased: Behold my Power

Rank: Novice rank six

You've managed to use this skill to great effect, but you don't use it enough. Get wild and show more people the true meaning of No Pain, No Gain. Spell now drains 1.5% of your group's health every second for ten seconds before transferring the damage done to your party to the chosen target of the curse. The Debuff provided remains unchanged.

Skill Increased: Cleanse

Rank Apprentice rank seven

When is poison not a poison? When it's a cleanse. Just don't use kale. You've used this skill to great effect, not only for poison but to clear toxins from the body. Cleanse now has an increased chance to proc, and on successful application of the skill, it will also apply a small heal to the target.

Skill Increased: Curse of Giving

Rank Novice rank five

If you want to see bigger increases, you need to use the spell more often. Cast this on anything that moves and keep your group in the fight longer. This spell applies a damage over time effect to the target, and 3% of the damage done is returned to your party as health.

Skill Increased: Dodge

Rank: Apprentice rank one

You've been pretty good about not getting hit, you know, except for that one time you lost your head. You now have a 5% chance of dodging an incoming attack. Because you have reached the apprentice ranks of this skill, any attack you can't dodge has a 5% chance of becoming a glancing blow and reducing the damage of the attack by 10%.

Skill Increased: Divine Light

Rank: Apprentice rank five

Come on, we all know you like dishing out the damage as much as you enjoy healing. Why try to pretend otherwise when you can wreak havoc across the battlefield in a multitude of ways? This spell's damage remains unchanged. Try to reach higher levels for better rewards.

Skill Increased: Healing Orb

Rank: Journeyman rank one

You've reached the journeyman ranks for the first time. Who knew constantly splashing people with water would make you so badass? Your Healing Orb is now 25% percent more effective than the base skill and applies 30% of the original heal as an additional heal overtime bonus. As a journeyman in this skill, it will also apply a cleanse to the target.

The cleanse will only work to clear the effects of novice level or lower aliments.

Skill Increased: Snare

Rank: Apprentice rank one

Who knew tripping a horde of ravenous werewolves would work so well at leveling this skill? Creatures at a novice level will no longer be able to dodge this skill. All others have to pass a successful check to keep moving. Some boss monsters and higher-level entities will remain unaffected.

Skill Increased: Sneak

Rank: Apprentice rank four

Your legendary ability to hide in the shadows has progressed a small amount. Now you might even stay hidden if someone sees you, but I wouldn't press your luck. Shadows cling to you like a second skin, giving you a 13% chance to avoid detection when someone is actively looking for you. Stay safe and stay out of sight for better results.

Skill Increased: Way of the River

Rank: Novice rank nine

It's easy to make great strides at lower levels. Continue using this skill to increase its effectiveness in combat.

Skill Increased: Way of the Boulder

Rank Novice rank nine

Why are you making me repeat myself? If you want to be a Grandmaster, you're going to have to kill more stuff.

Skill Increased: Weaken Undead

Rank: Apprentice rank five

Sometimes you need to soften a target up before you take it down. Using this skill in combination with other damage-dealing abilities is key to its success. You seem to have grasped the concept, but you don't use it every time. If you want to see journeyman in this skill, you are going to have to up your game.

Skill Increased: Who Needs a Shield

Rank: Novice rank five

This is a pretty awesome skill, and you don't use it nearly as often as you should, which seems to be a theme with you. As a healer, you'd think less damage to your group would be a good

thing. Oh, well, live and learn, unless of course you get hit really hard and have to see your caseworker again.

After he finished, Tim sat back for a moment, thinking about some of the snarky comments. Sure, most of his skills had increased, and he wasn't mad at the game for gently nudging him in the right direction. No one liked having their play interrupted with all kinds of popups. It ruined the immersion factor. He didn't check on his skills as often as he should, and when he did, it was always entertaining.

Not to mention he was a journeyman now.

It felt pretty good to level his first skill out of the apprentice ranks, but Tim knew things would only get harder from here. To become a Grandmaster was going to take a ton of effort. He was pleased his new skills seemed to level faster, now that they were taking on harder enemies.

He wondered if the game had a catch-up mechanic. Fighting level fifteen monsters with novice ranked skills would be almost impossible. It made sense not to leave the players twisting in the wind. No one wanted to log into a game and have to work at it like it was their job.

Although in this case, it was his job.

He wondered if any of the streamers in the real world woke up sometimes and said, fuck, I've got to play this same game for eight hours today. It always looked glamorous from the outside, seeing someone playing games for a living, but not nearly as exciting when you saw how much work they put in behind the scenes.

Thankfully for Tim, he got to wake up and play every day with what felt like his best friends. Playing with other people kept things fresh. If one person was having a bad day, the others could lift them up. Having partners in this industry was the key to success. The Blue Dagger Society was slowly growing, and it wouldn't be much longer before they would need to recruit a second group to join them. When the game started offering raids, they were going to have to have more people on their team to be successful.

The others must have been looking at their updates because Tim was the only one who noticed when Brother Colton walked back into the room.

The priest cleared his throat to get their attention. "I'm going to need a little help to get the defenses back up. From the scratching noises outside, sooner would be better."

Tim made sure he turned his notifications off before responding, "Tell me what we have to do."

"I need all of you back at the altar. The system needs a jump-start of sorts." The priest looked at the open keg of beer and licked his lips. "Maybe after."

Cassie finished off her beer. "We aren't going to have to pray or anything, right?"

"If prayer was all we needed, I wouldn't have disturbed you." Brother Colton looked at the tank, his expression saying he thought she should be a little more grateful Eternia saved her from becoming a monster.

Before Cassie could intervene, the priest continued. "The system runs on energy taken from those who come into the building to pray. Normally, the effect is easy to maintain because the temple is full. With only us in the building, it's going to need a bigger sacrifice."

JaKobi frowned. "Sacrifice isn't a very nice word."

Ernie shoved Brother Colton aside. "What the big idiot is trying to say is, it's going to suck on your mana like it's going out of style. Now get in there and get this done, so I can honor my debt to Seraphina."

Noticing the stress his friend was under, Tim motioned for everyone to get up. "Let's get this over with. Last thing any of us wants are the werewolves breaching the perimeter."

Brother Colton led the party back to the altar. "All we have to do is place our hands on the altar, and Eternia will do the rest."

One by one, the group stepped up to the altar. Each of them placed a hand on the clean white stone. Tim looked at the priest. "How will we know when it's working?"

A second later, he dropped to his knees as the altar ripped his mana out of his body with relentless hunger. He managed to open his eyes for a moment and saw that all of them were in the same state. He tried to flash ShadowLily a reassuring smile, but it felt more like a nervous tick. The last thing he saw before passing out was a bright white light.

CHAPTER THIRTY-EIGHT

"Why are you all glittery," Tim croaked as he was helped to his feet.

"Just a small amount of feedback from the altar. The effect should fade momentarily." Brother Colton smiled as he moved over to help JaKobi to his feet. "I can't thank you enough for all you've done here. Letting one of our temples fall into Vitaria's hands would have been an unmitigated disaster."

Tim wasn't as concerned with the temple falling into the hands of the dark goddess as he was with the loss of life. A hundred and fifty people had died here today. Not to mention how many people died to the werewolves when they tried to reach the city. This entire place felt like a graveyard.

It was time to change that.

They were lucky to have made it into the city without getting eaten, but the first part of their quest was complete. The city of Tristholm defenses had been restored, along with the temple. Now they had to enter the city proper and deliver Ernie to Seraphina. Tim wasn't sure what to expect but based on the damage to the city they'd already seen, he was sure there would be plenty of quests to complete.

With new opportunities on the horizon, Tim decided it was better to turn in his latest quest right away.

Quest Completed: Don't Stop Believing

You have returned the temple of Tristholm into the goddess' light.

Rewards: Fast Travel access between the temple in Tristholm and the temple in Promethia. Please select an item from the treasury.

A list appeared in front of Tim's eyes with text at the top saying to select one item. It took him a few minutes of scrolling, but eventually he found just the right one. With a thought, he selected Battlesworn Robes of Justice. It took him a few seconds to equip his new robe, and he couldn't believe how cool it was. The black fabric was a drastic departure from the white robe he'd been wearing before.

Still, the robe was trimmed with white. It almost made him look as if he were a witch hunter of old, ready to bring the minions of Satan to justice. The best part might not have even been the look, but the stats.

+4 Intelligence

+6 Wisdom

Special ability: Shadows to light. The Goddess Eternia's light shines eternal and yet manifests itself in different ways. Activating shadows to light changes the robe's color from black to white, and provides a 5% bonus to healing and 5% bonus to mana regeneration for twenty seconds.

A grin broke out on Tim's face, and he hoped everyone else found an item to their liking. By the look on their faces they were still searching through the list. Paul giving them a choice to choose a single item from the temple's coffers seemed incredibly generous. His new robe was awesome, and it would set him apart from the sea of traditional healers.

Just one more thing to boost my stream, and maybe get the rest of the guild their own contracts.

Tim's life had become incredibly less stressful when he'd had his pod fees taken care of. Knowing the extra money he made in-game would go to his parents so they could take care of his brother and sister did a world of good when it came to easing his mind. He didn't know how families could thrive when they didn't know where their next meal was coming from or if they could pay the rent.

He wished there was a way to help everyone.

For now, he'd work on providing great content for NPC Corp, so that it would be a no brainer for Barbara to set his guild up with their own streaming contracts. Tim had spent enough time watching streams and videos about gaming and raids to know it helped to see fights from multiple angles. The people his streams helped entice into the game would have a leg up on the competition if they ever fought any of the same bosses. So far, he hadn't seen any repeats, but the strategies he studied for years as a player of other games had certainly given him an advantage.

Looking at all the smiling faces around the room, Tim knew everyone was pleased with their quest rewards. It also meant it was time to go. He looked at Brother Colton. "Time to open up the gate."

The priest moved away from the altar. "Of course you're right. The sooner we get some parishioners in here, the sooner I can open the gate back to Promethia for reinforcements."

"Wait, the portal runs on people power?" Cassie gawked at the priest. "Isn't that against the rules or something?"

Leading them from the altar room and back toward the temple's gate, Brother Colton answered. "Eternia takes a small tribute of power from each of her worshipers. Nothing like what we just went through moments ago."

Pausing at the gate, Brother Colton turned to face the entire group. "Most people attribute the gift as just a small drop in mana, something easily recovered before they leave the temple. It takes a little more to get the ball rolling."

Tim wondered how powerful the goddess really was. If her temples all across the game provided her a boost in power for each person entering them, then Eternia was stronger than he ever imagined. It also meant to bring down a god, you had to strike at their power sources to even have a chance. Is that what Vitaria was trying to do now? Weaken the goddess before attacking her directly?

Sometimes it was nice being an average Joe.

There was a part of him that wondered how celebrities dealt with being famous. It had to be hard having the world monitor everything you said all the time. Tim knew he said a lot of stupid things, and getting his feet dragged over the coals by social media crusaders would drive him nuts.

Must be why publicists exist.

Someone has to take the heat and manage the profiles. It was no wonder once people started taking pictures of celebrities every waking moment that they dropped out of sight. The amount of pressure that came with something like that must have sucked, but it also had to have some perks. Being rich never hurt anyone.

Unless of course, you fell into the age-old adage *more money, more problems.*

Tim chuckled to himself. He had enough problems without the money. All he wanted to do for the future was to make sure he had enough not to worry about the essentials, and to take care of any emergency expenses.

Everything else was gravy.

A quick ready check showed that everyone was here and focused on the gate.

Brother Colton scowled at the Poison Master as he brought the horse-drawn cart into the temple. "Those horses better not shit on the tiles."

"Then you better get the gate open. Kat here," Ernie pointed at one of his horses. "Can drop a squishy at a moment's notice." The Poison Master was obviously feeling a little salty about being knocked unconscious.

Colton stared at the man for a moment longer before turning to look at the gate. "Please forgive the heathen for his disrespect," he mumbled as he moved toward a latch set to the side of the gate.

There was a loud click when Brother Colton pulled on something hidden inside of the wall. "That should do it." He scurried back from the opening, unsure of what waited for them on the other side.

Tim pointed at Cassie. "Get ready." He gave her a quick wink. "Just in case."

"Safe is better than sorry, especially when you're betting with your life." Cassie pulled her staff free and moved to the front.

It might have been odd, but Tim never got tired of seeing the tiny tank out in front of them. There was something to be said about seeing someone so small in stature ready to take on the world. Cassie had proved time and time again that she was more than up to the task, and her steadfast courage in the face of battle made things infinitely easier for the rest of them.

The gate rattled, and then there were a series of groans before it slowly started moving upward. Tim could make out the iron bars waiting for them on the other side. Maybe Tristholm had its own way of cutting off access to the temple. If they didn't, creating one might have been their first order of business after the Surgeon appeared.

As the iron bars inside of the temple started to rise, the wooden doors to the city also started to open. Tim wasn't sure if the two were linked or if the people on the city side just wanted the option to attack first if they needed to. As the wooden doors continued to open wider, he could see people waiting for them. All of them were armed with bows, and weapons were trained on every member of their group.

Torches flickered in the darkness outside, making it seem like the men and women were moving, but Tim knew they hadn't moved an inch. Cassie had her staff held in front of her like she was ready to charge in some kind of heroic last stand.

Moving forward, Tim placed a hand on Cassie's shoulder. "Dial it back a notch."

Lorelei had her own bow out but kept the nocked arrow pointed at the ground as she moved up to stand beside them. She scanned the group of warriors, looking for a familiar face. The archers parted, and a man strode down the opening. His eyes were alert as he looked for any sign of deception.

"I see Tristholm's greetings haven't improved since the last time I was here," Lorelei said with a smile on her face.

Jon put his sword away and held out an armored hand. "To be fair, you keep showing up in unexpected places."

Lorelei bumped her fist against the warrior's gauntlet. "This time, I brought friends." She motioned to the group behind her. "And one Poison Master as requested."

"Seraphina will be pleased. I only hope she will live long enough to see this through." Jon looked down at the ground and then back up as he tried to keep the tears out of his eyes. "Are any of you healers?"

The hope in his voice almost made Lorelei crack. Instead of risking her voice coming out full of emotion, she just pointed at Tim.

Guess this is what I signed up for as guild leader.

"I'm a healer," Tim said, meeting the warrior's eyes. "I'd be happy to help tend to your wounded."

Jon smiled. "In that case, welcome to Tristholm and thank you for restoring the temple's defenses."

Turning, the warrior motioned for his men to stand down. "I'm Jon, Seraphina's son and commander of the city's defense. We wouldn't have made it through the night without the walls."

Tim looked back at his group before making eye contact with Jon. "I'll do whatever I can to help her. If any of your men have been attacked by the werewolves and need to be cleansed by the goddess, Brother Colton would be happy to help."

"I would?" the priest spluttered.

Tim clapped the startled priest on the back. "Of course you would. The goddess demands sacrifices of us all."

Jon offered the men a sad smile. "She surely does, but never more than we can endure. Right, Brother?"

Colton looked between the men as he realized he wouldn't be getting back to his cozy little annex anytime soon. "That you are. Any men who need to be cleansed of the taint may come to the temple. I'm sure when they are cured, Tim will be more than happy to accelerate their healing." He gave the healer a look that said, "See, I can assign you work too."

Tim did his best not to laugh at the priest. He was a healer. It was what he did. He'd heal every man, woman, and child in this city if they needed it. It was crazy to think about what a difference of a few hours could make. Get to the altar and get cured or be cursed for life. With the temple closed, Jon had basically condemned his soldiers to death. It must have been a relief knowing they should all live if they hurried.

"Does Seraphina need access to the temple first?" If Jon's mother had been bitten, she might already be past the point of no return.

Jon motioned for them to follow him. He stopped by one of his men. "Get anyone who can still be saved from the curse here now. After they have been cleansed, have them wait here for additional healing."

The man nodded and sprinted off to carry out his orders.

Continuing their trek toward the castle, Jon continued. "All of this madness at the temple started when we brought her for healing. The brothers had just started working on her when all hell broke loose. We had to take her with us before they finished, and my fear is that it only bought us a few extra days. Each night she looks worse than the day before."

Jon bowed his head. "I don't know how much longer she has before the goddess calls her home."

"Then why are we walking?" Tim snapped. "Let's go."

The first genuine smile appeared on Jon's face. "I hope you're in better shape then you look." Jon took off running.

Tim shook his head as he started jogging after the man. "Why does it always have to be running? Just once, I'd love for someone to show up with a cart."

"Stop your bellyaching and try to keep up." JaKobi grinned as he sprinted past.

Tim grimaced and pushed himself to go faster. "Next time, I'm going to keep my big fat mouth shut."

"Why start now?" ShadowLily slapped his butt as she passed him.

Laughter made running a bit harder, but it kept his mind off the burning sensation he felt in his legs. At least he didn't have to work out constantly. In this world, how he felt was solely based on his stats. Maybe it was time to invest a few more points into things that would make his everyday life easier, and not just make him the best healer.

Gasping for his next breath, Tim managed to wheeze. "Fuck that."

CHAPTER THIRTY-NINE

Castle was a generous term.

Tim looked at the squat structures and couldn't help but think of the castle in Promethia. That was a castle straight out of a classic fantasy novel, with spires and a moat. The structure in Tristholm reminded him more of a battle fort. The building was assuredly more function than form.

The gate opened at their approach, and Jon led them inside. They moved through the building until the group entered the throne room. On the dais normally reserved for a chair, was a daybed with a single occupant resting on it.

Tim didn't wait to be told what to do as he crossed the room. He cast healing orb. The water splashed against Seraphina, and she groaned in pain as her wounds started to close. Dropping to his knees next to the woman, he cut away the bloody bandages so he could lay his hands directly on her.

With his hands in place, Tim started casting cleanse. He channeled the spell, hoping that any infection from her wounds would be gone before he finished healing her wounds. Greenish pus bubbled out from her ribs, eliciting another cry of pain.

"I need clean cloth." Tim held out his left hand while he kept his right firmly pressed against Seraphina's side.

A bolt of clean white linen was placed in his hands, and Tim used the cloth to wipe away the smelly pus as it came out. When he was satisfied, there wasn't anything left for his cleanse spell to accomplish, he went back to casting healing orb.

The sound of bones snapping back in place brought Jon rushing forward with his sword drawn.

Lorelei grabbed his arm. "Just wait."

"If she turns, we're as good as dead," Jon snarled.

"He won't let that happen." Lorelei held Jon's arm firmly in her grasp. "Trust me."

Seraphina's body arched, and she let out a scream before falling back onto the daybed in a heap. The last of her wounds closed, and Tim stood up, exhausted. He took a step down from the dais and then crashed to the ground. "Guess that was a bit much after the temple."

ShadowLily helped him to his feet. "You know that's why I love you. Not everyone would put someone else's health in front of their own like that."

Falling back in her arms, Tim batted his eyes up at her. "You love me?"

She dropped him like a box of rocks. "Don't let it go to your head."

Rolling to the side so he could climb back to his feet, Tim was beaming ear from ear. He knew what they had was special, and he was deeply in love with the woman in front of him, but they didn't say it much. They were about to reach the point in their relationship where that changed.

Jon's sword slid back into its sheath, and the entire guild turned to look at him. Their eyes lingered there for a split second before moving past him to Seraphina. She rose to her feet, and someone ran out of an alcove to bring her a robe. Before she had time to tie the robe about her waist, she was asking Jon for a battle report.

"We haven't fared as well in your absence as I would have liked." Jon looked down at the ground. "Once the temple's defenses went down, we had several new problems spring up."

Seraphina listened to his report, and then addressed the group of assembled warriors and the Poison Master. "Ernie and I have much to discuss. While we deliberate on the best course of action to save Tristholm from the werewolves, I have several tasks that need to be accomplished. Time is short, so I have assigned one of them to each of you. If you need help, Jon will assign some men to assist you in your endeavors."

Quest Received: Holding the Line

Seraphina has awakened to find Tristholm in a state of chaos. While there are other important tasks in the city, your job will be to heal and support the warriors manning the walls. Heal fifty of the city's defenders.

Accept Quest: <Yes/No>

Tim accepted the quest. Healing was what he did, and he could heal fifty people in a matter of hours if the wounds were light, days if they were severe. It felt good having a task that was one of his favorite things in the game. He wondered if everyone else was as happy with their quests as he was.

Looking around didn't show any upset faces, so their quests must have been fine. "All right, it looks like we've all got jobs to do. Stay safe and meet back in front of the castle when you're done."

All of them nodded, but Lorelei moved to the dais and dropped to one knee. "I have sad tidings to bring you about Camilla."

Seraphina looked down, the sides of her mouth pulling into a frown. "Don't keep me in suspense."

Lorelei held the ruler's gaze. "She's dead."

"It can't be." Seraphina took a step back and fell onto the daybed. "Tell me, how do you know this?"

"Because I killed her." Lorelei lowered her head in a sign of respect. "She found me on my journey to Promethia. When I refused to join her, she tried to force me."

"Lies!" Jon snarled. "My sister would never."

Rising to her feet, Seraphina descended the few steps until she was standing next to her son. "Of course she did, Jon. We know better than most what the change can do to a person, and how the first few years are the hardest to control the wolf inside."

"Vitaria be damned," Jon snarled.

Lifting Lorelei back to her feet, Seraphina searched her eyes for the truth. "A mother should never have to thank someone for murdering two of their children, and yet I find myself indebted to you." She pulled the Ranger into a hug. "You are now a daughter of Tristholm. If you are ever in need, we will do our best to help you."

Jon looked upset but nodded in agreement. "On my honor."

Lorelei pulled Seraphina into another hug. "This isn't what I wanted. Your daughter was an incredible woman."

"So she was, and so shall we celebrate her life." Seraphina looked at herself for the first time. "You have tasks to complete, and I need a bath." Without another word she turned and strode from the room.

Jon reached into a bag on his hip and pulled out five silver pins in the shape of werewolf heads. "These are the symbol of our house. Wherever you go, all you must do is brandish this pin, and no access will be denied you."

Moving toward Tim he clapped him on the shoulder. "I have work on the front lines, but I expect to see you there soon enough."

Tim nodded. "I thought I'd start with the men being taken to the temple and work my way through the city from there."

"As you will." Jon clapped him on the shoulder again in a sign of affection and left the room.

JaKobi looked at Cassie. "I'm not super happy about them dividing us. Something doesn't feel right."

"I'm sure it will be fine." Cassie snorted. "This is your chance to light shit on fire with impunity. Embrace it."

Rings of orange flames danced around his eyes. "I do like fire."

ShadowLily laughed. "Just remember our rules."

"No incinerating things that don't deserve it. I'm not a monster." JaKobi sounded annoyed.

ShadowLily started for the door. "Tell that to the sheep."

"That was one time," The pyromancer called out as he chased her out of the room. "And that cute little fucker had it coming."

Cassie let out a snort. "I got him this magical carving of sheep jumping over a fence, like the old kids' story for going to sleep. The first sheep jumps over fine, and so does the second. The third burst into flames."

Tim tried not to laugh but couldn't stop himself. They walked out of the throne room together. "But seriously, make sure he doesn't kill any more sheep."

Lorelei caught up with them. "Why does he hate sheep so much anyway?"

Cassie stopped walking. "It's not that he hates sheep. It's that his particular blend of magic makes him volatile. That's the thing with fire. It always wants to be used."

"Sounds like a line I'd use at a bar." Lorelei grinned as she started walking again. "No wonder I never find the right girls."

Tim found himself chuckling again. He looked at Cassie. "I want to be used."

"Good luck with that." Cassie left him behind.

Tim followed her out of the room. "Must only work if you're a hot girl."

"I heard that," Cassie shouted back.

"Shit!" Tim closed his mouth, determined not to get himself in any more trouble.

It was time for him to get to work, but he'd be damned if he was running all the way back to the temple.

Running is for suckers.

CHAPTER FORTY

At least the library didn't have sheep.

JaKobi wasn't sure what a library had to do with the war effort. It wasn't as if he could sit down and find some spell that would make everything better in a few hours. Still, his quest was to go to the library and help the Head Librarian with whatever task he needed accomplished.

There wasn't too much to be upset about. Any day surrounded by books was a good day.

Maybe Seraphina knew that while JaKobi might burn a digital sheep into ash to get back at a cursing farmer, he'd never burn a book unless it was an emergency. He actually hadn't been trying to hurt the sheep either, but he lost control of the spell, and he'd never been able to live it down.

It was like ShadowLily thought he was Smaug.

He wasn't even sitting on a pile of treasure. In fact, JaKobi had to pay the farmer for the damage and promise to never come back again just to stay out of the slammer for a day. "Fuck, it wasn't even a real sheep." How did you get in trouble for killing a bunch of ones and zeros? That being said, he made sure not to try out spells when living things that could go up in flames were nearby.

The library was the last place to start throwing around fire magic unless of course, you wanted to burn the building down. JaKobi didn't think Seraphina would take too kindly to him doing that. There had to be another reason for his trip. The only thing he had to do now was step inside and figure out what it was.

Opening the giant wooden doors, JaKobi stared at the interior in wonder. The building had more books than the Mage's College in Promethia. Why were there so many in a city designed for battle? Did people even have time to read?

After closing the door behind himself, JaKobi walked deeper into the library. He made it all of five steps when a man in a tweed sweater and glasses stepped out from behind a large desk.

"Are you the one I've been waiting for?" The Librarian asked.

JaKobi almost snorted. That was a loaded question. "I'm not sure if I'm the one, but Seraphina did ask me to come and speak with the Head Librarian."

"Frank's my name, and books are my game." Frank tittered to himself as he looked JaKobi over. "I'm the Head Librarian, and I've got a little problem I need handled discreetly."

"Discreet is my middle name."

"Excellent." Frank pointed to a small office to the side of the lobby. "Let me tell you what I need to be done."

JaKobi followed Frank into the small office and closed the door behind him. He sat down in a comfortable chair, still unsure of what he was doing here. When the librarian didn't speak, he decided to prod him. "So, you have a problem?"

"A big one. It's about nine feet tall with a streak of white fur down it's back. I lost four librarians to its claws before I got everyone else out and sealed the werewolf inside."

JaKobi let out a low whistle. "You want me to deal with your wolf problem?" He leaned forward. "Tell me, how flammable is the room it's locked in?"

"Under no circumstances will you be damaging my books!" Frank shouted before regaining some measure of composure. "The room in question has wards protecting the stacks, so the only way to harm one of them would be to remove it from the shelf first."

Frank's eyes narrowed. "Is that going to be a problem?"

"Not for me." JaKobi smiled. If Frank said the books were safe, it wasn't his fault if they got damaged.

Let's see ShadowLily poke a hole in that theory.

"Why don't you show me where you've trapped the werewolf so I can get to work?" JaKobi felt the flames calling to him, and he was ready to set them loose upon this world.

Frank stood up and opened the door. "I'm serious, no harm to the books, or it comes out of your pay."

"Me kill werewolf, no hurt books," JaKobi deadpanned. "I think I got it."

Frank moved up the stairs and continued further into the library. "I hope this works out. The last four men she sent weren't up to the task." He stopped in front of a giant wooden door with iron bars over it. "The restricted section."

The Head Librarian hit a switch, and the bars rose into the ceiling. "There is a bell on the other side of the door. Just pull the cord three times, and I'll let you out."

"Wait. You're locking me in?" JaKobi didn't like the sound of that one bit. It made him feel like a werewolf Scooby Snack.

Frank smiled. "I simply can't risk exposure to the rest of the library. You understand, of course. These books are my life."

He didn't understand, and he didn't really care. All JaKobi could think about was the fact there was an honest to goodness werewolf in the other room, and this man was about to lock him inside with it. Something about this didn't feel right. Kind of like when no one came to help the Tiger King when he was getting dragged around the pen. Sure the guy was an asshat, but no one deserved to be eaten alive.

Reaching out, JaKobi grabbed a handful of Frank's sweater. "Just be ready to let me out."

"When the beast has been slaughtered, your freedom will be restored." Frank reached out and grabbed the door handle. "Good luck."

JaKobi stepped inside the room, and the door slammed closed behind him. "Bastard might as well have rung the dinner bell."

This section of the library was almost as big as the one Frank had led him through. The big furry death trap could be waiting for him anywhere. It was times like these JaKobi wished he'd taken Gaston up on his offers of training. A little stealth could go a long way right now.

Fire was flashy, and that's why he liked it.

The flames also got him in trouble on more than one occasion. It was easy to take a little blast and make it bigger by accident. The key to being a pyromancer seemed to be controlling emotions. He'd never been too good at that, but he was starting to learn. If this werewolf pissed him off, that fucker was going to learn what it felt to be rotisseried.

Slowly JaKobi inched forward. He couldn't see anything out of place, but that didn't mean much. "I guess it would have been too easy for there to be a big sign with an arrow saying, werewolf here."

"So he sends me another," a voice called out from the stacks. "Hopefully, you last longer than the previous one. He was rather disappointing. Delicious, but disappointing."

The taunting voice seemed to come at him from all directions. There was no way for him to know where to look. What JaKobi really wanted was to make sure he kept a wall at his back. It the werewolf could only attack from a few different directions, he had a much better chance of living through this encounter.

Keeping the wall on his right, JaKobi started to move deeper into the stacks. If the only way out was by killing the monster, then he was going to do it and quickly. No one should have to ever enter a library thinking two men enter, one man leaves.

That shit only happens in dystopian novels.

Every noise he heard made him jump and spin to look. If he wanted to make it out of this alive, he needed to calm down. Better yet, he needed to get angry. Why shouldn't he be fucking pissed off? They just saved Tristholm's collective ass, and the first thing they did was send him on some menial chore without his group.

Fuck Seraphina, she should be grateful.

Flames rippled down his robes as his anger bloomed. Why was he stuck doing this worthless shit when he should be with Cassie? All he wanted to do was hold her and make sure she was really safe.

And that kiss.

Oh, boy, did he want a repeat of that. Hopefully, Cassie didn't have to be turning into a werewolf for her to want to kiss him. It had seemed like they were getting closer before the smooch happened, so maybe it was just a matter of time.

"Your fear smells delicious." The werewolf's voice echoed from somewhere deeper in the library.

JaKobi stopped walking and watched the area above and in front of him for any signs of movement. He began slowly shuffling forward again, but as he continued deeper into the restricted section, his steps became more confident. What did he have to worry about? He'd slaughtered more werewolves with one spell before they made it to the temple. Killing one monstrous fur baby couldn't be so hard.

Eventually, the stacks opened into a wide room at what must have been the center of the restricted section. Some of the tables had been overturned, and there were streaks of blood on the ground as if bodies had been dragged away.

Fuck. He'd always hated horror games.

It wasn't so much the blood or guts as it was the suspense. A great game always ratcheted up the suspense and then hit you with a scare. When JaKobi played with friends, everything felt right but playing in the dark alone, he'd let off a few more girlish screams than he would like to admit. If there was video, he would have been the next internet sensation.

The way he saw it, there were two options. Wait for the were-wolf to make the first move, and possibly fail to react. Or take the initiative and throw the werewolf off balance. When he really thought about it there wasn't much of a choice.

Striding into the center of the room, JaKobi grinned. "For such a cocky sounding fucker, you're kind of a cunt."

Oh, man. If his mother could hear him now, she'd slap the taste out of his mouth. Maybe it was his penchant for watching British comedies, but they seemed to throw the "C" word out a lot more than they did in America. One thing JaKobi knew for sure is that no one liked to be called a bitch with a capital C.

A roar sounded before he even finished the thought. JaKobi looked up in time to see five hundred pounds of flying fur coming at him. His flame shield slammed into place a second before the werewolf hit. The beast bounced off the shield and growled in fury at the singed spots on its skin. JaKobi's shield winked out of exis-tence, and the werewolf smiled at him.

"Meat for the beast!" The words tumbled from the creature's muzzle like gravel spilling out of the back of a truck.

"If you want to see my meat, you normally gotta buy me a few drinks first," JaKobi laughed as he let the fire inside of him take over.

The werewolf charged toward him again, and this time JaKobi held his ground without the shield. He saw the beast's teeth pull into a smile, and then he cast his favorite spell. The Phoenix launched from his upraised hands just as the werewolf jumped upwards for an easy kill. His spell slammed into the monster, igniting it in flames from head to toe.

Moving to the downed werewolf, JaKobi called on all the power he had. His hands moved in vicious concentric circles almost as if he were trying to conjure a tornado. Flames appeared in his hands, a swirling inferno of white-hot death. He released the spell and watched as it tore through the werewolf, like it was made out of tissue paper. The spell hit a stack at the far end of the room and detonated like a bomb.

"ShadowLily is going to be so pissed." Oddly, JaKobi's grin only got bigger at the thought.

From where he was standing, there was a three-foot-wide swath of destruction. The first thing his spell had hit was the werewolf. Its entire body had been turned to ash, except for one arm down to the elbow, and a foot. Then the spell had ripped through five tables and dented the stack at the end of the room. The magic protecting the books was stronger than he expected, lucky thing for the Head Librarian.

Turning away from the destruction, JaKobi started walking back to the entrance.

The Head Librarian ran into the room. "What in the hell was that?"

"I fixed your werewolf problem. I believe thank you is the proper response."

The man looked as though his head was about to explode. "Thank you, thank you." His words dripped with sarcasm. "Do you know how much this will cost to fix? I doubt someone like you even has enough to pay for it."

JaKobi's eyes had orange rings of fire around them when he responded. "Take it up with Seraphina." He reached out and stuck his hand inside the Head Librarian's robes, plucking the coin purse free. He counted out the two golden coins he'd been promised as a reward, then threw the remainder back at the man.

Turning on his heel, JaKobi strode out of the room. "You're welcome."

Now he could find Cassie and see if she wanted another kiss as badly as he did.

CHAPTER FORTY-ONE

Why do I always have to go into the werewolf infested forest?

Lorelei looked at the trees around her and wondered how long she'd be safe outside of Tristholm's walls. Maybe she was a victim of her own success, but there was always a chance Seraphina had assigned her this suicide mission as payback.

It wasn't fair to blame Lorelei for killing her kids, not when she'd been given a quest for one of them. That didn't mean there wasn't some resentment there though. No one felt worse about killing Camilla than Lorelei. It wasn't every day she found a kindred spirit in this game. Outside of the working girls, she hadn't noticed a lot of options for lesbians.

"Maybe if I got out of the fucking woods for once," Lorelei grumbled to herself as she crawled under a bush and started down the hillside.

The thing with being a Ranger was that it worked better if you were outside. Talking to animals, tracking, and using a bow like a legendary elf warrior all sounded cool on the surface. Covering yourself in werewolf shit and sneaking around wasn't exactly what she'd fantasized about when she signed up.

Her bow did come in handy, and she'd found a group of people to hang out with that were pretty freaking awesome. It wasn't what she had expected, but now that Tammy was gone, Lorelei was actually having fun.

Plus, it felt like these individual quests were building to something, and one rule always held firm in games. The bigger the quest, the larger the reward. This girl felt like it was about time she got something new and shiny.

It was funny how quickly she forgot about the Boots of Swiftness she just received from the quest at the temple. Her new kicks were pretty awesome. They added two points to her Strength and six to her Dexterity. Not to mention a handy once a day special ability that would increase her movement speed by ten percent for one hour.

Lorelei wouldn't have minded if the buff could be used a little more often, but a boost like that at the right time might be what saved her ass. If a rabbit could dodge a wolf, and a seal could dodge a shark, then surely, she could dodge a fucking werewolf with a little help from her boots.

The watchtower at the base of the hill looked deserted, but that didn't mean much when you were dealing with werewolves. Despite their immense size, shadows hid them pretty well. So would the stone walls of the watchtower. Why lighting this one tower was so important she'd never know. Thankfully, it wasn't her job to question why. Her quest was just to get the damn thing lit.

Sliding down the hill on her belly was about as fun as she expected. Her leather vest took the brunt of the damage and didn't make much noise. Lorelei slithered from one clump of bushes to the next like the Grinch worming his way around a Who's living room.

Slide.

Pause.

Wait for death.

Repeat.

This had been Lorelei's life for the last half hour. So far, she hadn't died and had managed to cover about two-thirds of the distance to the Tower. Maybe she was taking this too seriously. If the werewolves killed the guards, why would they stay? It wasn't like the nine-foot-tall killing machines attacked from a distance or needed a tower to sleep in.

Moving like she was being tracked by a spy satellite, Lorelei took her bow from behind her back and nocked an arrow. She could slither down the hill just as fast with her bow out. Looking through the branches only revealed one small problem.

There weren't any other bushes to hide behind.

All of the land between where she was and the tower had been cleared. Not a single tree or bush to hide behind, and at least three hundred feet to reach the tower. Lorelei planned on saving her boots for the return trip, but she might need them now. If she moved fast enough, there was enough time on the buff to get her almost back inside of the city.

Lorelei looked at the tower. One football field's worth of open space in front of her. *How fast did those guys run the forty again?* Shaking off thoughts of time well spent with a past girlfriend, she decided to save the full bonus of her boots for the run back. Once she lit the tower, every werewolf and their brother would be heading in this direction.

Rising into a crouch, Lorelei scanned the field in front of her, hoping to catch a glimpse of one of the monsters. It helped to know where your enemies were when you had to shoot them. Getting up close and personal with a werewolf was a bad idea. One scratch and she had to make it back to the temple on her own, or risk becoming one of them.

The world seemed to slow down as she sprang over the bush and started running.

A howl to her left let her know she'd been spotted. The echoing howl from her right told her the werewolf wasn't alone.

The two of them were boxing her in, forcing her toward the tower.

But why?

There wasn't time to think of anything except making her legs go up and down as fast as possible. She needed to channel her inner Bolt and run so fast it made every other sprinter cry. It was easy for her to put every last ounce of strength she had into her effort when the sound of the werewolves drew closer.

Lorelei rounded the corner of the tower fast enough, she slid on the hard dirt like it was ice. Waiting in front of the tower's only door was a giant werewolf. Did she turn around and try to take out her pursuers or keep running forward and hope for the best?

Sometimes two isn't better than one.

Her bowstring thrummed as she let the first arrow go. There was no stopping her now. She had to find a way inside, or she was going to die. The arrow slammed into the werewolf's leg, and it hit the ground hard. Before the creature could move, Lorelai added another two arrows to its chest.

The large wood and iron door loomed in front of her, but it didn't look open. Seraphina had given her a key, but there wasn't time to use it. Spinning around to face her pursuers, Lorelei nocked two arrows at the same time. These furry bastards weren't going to know what hit them.

A smile spread across her lips as she waited.

It was a big mistake to come around the corner of the building alone. One on one Lorelei knew her bow would always win the day. The bow was named Wolfsbane because it magically added the poison to the tips of all her arrows. One arrow from her would put enough toxin in the furry fuckers to drop them dead. Two or three just made it happen faster.

The lone werewolf charged at her and Lorelei flipped the second arrow to the same side of her bow as the first and let the shot go. The arrows crossed the distance in the blink of an eye, putting two holes in the monster one just above the other. Now there were two human bodies lying in the dirt.

Where was the third one?

There was a noise of some loose dirt falling from above her. Lorelei didn't hesitate. The second she heard the sound, the Ranger threw herself to the ground and rolled. The earth shook as the werewolf crashed into the ground where she'd been standing. *No wonder the guards had died. These fuckers can climb the stone.*

Her back hit the side of the tower. There was nowhere left for her to go. Lying on her back in the dirt Lorelei pulled her bowstring back. *I've got one shot.* The arrow almost seemed to sing as it flew through the air. It was more luck than any talent of her own when the werewolf turned, and the arrow embedded itself in his eye, the tip coming out of the back of the monster's skull.

Before the werewolf's final death throes were over, Lorelei was past it and pulling the key from around her neck. Who knew how many more of them were coming for her? She had to get inside and get the fuck out before they swarmed this place.

"Dying isn't on my fucking agenda." Lorelei slammed the key into the lock and gave it a hard turn.

A series of clicks moved upwards from the lock as some internal mechanism released the door. A howl sounded from the hill she'd just descended. If that was the closest one to her, she didn't have anything to worry about. The door opened, and Lorelei dove inside and slammed the door closed behind her.

It took her a second to find the bolt to close the door in the dark. Why didn't she bring a light? Swearing to herself, she pushed the one bolt she found in place and then started feeling the door for another one. Her eyes started to adjust to the darkness as she slipped the second bolt home.

The door shook like SWAT rolled up and tried to kick it in. The werewolf continued to batter the door, making it rattle in place. Her eyes fully adjusted to the dark, and Lorelei slammed the third bolt in place. The door stopped shaking. She was safe for now.

"That better hold them." The Ranger let out a sigh as she thought about how long she'd stumbled around in the dark just to earn a little night vision.

Lorelei almost laughed when she thought about how dependent they were on electricity. Back in the day, the world stopped at night, unless you were rich enough to afford a lamp or a candle. That was why in the old stories, people were always around a fireplace in a central room. Lighting the entire house was just too damn expensive.

Outside of *The Etheric Coast*, the world never stopped spinning. Having power and internet really made the world a twenty-four hour a day monster. Deals were getting done all across the planet at any time of the day. The wheels of commerce kept churning even if you went to bed.

Sometimes it made Lorelei think of a simpler time. Not that she'd ever seen one, but there was a certain sense of nostalgia for her regardless. It seemed odd to her there was a time when one member of a household could work, and it generated enough income for them to own a house, a car, and have a couple of kids.

Today, if both parents weren't working, you'd be lucky to get out of an apartment.

Not that she'd hated apartment life back in the day. Some of her best friends were people she'd met while living in her tiny box, and Lorelei had a penchant for finding hot single women as neighbors. There was something to be said about the community feel of a really good apartment complex.

But she'd never give up her house to go back.

Lorelei felt blessed that her career gave her the chance to make enough money to do crazy things like packing up and going on a trip whenever she wanted. It wasn't until recently she started to think about settling down. Maybe if she found a way to stay in one place long enough, it would increase her chances of finding the right woman. She might even find her in the game.

Putting aside thoughts of that new girlfriend shine, Lorelei looked for a torch. Her eyes adjusted so she could see the wall in front of her, but anything outside of a three or four-foot circle was just pure blackness. It was the kind of dark where you would run into the furniture when you went on a late-night bathroom run and couldn't turn on the lights.

Lighting a torch didn't make the tower less creepy. Blood was splattered on the walls, and there were a few naked bodies on the floor. Some of the werewolves had obviously made it inside before the door was closed. What Lorelei didn't see were bodies of any armed men.

If any of the men inside of the tower had been scratched, they would have turned by now. Maybe they had all killed each other already. It felt like wishful thinking to assume she'd make it to the top of the tower without running into something. The worst part was she couldn't carry the torch and use her bow at the same time.

Instead of pulling out her knife, she kept the bow in her left hand. A knife wouldn't do anything but get her killed, but if she saw a werewolf first, she could toss the torch and fire an arrow within seconds.

If Robin Hood could do it, so could she.

The tower didn't look like there was much to it. The bottom floor had several closed off doors and a staircase. Now wasn't the time to go exploring though. She needed to get this done and get the hell out of there. Moving up the stairs, Lorelei skipped past a small landing and kept moving up. Now there wasn't anything but stairs in front of her and darkness behind her.

It might have been a mistake not to clear the rooms below, but she couldn't go back now. Lorelei started running up the stairs, taking them two or three at a time. Her legs were tired after her mad dash to the tower, but they had enough juice to get her to the top.

She rounded the last corner and froze. There was a man in armor lying against the door. The rents in his chest piece let her know he wasn't going to be around much longer. She moved forward slowly so as not to disturb the fallen guard. He might have been dead already, but he could also be in transition.

Lorelei held the torch above her to get a better look.

The guard's hand held the same kind of knife she had in her belt. It was the kukri used by Tristholm's rangers. It looked like the soldier climbed to the top of the tower to light the beacon, and must have run back inside after being attacked. Instead of waiting for the transformation to make him a killer, the ranger had slit his own throat. That was some next-level dedication to the cause.

Lorelei didn't have to think about the choice. She'd rather get wolfie than get dead.

She also wouldn't like being a slave to the dark goddess Vitaria. Getting wolfie was a mixed bag, and one she'd rather avoid. Moving toward the corpse, Lorelei hung her torch in the sconce by the door and dragged the soldier's body out of the way.

"Rest well ranger and know that your sacrifice wasn't in vain." She closed his eyes before standing back up.

Grabbing the torch and using the key around her neck, Lorelei opened the door to the top of the tower. In the center of the open space was a pile of oiled wood in a huge iron fire pit. The wood was piled taller than she stood. Her torch announced her presence to anyone watching, so there wasn't any time to waste.

Lorelei tossed the torch into the pile and then turned and ran for the edge of the roof. She fired a special arrow Seraphina had given her into the stone of the tower. The magical arrow sank into the parapet, and Lorelei flung herself from the tower. Her second arrow arced out into the night and hit the ground somewhere in the distance. A rope magically pulled itself tight, and she was sliding down the world's fastest zip line hanging onto her bow for dear life.

Lorelei let go of her bow and hit the ground. She rolled three times before coming back to her feet. Pulling the arrow free, she grabbed her bow and started running. Three steps later, she activated her boots and disappeared into the trees. The werewolves wouldn't take long to find her scent, but by then she'd be long gone.

Mission accomplished.

CHAPTER FORTY-TWO

Why did assassins always get assigned tasks in the dirtiest, darkest corners of the kingdom?

It wasn't like assassins didn't have other skills that would come in handy. ShadowLily could pick a lock faster than a police officer with a snap gun, tumble like she was Simone Biles, and kill quicker than a marine raider.

At least she could visit beautiful places with the money she made.

No one had ever said, become an adventurer, and you can enjoy the experience of crawling through Eternia's sewers, and yet that was where she found herself. Sewer spelunking wouldn't have been much of a sales pitch for players. Still, she couldn't complain. Being a badass was too much fun. It wasn't every day you got to go from being a normal everyday person to becoming a super-assassin. For ShadowLily, it might as well have been a fairytale come true.

Her boot slipped in a pile of sludge.

Maybe fairytale was overplaying it a bit, but being a killer for hire was something she had always wanted to do. Some people had moral qualms about her chosen profession, but not her. Shadow-Lily wasn't some scum-sucking assassin working for the cartels, cutting people's heads off for shits and gigs.

Those were the type of people she accepted contracts on.

So while killing people might leave her on morally shaky ground, ridding the world of evil made her feel a lot better about it. That was the thing with killing. As long as you were more like Dexter and less like Escobar, there was a good chance you would come out on the right side of things when you died.

It was nice to be the executioner of justice.

Although her particular stance on being an assassin made it harder to find work. Most of the good people in this world weren't out looking to hire someone to kill others. It was just a simple fact. Good people didn't need hitmen. At least they shouldn't.

While the idea of an assassin working to take out the trash was new to a lot of people, it also created business opportunities. ShadowLily did what any young and headstrong entrepreneur would do. She got the word out about her services any way she could. The city guards weren't big fans of the flyers she put up, but with no proof of an actual crime, all they could do was cast menacing glares in her direction.

Thankfully for her clients, they could send her messages the guards couldn't see.

After ShadowLily received a message, she would do a little research on the target and name a price. When the person sent her half of the gold requested, ShadowLily got to work. The person in question wasn't assassinated immediately. First, she had to stalk them and come up with a plan. It normally took a few days of surveillance before she got anything accomplished.

More than once ShadowLily found from watching a target that whoever wanted them removed had lied. Jealous lovers mostly, but sometimes it was business partners, and once or twice a son or daughter looking for an early inheritance. In those situations, she liked to set up a meet and explain the error of their ways. It came with a threat of what would happen to them if the person in question died. Hiring someone to kill an innocent was a no-no in her book, and before they left her former clients understood exactly what she expected of them.

If not, well, payback was a stone-cold bitch.

Today her target was a small group of thugs who had decided wartime was a good time to attack the city's food stores and escape with enough grain to feed an army. In this case, the army needed to defend the city. Seraphina's agents were able to track the grain from the black market to the sewers but could never find the hideout.

That was why ShadowLily was stuck in the sewers instead of spending time with her man. After their near-death experience on the way into town, she didn't want to let Tim out of her sight. Sure, he had a few cool damage-dealing abilities now, but on the whole he was a much more effective healer. Someone needed to be there to protect him, but they'd been separated rather easily.

ShadowLily pressed her back against the wall and dropped into stealth. Waiting wasn't exactly her specialty, but Seraphina hadn't provided the final location, so she had to make do with hiding until someone walked by to point her in the right direction. Cleaning the smell off her clothes would be as simple as placing them in her inventory and replacing them, but getting the stench out of her hair and nose was going to take a lot more work.

The burdens of greatness.

A light started bobbing down the tunnel. Someone was walking toward her with a torch, she was sure of it. Her stealth wasn't to a level yet where she could stand in direct light, so she either needed to find a better place to hide or grab the fucker before he could make a noise.

She didn't know if whoever was coming was with the thieves, and she couldn't just kill them for being in the sewer. Once you had a code to live your life by, you didn't violate it. She killed bad people who did bad things, not randos just walking down the street.

Only a psycho would kill random people.

There was a small series of iron shelves above her head. At some point, they had probably stored supplies for repairs. The thieves of the city had long since cleared them away. The metal grating would leave her exposed, but it was better than walking up to the person and saying hey, I'm looking for a hidden underground lair, any advice.

ShadowLily jumped to grab the metal railing and then swung herself up onto the grate. She could see through the latticework of metal and hoped the person coming was so confident they were alone they wouldn't bother looking up.

The flames drew closer, and ShadowLily was forced to close her eyes to ward off the brightness. When she opened them again, the man with the torch was moving past her. He started to whistle a little tune as she climbed down from the grate and followed him.

When it came to killing, she was an equal opportunity employer.

It didn't matter if you were a man or a woman, fat, skinny, short, or tall. If you had been involved in dastardly deeds and she could prove it, you died. Stealing food during a crisis and selling it to the highest bidder on the black market made the list of reprehensible offenses.

Her fingers twitched by the handles of her daggers, and ShadowLily had to remind herself that she couldn't kill him yet. *Hideout first, killing later.* Making sure to stay a good twenty feet behind him, she worked on keeping her footfalls silent. A lot of people thought she just disappeared when she used stealth, but there was more to it than that.

Learning to walk without making noise was the first step.

Not that the slimy surface of the sewer floor made things easy. She was one step away from making a squelching sound that even the whistling idiot in front of her wouldn't miss. The torch stopped bobbing, and the man turned to stare at what appeared to be just part of the wall. Her target looked back in her direction and then satisfied that he was alone, he knocked on the wall like a door.

The first thing ShadowLily did was try to memorize the knock. If all else failed, she could repeat it at the door to gain entrance. For now, she settled on moving as close as she could and remain in full stealth. When the door opened, she would try to sneak inside with him, or fight her way in if she couldn't make it.

"Put that fucking torch out, you twit!" a voice called out from behind the door. "How many times do I have to tell you, no fucking lights?"

"Sorry, boss," the man in the sewer replied. He cast one last glance up and down the tunnel and tossed the torch into the slow-moving pile of sludge that ran down the center of the tunnel. The flames flared briefly and then went out, plunging them in complete darkness.

ShadowLily started moving as soon as the lights went out. As the door opened, she was so close to the man on the walkway that she could have been his shadow. A few steps later, they were inside of a room, and she was looking for somewhere to hide.

There was a small table against the far wall. She started running as one of the men moved to open another door. She didn't see him use a key, so they must not have kept the secondary entrance locked. Light streamed into the small square room just as she slid under the table.

No one could have seen me.

That thought wasn't enough to keep her heart from hammering away in her chest. Keeping her eyes on the two men, she was happy to see that neither of them looked back in her direction. *Overconfidence killed the cat*, Gaston told her. She'd made the mistake of entering a room not knowing what was on the other side. It could have been a disaster.

Thankfully, it sounded like the men on the other side of the door were more interested in drinking away their profits than worrying about the city guard tracking them down. The sound of mugs clinking and not so subtle laughter drifted in from the room. The two men went inside, and then ShadowLily was back in the dark.

Just the way she liked it.

There was no time like the present to accomplish a shitty task her dad used to say. This line usually came right before he made her clean the fryer while he worked on the grease traps on the hood vent of the diner. Cleaning the kitchen wasn't her thing. If she was in the kitchen, it was to cook, and she hoped like hell someone else would do the dishes.

ShadowLily didn't even like cleaning her apartment on campus. She'd pick up shifts at the diner just so she could pay someone to clean the apartment for her. On the occasions she had to handle it herself, she bitched relentlessly about it and ended up turning it into a drinking game. But she always got the job done.

Adulting was hard, killing was easy.

After spending enough time in the basement of the Blue Dagger Inn facing off against Gaston's murder ball, she'd honed her skills when it came to facing unpredictable attacks. The whole point of the master assassin's training regimen was to prepare her for a time when she might have to face multiple opponents in a well-lit environment.

Personally, she thought Gaston was crazy.

ShadowLily planned her jobs down to the last detail and had sworn up and down she'd never find herself in a situation like this. It seemed the master was right, and it was better to be prepared then found wanting. Today was the day her teacher's lessons would pay off.

The daggers felt good in her hands. It was the same feeling a soldier had when he came home after the war. Her knives were like family, and she always felt better when they were together.

There wouldn't be time to plan. The people inside would know she was coming as soon as the door opened. Maybe if she was quick, she could take out the first couple before they could draw their weapons. Guns didn't exist in *The Etheric Coast*, which made her job magnitudes easier than it would have been in the real world. ShadowLily was a hundred percent more like Garrett from *Thief* than John Wick.

Sliding one of her daggers back into the sheath, she turned the knob. Pushing the door open with her shoulder was easier than expected, and a second later she stumbled into the room full of thieves. Instead of trying to catch her footing she rolled, using the momentum to her advantage.

As she came back up to her feet, the first of her throwing knives found a target. She downed two more men before moving out of the way of an overzealous pursuer. As the man dove past her, she slashed his back, cutting him down to the spine.

"He won't be getting up again," she snarked as she spun around to get the lay of the land.

There was only one man left, but this one was different from the others. He had a boiled leather breastplate on, and a sword in his hand. "What do we have here, a mouse in the house?"

"Call me what you want, but you're not walking out of here alive," ShadowLily replied as she circled the man, looking for any weaknesses in his form.

"You may call me the People's Baron." He gave her a small bow and moved his sword into the ready position.

ShadowLily laughed. "Your parents must be so proud. Baron of the sewers, king of the soldier's food."

"So it was that bitch Seraphina that sent you," the Baron raged. "She has enough food for years. It's the people who suffer." His sword came down with enough force to chip the stone floor.

Grinning as the fight began in earnest, ShadowLily couldn't help but give him one last taunt. "All the gold doesn't hurt either."

"No, it doesn't." The Baron took another wild hack at her.

This idiot's sword was probably enough to keep the rabble

down here from attacking him, but for her it felt almost like an insult. It was clear the People's Baron had no real training. If she didn't know any better, ShadowLily would have thought he was a kid playing crime boss, and not someone smart enough to steal all this grain in the first place.

She let another wild swing slide past her and moved forward with the grace of a cheetah. Her dagger came up and slammed into the Baron's stomach just under his breastplate and up into his vital organs. The man gasped as blood bubbled on his lips. ShadowLily kicked him in the chest to get her blade free.

As the People's Baron bled out on the ground, ShadowLily bent down to pick up his sword. "Might be worth something at the market." She placed the sword in her inventory and marked the location of the thief's hideout on her map.

A quick message to Seraphina on where to pick up the grain and her quest was completed. Now she just had to track down Tim and make sure he wasn't getting into any trouble.

Yeah, right.

CHAPTER FORTY-THREE

Sorry you almost turned into a big furry bitch would have been a nice thing to say.

Instead, Seraphina had sent her on a quest. Not that Cassie would grumble too much. Questing was by far the best way to gain experience, and had led her to all the best loot. How Tim continually found these epic quest lines was beyond her. The most she'd managed before joining the Blue Dagger Society was kill twenty monsters and return type quests.

In other games, the kill, return, and repeat quest would have turned her off, but in *The Etheric Coast,* the mundane quests became fun. Mostly because the combat was awesome. It was one thing to be locked behind a keyboard and another to be inside of the game, feeling every hit of her staff against the opponent. It also gave her the incentive to get the fuck out of the way when someone took a swing at her.

That was how she settled on her class choice as an avoidance tank. Technically, Cassie's newest class was called Whirling Dervish. When she hit level twenty, she would have the chance to specialize again into a more DPS oriented class or more tank-y.

For now, Cassie was still a hybrid. She brought significant DPS but could also tank. A few solid hits from a boss level monster could destroy her, though, which made her main goal in life not to get hit very often.

If you could dodge a ball, you could dodge a giant fucking sword.

A smile broke out on her face as she thought about the old man from the movie, throwing knives at people instead of wrenches. What a world we live in where entire movies could be dedicated to taking road trips, playing beer pong, and dodging balls.

Not that she didn't have her fair share of experience dodging balls.

What was with college guys anyway? It was like they only thought of two things, beer and sex. Why even go to school? You could get fucked up and have sex if you worked at the drive-through at McDonalds your entire life. No one ever got a college degree in hit it and quit it.

Although underwater basket weaving was still an option depending on the school.

It surprised her how much work it was to find a decent guy. It wasn't that they were all bad dudes. It was more that she was already looking into the future, while most of the guys she met were just looking forward to Thursday night.

Only suckers scheduled classes on Friday. Three-day weekends were the best part of college.

Unless you picked a super intense major.

Then those three-day weekends were spent trying to figure out how to get all that classwork done, and still make some money for incidentals. It blew her mind that kids used to be able to work in the summer and make enough cash to pay for the next semester's tuition. The only way you'd be able to do that now was if you became a drug mule or a webcam girl.

At least there was one legal choice.

If Cassie was a little bit taller, she probably would have gone the webcam route. Instead, she learned how to mix drinks. People would be surprised how much money you could make as a bartender if you didn't go drinking every night after work. That was one thing she noticed about people who worked in the service industry. They tended to blow their tips on bullshit more often than not.

It also made them some of the best tippers in the business.

Now her business was kicking ass. Which was why Seraphina sent her out to the front lines. Someone had to teach these fuckers how to kick some werewolf ass, and she was just the one to do it. With power restored to the walls, every gate into the city became a weak point in the fortifications of Tristholm's defense. Her job was to plug the hole at the Eastern Gate and help the warriors there gain control of the perimeter.

The sounds of battle called to her and Cassie started jogging. It never paid to be late to your own party. The last thing she wanted to do was walk across the entire city just to miss the fight. What was with developers and making these giant ass cities anyways? All you did in the city was sleep and sell your shit. After that, it was back out into the world to grind.

Unless you were one of the suckers who still had a job.

Although a job being a bartender inside of a game wouldn't be half bad. You could mix drinks during the day and go adventuring before work. Play your cards right, and you could make a nice little living slinging drinks and return to the real with a fat wad of cash. Cassie liked to plan for the future.

Sometimes so much she forgot to enjoy the moment.

It scared her to think of how many people didn't have a backup plan. No savings and a lot of bills meant shit hit the fan quickly if you lost your job. It happened to her father once and almost sent their family into a tailspin. Thankfully he found another job, but it instilled in her a desire to squirrel away every last cent she could.

The hardest part was looking at the account and not spending money on bullshit. She didn't need two hundred dollar glasses, or a fifteen hundred dollar purse, to feel special. Cassie did most of her clothes shopping at Target and supplemented her wardrobe on Amazon when things went on sale. While she might not have the most current fashion, she did have a bright future.

At least she liked to think so.

Now that Tim and ShadowLily had basically made her family, there wasn't a lot left to worry about. All she had to do was be the best tank she could be. If Cassie had problems, she knew they would help her no matter what. That's what family did. The only wrench in the whole situation was JaKobi.

The man infuriated her to no end, but he also made that ice-cold spot in her heart melt just a bit.

Cassie could blame the kiss on her being wolfed out, but in reality, she had wanted to do it for a long time. She wasn't the most easily approachable person in the world, so it never hurt for her to make the first move. Now that she'd kissed him, the proverbial ball was in the pyromancer's court.

The next kiss was on him to initiate.

A man ran past her bleeding from a cut on his head, snapping her back into the moment instantly. Her eyes moved across the soldiers, looking for the weak spot in their defense. The only thing she could see was a hole in the gate. The werewolves were trying hard to make the breach bigger. The ragged hole in the wall was where she needed to be, but she had to find out who was in charge first.

Jon appeared on top of the battlements calling for archers.

Pushing through the press of men, Cassie climbed up the battlements to where Jon was standing. "Where do you need me?"

Jon turned around, and his eyes went right over her. Then he looked down. His eyes widened with surprise as if he'd found a child trying to play soldier in front of him. "We've got this under control, little one. Head home to your mother."

"Seraphina didn't seem to think so jackhole. If she thought you could handle the issue, I wouldn't have had to run down here to save your ass." Cassie glared at the man. "Unless you've got a better idea, I'm going to plug that hole in the gate for you."

"What pray tell is a jackhole?" Jon looked genuinely confused.

"It means you're a big giant asshole, and you wouldn't know how to accept help if it hit you smack dab in the face." She was done with this guy. It was time to get to work.

Jon's cheeks flushed red. "It's your life. Just know I won't be sending anyone to save you."

"Oh, my hero." Cassie pretended to swoon. "This damsel doesn't need saving." She thumped her staff on the stone-hard enough that the step showed a crack. "Just tell me how much time you need to fix the gate."

"I'm starting to like you." Jon's flush at his recent scolding turned into a smile. "If I had more men like you, we wouldn't be losing this fight."

"Maybe it's time to diversify your talent pool." Cassie pointed toward the female archers on the wall. "A few of them might be just the front-line warriors you need. Never underestimate the power of lady balls."

Jon gulped. "Lady balls." He shook his head to clear it. "Five minutes. We need five minutes."

"Don't leave me out there a second longer." Cassie checked the straps on her gear and started running for the edge of the parapet.

When she reached the wall, Cassie sprang over the edge. "Lick my balls, you furry bastards."

The tank landed in the middle of the werewolves attacking the gate. The shockwave created by her skill sent them all crashing to the ground. It was just the advantage the archers needed to plug the monsters full of arrows. The injured werewolves ran back to the forest but were quickly replaced by new healthy monsters.

A small timer started in the upper right-hand corner of her vision. Five minutes before she could go back inside if she could even get back in. Cassie pushed any negative thoughts to the side.

Her only job was to hold the line. Live or die, none of these monsters were getting past her.

There was a rustling along the edge of the forest as the werewolves mustered for a charge. Howls rang out across the tree line, making Cassie think she'd been overly optimistic about her chances for survival. Instead of a pack of werewolves emerging from the trees, a single warrior strode out of the forest.

The werewolf stopped at what must have been just outside of bow range and howled at the moon. Armored plate covered his thighs and shoulders, but it wasn't the armor that drew her attention. It was the massive sword and equally impressive shield. If he hid behind that hunk of armor, she'd never be able to touch him.

Ignoring the shouts from the wall, Cassie walked out to face the monster alone. She didn't care if the archers couldn't hit him. There were only four minutes left on the clock. There wasn't a bone in her body that thought about running away. She was pretty sure she could dance with the devil for five minutes and come away unscathed.

If a fiddle player could do it, so could she.

A roar escaped her lips, and she started to run toward the massive werewolf. The fucker started to laugh. No one laughed at her. That was where she drew the line. Smirk all you want, but if you laughed at this little lady, you were going to regret it. Cassie would make sure of that!

The warrior's shield came up in time to block the swing of her staff. Instead of following the blocked attack, she used the reverse momentum to throw herself into a roll. Cassie felt the air from the sword's passing on her back. The werewolf had the strength to wield the giant sword-like she would use a Nerf bat.

Must be nice to be as strong as the Rock.

"Not nearly as good looking though," she mumbled to herself as her staff smashed into the werewolves back.

Being big wasn't always an advantage. The bigger they were, the slower they moved, and while their longer reach could make up for that, it wasn't a perfect solution. Cassie didn't have to win the fight. All she had to do was keep him entertained for another three minutes.

Her life turned into a series of rolls, dodges, and leaps.

Each one of her hits kept the big ugly focused on her but did almost nothing to the werewolf's health bar. There was no way she'd be killing this guy without a little help. The only way he was going to die was if Cassie could get him back in the range of the archers. Plus, there was the question of what would happen when the timer wore out. Would the werewolves hiding in the forest charge and overrun her?

With time starting to tick down, Cassie knew one thing. Closer to the wall was better than further away.

There was only one minute left on her timer, and the boss was trying to press her. The last thing the giant mongrel wanted to do was lose in front of his people. It made him reckless.

Cassie didn't have to even worry about offense at this point. All she had to do was hit and retreat and let the big ugly come to her. Not having to win made the fight so much easier. No one would be disappointed if she didn't take down a boss level monster on her own. Her friends might even be impressed she lived an entire five minutes without heals.

For Cassie's grand plan to work, she had to make the mangy fucker madder than a dog fresh out of the Pet Cemetery. Cassie moved in close, dancing around the fur-hulk's feet. Each blow of her staff drove him insane. She could see a faint red outline around the boss, which let her know he was enraged.

Cassie's staff came up between the werewolf's legs, and the red glow changed from faint to bright red. She started running.

The timer in her window counted down as she sprinted toward the wall.

Ten, nine, eight.

She could feel the werewolf catching up to her. In a flat out run, her stubby little legs had no chance of winning, but she didn't have to win, she just needed to draw him in so the archers could do the work for her.

Five, four, three.

"Shoot him. Fucking shoot him!" Not the most dignified way to end her battle, but all that mattered was winning.

Arrows started to rain down around her, and Cassie knew the monster must be close. If she turned to look, there was no way she'd make it back to the wall in time so she just pushed herself as fast as she could.

Two, one.

Cassie leaped for the wall, holding her staff up to the men on the battlements. Jon's face appeared, and his hands closed around the staff. With a mighty tug, he pulled her out of the reach of the boss. The wall shook as the monster ran into it at full speed. With Cassie out of the way, the archers quickly finished the job.

Jon clapped her on the back. "Ladyballs indeed."

CHAPTER FORTY-FOUR

Getting a quick quest to heal people was awesome.

Tim was always excited to get a quest for something he was already going to do. It felt like he was just getting bonus experience for doing what he loved. If the soldiers fighting to save Tristholm from darkness needed a few hours of his time, he was more than happy to give it.

Healing was what he did best.

The entrance to the temple didn't look nearly as intimidating from the city side. In fact, it looked downright inviting. That was one thing Tim always thought churches missed out on. Most of them looked like scary places to go. If they made the buildings a little more appealing, more people might step inside.

Not that you needed a building to believe in something.

The Goddess Eternia must have been pleased to see all of the wounded men and the soldiers attending them inside of the temple. If she siphoned a small bit of mana from everyone who walked in the door, today was going to be a banner day for increasing her power. The influx of god juice might be enough to make a difference in the coming fight.

Tim knew for certain they weren't called here just to get the temple and the quick travel location opened up again. So far, every one of his quests had ended with a huge fight of some kind, and he doubted it would stop now. The game wouldn't be very rewarding if the developers just handed out loot for showing up.

He kind of liked the grind.

There was a delicate balance between grind and reward. If they made the rewards too hard to get, most of the people would stop playing, and if they were too easy just as many would quit. Developers had to walk a fine line between enough challenge to keep people interested, and enough of a reward at the end to make them hungry for more. One of the greatest things Tim had seen recently was game developers creating different difficulty levels of content in MMOs.

It was cool that they could introduce a fight to a group of total noobs and hardcore players, and both of them found the experience rewarding. That hadn't always been the case in games, and when you pushed too far in either direction, huge swaths of the player base were lost. It wasn't enough to have cool visuals anymore. The combat had to be lights out, and people who could only play twice a week needed to feel like they got something out of it just as much as the everyday player.

Tim hadn't noticed any difficulty settings in *The Etheric Coast*, but the game seemed to provide just enough challenge. He'd had plenty of brushes with death and even died a couple times. In most MMOs, dying in the first few levels took a certain amount of carelessness to accomplish, but not here. If a player stopped paying attention to a monster with a weapon, they were dead.

And dying fucking hurt.

Until you showed up in the little waiting room. That shit always made him feel like he was in a remake of *Beetlejuice*. You've died, here's what to expect next, and all the hoopla that came with it. At least he wasn't stuck in line behind an entire football team. Having to wait to see his caseworker would have really sucked.

All Tim ever wanted to do after he died was get back into the game.

It was time to put his thoughts on hold and get to work.

Everyone inside of the temple was crowded into the massive center room. Some men were waiting to see the priests, while others looked like they might be too injured to even move. Everything was chaotic, and not what Tim would have expected from military men and women. He'd seen enough movies about basic training to know all it took to get soldiers organized was a little motivation.

Lifting his hands above his head, Tim started clapping to get all eyes on him. "Gentlemen. I'm going to need a little help from you." His eyes moved around the room and noted there were plenty of female soldiers as well. "Same goes for you, ladies."

He pointed to the entrance leading into the temple's courtyard. "I needed everyone waiting to see a priest to remove the lycanthropy curse over there." Then he pointed toward the entrance back to the city. "Anyone who's already been seen by the priests but still needs healing, over here."

A man missing an eye looked up at him. "Who the bloody fuck put you in charge?"

Lowering his eyes to look at the man on the floor, Tim replied. "I did, you codgy old bastard. Since I'm in charge of who gets healed, it might be a good time to start listening up."

"If you're trying to sell me some kind of healing potion, you can fuck right the fuck off," the man grumbled as he got to his feet. "But I'm not willing to risk it." He gave Tim a glare that said, I doubt you've healed a single person in your entire life.

Tim was torn between helping the old guy and making him wait until he was done with everyone else. It was easy to become cynical when you were older and in pain. Seeing the worst of humanity tended to put you in a very skeptical place. Maybe it was time to ease the burden of a man who'd spent his life fighting for others.

Reaching out, Tim placed a hand on the man to stop him from lining up with the others. The old man swatted his hand away and received a splash of water in the face for his troubles. As the swearing and spluttering continued, he got to work healing the rest of the old soldier's injuries.

"I can't do anything for the eye, but I think you'll find the rest of you is doing just fine." Tim slapped the man on the back. "Thank you for your service."

Looking down at his hands and then back to Tim, the older soldier smiled. "I haven't felt this good in years. Randolph is my name, and getting soldiers in line is my game."

Randolph turned away from Tim and started barking orders. People jumped up as he jabbed and coerced them into moving. When someone was too injured to get up on their own, he had others help the wounded to the front of the lines. He had the entire temple sorted in a matter of minutes.

Tim felt like it was more than he could have accomplished in days.

Reaching out, he shook Randolph's hand. "Thank you for the help."

"Don't mention it." He gave Tim a winning smile. "And if you ever learn how to fix an eye, you know where to find me." He shook Tim's hand one more time and headed back into the city.

This was where the grind began.

He attacked the line, quickly healing any relatively small injuries first. After the first thirty minutes, he had everyone not grievously wounded back on their feet and off to help in the war effort. Then Tim moved onto the patients who needed a little more care.

Missing fingers or toes, not a problem. Apparently, at the journeyman level, he could reverse the effects. For a missing foot or a hand, he couldn't regenerate them, but he could make sure the wounds were healed, and the person didn't have an infection. Those cases took him another hour to finish.

Then it was time for him to move onto the people with internal injuries. Working with people's insides took a little more effort. He had to guide the magic once it entered their bodies. He didn't have a ton of experience healing more intricate wounds, but he was getting there quickly.

Four hours later, Tim was swaying on his feet, but all of the soldiers had been tended to.

Hundreds of soldiers had been healed. He should have asked Seraphina to make the quest repeatable so he could have an easy experience farm. Something to think about the next time he was going to help out. Screw the gold. All he wanted was the juicy experience. Once he hit level twenty, his skill set would make him enough gold, he'd never have to worry about money again.

Brother Colton appeared out of nowhere and handed Tim a hunk of crusty bread and a warm bowl of some kind of stew. "You need to eat something."

Tim tried to take another step and almost fell over. "Maybe you're right."

None of his group had returned yet, and that had him a little worried. He was in charge of keeping them safe and didn't enjoy the feeling of not knowing where they were. The soup and bread were bland but did more for his flagging energy levels then he would have expected.

"Do you mind if I take the rest of this with me?" Tim mumbled after slurping down some of the broth.

Brother Colton smiled in response. "Just bring the bowl back when you can." He patted Tim on the back. "Glory to Eternia."

"Thanks again." Tim waved his crusty bread at the priest and started making his way to the front of the city.

There would be more men who needed healing there, and he wanted to get the city's army back up and running before taking a break. The last thing he wanted was to grab some shuteye only to get woken up to the sound of the city falling to Vitaria.

He wondered, why now? Why did the werewolves want

Tristholm so badly? There had to be something pushing them, and the only answer he could come up with was the dark goddess Vitaria. She wanted to take everything from them, and the bitch had to be stopped.

The front lines looked about as bad as Tim thought they would. He started healing the wounded and encouraging those attacked by the werewolves to go to the temple to be cured. His presence seemed to uplift the men on the wall. It still sucked to get hit by an arrow, but it felt a little better knowing there was someone around who could instantly heal you back to full health.

He kept up his efforts until his favorite tank showed up.

Cassie grinned. "This shit is wild, right?"

"Sure, if you like the potential of getting ripped limb from limb hanging over your head." Tim sent a healing orb at a soldier who was falling off the battlements with an arrow sticking out of his leg.

Ignoring Cassie for a moment, he ran toward the man. "This is going to hurt." Tim yanked the arrow out and then healed the soldier.

Glaring at the healer, the man stood up. He tested out his leg, and a smile spread across his lips. "Thanks." He grabbed his fallen bow and ran back up the steps.

Cassie grabbed Tim's robe and turned him around. "Looks like the rest of the crew is here."

ShadowLily grinned as she walked toward them. "Ready to find out what's next?"

"I don't know about you guys, but I could use a bath and good night's rest before going back out there." Lorelei looked at Tim and frowned slightly as she picked a few stray pine needles out of her hair. "You can't seriously tell me none of you are tired."

He was tired, all right. Tired like a dog pulling a sled for a ten-hour trip. "I think you might be onto something."

ShadowLily nudged Tim. "A beer and a room with a bed sounds nice. The fur army will be there in the morning." She gave him a quick smile. "Plus, you know how cranky you get when you don't get enough sleep."

"Cranky." Tim looked appalled. "Name one time I was cranky waking up next to you?"

The woman he loved shrugged. "Maybe it's me who gets cranky in the morning, but a good boyfriend would never tell."

Tim didn't fall for the bait and switched topics immediately. "Let's track down Ernie before we do anything. I want to make sure he's safe and settled in before going to bed."

JaKobi smiled. "I know where he is. Bumped into him on my way out of the library."

"Figures. The pyromancer gets to go read a book while I have to go over the wall and fight a giant with a massive sword."

"Hey, I had to kill a werewolf," JaKobi whined.

Tim slapped him on the back. "You know reading about killing one and actually killing one are two different things, right?"

"Fuck off." JaKobi stomped away.

Cassie started to follow him. "After you then," she called out, earning her a little glare that softened instantly when he saw who it was.

Tim wrapped his arm around ShadowLily's waist. "Let's see what kind of trouble our pet Poison Master is up to."

"If you want to get kinky, I'm going to catch up with them." Lorelei laughed at the looks on their faces and then ran to catch up with Cassie and JaKobi.

Glancing down at his clothes, Tim whispered, "You're not a poison master. No, you're not."

ShadowLily laughed, then grabbed his hand to catch up with the rest of the guild. Their night wasn't over yet.

CHAPTER FORTY-FIVE

Ernie peered into the giant cauldron and sneezed.

"Fucking allergies," the Poison Master grumbled as he added the next ingredient.

There was something about making a giant batch of wolfsbane that made it unstable. A cauldron with enough of the stuff to kill an army of werewolves certainly qualified. One miscalculation and he'd ruin the entire thing. There weren't enough ingredients to start over, so he had to be careful.

It was almost time to add the last ingredient to the mix. He looked over at the assistant Seraphina provided and saw the man was sleeping. If he was the best alchemist Tristholm had to offer, it was no wonder they were in bad shape. He took a clean wooden spoon in his hand and chucked it at the unsuspecting sleeper.

There was a certain sense of satisfaction when the spoon hit his assistant in the chest. The man jerked awake and his chair tipped over, spilling him onto his back. Ernie couldn't stop himself from laughing as the man rolled on his back like a turtle.

"I wasn't sleeping," the assistant cried out as he scrambled to his feet.

Ernie chuckled. "And I didn't throw a spoon at you, Sean. Now, before this batch becomes totally worthless, bring me the last ingredient and be quick about."

Sean looked around the room with no idea where the last ingredient was. The man was so confused, Ernie wished he had another spoon to throw at the kid. Why was it when you needed something done right, you always had to do it yourself?

Climbing down from the little platform above the caldron, Ernie brushed Sean out of the way and grabbed the stabilizer to add to the poison. "See if you can find my spoon."

He moved back up the three steps and leaned out over the bubbling liquid to drop a trash bin's worth of the white powder into the cauldron. The black liquid took on a greenish hue, and Ernie knew he hadn't missed the window to make the perfect batch.

Snapping his fingers a few times for emphasis, Ernie held out his hand for the spoon. When the object didn't appear in his hand right away, he turned around and scowled at the young man.

"Bless Eternia, son, I don't know if you're dumb or just stubborn." Ernie jumped down and grabbed the large wooden spoon, and when he was back in place on the platform, he started stirring the concoction.

All of his attention was focused on the potion in front of him. He had to stir it just right and then reduce the heat almost completely within a few minutes. "Tell me you at least know how to turn off the fire."

Ernie kept stirring until a voice called out from behind him. "Stop!"

Turning, Ernie saw Sean about two feet away from him with his hands extended to push him into the poison he was so carefully brewing. The accident would have ruined the poison, but the death would have been explainable if Sean was the only witness.

He was actually impressed. Ernie didn't think the kid had the stones for murder.

His eyes moved past the would-be assassin and found a smiling group of his friends. "Just in time as usual."

"I see you still make a great first impression," Tim snarked. "What do you want us to do with him?" He glared daggers at the young man who had been about to shove Ernie into the vat of poison.

"Just say the word, and I'll make him disappear." JaKobi pointed a finger at the man, and his robes rippled with blue flames.

Ernie pulled his spoon free from the poison and rapped the man on the forehead with it. His skin hissed and bubbled. "So, it's not that you're dumber than a box of rocks, it's that you're one of them."

Walking past the would-be killer, Ernie placed a hand on JaKobi's shoulder. "Can you put out fires just as easily as you start them?"

"Of course." The pyromancer sounded indignant. "I am the master of flames."

Ernie grinned. "Good, put that out." He pointed to the cauldron. "And get rid of the traitor."

JaKobi looked at ShadowLily for confirmation, and the assassin nodded her head in response. The flames under the cauldron winked out of existence, and the man who tried to kill Ernie went up in flames.

"I probably should have asked him questions first, but it's easier to eliminate the problem." Ernie let out a sigh. "Now I'm going to have to take some of this batch and dilute it so we can test the guards. We can't afford to have any moles close to Seraphina." Ernie wasn't even looking at the group. He was just talking to himself as he thought about the work he had to do.

Smiling as he grumbled his way back to the vat, Ernie couldn't help thinking of how he got his own start, and where he was now. The thing with working on poisons was that you spent most of your time alone. The last thing you wanted was to share your secrets with someone who could use them against you. People tended to think of poisons as slow and methodical killers, but all of his worked instantly to do the deed.

Coming back to the moment, he looked at the group. "What are you doing here anyway?"

"We just came to check on you." Tim moved up the steps and peered over the side of the cauldron. "Good thing we did. I wouldn't have enjoyed explaining to Gaston how you were killed on my watch."

"As if. I knew where he was all along." Ernie's cheeks turned slightly red. "I've got to start getting this into smaller containers and out to the men on the front lines."

Tim turned and started walking for the door. "Good luck with that."

"What if I offered you a quest?" Ernie pleaded.

Why was it when he needed a few extra hands they were so hard to find?

Ernie saw Tim turn, and he thought maybe he had won the lad over to his way of thinking. One look at the remaining members of the group told him the truth of the matter. He was going to have to get more help, and after his last assistant went missing it wouldn't be easy to come by.

Despite the fact he needed the work done, Ernie understood how they felt. It had been a long day for all of them, and he didn't even have to do any fighting. If he could quit right now, he would go grab a beer and hit the sack just like they wanted to do.

Tim smiled as he delivered the bad news. "We're going to pass this time, but I'll send one of the guards back to help you."

"Fat chance of that." Cassie started moving toward the door. "After what happened to his assistant, I'd be surprised if anyone had the balls to come in here."

JaKobi hurried to catch up with her. "Lucky for Ernie, there's no evidence of his assistant's untimely demise. None of the guards will know until he reports it."

"I'd suggest not reporting it until after you get the work done."

Lorelei shrugged. "It's not like doing it sooner would change anything."

Tim grinned as ShadowLily took his arm and started to drag him away. "Don't worry Ernie, we'll be back in the morning. If you haven't found help yet, I'll take that quest."

"Don't come begging to me when you need wolfsbane, you ungrateful ingrates." Ernie scowled for a moment before he winked at the stunned group. He tossed ShadowLily a few vials of the poison. "Just kidding. Thanks for saving my ass."

Laughter erupted from the group. At least if they had to leave, Ernie could send them away with a laugh. For a second there they looked worried, and that gave him enough energy to start dishing out the poison into different containers.

Let them get their rest. If he knew Seraphina, tomorrow was going to be an even longer day for the adventurers.

CHAPTER FORTY-SIX

The throne room was the same as Tim remembered it.

With Seraphina in full armor, the tone of the room was drastically different. This was a woman ready to go to war. Not only to protect her city but to ensure the rest of *The Etheric Coast* didn't fall to evil. She looked like a Viking goddess, ready to enter the halls of Valhalla after killing half an army on her own.

When it came to Seraphina's plans to win, there would be no half measures. If it took sacrificing soldiers to save as many people as possible, she would gladly do it. The look in her eyes also said she would gladly give her own life to protect one of her people. It was a quality he wasn't used to seeing in the political leaders back in the real.

There was a time when people in power viewed their time in the government as a service to the people. It was their job to protect them, and to make sure their subjects flourished. Now it felt like it was more about sticking it to the other guy than any true sense of purpose to make the lives of their constituents better.

Things didn't work that way in *The Etheric Coast.*

Inside the game, you had the chance to be anything you wanted. If you wanted to tend bar and bang hookers all night, that was up to the player. You could also be a farmer, learn to craft, or run an inn or a restaurant. Not everyone had to be an adventurer to succeed. The best part about being here was that the effort put in directly translated to how successful you could be.

Knowing the right people or having the best connections didn't mean a thing. Life inside of *The Coast* was what you wanted it to be. Tim surrounded himself with people he enjoyed spending time with. The fact that all of them were competent and wanted to succeed was even better.

There was something to be said about the feeling of accomplishment he got while playing the game. It was a world where he could still be the first to do something. He would have never been the first stockbroker to make a billion dollars, the first writer to get a movie deal, the first college graduate to lead his family to a better life. Inside of the game everything was new, and he never had any idea what to expect.

That was the joy of being a gamer.

You could enjoy the classics, but there was always something new on the horizon. The visuals changed, but so did the stories. Being a gamer was like being the star of your own action movie. If someone wanted to experience what it felt like to be a Viking, a demon hunter, or a plumber from the Bronx, they could do it.

The real joy was letting your imagination go.

Tim loved games. It was like reading a book where the story came to life. He didn't know a reader on the planet who didn't envision the characters as they enjoyed the book. In games, you didn't have to imagine the characters as much as become one of them. Sometimes saving the world from annihilation was just the thing he needed to take the edge off a bad day.

Looking at Seraphina in her armor, Tim knew the opposite would happen today. He was going to be stressed. The tasks they were assigned were going to feel impossible, but they would find a way to win. The Blue Dagger Society always did.

Tim had the t-shirt to prove it.

Seraphina rose from her chair. "Thank you for coming. Our need for your services is great." She walked down the steps. "The city of Tristholm is the only thing protecting the Capital. We cannot fail in our quest to push back the darkness."

Stopping in front of Tim, she continued. "Tristholm stands on a razor's edge. One push by either side and the battle will be decided."

He quickly dropped to a knee. "Then we will be the tip of the spear, the group that changes the tides of battle in Tristholm's favor."

Kneeling might have been a little much, but Tim had always been a sucker for theatrics. It wasn't enough to say the words, you had to show people you meant them. Words were nothing but air, actions made the world turn. He chose to wake up, to be here, to serve the Goddess Eternia.

And so he would.

Seraphina smiled as she motioned for Tim to stand. "The spear you shall be. Tonight they will come for us, and with your help we have a chance to succeed. Are you ready to fight for the salvation of our city, to carry all of its inhabitants' fates on your shoulders?"

Getting back to his feet, Tim replied, "The Blue Dagger Society will answer Tristholm's call. All of us are willing to risk our lives to do what is right."

The blade of Seraphina's sword rang as she pulled it from the sheath on her hip. She thrust the weapon to the heavens. "Tonight, we are the light standing in the doorway. Our iron shall hold back the darkness. The evil that swarms around this city shall be laid to waste, and we will bask in the goddess' light once again."

"We're going to take evil by the balls and castrate that mother fucker," Cassie growled.

Seraphina laughed. "I like her."

Sheathing her sword, Seraphina moved back up to the chair that served as her throne. "The battle for Tristholm begins."

Quest Received: Defending the City

One of the greatest battles in history involved only three hundred warriors. Today you will be my three hundred. This is a multi-part quest that will lead to the final battle of Tristholm. The fate of the entire city is in your hands; don't let us down.

Rewards: Variable upon success

Accept Quest: <Yes/No>

Tim quickly accepted the quest and shared it with the rest of the group.

A smile lingered on Seraphina's lips as she gave them their first task. "The Eastern gate has been under constant assault since yesterday's incident." She smiled at Cassie. "Go and make sure that it doesn't fall."

Tim nodded. "It will be done."

Seraphina sat down and made a dismissing gesture. "You have your duty, see it through."

JaKobi started for the door. "I swear this game has no sense of scale. It's always do this, or the whole world dies."

Cassie slapped him affectionately on the back of the head. "Don't you like saving the world?"

Smiling, the pyromancer put an arm around her. "I like getting the girl better."

"That was pretty smooth," Lorelei quipped. "Soon you're going to be as bad as him." She pointed at Tim.

Tim's cheeks started to turn red, and he motioned for everyone to hurry the fuck up. The last thing he wanted was Seraphina listening to their witty banter. "For the record, I don't think I'm that bad."

"Little sappy sometimes, but that's why I love you." ShadowLily poked him in the ribs. "Don't change just because these guys can't handle it."

"Handle it? The dude is my mentor." JaKobi grinned.

Cassie's hand moved to whack him again, but she stopped herself. "Guess it could be worse. At least JaKobi is smart enough not to take love advice from Gaston."

"I'm just going to keep my mouth shut. The last girlfriend I had turned into a werewolf and tried to eat me," Lorelei pouted.

ShadowLily wrapped an arm around the Ranger's waist and pulled her close. "I'm sure when we get back to Promethia we'll find you someone a little less ravenous."

"I've always preferred ravishing to ravenous myself." Lorelei snorted at her own joke. "But I like to play things by ear. If you're actively looking for the right one, you're bound to miss opportunities right in front of you."

Tim grinned. "And there's always beer to help take away the pain when you fall flat."

"And friends to lift you up," Cassie chimed in.

JaKobi sent a blast of fire into the air, and glowing embers fell to the ground around them like fireworks. "Let's not forget about eating your feelings. When you don't gain weight, there isn't anything wrong with a little overindulgence."

"I swear if he didn't like girls, he'd try to marry Joe," Lorelei said with a laugh.

JaKobi grinned as he opened the door to the outside. "Might be worth it. That man can cook."

"Fucker." Cassie hit him with an elbow. "You're not marrying anyone but me." Her face turned white as a sheet, and she looked like she was about to have a panic attack. "I didn't mean that."

Pretending his hands were a scale, JaKobi moved them up and down. "Hot girl? Food?" He moved them up and down again, watching Cassie's eyes harden as the food started to rise.

Lorelei slapped his hand down. "Hot girl always wins."

"She gets it." Cassie shot the pyromancer a dirty look. "Try doing what we did last night with your food."

Tim couldn't help himself. "Wasn't there a whole movie franchise that started with a guy fucking a pie?"

They all started to laugh as they walked out into the noonday sun. It felt good to be together, it felt right. When the five of them put their minds to it, nothing could stop them.

Let the evil come. We're ready to hand out an economy-sized can of whoop-ass.

CHAPTER FORTY-SEVEN

They say heroes run toward danger while others run away.

Tim had felt like a hero since he entered the game. His time in *The Etheric Coast* had been spent saving innocent lives and healing people who couldn't afford the temple's services. Now the team was fighting the flow of people running away from the fight. There might be a time when they needed every man, woman, and child to stand and fight, but he was hoping it wouldn't come to that.

I won't let it come to that.

Casting a few healing orbs at the injuries he saw made him feel better about not stopping to help all of them. If he had the time, Tim would have gladly stopped and healed every injury he saw. The choice for him was stop and help a few or try to save them all. He was going to try to save them all.

Right now, they needed to heed Seraphina's warning and get to the Eastern Gate before the enemies took control.

"We don't know what to expect, so be ready for anything," Tim shouted above the fleeing crowds.

"Really helpful advice," Cassie grumbled as she shoved her way through a cluster of villagers who refused to move.

Tim quickened his pace. He wanted the tank to have something besides a villager to take her wrath out on. "Let's take it slow when we get there and get a feel for what we need to do before diving in headfirst."

"If that's a Zula joke, I might head-butt you." Cassie darted between two people to take her place at the front of the group.

He hadn't been trying to make a joke about the game, giving Cassie a headband named after the famous female warrior from the Conan movies. That she was still upset about what the game said when it gave the item to her made him laugh.

Tim quickly turned his laugh into a cough. "No puns intended."

"Whatever. I just want a new headpiece to drop, so I don't have to listen to you idiots snicker about my hard head." Cassie used her bō staff to push someone out of the way.

"But your hard head is why we love you." ShadowLily caught up with her best friend. "You just be you, and we'll be right behind you, kicking ass like always."

Tim smiled warmly. "Of course we will. We've got the best tank in the game. All those groups that passed on you because of your play style are wishing they didn't now."

"I may or may not hit you later." Cassie grinned. "You keep up those sweet words, and your chance of not getting whacked with my staff improves dramatically."

JaKobi pointed at a man on the wall above them. "Anyone else seeing the golden glow around that guy."

"He's lit up like a Christmas tree." Lorelei's eyes moved across the battlements. "I don't see anyone else with a glow."

Tim felt his smile widen. "Nothing says go here and talk to that guy like a little glow. Let's find out if he's in charge."

Cassie cleared a path through the rest of the people, and then the soldiers that followed. The men at arms started moving out of the way quickly after the first few got rapped on their shoulders by the tank's staff. Tim's healing of the wounded as they passed seemed to ease any hard feelings.

There weren't nearly as many wounded here as Tim was expecting. Seraphina had made the situation sound dire, but as far as he could tell the gate was holding, and there were enough soldiers to keep it that way for a long time.

If everything was this battened downed, why were they here?

They climbed up the stairs leading to the rampart and the glowing man. Tim moved to the front of the group. He loved Cassie to death, but he didn't think *why the fuck are you glowing* was the right way to introduce themselves. Something slightly more diplomatic would probably be beneficial.

"Excuse me, sir, Seraphina sent us to help you," Tim said as the man turned to glare at the new arrivals.

The man looked over the group, unsure of what to make of them. "At least you got the sir part right." He held out his hand for Tim to shake. "Captain Sullivan. As you can see, we've got things under control at the moment thanks to our new poison arrows."

Tim peered over the parapet and could see that it was clear up to the tree line. Naked bodies covered the ground between the trees and the wall—men who once fought as werewolves had returned to their normal state in death.

"I doubt Seraphina would have sent us here in error. Tell me, Captain, is there something out there that needs to be dealt with?" Tim looked at Captain Sullivan with a hopeful expression. He didn't want to beat the man over the head, but gently prodding him with Seraphina's name seemed like the right thing to do.

Gritting his teeth for a moment before returning his face to the stoic mask soldiers often wore in battle, Captain Sullivan responded. "There is something." He was too proud to say his men couldn't handle it. "We've been having some issues."

The leader of the Eastern gate had an expression on his face that said what he was about to ask next was more than one man should ever ask of another. "The enemy's commander is something we haven't encountered before, and we can't seem to kill it. If you could bring the commander down, I'm sure my men could mop up the rest of them."

"Don't worry, we'll fix your little problem," Cassie blurted out.

Captain Sullivan looked down at the tank. "Don't think you're the first adventurers to try to take the monster down. Many have fallen on the battlefield, but right now we seem to be at a bit of stalemate. When darkness comes, we might not be able to push back the tide."

Tim placed a hand on Cassie's shoulder hoping it would be enough to keep her quiet for a moment. "We'll do our best to take care of the problem for you."

"I'll have my men open the gate. May the Goddess Eternia protect you." Captain Sullivan made a motion with his hand to someone below. "They are ready when you are."

Tim reached out and shook the man's hand again. "Thank you, Captain."

"Just be ready to let us back in after we kick some major ass." Cassie stared at the Captain, daring him to say something else about how they might die.

Captain Sullivan grinned at her. "If you kill the commander for us, I'll be the first to heap praises upon your name. Just know that we can't risk opening the gate if you try to retreat."

"Retreat…" Cassie growled until ShadowLily pulled her away.

Tim decided it was time for them to leave. He wanted their tank's angst focused on what was waiting for them outside of the walls. "Thanks again, Captain."

Cassie led the way down the stairs and to the gate. She was agitated and ready to dish out some punishment. Her body seemed to be coiled with tension, and Tim wondered if she might be showing a few signs of the after-effects of almost being turned. Thankfully, the chance to kick the shit out of something always put Cassie in a good mood.

"Same plan as usual. Let's see what the boss does and react

accordingly." Tim got four nods in return. "If we take this slow and steady, we've got this."

The group reached the gate, and a nervous-looking bunch of soldiers held a door open for them so they could enter the battle-field. Tim felt like they were stepping into an ancient arena. This would be the first battle they fought with a live audience watching from the wall as they fought.

Tim didn't know how many people watched his stream, but he did know a couple hundred soldiers were about to watch them fight, and it made him a little nervous.

A quick check to make sure his stream was active, and he followed Cassie through the door. "Lorelei and JaKobi, try to stay grouped up. I'll stick with you as much as I can."

"What about us?" ShadowLily looked over at Tim with a devilish smile on her face.

If there was one thing he knew, it was not to fall into that trap. You never give your girlfriend orders, and you never ask her to do something you could do for yourself. "Cassie is going to do her tank thing, and you'll disappear and go stabby-stabby."

"I always love his intricate plans," Cassie quipped.

Tim found it hard to smile as they walked through the field of dead bodies, but the corners of his mouth tugged up just a bit. "Sometimes, the best thing a leader can do is get out of the way and let his people do what they do best."

Cassie looked like she was about to respond but stopped when the tree line at the edge of the forest parted. It wasn't so much like Moses parting the sea, it was more like a giant shoving trees to the side because they wouldn't get out of his way. Tim might have stopped moving forward, but at least he didn't back up. There were people watching. If the Blue Dagger Society was the city's only hope, then they had to be resolute in their actions.

The orc in front of them wasn't your average everyday orc. They'd fought enough of those on the outskirts of Promethia to know what they looked like. Even the orcish leaders their group had faced looked like babies compared to the behemoth in front of them. The boss' title didn't fill him with any confidence. Who in their right mind wanted to face off against a creature named General Smash?

The name Smash was exactly what Tim would expect from a General set to tear down one of the gates to the city. The nine-foot-long club in the boss' hand was a good indication of his intentions. Tim was pretty sure the five of them couldn't lift the weapon together, but Smash carried it in one hand like a baby with his favorite toy.

The orc general didn't have any armor except for a battered helm that looked like it had been beaten onto his head by a team of angry smiths, and a shield so big he could disappear behind it. No wonder the people had been running in fear. If he didn't have a job to do, Tim would have been thinking the same thing.

Time to fucking go.

Cassie standing in front of the group always gave him confidence. If the smallest member of their team was willing to go toe to toe with that thing, then he had to man up. At least all he had to do was stand in the back and make sure no one died. Their tank was the one who had to get close enough to smell the fucker.

"Is Tristholm really so weak that the best they can do is you?" General Smash's mouth pulled into a sneer. "I was hoping for a challenge."

An arrow pinged off his helmet and left a bright scratch across the dull iron surface.

The general let out a roar, and everyone on the walls watching in silence let out a cheer as the fight started. Men and women shouted from behind them, as werewolves howled from the tree line. A smattering of orcish archers came out of the trees, but not close enough to fire on the group. Tim got the feeling this was more of a one on five-fight to take place in the dead zone between both groups of archers.

Lorelei's arrow started the fight, but Cassie was the one

running toward General Smash. Her bō staff cracked against the General's shield as the tank tried to get his attention away from the Ranger. The massive spiked shield moved away from Cassie as a fireball exploded over it.

"There isn't a DPS meter to worry about. Just give me a fucking minute," Cassie snarled as a red aura enveloped her.

The tank's next three attacks came in rapid succession. The first bounced harmlessly off the shield, and her second effort was turned aside by the club. Cassie's third strike managed to sneak around the edge of the shield and hit the General in the leg. A small blade exploded out of the end of Cassie's staff, scoring the first real hit of the fight.

General Smash wasn't impressed. With a nudge of his shield, he forced Cassie to back up. He followed by bringing his club above his head to crush their tank like a watermelon meeting the business end of a sledgehammer.

Tim shouted as he started casting healing orb, "Cassie, look out!"

Their tank danced out of reach of the club with a smile on her face. When the club slammed into the ground, dirt erupted from the impact site and raced toward Cassie. She tried to flip out of the way, but the rolling mass of debris caught her by surprise. She flew back and hit the ground hard.

His next healing orb found her just as she hit the ground, taking most of the sting off of her fall. He quickly cast his buffs, even though it didn't appear that General Smash was harnessing any kind of dark energy.

It always paid to be prepared.

Cassie flipped back to her feet as the General slammed his shield into the ground. It quivered in place, but the boss seemed to have lost all interest in it. Slowly he started to spin his club, extending his reach to an almost impossible length. It wasn't more than a few seconds before the General became a whirling tornado of death.

ShadowLily appeared as she met the business end of his club. The assassin must have been sneaking in for an attack when the spinning started. Tim forgot about everything else and rushed to her side. He had to heal her, but more importantly he needed to get her moving so General Smash didn't finish them off.

Lorelei's arrows flew into the spinning cloud, but there was no indication if the arrows did any damage or not. The boss' health bar looked relatively unchanged, so Tim guessed the nots won the day.

The General just kept spinning.

JaKobi's phoenix didn't seem to have any effect on Smash except to make the whirlwind surrounding him a beautiful orange color.

Cassie was heading back into the fray as Tim stopped at ShadowLily's side. He cast healing orb on her and followed up with casting who needs a shield on the boss. As light returned to the assassin's eyes, Tim thought about what they needed to do next. There was no way the boss could keep spinning forever, and from experience he knew when you stopped spinning in circles, you were dizzy as fuck.

"Spread out and wait for him to stop!" Tim shouted as he pulled ShadowLily back to her feet.

The assassin gave Tim a quick kiss. "I didn't see that coming."

"Just be ready to dish out a little payback." Tim smiled as he cast curse of giving and behold my power.

Each tick of behold my power knocked health off his group, but his other spell was restoring their health. To make sure they didn't run into any issues, Tim cast a quick round of healing orbs on everyone.

General Smash continued to spin across the battlefield, and a roar of rage escaped the orc's mouth. He must have been used to easily winning fights once he started the spin of death, but so far, all of his targets were still alive. Tim counted down the seconds in his mind until behold my power took effect. When the curse finally activated, the damage pulled the boss out of his spin and applied a debuff to him.

"Hit him with everything you've got!" Tim cried out as he cast divine light.

Cassie moved to cut the General off from his shield. It was a smart move, but she needn't have worried about it. The boss was wobbling unsteadily on his feet. Any attempt to make it to the shield would have sent him sprawling.

Falling over now would have been a death sentence.

The first two arrows caught him in the chest while a third slammed into his thigh and spun him away from the group. JaKobi's phoenix hit General Smash in the back and forced him to his knees. Now it was ShadowLily's time to shine. Her daggers slammed into the general's back like pickaxes as she used them to climb his body.

When the assassin's head dropped below his shoulders, her arms crossed in front of his massive neck. A torrent of blood sprayed across the dusty ground as she slit his throat from ear to ear. With a kick to his back, she flipped off the General's corpse, and he hit the ground.

Cassie walked up and slammed her staff into the General's skull, and the iron helmet sounded like a gong as her bō staff bounced off it. "Now, that's what I'd call a hard head."

A trumpet sounded from the walls, and they saw Captain Sullivan waving them back to the city. Tim didn't know what was happening, but the last thing he wanted was to be trapped out here when something went down.

"To the city!" Tim shouted.

He turned away from the group to look at the General one last time. When Tim turned back, he saw the rest of his group was already running away. It took him a moment to come to his senses, and then he was running too.

There were sounds coming from behind him, and they were getting closer. Tim refused to look back. It would only slow him down. He watched as the archers on the wall aimed their bows into the sky and let loose a volley of poisoned arrows.

Please let me be fast enough not to die as a pincushion.

The arrows started raining down around him, and a wild cheer went up from the walls. He didn't stop to look at what had been chasing him until he was safely inside of the city gates. When he finally saw what was on the field, Tim wished he hadn't looked at all.

Dying not a hundred feet from the wall was something out of his nightmares. The giant eyeball with tentacles looked just as scary as he always imagined. It was the kind of thing that had been haunting his dreams since the first time he saw *Big Trouble in Little China*. He didn't know what the creature from his nightmares was doing here, but he did know that he had escaped its clutches for the moment.

He was about to say something to his group when an indicator flashed across his vision.

Quest Updated: Defending The City

The eastern gate has been secured, but our western flank is now under attack. Make your way to the western part of the city and find Captain Thomas.

Deep down, Tim knew this was going to be a long day. The sun began to dip on the horizon as he turned to look at his friends. "Looks like we've got more work to do."

Cassie started trudging forward. "All I'm saying is the loot better be worth it."

ShadowLily laughed. "So, it's not about the journey with you?"

"Fuck no. If I could get the loot and experience just for showing up, I'd be just as happy," Cassie replied pointedly.

Tim caught up with the rest of them. "They have a name for that where I come from."

JaKobi looked at Cassie and back at Tim. "Are you sure you want to tell her?"

"Maybe not. I mean, a warm body is better than losing to the roster boss," Tim replied. "And it's not like Cassie just fills a void on the roster. As much as she pretends to just want loot, I know she really loves kicking ass with us."

"Damn right, I do. I'm just saying new shiny things always make this girl feel special." Cassie pointed at her gear. "And this tank needs a few upgrades."

Lorelei shouted, "I hear that sister! I feel a serious shopping spree is needed when we get back to the big city."

"Did someone say shopping?" ShadowLily chimed in. She turned to Tim. "And I don't want to hear you complain, you loved those leather pants I got."

"Still do." Tim grinned. "Let's get moving. My lady has some tight ass pants she wants to buy!"

With smiles all around, the group started toward the next leg of their quest.

CHAPTER FORTY-EIGHT

The Western Gate wasn't much different from the Eastern gate.

If Tim had to wager a guess, in less troubled times the gates would have been used by residents to enter the city and avoid merchants blockading the main entrance to the city as the guards searched their wares. Now the gates just served as weak points that had to be protected.

Any inhabitants from this side of the city were already gone, so making it to the gate was relatively easy compared to their last trip. Despite the fact that they met no resistance on the way, Tim was heaving from the run. Before they could join another fight, he was going to need a minute.

Healers weren't runners.

It was in a healer's nature to stay put, sometimes to their detriment. The will to save someone in a game should never come at the expense of your own life unless the boss was in the burn phase. Losing a healer normally meant death for the entire party, especially if the game didn't have a resurrection mechanic.

Inside of *The Etheric Coast*, the only time he'd seen someone come back to life was the one time the goddess saved Cassie. Her gift came with a price, a promise he had to honor during his quest to kill Cardinal Jepsom. Things had worked out in the end, but Tim never felt great about making open-ended promises.

When the air in his lungs didn't feel warm and gross anymore, he started walking again. A few deep breaths and he was almost back to normal. Tim felt the sweat on his skin under his robes and wondered just how bad the soldiers of yesteryear would have smelled. When you were marching to war, bathing wasn't a priority, not when you needed the water for drinking and taking care of pack animals.

The thought of a couple thousand unwashed bodies made Tim gag. He liked to shower twice a day, and he made deodorant his best friend after each session. It didn't even matter if he was alone or locked in a marathon gaming session, there was always time for a shower.

Just not today.

Today was the kind of day that was going to be crazy and chaotic. After they secured the Western Gate, Tim was pretty sure they would be directed to the City's main gates to the north. The temple to the south should already be secured as long as Brother Colton called for reinforcements from the high priest.

The afternoon sun hit the horizon as their group walked toward the faint golden glow surrounding Captain Thomas. When they reached the man, he was laying into one of his men about having the courage to stand and fight. The boy looked like he couldn't have been out of high school. There would be plenty of time for him to learn to be courageous.

Tim cleared his throat. "Captain Thomas."

"This better be good." Thomas whirled around to fix his icy glare on the five of them. "What do you want?"

Cassie jumped in before Tim could answer. "Listen dillhole, Seraphina sent us to fix your little problem. So just show us where it is and maybe show just a smidgeon of respect."

"You're lucky I already heard about what you did for Captain Sullivan at the Eastern Gate, or else I'd have you flogged for your tone," Thomas replied.

Cassie got right up in his grill. "Try it! My guess is you couldn't fight your way out of a wet paper bag."

The man behind Captain Thomas snorted and then quickly found somewhere else to be.

Deciding he'd let Cassie have enough fun, Tim stepped forward. "Captain Thomas, just point us in the right direction, and we'll happily get out of your hair."

Thomas looked from Cassie to Tim and back again, clearly torn on what he wanted to do. In the end, his duty to the city of Tristholm won out, and he addressed Tim. "We've got a Succubus problem. Not just a succubus but an incubus, too. Damn things put their voodoo on my men, and they won't even lift a weapon in self-defense. We're getting slaughtered."

This wasn't going to be easy. Fighting two bosses at once was fine in a raid where you could split the groups, but it got a lot harder when you only had the one tank. If Cassie could keep one of them off balance, someone else had to try to tank the other one. At the very least, they would need one of them to get their attention and just run around in circles. Tim's mind was racing as he tried to think of another option, but he couldn't see one.

ShadowLily would have to be their off-tank. She was the only one who could do it.

"Just be ready to let us back in when it's over. Last time they sent a monster to take us out after we killed General Smash." Tim made sure to look the Captain straight in the eyes as he waited for a response.

Captain Thomas smiled. "You take care of our problem, and I'll throw you a fucking parade." When Tim didn't seem satisfied, he continued. "And the door will be open."

Placing a hand on Cassie's shoulder to back her up a step, Tim smiled. "It had better be, or we'll come back and haunt you."

"Damn straight!" Cassie clicked her teeth together.

Their tank was pretty hostile lately. Maybe her getting with JaKobi would be a good thing. Nothing calmed his nerves like a little romp in the bedroom—a distraction and an endorphin rush all in one.

It wasn't too bad in the burning-a-few-extra-calories department either.

Not that calories mattered in *The Etheric Coast*. He could eat as much as he wanted without getting fat. It was too bad that didn't work in the real world, not unless you picked up the unhealthy habit of an after-meal purge. The real kicker in the game would be if someone like Joe found a way to infuse food and drink with buffs. He was going to have to talk to ShadowLily's father about that the next time they saw him. Imagine sitting down for some carrot cake and getting a wisdom plus three buff when you finished.

That would be the shit!

Captain Thomas took their threats as his cue to lead them to the gate. When they arrived, he had his men open the door. For the first time since they'd met, the captain showed some courtesy by extending his hand. "Good luck."

Tim shook Thomas' hand. "I just hope to be of service." He motioned for the rest of his group to step outside before he followed.

The sound of the iron bars closing behind him had a sense of finality about it he didn't like one bit. He wondered if this was how the prisoners in Rome felt as they were marched into the coliseum to be fed to the lions. That must have been one of the most terrifying experiences in history. There weren't any lions waiting for them now.

Only a pair of demons.

There was a time when he thought a succubus was just a sexy woman who seduced men, or maybe a girl trapped in a box. Thanks to playing a ton of video games and doing some late-night reading after a funny brownie he ate at a party, Tim knew the truth. Incubi and succubi were denizens of hell, or whatever was considered hell in *The Etheric Coast*.

That wasn't exactly a ton of information to go on.

In some of the lore, a succubus would corrupt a person slowly. In other stories, they were more similar to sirens leading people to their deaths. The only thing he knew for certain was that they preyed on your desires. How that particular skill would translate in a fight, he didn't know. All of them would have to be careful.

"Just remember, whatever they tell you isn't true." Tim looked at the group. "We came here together as friends, and we will leave the same way."

Cassie snorted. "Seriously. Did you find that shit on the back of a cereal box? What did you think was going to happen? I'm too hard-headed to let some man tell me what to do just because he's hot as fuck. I think I'll be fine."

"So everyone else, keep your wits about you," Tim deadpanned.

"Dick," Cassie said with a smile of her own.

That was how things went with friends. They could bust your balls because at the end of the day, they were doing it out of love. Their tank could call him an asshole all day, and it wouldn't mean a thing. If someone from outside the guild called him an asshole, Cassie would be knocking out their teeth.

Being in a guild was like being family.

Some of his friends in other guilds liked their gamer buddies better than family. If Tim's parents weren't so damn awesome, he probably would have felt the same way. It didn't happen for every-one, but his family was pretty close. The hardest part about joining the game was knowing he couldn't see them on a regular basis. There was no way either of his parents was coming to join him in the game when they had his brother and sister to look after.

So the Blue Dagger Society was his family now.

All Tim wanted to do was make it through this fight and get to the final showdown. It didn't have to be a pretty victory, they just had to live. He quickly cast both his buffs on the group. The Succubi were going to be dark aligned, so having the goddess of light on their side was a must.

A man and a woman with large leathery wings, almost like a dragon's, flew from the trees and landed gracefully on the ground in front of them. They were the most beautiful demons ever created because all he wanted to do was fall to his knees and declare he'd do whatever they wanted.

The only thing keeping Tim from running toward them was the rapiers each of them had. Running into their arms would be embracing death. And his girl had demanded a shopping trip after this. It might have been weird, but he could watch her try on outfits all day. He was dating his very own cosplay model.

"Serena, they've brought us more gifts," the Incubus purred.

Laughter like the sound of falling rain rolled across the empty space. "Desmond, I think you've misunderstood. We are to be gifts to them."

Desmond's smile would have broken the political process during his first speech. "They do look rather scrumptious. It would be a shame not to indulge them."

"Suck on this!" Cassie made a very unladylike gesture toward the twins and started moving, ready to crack their heads open at the first opportunity.

JaKobi started running after her. "Oh, shit, here we go."

Serena launched into the air, while Desmond planted his feet and readied his rapier to battle with Cassie.

Flashing his million-watt smile, Desmond lifted his free hand and made a bring it gesture. "Beauty and anger, my favorite combo."

Cassie's staff whistled as it descended toward the incubus' head. "Foppish and arrogant, my least favorite."

Desmond moved the staff to the side with ease and stepped into Cassie's guard to give her a kiss on the cheek. He danced away before she could react. "Oh, the sweet taste of innocence. How I long to break you."

"Haven't you heard? No means back the fuck off creeper." Cassie ducked low, trying to sweep the incubus' legs out from under him.

He flew into the air and brought his rapier up in an arc. The tip of the blade cut deep into Cassie's chest. The tank screamed as the blade tore through her armor like tissue paper. Blood flowed from the wound as Tim cast healing orb to try to stem the flow.

It had better be enough to keep her going.

Cassie hit the ground hard and wasn't moving. Tim hit her with another heal as Desmond lifted his sword high. Rapiers were made for stabbing, and by the tilt of the blade, he was planning on plunging straight down into her chest to finish her off. The incubus started descending, and an arrow slammed into his chest.

The arrow did enough damage that his downward strike missed Cassie completely. Her eyes snapped open as Tim's third application of healing orb washed over her. Her staff came up between Desmond's legs, and the incubus went to his knees.

Realizing he'd forgotten about the succubus, Tim turned to see JaKobi walking blindly toward her. His eyes had gone blank. The power of Serena's magic was more than he could handle.

ShadowLily lay on the ground, bleeding from a cut on her head.

Fuck, he felt like the worst healer in the world. Tim started running toward the pyromancer while he cast healing orb on the assassin. Things were getting out of control quickly, and he hated that. Healers loved when things went by the book. Stay out of the red on the ground, and the damage was predictable in most games.

Here they didn't know the fights, and Tim had yet to see a bright red indicator telling him to get the fuck out of the way.

A quick glance showed Cassie back on her feet, with Lorelei moving to assist her. With their tank back up and moving, Tim had time to cast one more heal on ShadowLily before he slammed into JaKobi and tackled him to the ground.

Serena let out a scream of rage as her easy kill was denied.

Tim tried to climb back to his feet, but JaKobi grabbed a fist full of his robes and dragged him back down to the ground. The pyromancer's fist rose and fell. Each hit felt devastating, but he couldn't break JaKobi's grip.

Hitting him back didn't occur to him.

His nose broke on the third punch, and the follow-up punch cracked his cheekbone. The entire time JaKobi was screaming incoherent nonsense about how no one would stop him from reaching his love. Tim managed to block the next few hits, but he wasn't going to last much longer unless he was willing to hurt his friend.

The next punch didn't come, and Tim lowered his guard to peer around the pyromancer. He couldn't see much, but JaKobi's eyes started to clear up, so he knew things would get better soon. The mage looked at his bloody hand and then at Tim's shattered face. The realization that he had been pummeling his friend caught up with him, and he sat back in shock.

"Oh, fuck." JaKobi rose to his feet, looking scared. "Heal yourself, damn it."

The words sounded fuzzy in his ears, but Tim managed to move his hands through the motions for healing orb. The ball of healing water flew into the air and came down on his face with a splash. The pain was almost enough to make him blackout, but then the soothing waters went to work.

His face started to knit as JaKobi helped him up. Tim turned to see how ShadowLily was faring, but he needn't have been concerned. The succubus had been so focused on JaKobi that she'd forgotten about the assassin.

Big fucking mistake.

One of her wings lay in the dirt, and there was a deep cut down her other arm. Wounded and off-balance, Serena didn't stand a chance. ShadowLily danced around the rapier with ease before slicing the succubus' hamstrings with her daggers. With the demon down, she moved away to let the pyromancer finish her off.

A phoenix made of holy fire slammed into the demon, and she burst into ashes. It reminded Tim of the old vampire movies when a vampire was scorched by the sun, only this time it was JaKobi doing the scorching. With the succubus down, all of them turned their attention back to Desmond.

The incubus was in bad shape. His wings hung in tatters from the holes Lorelei had shot through them. There was also a giant bruise on the left side of his face from Cassie's staff. Desmond didn't look worried about the outcome. In fact, he looked like a cat Tim used to watch as it played with mice before it bit their heads off. The incubus clearly thought the final outcome was not in doubt.

"My love, why would you wound me so?" Desmond dropped his guard and held his bruised cheek. "I would give anything to be with you. Don't you want to be with me?"

Tim rocked back on his heels as he felt Desmond's power wash over him. Despite the fact he wasn't into men, he felt his feet moving. He tried casting cleanse on himself, and the effects lessened dramatically. He quickly cast the spell on JaKobi and Lorelei. He didn't know if orientation had any effect on the incubus' magic, but he thought it'd be easier to cleanse the people not interested in men.

Cassie turned away from Desmond and locked eyes with ShadowLily. The tank let out a roar and charged across the battlefield, intent on killing her best friend. ShadowLily's daggers shone in the setting sun as she rushed forward to meet the tank's charge.

"Kill that fucker!" Tim shouted as he prepared to cast divine light.

Lorelei's next shot hit the incubus in the throat, and a blast of fire knocked the demon to its knees. Tim's divine light shot a bolt of white light from the tip of his staff, and it ripped the incubus in two.

It seemed that the demons weren't that tough. Unless you fell prey to their magic, then all bets were off. Turning away from the sundered remains, Tim started casting heals on both of his downed group members. The two women rose to their feet, blood dripping from their fresh wounds.

Tears sprang from their eyes as they pulled each other into a hug.

One of the scariest things in life was the thought of someone you loved turning on you. That feeling was only amplified when they did it with a knife. Tim was happy the two women weren't holding any grudges. Their actions hadn't been their own, and neither of them needed to feel guilty.

JaKobi pointed toward the forest. "I hate to break up the love-fest, but I think it's time for us to go."

They ran for the city's gate, with hell on their heels. Tim started to smile. This was almost over. Soon they would face the final battle in the fight for Tristholm. He looked down at his notifications as he stepped through the gate.

Quest Updated: Defend the City

The east and west gates have been secured. Seraphina is asking for you to meet her at the main gate to the city. The final battle is upon us.

CHAPTER FORTY-NINE

Seraphina's silver armor shone brightly in the growing darkness.

The leader of Tristholm was a beacon of light amongst the worried faces around her. Every movement she made, every word spoken, filled the men and women around her with confidence. Following a warrior like her into battle would be easy. Her stoic grace would have stopped even the weakest hearted of soldiers from turning away from their duty.

A smile lit her face as she watched the group of adventurers pushing their way through the press of men at arms. Tim returned the welcome with a grin and a wave. There was nowhere he'd rather be at this moment. He'd never fought in a pitched battle to save a kingdom before.

This was going to be fucking awesome.

"Welcome, Eternia's Chosen. May the goddess' light shine down upon us all." Seraphina beamed, despite the fact some of the soldiers in the back looked nervous. "You've done good work today, but the job isn't over yet. This is our chance to push back the darkness. Tonight, we take the fight to them."

The soldiers around them broke out in a cheer. Tim had no idea what they were saying, but the men thrust their spears up into the air three times. Each time, they shouted the same word, and after the third cheer silence descended.

"I'm looking forward to it." Cassie had the look of a dog on the hunt. "After those incusluts, a real fight is just what I need."

Seraphina tapped Cassie's pauldrons. "Then a fight you shall have." She turned from the tank to look at Tim. "I don't know what is waiting for us out there, but I want you to handle the unexpected. My soldiers and rangers have been training their entire lives to take down werewolves. It's the unexpected we need help with."

Tim held out his hand and waited until Seraphina grasped his wrist in response. "The unexpected is what we handle best." They broke their shake. "The Blue Dagger Society never gives up, and we won't surrender."

Cheers rose up around them as Tim finished, but he heard JaKobi in the background making a funny alien noise. The sound almost made Tim laugh as he thought of the movie it came from. Just because the words might have been embellished from a cheesy science fiction comedy didn't make them any less true.

If he knew one thing about his guild, it was that only death that could stop them.

Seraphina pulled her sword free, and bright white light ran up and down the blade. "Tonight we fight for the very future of *The Etheric Coast*. If we fail in our duty, Vitaria wins. There will be no retreat, no surrender. Tonight the fight ends. Let's make sure we are victorious."

The soldiers repeated their cheer.

"If you wake up surrounded by the goddess' warm embrace, know that we are jealous of you and that we long to join you at the feasting table of Eternia's Golden Halls. There is no greater death than one in the service of the light." Seraphina gave the men a wolfish smile. "But don't go dying just to get out of clean up duty."

Laughter rippled out from the soldiers. All of them knew burying the dead from the battlefield was a grim task. In some societies, it fell on the religious or women to bury the dead, but in Tristholm, the work had always fallen on the soldiers. Those who created the bodies must tend to their needs for the next life.

It was a courtesy not often repaid.

Tim felt good. There was a buzz in the air. Was this how it always felt before soldiers stormed into battle? The only time he'd felt this same level of nervousness and excitement coursing through him was when he made the PVP finals in his favorite MMO. He didn't end up winning, but he learned a lot about himself in the process.

Today's battle wasn't about him. The stakes were so much higher. The fate of Promethia hung in the balance, as did the lives of his friends. He looked around at the Blue Dagger Society and saw the same nervous excitement that must have been etched in his own features. All of them were ready to do their part.

Seraphina gave Tim a quick nod and turned to face the gate. "Onward to glory!"

The large wooden doors swung open, and the iron portcullis started to rise. Torches had been lit along the walls, and Tim could see the burning towers in the distance. He was going to have to ask what they were for at some point, but now wasn't the time.

Flaming arrows fell from the heavens, filling the valley in front of them with enough light to see by. Seraphina moved to the front of the army and led them into the night. Tim and his group stayed clustered behind her, not wanting to interfere with the movements of her men. His guess was the battle would be raging around them, but there would be something for them to focus on.

The tops of the trees at the edge of the forest burst into flames to reveal the legion of werewolves hidden underneath them. Their howls rang together as one. It wouldn't be long before the beasts came for them.

Tim was impressed by the soldiers' training. Leaving the

protection of the walls to face an army of werewolves wasn't something everyone could do, training or not. Every part of him was screaming for them to turn around and do what they could from the walls where it was safer. He knew hiding wasn't an option, and that their place was out there.

ShadowLily pulled him in for a hug. "We've got this."

"And if we don't, I'll stand beside you and go down swinging," Cassie added.

JaKobi's robes burst into flames. "There isn't anything I would rather be doing."

"Says the guy who ran away from a giant gopher." Cassie hit him in the arm.

Lorelei snickered. "That's a story I need to hear."

"No one needs to hear that story. Just watch me kick ass today and know it couldn't possibly be true." JaKobi kept his eyes focused on the distance.

Tim felt better going into this battle not surrounded by friends but surrounded by family. This was where he belonged. On the battlefield fighting against the darkness. If their will remained resolute, they would win.

Flames erupted in the night sky, highlighting a dragon made out of bone. *Maybe I spoke too soon.* The dragon lit the night and let out a massive roar as it circled the battlements. It looked like there was someone riding the dragon's back, but he couldn't be sure from this distance. Thunder clouds started to gather overhead, but it didn't start raining. Instead, streaks of lightning filled the air.

The dragon landed in the field between the two armies, and the voice of the dark goddess Vitaria rang out. "Tonight life as you know it will end. The city of Tristholm is mine, and death is all that awaits you."

Seraphina stood as a lone figure in front of her army. The white flames of her sword made her look every inch of a holy warrior. "Your servant Abigale said the very same thing, and yet here we stand."

A scream of rage filled the night, and the dragon inhaled. Were they all going to be turned to ash before the real battle even started? Seraphina looked undaunted, so Tim kept his shoulders squared. If he was going to die in dragon fire, then so be it. He'd be back soon enough, and next time he'd have a better plan.

The dragon exhaled, and flames rushed toward Seraphina. She held her arms wide as if to embrace death. After the loss of her husband, son, and daughter to the werewolves, maybe she just didn't give a shit anymore.

A foot from Seraphina, the flames hit an invisible barrier and rose into the air. When Tim looked back, the Goddess Eternia was standing in front of Seraphina with a single hand raised. The look on her face said she could keep this up all day. Tim wondered just how powerful a person had to be to turn away the dragon's fire with just their hand.

The flames stopped, and Eternia took a step forward. "Vitaria, this land belongs to me. You have no claim upon it. Return to the deserts from which you came, and all will be forgiven."

"Forgiveness is a sin of the weak." Vitaria spat the words out like a curse. "I plan to take everything from you, sister."

Eternia walked toward the dragon without a weapon in hand. "Then you will have to fight for it, but now is not the time. This land belongs to me, and I banish you from it. Begone foul witch, and let your minions die as they may."

The dragon's wings started flapping, and Vitaria rose into the air. "Be thankful for the rules of this world, sister. They are the only things sparing you from my wrath."

"I'd rather embrace you as a sister than strike you down." Eternia had a sad smile on her face. "Leave now or suffer your fate."

The dragon tried to burn Eternia again. This time she walked through the flames, inching ever closer to the dark goddess. Screaming in fury, Vitaria rose into the night sky and disappeared in the direction of the cave under the mountain.

Eternia turned back to face the army. "May the light protect you all!" She vanished.

Seraphina lifted her sword high into the air. "For the goddess!" She ran forward to meet the werewolf army head-on.

Tim wasn't sure what their part in this would be just yet, only that he'd follow Seraphina's instructions. "Let the soldiers take care of the werewolves unless you can help without being distracted. The boss lady said they could handle it."

"What exactly are we looking for?" Cassie shouted over the sounds of battle.

Tim shook his head in frustration. "I've got no idea, so just keep your eyes peeled."

"There!" Lorelei shouted and pointed a finger for them to follow.

Tim saw what she was looking at. There was a woman riding a werewolf. She was raining down magical attacks on the men around her, trying to create a hole so the wolves could break their line.

Lorelei fired an arrow. The entire group watched the flight of the arrow until it slammed into the werewolf's eye. The beast dropped to the ground, but the woman riding it didn't fall. The witch hovered in the air for a moment and then gently lowered herself to the ground. Arcs of lightning shot out from her fingertips, and the men who tried to attack her fell to the ground writhing in pain.

Cassie started running. "Time to beat an evil bitch!"

Tim followed in Cassie's wake, making sure he healed any of the wounded soldiers he saw as they went to meet the boss. The last thing they needed was for part of the wedge to give in and to be slaughtered from behind.

His mind went to the fact the last time Cassie died it was due to a magical attack. He hoped since then she'd picked up some resistance. He really needed to do a better job of learning his team's strengths and weaknesses. It was going to be hard until they all passed level forty, and their final class changes. Who they were now wasn't who'd they'd be years from now. All he could do was try to keep up with the changes.

Not wanting to worry about an early hit taking Cassie out, Tim cast who needs a shield to reduce the boss' damage. His spell hit just as the two collided. Cassie's bō staff must have been insulated because it didn't drive her to the ground when it connected with the woman's shield.

"Did you really think you could break my shield?" Abigale snorted. "It's going to take a lot more than a wooden stick."

Cassie snarled in rage and started beating her staff against the shield, but Abigale only laughed.

Lorelei fired an arrow, but it burnt to ash before touching the mage. Tim wasn't sure what to do. He dropped into his Way of the River stance, and quickly cast curse of giving. There was no way to know if the curse would even work if she was shielded from attacks.

Abigale cried out in pain as the curse ripped away some of her life force and used it to heal his group. If his curses worked, maybe doing enough damage to her would break her shield so the group could take her down. Without a second thought, Tim cast behold my power.

ShadowLily staggered as the first bit of life was sucked out of her. "Little warning next time." Before she had fully recovered, the assassin was throwing a knife at Abigale.

The blade bounced harmlessly away from the mage's shield, but this time an arc of lightning lashed out as though the shield gave off electric feedback. A huge chunk of ShadowLily's health disappeared, and then Tim's curse took another.

He started casting healing orbs on the group. If Abigale could go on the offensive in her bubble, they might be in trouble. He watched as JaKobi and Lorelei both went down to lightning flashes from the dark mage's shield. Then it dawned on him what was happening. Her shield was reflecting damage, or just doing damage to anyone that hit it.

"Wait for her shield to go down before you attack," Tim shouted as he struggled to keep his wounded teammate's health topped off.

Cassie had no qualms about continuing her attacks. For some reason, her bō staff didn't get the same kind of feedback as the other attacks. Outside of pissing off Abigale and distracting her, the blows didn't seem to accomplish much.

Tim cast curse of giving again as the initial application was about to wear off and waited for the real curse to do serious damage. Abigale cried out when the curse hit her for the second time. Her hands started moving in a motion Tim hadn't seen before, and he knew he was in trouble. Cassie wasn't the only one who might have been lacking magical protection. He was afraid one hit by whatever spell the dark mage was casting would take him on a visit to see Barbara.

He wasn't ready to see another one of her t-shirts just yet.

Tim held his staff out in front of himself as if the wood would stop whatever was coming. If he was going to die again, then he would face it with as much dignity as he could muster and hope his group could finish the bitch off.

Behold my power hit Abigale as she released the spell.

Tim managed to throw himself under Abigale's wayward attack. He looked up from where he was lying in the dirt, coughing as the dust drifted up around him. He saw the dark mage take a brutal hit to the head from Cassie's staff. She tried to stand, but an arrow and a ball of fire blew her off of her feet.

Abigale hit the ground with a thud. She looked up at the sky, cursing herself for being so stupid. She should have just killed them all from the start. The last thing she saw was daggers coming down at her eyes.

ShadowLily pulled her daggers free from Abigale's head and wiped them off on the woman's robe. Her eyes were full of fire as she turned back to the group. "No one fucks with my man and lives."

"That's why I love you," Tim called back as he started topping off everyone's health.

A cheer rose up from the men at arms as the werewolves began fleeing into the night. The battle for Tristholm was over.

They were victorious.

CHAPTER FIFTY

The throne room had a celebration vibe.

It wasn't every day the people of Tristholm sent the dark goddess Vitaria packing and brought down one of her top minions. When Abigale died, her hold over the werewolves had broken. Three days after the battle, the first emissary from the clans showed up to re-pledge their clans' vows of service.

Seraphina could have told them to fuck off. Tristholm's leader had lost so much in the wars with the werewolves that no one would have judged her for it. Instead, she'd embraced the messenger as a friend and sent word back that all would be forgiven, and the old ways would be restored.

Tim was a little shady on the details of their alliance, but it seemed that the werewolf's intentions were pure. At tonight's feast, the heads of the werewolf's clans joined them at the table of honor, next to Seraphina and Jon.

The food was incredible, and the music playing in the background was jolly and fun. He'd never been to a celebration all about him unless you counted his birthday. Not that this was really just about him. It was the Blue Dagger Society as a whole receiving the honor. Tim wouldn't be able to do the things he did without his team, and he'd never forget it.

They were the most important people in his life.

Seraphina stood and held her glass aloft. The entire room fell silent and the musicians stopped playing a moment later. "Tonight, we celebrate a great victory. Vitaria has fled from our lands, and the werewolf clans have rejoined us in our fight against darkness."

She took a sip from her glass before setting it down. "Many of you have only known the werewolves as our hated enemies, and I am to blame for that. In my grief over my husband's death, I dishonored our deal. Every death on both sides of this war is my responsibility."

The heads of the thirteen werewolf clans looked at Seraphina, shaking their heads slowly. It was clear that the men and woman at the table with her clearly thought there was enough blame to go around. Seeing her take the blame for all of them had the added effect of strengthening their new bonds of fealty.

"There are others here today who have done great services for the kingdom and for the city of Tristholm. The Blue Dagger Society has made this night possible, and for that we must honor them."

Seraphina motioned toward the doors, and four men struggled forward with a golden chest held by four-inch-thick iron rods resting on their shoulders. The chest was so heavy the rods sagged as the men struggled to carry it in.

Cassie's eyes lit up like it was Christmas morning.

"Thank you for saving our city." Seraphina smiled warmly at the group and motioned for them to rise and accept their gifts.

Quest Completed: Defending the City.

You have saved the city of Tristholm from the forces of darkness. Not only that, but you helped to reforge the bond between the city and the werewolf clans. Each member of your

party will be given fifty gold coins and an item from the city's treasury.

Experience gain for this quest has been increased.

Tim smiled as he looked at his notifications. He'd gained another two levels. The experience was better than the loot to him. The gold would help him to continue rebuilding the slums in Promethia, and make sure that his future in the game was secure.

"Thank you for the kind words, Seraphina. I hope that you never have need of us again, but if you do, the Blue Dagger Society will answer the call."

The leader of Tristholm nodded her head and motioned for them to claim their prize.

Cassie was the first one out of her seat and in front of the chest. She looked back at the group. A smile appeared on her face as she touched the chest. "Jerkin of Unfathomable Might. It's got a bonus for close quarter combat."

She turned around and bowed to Seraphina. "Thank you for the incredible gift."

Tristholm's leader nodded and motioned for the others to hurry. "There is wine to drink and food to finish."

Lorelei was the next person to step up to the chest. Her face lit up with glee. "Fuck yeah. I got a pin that increases all my skills by one level when using a bow."

JaKobi was almost running as he placed his hand on the chest. "Bag of Bottomless Wonder. Not what I was expecting, but an amazing reward just the same."

The pyromancer turned, and Seraphina held up her hand to stop him. "A small token of affection from our head librarian." She tossed a spell book to him.

"Now that's what I'm talking about." JaKobi was grinning from ear to ear. "Flaming Missiles. It's like magic missiles but made out of pure fire. This is going to be so fucking awesome."

Tim walked up to the chest with ShadowLily. "Ladies first."

Reaching out, the assassin touched her palm to the chest. "Cloak of Shadows. It increases my stealth rating and damage bonus when attacking undetected. In short, it's awesome."

It was finally Tim's turn. He placed his hand on the chest, and nothing happened. He turned to look back at Seraphina, but standing just behind him was the Goddess Eternia. He almost backed up in shock but managed to keep still.

"Your service to the light has been noted adventurer, but your task here has not yet been completed. The passage under the mountain still holds a great evil. We must eliminate the threat and push into the dark goddess' territory so we can defeat her once and for all."

Eternia floated over to him. "Will you take up the mantle of light, and be a defender to those who cannot defend themselves?"

Tim found himself nodding along and forced himself to stop. "If there is an evil that needs to be defeated, you have my word we will do our best to do so."

"Take this gift as an acknowledgment of your sacrifice and know that I am counting on you." Eternia handed Tim a spellbook and vanished.

Quest Received: Clear the Mountain Pass

Evil still resides under the great mountains north and west of the city. The werewolf clans are responsible for killing anything that makes it out of the pass, but the darkness has been allowed to fester for too long. Find the source of evil buried deep below the mountains and rid *The Etheric Coast* of its contamination.

Accept Quest: <Yes/No>

Tim quickly accepted the quest and placed his hand on top of the chest before the guild could bombard him with questions. A necklace appeared in his hand a moment later, and he placed it over his head before turning to all the inquisitive faces.

"Necklace of Holy Light, something to help you see in the

darkness." It also had a nice Intelligence and Wisdom bonus, but he didn't have to rub it in.

There would be time to dive into the spellbook after the feast. For now, he placed the book in his inventory and returned to his spot at the table.

ShadowLily handed him a glass of wine. "The fun never stops."

"And we never want it to," Tim replied as he clinked her glass.

List of Tim's Current Stats and Skills.

"Tim" level thirteen magic user

Primary Stats
Strength: 12
Endurance: 12
Dexterity: 16
Intelligence: 23
Wisdom: 38
Perception: 5
Vitality: 3
Revitalization: 3
Luck: 5

Notable Gear
Simple Dagger of Dexterity +1 (X2)
Staff of Divine Retribution +4 Intelligence +5 Wisdom
Circlet of Wisdom +1
Boots of Swift Regeneration Increase base movement speed and Mana regeneration by 1%

Battlesworn Robes of Justice Intelligence +4 Wisdom +6

Belt of Wisdom +2

Wristband of the Goddess 10% damage reduction to dark based attacks

Gloves of Wisdom +2

Leather Wraps of Divergent Health 10% chance for single target healing spell to jump targets and heal the secondary recipient for 50% of the value.

Ring of Marginal Transcendence Wisdom +2

Necklace of Holy Light

Skills

Healing Orb: Journeyman rank one

Dodge: Apprentice rank one

Flame Burst: Apprentice rank three

Cleanse: Apprentice rank seven

Appeal to the Goddess: Novice rank one

Infiltrator: Novice rank three

Sneak: Apprentice rank four

Small Blades: Apprentice rank six

Throwing Knives: Apprentice rank two

Night Vision: Novice rank five

Back Stab: Novice rank seven

Weaken Undead: Apprentice rank five

Divine Light: Apprentice rank five

Healing Storm: Novice level one

Curse of Giving: Novice rank five

Behold my Power: Novice rank six

Who Needs a Shield: Novice rank five

Stance: Way of the Boulder, Novice rank nine

Stance: Way of the River, Novice rank nine

Buff: Armor of Eternia, Novice rank six

Buff: Armor of the Faithful, Apprentice rank one
Unidentified Spell book

420

Open Quests
Clear The Mountain Pass

CHAPTER FIFTY-ONE

"Something is coming out of the cave," Will said as his face turned white.

Justin peeked over the fallen tree they were hiding behind. "It's another one of those skeletons."

"It's fucking freaky, man." Will checked his gear to see if he had any holy water left. "The dead should stay dead."

Justin stood up. "Don't be such a pussy, bro. We're playing a game. Let's just go kill the fucker."

Holding out a vial of holy water, Will turned it upside down to show his friend it was empty. "Won't be easy."

Justin ducked back down. "Shit, I think it saw me."

Edging his eyes over the tree stump, Will watched as the skeleton changed directions and started shambling toward them. There was something about seeing the animated bones that put him on edge. How did bones just get up and start walking around?

Something about this didn't feel right.

He'd never thought to question it in other games. The skeletons in your everyday MMO weren't any scarier than giant spiders or fighting off hungry crocodiles. In *The Etheric Coast*, that wasn't the case. Going one on one with a giant spider was terrifying, and to a fifteen-foot croc, you were a snack on the way to grabbing an afternoon suntan.

The skeletons were the worst, though.

One touch of their fingers, and it was like ice tore through his veins. Will felt like when a skeleton grabbed him, it was trying to drain his very essence. Luckily for them, holy water made most of the skeletons one-hit wonders, making standing outside this cave an easy experience farm.

"Shit, mine's gone too," Justin said. "Guess we have to do this the old-fashioned way."

"What we need to do is go back to town and find a tank." Will was starting to freak out. "Or some more holy water."

Justin held his coin purse open and turned it upside-down. Five silver coins and three coppers fell out. "I don't have enough for another vial. You?"

Will's reserves were just as low.

"Fuck." One thing about skeletons: the experience was amazing, but they didn't drop shit for loot. Will had a feeling if they wanted to see any real loot from this place, they would have to go deeper into the cave instead of standing outside.

"Fine, we do this the hard way." Will made sure his buckler was tied to his wrist, and then pulled his sword free. "I'll distract the fucker, you knock its head off."

A smile spread across Justin's lips as his hand tightened around the grip of his massive double-bladed axe. "Let's go."

"Easy for you to say, you've got the easy job." Will snapped the retort as he jumped over the fallen log.

As soon as he was visible, the skeleton beelined to Will. He wondered how a monster with no eyes could even see him. Maybe they just felt out the living like bats hunting bugs in the dark. What if skeletons had life sonar? Justin was going to have one hell of a laugh at his new idea as they celebrated today's hunt over beers.

Moving away from the log, Will kept his shield in front of him.

Why he didn't practice more with his buckler was beyond him. He was torn between using his sword like a mythical duelist or having a little extra protection. All he was doing by failing to decide on a single path was hamstringing himself.

Could you still top the DPS charts with a shield on one arm?

The only way he'd find out was if he learned to use the buckler as more than protection. Shields could cause harm or be used to create openings. It was a pretty handy tool if you knew how to use it. What he hated was how everyone saw his shield and thought he was a tank. He wasn't a guy who liked to stand toe to toe with danger.

He didn't want the glory, he just wanted to live.

The skeleton was within ten feet of him. Will started to angle himself so the monster's back would be to the log. The last thing they needed was for the thing to figure out their plan. It might never happen, but it wasn't worth the risk.

So far, the skeletons hadn't shown much intelligence. They shambled toward the next living thing and tried to kill it. They didn't talk or moan. They didn't make any sound as they walked.

In short, they were the perfect silent killer.

His buckler managed to block the thing's hands for a moment, but then the skeleton grabbed the edges of his shield and tried to pull him closer. Will let out a scream that would have made a horror movie actress jealous and tried to loosen the strap of his shield so he could get away. His fingers fumbled with the clasp.

Will was jerked forward with a strength he didn't know the skeleton possessed. Off-balance, cold exploded across his shoulder as a skeletal hand grabbed him. His sword fell out of his grip a second later, and he started sinking to his knees.

Where in the fuck was Justin?

Will looked up into the dark soulless void that made up the skeleton's eyes and started to scream. His scream tapered off as he ran out of air. This was it. He was off to see his caseworker again.

Greg was probably tired of seeing him by now. Who else could have possibly died thirty-seven times already?

Maybe it was time to think of a new line of work.

Justin's axe cut through the skeleton's neck in a single stroke.

The icy embrace of death left his body almost instantly. Will backed away from the pile of bones, afraid they might knit themselves back together. As soon as he felt safe, he glared daggers at his partner in crime. "What in the fuck was that dude!" he raged. "I could have died."

Justin didn't look too worried. The guy kicked the bones with his boot. "That was easier than I thought it'd be."

"Not for me." Will picked up his sword. "Where in the fuck were you, anyway?"

Justin twirled his axe around like a pro golfer after making a putt. "Just wanted to make sure the thing couldn't see me." He grinned. "It totally worked though. I say we go into the cave and see if there is anything worth taking."

"Sure, but you get to go first," Will snapped.

Justin's cheeks turned red in anger. "Me! You're the one with the fucking shield."

Will unstrapped the shield and tossed it at Justin's feet. "Now you have a shield."

"Can't use it with this bad boy." He waved the two-handed axe around. "But if you're too chicken shit to go first, then I will."

Bending over, Will picked up his buckler. "Says the guy who hasn't been hit yet. I think it's about time we see how big your balls really are. So far, it's been all talk."

"Follow me, and don't run off like a little bitch," Justin said as he started moving toward the cavern's entrance. "These things are still easy to kill without the holy water, but we need to keep our wits about us."

Will started to smile. "Then going into the creepy cave of death might not be our best option."

Justin lit a torch and held it in front of himself. "I don't know about you, but five silver isn't going to cover next month's pod fees."

Shit.

Will hated it when Justin was right. While he had next month's POD fee already taken care of, the month after was going to be a problem if they didn't find some quality loot to sell. He wasn't sure if going into the cave would help. Maybe they should head back to Tristholm and take on a bunch of those repeatable quests.

It might be boring as fuck, but it paid the bills.

Screw it. Will tightened the straps of his buckler again and caught up with Justin. "I'm right behind you, buddy."

"Just don't get too close, this weapon has reach." Justin wiggled his axe as a reminder.

The entrance to the cave didn't look like much. It was just a jagged crack in the mountainside. The opening was wide enough for three or four people to walk through it at the same time, and nearly twice as tall as they were. It was big enough something huge could be inside, but so far, they'd only encountered the skeletons.

Justin stepped in the cave and gagged on the smell. Will smiled at his reaction until the smell hit his nostrils. It was a good thing he hadn't eaten in the last twelve hours, or he would have sprayed the cave floor with vomit.

Some brave adventurer he was turning out to be.

Part of him wondered why the cavern would smell so bad if there were only skeletons inside. Bones didn't stink. They didn't even have clothes. The only smell he could think of that was close to this stench was a dead deer he'd stumbled on while hiking out in the woods. Once he'd caught the scent, it had been easy enough to follow it to the animal, and he had left as quickly. The last thing he wanted to do was get murdered by a bear that thought he was there to steal its dinner.

Facing off against a bear might be easier than whatever was waiting for them inside the cavern.

The first skeleton went down to a one-handed swing of Justin's axe. Will snorted, realizing his excuse about the shield earlier was bullshit. Still, his buddy manned up when he really needed him to. Otherwise, they'd be back in town lamenting their bad luck. As much as he bitched about the fights, being out here was better than delivering ten packages or collecting a hundred chicken eggs.

Real jobs were for suckers.

Who in their right mind would want to work a nine to five when they could be playing video games for money? It was crazy to think that when he was a kid, gamers had been ridiculed. The school shooters played games, the terrorists played games, dropouts played games. But they weren't actually bad for you.

Will likened the way gamers were treated to the way people talked about porn. The porn industry didn't pull down six billion dollars a year because no one watched the stuff. Just like all gamers didn't go mad and start blowing shit up, or the people who listened to rap music weren't all in gangs.

People used those as scapegoats because the real issues were much harder to fix.

The next few skeletons went down easily enough. Now they were working together in tandem, as they had done so many times before. It felt good not to be bitching and to let his sword do the talking. They moved steadily deeper into the cave until his map showed only one room remained.

Will felt himself start to smile. "I think we've got this."

"Told you, dude. Never doubt me again," Justin replied as they stepped into the last room.

Ten skeletons moved to surround them. Will still didn't understand where the smell was coming from, but he had more immediate problems to deal with. Together, they moved around the room taking out pairs of the skeletons as they went. Soon all ten were lying on the floor in small heaps of bones. Both men looked at each other with excitement.

"We did it!" Justin cried out.

Will felt just as good, but he didn't see a chest anywhere, and his notifications didn't show any bonuses for clearing the cave. "I'm not seeing a completion update."

"Me either. What in the fuck? Everything is dead," Justin whined.

"Not everything," a voice called out.

Justin's torch snuffed out, plunging them into pitch black.

Two red eyes appeared in the darkness, ten feet off the ground. The distance between them would have meant the monster's head was fucking huge. Will thought about running, but if the thing was that big, he wouldn't make it out of the cave before it cut him down from behind. He turned for Justin and couldn't see him in the dark.

The eyes disappeared and Justin screamed.

Will started spinning in circles, slashing his blade around himself like a mad man.

The glowing red eyes reappeared. "I have a message for you. Krevus has awakened."

Will didn't even feel the blow that killed him. He only knew he was dead because the system message appeared across his vision. Instead of being pissed, he decided a quick death wasn't so bad.

"Maybe the thirty-eighth time is the charm."

CHAPTER FIFTY-TWO

Tim rolled out of bed and didn't smell any coffee.

He wasn't sure what it said about him that he was disappointed. It was just that back at the Blue Dagger, Liz would have already had a cup waiting for him, every morning since she started working there. Sure, it wasn't life or death, but he'd grown used to the creature comforts of the Blue Dagger Inn and missed it when he wasn't there.

"You're not going to like me without coffee," Tim said in his best Hulk voice.

Tim looked at the other side of the bed when he didn't get a response, and realized he was alone. *Coffee must also help my situational awareness.* How people got up in the morning and just started to function seemed crazy to him. He needed three cups of the good bean's nectar before walking out the door.

While coffee and a bath were both going to elude him today, at least Tim could take a warm bath before they used the temple's gate to get back to Promethia. Whatever was under the mountain could wait. The guild needed time to get some new gear for their next adventure. Plus, he hadn't been expecting to be gone for so long. If Tim was going to be away for longer periods of time, he had to make arrangements with his business manager, Mr. Applebottom.

Stumbling to the bathroom looking like one of the zombies they killed was a good first step. He got the door open on the first try, which seemed like a mini-miracle, and went to the nearest tub full of hot clean water. A quick thought and all of his clothes disappeared. He slipped into the tub.

As his muscles started to relax, Tim decided it was the perfect time to check out the spell book he'd been given and go over his skills. After drying off his hands, he summoned the book from his inventory. The second it landed in his hands a prompt appeared.

Spellbook: Quick Feet

The greatest adventurers always have a hidden advantage up their sleeves, or in this case, their boots. Quick feet increases your movement speed by 1% and your dodge chance by 1% for ten seconds.

Learn spell: <Yes/No>

Tim clicked yes.

The spellbook disappeared, and the knowledge of how to use it popped into his head. While the spell didn't seem to do much now, if he could get those percentages higher it could have amazing potential. Being able to move faster would make it easier to avoid getting pummeled, and the dodge component would be an extra bonus if he couldn't get out of danger fast enough. All in all, it wasn't his most useful spell, but it always paid to have a little utility on his side.

The biggest problem Tim faced right now was that he had so many skills he sometimes forgot to use the newest ones. He'd been so wrapped up in his curses and how they could heal the entire group, he'd ignored his healing storm ability. He vowed to use it more often going forward.

Being able to heal multiple people at once was handy, and not nearly as situational as his flame burst or snare spells. One thing healing storm would be great for was healing minor injuries at the Shack. It'd cut down on the time he had to spend there. Thinking about the Healing Shack made Tim feel a little guilty. It was time he got back to the slums and helped a few people.

Before he got out of the bath, Tim looked over his stat sheet and notifications. With his new gear, his Intelligence went over twenty for the first time and provided him with a little bonus. Not to mention the fact he had two stat points to distribute. The next closest stat to twenty was his Dexterity. If he put both unused points there, when he equipped his daggers, he'd go over the twenty threshold for an additional bonus.

Without putting too much thought into it, Tim placed the points in Dexterity. The extra should help him with his assassin skills and increase his chances to dodge and hide. There wasn't really a downside that he could see unless it was that he was passing on getting his Wisdom above forty.

The only reason Tim didn't go for the easy solution was that his next piece of gear would probably push him over forty Wisdom. There was no way of knowing when he'd get any gear to benefit his Dexterity. Healing gear didn't seem to come with a lot of supplemental stats, although that could change later in the game.

With the points in Dexterity, he'd also feel a little better if he had to use his daggers again. It wasn't long ago that those daggers saved his ass. Without Gaston's tutelage, he would have never made it this far.

"Fuck," Tim grumbled to himself as his mind started to wake up.

When they left with Ernie, Gaston might have needed help back home. Leaving his friend high and dry after all he'd done for the Blue Dagger Society seemed a little fucked up. When they got back to Promethia later, he vowed to make sure Gaston had whatever he needed before they returned to Tristholm to deal with the mountain pass.

Now that he was alone and had some time to himself, it seemed like a perfect opportunity to review his skills.

Both of Tim's stances had increased to the apprentice rank without much of a change. He didn't mind that two options didn't have huge increases. It was nice to know he could heal his whole group or focus on the tank just by changing them.

Skill Increase: Who Needs A Shield

Rank: Novice Nine

Try using this spell situationally instead of just casting it at random for better increases. Reach the apprentice ranks for additional benefits.

"Hey, that's rude. I know how to use my spells." Tim was shouting at himself in the tub. He started to blush. Who in the hell yelled at their games? Oh, yeah, that's right, everyone. Sometimes games pissed you off.

Tim smiled as he jumped out of the tub. At least the last message did something to boost his confidence. Sure, there were ways he could tighten up his rotation, and use a few more of the spells he'd been given, but the guild seemed to be doing fine in combat. Why screw with what worked?

He quickly re-equipped his clothes and decided it was time to head down to breakfast. It would be nice to meet up with everyone before they left for the big city.

They better have coffee, or I'm going back to Promethia without them.

CHAPTER FIFTY-THREE

There was a dented and battered teapot in the center of the table.

Tim looked at the pot. The last time he'd seen it, he'd been sitting at an unused campfire thanking Eternia that such a wonderful invention existed. Now his only hope was that the people sitting around the table were smart enough to fill the thing with coffee instead of tea. In Tim's mind, there were two kinds of people in the world. People who said tea would do in a pinch and people who would rather drink water than suffer through a sip of leaf juice.

He preferred to think tea didn't exist.

The words "but this one time in college" came to mind. Tim couldn't think of many things he wouldn't have done to impress a girl back then. Drinking tea was on the less controversial list. Jumping off the roof into a homemade ball pit during rush week was something not everyone could say they did.

Probably because they were too smart or too sober to do it.

If you couldn't look back on life and laugh at some of the stupid stuff you did, then it wasn't worth living. Tim didn't mind that he made mistakes, or sometimes did dumb things for the wrong reasons. What he did was learn from those incidents and promise not to make the same mistakes twice.

One of the best things about college for him was finding out how different everyone was, and yet they all managed to end up at the same place. Rich, poor, jock, geek, democrat, republican, it didn't matter. All of them were in school together. Once he learned more about the people around him, he placed less importance on his perceptions of people and focused more on their actions.

It didn't matter what color someone's skin was, who you loved, if you pulled yourself up from nothing, or had a silver spoon in your mouth. There was something he could learn from everyone.

Except the tea drinkers.

Tim pointed at the pot on the table. "Please tell me that's coffee."

JaKobi reached for the pot and a glass. Dark brown liquid poured from the spout, and Tim felt like one of the old forty-niners when they found a seam of gold in them there hills. He held out a shaky hand, almost unable to believe his luck. The jolt his system craved was only inches away. The first sip of steaming hot liquid rolled down his throat and exploded into his belly, filling him with warmth and a sense of purpose.

"Ah, that's the good stuff." Tim let out a contented sigh and sat down in an empty seat.

ShadowLily grinned. "I told you he's worthless without a cup of coffee."

Tim spluttered. "I wouldn't say worthless."

"Did you even notice we had a guest?" Cassie snorted. "I swear Liz has you so spoiled I'm surprised you ever leave the inn."

No one was going to ruin his first cup of coffee by talking about his lack of awareness or fondness for the server who had his daily joe waiting outside of his room every morning. "I'll never apologize for coffee, but I will say sorry to our guest."

Tim locked eyes with Jon. "So, what brings you here today?"

An elbow dug into Tim's side. "That didn't sound like 'Sorry, I didn't know you existed until I had my coffee,'" ShadowLily quipped.

"What she said." Tim held out his cup for a refill. "It is nice to see you again. Doubly so when we aren't about to be eaten by werewolves."

Jon looked around the table to make sure no one else was going to say anything before he spoke. A small smile quirked at the corner of his mouth. "I was wondering if you could deliver a letter for me. Something I'd rather keep private."

"Probably shouldn't have asked with Cassie here," Tim snarked.

This time he got kicked under the table.

"Dick," Cassie retorted. "You know I don't have loose lips."

Lorelei snorted.

Before they could devolve any further in front of their esteemed guest, Tim coughed into his hand to stifle his own laughter. "Sorry, Jon. I'm still trying to wake up. Of course, we'd be honored to get a letter to someone for you."

Jon looked unsure of what to make of the group, but his face told the real story. Jon didn't have any other options. "You are still going back to Promethia?"

Tim nodded and took another sip from his glass. "Yes, to resupply. I also have a few business things to take care of before I can leave for an extended absence."

Reaching inside his coat, Jon pulled out a sealed letter. "I expect this to still be sealed when it reaches its destination."

Reaching out, Tim accepted the letter. "You have my word."

"I will hold you to it." Jon's words were sincere, with the right undercurrent of, if you fuck this up, I'm coming for you.

Tim put the letter in his inventory and took another sip of coffee. "Who am I delivering the letter to?"

Jon's smile softened as he thought about the person he was

writing too. "Her name is Lucy Briarthorn. I can mark her house on the map for you."

"I know exactly where it is." Tim grinned. "We've had dealings in the past."

Standing up from the table, Jon smiled. "Then I can count on you, and your discretion?"

"You can." Tim nodded to the man. "We would never think of betraying your trust."

Thrusting out his hand for a gentlemanly shake, Jon said, "Thank you." His smile vanished in an instant. "In my haste to make sure my own needs were taken care of, I forgot to tell you that Seraphina is waiting for you at the temple. I believe she wanted a final word before you go."

Tim shook Jon's hand and looked longingly at the pot of coffee.

JaKobi grinned. "Don't worry, we can take it with us."

"What I wouldn't give for a travel mug right about now." Tim gave a longing look at the pot before setting his cup on the table. "Better not keep Seraphina waiting. Let's make sure we have all our gear, and then it's time to go."

The group nodded, and all went off in their own directions to make sure they hadn't left anything in their rooms. Instead of following them, Tim poured another cup of coffee and smiled to himself. He'd bought a couple of extra minutes to enjoy his favorite part of the day.

The entrance to the temple looked immaculate.

Brothers from the temple scurried over every surface like swarming ants. Once the portal between Tristholm and Promethia had been reestablished, Paul must have sent reinforcements to help with the cleanup efforts. Tim couldn't see a single drop of blood on the tiled floors, which was a welcome relief after healing the soldiers.

Seraphina smiled at their group and waved them over. "Ah, the heroes of Tristholm. How good it is to see you again."

Tim nodded. He felt the same way. Since the battle ended, Seraphina had been nothing but gracious. It seemed having her city back to normal, and the werewolf clans as partners again had removed a great burden from her. He liked the new Seraphina much better.

"Jon said you wanted to see us before we left." Tim stopped short of the woman. He wasn't much for bowing and didn't think a handshake was a better option, so he waited a little awkwardly for her to respond.

"Did he?" Seraphina winked at him, indicating she knew exactly what her son was up to. "I have other business to discuss."

Tim motioned for her to continue.

"There have been reports of animated skeletons around the mountains. Not all of them have been coming from the pass. It seems we are in greater need of your services than we thought. How long will you be gone?"

Looking back at his group, Tim saw them holding up either one, two, or three fingers. Tim hoped they meant days because by the nervous look on Seraphina's face, they didn't have weeks.

"Just a few days," Tim answered in his most non-committal voice. He was pretty sure he could wrap up most of his business in a day, but it would be nice to have at least one day where he didn't have to worry about dying and could relax before rushing into danger again. Everyone needed a mental health day every now and again.

"When you return, come and see me. I'll have an update waiting for you and maybe a quest to fulfill." She lowered her head and leaned closer as if she wanted to share a secret. "Other adventurers have arrived, but I am not sure they are up to the task. Please do your best to return quickly."

"Flattery like that will get you everywhere with me." Tim smiled. "I promise to return as soon as humanly possible."

Seraphina nodded and stepped back before pointing to Ernie. "Maybe leave him back at home. It seems several of his apprentices have disappeared during his time here, and I'd hate to have another incident."

Looking at the poison master Tim thought, *You sly dog.* "I'm sure Ernie has more than enough to keep him busy back in Promethia. You can only leave an assassin in charge of your inn for so long before the number of guests goes down."

A chuckle escaped Seraphina's lips. "Because he kills them, oh that's rich."

Tim had been thinking more of his surly disposition and fondness for alcohol and hadn't meant to make a pun.

"Thank you for all you've done for my city." Seraphina gave Tim the smallest of bows, before waving to the rest of his group and striding back into the city with purpose. She had damage to repair, soldiers to honor, and a city still very much in need of protection to run.

Tim didn't envy the task in front of Seraphina at all. Thankfully, they were going to put Tristholm's problems out of mind for a few days. When they returned to Promethia, it was time to shop, resupply, and rest.

Business as usual would resume upon their return to Tristholm.

Cassie brought Tim's attention back to the group. "How do we get back?"

That was a good question. Tim didn't know the answer, but he knew where to find the man who did. "Let's track down Brother Colton."

The group walked through the gates and into the temple. A few moments later, Brother Colton appeared. His cheeks were red, and he was slightly out of breath as if he'd run down the stairs from the top of the tower to meet them.

"Thank the goddess, I've been waiting for you to return,"

Brother Colton puffed. "I have business with the high priest but wanted to escort you back myself."

JaKobi grinned. "Then let's get this show on the road."

"Couldn't have said it better myself." Lorelei looked at the coin purse dangling off her hip. "I've got gold to spend and beer to drink."

"Very well. Please follow me." Brother Colton turned on his heel and led them into a small antechamber.

"Since all of you have been granted access except Ernie, all you have to do is touch the crystal, and you'll be back in Promethia. Ernie will have to hold my hand." Brother Colton held out his hand for the Poison Master.

"Are you sure there isn't another way?" Ernie looked at the priest's outstretched hand. "I'm not much for hand-holding."

Brother Colton grabbed Ernie's hand and then touched the crystal. There was an audible pop and the two men were gone.

"Better get there and make sure Ernie doesn't poison him in the temple." JaKobi placed his hand on the crystal and vanished.

One by one, the rest of his group left. Tim turned and looked at the temple they'd liberated from The Surgeon, and then placed his hand on the crystal. His gut heaved like the first time he'd entered the game, and then everything went black. One thing kept repeating in his mind as he waited for the journey to end.

I hope I don't get sick.

CHAPTER FIFTY-FOUR

It felt good to be home.

Tim smiled as he stepped into the sunlight of Promethia. Part of him wondered if it was weird that this city felt like home now. There were always people who would condemn others for taking games so seriously or having more online friends than in the real world. He would have bought that explanation at one point, but he'd seen firsthand how much gamers cared for one another.

The lives people led in MMO's felt real, but he'd seen real-world good come out of them. People had gotten married, lifelong friendships formed, and once he even watched a funeral procession in-game to honor a fallen guildmate. He'd played games with people with disabilities or conditions that kept them isolated. Gaming was their way to feel normal, to feel included, and to not feel judged.

No one cared what you looked like, if you had a good job, or lived in a house or an apartment. The only thing that mattered to gamers was that you had mad skillz and weren't a total dick. Now that the POD technology was out, you didn't even have to be a keyboard guru. You just needed a sharp mind and a will to succeed.

If you had those things, no power in the 'verse could stop you.

Tim felt blessed that he'd found such good people to be around. He'd been a part of a few toxic guilds in his day. There were people who put progress in front of everything, and those who just liked being in charge because it was the first time they'd ever been empowered. Since starting his own guild, he realized it was the people that needed to fit. If a guild master could accomplish that, the gameplay would follow.

He would always be willing to grind with players who wanted to get better.

That was kind of like his gamer creed. It didn't matter where you started. If you had a desire to get better and improve yourself, he was happy to help you get there. Tim was also just as happy to take advice from other players who played a class better than he could. That was back in normal MMO's.

In *The Etheric Coast*, things were different.

It wasn't like you could hop on Google and search for class tips or rotation guides. There weren't any videos of boss fights or dungeon maps. How each person played a class made it different. No two healers would ever be exactly the same. Different weapons, subtle changes to armor and stats, and player's skills only leveled when they used them.

The best part was the game was like that for everyone. It wasn't like two assassins could be put side by side and told show me what you've got on the DPS meter. Depending on their play styles, each one could shine in vastly different situations. Tim felt like that was something that made *The Etheric Coast* special.

You really could create your own future.

"Are you going to stop staring into the sun or what," Cassie snapped.

Tim snapped out of his thoughts in an instant. He was getting better about not zoning out around others, but every now and again his mind went down a rabbit hole and he couldn't help himself. Thinking about gaming was one of those things that could keep his mind occupied for hours.

"Didn't they teach you staring into the sun is bad for your eyes in school?" JaKobi grinned. "It's like one of the basic principles. First is don't eat glue. Next comes the sun thing."

Lorelei snorted. "No one should have to tell you not to eat glue."

"Tell that to a room full of preschoolers. Eventually, everything gets in their mouths." ShadowLily laughed at the thought of a bunch of kids sitting around eating glue off construction paper with wooden sticks.

"If they eat all the glue, how will they make the hand turkeys?" Tim joined in on the fun.

Cassie smashed the butt of her staff on the ground to get their attention. "The only hand turkey I see here is you." Her face softened. "Just tell us we can go shopping already."

The three women looked at him with expectant eyes. Tim knew better than to keep them in suspense. "Don't let me stop you."

Apparently, the ladies in his life weren't past the squealing in delight stage of life.

ShadowLily rushed in to give him a quick kiss. "See you soon."

The women started to head toward the market, but ShadowLily turned, shouting, "Let's all meet at Joe's for dinner. I'm sure he's dying to see us."

Tim waved for her to go and have fun. "See you then."

Turning from the women in his life, Tim found himself looking at Ernie and JaKobi. "Any plans for the day, gentlemen?"

Ernie huffed. "I've got to go back to the inn and make sure Liz and Gaston didn't destroy it in my absence." He pointed at Tim. "You should come back and open the Healing Shack before you go running off again."

Tim felt the tug of responsibility, but he had a few other things to handle first. "Put a sign on the door letting everyone know we'll be open this afternoon. I need to check in with Ironbeard and Lady Briarthorn before heading back."

Ernie grunted in response and started back to the inn.

"You need me with you, boss, or can I head to the library?" JaKobi asked.

It was good to know his buddy wouldn't leave him out in the cold if he was planning on walking into a bad situation, but he shouldn't need any additional protection for the tasks he needed to carry out. "I'm good. I'll either see you at the Shack later or at Joe's for dinner."

"Awesome. I can't wait to see my class trainer's face when I tell him how well that little surprise he gave me worked out." JaKobi was grinning from ear to ear. "Who knows, maybe he has something else for me, something more explode-y."

Tim shuddered. "I think the last explosion was big enough."

"Better to have a bomb and not need to use it, than to need one and not have it," JaKobi said sagely. "That and I like lighting shit on fire." He gave Tim a casual wave and headed off in the direction of the Mages' College.

Alone for the first time in what felt like forever, Tim started walking to Lady Briarthorn's residence. He had a letter to deliver. It was funny how his life changed dramatically the first time he took a letter from the high priest to drop off at Lucy's house. One single piece of parchment had set him on an adventure that was still progressing.

Which reminded him that he needed to see Mr. Applebottom to talk about the future. Tim wanted to check on the progress being made to the buildings he owned and find out where it was best to spend some of his reserves.

Knowing he would have a steady supply of cash sent to his family via his streaming contract freed up a lot of his funds in-game. It meant he could afford to put more money into his projects. Cobblestone streets instead of mud, maybe a system to catch the rainwater and use it for farming. The possibilities were endless as long he could put someone else in charge of the small details.

Tim felt like that was the key to his success.

He was good at finding the right people for the job, or at the very least, finding out what people were good at and putting them in a position to succeed. There wasn't a person on this planet who didn't bring a skill to the table. Sometimes you just had to find it before you could harness its potential.

Mr. Applebottom had proved to be resourceful and trustworthy. He was the type of man Tim could put in charge of making sure his visions were carried out. Yes, he wanted to revitalize the slums, but he also wanted to do it in a way so that the people who lived there still had a place to call home. He wanted them to feel welcome, and not as if they'd been priced out of their own neighborhood.

So far, they had done a good job. Fifty percent of the properties he owned would go to shop owners in the slums, at reduced rents. He hoped that putting their amazing products in a nicer store might give them the edge they needed to attract new business. The same went with the housing.

The rooms Tim rented weren't free. He didn't believe in giving people free stuff. Maybe it was the way his parents raised him, but it felt like you never treated something free with the same respect as something you had to earn. Having to work for something gave it a value more important than money.

If a person worked hard and gave whatever profession they picked everything they had, it only seemed fair they should benefit from a job well done. Those were the type of people he wanted to help. He didn't care if they sold salted fish, farm-fresh veggies, or newly made pots, he'd give them a shot to sell in style.

People liked to look down on people in the trade industries, but he never understood why. Talented people occupying in-demand skills could make a lot of money. People scoffed at certain jobs, but there was a lot of money to be made doing dirty shit. Not everyone was wired to be tech savvy. Some people could build, others could use a wrench, and there was no shame in going to a technical school instead of college.

The world takes all kinds to keep turning.

Tim grinned as he rounded the corner to Lady Briarthorn's abode. There was a lot of good to be done in the world if you had the means and the desire. All you had to do was work your ass off, or as his dad liked to say, "Sometimes you just gotta pay your dues."

Good things took time to build, and Tim was as patient as the mountains.

CHAPTER FIFTY-FIVE

Reginald answered the door with a smile.

Seeing as how the man almost never smiled unless something bad was about to happen, Tim turned and looked for an attacker. Not seeing anyone behind him, he whirled back and was enveloped in the man's arms.

Reginald hugged him with enough ferocity to snap a rib. "Thank you for all you've done."

Not sure what he'd done to deserve the hug, Tim tried to return the man's affection as best he could. "Mind telling me why I'm so great?"

"For sending Gaston to her, of course." Reginald let Tim go and gave him a more manly slap on the shoulder. "He's made the lady of the house extremely happy."

Tim still wasn't sure if that was a good thing. If Gaston was sleeping with Lady Briarthorn, who knew what sorts of problems that would cause in Royal circles. Although, it might be an even bigger problem if he wasn't sleeping with her. Killing off her suitors to make the others back off would be much, much worse.

Even in *The Etheric Coast*, killing nobility was a risky business.

No one but nobility would meet the standards Lucy's parents set for her. Tim thought it was almost barbaric to arrange a marriage, but at least her parents were giving her a choice between suitors. He almost laughed at the thought of anyone forcing Lady Briarthorn to do something she didn't want to do.

One thing people learned quickly about Lucy was that she always got her way.

"Care to enlighten me on what the pair have been up to?" Tim was hoping to get a sense of how big of a puddle of shit he was about to wade into.

Reginald kept his smile in place as he guided Tim inside. "I think I'd rather have her tell you."

Now the man was putting the screws to him, which made Tim feel a little better. When Lady Briarthorn's manservant and guard was being nice, there was probably a good chance he'd stab you in the back.

Thankfully, Reginald was leading the way to the study. Tim felt good about that. His continued service to Lucy and the temple had purchased him more than a bit of good faith. Now the only question he had to answer was, would she be happy about the letter from Jon or just exasperated?

The door to her study was open, and Lucy Briarthorn was standing in front of the fireplace nursing a glass of wine. "So, the hero of Tristholm returns."

She turned, and Tim got the first good look at her dress. Whoever Lucy's seamstress was, she either used magic to enhance her work or was the best damn designer in the world. The dress hugged Lady Briarthorn like a glove, but it wasn't that which made it so stunning. It was that it seemed to move.

He looked her over again, hoping that it wasn't rude. The navy dress was covered with a mesh of white diamond cutouts. As Lucy moved, so did the diamonds, but the navy underneath stayed constant. It gave the dress a sense of being alive, and Tim had the feeling it cost more than he'd spent revitalizing his little slice of the slums.

Lady Briarthorn poured a second glass of wine and extended it to him. "Please do come in."

Tim accepted the glass and saw Reginald close the doors to the study before disappearing. "Thank you for the drink."

"You are more than welcome." Lucy motioned for him to sit down. "Now, tell me what brings you to my humble abode."

Tim wondered how rich her family was if this house was considered humble by their standards. "I have a letter for you from Jon in Tristholm. He asked that I didn't read it."

"Just when I thought I had this suitor business under control, there is another." Lucy frowned at the letter as she accepted it.

Attempting not to anger her, Tim tried to be honest about the situation. "There was a lot going on in Tristholm. He might not have gotten the memo."

"So you've heard about our exploits." Lucy grinned. "The idea didn't hold much merit for me at first, but it has been rather successful at getting all these bastards to back off."

Her face hardened into the look Tim had only seen her use when she was going to demand something. "You would think a simple fuck off would be enough to dissuade a man from continuing his pursuit of me, but it only seems to invigorate them."

Tim felt like he'd been on both sides of that equation. There was no doubt in his mind he'd been too stupid to take the hint more than once, but he'd also been pursued by someone he wasn't interested in.

"How much trouble am I going to be in if someone links these murders to Gaston?" Tim tipped his glass back, almost finishing the wine in one giant gulp.

Lucy moved forward to refill his glass. "Murder? Who said anything about murder?"

"He's an assassin. I assumed you had him do what he does best." Tim reminded himself of what happens when making assumptions.

Gentle laughter escaped her lips before she could stop it. "It almost came to that." She paused as if thinking about an unpleasant experience. "But we had a little fun at their expense."

"You're going to have to tell me about it sometime." Tim took a much smaller sip of wine.

"Oh, I never kiss and tell," Lucy mocked. "But I do have something I need you to do for me."

Tim almost cringed but managed to keep his composure. Every mission he'd undertaken from Lucy had been harder than the last. What sounded like something simple often turned into a huge ordeal.

He tried to smile but ended up taking another sip of wine to calm his nerves. "And that would be?"

"You are returning to Tristholm, correct?" Lady Briarthorn's eyebrow went up in question.

"I am."

Lucy nodded once. "Good. Then you can return my response to Jon."

Tim wanted to back out of the room, but the doors were still closed. The last thing he wanted was to be the go-between on love letters unrequited. "I'm not sure that is such a good idea. We have a quest to complete there, and I'd really prefer not to make an enemy of the man."

"An enemy, for delivering a letter?" Lucy clucked her tongue against the roof of her mouth. "Very well, I shall make it easier for you."

Quest Received: Turning the Tables

Lady Briarthorn has requested that you take her response back to Jon in Tristholm. She asked politely, so don't be a dick about it.

Reward: One gold coin
Accept Quest: <Yes/No>

Tim reviewed the message for all of a second. He knew when to take a hint and accepted the quest.

Lucy tossed a golden coin at him. "See that you get it done."

The doors behind him opened and Reginald appeared, ready to usher him out. Tim took that as his cue to leave and quickly finished his drink. "I won't fail you."

"I never expected that you would." In an unexpected show of emotion, Lucy pulled Tim into a hug. "Thank you again for everything." She pulled away and straightened her dress. "Please don't die in Tristholm. I am sure to have need of your services again."

Tim gave Lucy a small bow. "If you call on any member of the Blue Dagger Society, they will always do what they can."

Reginald placed a hand on Tim's shoulder and turned him toward the door. This time Lucy's servant kept Tim in front of him to make sure he didn't wander off on his way out. He was so nervous he realized that he never got a letter from Lady Briarthorn.

As Reginald shoved him outside, Tim managed to squeak. "I seem to be missing the required correspondence."

"I'll have her response dropped off at the inn as soon as it's ready." Reginald shooed him out of the house. "And if you run into Gaston, ask him to stop by the house to provide the good lady with an update."

Tim didn't want to know what the update was about. He promised to give the assassin the message and bounded down the stairs before he got pulled into another questline. The guild had enough on their plate right now. The last thing they needed were angry nobles sending guards to arrest them.

Although, there seemed to be a lot more money in delivering letters than he thought. Maybe Tim should have become a messenger instead of an adventurer. But what would be the fun in that? He picked up his pace as he headed back to the inn. If he didn't hurry, he'd be late opening up the Healing Shack. As he ran, a song sprang into his head, but he changed the chorus a bit.

"Toss a coin to your healer," he crowed to himself, wishing he had learned how to carry a tune.

CHAPTER FIFTY-SIX

Gaston was sitting in a chair outside of the Healing Shack.

The burly assassin had one of his daggers out and was picking idly at his nails while the people waiting in line gave him nervous glances. When he saw Tim, he flipped the chair down on all four legs and stood up. His dagger disappeared so fast if Tim hadn't seen it moments before he would have thought he imagined it.

"Thought you might like a little help in case things get unruly." Gaston pushed the door to the Shack open for him.

Judy was waiting for him inside and had the room cleaned and ready to go. Tim was happy to see that the vertical garden was still alive, which meant she'd come to take care of it in his absence. It was a blessing to have an assistant who anticipated your needs and obviously cared about helping others.

"I was starting to think you weren't coming back," Judy said with a warm smile.

Tim wasn't sure exactly what to say. He couldn't die anymore. Well, he could die, but now it wouldn't reset his character, so he'd always come back. Instead of explaining, he decided to play his part. "Almost didn't. Tristholm was a little bit more complicated than we expected."

"I always say, anything happening outside of Promethia is trouble." Judy handed him a basin to wash his hands in. "Should I bring in the first client?"

Laughter almost escaped Tim's lips. He didn't think of these people as clients, just folks who needed healing. Unlike doctors back in the real world, he would never turn someone away even if they couldn't pay. He also didn't have a set price for his services. He only asked people to give what they could. While a few people tried to take advantage of the situation, most of the folks were good honest people who needed a little help.

"Did the high priest have anyone here in my absence?" Tim asked as he prepared himself for a long afternoon.

Judy frowned and looked at the ground as she spoke. "He did send someone."

"Let me guess, the guy tried to charge people the normal rates for healing." Tim started to feel angry.

His assistant stopped by the door and closed it before coming back to stand next to him. She whispered in a tone that said, I don't like to speak ill of people but— "And he wasn't here on time or for a full day. I got the impression he thought this job was beneath him."

Tim placed a comforting hand on Judy's shoulders. "I'll send Paul a message and let him know the situation. I have to leave again for business, and he assured me this would be handled."

The door to the Shack flew open and a man walked in. He sneered when he saw Tim's black robes, and then turned his scowl onto Judy. "Make sure these hicks can pay or tell them to leave."

Tim smiled at Judy, ignoring the man in the light blue robes of the priesthood. "Judy, can you step outside for a moment."

She nodded her head as she looked at the serious expression on her boss' face. "I think that might be best."

"Now listen here, I don't know who you are, but you can't tell my people what to do," the foppish priest declared. "She will stay here."

Judy moved past the man and out the door. The priest turned to grab her arm, infuriated by her ignoring him. Instead of her arm, his hand smashed into Gaston's chest.

The man spluttered. "See here you brute, I am a man of the cloth and you're interfering with temple business."

Gaston looked past the priest, his face a mask of stoicism. "Can I kill him now?"

"My name is Martin Emory the Fourth, and you will get out of my way, or I will have you put in chains," the priest blustered even as he took a step back.

A dagger appeared in Gaston's hand, but Tim quickly waved for him to put it away. He had a better idea of how to handle things. "Martin, is it?" He moved toward the priest. "Whatever gave you the idea you could order around my assistant?"

"Your assistant? She is here to serve at the temple's behest." Martin pointed at himself and looked at Tim as if he were stupid. "And I am the only representative of the temple here."

"Maybe I should let you kill him," Tim quipped.

Gaston shrugged. "Just say the word. It's not like it would take any effort."

"There will be repercussions if I die," Martin whined. "My father will see to it."

Tim laughed. "My guess is the third son of a noble isn't very high up on his father's priority list. As to the question of who owns this building and who Judy works for, the answer is simple. I do."

"But the high priest sent me here himself." Martin sounded indignant.

Tim knew he had him now. "And what were his exact orders?"

"I don't have to tell you." Martin's face paled as Gaston placed the tip of his blade against his back. "Ok fine. He told me to come down here and heal, but he didn't give any specifics as to how I should handle the task."

Not in the mood to laugh anymore, Tim sneered at the man. "So instead you showed up late, left early, and refused to heal anyone who wouldn't pay you a king's ransom. I think Paul will be rather disappointed in you when I give him my report."

"Paul." Martin tried the word on for size. His face fell when he realized the man in front of him was on a first name basis with the high priest. "Like I care. You probably don't know him."

Breaking through this man's arrogance was a waste of time. He'd delivered a subtle threat without effect, and now it was time to take a firmer hand. "Gaston, throw this piece of shit out of my office."

"You can't," Martin screamed as Gaston picked him up by the robes. "My father will hear of this!"

The assassin didn't even slow down as he tossed Martin down the stairs and into the dirt. "Fuck off."

Brushing off his robes, Martin glared at Gaston. "This isn't over."

Tim stepped outside. "You're right. I'll be sending a message to the high priest about your lackadaisical performance. Paul and I are friends, so I wouldn't expect a warm welcome back at the temple."

"We'll see!" Martin Emory the Fourth spat before stomping off.

Tim shouted after him. "Remember that humility is one of the goddess' many blessings."

The crowd in front of the Shack wasn't sure what to make of the situation, but a few of them were smiling as they watched the disgraced priest walk away.

"Judy, please bring in our first guest," Tim said in the most pleasant voice he could muster.

He always started healing with the worst cases and then moved to the others. Today, he thought about trying something different. "Gaston, can you separate anyone who has a minor injury and put them in groups of five off to the side?"

"Of course I can." The assassin moved down the line, pulling people out with light injuries as Tim watched.

Moving to the front of the Shack to address everyone, Tim tried to put a smile back on his face. These people deserved better, and today he was going to make sure they had the best experience possible. "I promise that anyone with an injury will be seen today. Because of the way you were treated in my absence, all healing provided today will be free of charge."

Those well enough to cheer did so. The rest stared at Tim with unbelieving eyes. He'd worked so hard to build up trust in this community, only for that idiot to ruin it in his absence. There was a bubble of rage building inside of him. It wasn't only his business Martin tried to ruin, but his reputation.

Gaston had six groups of five lined up in the street. One of the men in the first group looked up in confusion. "Why did we get separated?"

This time his grin felt genuine. "Because I thought you had better things to do than stand around all day." Tim quickly cast healing storm on each of the six groups. He was happy to see the spell worked as intended, and all six groups were healed of their minor injuries almost instantly.

He wouldn't be able to use the spell effectively in combat until he leveled it up, but this was the perfect setting for him to practice. He waved at the groups. "Thank you for your patience." Without waiting to hear a response, Tim turned and headed back into the Shack. Now it was time to take care of the truly needy.

The next four hours were a blur of broken bones, infections, and lacerations. More people came as the word got out that he had returned, and Tim healed every single one of them. He wasn't doing this just for a skill increase though. These people deserved access to the same magical healing as the wealthy. When it came to saving lives, money shouldn't be a factor.

When the last patient had been attended to, Tim turned to

Judy. "Thank you for your help today." He flipped her the golden coin Lady Briarthorn paid him earlier.

"I can't accept this," Judy stammered.

"You can." Tim closed her hand around the coin. "And you will." He let her hand drop. "Judy, I really couldn't do this without you."

The older woman smiled at him. "That's kind of you to say."

"I mean every word." Tim frowned for a moment. "And I promise if Paul sends someone else to help in my absence, they will be the right type of person for the job."

Judy tapped a finger to her chest and pointed it at the sky. "Praise Eternia."

Pulling his assistant into a quick hug felt right. "I'll see you tomorrow." Tim pointed to Gaston. "Can you make sure she gets home safe?"

"I'd be delighted." Gaston held out his arm for the older woman.

Tim watched as the two of them left. It only took him a few minutes to put a message together for Paul. Once the letter was sent, Tim locked up the building and walked around to the main entrance of the inn. After a long day, all he wanted was some good food and a beer.

Maybe a couple beers.

CHAPTER FIFTY-SEVEN

Tim couldn't believe his eyes.

Their new suite at the inn was complete, and it even had a shower. How people lived always taking baths, he'd never know. After a day of adventuring, the first tubful might as well have turned to mud. The thought of sitting in all the filth he was trying to get rid of never appealed to him.

Showers were the way to go.

It seemed magic also had a place in the plumbing industry because his water never got cold. How cool was that? Unlimited hot water and a shower that could run for days without getting an email from the conservation police. Tim took full advantage of his very first shower inside *The Etheric Coast*.

His shower lasted thirty minutes.

Thankfully, it didn't take long for him to dry off and get dressed. Then it was down a quick flight of stairs to the bar. When Joe's had become super popular, the restaurant inside of the inn turned almost exclusively into a bar. They still served a few items, but most of the business they drove right into the diner.

Ernie didn't seem to mind.

Not that he'd ever been that interested in the kitchen for cooking. The Poison Master made his concoctions in the inn's kitchens. When the chance to claim his workshop back for a majority of the day came along, Ernie snapped it up. There was an unspoken pact between the two businesses. Joe wouldn't serve booze, and Ernie wouldn't serve anything but cheap filler for people too drunk to make it to Joe's.

ShadowLily's dad also picked up all of the room service business.

In the end, it wasn't a bad deal for either of them, and it was more profitable than if they fought each other over the same customers. Tim didn't know a lot about the restaurant business, but he did know it was cutthroat. If the food sucked or the service was bad, people found other places to go.

His own dad liked to say you never get a second chance at making a first impression.

It was a line Tim tried to take to heart when meeting someone for the first time. Once, at a job interview, the employer asked to see the inside of his car. The man told him you can tell a lot about a person by the way they keep their car. Thankfully for Tim, he'd cleaned the car out that morning, and the job was his.

You never know when people are judging you or why. Maybe that hiring manager had a bad experience with an employee with a messy car. If it happened more than once, he might have decided that was his litmus test for hiring someone. A lot of people talked a good game, but it was always a person's actions that defined them.

Tim tried not to judge people by their cover. He'd seen kids that looked like stone-cold gangsters help an old lady across the street and men in business suits beat each other up over a cup of spilled coffee. One thing he knew for certain was that nice clothes and a fat wallet didn't make you a great person.

Just like being poor and wearing knockoffs didn't make a person worthless.

Some of the best stories in reality and in fiction were about someone who started with nothing and ended up with everything. Everyone loved those stories. It gave them hope for the future. It was never too late to do something incredible.

He felt that way about being inside the game. Every day since he'd made the decision to enter *The Etheric Coast* had been better than the one before. Sure, some days were harder than others, like when he died or got roped into delivering break up letters, but every day was exciting.

Having the right people around him made it so much better.

Taking a seat next to ShadowLily, Tim couldn't help but grin. He'd worked his entire life to go to college for a business degree and now here he was playing a game for a living. "How's the beer?"

JaKobi held out a hand and wiggled it from side to side. "It's good, but not like that stuff we found in the temple's kitchen."

Laughter spilled from Tim's mouth before he could stop it. It wasn't what JaKobi had said that had him rolling, it was the fact the priests had the best beer in town. When he got himself under control, Tim responded, "Maybe I can ask the high priest for a barrel."

"Hell yeah!" JaKobi clinked his glass against Tim's.

Now it was time to get everyone back on track so they could wrap up their quick meeting and go out for some food. "Did you get everything you wanted from your shopping trip?" Tim looked at ShadowLily first but slowly moved his eyes around the table.

Cassie showed off a new set of rings and a necklace. "A little bit better magical defense for me, not that I need it."

"Damn straight, you don't." JaKobi grinned as he polished off his beer.

Cassie stood up and grabbed JaKobi's hand, pulling him away from the table. "I think we're going to head upstairs before this guy passes out on the table."

"Hey, you were the one that said I could beat Gaston." JaKobi's eyes were downcast.

"Obviously, I was wrong." She helped him up and started toward the stairs.

Tim looked at the two ladies still at the table. "And then there were three."

"Two actually. I met this cute thing at the market, and I'm going to go buy her a few drinks." Lorelei smiled. "We aren't leaving early in the morning or anything, are we?"

"Nope, we've got the whole day in the city tomorrow. I was thinking of leaving the following morning," Tim replied. He hadn't checked, but he was pretty sure no one would say no to an extra day off. The Mountains would still be there when they returned to Tristholm.

Lorelei jumped up from the table. "Then I'll see you two crazy kids in the morning." She winked. "Maybe late morning."

The ranger left, giving the couple a jaunty wave.

Tim turned to ShadowLily. "Well then, I guess it's just you and me for dinner."

"And my dad." The assassin laughed. "But don't worry, I've got a few things to show you later."

Tim stood and held out his hand. "Dressed and then undressed happens to be my favorite way to spend an evening." He knew she was talking about showing him her new armor or casual clothes, but he could make it about something else if he wanted to.

She took his hand and Tim escorted her out of the inn.

Dinner was amazing.

That was the thing with Joe's. The food was always amazing, but tonight the company matched the meal. Joe was so happy to see them back in Promethia he practically gushed over them the entire evening. Despite how many times ShadowLily told him not to worry, that she couldn't die in the game, Joe wouldn't stop fussing about their dangerous lifestyle.

Now that their meal was done, Joe appeared with three slices of carrot cake, and what looked to be vanilla ice cream.

"Holy shit, is that really ice cream?" Tim blurted out as Joe slid the plate in front of him.

The chef nodded his head. "I found a dairy farmer to buy cream from, and you don't want to know how much the sugar costs."

"But how did you?" Tim swirled his hands around and then pointed at the bowl.

Joe sat down at the table. "I found a woodworker and told him what I wanted. He made me an old-fashioned ice cream churn. From there, I just needed ice and salt."

When Tim still looked confused, Joe continued his explanation. "Basically, the cream, sugar, and vanilla beans go in a bowl I keep in the icebox. That bowl goes in my wooden contraption that is lined with ice and salt. The lid goes on and you crank the handle until you've got ice cream."

Tim took a bite and let out a groan of pleasure. ShadowLily kicked him under the table and mouthed, "Why don't I get a response like that?"

After almost choking on his next bite, Tim tried to steer the conversation in a different direction. "Why the salt?"

Joe took a bite and then leaned back in his chair looking satisfied. "Salt helps lower the temperature of the ice." He held up his hands to forestall any questions. "I don't understand the science of it, I just know that it works."

"It's amazing, Dad," ShadowLily jumped in before Tim could keep harassing her dad about the ice cream. "So tell me, how are you doing?"

"Things are going great. We've had a few run-ins with some unfriendlies who are mad I'm taking their business, but that big fellow you hang out with has been running them off."

ShadowLily's face turned hard as winter's ice. "Tell me who it was!"

"Let's not get ahead of ourselves." Joe held up a hand to stop her. "It isn't anything I can't handle."

"Handling bad people is what I do. Threatening my father makes you a shit person in my book." She looked around the restaurant for a potential target.

Joe smiled as he took another bite of his carrot cake. "Don't go breaking your code for me. I've been threatened by other people my entire life. Success tends to bring out the haters."

Tim patted ShadowLily's leg under the table. "Joe, if this ever gets past the idle threat stage, you better let us take care of it for you."

"Of course I will." He looked at his daughter with pride. "I know my baby can kill anyone I can't handle."

"Damn straight I can." ShadowLily grinned. "No one fucks with pops!"

Tim was about to remind her about language in front of parents when a gasp came from the door. He turned and saw a blood-soaked man stumbling toward them. Without thinking, he cast healing orb on the man and ran to see how much healing was needed.

His second healing orb caught the man in the chest before he fell on the floor. Tim reached his side and flipped the traveler onto his back. "Shit."

Gaston had stab wounds all over. How he'd made it from wherever he had been to Joe's was a miracle. Tim started healing the lacerations, but it was the giant welt on the assassin's head that had him worried.

Slowly, the wounds started to close, and Gaston's eyes snapped open. Tim and ShadowLily held him down while Tim continued to heal him. He heard Joe calling for cleaning supplies in the background. It felt good knowing Joe knew he would handle the healing, and he didn't need to get help. All there was to worry about was cleaning up the blood.

The swelling on Gaston's head went down to almost nothing,

and his eyes seemed to focus as he reached out for Tim's arm. "I need your help."

"What do you think I've been doing?" Tim gave him a weak smile. "Just give me a few more minutes and you'll be fine." He placed a hand on his chest and continued to heal.

Gaston swatted Tim's hand away. "They took her, we have to get her back."

ShadowLily let go of Gaston. "Took who?"

Tim and ShadowLily shared a look, thinking of a certain proper lady who had recently been using the assassin's services.

Looking indignant, Gaston struggled to his feet. "Lorelei. They took her before I could stop them."

Tim was pissed off. No one fucked with one of his people. "Who snatched her, and where the fuck are they?" He felt his heartbeat thrumming in his ears and tried to calm down.

"Knights of Malvonis." When Gaston noticed their confused looks, he explained, "Offshoot of the assassins Guild that's unhappy with my leadership."

"But why take Lorelei?" ShadowLily asked. "She isn't an assassin."

Gaston started for the door, and Tim stopped him. "Let's get you a change of clothes before we go out into the city. The last thing we need now is the guards chasing us because you look like a murder victim."

Turning on a heel, Gaston headed for the inn. "They took her to get to me." He sounded disgusted. "When you can't get at a target, you have to lure them out."

"But you're all fucked up. Why didn't they just finish you off?" Tim asked without thinking of what the answer might be.

"Because I ran!" Gaston roared. "When I couldn't save her, I ran like a fucking coward."

ShadowLily pulled the blood-covered assassin into a hug. "You did the right thing. If you hadn't come here, we would have never known."

Tim wrapped both of them in his arms. "Let's go get her."

They followed Gaston to his rooms below the inn, where the assassin quickly changed and then started grabbing weapons off the shelves. "We have to hurry, but we also can't leave the inn or Joe's unprotected."

It took him a second to decide what to do, then Tim typed an emergency dispatch to Cassie and JaKobi.

Cassie, get JaKobi sober enough he can stand guard over the inn. I need you at Joe's to make sure no one screws with ShadowLily's dad. Lorelei has been taken, and we're going to get her.

Tim saw that Gaston was ready to roll. "Lead the way!"

The burly assassin didn't hesitate as he ran for the stairs. "Tonight, we end this!"

ShadowLily and Tim exchanged quick glances and knew they were on the same page. It was a look normally reserved for people who had been married for years that said, "We're in this together and I love you."

"Let's go get our girl." ShadowLily started running, and Tim was right behind her.

CHAPTER FIFTY-EIGHT

"Is this the place?" Tim hissed.

Gaston looked out over the lawn of the estate and nodded his head once. "Lord Astor was one of the guild's best clients and didn't approve of the changes I've made."

"Which means he's an evil prick." ShadowLily pointed her dagger toward the estate. "And tyrants always get what's coming to them."

"Let's try not to kill any nobles tonight." Gaston sounded worried. "Unless you're about to die, Astor is off-limits."

ShadowLily slammed her dagger back into its sheath. "Fine, but if he's hurt Lorelei or she's dead, all bets are off."

Tim knew better than to stand in the way of a moving freight train, and when ShadowLily put her mind on something, she might as well have been the Snow Piercer.

"Maybe they'll get lucky," Tim mused out loud. "Let's hope he doesn't make an appearance."

Both assassins looked at Tim as if he'd become delusional. He shrugged. It never hurt to be optimistic as long as you had a backup plan. Charging blindly into the future with no plan and hoping for the best was reckless. It was the kind of thing that normally ended in disaster.

As they started to run across the lawn, clinging to shadows from trees, bushes, and topiaries, Tim thought about one of his favorite shows back in the real world. While he'd never been a cook, he'd always been fascinated by restaurants. It shocked him how many people bought them with zero experience and wondered why they failed.

One thing about Tim was that he liked to have a plan. No way would he buy a restaurant without doing research on it first. Like now. He wished they had time to check out the estate before running onto it, blindly looking for Lorelei. Gaston seemed to know where he was going, so Tim decided to put his faith in him, and hope the assassin had a plan.

Gaston paused behind a thick tree and motioned for them to crouch down. "There is a cellar door about twenty yards ahead of us. Two men are standing beside it, but they don't look too worried. Idiots probably think I died."

"If you'd gotten to Joe's a few minutes later, you would have," Tim snapped. "Let's not get complacent now."

A grin formed on the assassin's face, and Tim knew he was in for news he wouldn't like.

"Fair point." Gaston's eyes shone with mirth. "That's why I'm going to have you two kill the guards while I keep an eye on things."

"But wouldn't it be better if I..." Tim started saying before being cut off.

"No." Gaston's voice was firm. "If we get into trouble, I'll be able to handle it faster."

ShadowLily huffed. "As if."

"My guess is there is at least one we can't see, so unless your stealth has reached the Master ranks yet, my point stands." Gaston looked into ShadowLily's eyes.

Tim felt a smile spread on his lips. It was bold to stare his woman down. Not many men could do it and survive. Thankfully, Gaston was like family, and Tim was pretty sure that put him on the exempt from getting stabbed list.

"We'll do your plan, but I want additional training after this," ShadowLily groused.

Gaston's disembodied voice called from the shadows to their right. "The best training is experience."

"Sounds like someone trying to get me to work for free," ShadowLily grumbled. "You ready?"

Tim compared Gaston's line to one of his friends who was an artist. She was always telling him about how people tried to get her to work for free like she didn't have bills to pay. No one wants to be living off ramen for the rest of their lives.

"Let's go save our friend." Tim activated his own sneak ability and made sure to equip his daggers and leather armor before heading into position.

ShadowLily didn't respond, but Tim felt her take the lead. He did his best to follow her and not make any noise. It wasn't as easy as he thought, even on the grass. If he wanted to keep his assassin skills relevant, he was going to need to spend more time using them.

After a few minutes of very intense stealthing, Tim was in position behind one of the guards. He wasn't exactly sure when to attack. Maybe ShadowLily would wait for his clumsy attempt at a backstab before she made her own. Standing behind the guard and not acting was making him nervous. Eventually, the guard would notice him and then all hell would break loose.

A countdown appeared in the upper right-hand corner of his vision.

3

Oh, shit.

2

Tim adjusted the grips on his daggers.

1

Lunging forward, he sank both of his blades into the man's back. Quickly pulling the daggers free, Tim slipped his left hand around the guard's chest and slit his throat with the knife in his right hand. He lowered the man to the ground and waited for the alarm to sound.

Nothing happened.

Tim's heartbeat started to slow down, and he looked back toward ShadowLily. Her guard was down and she was scanning the area. A sound behind them made them both spin around, but it was only Gaston dragging two bodies.

He dropped the bodies by the cellar door. "Never leave any evidence if it can be helped. A missing guard is one thing, finding a dead body is another."

Solid advice, Tim thought. It reminded him of some of the earlier stealth games he'd played. Staying hidden was always the key. It didn't matter if you were a ninja, a thief, or hitman, leaving bodies behind was a sure-fire way to get caught by a patrol you hadn't noticed.

"Let's get them inside before someone sees the three of us standing over their corpses." ShadowLily reached down to pull the cellar door open.

With the door open and no one springing out, she turned and grabbed her latest kill by the wrists and started dragging him to the entrance. A small grunt escaped her lips as she pulled the man over the lip of the cellar door and onto the stairs. With each step she took, there was a small thump as the man bumped along the wooden stairs in her wake.

Not one to waste time, Tim grabbed his own body and started moving. His attempt at dragging the man was a little more awkward. It wasn't the first time the game reminded him how much stronger his girlfriend was than him. At some point, he'd focus on getting his strength up to at least twenty, but other stats needed his attention first.

Tim dumped his guard behind a box at the bottom of the stairs and thought about how much less messy it was to kill someone with magic. Oftentimes, there wasn't any blood. Killing someone with a knife left so much more to clean up.

Gaston brought his two corpses down the stairs without making a sound. He added them to the pile and then moved back up the stairs to close the door. When the assassin returned to the cellar, he looked at the torches lining the walls every six feet. "From here on out it looks as though stealth probably won't be much of an option."

Tim changed out of his leather and back into his robe before pulling out his staff. "I'll be better off like this. If I can't sneak up on a target, my dagger skills are pretty useless."

ShadowLily poked him in the gut with a finger. "Just stay behind us, and don't let us die."

Gaston grinned. "Actually, this might work out perfectly."

"Is that the look I get when I have a plan?" Tim pointed at Gaston. "Because I don't like it one bit."

"Your look is a little less tie the sacrificial goat to the stake, but other than that it's about the same," ShadowLily said, clearly trying not to laugh at his discomfort.

Placing a hand on Tim's shoulder, Gaston pulled him closer. "How do you feel about being the bait?"

Fuck.

Tim tried to push his nerves down as his hand closed on the door handle.

Walking into the unknown was something he wasn't exactly comfortable with, but despite his feelings, he knew Gaston's plan made the most sense. Tim would never be able to stealth his way past trained assassins, and if walking into the room alone let them take out a few of the guards before an all-out brawl started, then he would do what he had to.

The door handle slipped a bit against his sweaty palm, but he managed to turn the knob on the first try. As he walked into the room, he felt Gaston and ShadowLily slide by him. The assassins gathered inside turned to look at him. As they spread out, Tim could see Lorelei tied to a chair behind them.

The ranger's head was bleeding, but her eyes looked alert enough. When she saw Tim, Lorelei bucked against her restraints but couldn't break free.

One of the guards turned and slapped Lorelei to make her stop. "Shut up, bitch."

"No need for that, gentlemen. I've come to collect my associate, and I'd prefer for her not to be damaged, if possible." Tim advanced a few steps into the room to make sure their attention was focused on him.

One of the assassins pointed a dagger at Tim. "So, you're that asshole who bought the inn and screwed up Malvonis' plans."

"The very same." Tim shrugged. "As for Malvonis' plans, well, we didn't ever really sit down and discuss them. The guy wasn't much of a talker."

One of the men moved to guard Lorelei while the other four advanced on Tim. The same little countdown timer appeared in his vision, and Tim knew it was almost time. His primary focus was going to be the man guarding Lorelei, while his friends focused on the others. He made sure his buffs were active and prepared to act.

When the countdown hit zero, Tim cast divine light at the man holding Lorelei. The blast of magic knocked him off his feet. Then he cast flame burst as a distraction. The flames roared out of his hands, forcing the other four men to back up a step. ShadowLily and Gaston took them down within seconds.

The man behind Lorelei groaned and started to climb to his feet. Tim was a little out of practice, but throwing a knife had to be like riding a bike. When you knew how to do it, you just knew.

Summoning a throwing knife from his inventory, he thought about his lessons with Gaston and let the blade fly.

Lorelei's eyes went wide as the blade missed her head by only a few inches before hitting her assailant in the chest. The three of them quickly checked to make sure everyone was dead, then converged on their wounded friend's chair like vultures on a carcass. A few moments later, she was free.

After ripping the gag out of her mouth, Lorelei stared at Tim. "Never do that again."

"Hey! What's a few deaths between friends?" The healer chuckled at the dark look on her face before relenting. Holding up his hand, Tim made a proclamation. "I solemnly swear not to throw knives that close to your head."

Gaston laughed. "The best part is, it wasn't even close to where he was aiming."

Tim punched Gaston in the shoulder. "At least if I fucked up, I could have healed her."

"No healing needed if you don't throw knives," Lorelei smirked. "But I also believe a thank you is in order."

ShadowLily waved off her thanks. "Friends don't have to say thank you. All they have to do is show up when you need them."

"Thank you, just the same," Lorelei replied as she looked around the room. "Now I want to know where that bitch is who set me up."

Tim tried not to laugh. "It was your date who did this?"

"I really do have the worst luck with women." Lorelei sighed.

Gaston flexed. "Maybe it's time for a change."

"Just keep it in your pants, big fella. I'm not down with the Dick." Lorelei patted Gaston on the chest. "But if you know any ladies who aren't crazy as fuck, I wouldn't mind an introduction."

"Maybe we can worry about your dating life later? We still need to get out of here." Tim pointed back the way they'd come. "I, for one, don't want to be here when Astor and his cronies show up."

Lorelei summoned her bow from her inventory and nocked an arrow. "Let's get the fuck out of here then."

The four of them ran down the corridor and up the steps. The cellar doors creaked open, and they stepped out into the cold night air. It didn't look like any guards had found their dead friends yet, so they had the opportunity to flee without being seen.

Tim finally let himself smile as they slipped back over the wall to the estate. Now that they were back in the city and not on private property, all they had to do was make it back to the inn. Not wanting to be on the streets any longer than possible, Tim stepped up to a kiosk and ordered a carriage ride.

The four of them piled into the carriage and started the long journey back to the Blue Dagger Inn.

Tim looked at his hands and wondered how bad of an enemy Lord Astor was going to be going forward. He had to find out more about what Malvonis was planning in the city and stop it. He didn't save Tristholm from the werewolves only to watch Promethia fall to an unseen threat.

Looking up from his hands, Tim focused his stare on Gaston. "Time for you to tell us what Malvonis wants and how we can help you stop it."

Gaston looked out the window and then at the floor before he started speaking. "He wants to run all of the crime in Promethia, and I want to stop him."

Reaching out, Tim placed a hand on the assassin's shoulder and waited until he looked up to speak. "We're with you. Just tell us what you need."

They spent the rest of the carriage ride coming up with a rudimentary plan to limit Malvonis' influence in Promethia until they could take him out of the equation for good.

CHAPTER FIFTY-NINE

"My spies tell me Malvonis is at Lord Astor's mansion," Gaston rumbled.

Spinning a dagger around one finger, ShadowLily smiled. "We were just there, so it's probably a trap."

"Of course it's a trap!" Ernie roared. "Malvonis isn't dumb enough to tell anyone where he is without a reason."

Having met the man himself, Tim had to agree. Malvonis wasn't the type of guy who took chances. If he wanted you to know he was somewhere, then he was probably somewhere else. They had heard the half-orc assassin's name mentioned more than once around Tristholm.

Tim was starting to think Malvonis might have been turned into a wraith. From his few interactions with the man, he didn't seem like the type to take orders from anyone. Jepsom had the assassin under his thumb before the wraiths killed him. If Malvonis tried to stealth his way under the mountain, he could have been turned.

Or maybe he just saw an opportunity for power.

It was hard to judge a man's intentions until you knew what

motivated him. Malvonis seemed to want money and respect. Taking orders didn't seem to be something that concerned him, so Tim was willing to put his money on the half-orc being corrupted by Vitaria somehow.

"I agree with Ernie. Storming Lord Astor's compound again doesn't seem like the right call." Tim tapped a finger on his chin as he tried to puzzle out the situation. "Could it get us in trouble with the other nobles?"

Ernie looked at Tim. "It depends on how it's presented. Most of them hate Lord Astor, but if they think they might be next on the chopping block, you can expect them to band together to wipe you out."

"Fuck that guy," Cassie snarled. "He took one of ours, and he has to pay."

Lorelei grinned. "A little payback wouldn't hurt my feelings any."

They were going to attack. You didn't kidnap a member of their guild without facing serious repercussions. He just wasn't sold on the idea they had to walk into a trap to do it. "What if we lured him to somewhere of our choosing?"

"Why would he come?" Gaston took a sip of his beer. "He controls the variables at the estate, and if Malvonis really *is* there, he's got one hell of a weapon on his side."

Remembering how quickly Malvonis had moved when he stabbed Ernie, Tim had to agree. The half-orc was more like a boss monster, and if he had help at the manor, there was no reason to leave. Lord Astor and his guards were a wild card.

Tim hated surprises.

He let the conversation around him fade into the background and focused on their options. To go or not to go, that was the question. The smart money was on avoiding the trap, but what kind of message would that send to others? That it was okay to kidnap their members.

Not on his watch. People needed to be made aware that if you screwed with the Blue Dagger Society, there would be swift and severe repercussions. Still, they had to find a way to do this as safely as possible. Gaston couldn't come back to life like the rest of them.

So what were they going to do?

They couldn't protect the bar and the inn forever, not without hiring guards. Guards didn't work for free, and mercenaries would always take a few extra coins to betray you. Tim doubted Lord Astor would let them just leave without retaliating, which put them in a tougher spot. How could they go back to Tristholm with so much to lose at home?

When Tim thought about the choices, there really wasn't a choice at all. "We take the fight to him."

Ernie looked shocked. "Tell me you didn't just say that?"

Standing up from his chair, Tim looked around the room to meet everyone's eyes before addressing Ernie. "We take the fight to him." He waved away the Poison Master's objection. "The fact is, we can't afford to leave such a powerful enemy behind. What good is saving Tristholm from Vitaria if Promethia falls to her advances in our absence?"

JaKobi stood up. "I'm with you, boss. Can't have this guy breathing down our necks while we're trying to save the world."

"Of course I'm with you, but I still think it's a trap." ShadowLily slammed her dagger back into its sheath. "I'd put money on Malvonis not being there, and Lord Astor being a pawn for Vitaria."

Tim knew as soon as she said the words she was right. "Then let's plan accordingly. It's only a trap if you don't know you're walking into it."

Cassie gave Gaston a brief glance before looking back to Tim. "Maybe we should send our burly friend to speak to a certain noble that we know. Having Lady Briarthorn on our side to deal with the fallout would be huge."

"And it'd keep him from dying." Lorelei stood up and gave

Gaston a hug. "Thank you for trying to save me, and then actually saving me."

Gaston looked a little shocked by her show of affection. "If Malvonis is there, you're going to need me." He patted the ranger on the back. "And you're welcome."

Tim didn't ask why Gaston had been following Lorelei in the first place. There was something deeper going on with his battle for the city's assassins. Fortunately for their burly compatriot, they didn't have time to dig into all the subtle nuances right now.

"We are going to assume that he isn't there. If Malvonis shows up and we all die, then you can count on the fact I'll be bringing you with me next time." Tim smiled. "Don't get bent out of shape just yet."

Gaston gave Lorelei one last squeeze. The look in his eyes was one of brotherly affection. The assassin really did care for all of them. "You mean I get to spend the rest of the night in Lady Briarthorn's company drinking wine, while you have to fight the unknown? And you think I'm upset."

Tim took his point. Drinking in the company of a beautiful and brilliant woman was hardly a burden. "Thanks for taking one for the team."

"We all have to do our part." Gaston waved at them as he strode from the room. "See you in the morning."

Cassie waited for the door to close behind him before speaking. "There is something going on between those two, I just know it."

"*Real Housewives of the Etheric Coast*, tonight at ten," Lorelei snarked.

Tim felt the same as the rest of them. There was a story there. They didn't get to know the details, and missing out on those sweet nuggets of information only made them even more curious. They'd left Promethia when Gaston had an assassin guild problem and Lady Briarthorn had a suitor problem, and now one of those issues seemed largely resolved.

Maybe one day he'd be able to pry the truth out of one of them.

Until then, it was time to focus on what they needed to do tonight. "Looks like we're headed back to Lord Astor's manor." Tim looked at the group. "Everyone ready?"

"Let me get this straight," Cassie said with a smile. "We don't know who's waiting for us, how many of them there are, and we're pretty damn sure it's a trap." When everyone nodded, she continued. "I like those odds."

JaKobi put an arm around Cassie's shoulders. "And I like her, so I'm in."

"No one fucks with one of us." ShadowLily looked at Lorelei. "And you *are* one of us."

The ranger looked as if she were about to cry. "Just know I'd do the same for any of you."

Tim nodded. "I think we all feel the same way, that's what makes us guild. We ride together, we die together."

"Blue Daggers for life." JaKobi thrust his fist into the air like a bad boy from an eighties movie.

Ernie frowned at them. "I'm going to make sure Joe is okay. Liz will take care of the inn." The Poison Master stalked out, clearly unimpressed with their decision-making skills.

The rest of the group started to laugh as Tim pulled them into a quick huddle. "This is what we have mapped of the estate. We don't know much else, so it's going to be interesting. The only thing I know for sure is I don't want to enter from the same spot we did last time."

"That's not much of a plan," Cassie quipped.

Tim shrugged. "It is what it is. Let's go dish out some justice."

CHAPTER SIXTY

Torches covered Lord Astor's lawn.

"That's a bit of a change," Tim grumbled as he looked out over the massive yard that led to the house.

ShadowLily crouched on top of the wall next to him. "At least we don't have to hide now."

Looking at the sea of flickering lights, Tim thought that even if they had arrows that could splash water on the torches, the amount of time it would take to carve out a path wouldn't be worth it. Not to mention, anyone watching from the house would probably notice hundreds of torches going out in a line.

Cassie jumped down into the yard. "Let's hurry this shit up, I'd still like to get some sleep tonight."

"Sleep is for the weak," JaKobi replied as he landed next to her.

Turning, Cassie poked him in the chest. "Says the guy who was passed out cold a few hours ago."

"Being passed out doesn't count as sleeping." JaKobi looked back up at the wall. "Help me out here."

The three remaining members of the group all jumped off the wall to land on the finely manicured lawn. Tim clapped JaKobi on the back. "I think the best thing we can do is get this fight started, so you don't dig the hole any deeper."

"Spoken like a man who's had to dig himself out of a lot of holes," ShadowLily quipped.

Tim nodded. He had his fair share of experience saying the wrong thing at the wrong time. It was funny for someone who liked to plan things out, how often he screwed up when speaking to people. If the worst thing someone could say about him was that he was a little awkward, then life wasn't so bad.

A chanting sound started from somewhere deeper in the estate's grounds.

"Well, if that isn't ominous, I don't know what is." Lorelei gazed across the open space. "I don't see anything yet."

Cassie started walking forward, angling herself toward the main path that led to the house. If they weren't trying to be subtle, there was no reason to walk through the grass. Tim kept his head on a swivel but didn't see anyone rushing toward them. The entire time, all he could think of was, how did they set up the torches so quickly?

There must have been thousands of torches set in the ground, and they'd only been gone for a few hours. Either Lord Astor had an army, or there was something magical going on here. The chanting grew louder and picked up speed.

"I don't know about you guys, but I'd like to get to wherever the chanting is coming from and stop it." Tim had never played a game where chanting in the dark was a good thing.

Cassie turned to look at Tim. "Just don't bitch about the running." She started to jog.

"No promises," Tim huffed as he picked up his pace. One of the good things about being a healer was that he was always in the back of the group, so they couldn't see how much he hated running.

Not that they didn't know already.

They reached the manor, and Tim gawked at the size of the

place. He'd only gotten a small glimpse from the side of the house when they'd entered the cellar. From his sneak peek he knew the house was big, but this was more than he'd imagined. There was no reason a person needed a ten thousand square foot residence, not unless they had a family of thirty.

He laughed at the idea of his family owning a place like this. There would probably be wings of the entire house they never used. That or they would live in a different part of the house every day. If you decorated each section differently, it'd be like going on vacation in the same house.

Sometimes he watched people remodel giant houses on TV and marveled at the stuff people put inside. Pools, movie theaters, bowling alleys, basketball courts, and sometimes even more exotic features. While it was super cool, he couldn't imagine paying the upkeep on something like that.

Not to mention the cleaning.

Tim had enough trouble keeping his room clean, and the cost of hiring someone to keep a house that size cleaned seemed crazy. It was the type of place that would require permanent staff. If you were rich enough, it didn't matter, but he'd rather have a smaller house on just as much land.

No full-time employees required.

Cassie started making her way around the house. The tank kept her head moving from side to side, but there was nothing to see except more torches. The chanting stopped, and they froze in place as though one false move would kill them instantly. When death and destruction didn't rain down upon them, Cassie started creeping forward again.

The chanting took on a new rhythm. The people's voices moved up and down in volume, almost as if they were making music. Tim couldn't make out the words, but he had a feeling that whatever was going on wasn't for their benefit.

The group came around the corner and froze again.

Behind the house was a circle of thirteen torches. Standing in front of each torch was a person in a red robe trimmed with gold. Hoods covered their faces, so there was no way to know who they were. As their voices rose in harmony, a man walked out of the house and approached the circle.

Five torches in the center of the circle lit in unison. Fire spread between the five points, leaving a burning pentagram on the ground. The robbed figures fell to their knees, their voices never wavering. They started to bow and rise as the chanting continued. Tim knew they should try to stop whatever ritual was taking place, but he had no idea how. Just as he was about to nudge Cassie, the man outside of the circle's voice rose above all the others.

"Vitaria! I am your loyal servant. In my time of need, I beseech you to send me a guardian." The man thrust his arms into the air, and a dagger in his right hand gleamed in the torchlight.

The dagger moved quickly as the man slashed his left forearm nine times with the blade. "Three times three, the offering has been made." Blood dripped from his wounded arm as he walked around the circle and sprinkled the thirteen chanters with his blood. "My blood for you, my life for you."

The chanters stopped and repeated what their leader said.

"All will bow before your will. May the darkness consume them." He strode into the pentagram and slit his own throat.

The thirteen chanters around the edges of the outer circle all stood as one and repeated the gesture. One by one, they fell to the ground as their life's blood poured out, staining the grass crimson red. Tim thought about saving them, but fourteen less Vitaria worshippers in the world didn't seem like such a bad thing.

"Oh, shit," Cassie stammered as she pointed at the center of the circle.

The man who killed himself first was rising into the air, his body spinning in a slow circle. He landed on his feet a moment later, and his eyes found their group instantly. "Welcome to my manor. Sadly, you won't be around long enough to enjoy the hospitality."

"If this is what passes for good manners, I think I'll skip the dinner invitation." JaKobi looked over the other corpses, making sure none of them were standing up.

"Such rude little creatures," Lord Astor said with disdain. "You know, none of this would have been necessary if you had just gotten out of the way. Your assassin friend sealed your fates the moment he stood against us."

Lord Astor looked over the group and snorted. "And in the end, he didn't even show up to help you. Now you know what friendship is really worth."

Tim was about to snap a witty line about how friendship is what you make it, but something started forming in the pentagram as Lord Astor moved to the outer circle. A huge cloud of swirling darkness spun around like a tornado before pulling into itself. There was a shape in the middle that he couldn't quite make out.

"Cassie, get ready!" Tim cried as the inky darkness started to dissipate.

A demon of some kind formed in the circle as they watched. The ugly fucker had red skin and golden hair. Tim had never seen a monster like it in any other game. Maybe it was the colors that were throwing him off. The demon's body finished forming, and Lord Astor started to laugh.

"I hope you enjoy my little surprise," Lord Astor smirked at them as the demon roared into the night.

The creature's body was man-like in that it had two legs, and a head-on top of its shoulders. The similarities stopped there. The tail had him worried. It looked more like a crocodile tail than something from a mammal, and then there were the wings.

Why did really scary shit always have wings?

The demon's wings unfurled and flapped a few times. The beast towered over Lord Astor, easily three times the height of a normal man. Muscles rippled as the creature pulled a massive double-bladed axe from out of thin air. Tim wouldn't have been surprised if the axe weighed as much as the house.

Lord Astor turned and looked up into the face of the creature he'd summoned. "Kill them!" he commanded.

Laughter bellowed from the demon's mouth as he looked down on the tiny human in front of him. "I have risen from the seventh gate. The seals have been broken."

The demon reached out and grabbed Lord Astor around the waist. As Lord Astor struggled, the demon laughed in his face. "No one commands me, but Vitaria. Especially not someone as delicious as yourself."

Lord Astor's screams were cut off abruptly when the demon bit off his head. The crunch as he chewed made Tim think of someone biting straight to the Tootsie Roll center of a Tootsie Pop. The demon sucked at Lord Astor's neck like someone sucking the meat out of a crawfish and then tossed the rest of the body aside.

Looking down on the five mortals, the demon spoke again. "The lambs always come so willingly to the slaughter. Have you also come to offer yourselves to Azak, The Defiler?"

"I've got something to offer you." Cassie flipped Azak the bird and started running forward.

JaKobi grinned as he moved into position. "Oh, shit, here we go again."

Lorelei moved to follow JaKobi, and ShadowLily winked out of existence. Tim cast both his buffs on the party and followed it up with curse of giving on the boss. Before Cassie's first blow landed, he dropped into his Way of the Boulder stance, thinking the tank was going to need all the healing she could get.

Azak launched into the air. The wind he created buffeted Cassie back a few steps and gave the demon room to operate. His axe whistled as he brought it down to cut her in half. Rolling to the side, their tank missed being split down the middle, but the lawn exploded from the impact and sent her crashing to the ground.

Tim quickly cast a healing orb on their fallen tank as he shouted to the party, "Light him up!"

Arrows slammed into the demon's chest but bounced away,

doing very little damage. Tim looked at Lorelei and sensed her frustration. His head turned to follow JaKobi's phoenix as it flew across the estate before slamming into Azak.

The Demon laughed as the fire burst over him.

"So fire is out," Tim mumbled to himself as he tried to work out a plan.

"Is this the best you have to offer?" Azak beat his wings as he lifted another few feet into the air. Flames erupted from his mouth like he was a dragon.

Lorelei cringed as the flames headed straight for her. Tim watched in horror as the ranger held up the bow like a shield, but it wouldn't be enough to save her. The flames reached her position and hit some kind of barrier.

Screaming, "You shall not pass!" at the top of his lungs, JaKobi stood with one hand extended toward the fire. Sweat dripped off his brow as he fought to shield Lorelei from the flames.

Knowing there wasn't a lot of time to act, Tim fired off his next two spells. Weaken undead slammed into the demon, quickly followed by who needs a shield. He didn't know if the reduced damage and the extra damage received to the demon would make a difference, but every little bit had to help.

They weren't going to lose. It just wasn't possible.

The flames stopped, and Azak lowered himself to the ground. Cassie was there a moment later, harassing the demon with her bō staff. Cuts appeared on his legs as the spikes embedded in the end of her staff activated, but the boss' health didn't seem to be dropping by all that much. The demon lifted his axe and then slammed it into the ground, using the giant double head as a shield to keep Cassie away from his legs.

The giant axe head was enough to keep the tank out of reach, but it also meant the demon couldn't attack them. So far, all of their attacks didn't seem very useful. Lorelei's arrows remained ineffective, and JaKobi might as well have been sitting this one out. In the future, they were going to have to find some way to diversify his skill set. They couldn't afford to have one party member be completely worthless against any enemy.

ShadowLily appeared as her blade tore through one of Azak's wings. It was a crippling blow based on how fast the boss' health dropped from the strike. With Azak reeling, Tim decided it was his chance to go on the offensive. This seemed like the perfect battle for a warrior of light.

Behold my power attached itself to the boss like a ticking time bomb. All they had to do was make it another ten seconds and they would have a real shot at winning this fight.

Tim started casting divine light as rapidly as he could. Each time behold my power stole a portion of his health, his attacks faltered, but he managed to hit the demon five times in a row before the demon's attention turned away from the tank and focused on him.

Oh, shit!

Azak swatted behind himself and sent ShadowLily crashing to the ground. A flick of his axe to the side had the same effect on Cassie. While neither of the women had been seriously injured, they also wouldn't be able to help Tim before the demon cut him down.

The boss lowered his shoulder and started to charge.

Not knowing if he'd make it through the fight or not, Tim quickly cast healing storm. He ducked, hoping in some way the demon might miss him if he was a small enough target. With one last desperate breath, he cast divine light and gritted his teeth as he waited for impact.

Barbara was going to get a kick out of this death.

Hearing the sizzle of fire all around him, Tim opened his eyes. JaKobi had covered him with his flame shield. Thankfully, they didn't have to see if it worked. Tim's hastily cast divine light clipped the boss in the shin right as behold my power took effect. Azak hit the ground hard, screaming in rage as he tried to get back up.

The demon clearly wasn't used to fighting without the use of one of his wings, and the loss of that limb was throwing his balance off. ShadowLily was on him a moment later, slashing her way up his legs with her daggers. Cassie kept her attacks focused on the boss's arms as he tried to push himself up from the ground.

A third fighter leaped into the mix, and Tim was surprised to see it was Lorelei. She had her kukri out and was slashing at Azak with reckless abandon.

The demon looked up at Tim, hate burning in his eyes. His mouth opened to curse the healer and a blast of divine light slammed into the demon's open mouth, ripping out chunks of flesh. When the light dissipated, Azak's face was charred.

ShadowLily finally reached Azak's head. Her legs slid around the demon's thick neck and her arms swung out wide. Her hands came down like dueling pendulums, the blades only stopping as they sank into the sides of Azak's skull. The last of the demon's health bled off as she pulled her daggers free.

"Not so delicious now, am I, bitch?" ShadowLily roared as she lifted her ichor encrusted blades into the air.

Tim felt his legs weaken as his mana dipped to dangerously low levels. He took a seat on the grass and watched Azak's body exploded into beautiful swirling motes of light. Hands slid under his shoulders, and someone lifted him into the air.

"That was a little bit closer than I would have liked." Tim smiled at JaKobi and motioned for the man to let him go.

"Any fight you can walk away from is a win in my book." The pyromancer clapped Tim on the back, almost making him stumble. "But, I'm going to have to talk to my trainer about how to deal with fire-resistant monsters."

Lorelei flicked black goo off her blade. "It wasn't just you. All of our attacks were ineffective. I bet his resistances were through the roof."

"Demons." Cassie sighed as she looked at Lord Astor's remains. "Can't trust 'em even if you make a deal."

ShadowLily snorted. "The devil only wins until he doesn't." She looked at the chest that now rested where Azak's body had been and placed her hand on it.

Smiling as the coins appeared in his inventory, Tim addressed the group. "Let's head back and make sure nothing is happening at the inn." He looked around the estate. "I don't want to be here to answer questions when the guards show up."

"At least they can't hold us responsible for killing Lord Astor. That idiot got his own head ripped off like the first bite of a freezer pop. It wasn't our fault this time." Cassie kicked the top half of the Lord's corpse over before poking him with her staff. When she noticed everyone looking at her, she shrugged. "Just making sure."

Tim chuckled. He'd seen enough films in his life to know that you should never leave an enemy behind. It was always that one case of misplaced generosity that got people killed. Thankfully for them, everyone here had either killed themselves or been killed by the demon.

Knowing the easiest way to get things moving, Tim pointed toward the exit. "The first round is on me."

No one needed to be told twice.

CHAPTER SIXTY-ONE

"**F**uck!" Gaston roared as he slammed his fist on the bar.

The glasses on the bar bounced in the air from the force of the assassin's strike. "I really hoped Malvonis would be there, and all of this could have ended quickly."

Tim knew better than to try to comfort Gaston right now, so instead, he fell back on the time-honored tradition of talking shit about the other guy. "Malvonis doesn't strike me as a man who fights his own battles."

"You'd be wrong about that." Gaston took a shot of whiskey. "But he does always try to get someone else to fight them first."

Turning away from the bar, the assassin locked eyes with Tim. "There will always be a threat to the assassins guild as long as Malvonis is out there, and there will always be people who say his way was the right way."

Tim knocked back his shot of whiskey. "The only thing I care about is how we can help."

ShadowLily tipped her glass back and made a face as the fiery liquid coursed down her throat. "You've done so much for us. Tell me how we can help before we have to leave town again."

Gaston poured himself another shot. "There is only one thing left to do." His eyes locked onto the innkeeper's. "Send the message."

Ernie's face went pale. "Are you sure?"

"Can't be helped now." Gaston nodded, and Ernie ran out of the room.

Tim looked at ShadowLily, then back at their burly friend. "What message?"

"If Malvonis isn't going to show, I have to…" Gaston poured another shot. "Tomorrow night is going to be a real bitch."

Standing up from their table, ShadowLily crossed the room to stand by Gaston's side. "Our offer stands. Tell us how we can help."

"Qwark is one of our most ancient rituals, but we have another for disputes that can't be solved so easily. When the hatred between members goes so deep the ritual is insufficient, we solve the problem in the only way assassins can: with death."

Gaston had a hint of a smile on his face. "The first time I saw the ritual of death, I was seven. The men fought for what seemed like hours until finally, one of them was cut down. With his death, the guild was made whole."

Shocked by Gaston's story, Tim poured himself another shot. "Seems like there would be an easier way."

"The ritual is a last resort, but one that is needed." Gaston put his glass down. "The guild comes before us all, and having unsettled disputes causes dissension in the ranks. Instead of letting individual grievances fester, we let the gods decide."

Pouring the last of the bottle into his cup, Gaston frowned. "There was a time such a thing was reserved to balance the scales when someone went off the rails and attacked the families of other members, or took jobs not sponsored by the guild to create chaos. Malvonis has polluted our order, and I will not let it stand!"

Tim took his empty glass to the bar and set it down. "So, what do we have to do?"

"Our side will need to have a witness." Gaston placed a hand on each of their shoulders. "I would like it to be you."

"Of course we'll go." ShadowLily smiled.

Tim felt good about what Gaston was asking them to do, but one question kept darting around his mind. "What happens to the witnesses if their champion loses?"

The assassin smiled. "Death is the way."

ShadowLily looked excited by the prospect. "Get ready for a shit storm."

"I won't lose." Gaston rumbled as he started swaying his way toward the basement stairs.

Tim wondered how much someone with Gaston's dexterity had to drink before they actually fell over. "Live or die, we stand with you."

The door to Gaston's training area opened and closed without a word.

ShadowLily nudged Tim in the side. "If we're going to die tomorrow, we might as well make the most of tonight."

"You had me at 'Let's go to the bedroom,'" Tim replied as he started making his way to the stairs.

"Hey, I never said that!" ShadowLily pouted.

Tim held out his hand for her. "A good man anticipates his woman's desires."

"A good man would already be waiting in bed." She laughed at the expression on Tim's face. "I guess the search for perfection must continue."

Tim started up the stairs two at a time, his clothes disappearing halfway up. "I'm in bed, I'm in bed."

ShadowLily snickered. "Sometimes it's too easy."

"Seems as if your travels have made you weak," Ironbeard said with a chuckle.

The hammer in Tim's hand went up and down relentlessly as he pounded the steel blade. Pumping the bellows was one thing, but working the hammer was something else. If he ever wanted to become great at crafting steel, he was going to have to get stronger. Maybe there was some way he could train to increase his strength, so he wouldn't have to waste his skill points leveling it.

As it was, Tim had enough strength to hit the steel hard enough to shape it, but not much else. If working the metal became harder when you wanted to add enchantments, he wasn't going to be able to do it without some upgrades. For now, he was satisfied to be learning something besides making gold bars.

"I've always been weak. I'm shaping this steel with nothing but determination." Tim grimaced and reminded himself to let the hammer do the work.

That shit was heavy for a reason.

IronBeard laughed. "Grit and determination have seen a lot of men through hard times, but sometimes at the forge, you need more than strength of character."

Reaching out, the smith caught Tim's hammer before it could descend again. "I think that's enough."

Tim donned his heat resistant gloves and picked up the blade. His arms were so tired the blade almost crashed to the ground, but he managed to keep it up until he reached the barrel of salt water. He sank the blade in, enjoying the sound of the metal hissing as it cooled.

As he removed the blade from the water, he moved it back over to the forge. The key now was to not heat the metal to the point where he could shape it again, but hot enough that some of the durability would return to the blade.

The first sword Tim made had shattered on contact, the second one lasted exactly four hits. The third held up on the dummy but shattered when IronBeard smashed his dwarven hammer against it.

This time he had to do it right.

He waited for the moment he thought was right and pulled the blade free. A second later, he stuck the blade into a pile of coarse sand. It wasn't the traditional way of cooling the metal after it had been reheated. Normally you did it in the air, but the dwarf had his little tricks and Tim wasn't going to complain as he learned them.

A smile stretched across his lips. He was pretty sure he did it right. "I've got this."

"Guess we'll find out tomorrow." IronBeard pointed to a clock on the wall. "Don't you have places to be?"

Tim glanced at the clock. "That can't be right?" He was late.

"Before you go sprinting off like a fox escaping the hen house, I've got something for you." IronBeard held out a perfectly curved dagger.

It was the nicest blade Tim had ever seen in the game. "Is this the one I commissioned?"

"It is." The dwarf handed Tim the dagger. "It's some of my best work."

Was it wrong to want the knife for himself if he still gave it to Gaston? "The blade is beautiful." Tim placed the weapon in his inventory. "Would it be possible to order a twin?"

"Thankfully for you, I anticipated your needs." Ironbeard pulled out a twin of the beautiful dagger he'd already presented to Tim. "Ten gold and it's yours."

"Extortion," Tim replied as he forked over the additional gold. They both knew the price was a bargain.

Fuck, he still had to go.

His feet were moving before his mouth could catch up. "See you in the morning," Tim shouted as he ran from the building.

A lot depended on how tonight went, and his late arrival wouldn't help. Tim knew he should have set an alarm when he walked into Ironbeard's shop. Time had a way of slipping past him when he was working at the forge. The only other time that happened to him was when he was playing video games.

Tim always thought slipping into the zone was like a marathon runner's trance. His brain was normally so active that it didn't happen. Finding another place he could quiet his mind was amazing, unless he had an important appointment to keep. Then it was more like that song about missing things because you got high.

I wanted to help my friends, but then I got to smithing.

It didn't have the same ring to it as the original ditty, but Tim didn't mind. No one else was going to hear it. It wasn't like he was trying to make a living off creating parody tunes. As far as he knew, only one man was successful at that, and Weird Al wasn't sharing his recipe to success in a Master Class.

As he was running through the market, Tim switched out of his work clothes and into his robes. A stall selling rumpleberries grabbed his attention. Something about being a kid playing soccer and eating tons of orange slices came to mind as he bought three before moving on. A few moments later and he was out of his robes and into his leather outfit cutting open the rumpleberry with his dagger as he walked through the streets back to the inn.

Tim had finished his last rumpleberry when the familiar arch to the slums appeared, along with his favorite two guards. "What's shaking, gentlemen?"

"Certainly not Chris' knees," Barry snorted.

Chris glared at the man. "That was one time, and that guy was scary as shit."

Fighting down his urge to laugh about a guard being scared of someone, Tim decided he was more curious about who it was. "What happened?"

"Not one word, Barry!" Chris snapped. "Guards don't throw guards under the carriage wheels."

Barry chuckled. "In your defense, that guy was huge."

"And rather muscly," Chris added.

At the mention of huge and muscly, Tim's stomach clenched. He could think of one half-orc that fit the bill of scary as shit, and he really hoped he wasn't waiting for him at the inn. "When was this?"

Barry looked at Tim with a smirk. "Look Chris, you got the new guy scared just by telling a story."

"At least I actually had to be intimidated before I got scared." Chris looked at Tim as though wondering how the man was still alive.

He almost lost his cool, but at the last second Tim was able to rein it back in enough not to look too deranged. "Just tell me if it happened tonight?" Tim snapped.

"Nothing to worry about, sir, this was weeks ago." He lowered his voice in a conspiratorial whisper. "Crazy thing. I swear the guy had fangs."

Chris frowned. "Looked more like tusks to me. Not something I ever expected to see inside the city."

Tim felt the pit of dread in his stomach start to disappear. At least he hadn't missed the fight. Looking over the two guards, he thought they had every right to be scared. Malvonis wouldn't have given a second thought to slaughtering these two men where they stood.

It felt like it was time to steer the conversation back to something less dastardly before he left. "Have you two tried Joe's yet?"

"I don't trust any business that operates out of the slums," Chris said, looking offended at the very suggestion.

Barry looked slightly more hopeful. "Haven't been there yet, but I hear good things."

Tim smiled. These two guys were in for a treat if he could actually get them through the door. "If you guys ever want to go, your first meal is on me." Despite the fact these two were normally a pain in the ass, having a few guards on the other side of the wall wouldn't hurt anything.

"Sweet." Barry nudged Chris. "Now we really have to go."

Chris frowned at his partner.

"I'll set it up with Joe and tell him to expect at least one of you." Tim started walking through the arch. "I promise you won't be disappointed."

Chris pouted. "Well, it does look a little less trashy in there."

"Just don't screw up our chance for a free meal," Barry quipped. "Not all of us are made out of gold."

"As if. I get the same damn pay as you do," Chris retorted.

Tim grinned as he walked down his newly cobbled street. Even the slight mist that had started couldn't take away his feeling of accomplishment about what he'd done in the slums. His morning meeting with Mr. Applebottom made things even better. With Tim's parents getting money from his contract, Tim was able to spend more of his in-game resources to speed up his projects.

It felt weird using so much of his wealth to do something that would only pay off in the future. Money had always felt like a right-now thing, but in *The Etheric Coast*, he had the opportunity to do so much more thanks to the high priest's quest. It felt good to know he was helping people with more than just healing.

Giving people the opportunity to not live paycheck to paycheck was huge. Sure, they had to put the work in themselves to start a business and to make it thrive, but he felt like a small part of their success for giving them the tools to do it. A good-looking storefront, access to a market kiosk, and a freshly cobbled street was just the start.

Eventually, the reputation of this part of town would change. There were good people living in the slums of Promethia. People who worked hard and took pride in what they made. All he was doing was giving them the chance to be the driver of their destiny, instead of being beholden to their station.

And if he made a nice little profit along the way, even better.

No one said you couldn't make money and not be a giant asshole. He was a firm believer that if you treated people right, and paid them accordingly, they would work their asses off for you. If an employer offered the lowest salary, most people would look at the job as a stepping-stone to get them to their next opportunity.

It seemed like a losing policy for companies to spend so much money training people only to let them walk out the door for a few thousand dollars more a year.

Thankfully for him, he didn't have to train anyone. All he had to do was pay Mr. Applebottom to collect the rents he set, and the earnings from the kiosk went directly into his bank account. He hadn't checked on his total funds in a while and made a mental note to do it soon. Tim's only responsibility was to live up to his end of the deal. He would have to keep the freshly cobbled main street in good repair, as well as the storefronts. Any problem a tenant in one of his buildings had was also his responsibility if Mr. Applebottom couldn't resolve it first.

It felt good being the one designating assignments, instead of receiving them. It freed up his time for adventuring quite nicely.

Tim laughed as he opened the door to the inn. Who was he kidding, he didn't do any of the work. "Money for nothing and rent's not free."

Mr. Applebottom was more than happy to coordinate and run his business for him in his absence, and his fee was reasonable. Hiring the right person for the job was the key to any business longevity. There would always be turnover, but filling those spots with amazing people was paramount. Hopefully, he was paying him enough not to want to leave, and if not, he'd be getting a raise.

"On time, as usual," ShadowLily groused as he walked in the door.

Tim didn't have a defense. He knew he was late, and there was only one thing he could do. "Sorry."

"Good thing I told you to be here an hour earlier than we needed you." ShadowLily smiled like she'd just pulled off a miracle.

Sneaky and devious she was. Thank God she was on his side. "You know me so well."

Gaston emerged from his room. "Let's go, and keep your mouths shut."

"Before we do the whole broody silence thing, I have something for you." Tim pulled the daggers from his inventory and held them out to Gaston. "I had these made for you, for helping us with the wraiths."

Gaston took the weapons and took a few practice slashes with them. "These are amazing."

"I'm glad you like them. I hope they help with the fight." Tim flipped up his hood. "I'm ready to go."

"Like I said, mouths shut, eyes open," Gaston growled as he started for the door.

Tim knew better than to interrupt the assassin again. He gave ShadowLily a quick nod and hurried to catch up.

CHAPTER SIXTY-TWO

Gaston grinned as he entered the Temple of Blades.

This place felt like home to him. It was where he passed the trials and earned his first kill. Since then, he'd been challenged four times in single combat, and won every match. The only person he'd ever hesitated to fight was Malvonis. After seeing the way the half-orc ripped apart the Grandmaster, it had been an easy call to make.

How I wish I'd struck him down then.

It was funny how the problems left for tomorrow turned into problems for today if you let them. Malvonis had been weakened, the council in shock. No one would have questioned if he stepped forward to end the bastard as he bled on the ritual room floor. It was only his pride that had stopped him. That and his belief in the code.

Back then, he thought there would be plenty of time to bring Malvonis down, but instead, the man only grew stronger. He brought in worthless thieves to swell their ranks, and to steal votes. He changed the code, but there were always those who honored the old ways. They lined up behind Gaston now.

Those men who only cared about gold, and had no honor, lined the other side of the room. Gaston wasn't sure who they would select as their champion, but as long as Malvonis himself didn't show up, this fight was his. There wasn't another assassin in the guild who could hold a blade to him.

He'd been training for the last ten years to kill the man who polluted their order. If he wasn't here, then one of his henchmen was the next best thing. He looked at the growing number of men and women across the room and wondered if any of them had the balls to step forward.

He'd kill every single one of them if the situation demanded it.

The raised rectangular mat dominated the center of the room. Twelve feet wide and thirty feet long, the mat was designed to give the two fighters enough room to maneuver, but not enough that they could avoid each other for long. Not that avoidance in the arena was ever a problem. If things had gotten to the point they needed to be solved here, then death was the answer.

Some of the men lined up across from them had never seen a duel in action. Malvonis got rid of the rituals as a way to make entering the assassins Guild easier. Gaston remembered a time when you had to kill your way into the guild. He still felt the sting of the blade as it pierced his thigh like it was yesterday. He'd given up his limb to make sure he landed the killing blow.

Pain was something that could be tolerated, death was the end of the line.

Fifteen years old seemed like a young age for a man to become a killer, but when you grew up on the streets of Promethia, if you hadn't done worse, you were blessed by the goddess. Killing kept him fed, it kept coins in his pocket, and eventually he was invited to try out for a spot in the guild.

Four months he'd spent locked in a cell only slightly wider than he could reach. Outside of the locked room, he was taught how to hold a blade, and where to pierce a man to kill him as quickly as possible. Each day he pushed his body harder than the day before.

Sit-ups, pushups, knife skills, food, repeat. When he emerged from his cell, he was stronger than he should have been, and his mind only screamed one thought.

Freedom.

He would do whatever it took to make sure he didn't have to go back into the cell, and the trainers knew it. The next few months were spent getting individualized training. He limped back to his cot every night, convinced he wouldn't be able to continue in the morning. It was also the first time he noticed some of the other boys had gone missing.

The thought of being cast out only made him train harder. Back then, he didn't know that the ones too weak to make it through training were executed. The guild wouldn't suffer a half-trained thug tarnishing their name. Once you were in the guild, you were a member for life.

The final test was the hardest for Gaston. He'd killed men in anger, for stealing, or even in self-defense, but he'd never killed someone he didn't know. When he stepped onto the mat, his instructions were simple. Kill or be killed.

Death is the answer.

That was the day he became a man and an assassin. It was the day his life started, and for the first time it felt like he'd found a family. Malvonis had taken that from him, and he wanted it back.

A man walked out onto the center of the mat, and the restless crowd fell silent. "Tonight we have a battle for the future of our guild. Malvonis is gone, but there are those who wish to keep his decrees intact."

The speaker turned to Gaston. "And those who wish to see the old ways restored."

"Tonight the fate of the assassins Guild will be decided. Death is the answer." He motioned for Gaston to step onto the platform, and then turned and motioned for his challenger to step up.

Watching the crowd intently, Gaston snorted as they parted for Matheus. Was this the best they could do without Malvonis pulling their strings? He wanted to laugh, but the words of The Grandmaster echoed in his head. "Overconfidence is the harbinger of trouble."

He knew Malvonis was a sneaky shit, and if this man stood for him then looks would be deceiving. It was time to let his training take over. There was nothing to do now but pull his new daggers free and see what his competition brought to the table.

The blades felt good in his hands, they always did. Just wrapping his fingers around the daggers brought a smile to his face. Gaston had never fit in the world, a square peg forced into a round hole until he found the guild. Killing had given him the freedom his heart truly desired.

Death was the answer.

The speaker jumped off the stage and then cried out a single word. "Begin!"

Matheus started sprinting toward him, and Gaston waited patiently. If the idiot was so quick to meet death, who was he to get in his way? Each heartbeat felt like an eternity. He willed Matheus forward, knowing the ultimate outcome was already foretold.

Death was the answer.

Gaston ducked under a wild swing and brought his dagger up into the man's gut. At the same time, he danced around him like a boxer fighting a man with a longer reach. His other blade should have torn through Matheus back like tissue paper, but instead the weapon barely left a scratch.

What in the fuck was going on?

Back peddling away from a man whose guts should have been spilling out on the mat, Gaston tried to buy himself some time. "I wondered why they would have picked you. It seems the sacrificial goat has magical protection."

"You act as if the rules matter." Matheus winked at him. "The only rule I believe in is winning."

Gaston sheathed his dagger and pulled a throwing knife from

the bandolier on his chest. "I want everyone to see this, so they remember how you died with no honor."

Matheus held his arms out wide, exposing his entire chest to Gaston.

The idiot wasn't scared at all, and that was a mistake. Gaston had killed men with magical protection before, it just took a little longer. Still, there was a lesson for the crowd to witness here, and he was going to take full advantage of the opportunity to teach them. The man in front of him now was the reason they needed to follow tradition and not the perversions Malvonis heaped upon their order.

The blade flew from his hand. Before the knife struck, he had three more following its wake. The first knife hit and skittered away. Two and three didn't fare much better, but the fourth created a tiny pinprick of blood. The wound was so small he didn't even think his opponent noticed it. Now that Gaston knew Matheus could bleed, he knew the man could die.

"It seems death is not on your side today," Matheus snarled. "But when you meet him, tell the bastard I said hello."

Gaston started toward his opponent. "Tell him yourself!"

When he was five feet away from the weaselly little fucker, Gaston threw himself into a slide. Just as he thought, Matheus didn't react in time, and Gaston sliced at the man's inner thighs as he slid between his legs. The blows that should have crippled the man barely left a scratch, but at least he knew the idiot felt it.

Flipping back to his feet, Gaston found himself parrying a set of wicked slashes. Somehow, he managed to turn the blades away. He hadn't expected Matheus to recover so quickly. Maybe the assassin had a few more tricks up his sleeve. He teetered on the edge of the mat before finally driving the man back.

It was time to see what his opponent brought to the table.

Gaston set his feet and began the dance of death. His blades moved with a dancer's grace as they sought out any opening in Matheus' guard. By the time they reached the middle of the mat, his opponent was bleeding from four different wounds, the worst of which left a flap of useless skin hanging from his shoulder.

The room grew silent as the cheers that had accompanied the fight until that moment were forgotten. Everyone gathered could sense that the battle was drawing to a close. Matheus tried to lift his right arm, and when it didn't move, he tucked his wrist into his belt and set his feet so that he could attack with his left hand.

Gaston sauntered forward, in no hurry to end the bastard's suffering. "Tell me, can you hear death's whisper? I can hear your name on the tip of his tongue."

"Gloat all you want, dog. The old ways are over, and there are more of us ready to challenge you. You won't see another peaceful day until we put you in the dirt. Malvonis' Chosen will prevail."

It was hard not to smirk, but his old master would have said, *"It's when one feels victory is inevitable that it is often snatched from their grasp."*

He wasn't going to fall victim to one of the classic blunders.

Watching the room for signs of a trap, Gaston willed his feet to keep moving forward. The distance between Matheus and him shrunk until they had no choice but to fight. It was easy enough to dodge the strike from Matheus' offhand, and almost effortless to slice through his throat as he spun behind the man.

His follow up slash down Matheus' back sealed the man's fate. Gaston kicked the dying man off the mat and turned to face the men who opposed his ascension to the head of the guild. "You have one chance to save your lives. Submit to the trials or die where you stand."

Blood dripped from the tips of Gaston's daggers as he waited for an answer. A man stepped forward to address Gaston. The move was so quick it was almost enough to pull his attention away from his surroundings.

Almost.

Launching himself into the air, Gaston dodged the stealth attack aimed at his back. He flipped at the apex of his jump and came down behind the would-be attacker, driving his own daggers into his opponent's back. Two down, how many more until they see reason? Maybe it was time to be more assertive.

"Death is the answer!" he bellowed to the heavens. By the goddess, they would understand the meaning of the words or he'd slaughter them all.

A few of the men dropped to their knees in submission. The rest of the worthless little shits reached for their weapons. If they wanted to desecrate the great hall, then it would run in rivers of their blood. He would not be stopped. This was his destiny.

"Spare any that submit to the trials, kill the rest." Gaston watched as the men and women behind him charged into the fray. Most of them had been trained in the old ways, and these worthless thieves would be no match for them. Malvonis knew it was easier to stay in power when everyone who worked for you was worthless.

Tim appeared at his side, and Cassie stepped in front of him. The tiny tank smiled up at Gaston. "Damn good show big guy. What do you say we get out of here?"

"Not until it's over," Gaston rumbled as he tried to shove her out of the way.

Cassie didn't budge until she received confirmation from Tim. "Then point out who to hit and follow my lead."

Laughter spilled from Gaston's lips like a dam bursting after the summer floods. "Just make sure no one can sneak up on me." He placed a hand on Cassie's staff and used it to vault over the tank and back into the battle.

He didn't bother to see if they followed. The bloodlust was upon him, and it was time to bask in its bliss.

Death is the answer.

CHAPTER SIXTY-THREE

The inside of Tim's mouth felt like sandpaper.

Why was it that drinking too much always made you feel like you were going to die? Something so fun shouldn't have such horrible consequences. Thankfully, inside of the game he didn't need to get an IV. All he had to do was cast cleanse on himself. His fingers fumbled through the first cast, but the spell still managed to take the edge off.

Now that he felt like every movement he made wasn't going to make the world spin, Tim cast the spell on himself again. This time he felt damn near normal. The only thing missing was his morning coffee. The scent of freshly brewed beans reached his nose, and Tim thanked Eternia for putting Liz in his path.

That woman deserved a raise, just for being awesome.

ShadowLily was still curled up in bed. The shot contest the assassin in training had with Gaston was a really bad idea. Say one thing about his girlfriend, she never backed down from a challenge. That was part of the reason he loved her. Nothing would ever be too much for her to handle. She was so strong.

She was his rock.

That didn't mean his rock needed to wake up with a hangover. Tim cast cleanse on ShadowLily before making his way to the steaming pot of coffee in their living space. He sat down in the chair and poured himself his first glass of deliciousness. Now the biggest decision facing him was if he should go to Joe's before she woke up or afterward.

Tim took a sip of coffee and thought about the battle the night before. It had been a bloody mess, but having a healer turned the tide in their favor. It was easy enough to keep most of the assassins on their side alive and well. A few fell to catastrophic damage he couldn't repair, but most of the men and women who fought with Gaston survived.

He didn't understand all the "death is the answer" business, but he did feel good about supporting his friend. Plus, it never hurt to have the head of the assassins Guild on your side. Still, there was always a chance their victory would bring Malvonis back to town, and if that happened, Gaston needed to be ready.

Tim finished his cup of coffee and decided it was best to get his day started. They needed to return to Tristholm today. It felt like they had already been gone too long. The last thing he wanted to do was find out the city they had just liberated from evil was back in Vitaria's clutches.

Before they could leave, the group would need a good solid meal, and it wouldn't hurt to check his pending notifications.

System Message: You have reached level fourteen and have one undistributed stat point.

Tim quickly dumped the spare point in Dexterity, bringing his total up to seventeen. Once he hit twenty, he'd probably try to get his Strength up to a more reasonable level. A quick glance at his stats also confirmed he'd received a +1 bonus to Luck, bringing that stat up to six. He scrolled through the system messages looking for a snarky note about why he received the increase but couldn't find one.

No reason to worry about it now.

Thankfully, he didn't just gain a level, but he also increased a few of his less-used skills.

Both of Tim's buffs had reached apprentice rank two. Not a lot had changed with those, so he scrolled past them to see if he had any other notifications. Not seeing anything else he needed to address immediately, Tim's thoughts turned toward food. Their meal the previous night had been interrupted, and his belly needed to be satisfied before the day got away from him.

Standing up from the table, Tim scrawled a quick note to ShadowLily to tell her where he was going and then headed out the door. He bounced down the stairs with a cheerful gait until he heard a groan coming from the common room. Not sure if something was wrong, Tim moved faster.

He sprinted around the corner and skidded to a halt.

Gaston was draped over the bar like he'd died there. Knowing how much the man drank last night, Tim wasn't surprised that he hadn't made it to his room. He *was* surprised there wasn't a puddle of vomit or urine.

Liz was poking Gaston with the end of a broomstick, trying to get him moving. She obviously didn't want any of the guests coming downstairs to see someone passed out on the bar. It wasn't the kind of thing that should happen in public places, but he'd been there before. Sometimes overindulgence left you in weird places. Tim had a cure for that.

"Good morning, Liz." Tim smiled at her frown. "Thank you for the coffee."

Liz jabbed Gaston with the edge of the broom hard enough to make him grunt in pain. "Just help me by getting this oaf back to his room."

It took three casts of cleanse to get Gaston back on his feet. Then Tim spent a minute healing the man's bruised ribs. Ernie emerged from the kitchen a moment later and placed a bowl of steaming liquid in front of the assassin.

"By the dead, what in the hell is that?" Gaston roared as he jumped out of his seat.

Ernie nudged the bowl toward him. "Just a little something to cure what ails ya."

"Ernie, I just need some sleep. You know, the kind I can wake up from." Gaston pushed the bowl back toward the innkeeper. "Let me know when there is actual food." The assassin rose from his spot at the bar and disappeared through the door to his private sanctuary.

Liz looked at the bowl and then at Ernie. "What in the hell is that?"

"I call it, get the hell out of here juice. It won't kill you, but it sure stinks like hell." Ernie grinned. "Easiest way I've found to clear out the bar."

"Ugh, get it out of here." Liz ran off to open a few windows.

Tim started making his way for the door before he could get roped into anything else. He wanted to order a bunch of food from Joe's and have it ready for the guild when they climbed out of bed. Then he'd go to Ironbeard's shop and see if his metalsmithing skills had improved enough that the blades he created wouldn't shatter on contact.

Joe said the food would be ready in about an hour and a half, so Tim had a firm timetable for how long he could spend in Ironbeard's shop. He needed to get inside and find out if he succeeded and get the hell out. Somehow it was never that easy. His thirst for learning something new often made him late. It was like watching fail videos back home. You looked up to realize you'd wasted an entire hour doing absolutely nothing.

Technically, he wasn't wasting time if he was learning a skill, but it felt that way with the fate of the world on his shoulders. No one ever really talked about how exhausting it was to be a hero.

The closest thing he'd ever seen on TV was a documentary about Michael Jordan and the constant pressure of carrying a franchise on your back.

That kind of pressure weighed on a man.

At least here, if he wanted to give it all up and earn a living as healer or a smith, he could. With the buildings he had and his skills, Tim was pretty sure he could make a good living without all the fuss. So what was it that was driving him to continue? He had to think about it. When it came down to it, it was the desire to experience something new.

As he moved through *The Etheric Coast*, there was always something new and exciting about to happen. It didn't matter if you followed the road most traveled or decided to venture off the beaten path, there was always something exciting on the horizon. Right now, that was the passage under the mountain.

He felt the adventure calling to him like a siren's song to sailors. There was a pull deep in his soul to find out what was next, and it filled him with a sense of excitement. So far, the dungeons had been the most rewarding content they'd encountered, and he was ready to face another one.

There was no way to know what was waiting for them under the mountain, but it was time to find out.

The bell over the door jingled as Tim entered Ironbeard's shop, instantly snapping him back into the moment. There was enough time to find out if he'd finally succeeded or not, but by tonight he wanted to be back in Tristholm gathering anything they would need for their adventure.

"Ah." The old dwarf smiled warmly at his apprentice. "Ready to see if that sword will shatter like the rest of them?"

Tim waved away Ironbeard's concerns as if he already knew the outcome. "It'll work."

There was no way for him to know if the sword would work or not, but he was full of hope. Soon he would test it against the dummy and then one of Ironbeard's weapons. Tim felt like this had to be the one. No other skill at the forge had taken him nearly this long to master. Turning steel into a weapon was harder than he imagined.

Picking the sword up off the rack, Tim was surprised by how heavy the weapon was. If he had to use the bulky blade in a battle, he would have been worn out after a few swings. How some of the warriors used them relentlessly and without effort, he'd never know. It just showed him once again that there was something for everyone inside of the game.

Once they entered *The Etheric Coast*, a player chose their destiny.

No one cared how you got into the game. The only things that mattered in the game were where you wanted to go and how hard you worked to get there. Everyone started with the same blank canvas, making the game the ultimate equalizer.

Tim stepped up next to the training dummy and swung the blade at it with both hands. The sword whistled through the air and slammed into the dummy hard enough he almost dropped it. Hoping Ironbeard didn't notice, Tim proceeded to strike the dummy again and again until he ended his wild swings with a jab to test the tip of the blade.

"At least you don't have to rely on your swordsmanship to make a living," Ironbeard chuckled.

Tim was struggling to catch his breath after hitting the dummy so many times in a row. "Nope, I do this simply for enjoyment."

Ironbeard laughed with him. "Steel has a voice. If you work with it long enough, you will start to hear it sing." He motioned for Tim to stand up straighter. "Now, let's see if your steel is up to the test."

The dwarf grabbed a blade from the rack and took a swing at Tim. Somehow, he managed to get his sword up in time to block the strike, but Ironbeard was relentless. The old dwarf battered the sword in Tim's hands until it dropped to the ground with a clang.

"I think you've finally mastered the basics, but the real question is, can you repeat it." The dwarf watched him, clearly hoping the answer would be yes.

Tim found himself smiling despite the fact he'd almost lost a limb to the dwarf's practiced swings. "That will have to be answered another time." He picked the blade up from the ground. All he had to do now was sharpen the steel and wrap the grip.

Placing the unfinished sword back on the rack, Tim asked the question he'd been longing to know. "How much does a sword like this sell for?"

Ironbeard grinned like a used car salesman. "I'd buy it from you for three silver and sell it for seven."

Tim thought about all the hours it took him to make the blade. To only be able to sell it for a few silver pieces seemed wrong. Still, if he could master the basics, he could learn how to make better blades, and maybe even enhance them with magic. Enchanted swords had to sell for a lot more.

"Now that your dreams of getting rich have been thoroughly squashed, will you be coming back?" Ironbeard turned and started leading Tim to the front of the shop.

He had to think about it for a moment. Was he doing this for the money or because he loved it? Then he also had to decide if putting the work in would make him better at his craft. Tim thought about one of his favorite authors, Stephen King. In the beginning, King wrote his books after teaching all day, cramped in the back of his trailer so he wouldn't disturb his family. At that point, he was writing because he loved it, and he hoped to make money.

We all know how well that worked out.

What you didn't hear a ton about was King's relentless pursuit of his goals. He attacked his books with a passion only harnessed by the greats. That singular focus and passion shaped the way many people viewed horror now and in the future. Long after his death, people will still be making his books into movies.

So, would he come back to finish his sword and learn how to make other things at the forge?

Of course, he would.

Tim stuck out a hand for a shake. "I'll be back, but first I have business to attend to in Tristholm."

"Don't dawdle. Life at the forge is a skill that needs to be practiced to achieve greatness. You can't just put down the hammer and expect things to work out for the best." Ironbeard clasped Tim's hand and gave it a firm shake. "See you soon."

Walking out of the shop, Tim felt accomplished. Who would have thought a kid from the inner city would ever learn how to forge a sword? Part of him wondered if the skills he was learning in the game would come back to him when he had to return to the real world. His guess was there weren't a ton of custom armor and weapons makers out there.

Maybe he could corner the market.

Tim stepped out into the sunlight and quickly changed his clothes. From there, he made his way through the market with another couple of outfit changes before exiting and heading back to the inn. One could never be too careful, and after trying to wipe out half of the assassins guild, he was bound to have a few enemies in Promethia.

Thankfully for him, he also had friends he could count on.

CHAPTER SIXTY-FOUR

Buttermilk pancakes fixed a lot of ills.

Tim was starting on his second stack when a groan from the stairs drew his attention. He held the hot maple syrup over his pancakes and waited to see who emerged. Cassie came into the room, her vest on backward. Tim didn't even know how she could do that. Whenever he took off his clothes and re-equipped them, they always went on the right way.

Knowing there wasn't a moment to spare, he cast cleanse on the tank. For good measure, he cast the spell a second and then a third time. No one should have to deal with a hangover all day. One would think by now someone would have come up with a cure in the real world besides greasy food and a lot of water. If he saw another commercial promising a hangover-free morning, he was going to vomit. Tim knew what the promises of infomercials were worth.

A big fat nothing burger.

Anytime you could buy one item for nineteen ninety-nine, and they were willing to throw in a second one and free shipping, you knew you were getting something from the dollar store in a box.

Not always, but most of the time what you saw on TV only worked on TV.

What you saw in *The Etheric Coast* was what you got. If the item's description said it did something, it did it, and the durability or lack thereof was clearly stated in the description. It was a welcome change to everyday life.

Plus, cakes always made things better.

Tim finished pouring his syrup on the pancakes. "Where is your fiery half?"

"I'm going to let that slide because you cured my hangover, but JaKobi isn't my other half. We're just trying things out right now." Cassie grabbed a plate and started to load it up with bacon and eggs.

Tim finished off a bite of his breakfast with a huge sip of coffee. "I tried to take things slow, but ShadowLily wouldn't hear of it."

"That's because you're all in, or it's bullshit," ShadowLily whispered in his ear as she appeared out of nowhere.

Tim didn't jump, which was a huge improvement. He gave himself a mental pat on the back before responding. "You can be all in, and still not be sure."

"Is that what you are, not sure?" ShadowLily placed four full-sized pancakes on her plate and a handful of breakfast sausage.

Tim was too accomplished in navigating woman speak to fall into that trap. "Oh, I'm sure about us, but that doesn't mean people shouldn't date first. Once you start living together, it's a whole different ball game."

"A smellier ball game, maybe." ShadowLily grinned.

The tips of Tim's ears burned red. "That was one time, and it wasn't that bad."

"Even the chairs tried to run out of our room to avoid the cloud," ShadowLily replied with a chuckle.

Everybody farts.

The thought still didn't make it easier for Tim to get over his embarrassment, so he decided to stick with the classic farter move.

Blame somebody else. "I had one of Joe's new bean burritos. It was clearly your dad's fault."

"What was my fault?" Joe said as he came into the common room carrying another two trays of food.

ShadowLily looked mischievous. "Oh, nothing, Dad. Tim was just blaming you for his flatulence."

Joe chuckled as he set down the covered trays of food. "It was those damn beans. They tasted great but had other side effects." He patted Tim on the shoulder. "We're using half as many now and filling the rest out with veggies. Trust me when I say you weren't the only one having problems."

Tim tried to sink into the floor. Had he just had a fart conversation with the man who might become his future father in law? "It's nice to see you again, Joe."

Cassie giggled. "So the moral of the story is, if you can stand your man's farts, he's a keeper."

"Or maybe if he can light them on fire," JaKobi said with a smirk as he entered the room. He was holding his head. "Coffee, need coffee stat."

Tim took pity on the pyromancer and cured his hangover before taking another bite of his pancakes. "We were just sitting down for breakfast, and Cassie was telling us how you aren't a couple." He glanced at the tank and then stuck his tongue out, blowing her the nicest of raspberries.

"Gotta try it before you buy it," JaKobi said as he took his first sip of coffee.

Tim ducked reflexively. If he had said something like that to ShadowLily, she would have taken his head off. He'd already had that happen once in the game and didn't care to suffer the same fate because he couldn't control his mouth.

Cassie just grinned. "That's what I'm saying. Sometimes you just gotta kick the tires a bit before you make a decision."

"I heard a whole lot of kicking last night," Lorelei said with a yawn. "Had to get up and close your door to make the sound charm kick in."

The young lovers looked embarrassed, but Tim was just happy they were on the same page. Having relationships in the group could be a good thing and also a bad one. If things got off-kilter in the relationship, it would affect every member of the Blue Dagger Society, not just the couple involved.

"Lorelei, my dear, it's good to see you." Joe gave the ranger a hug and poured her a cup of coffee.

It was easy enough for Tim to smile now that they weren't talking about his farts anymore. Plus, it was awesome to see the two of them bonding. Tim got the feeling Lorelei didn't have her dad around anymore, or their relationship wasn't that great. Joe had become the perfect stand-in. He was just an all-around great guy, and he treated all of them like family.

Tim went back to work on his pancakes as Gaston bellied up to the bar. He still looked tired, but Tim had the feeling that had more to do with becoming the head of the assassins Guild than anything else. It was easy to be a member of an organization but running one was a whole different ball game.

Running a guild or group was stressful.

Everyone thought whatever they wanted to do was the most important thing. Tim could imagine that with assassins, it was even more difficult. Walking into a room of hardened killers and earning their respect wasn't for the faint of heart.

JaKobi opened up one of the covered trays and pulled out a slice of carrot cake. "So when are we leaving for Tristholm?"

Tim didn't have to think about it for long. "Right after breakfast if everyone is ready. If not, the latest I'd like to leave is midday. It would be nice to get outside of the walls before dark. Might save us a little trouble."

"Shouldn't be too much trouble, not with the werewolf clans working to keep things in line," JaKobi said with a hopeful tinge to his voice.

Lorelei took a few breakfast sausages and rolled them up in a pancake. She dipped her creation in syrup and took a bite. "We can hope, but I doubt Vitaria just gave up after her sister sent her packing."

"And whatever is waiting for us under the mountain is probably worse than what we faced in Tristholm," ShadowLily said flatly. She looked at all the unhappy faces. "If you haven't noticed yet, things haven't exactly been getting easier as time goes on."

Tim stuck his fork in what remained of his second tower of cakes. "As the challenges increase so do the rewards. A little more challenge might not be a bad thing."

"Never said it was. I just don't expect things to be easy." ShadowLily grinned. "I find less disappointment in life when I try to set realistic expectations for people."

"No one likes to be honey-potted," JaKobi said with a grin.

Cassie poked him in the ribs. "He's just full of good advice today."

Joe cleared his throat bringing the conversation to halt. All eyes turned to him. "Do you mind if I tag along?"

The confusion in the room was palpable, but Joe soldiered on. "As the players spend more time in other places, it dawned on me that expansion is going to be key to my business survival. I've got a guy working the kitchen here in Promethia who can handle it. I'd like to set up the new place myself."

ShadowLily climbed off her stool at the bar and gave her dad a hug. "I think that's a great idea. We might even be able to help you find a spot."

"What she means is, we have connections," Lorelei stated. "Seraphina owes us one."

Joe started making his own plate of food. "I'm ready to go whenever you are."

Tim looked around the room and smiled at his friends. They were really creating something special for themselves inside of this game. Every day they continued playing, this world felt more like home, and the burdens and responsibilities of the real world seemed small and insignificant.

That's how gaming should feel, like the great escape.

There was something to be said about putting down the nine to five and living out your fantasies. Being a gamer meant you could be whatever you wanted. If you wanted to be at one with the force or an NFL superstar, the feeling was only a click away.

Things were starting to fall into place. Tim was excited to see what waited for them under the mountain. Seraphina had also called it the mountain pass, so there was something on the other side. What new wonders awaited them on the other side of the mountains Tim didn't know.

The one thing he did know is he wanted to find out.

"Let's finish up and get ready. The Blue Dagger Society has a quest to complete." Tim felt good as his group members nodded along.

Cassie summed things up best. "Let's go kick today in the balls."

Tim couldn't help but laugh. That was a whole new way to say *carpe diem*.

CHAPTER SIXTY-FIVE

Tim felt the urge to get moving.

As much as he needed to come to Promethia to get his own house in order, he knew instinctively it was time to go. Healing the needy and making his first sword wasn't exactly the streaming content people were excited to see. They needed to be out in the world doing quests and killing bosses.

It wasn't just the fact that he knew what people wanted to see that drove him. Deep down it was what he wanted too. There was an immense feeling of accomplishment that came with beating a boss for the first time or clearing a dungeon. Just like in sports, there was a moment of triumph when something you'd been struggling to accomplish finally came to fruition.

Nothing since entering the game had been handed to him. Tim worked hard to become a healer his group could depend on, and a leader they could trust. Normally, he liked to sit back and just quietly do his part. Gaming could be stressful enough without having to worry about other people or running a guild, but now that he was doing it, he understood why some people loved it.

Every time someone in his group succeeded, Tim felt like he was part of their victory.

He wondered if this was how teachers felt when they saw their students go on to do great things in the world. There had to be a moment where they thought, *I helped them do that*. He'd had a few teachers in his life that really pushed him to be better. One of the best lines he ever received was from a computer sciences teacher during middle school.

The man looked at him point blank and said, "You better get comfortable asking one question." Tim, of course, had asked what that question was and the teacher responded. "Do you want fries with that?"

If only they could see him now. Not only was he a college graduate, but he was leading a team of incredible people in a game. He wasn't just a guy they didn't trust to work the register so they put him on fry duty. Tim felt like he was making a difference with his life.

The people of Tristholm certainly seemed to think so.

Being a leader also came with a certain amount of extra pressure. It was his job to keep the team firing on all cylinders. Sometimes that meant taking time off even when they had important things to do. Keeping the group focused on the end goal while giving them time to breathe was important. They'd had enough time to breathe.

Now it was time to get back to work.

On the plus side, they wouldn't be wasting any time traveling back to Tristholm. The high priest had given them access to the temple's portal between the two towns. Once they made it to the temple, they were only minutes away from being right back in the thick of things.

It wouldn't be much longer before some of them started hitting level twenty and got to specialize their class again. Tim had no idea what his options were going to be because they were still hidden from him. With a little simple deduction, he figured he would have between two and three options. One would be more healing intensive, while the other would be more DPS. If a third option presented itself, it would be a hybrid of both, offering a ton of utility during fights.

If he had to pick now, Tim would choose healing. Keeping people alive in combat was his passion. Healing was the thing that kept him coming back. It was one of the most important roles in any group. No group in any game was successful without a good healer. The pressure of it excited him and helped to keep him focused. It was like hitting free throws with your eyes closed.

Only the greats could do it.

Tim double-checked his inventory to make sure he had what he needed for the trip and headed back downstairs to the common room. Everyone else was already waiting for him, including Joe. It seemed his extra-long shower had put him slightly behind. There was no reason for him to worry about it now. It was time to go.

With his arrival downstairs, everyone stood up and headed for the door. Liz waved cheerily from behind the bar. "Have fun saving the world."

Tim grinned as he stepped out into the light drizzle. He was going to have fun. Sometimes, he got so stressed out about what he was doing that he forgot to enjoy the moment. Something he always tried to do was celebrate his successes and minimize his failures. Life was complicated, and failure was inevitable. Some people got back up and tried again.

What a person chose to do after failing was what shaped them as a person.

He'd never been the kind of person to shy away from a hard task. Pressure brought out the best in Tim. Sure, sometimes he took on more than he could chew and ended up with metaphorical egg on his face, but sometimes his risks paid off. Without taking a risk, he wouldn't be with the woman of his dreams right now.

All he had to do was remind himself to be bold.

Love wasn't a game for the weak of heart, but when you found the right one, things just fell into place. How did he know Shadow-Lily was the right one? It was a simple determination for him. At some point, he stopped caring about his needs first and thought about what would be right for them as a couple. Knowing that she was happy bolstered his own mood more than he would have thought possible.

The temple came into view and Tim once again marveled at the size of the place. The building might as well have been its own damn city, like the Vatican back in the real world. He wondered just how many priests worked for Eternia. There was no way to know unless Paul told him, but Tim thought it was easily in the thousands.

People moved in and out of the temple as they approached. Some of the citizens were looking for healing, while others had come to pray to the goddess. Tim hoped all of them would find what they needed to get through the day. A little hope went a long way to making someone feel good about themselves.

Their group climbed the stairs and reached the front doors to the temple. A young boy approached them, looking unsure whether he was in the right place. He stopped in front of the group and was working his hands together in a nervous gesture no young man should have to make. It was the sort of thing that happened when a kid did something wrong, and his parents made him go apologize.

"Excuse men are you Tim?" the young man asked.

Tim motioned behind him for the group to stand down. He didn't think the young man in question was here to take them out. "I am, and you are?"

Relief flooded the boy's face. "Bless Eternia, I thought I'd missed you." The worry the boy had been carrying disappeared in an instant. "I'm Brian. The high priest asked me to bring you to the portal as soon as possible."

"All right, Brian, lead the way." Tim looked behind him. "Keep up. The temple is a tricky place to navigate on your own."

The group made their way through the winding temple passages. Tim could have sworn they were going a completely different way than he had last time, but eventually they reached the room with the portal. Using the quick travel method was going to save them a day or two on the road.

Brain ran to stand next to a man by the portal and tugged on his robes until he looked down at the boy. They shared a few words, and then the man turned around. A smile spread across the high priest's lips as he locked eyes with Tim.

It was a look that meant trouble.

He'd seen that same look in his father's eyes right before he was given something to do. It was the look that said if you wanted twenty bucks to go out this weekend, then you better have your room cleaned, the garbage out, and the yard work done. In other words, you were going to work for your money.

Paul walked across the room, extending his hand toward Tim. "The goddess always provides. It's nice to see you again, Tim."

Making sure to meet the high priest's eyes, Tim shook his hand. "And you."

"I did hope that before you left, I could have a brief moment of your time." Paul motioned for Tim to join him off to the side of the room.

"Of course you can." Tim followed the high priest after giving ShadowLily a quick look that he hoped said we're about to get some additional work.

Paul stopped when they were just out of earshot of the others. "I have something I need you to do." When Tim nodded, Paul continued. "There is a tomb set along the mountains of Tristholm. Inside of it are artifacts blessed by the Goddess Eternia. We thought the tomb sealed forever, but there are rumors that it has opened."

Tim had a pretty good idea where this was going. "You want us to secure the tomb, so you can take back the artifacts?"

"Yes, and to destroy whatever is lurking inside." Paul looked nervous. "I know you have other things to do upon your arrival, but if you could make this a priority, I'd appreciate it."

Reaching out, Tim placed his hand on Paul's shoulder. "We'd be happy to look into it as soon as we get there."

"Eternia always provides." Paul's nervous manner was replaced with a smile. "Here you go."

Quest Received: Tomb of Krevus

Once considered the best healer of his generation, Krevus was corrupted by the dark goddess Vitaria. When it became obvious the priest was beyond saving, the temple brought the mountain down upon him, sealing him inside of his sanctuary. The items he stole from the temple were thought lost forever, but now the tomb is open. Reclaim the stolen holy artifacts for a reward.

Reward: Ten gold coins, and an item from the high priest's personal stores.

Accept Quest: <Yes/No>

Tim quickly accepted the quest. They were going back to Tristholm anyways, and the key to efficient questing was to get multiple quests in the same area and to farm them all at once. Knocking out multiple quests per trip was so much better than walking back and forth to town for each and every one.

Paul quickly shook Tim's hand. "May the goddess protect you on your journey."

Releasing Paul's hand, Tim returned, "Her light shines upon us all." He was starting to develop a knack for this stuff.

Paul quickly left the room, and Tim returned to his group.

"What was all that about?" Cassie looked a little peeved to not have been included in the conversation.

Tim grinned back at her. "Oh, just another quest for us." He shared the quest with everyone in his group.

"Far out." JaKobi laughed. "It's like everywhere you go, quests just rain from the heavens."

Motioning for everyone to move toward the portal, Tim

responded, "It feels that way sometimes, but it's the guild's reputation that does the trick. Our combined success rate makes the Blue Dagger Society a no brainer when it comes to getting shit done."

"I'm not complaining." JaKobi created a ball of flame in his hand and gently tossed it back and forth like a game of hot potato. "I'll take every quest you can get and then some."

Lorelei pulled the pyromancer toward the portal. "Let's try knocking out a few of the ones we have first."

The two of them disappeared in a flash of light.

Cassie smirked at Tim. "It's so much easier when I don't have to train him myself." Turning away from the portal, she extended her hand for Joe. "Come on big guy, I'll show you the way."

Smiling in wonder at the portal, Joe took Cassie's hand and let her lead him through the shimmering light.

ShadowLily held out her arm to her boyfriend. "Care to join me?"

"As you wish." Tim clasped her arm and they walked through the portal together.

CHAPTER SIXTY-SIX

"Stop, thief!"

Tim whirled around as a man by the city exit cried out in pain. He managed to get eyes on what was happening fast enough to see a man with long black hair stab another man in the chest and start running. His feet were moving before he had a chance to see if the others were following him.

A quick cast of healing orb on the injured man as he ran past should be enough to stabilize him until the priests could get there. Normally he would have stopped and stayed with the wounded man, but Tim's blood was up. What kind of person would steal something and stab someone at the temple?

This was the perfect time to use his newest spell. Tim cast quick feet and took off like a rocket. The thief's lead started shrinking rapidly. A person who would kill someone else just to try to get away with stealing a few coins had to be punished. You just couldn't go around killing people who got in your way.

His feet thundered against the cobblestones as he chased after the thief. The city guard missed their chance to stop the man as he left the temple and entered Tristholm. Despite the desperate situation, Tim found himself grinning. He felt like Bond at the start of *Casino Royale*, chasing a man through the streets of the city.

The thief in front of him was faster than he was, but Tim had the advantage of not having to dodge the people. He was far enough behind the man that it felt like he was riding in his wake. The people who were shoved out of the way or knocked to the side were the very ones he ran by without incident.

Two turns to the right, quickly followed by one to the left, and Tim found himself in a darkened alleyway. He cast a quick glance behind him and didn't see any of his friends. Had he really just run off without backup? The last time he left without them, he got stabbed in the chest. He hoped he wouldn't be repeating the process shortly. He wasn't ready to see Barbara again just yet.

The thief turned to face Tim. There was about twenty feet of space between them. They were close enough that it was easy for him to see the bloody dagger in the man's hand, and the look of cold confidence on his face.

"When they told me you'd be this gullible, I couldn't believe it," he smirked at Tim as he pulled another dagger free. "But here we are and you're all alone."

Tim wasn't going to be intimidated by some thief. He'd liberated this city from annihilation. Surely, he could handle himself against one man. He decided bravado was the right course of action. "Before I kill a man, I like to know his name."

"Carver," The man sneered. "They call me The Carver."

Two men slipped out of the shadows behind The Carver, and Tim thought that he might be in over his head. A quick glance behind him showed the alleyway was free. Not that he could just run away. The Carver was faster than him, and he wouldn't give the man the satisfaction of killing him when he tried to flee like a coward.

If Tim was going to die, he was going to go down fighting.

He summoned his staff from his inventory and squared his

shoulders for battle. "So tell me Carver, what person thought so little of your life they sent you to face me?"

Was it bluster? Yes. Was it over the top? So far over, it could have gone to the moon and back. Was it just what he needed to say to buy a little time for his friends to find him? Tim really hoped so.

Carver's sneer stayed in place as he motioned the men with him to move forward. "The bounty on your head is enormous. Frankly, I like it better that way. They post the job to the board, I cash in, no loose ends."

"No one wants to end up as a loose end," Tim said as he quickly cast his buffs.

With a thought, he cast snare on one of the men and then quickly followed the spell with a blast of divine light at the other. His spell ripped a nice little hole through the man's chest, and he fell to the ground. The second thief broke free of Tim's weak version of the snare spell and sprinted toward him.

Tim let out a squawk and ducked to avoid a wild swing of the man's dagger. When he stood up, the man had an arrow sticking out of his chest. He blasted him with a bolt of divine light and watched with horror as the back of the man's chest exploded out in a shower of gore. The spell had never seemed so violent before, but then again, he'd never used it this close to an enemy.

Carver dodged one of Lorelei's arrows and snapped his wrist forward. A knife flew from his outstretched hand right for Tim's chest. A slow smile spread on the thief's face as he thought about his reward for completing the job.

It felt like everything was happening in slow motion. Tim watched the dagger coming toward him but couldn't think of anything he could do to stop it. He started to bring his staff up but he knew it was too late. As he prepared to die, he made a mental note not to run off without his friends again.

Time jerked back into full speed as someone slammed into Tim. The knife that would have slammed into his chest hit him in the shoulder instead. A cry of pain escaped his lips, followed by a wail as he hit the alley wall and fell to the ground. Hands grabbed him under the shoulders and started to lift him up.

Forgetting about the knife, Tim focused on the battle playing out in front of him. ShadowLily must have lost her mind when he almost died. She was going toe to toe with The Carver and bleeding from several lacerations. His strikes didn't seem to slow her down. If anything, they only heightened her blood lust.

She dodged two more quick slashes and let out a scream of rage. "Just die already."

It was hard for Tim to follow what happened next. ShadowLily seemed to blur for a moment, and then she was behind Carver with her blades buried in the man's back. She jerked the weapons upwards, like someone skinning a deer. The scream The Carver let out as she drove the weapons in deeper pierced the night.

ShadowLily kicked the corpse off her blades, and then spit on it. "No one fucks with my man but me!"

JaKobi whispered in Tim's ear. "Don't forget to heal yourself."

The pyromancer held Tim still while Cassie reached up and wrenched the knife out of his shoulder. He felt the blood pour down his robes. The Carver's blade must have hit something important. Tim managed to cast healing orb on himself and the bleeding stopped. As the heal over time portion of the spell kicked in, he started to feel better.

Now that Tim didn't feel like he was about to keel over, he cast healing orb on ShadowLily before pulling her into a hug. "Thanks for saving my ass."

"Just promise me that next time you run off to play hero, you let me go first." She gave him a kiss. "Promise?"

It was the easiest promise Tim ever made in his life. "I solemnly vow to let my girlfriend run into danger in front of me." Now that he'd been thoroughly emasculated, he gave her another kiss. Not being the alpha in the relationship had its benefits.

"Uh-hum," Cassie said gruffly. "We might have another problem."

Tim turned to see what she was pointing at and saw the city guard had filled the alleyway from side to side. Five men knelt in front with crossbows leveled at them, and there were at least twice as many swordsmen lined up behind them.

"Gentlemen, I think you'll find that we've already dealt with the thief." Tim quickly put his robe in his inventory and then re-equipped the clean garment.

"Please sheath your weapons and come with us for questioning." A man moved in front of the archers. "I hope you understand that with three deaths, I can't just let you go."

Tim motioned for the group to put their weapons away. They hadn't fought to save Tristholm just to start killing the city guards. "I have a letter to deliver to Jon. Maybe you could take us to him, and we can resolve both our problems at the same time?"

The captain of the guards motioned for his men to stand down. "I hope you're not wasting my time with this. Jon isn't exactly known for being friendly to people who lie about knowing him."

Cassie smirked. "This guy must not have been invited to the feast. You know, the one where the entire city honored us for saving its ass."

Tim grinned as he placed a calming hand on Cassie's shoulder. "Don't worry, I'm sure Jon will take care of this, and we'll be out there completing Seraphina's quest soon enough."

The captain watched Tim for a moment looking for any deception. Not seeing anything that made him more suspicious, he waved for them to follow him. "Let's go. I want this done before lunch."

***

"What do we have here?" Jon asked with a cocky smile.

The captain squared his shoulders. "These travelers murdered three people in an alley."

Jon laughed. "If these folks did it, then I'm sure they had a good reason." Jon turned his head to Tim. "Go ahead, tell him why we have three bodies to clean up."

Maybe this situation was a little more serious than Tim assumed. "We just came through the portal inside of the temple when a man was stabbed. We chased the assailant into the alley and were attacked."

He didn't think it was the right time to bring up the bounty. You never knew who would be willing to turn a person in if there was enough money on the line. The fact that whoever put a bounty on his head was okay with dead or alive didn't make him feel any better. Tim wondered if there was some way he could pay off the bounty to make it disappear.

Jon nodded along with Tim's statement. "I think that will do, Captain. If I'm not mistaken, these adventurers have some business to complete outside of the city walls."

"Of course, sir." The captain snapped a stiff salute. "We'll make sure everything is taken care of and check on the man at the temple."

"As you were." Jon turned away from the captain and motioned for Tim to come closer. "Do you have something for me?"

Tim looked into Jon's expectant eyes and wondered how bad Lucy Briarthorn's letter would crush him. "Lady Briarthorn placed this letter in my hands herself." He pulled the envelope free and passed it to Jon. A small embellishment, but he trusted that Reginald had the right letter delivered to his room.

Quest Completed: Turning the Tables

You successfully delivered the letter without looking inside, and you've already been paid for the job. Why are you wasting my time with these updates?

Tim couldn't help smiling. He loved it when the game got a little sarcastic. It made it feel like someone was actually paying attention to what he was doing in the game, instead of everyone just getting the same boring text.

"Thank you for this." Jon grinned. "I know running letters back and forth is a little bit below your station."

Tim reached out and shook Jon's hand. "If you have any other quests that need to be accomplished, all you have to do is ask."

"That's very nice of you." Jon looked at the letter in his hand and then back at Tim. "If you'll excuse me, I need a private moment in my study."

Tim tried not to give anything away. "I'll stop by before we head back to Promethia, to see if you need anything else."

Jon shook his head. "If you're so insistent on finding more work, see Gerald by the gate. He'll have something for you." Jon didn't wait to see if Tim heard him or not and just turned and walked away.

Joe stepped forward. "Excuse me, Jon is it?"

Tristholm's second in command turned with a look of irritation on his face. "Yes!" he snapped. When Jon saw that it wasn't one of his men bothering him, his eyes softened just a fraction. "What can I do for you?"

"That woman over there is my daughter." Joe pointed to ShadowLily, who waved back at them. "She has to run off on an adventure, while I need help with something more practical."

Jon seemed to consider his options for a moment but didn't shut Joe down right away. "And that would be?"

"I'm looking to start a new restaurant and need help scouting locations," Joe said matter of factly.

A smile spread on Jon's face. "And does the person who helps you get a meal out of it?" Jon inquired.

"You help me find the right place, and I'll cook you something amazing." Joe turned to look at the group and made a come-on guys gesture.

Tim started to grin. "His food really is the best."

"Fine, I'll do it." Jon looked a little flustered. "But, I do require a moment before we go." He turned and headed inside the building.

"Did he just sniff that letter?" JaKobi asked as he moved next to Tim.

Cassie let out a low whistle. "Guy has got it bad."

"Well, his day isn't going to be getting any better then." Tim motioned for the group to start moving toward Tristholm's main gate. "Let's find Gerald."

Lorelei ran up. "What did you mean by his day won't be getting better? If you've got gossip, you better dish it out."

Looking around to make sure no one was eavesdropping on their conversation, Tim whispered, "I think Lucy has a thing for Gaston."

"No," ShadowLily giggled. "Are you sure?"

Tim stopped walking and drew everyone in closer. "They sure got up to something while we were here. It could have been nothing, but it sure didn't feel like that."

Lorelei snorted. "Men, what do they know about love?"

"Enough to know when someone's got the hots for them." JaKobi made a little heart of flames and pointed at Cassie.

Cassie grinned. "Keep it in your pants, fire boy. We've got work to do."

"Hope that was juicy enough for you." Tim started walking again but stopped when he realized they were leaving Joe behind. "Are you sure you'll be ok?"

Joe waved away his concern. "I'll be fine. I could have done it on my own, but why not take advantage of an opportunity."

ShadowLily bound over to her dad and gave him a hug. "See you soon." When she returned to the group, they left the small courtyard together.

It took about five minutes for the gate to appear and another two or three to track down Gerald. By the time they found the soldier, Tim was about ready to snap in frustration. Being sent in all sorts of different directions had him riled up.

"Jon said you might have some work for us?" Tim asked after shaking the man's hand.

Gerald looked their group over. "Well, you certainly appear to be capable enough. I don't like hearing from the widows when people don't return, so I have to be discerning about the tasks I hand out."

Tim could understand that. The saddest part of any war movie was when they brought the folded flag to the family. It was crushing to see those folks break down. He could imagine the feeling was the same for Gerald, except he also had to live and work alongside the people left behind.

"I understand completely." Tim tried to nudge the man along.

"First time, I try to give you something easier. You live through it, and I'll think about upgrading you to something else." Gerald watched Tim to make sure he understood before offering him a quest.

Quest Received: Stomping the Skeletons

Normally the occasional skeleton ventures out from under the mountains, but recently the flatlands leading to the mountains have been swarming with the fleshless bastards. Kill twenty-five of them and return for your reward.

Reward: One gold coin

Accept Quest: <Yes/No>

The reward wasn't much, but the quest seemed pretty easy. Tim expected the five of them could knock it out on their way to try to find the tomb. Instead of just accepting the quest like he normally would have, Tim made sure the rest of the group was on board. When no one looked upset, he accepted the quest and converted it to the group.

"Thanks, Gerald, we'll see you soon." Tim reached out to shake the man's hand.

Gerald returned the shake. "I hope so. The last few groups didn't return for the reward."

They started to walk away and ShadowLily wrapped an arm around Tim's waist. "Sounds ominous."

"Ominous is what we do, baby!" Tim fired back.

He got a couple good laughs from the group as they exited the city. This was it. After days of rest, they were finally back on track. It wouldn't be long now until they discovered what secrets were buried under the mountain, and why it took thirteen werewolf clans to keep the evil out. Malvonis was also out there somewhere, looking for them. The next few days were going to be intense.

Just the way he liked it.

CHAPTER SIXTY-SEVEN

The skeletons didn't make any noise as they moved.

Tim would have thought with all the bones they would have made some noise, but they just didn't. It was as if the dark magic that held their bodies together also made their joints work perfectly. His grandpa's ankles squeaked more when he got up from the recliner to go to the bathroom.

"I can see why these things are a problem," Tim mumbled to himself.

He could imagine players and even townsfolk excited about the bounty, setting up camp out here and then being overrun by the silent menace. By the time they woke up to fight, the skeletons would have had their icy fingers dug into them, sucking out their life force.

What a shitty way to go.

When it came to dying, Tim didn't think about it much, but he knew that he never wanted to drown, freeze to death, or be burned alive. If he had to pick, he would just like to fade away in his sleep, but anything not horrific would be a plus. Having his life drained by animated skeletons also didn't make the list of acceptable ways to depart this world.

Thankfully, the skeletons were easy enough to kill.

One blast of divine light had the bones back in a pile on the ground. It seemed everyone in the group could basically one-shot the creatures. It reminded him of the zombies from earlier. It wasn't that they were hard to kill, it was that they overwhelmed people with sheer numbers.

Cassie ducked behind a fallen tree. "See that crack in the side of the mountain? That seems to be where they are coming from."

Peeking over the tree, ShadowLily smirked. "What are we waiting for then? Let's take them out and see what's inside."

"Just remember what's inside might not be friendly." Tim hopped over the fallen tree. "So once we're inside, take it slow."

Lifting his staff in the air, Tim started casting divine light as rapidly as he could. He watched other skeletons burst apart in showers of flames. Lorelei even took a few out with arrows to the head. There were ten skeletons left, and Tim held his hand up to stop the ranged players from stealing all the fun.

"Go get 'em, ladies." Tim grinned. "You deserve to have some fun, too."

The two women worked together as a perfect team. Cassie kept the skeletons distracted while ShadowLily tore them apart. When all ten lay in heaps, the two adventurers turned to look for more. Not seeing any left, they both looked disappointed.

"Do you really think people died to these one-hit wonders?" Cassie asked as she looked over the carnage their group had accomplished in a matter of minutes.

JaKobi kicked at some charred bones. "Unlikely, unless they were caught with their pants down."

Tim had been thinking the same thing. The only way these skeletons could take someone down was if they caught them sleeping or managed to sneak up on them. Taking out a skilled group of adventurers who were ready for a fight seemed unlikely. There had to be something bigger waiting inside.

It would be easy enough to lure people into a false sense of security by giving them such easy targets. Set up a group of adventurers looking for treasure, and make them think the whole experience will be as easy as killing the skeletons, and then wham-o. A boss drops out of the sky and slaughters everyone in sight.

Or in this case, crawls out of a hole.

"Just remember, we were sent here for a reason. Whatever is waiting for us inside is going to be harder than these trash packs." Tim made sure everyone was paying attention. "So stay focused and expect the unexpected."

"Heads on a swivel people," ShadowLily said in her best drill instructor voice.

Lorelei let out a little giggle. "Yes, ma'am!"

Cassie snorted. "Let's get in there and see what's what."

"Did anyone bring a torch?" Tim asked, even as he started cursing himself for not planning that far ahead. After this, they were going to go under a mountain, and for that they were going to need some light.

"I feel insulted," JaKobi said with a cocky smile that implied he was anything but. "I'm a human torch."

The pyromancer tossed a small orb of fire into the air, and it hovered about three feet above his shoulder. "On our off days, I spent some time in the Mages' College Library and found some cool new spells. This one remains active for over an hour, and I can cast it on all of us."

Moments later, little balls of light appeared next to each member of the group.

"Tim's always bringing so much utility to the fights, I thought it was time I contributed a little more than DPS." JaKobi grinned. "Not that I won't be lighting everything I can on fire."

"Thanks for looking out for us." Tim was happy to see the pyromancer taking on more responsibility in the group. It also reminded him that his new necklace gave off light too. He activated the feature.

The way Tim ran the guild required everyone to be self-driven. He wasn't the kind of leader who tried to force people to do things. Instead, Tim expected everyone to be as motivated as he was to win. If you wanted something badly enough, then putting in the work felt as easy as breathing.

Cassie slapped JaKobi's butt. "If Sparkles here is done showing off, let's see what's inside of the creepy tomb."

"Sparkles, really?" The pyromancer frowned at the tank.

"I'll make it up to you later." Cassie winked.

JaKobi's frown turned upside down. "Then Sparkles is ready for combat, ma'am."

Tim wondered if he should grab some popcorn or if they would just get back to work. The thrum of Lorelei's bow answered the question for him as a skeleton in the entrance to the cave fell into a pile of bones. It was time to get moving or they'd have to waste even more time killing the skeletons again.

"Into the tomb!" Tim ushered them forward like a goose making sure her goslings stayed on the right path.

"Like those words never ended badly for anyone," Cassie mumbled as she took the lead.

ShadowLily moved up next to the Tank. "Just be happy that whatever is in there doesn't smell as bad as the fish people."

Cassie huffed and then started forward. "Nothing smells as bad as the fish people."

Now that they were closer to the entrance, Tim could make out more of the details. What looked like a crack in the mountain from far away was actually a huge stone door that had split open down the middle. So while it was still a crack this made a lot more sense. He'd never seen a cave turned into a tomb before.

At least not for a priest.

There was writing carved into the door, but all Tim could make out was the word "Krevus." Pictures carved into the door were odd. He'd always thought the outer door of the tomb would show what someone accomplished with their lives. What he saw here looked more like a warning. If he was getting the meaning right, it said death awaits all who enter. The sentiment wasn't exactly welcoming.

At least I'm not in front.

Cassie didn't look perturbed by the pictures on the walls. She was probably too busy making sure something didn't jump out of the shadows to slaughter them all. Tim had no such problems at the back of the group. He kept his eyes on the walls, even as he cast his buffs and dropped into his Way of the Boulder stance.

They were moving slow, which made him happy. They spent a lot of time running into battles and then hoping for the best. Now they might get a chance to feel things out before they had to fight for their lives.

Tim tried to squash his nerves down. He knew the game wouldn't send them into the tomb just to have the entrance collapse. There wasn't anything fun about starving to death. Still, the darkness felt like it was closing in from all sides until he saw the first picture.

The mural covered the wall from the floor to the ceiling. The damn thing had to be thirty feet tall and a good twenty feet wide. The images painted on the stone depicted a man floating above the ground with a halo of white light ringing his head. There was a line of parishioners coming to him for healing.

The next part of the image showed the man healing the people, and them leaving him gifts of thanks in return. Tim kept his eyes moving to the next image, and he gasped when he saw what was happening. The priest was now taking organs from people in payment for his service. It was unclear if the parishioners knew it or not.

Moving further down the hallway, the next image showed Krevus feeding the organs to something inside of a cave. The last image showed two massive red eyes in the darkness.

What in the fuck happened down here?

If Tim was reading the situation correctly, somewhere along the way the priest had been corrupted. He fed and nurtured the evil before eventually being sealed inside with whatever the evil was. All Tim knew from the lone picture of the red eyes was that it looked big and angry.

They were in for a surprise.

The long hallway narrowed and then ended at what would have been a second doorway. Tim couldn't exactly call it a door anymore because massive chunks had been gouged out of it, or maybe clawed, based on the deep gouges. The scratches left in the door must have been ten feet off of the ground. Not something a human could have done.

Whatever was in the room beyond was Krevus' pet, and not the man himself.

At least that would be the easy version. The hard version would involve having to take both of them on at the same time. And what was the deal with the skeletons? Unless they were left over from the monster's feeding, Tim wasn't sure how they tied in.

Cassie started making her way into the next room as Tim shouted, "Be on the lookout for a big ass monster."

The tank looked back at him for a moment. "Trust me, if I see something, you'll know about it." She disappeared through the doorway.

One by one, the entire party made their way after her. Tim understood why the monster might be upset. Besides being sealed inside by the priests, even if it made it out of this doorway, there was nothing but more rock to climb through. He wondered if the creature was smart enough to send the skeletons out to lure people in.

"How about a little more light?" Tim asked, hoping the pyromancer had a spell that would fill the entire cavern.

Never one to hesitate to show off his skills with fire, JaKobi grinned in the muted light provided by the orb floating over his shoulder. "Thought you'd never ask." With a flick of his wrist he sent the ball of flame up into the air. As the ball rose, it changed from orange to white and grew in size.

It was like someone had plugged a giant daylight bulb into the roof of the cavern. There were a few skeletons roaming around the cave, and a giant crack in the back wall. The skeletons could have come through, but nothing much bigger than a person could make it out of the gap. The monster he had seen in the pictures wouldn't fit in the opening, so he dismissed it as an option and kept his eyes moving.

There had to be something missing. As far as he could tell, there wasn't a grave in here. If there wasn't a grave or a burial site, where in the hell would the artifacts Paul asked them to find be? The high priest wouldn't have sent them here just to run around in circles. There had to be something he was missing.

Tim moved around the massive cavern looking for some sign but didn't find anything. "You think Paul would have mentioned if there was a secret door we had to find."

"This game never makes things easy," ShadowLily said as she pushed on a few stones that could have been buttons. When nothing happened, she continued. "Remember how long it took us to find the entrance to The Surgeon's room?"

Lorelei laughed. "Hopefully, this will be easier. It's just one cavern, not an entire tower."

The only thing that made sense to Tim was the gap in the wall. It shouldn't have been big enough for the monster, but in a world filled with magic anything was possible. They could probably walk through it in single file if they wanted to. Walking into a dark hole that might have a huge monster in it didn't seem like such a great idea.

Tim stared at the opening, trying to decide what to do.

Wait, were those fucking eyes?

Looking at Cassie, Tim called out, "I think we're going to need a bigger boat."

The tank whirled around to stand in front of Tim instantly. "You've got to be kidding me." She motioned for everyone to back up as the monster wriggled its way out of the crack in the wall.

Not sure if he should be disgusted or terrified, Tim watched in fascination as the monster revealed itself. The creature's head was clearly reptilian. He would have said like a crocodile, but the snout wasn't that big. It was more like the head of a Komodo dragon or a Gila monster. What had him worried was the body the head was attached to.

It was like a giant rat.

Now the smaller opening at the back of the cavern made sense. Rats could crawl through tiny spaces and were incredible diggers. A giant rat would have been scary enough. They have big sharp teeth they use to chew through just about anything. Plop a Gila monster head on one and make it ten feet tall, and that was some scary shit.

Weren't Gila monsters poisonous?

"Cassie, watch the teeth. It could be poisonous," Tim called out as the giant rat-lizard finished pulling itself free.

"Like I don't always watch the teeth," Cassie quipped as she spread her feet into a defensive stance.

A glowing light shot out of the crack and hovered in front of them. Slowly, the light formed the shape of a man.

Krevus had arrived.

The priest floated above the creature and looked down on the band of adventurers. "Why do they not come? My brothers have abandoned me."

Tim wasn't sure which way to go with this. If Krevus held a grudge against the temple, then mentioning he was here on their behalf could make things worse. If the man had a soft spot for them it might deescalate the situation. His money was on there being bad blood, but they came here expecting a fight, so what did he really have to lose?

"Krevus, the high priest himself sent us here," Tim called out.

Stripes of darkness pulled away from the walls to wrap around Krevus. He cried out in torment before looking down at their group with black eyes. "It's been so long since I've basked in the light. Here there is only darkness. Here, I am the darkness."

"Help us with our quest, and I am sure that all will be forgiven. It's never too late to return to Eternia's light." Tim felt like he was walking out on a thin branch, waiting for the moment it snapped and dumped him on his ass.

"The goddess has forsaken me and my companion. Tell me, why bring such a creature into this world, if not for it to thrive? I only did what had to be done." Krevus sounded petulant. "And for that, I was ridiculed."

Tim had heard enough of this happy horseshit. It was one thing to be shunned by the goddess for doing something right, and another to abuse your position as a healer to feed a monster off your parishioners.

"I've seen the pictures. I know what you've done. If you are looking for sympathy, you've come to the wrong place. Redeem yourself by helping us, or don't. The choice is yours." Tim stared up at Krevus, hoping for the easy way, but knew they were about to fight.

He motioned for the group to spread out and get into position as they waited for a response.

"So, you've come to offer me salvation? How very noble of you." Krevus' words dripped with sarcasm. "I handed out the same offer for a hundred years and look at my reward." He started flying back to the crack in the wall. "I must return to my great work, but my friend George here is hungry, always so hungry."

Krevus' light faded into the crack.

Lorelei looked at Tim. "George?"

All Tim could think of was a book they had to read in school called *Of Mice and Men*. George was a big guy, but not so bright. The guy had a thing for pets but didn't know his own strength. Shit went downhill from there. The creature in front of them could have been named because of the book, or Krevus could just be as crazy as he sounded and had named the thing George so he could have a friend.

Tim guessed it was better than talking to a volleyball.

Why the creature was named George didn't even matter as George opened his mouth to reveal rows of razor-sharp teeth and let out a roar.

The lizard was ready to rumble.

CHAPTER SIXTY-EIGHT

Cassie laughed in the face of danger.

The little tank stared defiantly at George with a smile on her lips. Tim didn't know how she did it. The pain receptors in the game made everything feel real. Getting stabbed hurt. Getting squished by one of George's massive rat claws, well, he'd never wanted to know what it felt like to become a pancake.

Using her bō staff to get the boss' attention, Cassie tried to turn him away from the group. George reversed his path and used his tail to stop Cassie from getting behind him. The giant lizard head snapped at her. One bite from those jaws would be catastrophic. Tim didn't want to find out if he could reattach an arm in the middle of combat.

Chances were the best he could do was stop the bleeding and take the pain away. Cassie wouldn't be very effective with one arm, so he had to keep an eye on her. Tim cast curse of giving and followed it up with who needs a shield. Less damage to Cassie now might save their asses at the end of the fight.

An arrow plinked off the boss' head. "Shit." Lorelei lined up her next shot and smiled as her arrow sunk into the fur-covered part of the boss.

JaKobi, seeing what happened to Lorelei's attack, started throwing fireballs at George's flank. The monster screamed in rage as the pyromancer's magic singed his fur.

The battle was going pretty well so far.

Tim felt better about the fact George was taking damage. Some of their more recent fights required them to break some type of shielding before the boss could be hurt. Worrying about those kinds of tricks with a twenty-foot-long rat who happened to have a Gila monster head just seemed insane.

Cassie dodged another swipe of George's claws and then dove forward to avoid his tail. Her health dipped enough that Tim cast a healing orb just to make sure she wasn't going to have any issues. The ranged DPS kept up the pressure, but where was ShadowLily?

The assassin appeared out of thin air and sank her blades deep into George's rear leg. Wrenching the blades free, she took a few hacks at the boss' tail before disappearing again.

George spun around snapping his jaws, but the attacker was gone. All he received for his troubles was a thorn-laden strike from Cassie's staff. The rat flipped around so quickly their tank never had a chance to move. George's beaklike mouth shot forward and snapped down on Cassie's bō staff.

"Oh, fuck." She was face to face with a monster that could eat her like she ate an M&M. Yanking the staff free didn't seem to be an option, but she tried again. Just when she thought she'd had it, there was a loud snap.

Tim watched as Cassie fell backward with half of her staff in each hand. He really hoped the old inventory trick would work to repair it, or they would have to secure her a new weapon before coming back to finish off Krevus. Of course, he should probably focus on making sure they lived through this fight before making future plans.

George rushed forward, jaws snapping in anticipation of his

first snack. A phoenix made out of flames slammed into his face. The boss shook off the blow to the head, but by the time he did Cassie was gone.

Before George could recover, ShadowLily reappeared. This time her stealth attack finished the job she'd started on the tail, severing it completely.

Tim started to smile. Despite Cassie going down, it looked like they might still have this fight in hand. He hit Cassie with a healing orb and fired another one at ShadowLily. George was fast and pissed off, so there was a good chance she'd get hit before all this was over.

He cast a quick reapplication of curse of giving. He wanted to use behold my power, but causing damage to his team when their tank might be ineffective for the rest of the fight seemed like a bad idea. It also dawned on him that George probably did most of his fighting in the dark, so having the room lit up for them was probably making this easier than it had been for the other adventurers.

ShadowLily rolled away from George's attacks, but the boss stayed on her. Without Cassie to grab the boss' attention, she was in trouble. Tim only knew one way for her to survive and it wasn't in a straight up battle. There was a chance she could dodge all of his attacks, but it just wasn't worth the risk.

"Kite him!" Tim screamed.

Not sure of exactly the best way to help, he fired off a blast of divine light which struck the boss in the head. The spell did some damage, but George kept thundering after a fleeing ShadowLily.

"I'm so stupid sometimes." Tim would have smacked himself in the forehead, but he was too busy casting snare.

George slowed down just as he lunged forward for a strike. The loss of momentum let ShadowLily escape the snapping jaws of death by a few inches. This was it. They had to give the boss everything they had right now, or he'd pick them off one by one.

Tim cast behold my power and followed it with healing storm. His AOE healing spell took care of the first wave of damage, and a quick round of healing orbs on everyone should mitigate the rest of the effect. Tim's mana was running low, but he had enough for one more root spell. He just had to time it right.

"Anyone want to get this guy off my ass?" ShadowLily screamed as George started to catch up with her.

Cassie ran in from the side and slammed both of the jagged ends of her staff into George's side. The boss spun around, snapping at Cassie. She got up limping, her face contorted in pain. Tim didn't know if Gila monsters could smile, but if they could he had a pretty good idea of what it would look like.

He could have cast his snare spell again, but it might not have helped. Instead, Tim cast cleanse. The tension and pain on Cassie's face smoothed out, and he knew he made the right call. His eyes stayed locked on her, willing the tank to run just a bit faster.

JaKobi grabbed Cassie around the waist and then they blurred for a moment as they sped away. Flames shot out from behind the pyromancer. When JaKobi stopped running, he fell to the ground, heaving from the effort of the cast. For now, the two were safe behind the wall of fire.

Lorelei was doing her best to do as much damage as she could to George's flank, and ShadowLily had disappeared again. The boss' health was dropping lower by the second. They had him down to fifteen percent. They just needed to hold out a little bit longer. Tim's mana was on its last dregs. He'd managed to replenish enough for one more cast, but that was it.

Should he wait for the right moment or just let it rip?

"Screw it," Tim mumbled to himself as George turned away from him and started chasing Lorelei.

"Guys!" Lorelei screamed as she activated her boots and started to move just fast enough to stay in front of George.

ShadowLily snapped into existence and severed one of George's tendons with a critical hit, just as Tim's divine light spell hit his other leg. The boss spun, ignoring ShadowLily completely as he focused on Tim.

"Not good. Not fucking good!" Tim yelled as he turned and ran toward the wall. He activated quick feet, hoping the small burst would be enough to keep him alive.

Maybe it wasn't the kind of content people would want to watch, but sometimes you just had to try to buy yourself a little time. Sadly for him, it seemed space was rapidly becoming a bigger issue than time as the cavern wall threatened to cut off his escape.

When he reached the wall, Tim turned to face George. If he was going to die, at least he wanted to see it coming.

The Gila monster head snapped its jaws in triumph as it closed the distance between them. Forty feet away, and then thirty. The boss made a face as Tim's behold my power curse took effect. He wasn't sure if the boss died instantly or not, but it crashed to the ground and began sliding right toward him.

Could you still get crushed to death after a win?

Tim watched as the body kept coming. With five feet to go before reaching the wall, there wasn't anywhere left for him to run. Not wanting to see his fate, he closed his eyes.

He didn't want to see death coming after all.

When the **You have died** screen didn't fill his vision, Tim stuck out a hand. It bumped into something hard and scaly less than a foot in front of him. Opening his eyes one at a time, Tim looked into George's open jaws.

"That was fucking close," he mumbled as he started edging around the fallen boss.

The fight had been enough to get his heart racing, and their day wasn't even close to being done yet. Tim made it around George's corpse and saw the rest of his party.

JaKobi was the first one to spot him. "I thought you turned into lizard snacks."

Holding out his fingers a few inches apart, Tim started to grin. "It was close."

The body started to break into golden motes of light and faded away. Tim's notifications showed him that he'd received five golden coins. The reward seemed a little small for what felt like their hardest fight yet, but the single kill had netted him a ton of experience. He reminded himself that Paul had promised them a reward, and the last time that happened it had been one hundred percent worth it.

The real question was, would they be able to continue, or did they have to leave to get Cassie a new weapon?

"How's the staff?" Tim asked as he turned to look at the tank.

Cassie pulled the weapon from her back and thumped it on the ground. "Good enough for now. The damn thing says I need to take it to a repair shop as soon as possible. So, not as good as new, but good enough to keep going."

Tim nodded. "Then let's find out where the rat kept its nest."

Cassie looked at the hole in the wall. "You know those movies where people go caving, they never end well."

JaKobi put an arm around her as they walked toward the crack. "Sometimes it's snakes, or it could be sharks, and every so often it's a long-lost race of cave people. What do you think we'll find today?"

"Might be your teeth on the floor if you keep on talking," Cassie snapped as she pulled away.

The pyromancer turned to look at Tim and mouthed. "She's not scared anymore."

He was right, of course. Cassie *was* too pissed off to be scared. JaKobi might pay for it later, but Tim was happy that he snapped her out of it. The tank disappeared into the darkness, and the others followed.

Krevus was about to go down!

CHAPTER SIXTY-NINE

"It's beautiful!" Lorelei said as she spun around, looking at the room.

It would have been hard for Tim to argue that with a straight face. The room would have made the pharoahs of Egypt envious. It wasn't just that there were carvings or treasure piled around. The entire room was chiseled out of solid rock.

Statues with perfect details dotted the landscape, their feet still attached to the polished cavern floor. To do all of this work without making a single mistake must have taken a lifetime. *Or lifetimes*. And there was light. Where was all the light coming from?

Tim felt his mouth hanging open in wonder and snapped it closed. This room was amazing, but the man who'd made it didn't get a free pass just because he could create beautiful things. Not when he spent his life taking from others instead of healing them. Not when his best friend was a giant lizard rat.

There had to be an atonement for the wrongs Krevus committed. His sins apparently hadn't stopped with his death, and neither had his ambition. This tomb was a symbol of how talented the bastard was, but talent didn't excuse people's actions. You didn't get a free pass on morals just because you were amazing at something.

"JaKobi, toss your light up there. I don't want to be caught with our pants down if the room's lighting fails."

An orb flew up to the ceiling to illuminate the room further. "You got it, boss."

Tim hadn't realized just how big the space was. With JaKobi's extra light he had the feeling he was seeing only about a third of the space. It seemed impossible that someone could have built this tomb under the mountain. If the tomb stretched as far as he thought, it was as big as an NFL stadium times two.

They were standing on a wide thoroughfare that ran through the center of the room. Tim refused to call it a road, although the twenty-foot strip of ground they were on could have been a two-lane road just about anywhere. The thought of having a road leading to a grave seemed crazy to him. What was next? Were they going to have drive-through cemeteries for celebrities' graves, so people could take pictures as they passed and listen to an audio recording about the person?

It was the next evolution for the look-at-me generation.

Tim almost laughed out loud. He managed to turn it into a cough at the last second and pretended he was clearing his throat. *When did I turn into my grandpa?* He didn't care how people had fun. If the worst thing someone could say about you was that you took annoying pictures with your phone on a stick that wasn't so bad.

It was easy to forget that different things made people happy. If taking a picture in front of everything or blogging about life makes them happy or feel more in touch with people, then let them have their moment. As he got older, it was easier to see that not everyone liked the same things, and it was okay.

Some of his friends were into sports and could fix cars, while his coder buddies couldn't tell you a thing about their car except where to put the nozzle in for a fill-up. There were no bullshit standards anymore. Women dominated fields traditionally held by men, men had branched out into fields held by women. It was a brave new world out there. Now Tim tried to find joy in things that made others happy and tried to stop himself from telling others what they liked was stupid.

But it wasn't always easy.

Tim nudged Cassie. "Care to lead the way?"

"Hiding behind a woman, typical." Cassie grinned as she pulled his leg. "Don't worry, I'll protect you."

"Yeah, you will," JaKobi shouted from behind.

Tim mumbled, "It's kind of your job." He paused and looked from the pyromancer to the tank. "And was that some sex thing?"

Holding up his hand to stop any comments, Tim quickly added, "Wait, I don't want to know."

"You don't know what you're missing out on." Cassie winked at him before moving forward.

ShadowLily smiled at Tim and purred, "If you want me to protect you later, all you have to do is ask."

Tim coughed again. "Nothing wrong with protecting the ones you love."

"Sounds like something they would say on *Game of Thrones*." JaKobi grinned.

Something moved at the side of the room and Tim froze in place. The look on JaKobi's face said, come on that joke wasn't too bad, but all he could do was look past him toward the walls. There were hundreds of skeletons, maybe even thousands of them. Their bones matched the stone so well that without the additional light, he might have never seen them.

Everyone else stopped to follow Tim's gaze, and a gasp escaped from someone.

"What are they doing?" Lorelei asked as she moved her bow from target to target.

Tim watched the skeletons for a moment before answering. "I think they're cleaning?"

"Some of them. Others are working on the stone." JaKobi

looked like he wanted to bolt but wasn't willing to leave without the rest of them. "What do you say we find Krevus, and get this show on the road?"

"I second that." Cassie nodded as she spoke. "This place is creepy, and I need to get my bō staff looked at."

Lorelei pointed to the center of the room where the actual tomb was resting. A twenty-foot-tall statue of Krevus stood at the head of the giant slab of stone. "My guess is we should start there."

Tim motioned for Cassie to lead the way. There was no chance in his mind that Lorelei was wrong. If you wanted to kill a spirit, the logical place to look for it was in its grave. He kept his head moving from side to side, ready to call out if the skeletons decided to charge. So far, all of the monsters seem preoccupied.

Now he understood how so many of the skeletons had made it to the surface. Keeping track of thousands of them, and a giant lizard-rat would have been nearly impossible for one man. At least Krevus' pet was dead. Fighting a couple thousand skeletons, a giant rat, and the spirit of an evil priest all at once seemed like a little much.

Cassie stopped a hundred feet from the tomb as a scratching sound came from in front of them.

Tim's first thought was, if it's a hundred of those rat things, we're totally fucked, but soon it became apparent that the source of the sound wasn't scratching at all. Something was shifting the giant slab off the tomb.

From the inside.

The lid shifted again. This time Tim could see the slab itself shift. How strong did the man inside have to be if he could move the lid? The strength it would have taken seemed almost unbelievable. The stone lid had to be fifteen feet long, eight feet wide, and at least a foot thick. The damn thing must have weighed a couple tons.

A cloth-covered hand rose up from inside of the tomb. The mummy's wrappings fell away as it worked to make the opening bigger. Slowly, a head came out of the tomb followed by a wide set of shoulders.

The mummy's gaze turned on the group. "It's been so long since I've had visitors."

Krevus climbed out of his tomb. The cloth bandages that had covered him since his entombment had seen better days. The priest looked down at his tattered wrappings and frowned. "This won't do at all."

The shadows clinging to the outer edges of the room started to swirl, then moved toward Krevus as if he called to them. They flew across the tomb, almost like strips of cloth in an animated Disney movie. The shadows covered Krevus from head to toe as the whirling maelstrom of darkness grew outwards, and then with a flash of light disappeared.

Blinking the haze from his eyes, Tim could see that Krevus was now covered in a robe of shadows. His outfit almost made him look like death. All he was missing was the scythe.

The massive weapon appeared in Krevus' hands a moment later.

"I just had to think it," Tim mumbled to himself.

Krevus looked down at himself and grinned. "That's better." His head turned to the group, and little red flares of light were where his eyes used to be. "Have you come to pledge your lives to me?"

Thrusting her middle finger forward defiantly, Cassie screamed, "We've come to take yours, you skeletal piece of shit."

Laughter rumbled, seeming to fill the tomb from all angles. "If you choose to throw your lives away instead of joining me in ascension, then so be it."

"George!" Krevus called out, making dust fall from the ceiling. The embodiment of death turned his head, looking for his pet.

"George won't be joining us," Cassie snarled. "We killed that rat mother fucker in the other room." She twirled her staff. "Now stop stalling and get your ass down here."

Tim couldn't help but grin. Cassie was taking her taunts to a whole 'nother level. Keeping up with agro from this group was no easy chore, and yet for the most part, their tank handled it pretty well. He'd only had to run for his life once.

Krevus let out a wail of anguish and leaped from the tomb. The floor shook as he landed on the polished floor. A huge swipe of his scythe let all of them know just how devastating a blow from the weapon could be. The priest came forward, eyes burning with hatred.

Cassie didn't give Krevus time to get settled. She sprinted toward the priest with reckless abandon. Ducking under the first swipe of his scythe, she rose up and then rolled to the side as he tried to stomp on her. The big weapon was no use against her when the tank got inside of his range. Her staff hammered against the boss' legs, letting the others start their attack.

A quick check confirmed that his buffs were still active and that he was set in his Way of the Boulder stance. He cast a quick healing orb on the tank just to keep her topped off and thought about how he could help in this fight. His heals would be needed of course, but fighting against undead things, and dark magic, was kind of his specialty at this point.

Tim jumped into the fight officially by casting weaken undead. He waited to see the spell take effect and then followed up with a series of divine light casts. The damage-dealing abilities ate up huge chunks of his mana, but the chunks of health he was knocking off made it worth it.

The boss' health dipped under seventy percent.

"Death calls and you must answer!" Krevus shouted as he floated into the air and away from Cassie's unrelenting attacks.

Tim heard ShadowLily swear as her stealth was forcibly broken. She managed to throw one of her knives at the boss before some kind of spell hit her.

"I can't move!" the assassin screamed.

Tim started casting cleanse as he ran to her. The spell didn't seem to have an effect. The skeletons from the side of the room started closing in. If the root wasn't cleansable then the spell had to be a mechanic, and that meant they needed to protect her.

"Cassie we're going to need you!" Tim cried as he reached his girlfriend's side. Placing a hand on the back of her head he pulled ShadowLily's forehead against his own and stared deep into her eyes. "We'll get through this."

The tank took up position, blocking the boss from them just in case as the others surrounded ShadowLily in a triangle, each of them facing away from the trapped assassin as the skeletons continued toward them.

"Don't wait on me, burn them to ash!" Tim screamed as he let his first blast of divine light go.

The spell wasn't an AOE, but the skeletons had so little health, each cast seemed to destroy ten of them if he lined it up just right. Sadly, he couldn't keep casting the spell indefinitely. He would need his mana for other things.

Hundreds of the skeletons crumbled around them as the group continued fighting. Even ShadowLily helped by throwing her knives at any of the monsters who made it past the group's assault. Just when it felt like they were going to be overwhelmed, the skeletons formed a wide circle around them and stopped advancing.

Krevus' laughter drew everyone's attention back to the boss. "In death, we find purpose. Your deaths will serve to further my great works."

"Shield Wall!" Tim screamed. He didn't know if the group would get the reference, but he hoped that all of them had at least watched an episode of *Vikings*.

He knew they didn't have shields, but he didn't have time to explain why they needed to get together, only that it felt right. One person might die from what was coming next, but if they all stood together and spread out the damage they might live. Or he was wrong and they were all about to die.

Game mechanics were a real bitch to figure out sometimes.

Tim only hoped he'd made the right call. It didn't seem like the developers would lock one person in place for certain death, when respawning took so long. No one wanted to lose a day seeing their caseworker when they could be out kicking ass. Only a real dick would design a fight like that.

The group crowded around ShadowLily, and Tim quickly cast who needs a shield to try to minimize the damage even further.

Krevus rose in the air almost to the top of the cavern. The shadows that covered him spread out to make a sphere of dark energy below his feet. "Death comes!"

The tainted priest fell from the sky like a comet, the sphere of darkness at his feet, pulling him toward ShadowLily like two magnets coming together. Tim felt the rush of air as Krevus drew closer. With a grunt of exertion, he jumped up and covered ShadowLily with his body.

Tim's world exploded in pain.

If things were this bad for him, then he knew the rest of his group was feeling it. Before standing up, he cast healing storm on the group. The other members were climbing to their feet and slowly coming back to their senses. Another blast of healing storm had all of them feeling a little bit more like themselves.

It helped that they weren't being attacked. Why weren't they being attacked? They might be missing out on a huge opportunity.

Tim spotted Krevus kneeling on the ground. "The boss is stunned!"

The first one into the fray was ShadowLily. Krevus' explosion must have freed her at the same time it sent the rest of them crashing to the ground. The assassin smiled as her daggers tore into Krevus' unprotected flesh like a pit bull with a tennis ball.

Tim grinned as Krevus' health started to plummet. He quickly cast weaken undead, curse of giving, and behold my power. He staggered a bit from the quick use of so many spells, but it was worth it.

As his spell ripped the life from his team, Tim started casting a round of healing orbs. It was his most cost-effective heal, but with him putting out so much DPS it felt like a drain. He would have cast healing storm instead, but the group didn't need a one-time lift right now, they need periodic healing.

Krevus' health dipped below thirty percent, and he started to stir. The shadows that had torn loose from the priest's body started to move to reform his robe. Tim looked at his mana, not sure if they could survive another one of the boss' special attacks. With a few more levels, they could have probably survived a few rounds, but right now, he'd burned through almost all of his reserves.

"Burn!" Tim shouted as he released the last of his mana in a shower of divine light.

Oddly enough, it was Lorelei who ended the fight. Up until now, the ranger hadn't done much damage. Her arrows did well enough to keep the skeletons at bay, and the poison on her arrows added a small amount of damage to the boss, but she'd been mostly ignored.

Tim grinned as he watched the tip of Lorelei's latest arrow flare to life with white light. The ranger took her time to line up the perfect shot and let the arrow fly. Her shot flew true and slammed into one of Krevus' empty eye sockets. The arrowhead exploded in a shower of holy brilliance, and the priest fell to the floor.

The shadows wrapped around Krevus fell away and sank into the ground. The sound of the skeletons falling apart filled the chamber like a summer rain. The priest's body broke apart into golden motes, and a small chest waited for them in the center of the room.

Tim smiled as the notification for completion filled his vision. He looked at ShadowLily. "I think you deserve to go first."

The assassin walked to the chest. "Don't think that I didn't feel you jump on top of me, Mr. Hero."

"We've all got our parts to play. Mine just happens to be a hero!" Tim said with mock bravado.

Cassie nudged JaKobi. "She must have missed the part where he screamed like a girl."

"That might have been me." JaKobi looked slightly ashamed. "What? I'm squishy."

ShadowLily placed her hand on the chest and turned toward the group. "Twenty gold coins. That's one hell of a haul."

"And don't forget we each get an item when we turn in the quest," Lorelei added.

Tim started ushering everybody out of the tomb. "Let's turn in the quest here so Paul knows it's safe to send a team for the artifacts. Then we can head back to Tristholm for the night. Tomorrow we head under the mountain."

"You would think adventurers would learn that nothing good comes from going underground. Just look at Bilbo. One trip underground and he found the damn one ring." JaKobi shook his head.

Cassie just smiled. "The best loot on his first adventure, what a lucky guy."

Tim smiled as he listened to the others talk about what was going to happen next. He turned in his quest to alert Paul and decided to wait on looking over the list of loot until they returned to town. Depending on the experience, he might get another level for turning in the kill quest, and he wanted to make sure the loot he received was based on his progress.

It was almost time to end the threat to Tristholm once and for all.

CHAPTER SEVENTY

Gerald grinned as the adventurers returned. "Back, and on your own two feet I see."

"The skeletons were easy. It was the giant lizard rat and Krevus that were the problem," Tim said casually as if he killed a centuries old demonic priest every day.

Pulling back the coin, he was about to hand Tim, Gerald eyed the adventurer skeptically. "You did all of that?"

"We sure did, bud." Cassie stepped forward and poked Gerald's chest. "Pay up."

ShadowLily rushed to corral her best friend. "Don't mind her. She doesn't play well with others."

Gerald reached in his coin purse and pulled out two additional gold coins for each of them. "In light of the events, and in hopes that you'd accept another quest on behalf of Tristholm, I think an additional reward is in order."

Quest Completed: Smashing the Skeletons

You not only completed the quest but ensured that the source of the skeletons was destroyed. Good job, enjoy the extra coins.

Reward: Three gold.

Tim smiled as he accepted his reward. "You said something about an additional quest?"

Now the gate guard didn't seem so confident. He looked over their group to figure out just how much of a challenge they could handle. "As you know, the passage under the mountain remains open. What you might not know is that no one has been able to make it inside."

Gerald started pacing. "What we really need is someone to eliminate the threat. Once whatever is keeping the adventurers out is vanquished, we'd at least stand a shot at turning back the tides of darkness."

"This is more than I have any right to ask of you, but it needs to be done, so here we are." Gerald extended his hand.

A prompt appeared in Tim's vision.

Quest Received: Slaying the Ghost

We don't know what is keeping the adventurers from entering the passage under the mountain, but we do know it needs to be stopped. Whatever it is moves like the wind and kills without remorse. If these things aren't enough to scare you off, then know also that no one else has survived their first encounter with the ghost. Good luck.

Quest Rewards: An item of your choice from the city guard's stockpile.

Accept Quest: <Yes/No>

A quick check with the group showed them all nodding vigorously. The best rewards they'd gotten in the game so far seemed to come when the quest givers opened up their coffers. Tim accepted the quest by shaking Gerald's hand.

The Gate Guard only shook his head. "I really do hope you succeed, but I'll be giving this quest to others just in case."

Cassie poked the guard in the chest again. "You won't need others. The Blue Dagger Society is on it."

"Obviously, we'll let you know how it turns out." Tim smiled at Gerald's shocked expression. "Have a good night."

The group turned to leave when a man in the Tristholm city's guard uniform stopped them. "I have a message for ShadowLily from her father."

Tim read the concern on her face as ShadowLily stepped forward to accept it. She looked down at the document and read it twice before looking at their expectant faces.

"You're never going to believe this," ShadowLily finally said. "Dad made a new friend."

"So, how did you end up cooking for Seraphina?" Tim asked.

Joe laughed. "When you left me with Jon, I told him what I was doing, and he told me his mom would love to try something new. He seemed like an important guy, so I thought it might be a good way to drum up business for the new restaurant."

Tim looked at the happy smiles on everyone's faces as they ate some of Joe's lunch options. One particular gentleman looked disgusted and then delighted as he bit into a Monte Cristo. Seraphina was inhaling huge forkfuls of a chicken chimi slathered in sour cream and guac.

Having sampled some of the game's offerings before Joe came along, Tim could understand how impressive this spread must have looked. If you were used to stew and bread, and maybe a fully roasted animal on the holidays, diner fare had to seem like a smorgasbord of options. Not to mention a good diner always had dessert.

Tonight was no different.

Joe got up from his seat and disappeared for a few minutes. When he came back, he had a carrot cake in one hand and an apple pie in the other. Tim saw a few servers appearing with additional cakes and pies. He'd been worried JaKobi wouldn't have left any for the guests to try.

A good homemade carrot cake was something to die for.

It wasn't anything like that shit that came out of a box. With canned frosting between the layers, a person might as well have just been eating sugar and flour. The homemade version was rich and moist in a way a big box brand couldn't replicate. Tim didn't care what anyone said, no creamed cheese frosting from a can tasted as good as the real thing. If the restaurants aren't making things from scratch, they aren't doing it right.

After a day of adventuring, getting to sit down to a good quality meal and not just some slop from the local inn was a blessing. Tim should have thought of inns earlier. They'd been in such a hurry to get out of town, he hadn't reserved them any rooms.

Seraphina motioned to Tim. "This is too good of a dessert to have such a long face at the table."

"Sorry," Tim mumbled. "I was just thinking of how I forgot to reserve rooms at the inn."

"Nonsense," Seraphina responded with a dainty wave of her hand. "You can stay here." She looked at Joe. "I'd be delighted to entertain this amazing man while you handle our other business."

Joe looked blown away by her kindness. "Seraphina." He started to bow and then stopped, unsure of the right form of address. "I couldn't possibly take such advantage of your hospitality."

"You can and you will," Seraphina smirked. "I expect you to cook for me every night, so you'll be working for your room."

Joe looked like he felt better about the situation, knowing he was going to work for room and board. "I would be delighted to be your guest then." He sat back down. "And you'll have someone show me around tomorrow?"

"I think I might handle that responsibility myself." Seraphina took another bite of her carrot cake. "This is really good."

Tim leaned over and whispered to ShadowLily, "It really is cute watching old people flirt."

"Only when it's not your dad." The assassin fake-barfed.

Lorelei was grinning like the Cheshire Cat. "You should be happy for him. It's gotta be hard being single at that age. Then again, maybe it's a million times easier because you know exactly what you want."

ShadowLily shrugged. "I'm happy for him, I just don't want to watch."

Tim stood up from the table. "Seraphina, would it be too much trouble if we adjourned to our rooms now?"

"Of course not." She clapped her hands, and two servants appeared to escort them away. "I'll have someone come and collect you in the morning. I've got a little surprise for you."

Joe stood to join them, and Tim motioned for him to sit down. "Stay and enjoy yourself, Joe. We'll see you in the morning."

ShadowLily gave her dad a wink of support before grabbing Tim by the arm and leading him out of the room. "Well done, sir."

"In all honesty, I did it for myself." Tim laughed at the look on her face. "How else was I going to get you alone before your dad was sleeping down the hall?"

It was one thing to have sex with your girlfriend, it was another to do it when her dad was sleeping in the room next to yours. In this game, Joe could actually kill him and not get in trouble. At least the cook hadn't started asking Tim about making an honest woman out of his daughter yet.

If he could postpone that conversation indefinitely, he would.

Not that he wouldn't marry her in a heartbeat, but they were young and needed to do things in their own time. Right now, they were living together and kicking ass. That was enough for him, and it seemed to be enough for her. There was a lot of life left to live before they talked about settling down and having kids.

Oh, shit. He'd just freaked himself out.

Instead of worrying about it, he took solace that for now they were living inside of the game. When they emerged from Eternia, they would have twenty-one years of marital experience, but only be three years older. That was when they could talk about the future. For now, all they should focus on was having fun.

The servant opened the door to their quarters. Stepping inside, the man lit the sconces around the room and then left.

Tim closed the door. "I thought that guy would never leave."

"Tell me about it." ShadowLily sighed dramatically as she threw herself onto the bed.

Tim jumped into the air and landed on the bed next to ShadowLily. The assassin flew up with a squawk. Her amazing Dexterity saved her from taking a bad fall.

She stood up glaring, but with a look that also said, I'm going to eat you up. "Now you really are going to need protecting." ShadowLily dove on top of him, hands tickling faster than Tim could ever hope to block.

He hated tickles.

And he loved them.

CHAPTER SEVENTY-ONE

"Holy shit," Tim whispered as they walked out into the courtyard.

When they woke up that morning, the last thing he expected was the spectacle before him now. Seraphina stood in full battle dress, flanked by the thirteen alphas of the werewolf clans. It made him feel like they were going to war.

Maybe they were.

He kept his feet moving, afraid that if he stopped to take in the entire scene, he might never get moving again. The only thing they were missing were trumpets. In the fantasy movies the heroes always entered to fanfare. The same happy tones followed them out of town as they left to face down evil.

Seraphina motioned for them to come closer. Her son Jon moved from the side of the procession to stand next to her. He was also dressed for battle. Tim wondered how a simple day of adventuring had turned into something so cool. He almost felt like this was an award ceremony, but they hadn't even made it to the mountains yet.

Tim stopped in front of Tristholm's ruler. "Not what I expected."

"I told you it would be a surprise." Seraphina grinned. "This ghost character has been killing everyone we send to the mountain. If we ever hope to contain Vitaria's evil, we need to cleanse the passage. We can't do that if we can't get there."

"So, these guys are here for what?" Cassie asked bluntly.

Seraphina winked. Tim almost thought it couldn't have happened. Despite winning the war against the werewolves, she had been unhappy when they left a few days ago. What could have changed in such a short period of time?

Joe!

Tim grinned like an idiot. ShadowLily's dad was a stone-cold player. Not one full day in the city, and he was dating royalty. He forced himself to wipe the goofy-ass grin off his face as Seraphina continued speaking.

"These, my brash little friends," Seraphina motioned to her son and the alphas, "are your escort. I told them in no uncertain terms that if they got you there, you could handle the issue."

ShadowLily pulled one of her daggers free. "I've been waiting to kill that fucker since the first day we met."

Nodding, Tim remembered the day Malvonis had come into the inn. He'd stabbed Ernie, and the innkeeper had almost died. That event had led him to get the deed to the inn and start his little empire in the slums. Things were coming full circle.

"You know who the ghost is?" Seraphina looked intrigued.

"We have an idea." Tim saw how tense ShadowLily was and knew instinctively the best thing they could do was get in a fight. "I think it's time for us to go."

"Of course." Seraphina nodded as if she knew a thing or two about the rage of battle. "My son and the alphas are at your disposal."

Lorelei couldn't help herself. "Where will you be?"

Seraphina smiled. "I will be showing that delightful chef from last night a few buildings that might suit his needs."

"You go, girl!" Lorelei exclaimed, enjoying seeing the two of them connecting.

Jon made a motion with his hand, and men ran forward with a horse for each of them. He climbed onto his mount and motioned for the ranger to join him at the front. "At first, I was angry that she could be happy after we'd lost so much."

Jon closed his eyes as if remembering the faces of his brother, sister, and father. All of them had been killed in Tristholm's fight against the werewolves. "But then I realized she deserves to be happy. It's nice to see her smile again."

Lorelei leaned out of her saddle and gave Jon a quick hug. "She does have a nice smile."

She squeezed him one more time and then Jon lifted his hand into the air. The thirteen alphas of the werewolf clans sprang into action. They ran out of the courtyard, and the party followed on horseback. This was it. They were off to face their final test.

It was going to be awesome.

Jon held up a hand to signal for them to stop. "We've taken you as far as we can go."

Turning, he pointed a gauntleted hand. "The entrance to the passage under the mountain is three miles in that direction."

Tim slipped off his mount. "Thank you for clearing the way."

"Just take care of the issue and hurry up about it." Jon frowned. "I'm not sure how long I can be in the castle alone with the two of them."

Huffing laughter from the werewolves made everyone start smiling.

"We'll do our best, Jon." Tim gave the man's hand a quick shake.

ShadowLily reached out to do the same. "Don't let them get into any trouble."

Jon turned his horse and started back to Tristholm. "Like I've ever been able to stop my mom from doing anything." He gave them a hearty wave and then kicked his horse into a trot to catch up with the others.

They were forty miles from Tristholm and all alone. It wasn't much past noon so they'd made good time to this spot. The three miles to the mountain pass shouldn't take more than an hour if they took their time. Tim didn't fancy meeting Malvonis winded and not ready for a fight so they would be taking their sweet ass time, no matter how antsy they were.

"Let's get moving but keep sharp. He could be anywhere up ahead." Tim moved aside so Cassie could take the lead. "Hey, is that a new staff?"

"Sure is." Cassie whirled it. "I told Jon what happened to mine and he let me pick one from the armory. It's more defense-oriented, but the stats are about the same."

"Nice!" Tim gave her a high five. "I'll have to thank him when we get back."

"So, what do you think we'll be facing?" JaKobi asked, clearly wanting to change the subject from how great Jon was.

Tim kept his eyes scanning the lowlands around them. There were trees to the side, but the path they were on was wide and clear. No one would be sneaking up on them without luck and a significant amount of magical help.

"Malvonis is strong, and that was before he maybe became a wraith." Tim frowned at the thought of facing the assassin head-on. Even with the five of them, the outcome was in question. "The one thing we might have going for us is that he's a wraith now."

"How exactly is that a bonus?" ShadowLily looked at Tim with confusion etched on her face. "Aren't wraiths even stronger than they were as people?"

"They are," Time replied casually. "But it also makes them weaker to my kind of magic."

"And since your buffs convert a portion of our attacks to light, we also do increased damage." JaKobi started to smile. "I like the sound of that."

"I don't know, this guy still sounds scary to me," Lorelei said as she scanned the horizon. "How will I even know what he looks like?"

"He's like Gronk but green." Cassie grinned. "I like the muscles, but I pass on half-orc relations."

"What's a Gronk?" Lorelai looked thoroughly confused.

Cassie groaned. "You don't watch football, got it." She tapped a finger against her lip for a moment. "Think of the orcs from *Bright*, but big, like Dwayne Johnson."

"Ah, the Rock," Lorelei said with a laugh. "He's got a nice smile for a guy, but I'd rather pretend it was Ruby Rose. You know, even if she was all orcified."

"Just look for something big, green, and scary," JaKobi replied.

"I like the sound of that," Malvonis hissed before plunging his dagger into JaKobi's back. "I think green and scary sums me up perfectly."

The pyromancer went down faster than a twenty-one-year-old celebrating their birthday at Mardi Gras. He let out a weak gurgle as he clutched his back it sounded something like, "See, I told you he was scary."

Tim ignored Malvonis, trusting Cassie to do her job now that the assassin had revealed himself. All he could do was focus on JaKobi. A healing orb flew from his hand even as the words to his cleanse spell issued from his lips. It would have been nice if he only had to heal, but he had to expect the assassin to have some type of poison on his blades.

Skidding to a stop next to his friend, Tim cast another round of cleanse and healing orb. In his haste to heal JaKobi directly, he almost forgot about what he could do with his class spells. A second later, he dropped into the Way of the River stance and cast curse of giving on Malvonis.

The pyromancer climbed to his feet. "That was not a pleasant experience."

"If you want to avoid feeling it again, I suggest you start throwing some fire around," Tim shouted as he turned to see who needed him the most.

"Now you're speaking my language." JaKobi lifted his hands above his head and clapped. A bright red and orange phoenix made out of solid flame flew at Malvonis, crashing against the wraith's leather armor.

Tim cast healing storm on the group seeing as they all had suffered a little bit of damage. It looked like ShadowLily was giving Malvonis a run for his money. Their daggers clashed together so quickly it sounded like the staccato bursts of automatic fire. Cassie was circling them, unable to contribute much to the fight beside the occasional deflection of the wraith's feeder as it snapped out to weaken them.

He was happy to see a few arrows sticking out of Malvonis. The ones in his legs seemed to be slowing him down just a bit. Still, he wondered just how long ShadowLily could keep up her amazing performance. Tim wasn't sure if the wraith would ever tire, but people did.

Even ones with something to prove.

Malvonis' health dipped below fifty percent and he disappeared again.

"Oh, shit, just let it not be me." Tim looked around wildly. As the only healer, if he went down, everyone would probably follow him quickly.

Not knowing if he'd be able to in a few seconds, Tim cast healing orb on himself.

"I never liked you," Malvonis whispered as he slid his dagger into Tim's ribs.

The healer went down, the only thing saving him from dying

being the heal over time effect on his healing orb. Getting damn near sliced in half felt about as good as he thought it would. The shock was numbing out the pain, but that wouldn't last for much longer. He quickly cast another healing orb on himself, hoping the built-in cleanse would be enough for now.

A scream of rage and anguish stopped Tim's mind from racing, and he looked around wildly for the source. If someone else was hurt he had to try to save them before worrying about himself.

ShadowLily must have seen Tim get stabbed because she totally lost it. She was going toe to toe with Malvonis and winning. Tim couldn't believe it as he climbed back to his feet. The boss' health was plummeting. As long as he didn't disappear again, they were golden.

When Malvonis' health hit ten percent, he started to shimmer. Tim started to prepare himself for what was to come next. His guess was that it would be ShadowLily he took out next. Almost all of their damage had been done by the enraged assassin.

The wraith's feeding tube shot out at Cassie, and instead of blocking it, this time she dropped her staff and grabbed onto the tube. Not being able to break free stopped Malvonis from disappearing, but Cassie was taking a shit-ton of damage. It took him a few seconds to adjust his thinking from attack back to healing. He made sure his curse of giving was active and cast a healing orb on Cassie to make sure she stayed alive.

Malvonis was so preoccupied with trying to suck the life out of Cassie, he forgot about the most dangerous person in the fight. One of ShadowLily's blades cut through the feeding tube while the other found a place in Malvonis' chest. The last few percentages of the health ticked off of the boss' stats, and the fight was over.

Tim jumped up and down like he'd just won a title game. It felt so good to kill that rotten piece of shit. Part of him felt bad like he missed the chance Gandalf gave to Frodo when he told him to let Golem live. Part of him felt if Malvonis had ever found a place he could truly be himself, he wouldn't have been such a huge douche.

But he was a douche, and now he was dead.

Golden motes of light swirled up from Malvonis' corpse, and sitting in its place was a chest.

Tim walked forward and placed his hand on the chest. Five gold coins appeared in his inventory, as well as a necklace.

Necklace of Unshakable Will

Maxis RedFinger showed everyone that sometimes you had to sacrifice yourself to save others. This necklace provides a +3 bonus to Wisdom, and +1 to Intelligence, as well as the special ability Self-Sacrifice. One per battle, you may immediately take ten percent of your health and transfer it to an ally in need. This spell is instant.

"Sweet, I got a necklace." Tim slipped his newest acquisition over his head as the others moved to collect their loot.

JaKobi slipped a ring on his finger. "Ring protects against magical attacks and increases my intelligence."

"I'm kinda finding I like the dorky ones," Cassie said as she reached for the chest.

ShadowLily grinned. "See, I told you."

"Nice! A new set of gloves." Cassie slipped on the black leather gloves with silver studs over the knuckles. "They add a bonus to my parry chance and increase my strength."

ShadowLily tilted her head to the side and put on a new earring. "Increased critical hit chance. Practical and pretty, just my kind of jewelry."

Walking toward the chest, Lorelei smiled with the others. "You guys really do kick a certain amount of ass, ya know?" Reaching down, she touched the chest and her smile turned ten watts brighter. "Weapon augment. Increases my accuracy while shooting on the move."

"Let's turn in the quest so the Gate Guard will tell everyone it's safe, and then we'll move into the passage." Tim looked at his party, feeling confident after their latest battle. "I don't know what's waiting for us down there, but I do know it's going to be a long night. I hope you're ready."

"Like you even have to ask," Lorelei snorted. "Have you seen me in action?"

ShadowLily grinned. "I have, girl, and it's hot."

Cassie joined the other ladies. "Let's let the boys worry about the quest, while we show them how to get things done." They started to giggle and walked away.

Moving to stand next to Tim, JaKobi watched the women leave. "Am I ever going to understand them?"

"Probably not, but that's what makes it fun." Tim clapped him on the back. "Come on, we don't want to get too far behind them."

Quest Completed: Slaying the Ghost

You killed the ghost so quickly we almost don't believe it. Thankfully, you can't fool the system. When you return to Tristholm, each member of your party can select one piece of gear from the city's stockpile.

Getting so much loot kind of felt like winning the lottery.

CHAPTER SEVENTY-TWO

The entrance to the passage under the mountain was in front of them.

Just off to the side of the entrance was a black obelisk. It looked like it had a button in the center, like the ones they have to play recordings at national monuments. There was a time when the exhibits had actual people at them to answer questions, but they had disappeared as technology made it cheaper to play a recording.

Tim wondered if this was going to be the first cut scene he'd found in the game. It seemed like in every MMO, before you got into a dungeon or a raid, there was a little cut scene to set up the story. They hadn't run into one yet, but he really hoped this was their first.

"What do you guys think, push it or don't push it?" Tim asked, looking back at the group.

Cassie stomped forward and slammed her hand against the button. "Don't be so dramatic."

"Just know that if something big jumps out and kills us all, it was your fault." Tim spun around, trying to make her think something was coming.

Music blared from an unseen source and made him jump.

"What in the fuck was that?" Tim snapped his focus back on the tank, thinking she'd played some kind of trick on him.

Cassie just pointed at the projection on the wall. "I think it's called a movie."

"Far out!" JaKobi shoved himself to the front.

Grinning from ear to ear, Tim leaned back to find out just what was in store for them.

The underground city of Elmore's Hallow controlled the trade between Promethia and the Deserts of Naroosh for centuries, until one day a great evil befell them…

Downward was the way to go. There was nothing but trouble in the outworld. Liars and cheaters, all of them were. They wanted to travel through our city, but they didn't want to pay the tax. If you didn't want to pay the tax, then you had to float your goods on the big blue ocean.

It was cheaper to come through The Hallow, and there was no risk of piracy.

So they came. People from all around. They came and they left. No one ever stayed in Elmore. It was just a stop on the way to better things. That's what Doug thought twenty years ago, but then he'd met a girl. So the wayward traveler became a part of The Hallow, and it became a part of him.

Things were fine in the beginning. The steady traffic of the travelers had been enough to feed the entire city. Then the troubles started. Something evil was spreading across the Deserts of

Naroosh. The flow of traffic stopped, and so did the flow of coin.

A lot of people left, but not Doug, never Doug.

He would stay in The Hallow until the day he died. His home would flourish again. All they needed was a little boost. There had been rumors of course, about hidden treasure in the depths. More than one of their rulers had gone loopy throughout time. Living in the darkness could do things to a man, but not to Doug.

The darkness was a welcome relief to him. The troubles in his life had all faded to nothing when he'd found Elmore's Hallow. Now he was a proud father twice over. He wanted his children to grow up knowing what a special place this was, and not fearing where their next meal would come from.

Like so many others before him, he went down into the darkness in search of his fortune.

For three days, he toiled through the endless caverns. Doug left marks on the wall. He wasn't an idiot. It wouldn't do him any good to find the treasure only to get lost on the way back. For three days, he went deeper and deeper.

On the fourth day, he found something.

"Holy fucking shit, I actually did it!" Doug stomped his feet into a shuffling jig. "Take that and stuff it in your ass, Trevor."

Oh, it was crazy to go down there. You're going to die and leave your family with nothing. Why are you such a fool?

"Who's the fool now, motherfucker?"

All that was left was for him to find a way inside whatever he was looking at and haul out the loot. They'd have to respect him now. Savior of the entire goddamned city. Hopefully, it would be enough.

"Please, Eternia, let it be enough." Doug made the sign of the lady over his chest and got to work.

The solid stone slab looked like something used to cover a giant stash of something amazing and not the kind of thing a person would put over a body. Who in the hell would get buried down here anyway? He'd had enough trouble getting here on his own. Carrying something that weighed a few tons would have been damn near impossible.

Although with magic, anything was possible.

Doug used his chisel and prybar to work at the seals on the stone. One by one, they popped off. He walked around what he affectionately thought of as the chest of endless loot looking for anything more. Satisfied that he'd gotten it all, he bent down to examine the first of his finds.

The seals could just be made of rock, but they could be made of gold instead? He brushed one of them off and noticed the gold hue.

Maybe he was wrong.

There was always a chance he was seeing a lesser metal. The seals were so dusty it would be an easy mistake to make. The metal didn't even matter since each of the seals was set with precious stones. Some had diamonds, other emeralds or rubies.

If these seals were real, he didn't need to find out what was in the chest. All he had to do was go back to Elmore's Hallow, and from there to Tristholm. Once he made it to the city, he could sell his wares and return with enough food to see them through the year. Surely, the troubles in the desert wouldn't last longer than that.

"If they put this much treasure on the outside of the damn thing, there has to be something amazing inside." Doug slipped his prybar into a crack between the two stones.

Slowly, he worked the bar until it was inside of the lid, and then he wrenched it to the side. It took all of his strength to move the lid a few inches. Another hour of work and he had created a gap big enough for him to reach in.

Doug went back to grab his lantern. Holding it above the opening he peered inside. He couldn't make out anything. He hoped he hadn't wasted all that energy for nothing. He leaned over the gap, getting his head as close to the opening as possible. There was a glint of something white, no, maybe it was silver.

Whatever it was didn't look like it would be out of reach. All he had to do was climb up there and reach inside. It wasn't like anything could be alive down here. There wasn't anything to worry about.

With a grunt of effort, he pulled himself on top of the stone. Lying flat on its surface, he reached his arm inside and started patting around for whatever it was he saw. His hand brushed against something and he swore it moved.

Pulling his arm free, Doug cursed at himself for being such a scaredy cat. Still, there was no reason not to be safe. Prudence was the adventurer's best friend after all. He lifted his lantern to look in the gap again. Now he could make out something silver, and it was right below the gap. Lying back down, he shoved his arm back through.

What the fuck?

"Arguahhhhh!" Doug screamed at the top his lungs.

Something had his arm and it was pulling it. No, pulling him—trying to drag him inside. News flash: he wasn't going to fit. That small fact didn't seem to matter to whatever was doing the pulling.

"Let me go!" Dog cried as his shoulder popped out of its socket. "I'll get you out, I swear it."

A voice echoed from inside of the chest. "Yes, I believe you will."

With a wet pop, Doug's arm tore free of its socket, and blood poured from the wound. He managed to fall off the stone slab without breaking his light and looked at the stump where his arm used to be, unsure of what to do. He wasn't going to make it to a doctor. Maybe Trevor had been right, and he should have stayed near the surface.

The slab over what Doug now knew was a tomb shuddered and then flew into the air. A skeletal creature rose out of the crypt, gnawing on the end of Doug's arm like it was a chicken wing from the harvest fair.

Seeing that the rest of his meal hadn't made it very far, the lich tossed the limb aside and closed on the helpless man. "Tell me, mortal, are there more of you?" The lich's lips twitched into a grin, revealing rows of razor-sharp teeth.

"I came here alone," Doug rasped. The least he could do was try to save his family. This thing could never know they were above.

"We shall see." The lich rushed forward and plunged a hand into Doug's chest, then took a bite out of his heart as Doug looked at him helplessly. "You can tell a lot about a man from the taste of his heart."

The last thing Doug saw was the lich licking its lips in delight.

"Whoa, that was pretty dark," Tim said.

JaKobi looked at the entrance and then back at the obelisk. "I think it's safe to assume things haven't gotten better in Elmore's Hallow since this happened."

"Fine by me." Cassie huffed. "I like kicking evil's ass."

ShadowLily wrapped an arm around her best friend and Lorelei. "And we look damn good doing it."

"Yeah, we do," the ranger exclaimed.

Tim smiled at his group.

They were about to head into the darkness to face at least one boss. While he was nervous, this was what he played for. The best part of gaming for him was facing danger with his friends. He knew that no matter what, they would find a way to win.

The Blue Dagger Society always did.

CHAPTER SEVENTY-THREE

Why couldn't the passage under the mountain be a happy place?

Just once, Tim would love to see some people living under a mountain who were happy as shit. Why did it have to be all doom and gloom, orcs and goblins? Wasn't there a race of subterranean people that just wanted to make little cakes and share them with anyone who happened by? That would be so much nicer than caverns full of people trying to rip their faces off.

The life of an adventurer was never easy.

No one was going to pay you to go to the village and eat cake with people. If there was a job where eating cake and talking shit were the only requirements, he could probably handle it. It was like watching a sports stream on the internet. Those guys talked shit non-stop. Back in the real, there was a mute button, and Tim could just play his tunes.

Why was it no one popped in to chat and said nice game?

It was always, I'll beat you next time, or You ain't shit. Whatever happened to losing a close match and just wanting to play the person again to test yourself? The best PVP games always had the best matchmaking. No one wanted to get blown out every match or win by a million.

Winning without the struggle never felt as good.

Everything since Tim entered the game felt like a struggle as it happened. First, they had to find a tank, then it was clear out a dungeon. Since then, he'd been arrested, killed, and attacked by supernatural forces. All of that was just the preamble to walking under the mountain to face off against a lich.

At least they didn't have to fight a Kraken or speak the elvish word for "friend" to enter.

All that was required of his group was to have the guts to walk into the darkness. JaKobi's light spell made the journey easier to stomach. Being stuck down here with only a few torches or a lantern would have been scary as shit.

On the plus side, the passageway seemed to be carved out of the mountain, and they weren't walking across rotted rope and wooden bridges to get places. In fact, they hadn't walked past a single separate path since entering. There was no road less traveled, only one road, and it only went down.

The path they were on was wide enough for three or four carts with a little room to spare. It made sense if this was originally set up as a trade port between the people on either side of the mountain. Moving a caravan through here one cart at a time would have been a nightmare. At least they had plenty of room to spread out.

The downside of this path was that with no offshoots, they could only go one way to get back to the surface. They'd been walking for about an hour, so running all the way back while being chased by Vitaria's minions probably wouldn't lead to anything except death.

This was a one-way trip.

It would have helped if there was something to look at.

The smooth cavern walls made Tim feel like he had been swallowed by a giant monster and was currently working his way through their intestinal system. Oddly, he wasn't too worried.

What he really wanted was a change of scenery or maybe a pack of trash mobs to tangle with. Walking into a dungeon and seeing nothing to fight was worrisome.

Eventually, there would have to be a monster of some kind. With the first cut scene of the game leading them here, there was too much pre-amble for a boss in a box type scenario. In some games he loved that. Sometimes raiding felt tedious when you had to spend hours clearing out trash just to unlock the boss fights. Finding the right trash to boss ratio was key.

Not that boss in a box didn't have its place.

Raid bosses in a box were a nice alternative to provide people who maybe didn't have time to do full raids, or a chance to test new raiders out without committing to carrying them for four hours. Sometimes it was just fun to have a boss you could kill together after completing a raid or to gear up an ALT.

In *The Etheric Coast*, Tim didn't have to worry about creating alternate characters. He was pretty sure all you had to do to learn a new skill was to find a class trainer and get started. How far you could go without oodles of gold for spell books, and with potentially suboptimal stats, well, that was up to the player.

He'd decided to play a healer this time, and so far, he was incredibly happy with the choice.

It felt good to be one of the core pieces to his team. Not that all of them weren't valuable. You couldn't kill a boss without three DPS who were on their game, a tank who wouldn't die, and a healer. Take any one of the pieces away and life got infinitely harder. Every gamer had carried a rando through content where a person didn't even try.

Tim could hear his buddies screaming into chat, "Your auto attack would have one more damage than that, it's like you're playing with your dick." They got banned from chat for a week after that, but it was worth it.

I mean, how hard is it to just click the buttons in a certain order?

At least in this game, there wouldn't be many slackers. Not in the pool of players who decided to become adventurers. It was easy enough for anyone with an eye for talent to see who was doing the work, even if they didn't have DPS meters. In this world, you either worked your ass off or you didn't survive. They had to be ready for anything all the time.

"Oh, shit. I wasn't ready for that," Tim blurted out as they came to a cutout in the wall.

JaKobi grinned. "It's beautiful in its own way."

The group stood in the cut out looking down on the once prosperous city of Elmore's Hallow in awe. It must have taken thousands of years, and a talent for earth magic to create the city. All of the buildings were made out of stone. It looked as though they had been carved from the inside of the mountain themselves. It could have been a trick, just a perfectly built house covered in stone to make it look built-in, but Tim didn't think so.

He thought about his own spells and how much power it would have taken to do something like this. It almost didn't seem possible. This was god-level magic. Shaping the world wasn't something just anyone could do.

In short, the city took his breath away.

JaKobi sent his orb of light floating out over the city. There was illumination coming off the buildings, and a few magical lamps were still running. Without the additional light from the pyromancer, the place would have been downright creepy. It was the difference between searching an abandoned building with a flashlight or having a spotlight.

The city of Elmore's Hallow felt like a place that should have been alive, bustling with people and laughter. Despite being miles underground, the place must have felt warm once. Tim could imagine the people living down here and prospering. Vitaria had put an end to that, along with whoever the lich was.

"It looks so tranquil," ShadowLily said as she moved next to Tim. "Not what I expected at all."

Cassie tapped her staff on the ground. "I thought we'd be

looking down on a sea of trash mobs and trying to plan our way through them. This seems sadder somehow."

"Whatever happened down there happened a long time ago." JaKobi started to call his light back to him. "We can't save them, but we can make the monsters that did this pay."

Lorelei slammed her fist against the cavern wall loud enough to startle them all. "Damn right, we'll make them pay."

Tim started to smile. He'd never been so happy to be surrounded by people. His team, their guild, was an amazing thing. Together, the Blue Dagger Society would work to set this wrong right. There was only one more thing for them to do.

"Let's keep moving." Tim pointed down the passageway. "I'm ready to push back the darkness and bring life back to Elmore's Hallow."

"Fuck yeah!" Cassie took one last look at the city and then started following the passage again.

Tim watched from behind the group as they all checked their weapons and equipment without being asked. Each one of them felt like a veteran. People you could count on to do the work without being told. He couldn't be any more excited to walk into danger with these men and women by his side.

The Blue Dagger Society could overcome any obstacle.

***

The gate to the city was a massive thing.

Whoever built the place had found a way to use the stone as a natural defense. The gate was made out of eight-foot-thick blocks of solid rock. The only way something like that could have functioned in the space was with a heavy dose of magic.

Tim didn't think there was an army in the world that would be able to breach that gate. Not without some kind of explosive device. A ram would be about as effective as a toothpick. You couldn't burn stone, at least not with a simple fire. The city of Elmore's Hallow was like a fortress.

It looked like there was a massive courtyard past the stone gate, and then another set of smaller iron gates leading into the city. It was the kind of thing that screamed trap or boss fight. He couldn't recall how many times he'd walked into a room only to get sealed in for the fight of his life.

But they hadn't come here to sightsee.

If the courtyard was going to be the first of their battles, Tim thought, bring it the fuck on. They were ready. Malvonis went down. Krevus bit the dust. Whatever they ran into down here, Tim was sure they could handle it.

"Be ready. I've got the feeling things are about to go downhill." Tim motioned toward the second set of gates.

"Yeah, like that ball in *Indiana Jones*." Cassie laughed to break the tension. "Or like the *Pirates of the Caribbean* series."

The group started to fan out, Tim in the back. "Hey, Jack Sparrow is a legend! Anyone who says different is a monster."

"I liked Jack in one and two. Possibly even in movie three, but then things got a little weird," Cassie replied. "Like I said, downhill fast."

Tim nodded. He could see her point. Maybe not about Captain Jack, but about series and shows altogether. It seemed like every great franchise had a dud episode or season that just left the viewers going, huh? He wasn't even going to get started talking about that show with dragons.

They didn't have that kind of time.

The group started to enter the closed courtyard and Tim could tell they were all on edge. They knew something was off down here. The game didn't hand out quests and then go oh wait, nothing to see here. Something was going to happen, and it would be soon.

It wasn't like he hadn't expected it, but when the stone gate behind thumped closed Tim jumped into the air. Thankfully, there wasn't anything rushing straight at him. There was only a wall of stone behind him and not a monster. The other members of his group seemed to feel the same way.

It was like they let out a collective sigh of relief.

The Blue Dagger Society was ready for battle, and it was the waiting that was killing them. So far, they hadn't faced a single trash mob, and now it felt like they had arrived at their first boss fight. Tim looked around wondering if there was some trigger. Not seeing anything, he motioned for Cassie to continue forward.

A man leaped on top of the gate in front of them. His clothes were torn and covered in dried blood. The man's face looked like plastic skin had been pulled over the bone, and his expression was that of someone gone feral. A little bit of drool leaked from the corner of his mouth as he looked down on the group of adventurers.

Was he holding someone's arm?

Tim had to double-check what he was seeing, but the man perched on top of the gate definitely held a severed arm in his hand like a wooden club. All he could think of was poor Doug. Was it too dark for him to wonder if it was the arm from the video?

"It couldn't be," Lorelei said. "Could it?"

Tim was glad he wasn't the only one thinking it. "Let's find out after he's dead."

An inspection revealed that the man on top of the gate was Trevor, The Gatekeeper. Tim thought that must have been an important job when the town was in full swing, but the prestige would have evaporated damn near instantly as trade withered up. It was the kind of thing that could make a person bitter and angry.

"All who come must pay the toll!" Trevor screamed from atop the iron gate. "Tell me which one of you will it be?"

CHAPTER SEVENTY-FOUR

"What the fuck is this guy going on about?" Cassie snapped.

Tim wasn't sure. Did the Gatekeeper really think that they would let one of their number be killed just to enter the city? That wasn't going to happen. If they left and came back after the person respawned, they would probably be forced to make the same choice. It'd be better for them to all go down fighting than be forced into playing this monster's game.

"Who will pay the toll?" Trevor screeched.

Tim stepped forward so he was standing just behind Cassie. "What are you demanding as payment?" He was pretty sure he knew what Trevor wanted, but it never paid to make assumptions when death was on the line.

Trevor took a bite out of the arm he was holding. He chewed the meat and swallowed as he looked over them with the dispassion of a butcher. "One of you must be given to feed the family, or all will become food."

Looking at the stone floor of the courtyard, Tim could make out dark stains under the dust. He wondered just how many men Trevor had killed down here to feed his family, and what kind of a family ate human flesh anyway? Unless you were trapped on a desert island or in the Alps, you didn't even consider it.

Not when all you had to do was walk to Tristholm for a snack.

Tim tapped Cassie on the shoulder and started to back up. He didn't know what was going to happen when they refused Trevor's offer, and he wanted to be far away when it did. That's why Cassie made the big bucks, she took the brunt of the risk.

"I think we're going to pass on the dinner invite. None of us are interested in being food for your family." Cassie spun her bō staff around in a swirl of circles and motioned that she was ready to rumble.

Trevor leaped from the wall landing in the courtyard. He took another bite of the arm. As he chewed, he held the arm up and the shoulder socket made the entire thing sway like some sick marionette.

The Gatekeeper took another trip to chow town, and this time he grew a little bit larger. The muscles on his arms bulged out, and his eyes changed from a soulless black to ember red. "No one ever wants to pay the toll, but if you want in or out, you have to pay."

He took another bite of the arm and then tossed it away. Now Trevor was almost eight feet tall and built like a mini version of the Hulk. "I'm so hungry. The others didn't understand, but I did what I had to."

Marching forward, Trevor pulled a hatchet from his belt, and a hunting knife from behind his back. "Try not to run, fear spoils the meat!"

Cassie rushed to meet Trevor's attack. "This guy thinks we'd run, he obviously hasn't been paying attention." Her bō staff moved like the wind as she parried Trevor's attacks.

Sending a healing orb her way, Tim started to frown. The fight couldn't be this easy, not in their first dungeon with a cut scene. Cassie was taking a few hits, but nothing his healing couldn't keep up with, and Trevor's health was going down quickly. He'd learned a long time ago when something felt too easy, it was a trap.

"Get ready for something!" Tim shouted as he cast weaken undead on The Gatekeeper.

An arrow appeared in Trevor's chest, dropping the boss' health to just under sixty percent. He abandoned the fight with Cassie and ran off to get his arm. As he chewed on the limb, his health went back up. When his health bar hit eighty percent, Trevor started stalking back toward the group.

"Time to meet some of the family," the Gatekeeper screeched.

Hidden doors on either side of the iron gate slid open and a person ran out of each. The two had the same skin-pulled-over-a-sack-of-bones look Trevor had. One of them was an older boy and the other a woman.

Was this Trevor's family?

"Cassie, keep Trevor busy. Lorelei, see if you can slow the boy down." Tim barked out orders like a practiced raid leader.

He was counting on ShadowLily to take out the woman, and he hoped by redirecting the other's attacks, he could free up space for the assassin to do her thing. Stepping forward, Tim tapped JaKobi on the shoulder. "Keep an eye on Cassie's and Lorelei's targets and make sure they don't get into trouble."

The pyromancer nodded as he sent a phoenix flying at Trevor's son.

The boy was already hobbled by arrows through each knee when the phoenix slammed into him. The teen was lifted off his feet and landed on his back. The fire that hit him in the chest spread rapidly over his body. A second later, he was turned to ash as his hit points expired.

The woman let out a howl of agony and changed direction straight for Tim. Maybe she had singled him out as their leader, or she could have just confused him for JaKobi. Either way, she was coming at him faster than he would have liked. The tips of her fingers looked more like claws than nails.

Tim's fingers twitched his snare spell. It hit the woman but shattered a second later. It was a good thing a second was all ShadowLily needed to make her move. The assassin appeared behind the woman and slammed each of her daggers into the back of her knees before slicing down to her ankles. Her calves split like Uncle Leo's pants after a Thanksgiving dinner.

Standing above her prey, ShadowLily brought her dagger down on the back of the woman's head, ending her suffering instantly. Without waiting to be told, all of the DPS refocused their efforts on Trevor.

The Gatekeeper tried his best, but their continued onslaught proved too much for him. Tim had to cast a few timely healing orbs, but his curse of giving spell seemed to be keeping everyone up just fine. He watched as Trevor's health dropped to fifty percent, then forty, and finally thirty.

This was normally when a boss made his final push to destroy a group. Tim didn't know exactly what to expect, but he did know that he didn't want Trevor to regenerate any of his health if it could be helped. Maybe there was a way to destroy his food.

Trevor's skin flashed briefly, and Tim noticed immediately that he was taking more damage. This was their moment if they could just pull it off.

"Why am I so hungry, always so hungry?" Trevor turned and started walking back to the arm.

Tim pointed at the arm. "JaKobi, see if you can destroy that thing."

The pyromancer launched a series of attacks. Tim saw an arrow or two fly into the maelstrom of fire. Their actions must have been working because Trevor started running for the arm. As the Gatekeeper reached the limb, he lifted it up and the last of the meat fell to the floor in a burnt chunk.

"Arguahhhh!" Trevor started pulsing red. "My food! That was the last of him. Now they will all starve unless I set them free."

"Burn the boss! Burn the boss!" Tim shouted as he cast weaken undead, followed by divine light.

Trevor shrugged off the damage as he lifted his hands. Doors all around the courtyard opened and children poured out. Some of them were toddlers, others were missing limbs, all of them looked as bad as Trevor did. It was something from a nightmare. Who wanted to hack apart kids?

Lorelei was looking around, trying to pick off the oldest and fastest of the new arrivals. "I don't think I can do this. They're just kids."

JaKobi cracked a whip of flame, instantly killing five of them. "I think the morality test can be bypassed with one simple question. Are these little shits trying to kill us?"

"They sure don't look like they are coming to give us hugs," Lorelei quipped.

Using the whip again, this time to hit Trevor, JaKobi continued. "When something is trying to kill you, you have the right to save your own ass. Better off alive and morally lacking, then dead and full of moral fiber."

Trevor fell to his knees as his health dipped under ten percent.

"Normally, I'd say it's a slippery slope, but when the children in question are undead cannibals, I think it's okay to be flexible," Tim said through strained teeth as he fired off a blast of divine light.

"I'm not going to let them eat me." Lorelei fired an arrow into Trevor's chest. "It just feels weird. Creepy little fuckers caught me off guard."

Trevor's health hit zero percent, and he fell over with a gasp as his red eyes faded to nothing. With the boss down, it was easy enough for them to mop up the rest of the kids. It was grisly work, but it had to be done. As the last of the children fell, the gate rattled open.

There was a golden chest waiting for them just on the other side.

"Loot makes everything better," Cassie said as she placed her hand on the chest. "Even this depressing place. I'd come back a million times if the loot was good enough."

She smiled at whatever appeared in her inventory. "Belt of

the Savior. When under ten percent health this item will instantly restore you to twenty percent. Can only be used once per battle."

"It'd buy me enough time to heal you up." Tim might have liked the item even better than Cassie did.

JaKobi moved to touch the chest. "Ring of Fire. Not real original on the name, but the ring increases my intelligence, and damage with fire magic by one percent."

Tim motioned for the others to go first. "I went first on the last chest, so I'm okay waiting."

"I'm up." Lorelei touched the chest. "Gloves of Accuracy. Boosts damage with all ranged weapon types by one percent and increases accuracy while moving by five percent."

Surprisingly, he'd never really thought about his accuracy. Tim just pointed at things and cast. Sure, he'd missed with some spells, but most of his magic seemed to target things automatically. Maybe it was different for each magic user, or maybe in this case, ignorance was bliss.

"Dagger of the Depths." ShadowLily looked the weapon over. "Same stats as my daggers except that it also adds a half a percent of life steal."

That wasn't much, but her attacks were so quick and devastating that every tiny bit of health she siphoned with them might be enough to get her through his behold my power spell without additional assistance, freeing him up to do other things. He guessed this was the developer's way of making up for having to be a melee class without very many defensive cooldowns. Steal a little life, and you wouldn't die nearly as often.

Not that he let people die.

It was his turn. Tim stepped up to the chest and placed his hand on it. A notification appeared in his vision.

Item Received: Pants of Recovery

These pants boost your mana recovery by ten percent while in combat. While they don't offer additional stats, they will

stop that cold little breeze from wafting up against your nether region.

But I like the breeze.

In fairness, the mana recovery would be nice. The last few fights he'd been running on fumes. Whether that meant he needed to tighten up his rotation or just needed some better gear remained to be seen. Tim equipped the pants and was excited to see how much the additional regeneration would help during their next fight.

Everybody had their new gear on, and they were ready to move to the next stage of the fight. Things hadn't been easy, but Tim had a feeling they would get harder from here. A good game designer always built up the difficulty as an instance went on. The last thing you wanted was players getting stuck too early and quitting in frustration.

The next fight being tougher than this one excited him. It was the challenge that kept him playing. He didn't want things to be too easy or too hard. Finding that balance is what made him want to play. As he grew more comfortable in his role and the people around him, Tim was starting to feel like it was time to push some boundaries.

No one ever attained greatness by playing it safe.

CHAPTER SEVENTY-FIVE

Elmore's Hallow was deserted.

Tim could see how the city could have been beautiful once. The buildings carved out of stone had amazing designs etched into them. Gas lanterns hung from the outside walls, illuminating the area. Half of the lamps were extinguished now, but Tim tried to imagine the city as it was.

It would have been a cool place for a vacation.

The entire city felt like you were on a caving adventure. Instead of having to crawl through tight spaces and sleep in a crappy tent, there would have been hotels. At one point, they might have led adventure tours through the lower caverns. Although seeing how that worked out for Doug, maybe tours weren't such a good idea.

Still, there was a sense of wonder about being underground, standing inside a city that would never have been possible in the real world. If they had some hot tubs down here, and a spa, it would have been the perfect retreat. Sometimes it was nice just to get away.

Although he didn't travel anywhere devoid of two-day delivery.

Everyone else looked a little worried. The city was bigger than it looked from their hidey hole on the way down. They were all wondering how long it would take to search this entire place for their next clue. If they had to go building by building, they would be here for weeks.

Their quest was to clear out the mountain pass, so there was no reason to be worried about searching for monsters. The quest would let them know when they found them all. Thankfully for them, it seemed there wasn't any trash to deal with. If that held true, they wouldn't have too much longer to wait before they had a showdown.

ShadowLily placed her hand against one of the buildings. "This place is amazing."

"Sure, if you like the whole living underground vibe. I always wanted to live in a treehouse," Lorelei said with a grin as she thought about a memory from childhood.

"For me, it's being by the water. Ocean, lake, river, it doesn't matter," JaKobi said.

Cassie looked at the pyromancer. "A cabin by a river sounds awesome."

Tim couldn't help but think of how awesome it would be to do any one of those things. In the game, they could do almost anything, but out in the real world, you needed money to make your dreams happen. Money didn't always come from just putting your nose to the grindstone and working hard. Sometimes you also had to get lucky.

Deciding to enter *The Etheric Coast* had been his lucky moment.

His parents were being cared for with a little extra money. He was having the time of his life while his student loans were paused. He wasn't incurring any additional debt with his streaming contract covering his POD fees. The project in the slums was rolling along, and he was finally starting to recuperate some of the costs with his rental income.

Life felt pretty darn sweet right now.

The sound of metal hitting metal rang through the city. All of them looked around, unsure where the noise was coming from. Then it came again, and again. After a few minutes of the sound, they zeroed in on the direction and started that way. Cassie moved toward the front of the group, while Tim dropped to the back.

It wouldn't be long until they were right back in the thick of it.

Cassie led them deeper into the city, never wavering from the direction the sounds were coming from. The further they moved into Elmore's Hallow, the louder the sound became. Now every third or fourth time the clashing noise sounded, there was also a low moan. Tim couldn't tell if someone was being wounded or if they were crying out with the effort of whatever they were doing.

The group moved down a narrow alleyway that emptied out into a square. On the far side was a huge open forge. In front of the forge was a blacksmith. Tim wasn't sure the man was human. He could be a thing like Trevor, or even something else. All he could make out was that he had a hammer and was using it to hit something on the anvil.

Cassie moved them forward slowly, and Tim was thankful that for once she didn't just scream fuck off and charge into battle. There were too many unknowns. Was the Blacksmith alone? Did he have a weapon besides the hammer? Who was he forging something for anyway?

The Blacksmith turned away from the anvil, and Tim gasped. He looked like one of those creatures from Silent Hill with the giant metal heads. Only his helmet wasn't much bigger than the head it was covering. It looked like it had been beaten and shaped while he was wearing it. While the monsters in the movie looked good, the Blacksmith looked like nine pounds of ground beef shoved into a three-pound container.

It also didn't help that the Blacksmith didn't have hands. One of his arms had been amputated just below the elbow and had been replaced with a hammer. The other arm was just as mangled but had been replaced with a sword blade. Replaced might have been too kind of a word. It looked like the items had been shoved into the stumps of his flesh and cauterized in place.

A moan escaped the Blacksmith's mouth, and Tim realized the creature didn't have a tongue.

It was hard not to feel sorry for the guy. *Town is going broke, some idiot named Doug releases a lich and everything goes to shit. Next thing you know, you're waking up with a bucket mashed over your head and no fucking hands.*

Talk about bad luck.

It would be a kindness to put the poor thing out of its misery.

Lorelei let out a gasp. She'd been creeping around the side to get a view of what was on the anvil. Tim was about to ask her what it was when something moved. Tim watched the Blacksmith for a moment to make sure he wasn't going to start the fight and then moved to get a better view himself.

There were two people stuck on hooks in the back of the Blacksmith's shop. Both of them looked to be alive. At least, they were alive in the same way Trevor was. If they were in the mountains, Tim would have called these monsters wendigos, but under the mountain they felt more like revenants.

A third man was lying on top of the anvil, his legs hacked off at the knees. When they had walked into the square, the Blacksmith had been in the process of replacing the man's lower legs with sword blades. Somehow the new creature flopped off the anvil and then pulled itself up until it could get its sword legs underneath it. The thing tottered from side to side like a drunken gingerbread man, its blades clicking against the stone with every step.

If death on two sword legs didn't signal the start to a fight, Tim didn't know what did. "Light 'em up!" he shouted like a cop who just had a hunch about a traffic stop.

A whoosh sounded from behind him, and a giant phoenix slammed into Scissor-legs. The blast blew the creature off its feet, but it wasn't dead. The damned thing was having the hardest time getting back up. The Blacksmith extended his hammer to let Scissor-legs use his arm to pull himself back up.

The Blacksmith pointed at their group and grunted something. Turning away, he moved to one of the people on the hooks. They started to shake and kick, but there was no getting away. The woman he grabbed was going to be next on the anvil, and they couldn't stop it until they dealt with old Scissor-legs.

Cassie intercepted the monster born out of nightmares with her staff. It took everything she had to keep the thing off of her. Somehow once the fighting started, the bastard seemed a lot more coordinated. Knowing he might not have time later, Tim reapplied his buffs and sent a quick healing orb in the tank's direction.

"Lorelei, see if you can slow the Blacksmith down!" Tim refocused on Scissor-legs and cast curse of giving. "Everyone else, take that thing down."

ShadowLily appeared on the scene, her blades cutting deep slashes into Scissor-legs' back. A spinning roundhouse kick almost took her head off, but the assassin managed to roll away just in time. Cassie was back on the thing a moment later.

"Duck!" JaKobi screamed.

Cassie didn't hesitate. She jumped away from the monster and hit the deck faster than a runner stealing second. A huge fireball slammed into Scissor-legs, knocking him onto his back. He was trying to buck himself back up when an arrow appeared in the side of his head with a wet plop.

When everyone turned to look at the ranger, she just shrugged. "Wasn't having much luck with the big guy."

The Blacksmith pulled the woman from the anvil and tossed her on the ground. She pushed herself up on the blades where her arms used to be. He pointed toward the group and growled, before turning back toward his forge and the man hanging next to it.

"Let me handle this." ShadowLily stepped in front of Cassie holding both her daggers so the blades rested against her forearms. "Finally, get a chance to work on some of my defensive skills."

The woman screeched something unintelligible and charged for ShadowLily. The two were instantly locked in a dance of blades. They moved so quickly Tim almost couldn't follow. He also forgot to keep an eye on her health as he followed the battle. With a quick cast of curse of giving, the assassin's health went up to almost one hundred percent.

Their blades clashed against each other, sending sparks of light through the cave like lightning on a summer evening. It looked like the assassin finally had the upper hand, but an arrow to the lady's knee made sure of it. ShadowLily turned to glare at the ranger, her look stating she didn't need the help.

"What? It was taking too long." Lorelei pointed toward the Blacksmith. "The next one's almost done."

With the woman hobbled it was easy enough for ShadowLily to finish her off. She danced around the woman's wildly flailing stabs and buried her blades into her from behind. Just like that, the fight was over—just in time to see his next creation.

The Blacksmith must have been adapting because the man had all four limbs replaced. Instead of swords, there were daggers in each of his appendages. It would decrease the man's effective killing zone, but make him faster, and Tim wouldn't be surprised if he could climb shit and then drop down from above.

Pointing his sword arm at the group, the Blacksmith gurgled something that almost formed a word and then turned back to the forge. There weren't any more bodies back there, so Tim had no idea what to expect next.

The newly created monster didn't waste any time. It charged straight for the group of adventurers. ShadowLily looked at Lorelei. "Don't wait for me."

The ranger grinned from ear to ear. "Wouldn't dream of it."

An arrow flew straight at the man, but he dodged it at the last second by somehow flipping onto all fours. He cleared the remaining space between himself and the tank in four mighty leaps. Cassie's bō staff was working overtime to keep the blades from ripping her apart. She was already bleeding from a number of serious wounds by the time Tim got his first healing orb off.

Curse of giving was an easy choice for his next cast. The extra healing over time would have a nice effect on the tank. One thing he loved in games was a good HOT. He liked to call them the set 'em and forget 'em spells. Of course, you couldn't forget them forever, but for the duration of the spell, you didn't have to worry about a thing.

Unless everything turned to shit.

Thankfully for their group, it was five on one. The Blacksmith's newest creation didn't stand a chance. Tim couldn't imagine what it would be like to fight more than one of them at the same time. If a horde of these descended on Tristholm, the city would be wiped off the map by morning.

And he thought werewolves were bad.

The five of them working together managed to get the four-daggered freak down to ten percent health. Surprisingly, it was JaKobi who dealt the final blow. He created a sword made out of flame and drove it through the man's heart.

All of the Blacksmith's creations were dead.

Flames erupted from the forge and the Blacksmith turned to face them. The fire sparked behind him like a volcano. His sword arm had been replaced by a whip made out of a steel chain. The metal was still so hot it glowed. The hammer was still there, but on one side there was a wicked looking spike. It was the kind of thing you would use to pop a knight's head open like a watermelon.

Shuffling forward, the Blacksmith let out a moan. His chain flashed out, slamming against the cavern floor and leaving a trail of flames as he readied the weapon for another strike. Tim could tell Cassie was trying to decide how best to handle the weapon before running into the fight. This was the time of every battle when he didn't envy her.

It was easier to stand in the back than go toe to toe with the big uglies.

Waiting for the Blacksmith's next attack to miss, Cassie followed the chain back as he readied for another strike. Before he could lash out with the chain, she was hitting him with her staff. The bō rose and fell, smashing into the Blacksmith relentlessly. The man only grunted.

It was almost insulting how little he cared about the hits he was receiving.

Tim thought about it for a moment. If you just pulled a sword out of your stump and replaced it with a whip made out of an iron chain, would getting hit with a stick even register? Was there a point where so much pain could be inflicted on a person, they just didn't feel it anymore?

A quick check of the boss' hit points showed that while he might not feel the attacks, they were still hurting him. Tim cast a healing orb on Cassie, quickly followed by curse of giving. Now they should only be facing damage from one source, so Tim switched stances back to the Way of the Boulder, providing Cassie with extra healing.

JaKobi was igniting Lorelei's arrows as they plunged into the boss for additional damage while keeping up a constant onslaught of fireballs with his other hand. Somewhere along the way he'd leveled up and was now casting more than one spell at a time. It was damned impressive magic.

The Blacksmith hit sixty-five percent health and a shockwave rippled out from him, knocking them all down. Before even looking up, Tim cast healing storm. Any damage from the fall should have been negated.

It took him a second to roll to his feet, but it was in time to see the Blacksmith's chain flash out and wrap around JaKobi like a lasso. With a grunt, the Blacksmith started to reel the trapped mage back to him.

Tim didn't know what to do. JaKobi's eyes looked frantic, but he couldn't think of a way to help him. Fuck it, he had to do something. Tim cast weaken undead, hoping for the best. His friend continued to get reeled in like a fish at a trophy pond, so he continued to troubleshoot the situation.

The rest of the group was busy doing whatever they could to stop JaKobi from reaching the Blacksmith. Cassie was pulling on the chain, trying to slow his progress. Lorelei was filling the Blacksmith's arm full of arrows. Even ShadowLily was in the mix, hacking at boss' legs.

None of it seemed to make a difference.

Tim reapplied curse of giving just as the Blacksmith pulled JaKobi against him. With a last second thought, he managed to cast who needs a shield. As the hammer started to descend toward his friend, Tim switched his stance from Cassie to the pyromancer and prayed for the best.

The hammer came down and Tim knew whatever he did wasn't going to be enough to save him. Cassie's staff snapped up, somehow clipping the Blacksmith's arm. The spike that was coming down to pierce JaKobi's skull was turned to the side, and the flat side of the hammer dealt him a glancing blow.

A healing orb hit the mage as soon as the Blacksmith set him free. ShadowLily helped JaKobi up and pulled him back toward Tim. It took him a split second to switch his stance back to Cassie, and then he hit JaKobi with another blast of healing. Having deposited the wounded at his feet, the assassin returned to the battle.

The Blacksmith's health was under fifty percent.

Shaking his head as if to clear it, JaKobi grimaced. "Why am I always getting hit with shit? It's like the game decided I'm the team's punching bag."

"Trust me when I say, I hope I never get to have the experience." Tim pointed at the boss. "Go get some payback."

"Yippee-ki-yay, motherfucker!" JaKobi screamed like it was nineteen eighty-eight.

Flames erupted over the Blacksmith like the 4th of July at a private country club. The pyromancer really hadn't enjoyed almost having his brains dashed out. Tim could understand. He checked everyone's health and cast healing spells where they were needed.

The Blacksmith had his hands full with Cassie and ShadowLily up close and JaKobi and Lorelei providing ranged support. His health started to plummet. Maybe they would get out of this without him doing another cast. It had taken almost everything they had to save JaKobi the first time. Whoever got pulled in next might not be so lucky.

Fifteen Percent.

Ten.

Another shockwave slammed them all to the ground. Tim cast healing storm again before trying to stand back up. As he got to his feet, he realized that none of them had been grabbed by the chain attack. Instead, the chain had split into ten smaller whips and was smashing everyone in the group repeatedly.

This was his time to shine. Tim switched to his Way of the River stance, and cast curse of giving. He followed up with a round of healing orbs, and one last blast of healing storm. The burst of group healing left him winded, and his mana reserves dwindling, but so far everyone's health was staying steady.

The Blacksmith's attacks started to slow, but it wasn't the time to throw caution to the wind. Before anything could happen, he started using the last of his mana to cast another round of healing orbs on the group. Their health started to drop as his healing was no longer able to keep up with the stacks of Blacksmith damage. Their party hit fifty percent health, and then the attacks stopped.

The Blacksmith was dead.

CHAPTER SEVENTY-SIX

The loot from the Blacksmith wasn't what they expected.

Instead of an item, each of them was granted a hunk of Elmorian metal. Tim had never received a crafting item from a boss before, so he was intrigued. The description simply said in the hands of a skilled craftsman, it could become many useful things. He wasn't sure he wanted to know what kind of bonuses something crafted from the metal would have considering the source.

Maybe Ironbeard could make him a weapon attachment to make his curses stronger. There had to be a useful purpose for it. The game wasn't in the business of handing out useless shit. It'd be fun to see what everyone came up with. Maybe Tim could get them a discount at Ironbeard's shop if he put in some of the labor.

Elmore's Hallow was the creepiest thing they had encountered in the game thus far. He wondered if the game would get darker after this or go in a different direction. He got the feeling there would be something different waiting for them in the next phase of their saga, whenever they got there.

Things down here were creepy enough, but knowing that they

were going to face off against an actual lich was scary as fuck. The guy would either be skilled in dark magic or in necromancy or both. They hadn't faced a lot of magical adversaries yet. Each time they had, the battles had been fierce and come right down to the end.

Cassie stopped at an intersection. "My guess is this way leads out of town, and this way leads down." She pointed in the different directions as she spoke.

Looking up at the sign, Tim decided there was only one answer. To complete their quest, they had to clear the dungeon and that meant… "We go down."

The tank turned to her right and took the street leading toward their fate.

"JaKobi recast those little lights. I don't want them running out in the middle of a battle." Tim took a moment to recast his buffs and made sure he was in the Way of the Boulder stance.

"You got it, boss." Each of their lights winked out and was replaced by a slightly brighter set.

The road they were on started winding down into the mountain depths. The smooth city streets quickly turned into a rough cavern floor. The dim lanterns of the city completely faded from view, to be replaced with a faint bioluminescent moss on the walls.

Tim didn't remember seeing that in the video and started to wonder if it had been placed on the walls to guide them to their next fight. "Let's follow the green stuff."

"Sounds like something you'd say right before going to White Castle," Cassie snorted.

"Or when taking a trip to the Shire. Those fat little Hobbits all had pipes, and they made the best leaf and beer in all the land," JaKobi said as he mimicked smoking a pipe. "See, now I'm ready for elevenses."

Tim chuckled. "I think it's more likely that they all smoked tobacco pipes, you know because Tolkien did. That being said, follow the glowy stuff and stay sharp. Just because we haven't seen any trash mobs yet doesn't mean that we won't."

"I'd love to run into something, just to know we're going the right way," Lorelei called from the back of the group as she looked around. "These tunnels could be taking us anywhere."

A scream of pure terror ripped through the darkness.

"I guess that means we're headed in the right direction," Lorelei huffed.

"And there isn't something like a teddy bear with a free hugs shirt waiting at the end of the line," ShadowLily snarked.

Cassie started moving again. "Let's just find this fucker and get out of here. I'm sick of this place."

"I kind of like it." Tim shrugged at all the stares. "You know, minus all the monstery stuff. You can't tell me this place isn't cool as shit."

"Maybe, but all it is now is dirty and full of dead things," Cassie grumbled. "The longer I'm down here, the more I like the beach and treehouse idea."

JaKobi changed the color of his light to make it look more like the sun. "You can't really go wrong when you're outside."

"Yeah, except for all the bugs, and grossness," ShadowLily griped. "I'd rather be inside getting served ice-cold drinks and watching movies."

A scream echoed from below, louder than before.

"Maybe we save the chit-chat until after we kill this asshole." Cassie started moving faster, and the group followed behind her at a steady jog.

They reached the bottom of the tunnels five minutes later. Tim was gasping, but everyone else seemed to be just fine. He was really going to have to find a way to up his physical just a bit. Running such short distances shouldn't have made him feel so tired.

But it was running. Did anyone really love running?

The chamber they entered looked different than it had in the cut scene. This room had been widened to give them plenty of room to fight. There were also pillars of stone throughout the space, almost set to break the room up into quadrants. Tim filed that fact away for later and tried to be in the present instead of thinking too far ahead.

At the back of the chamber was something they had seen before, the lich's tomb. Kneeling in front of it was a woman. The screams they heard had to have been hers, but she didn't look hurt. Instead, it seemed as if she were crying over something lying propped against the tomb. As they continued to get closer, he realized it must have been Doug's body. After all these years, she still missed him so much it ripped her apart.

That's what love is.

Caring about someone so much that losing them would tear your life down to its very foundations. It was never easy to lose someone you loved. It didn't matter how they died, only that they were no longer around. Losing someone sucked, that was all that could be said about it.

The lich appeared over his tomb, dressed in hooded black robes. The part of his face left uncovered by the fabric looked just like the gaunt dry skin they'd seen covering all of the people of Elmore's Hallow.

Hovering in place, he turned from the scene before him to face the group. "This is my favorite part of the day. Isn't her suffering delicious?"

Landing on the cavern floor with his tomb and Doug's wife behind him, the lich continued to address them. "Such brave adventurers you must be. There hasn't been a party of warriors who made it this far in nearly a hundred years."

"Get a good look at the last faces you'll ever see." Cassie flipped off the lich.

Laughter rumbled from the lich's undead chest. "So brave, so stupid. Come child, let us see which one of us prevails."

"I know where I'm going to shove my staff," Cassie growled as she charged forward.

A wall of spirits formed in front of Cassie, forcing her to slow down or run face first into the evil mishmash of ghostly spirits. She skidded to a halt and waited for Tim to blast the lich's spell out of the way with divine light.

As soon as the wall dissipated, Cassie was on the move to catch the boss. It was always easier if they could keep the boss relatively still while the DPS went to work. If she couldn't catch him to get agro, they would be on their heels early in the fight.

Tim watched as Cassie grabbed something from her belt. She tossed out a hook, catching the lich's floating foot. She snared him in place long enough to close the distance. Tim forgot all about the hook she had. It was such a cool move he was going to have to watch her in fights to see how often she used it.

With the boss pinned down, the group let loose. Tim wasn't sure how this was going to go healing wise, so he was playing it conservative early on. He cast curse of giving on the boss and watched Cassie's health for any serious fluctuations. Not seeing anything jump out right away, he almost cast weaken undead on the boss to bring a little extra utility to the fight.

The lich growled in anger. He lifted a hand in the air, and a skeletal knight appeared, charging toward the group.

Cassie had to abandon the boss and divert all her attention to the crazed swordsman rushing to kill her friends. Their tank paid for changing targets by taking a magical blast to the back.

Seeing Cassie stagger like that pissed Tim off. He quickly cast healing orb on her and curse of giving on the skeletal knight. With the triple healing over time effects, Cassie's health wouldn't be a problem.

The knight's sword hit Cassie's staff so hard it lifted her in the air. Tim cast weaken undead on the knight, hoping that it hit in time to prevent their tank from getting battered around. His spell hit the knight at the same time ShadowLily entered the fight from the shadows. Her daggers made short work of the last of the knight's health, and they all turned back to face the boss.

The lich hadn't been idle while they were busy with the knight. He was standing by his tomb, hunched over the lady crying over Doug's corpse. "I've found the ones responsible for killing your husband. They are here now, just behind us."

Tim wouldn't have called it a premonition, but he certainly had an inkling that something wasn't right. The lich had killed Doug, which meant they were in for a terrible surprise. He looked around the room and remembered the four stone outcroppings.

Oh, shit!

"Follow me!" Tim cried as he started running toward the nearest pillar of rock. He slid behind it and peeked around to see the woman getting to her feet. She looked at them, and her mouth opened. The force of her anguish started tearing the rock apart. Tim had no problem believing anyone caught directly in the blast would have died.

The last of the rock fell away, and the woman crumpled to her knees by the body, sobbing.

It didn't take him long to do the math. They had to kill the lich before the woman screamed for the fifth time. If they didn't, there wouldn't be anywhere left for them to hide. "We need constant DPS on the boss, we are way behind the numbers right now."

So far, they'd only managed to whittle the boss' health down ten percent. If they stayed at this pace, they would all die after only managing to take half of the boss' health. It was time for all of them to up their game. The conservative approach wouldn't work in this fight.

Not anymore.

Tim cast behold my power and curse of giving and watched as a fireball slammed into the lich, followed by a volley of arrows. Before anyone needed healing, he managed to reapply weaken undead and get off a blast of divine light.

They were starting to catch up.

Healing storm took the edge off the group's loss of health due to his curse. Behold my power hit, and the lich cried out in frustration. He flew back toward the lady once again.

"We all need to go to Lorelei's pillar." The ranger was standing next to one of the formations, making it the logical place to run. Tim pointed at her as he started sprinting to the lifesaving rocks.

During this interval, they managed to take another thirty percent off of the boss' health. Now they had a chance of completing the fight. The question was, would they be able to keep up the DPS. He was sure the lich wouldn't just keep letting them hammer away at him.

Sliding to a halt behind the pillar, Tim took a second to catch his breath as the stones in front of them absorbed the banshee's screams. What they needed now was one more big push. If they could knock the lich's health in half during this part of the fight, they could have one easier round before finishing him off.

The Blue Dagger Society looked tired, but they were not defeated.

"I want to see who's going to bring it. Winner of the DPS trophy gets free beer at the inn for a week!" Tim screamed over the howl of the banshee.

Sometimes you just had to find the right way to motivate people. It couldn't always be if you fuck this up, we're all going to die. Nobody needed that kind of tension in their lives.

The rock wall crumbled away and they sprang into action. Cassie used her hook to trap the boss and the DPS show began. Tim couldn't contribute as much this time because his biggest curse had an ultra-long cooldown. He might be able to use it again by the end of the fight, but he wasn't sure.

This time the lich summoned three skeletal archers. There was nothing they could do to avoid the first volley of arrows. Tim ran around the battlefield, pulling the arrows free and casting healing orbs on people so the DPS could do their thing. When a fight had a strict DPS check, there wasn't anything you could do, but go for it. The last thing you wanted to happen was to hit the enrage.

Or in this case, scream.

The archers fell to Lorelei one at a time. The rest of the group stayed on the boss. As his health started to dip, the lich cast a wall of spirits again and started floating back to his pet banshee.

A quick check of the boss' health showed it at twenty-nine percent. They'd made their DPS check so far. "How's everyone looking for the next round of the fight?" Tim asked as they hid behind the third rock formation.

"I'll be good as long as there aren't too many surprises," JaKobi said with his hands on his knees, sucking in air like it was going out of style.

"Same for me," Lorelei added.

Cassie grinned. "I'm fine as long as you can keep me up."

"Then you're going to be fine all night." Tim didn't have unlimited reserves, but his new mana regeneration was helping. Plus, a little bravado never hurt anyone's confidence.

ShadowLily looked like she was raring to get back in the fight. "Whatever he summons this time, just let me handle it and keep pounding his ass."

Tim nodded.

He knew better than to stop her from something when she put her mind to it. It just meant he'd have to be Johnny on the spot with the heals if shit hit the fan. He could handle that. It was what he was made for.

The rock shattered into dust, and they were all moving in unison.

The lich rushed out to meet them, not wasting a single second before casting his next summoning. A giant of a corpse with two daggers appeared in the chamber.

It couldn't be?

The only man Tim had seen that big was Malvonis. Had the lich somehow been able to summon his spirit here to fight? If it was him, ShadowLily was going to need some help, and they had to knock at least twenty percent off the boss if they wanted to cruise in on easy street.

Tim cast curse of giving on both of his targets, and then a healing orb on ShadowLily and Cassie. He saw an arrow hit ShadowLily's target and shouted, "Stay on the boss."

"You watch her," Lorelei stated flatly as she returned her attention to the lich.

"As if my life depended on it," Tim replied as he cast weaken undead on ShadowLily's target.

It was amazing to watch her duck and weave. It was almost as if she were dancing the way she moved with such grace. This projection of Malvonis wasn't as good as her, and they needn't have been too worried. Tim watched as she hacked one of the skeleton's arms off before dodging away from another attack.

He was so engrossed watching ShadowLily's deadly dance he almost missed it when the lich started moving away from them.

"Get to the pillar," Tim cried as he started to run.

The fake Malvonis was still on his feet. ShadowLily jumped into the air, planting both of her feet in the creature's chest and shoving it away from her. She got up and started to run after the others.

Tim didn't know where to look. Should he watch the lady as she stood up or the creature trying to chase down his woman from behind? Tim cast snare on the fake Malvonis and got his healing spells ready.

ShadowLily dove for them, but she was going to be too late. Cassie darted out like a flash and grabbed her, pulling her almost back to safety. The edge of the scream hit both of them and almost tore the assassin out of the tank's grip.

Their health bars plummeted as Tim started casting healing orbs like it was going out of style. After that, he wasted his extra mana casting healing storm even though only two of them needed healing. The breaks before boss phases weren't very long, and he needed them back on their feet for the final push.

It didn't take long to get Cassie stabilized, but ShadowLily's injuries were worse. Both of her legs had been shattered by the blast. Tim was healing them, but he had doubts about her effectiveness for the rest of the battle.

The boss' health sat at nine percent.

They could do this, even if she was out of the fight. "Guys, we've got this. Just hit him with whatever you've got, and let's end this." Tim held out his hand. "All for one, and one for…"

"Yeah, I'm not going to do that." Cassie huffed.

JaKobi held out his hand, then yanked it away as they said the word "all." He looked at Tim, said, "I got you, bro!" and tapped his chest with his fist.

Tim cast another healing orb on ShadowLily, hoping it would be enough to get her back in the fight as their last rocky hiding space faded away.

This time the lich was right in front of them. He sprayed a cone of some type of dark magic, and the entire group started taking damage.

Tim cast curse of giving, followed by healing storm. His mana reserves were fumes, but he decided to follow his own advice and just go for it. A quick blast of weaken undead followed by divine light had the boss on his last legs.

Appearing out of nowhere and looking like she'd been hit by a runaway truck, ShadowLily sank her daggers into the lich's back. The boss fell to the ground, his expression one of pure disbelief.

Tim hoped they didn't have to face the woman now since he was completely spent. He managed to cast one last healing storm, but he needed to recharge before he could do anything else.

A tiny blue orb flew out of the boss and toward the woman. When it approached, the orb turned into an image of Doug. The man lifted his wife up by the arms and kissed her. They hugged for a moment, and the skin she'd been trapped in fell away. Both blue ghosts turned back into orbs and shot into the sky.

They were together in death as they had been in life.

The tomb behind Doug's body turned to gold, and Tim grinned like a kid at Christmas. This was the biggest chest they'd ever seen. There had to be something good inside.

Today was an awesome day.

CHAPTER SEVENTY-SEVEN

The gold tomb called to him like no other prize they'd seen.

His general feeling about opening these was that everyone received something, so it didn't matter who went first. As much as he wanted to run up and touch the tomb, he felt like the honor should go to JaKobi.

The pyromancer had suffered the most in their recent fights, and a cold hunk of metal from the Blacksmith didn't feel like much of a reward.

"All right, fire guy, lead us to the promised land." Tim clapped the pyromancer on the back and shoved him toward the tomb.

"Don't mind if I do." JaKobi ran forward and placed his hand on the golden chest.

Coins appeared in Tim's inventory, and he smiled at the amount of gold he'd just received. There was something to be said about being fairly compensated for a job well done.

A circlet set with a single red stone appeared on JaKobi's head. "Crown of the Flaming Mind. Increase all damage with fire magic by one percent at the expense of losing one percent of my health every thirty seconds during combat."

"Not a gift for the healer then," Tim chuckled. In actuality, JaKobi didn't take very much damage, and Tim's curse of giving spell should be able to handle that much damage on its own if he was in the Way of the River stance. If he couldn't be in that stance, a healing orb would solve the issue just as quickly.

"I'm going next, and then I'm going to sit down for a minute." ShadowLily marched up to the tomb with a determined expression on her face.

Tim realized that while their health was regenerating, he could still speed the process along. He cast healing storm twice in a row and was happy to see ShadowLily standing a little straighter than she had been.

"Leather Vest of Shadows." Her armor disappeared and was replaced by a leather vest with a deep crimson slash down the front. "Ten percent additional damage from critical hits, and some nice stat upgrades."

Instead of giving her a high five, Tim helped ShadowLily down from the tomb. As soon as he was able, he cast a healing orb on her. His mana was still almost completely drained.

Cassie took advantage of the situation and placed her hand on the tomb next. "Wrist Guards of Unreasonable Strength."

She slipped the wrist guards on, and her forearms bulged like those of a fictional sailor who liked to eat spinach. "Ten percent strength bonus. Just a flat-out increase."

"You could probably also win an arm-wrestling contest," Lorelei snickered as she walked up and placed her own hand on the tomb.

The ranger grinned. "Quiver of Duty. This quiver was once owned by the famous archer Renault Dupree. His unrelenting skill with the bow empowered this quiver and whoever uses it to this day. Says it provides a damage bonus for every arrow fired. It also says that the item is level one, and it has four additional levels that can be unlocked."

"Holy shit, the game has gear that can be leveled up," Tim exclaimed. "That's fucking awesome."

"It's your turn. Maybe you'll get something cool too." Lorelei motioned for Tim to get his ass up to the tomb.

He didn't have to be told twice. Tim bounded up the few steps and placed his hand on the tomb.

Item Received: Jerkin of Unmeasurable Delight

Sam was a man who took pleasure in all things. Sadly for him, the mayor's daughter shouldn't have been one of them. Despite the tiny tear where the spear pierced him through the back, the shirt is in otherwise pristine condition.

+1 to all base stats.

That was a weird fucking story.

Thankfully, the rip wouldn't matter because the jerkin was something he could wear under his robe.

Cassie laughed as she read the description. "You always get the weirdest shit."

"Weird, but incredibly useful," Tim smirked. "Now, let's get out of here."

JaKobi sighed. "I'm not looking forward to the walk back."

"Maybe we can send for a carriage after we get out of Elmore's Hallow," ShadowLily griped. "They brought us out here on horses, and it'd be nice to have a ride back."

Tim noticed something shiny at the base of the lich's tomb. While the others were talking, he picked up the object.

Fast Travel Location Elmore's Hallow unlocked.

Access has been granted to the Tristholm gate portal and the portal at the gates leading to the Deserts of Naroosh.

"Guys, I think I solved the walking back problem. All we have to do is make it to one of the quick travel gates." Tim tossed the crystal to ShadowLily.

She grinned before passing the crystal to Cassie. Once the crystal made it to the final person in their group, it disappeared.

"Let's start moving. I want to find this portal and get back to

Tristholm. We've got quests to turn in and celebrating to do." Tim surprised everyone by starting to jog back the way they came.

Everyone knew how much he hated running, so they followed him without complaint.

———

The city of Tristholm was in full celebration mode when they appeared in the portal.

Fireworks erupted overhead as the Blue Dagger Society walked back to Seraphina's castle. The people of the city were too busy rejoicing to pay much attention to the weary travelers.

At least someone was enjoying their work.

This might have been the one time Tim didn't feel like turning in a quest in person. He wasn't looking for any more work right now. All he wanted to do was rest. The group deserved a few days off to pursue whatever they wanted to do for themselves. Once they all scratched their personal projects itch, they could head off to the Deserts of Naroosh. Until then, he was going to take the lazy way out as much as possible.

Unfortunately, there was no getting out of meeting with Seraphina to complete their major questline. It wasn't so bad though. They all needed to eat, and it would be nice to have rooms at the castle, even if they didn't come with coffee delivered to his chamber daily.

Tim hoped over the next few days he'd get a chance to go back to Promethia and get his affairs there set up in a long-term holding pattern while he continued his adventures. That and he really wanted to spend a few days eking out the last few secrets to shaping steel. He was so close to mastering the basics he could almost taste it.

When they reached the castle, the city guard parted to let them inside. It seemed they had done enough around the city that people had stopped questioning their identities, recognizing them and their pins. A servant showed up to lead them through the castle to the great dining hall. Tim was starting to get used to the idea of being the guest of honor.

As they entered the room, Seraphina stood. "Three cheers for the saviors of Tristholm!"

"Huzzah!"

"Huzzah!"

"Huzzah!"

Drinks were poured and glasses shoved into their hands. Seraphina motioned for them to join her at the head table, but Tim noticed Paul standing in the corner. "I'll catch up with you in a minute."

Tim approached the high priest. "It's good to see you again."

"And you." Paul motioned for Tim to follow him into a little alcove. "I noticed you haven't selected an award from your quest yet."

Tim blushed. "You know, with all that has been going on, I forgot about it."

Paul reached inside his robes and pulled out a package. "I thought you might have, so I took the liberty of selecting something for you myself."

Accepting the package, Tim eagerly tore away the wrappings and peered inside. There was an old pair of gloves with the fingers cut off lying in the box. Not exactly what he expected, but maybe they were awesome.

Item Received: Paul's Gloves of Mending.

Before the high priest attained his position, he was just a man serving out his daily duties to the Goddess Eternia. Healing the masses was something Paul took great pride in. These gloves bear the enchantments of years of his dedicated works, and love for the people.

+4 to Wisdom +7 to Intelligence and a ten percent bonus to direct healing spells.

Tim equipped the gloves and then pulled Paul into a hug.

"Thank you so much. These are more than I could have ever asked for."

"You deserve them." Paul gave Tim a warm smile. "I thought you'd also be happy to know the man I sent to take your place at the Healing Shack obtained Judy's firm approval."

Tim felt as if a weight had been lifted off his shoulders. "Thank you for checking in with her."

"It was my pleasure." Paul motioned for Tim to go to his friends. "That's enough from me for one night. Go enjoy yourself. This party is in your honor, it'd be a shame to waste it."

Paul made his exit from the room, and Tim started to make his way toward the head table and the food that smelled so damn tasty. He was halfway across the room when the world around him seemed to come to a complete stop. That could only mean one thing. The Goddess Eternia was on her way.

Sure enough, the goddess appeared moments later. "Warrior of the light, I have need of your services."

Tim dropped to one knee. "You have but to ask."

"My sister consolidates her power in the desert kingdoms of Naroosh. We must make sure that doesn't happen. Now that we have her on the run, we need to end this once and for all. I love my sister, but I will not see people's lives ruined just to please her whims. Will you help me?"

Quest Received: The Deserts of Naroosh.

Now that the way under the mountains has been cleared, we can attack Vitaria in the heart of her realm. Seek out her sources of power and destroy them to weaken her before the final battle.

Accept Quest: <Yes/No>

Tim accepted the quest. "It would be my pleasure to help."

The goddess smiled as she drifted back to the heavens. The world sped back up and he noticed everyone in his group staring at him.

Tim shrugged. At least they knew where they were heading next.

A notification appeared in his vision.

Quest Completed: Clear the Mountain Pass

Your service to the realm has been noted and will be well-rewarded. Thank you, adventurer, for securing the health and wellbeing of my people.

Reward: Fifty gold coins and the undying gratitude of Seraphina and her people.

"And a shit-ton of experience." Tim smiled as he gained another level. Things were really starting to move now. It wouldn't be long before he hit level twenty.

Tim decided on the spur of the moment that he should try to get his Endurance to twenty next. While being stronger might be more beneficial when he used his daggers, because they had to run so much, Endurance seemed like the logical move. He dumped his extra point there and gave his stat sheet a quick look over.

Things were looking good.

Tim grabbed a beer from one of the passing trays and went to the woman in his life. He didn't know what the future had in store for them, but he knew if they faced it together, they would always come out on top.

Blue Daggers for Life!

<u>List of Tim's Current Stats and Skills.</u>

"Tim" level fifteen Battlesworn

Primary Stats
Strength: 13
Endurance: 14

Dexterity: 20
Intelligence: 32
Wisdom: 44
Perception: 5
Vitality: 3
Revitalization: 3
Luck: 6

Notable Gear

Simple Dagger of Dexterity +1 (X2)
Staff of Divine Retribution +4 Intelligence +5 Wisdom
Circlet of Wisdom +1
Boots of Swift Regeneration Increase base movement speed and mana regeneration by 1%
Battlesworn Robes of Justice Intelligence +4 Wisdom +6
Belt of Wisdom +2
Wristband of the Goddess 10% damage reduction to dark based attacks
Leather Wraps of Divergent Health 10% chance for single target healing spell to jump targets and heal the secondary recipient for 50% of the value.
Ring of Marginal Transcendence Wisdom +2
Necklace of Unshakable Will +3 Wisdom +1 Intelligence.
Pants of Recovery Increases mana regeneration
Jerkin of Unmeasurable Delight +1 to all base stats
Paul's Gloves of Mending +4 Wisdom +7 Intelligence
Necklace of Holy Light

Skills

Healing orb: Journeyman rank one
Dodge: Apprentice rank one
Flame Burst: Apprentice rank three

Cleanse: Apprentice rank seven
Appeal to the Goddess: Novice rank one
Infiltrator: Novice rank three
Sneak: Apprentice rank seven
Small Blades: Apprentice rank six
Throwing Knives: Apprentice rank two
Night Vision: Novice rank five
Back Stab: Novice rank seven
Weaken Undead: Apprentice rank five
Divine light: Apprentice rank five
Healing Storm: Novice level one
Curse of Giving: Novice rank five
Behold my Power: Novice rank six
Who Needs a Shield: Novice rank five
Cleanse: Apprentice rank one
Stance: Way of the Boulder, Novice rank nine
Stance: Way of the River, Novice rank nine
Buff: Armor of Eternia, Novice rank six
Buff: Armor of the Faithful, Apprentice rank one
Quick Feet: Novice One

Open Quests
The Deserts of Naroosh

The story continues with book three, *Deserts Of Naroosh*, available now from Amazon and through Kindle Unlimited.

Grab your copy here.

When I started writing The Trials of Tristholm, we lived in a world where nobody heard of COVID-19. Since then, the word has changed. As an author, it's always hard to resist the pull of writing things like a deadly virus into your work, but I love my virus stories when the world isn't in the grips of one. Books like The Stand and Andromeda Strain are some of my favorites, but right now, I'd rather be escaping when I read.

The real world is strange enough.

One positive that's come out of this for us is my wife has been working from home. It's been nice to have her around the house more, and I know the four dogs have enjoyed it as much as I have. The downside for me is I haven't been able to see my Dad. He's in the high-risk age group and taking things safe. I'm going to sneak over for a six-foot away conversation and to give him a UofA shirt for father's day.

#BearDown

This book was a fun one to write. I thought about all the fun I've had battling monsters in all kinds of different gothic settings. There are so many incredible games set in a dark gothic environment, and every MMO has some sort of zombie, vampire, ghost, map, castle, or zone. The entire game of Secret World is one big supernatural surprise.

Before rambling on any further, I need to give credit where credit is due. I wanted to give a special shout out to my beta readers on the JIT Team, and my editor. Without the team's helpful hints and encouragement, this book wouldn't have been nearly as good. Trust me when I tell you that my editor always works wonders on the final product, and for that, I am genuinely grateful.

And there is always the man that made these books happen, Michael himself. I came to Michael with a passion for writing and a few books under my belt that had done ok. We sat down and talked, and he said, *show me what you've got.*

What came out was a very early first few pages of Rise of the Grandmaster.

Just like that, we were hooked on the concept and set out on this wild adventure together. Now with two books out and the first audiobook on the way, this series is really coming together. I hope all of you are enjoying it as much as we are, and I can't wait to introduce you to The Deserts of Naroosh later this year.

I know I mentioned her earlier, but I can't thank my wife enough. When I came to her five years ago and said I wanted to be a writer, she was a bit skeptical (who wouldn't be), but always supported me. Without her love and faith in me, I wouldn't have grown from a guy who's first draft of a book was twenty thousand words of rubbish into the man who turned that same book into a novel called Ascendancy The Arena.

It was work. Hard work. A lot of nights asking myself if I made the wrong choice? What if after having a taste of the dream I had to go back to my cube and start the daily grind again? There is so much more that goes into self-publishing than just the writing. It felt like there weren't enough hours in the day.

Working with Michael fixed that for me. I get to focus on what I like doing best crafting and revising a story. While he hires the best people in the world to take care of the rest of the stuff, and talks me through any hurdles or story stumbling blocks I might have. It's surprising how much a small nudge in the right direction can get a story where it needs to go.

Anyways, I'm stuck in the writer cave for the summer, or as my wife has named it The Cave of Nefariousness. It gets hot in Phoenix real, damn hot. So during the summer, I typically walk the dogs in the am and stay inside most of the day. Extra time inside should be good for the writer mojo.

Maybe not so good for the old waistline.

In closing, I hope all of you have a wonderful summer and that your families are safe and healthy. I'll do my best to get the Deserts of Naroosh to you as soon as I can.

I have to agree with Bradford—supportive wives are the world to us and mean so much. Fortunately for me, I've been mentioning my wife Judith in my *Author Notes* since the beginning in 2015 (my first books).

It wasn't until much later (2017, I think) when *she* realized *what* she was mentioned for—shoe selection requests and fashion knowledge—where I would sneak questions to her without context. When she saw she had paired Coach with a fashion brand 10x the cost (or rather, I did when asking two questions at different times), she had a small cow. Seems that context is very important when discussing fashion.

I don't forget that important part now.

I'm with Bradford on the no pandemic stories. Unlike Bradford, I didn't like them before the pandemic, either, so at least I'm consistent. Either in or out of a pandemic, I don't like pandemic stories.

Don't ask me how I got involved in The Age of Madness. *The fans made me do it.*

I'm looking forward to building a man-cave with a game

system(s) in it over the next three years. With the new systems coming out (and possibly the last major game systems to arrive for years), I might spend a few nights playing.

You know, for research purposes.

Diary June 28 – July 4, 2020

I used to do this for a living. Now? You might be forgiven for wondering if that is true.

In my past life (10+ years ago), I was a professional computer programmer / database guy and messed with different software packages. There was an ISBN file I needed to load into a database was three (3) gigabytes.

Not a big deal anymore. The laptop I am using has 4,000 GBs of SSD storage and 32 GBs of RAM. That means it is MORE than big enough to handle a (fairly sizeable) file.

Well, the file was a RAR (a compressed file; it's smaller than the real file to save on download speed and costs.)

I had to go into Windows (I am typically on a Mac) to play with the file because a partner I'm working with uses Windows, and I didn't think it would be challenging for me vs. the opposite. I'm pretty familiar with the Microsoft Access database program, so no problem, right?

Wrong.

After twenty minutes of screwing around with my Microsoft Office license and downloading Access, I learned it has a 2GB limit.

I'm going to compress this story a little. About four major downloads later of Microsoft SQL Server, MySQL, and Microsoft Visual Studio later…

I finally download SQLite and locate a front-end program to have a look-see into the file I have.

Here are a few interesting facts:

• The 3GB file un-compressed to 32 GB (killing the option of using Microsoft SQL Server personal, which is limited to 10GB.)

• I could not load the latest MySQL to my machine, not because I'm ignorant (maybe that's true as well), but rather because the latest MySQL install *didn't.* Install, I mean.

• SQLite has a 2,000 GB limit to the database (I only need about forty.)

• I found a suitable front end, imported over 18 MILLION records into the file (this took about ten minutes on my super-duper-Mac Pro-running-Windows laptop), and I can now find the +/- 50,000 records I need.

Talk about overkill.

I have NO idea if I will need this data in one (1) month, and I know I'll never get some of those files I downloaded to try off my hard drive. In fact, if this computer is EVER in a museum for Michael Anderle, you will know the latest Visual Studio install is right there in the Parallels Window partition.

Not being used.

The 4th is on a Saturday?

I'm sure for many of you, July 4th (for those here in America, where it is a holiday) being on a Saturday is not news. I just figured this out like yesterday, which is a week from July 4th exactly.

I heard someone call the lack of knowing what day (or time) it is the new "Corona Calendar," and I completely agree. I have a real hard time knowing what freaking day of the week / month / year it is these days.

HAVE FUN! Life is hard enough right now. Take a moment for a few deep breaths and your favorite calming influence, then crack open that next book!

Ad Aeternitatem,

Michael Anderle

BOOKS BY BRADFORD BATES

<u>Ascendancy Legacy</u>

The Arena

Jar of Souls

Guardian of the Grove

Demon Stone

The Rising Darkness

Redemption

<u>Ascendancy Origins</u>

Rise of the Fallen

Butcher of the Bay

Night of the Demon

<u>The Bozley Green Chronicles</u>

Possessed

<u>The Galactic Outlaws</u>

Forced Compliance

Genetic Purge

Smuggler's Legacy

<u>Fortune Hunters</u>

Star Talon

Lost Signal

<u>A Galactic Outlaws Story</u>

The Marchenko Incident

Smuggler for Hire
Origin Ice

<u>The Fairy of Salem</u>
Witching Hour
The Wild Hunt

<u>Standalone Titles</u>
Crimson Stars

BOOKS BY MICHAEL ANDERLE

For a complete list of books by Michael Anderle, please visit:

www.lmbpn.com/ma-books/

All LMBPN Audiobooks are Available at Audible.com and iTunes

To see all LMBPN audiobooks, including those written by Michael Anderle please visit:

www.lmbpn.com/audible

CONNECT WITH THE AUTHORS

Connect with Bradford Bates

Facebook:
https://www.facebook.com/bradfordbatesauthor/

Twitter:
https://twitter.com/Freetheblizz

Website:
http://www.bradfordbates.com/

Connect with Michael Anderle and sign up for his email list here:

Website: http://lmbpn.com

Email List: http://lmbpn.com/email/

Facebook:
https://www.facebook.com/LMBPNPublishing

ABOUT BRADFORD BATES

Bradford Bates is a full-time author, husband to an incredible wife, and father to four furry rescue dogs. He lives in sunny Phoenix, Arizona, trying to not melt in the oppressive heat of the summer. When he isn't busy writing the next book, you can find him playing video games and watching scary movies.

www.ingramcontent.com/pod-product-compliance
Lightning Source LLC
Chambersburg PA
CBHW020224110726
47898CB00004B/1135